Hockey
Girl
Loves
Drama
Boy

Hockey Girl Loves Drama Boy

FAITH ERIN HICKS

:01

First Second

NEW YORK

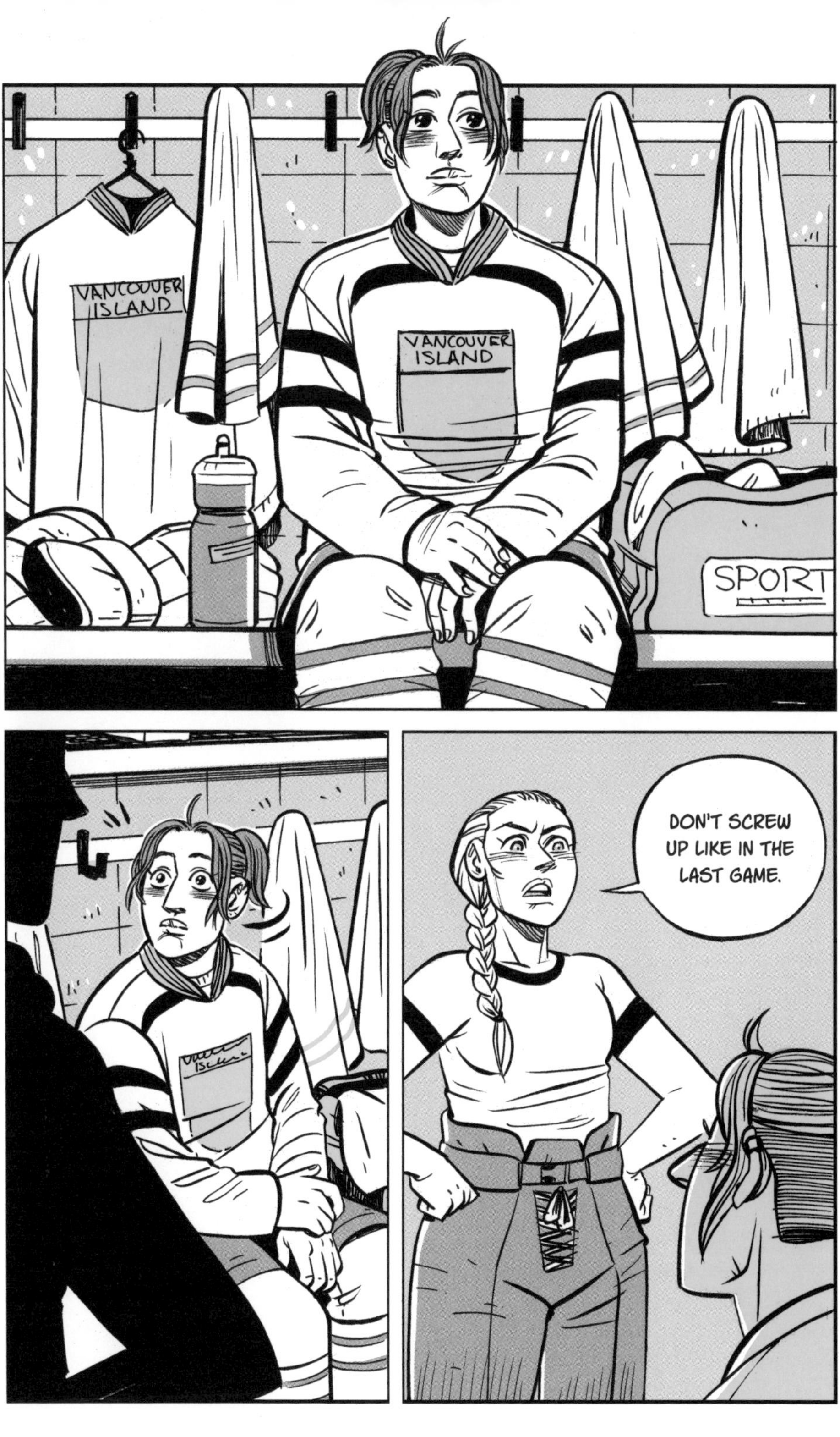
VANCOUVER ISLAND
VANCOUVER ISLAND
SPORT
DON'T SCREW UP LIKE IN THE LAST GAME.

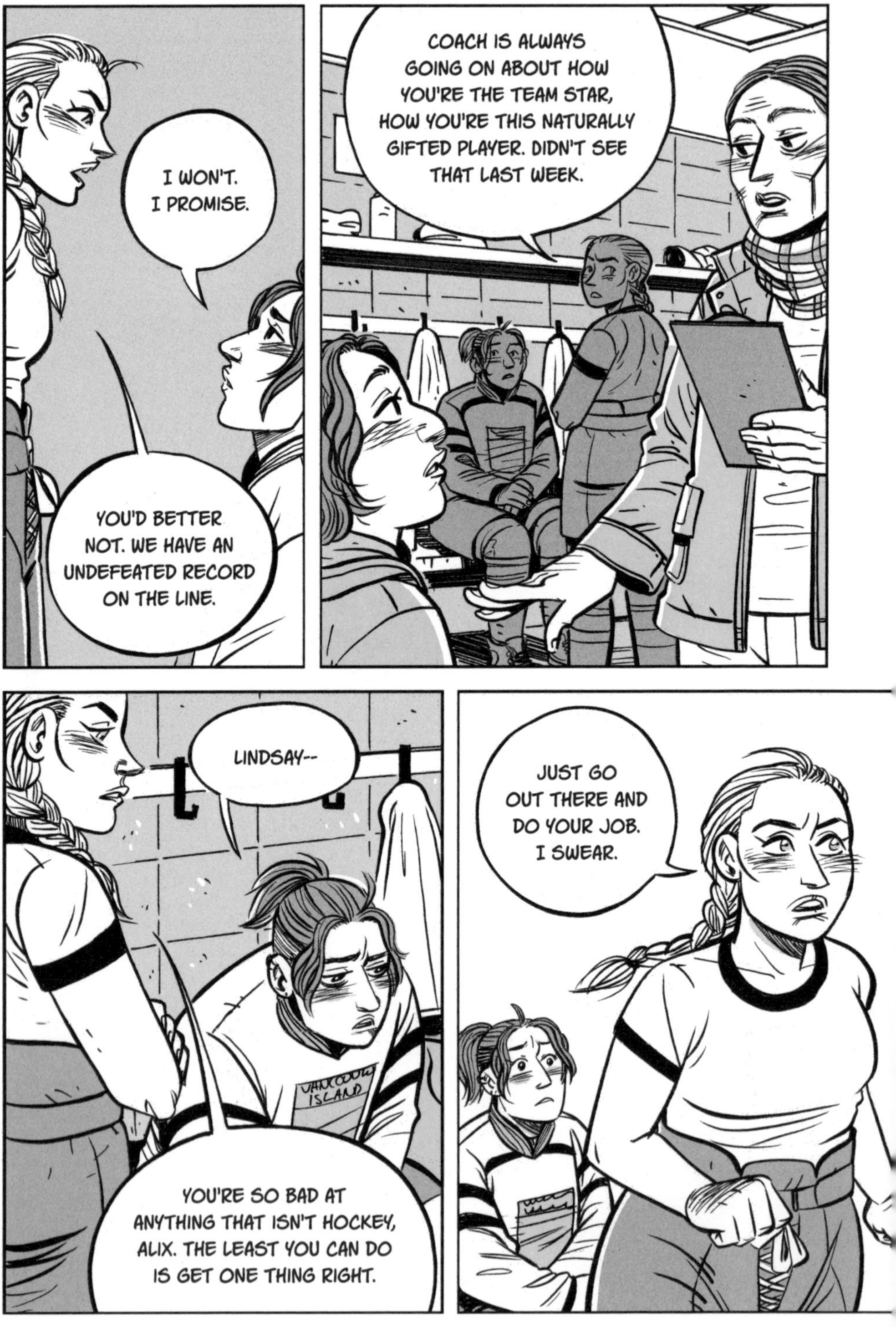
I WON'T. I PROMISE.
YOU'D BETTER NOT. WE HAVE AN UNDEFEATED RECORD ON THE LINE.
COACH IS ALWAYS GOING ON ABOUT HOW YOU'RE THE TEAM STAR, HOW YOU'RE THIS NATURALLY GIFTED PLAYER. DIDN'T SEE THAT LAST WEEK.
LINDSAY--
YOU'RE SO BAD AT ANYTHING THAT ISN'T HOCKEY, ALIX. THE LEAST YOU CAN DO IS GET ONE THING RIGHT.
JUST GO OUT THERE AND DO YOUR JOB. I SWEAR.
VANCOUVER ISLAND

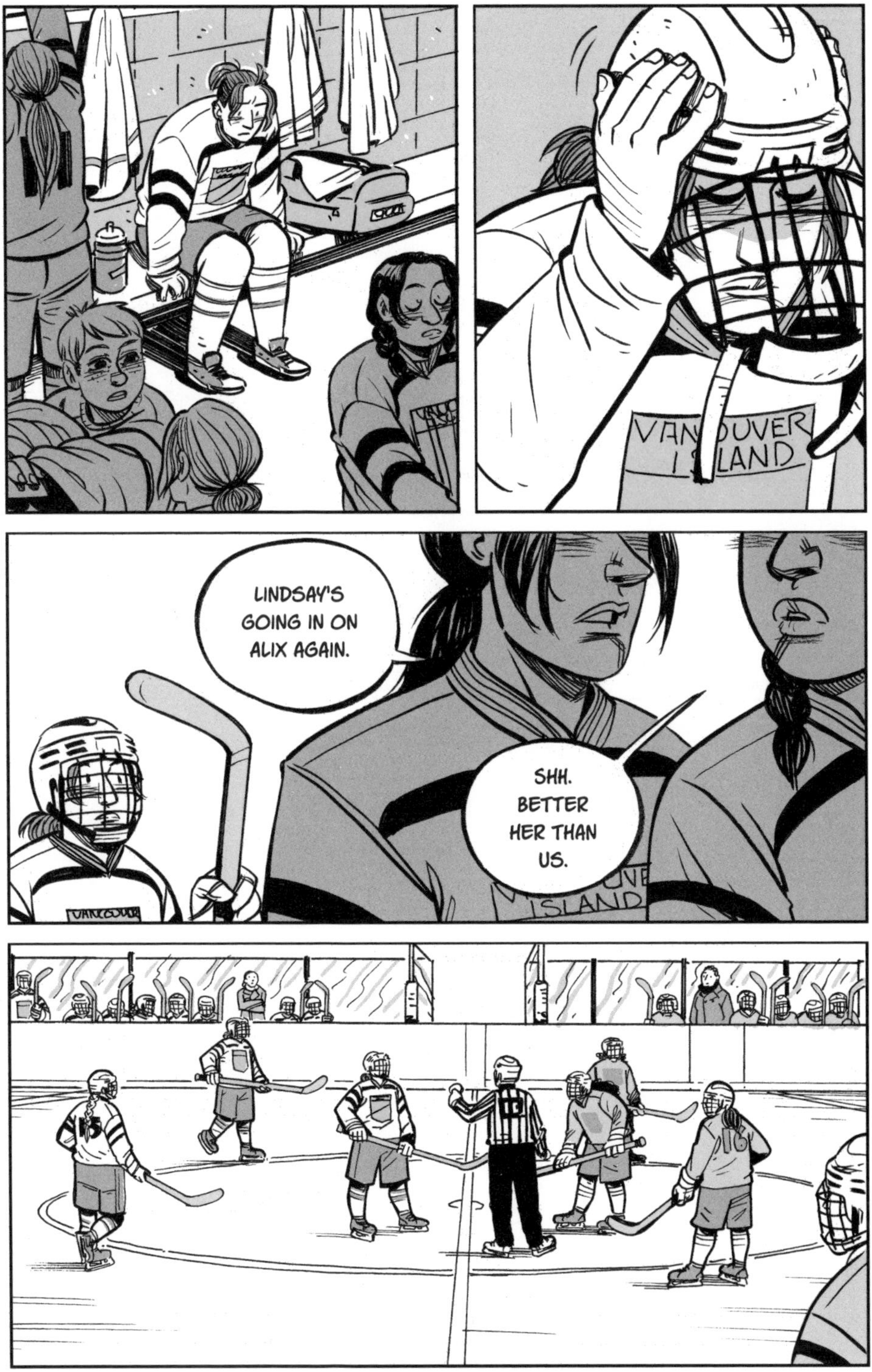
VANCOUVER ISLAND
LINDSAY'S GOING IN ON ALIX AGAIN.
SHH. BETTER HER THAN US.

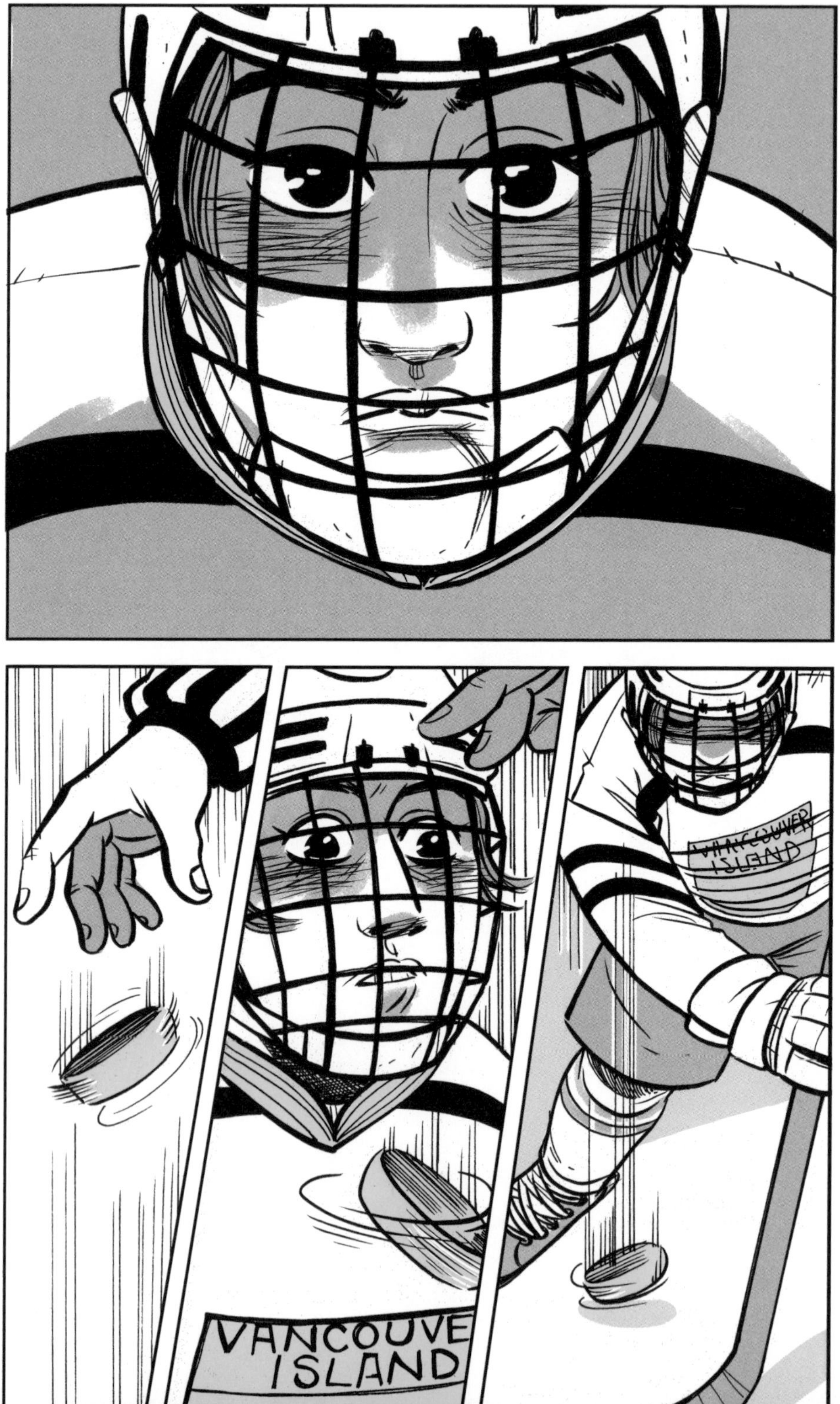
VANCOUVER
ISLAND
VANCOUVE
ISLAND

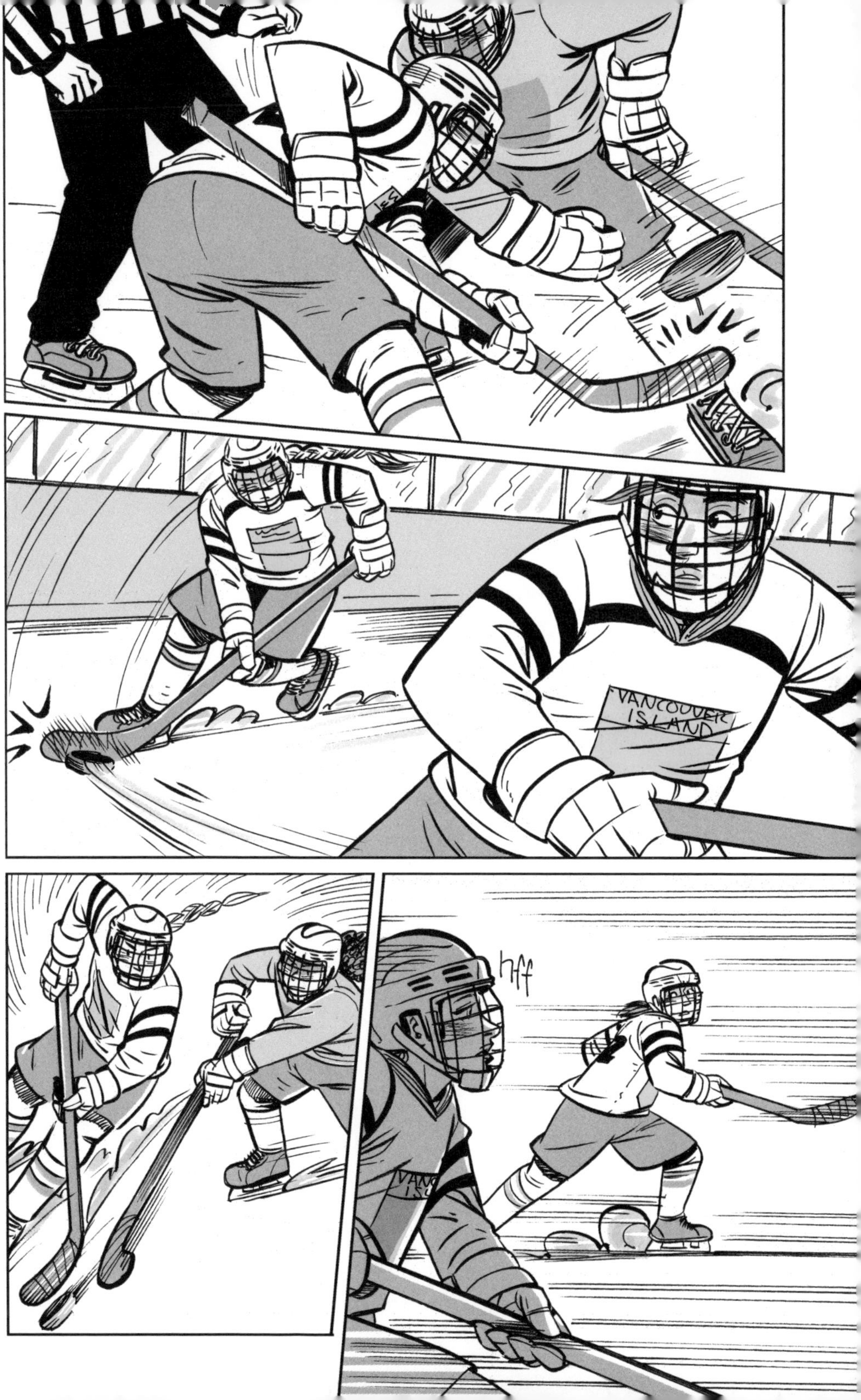
VANCOUVER ISLAND
hff

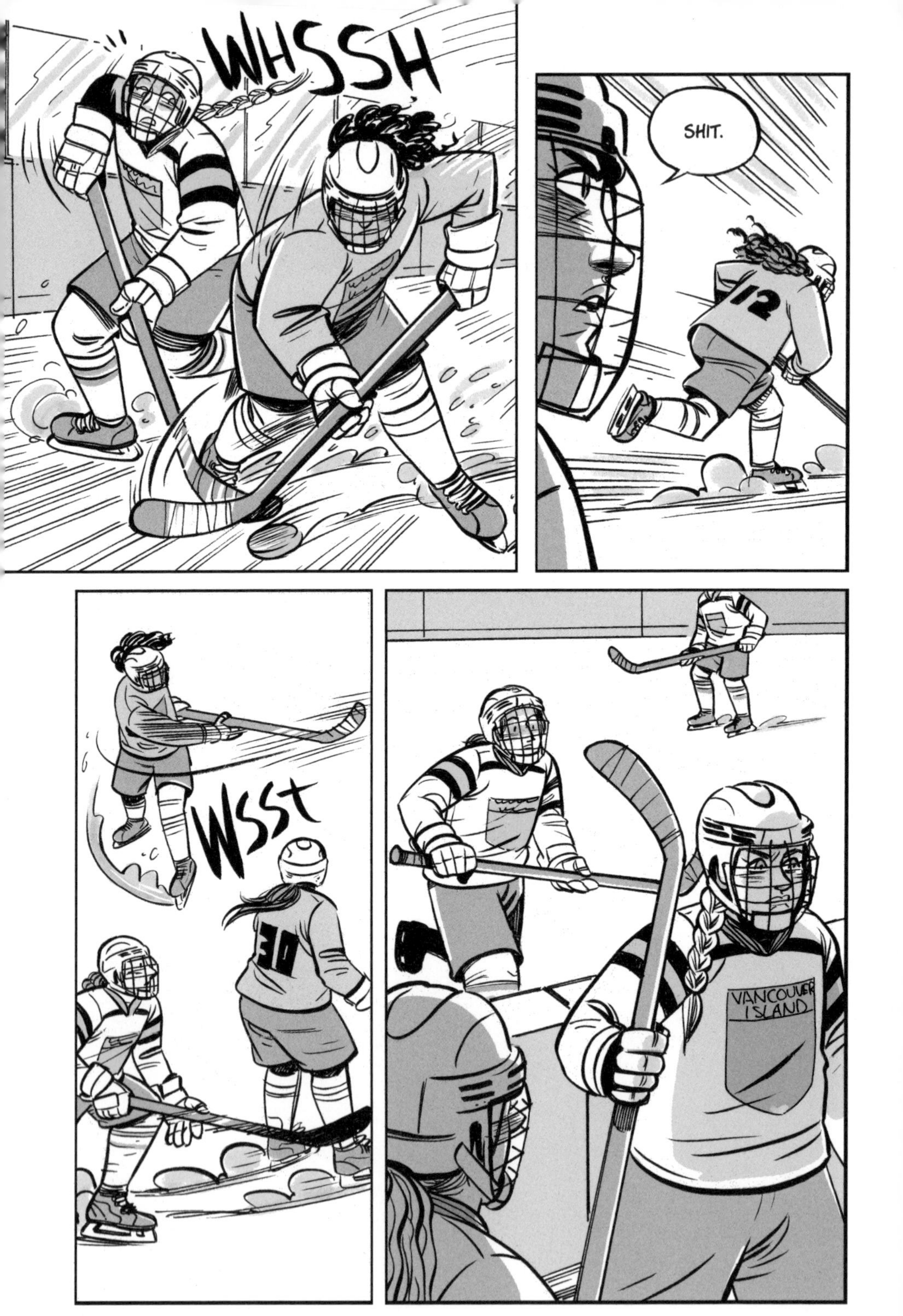
WHSSH
SHIT.
12
WSSt
30
VANCOUVER ISLAND

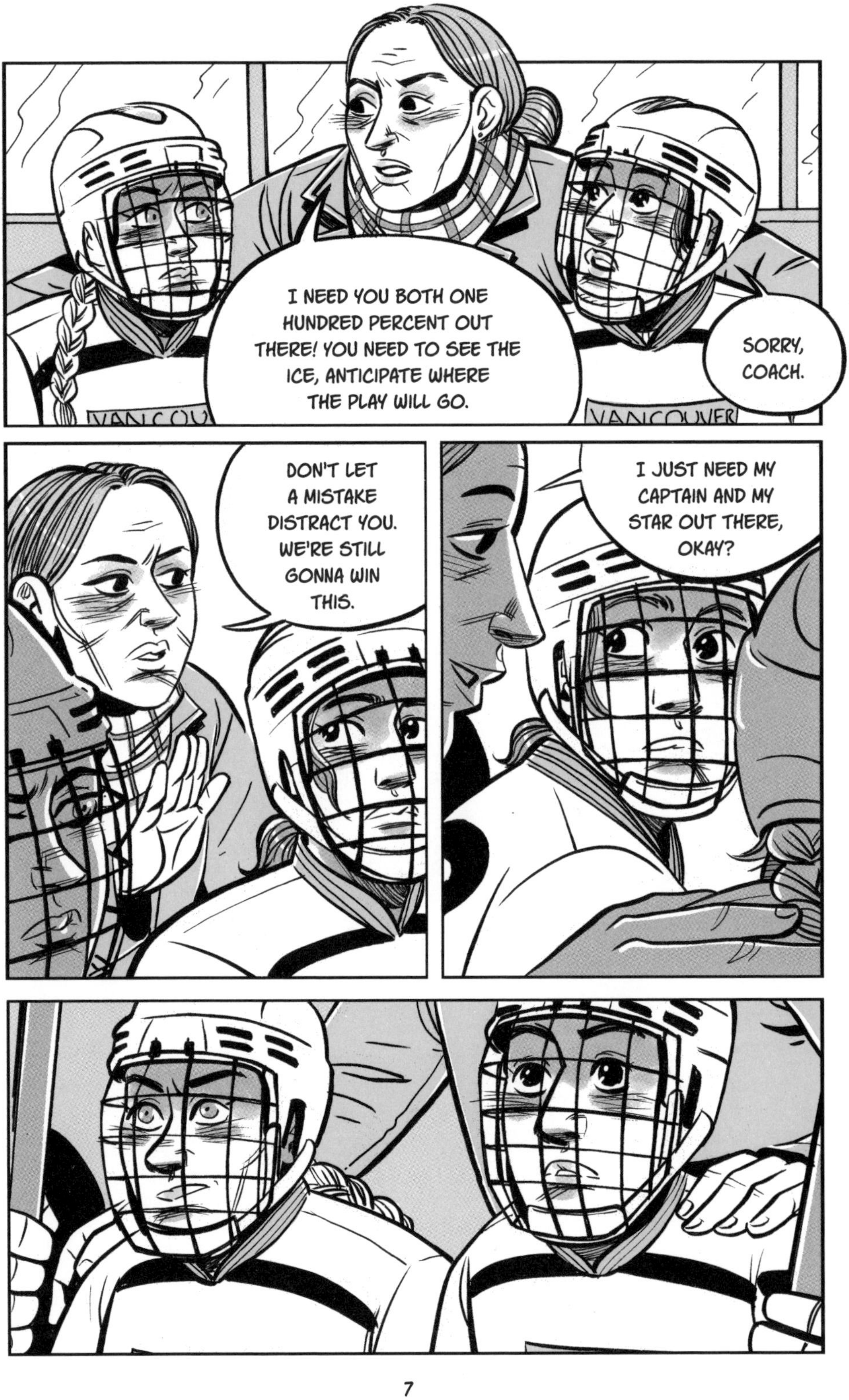
I NEED YOU BOTH ONE HUNDRED PERCENT OUT THERE! YOU NEED TO SEE THE ICE, ANTICIPATE WHERE THE PLAY WILL GO.
SORRY, COACH.
VANCOUVER
DON'T LET A MISTAKE DISTRACT YOU. WE'RE STILL GONNA WIN THIS.
I JUST NEED MY CAPTAIN AND MY STAR OUT THERE, OKAY?

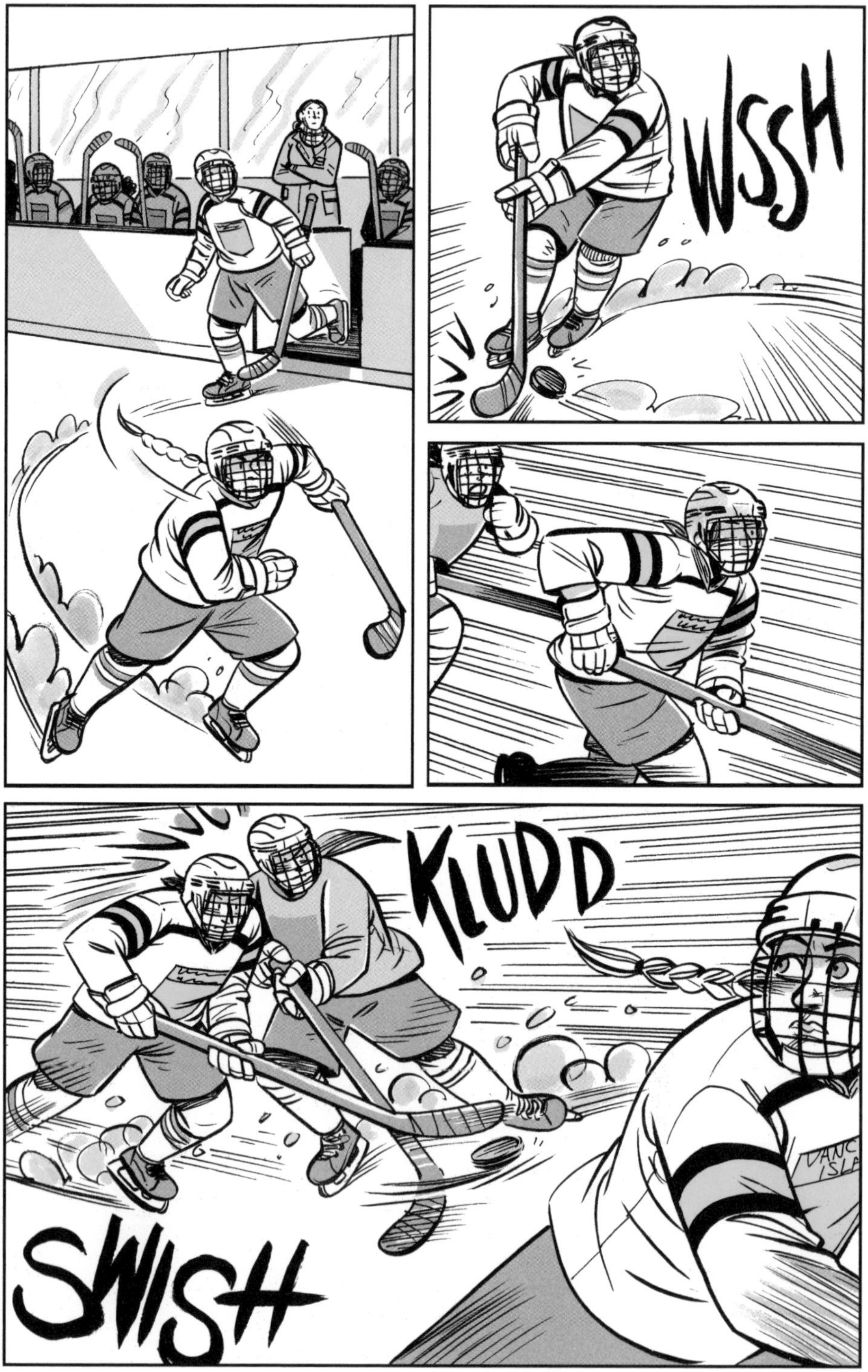
WSSH
KLUDD
SWISH
DANC
ISLA

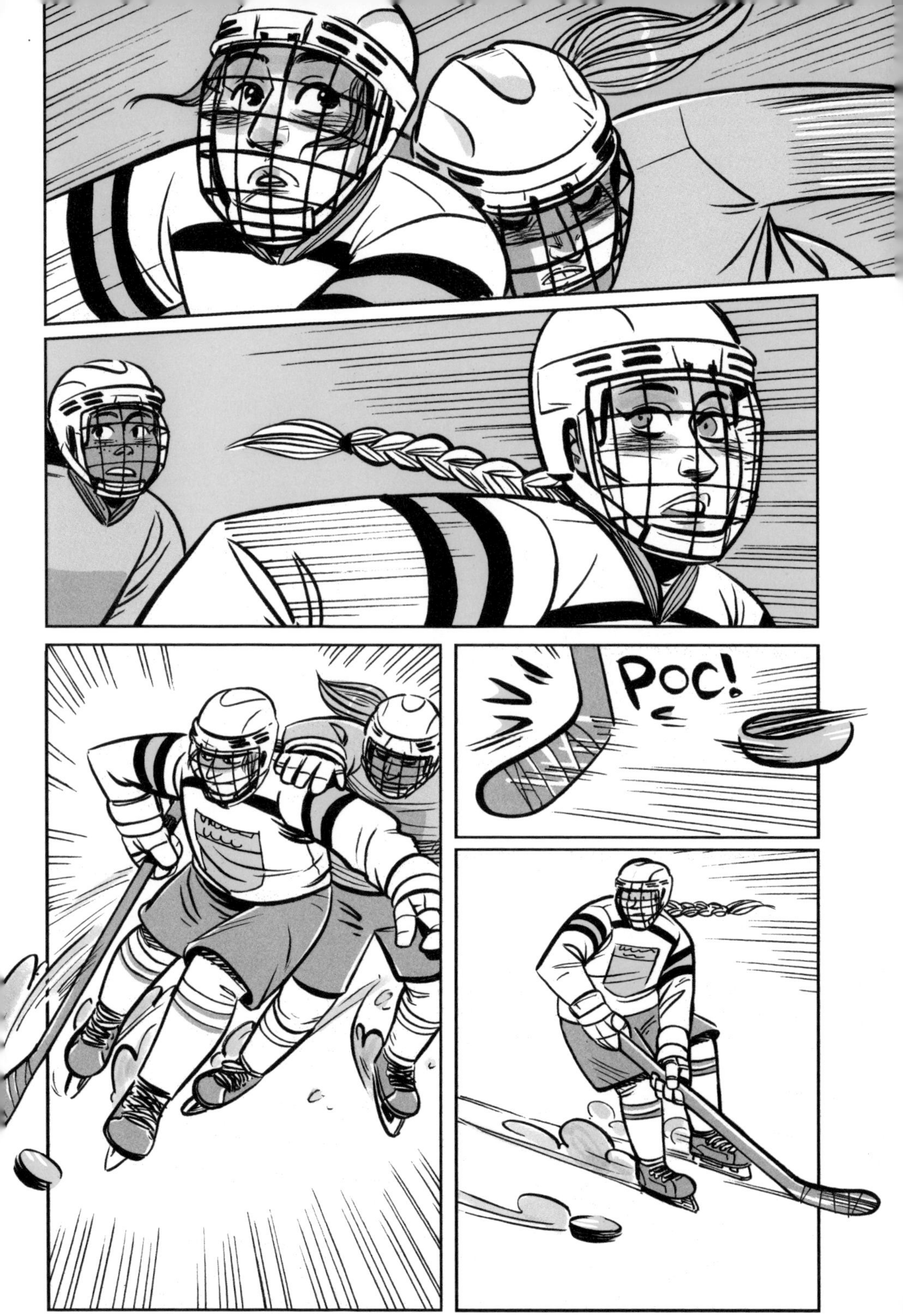
POC!

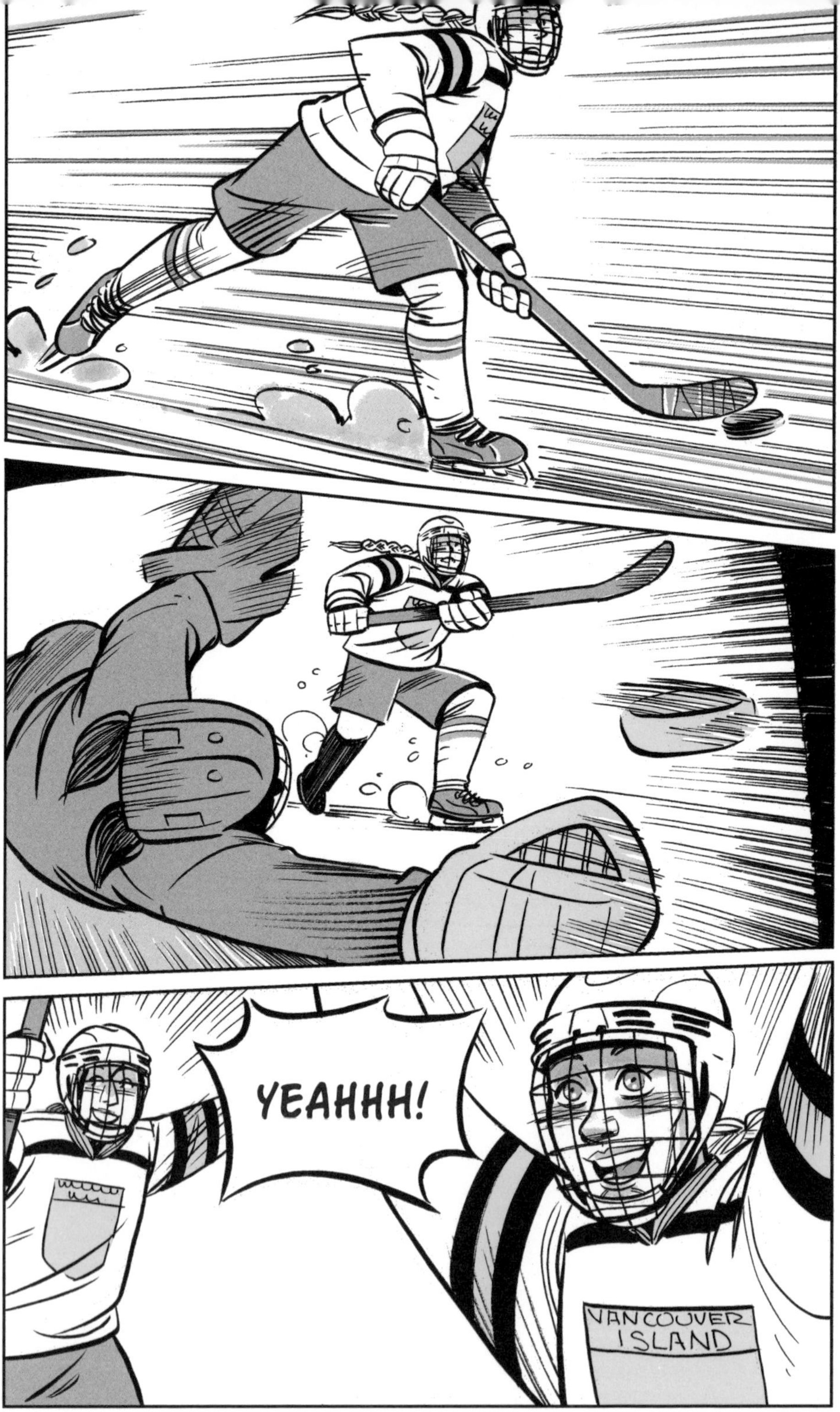
YEAHHH!
VANCOUVER ISLAND

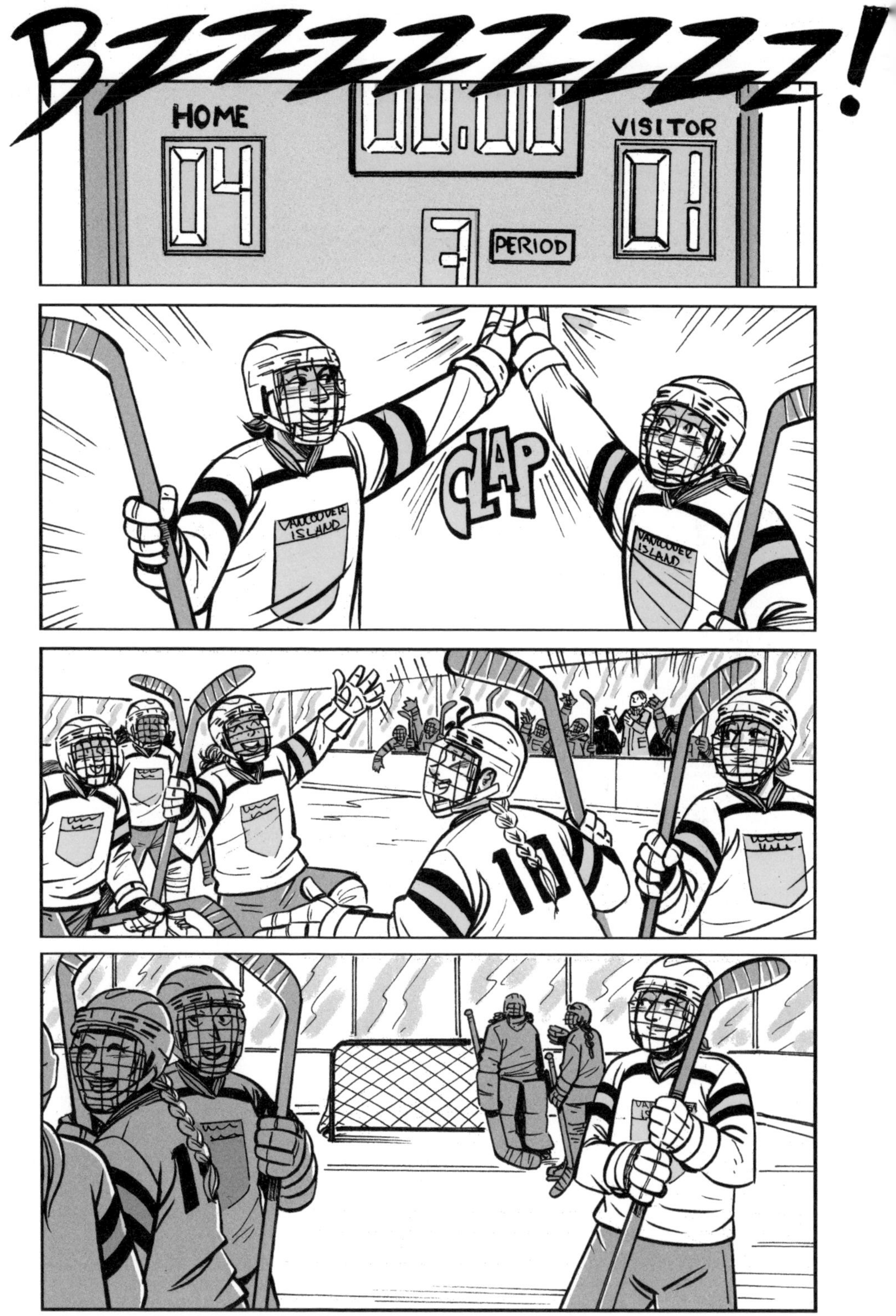
BZZZZZZZZZ!
HOME
04
00:00
VISITOR
01
3
PERIOD
CLAP
VANCOUVER ISLAND
VANCOUVER ISLAND
11

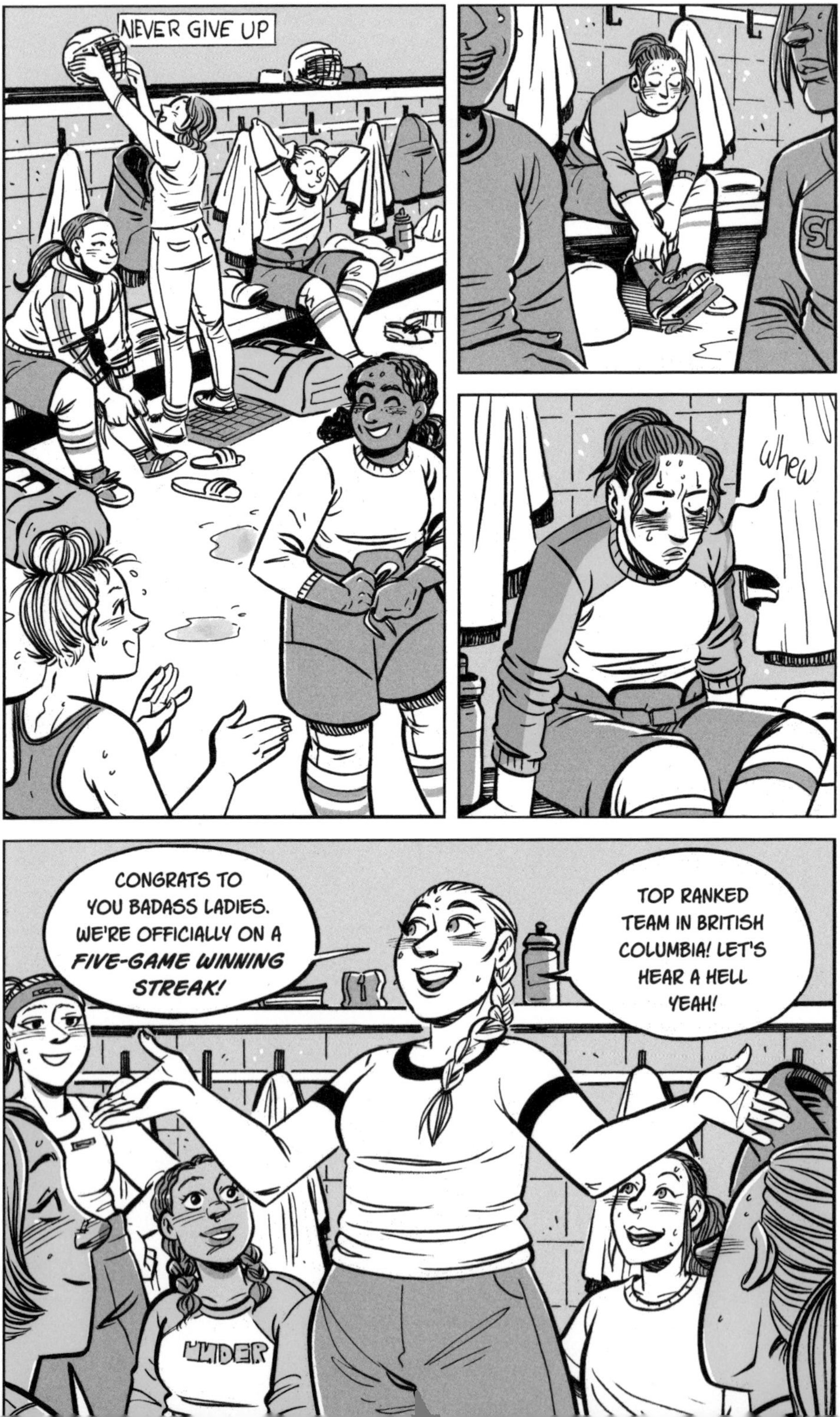

NEVER GIVE UP
Whew
CONGRATS TO YOU BADASS LADIES. WE'RE OFFICIALLY ON A *FIVE-GAME WINNING STREAK!*
TOP RANKED TEAM IN BRITISH COLUMBIA! LET'S HEAR A HELL YEAH!

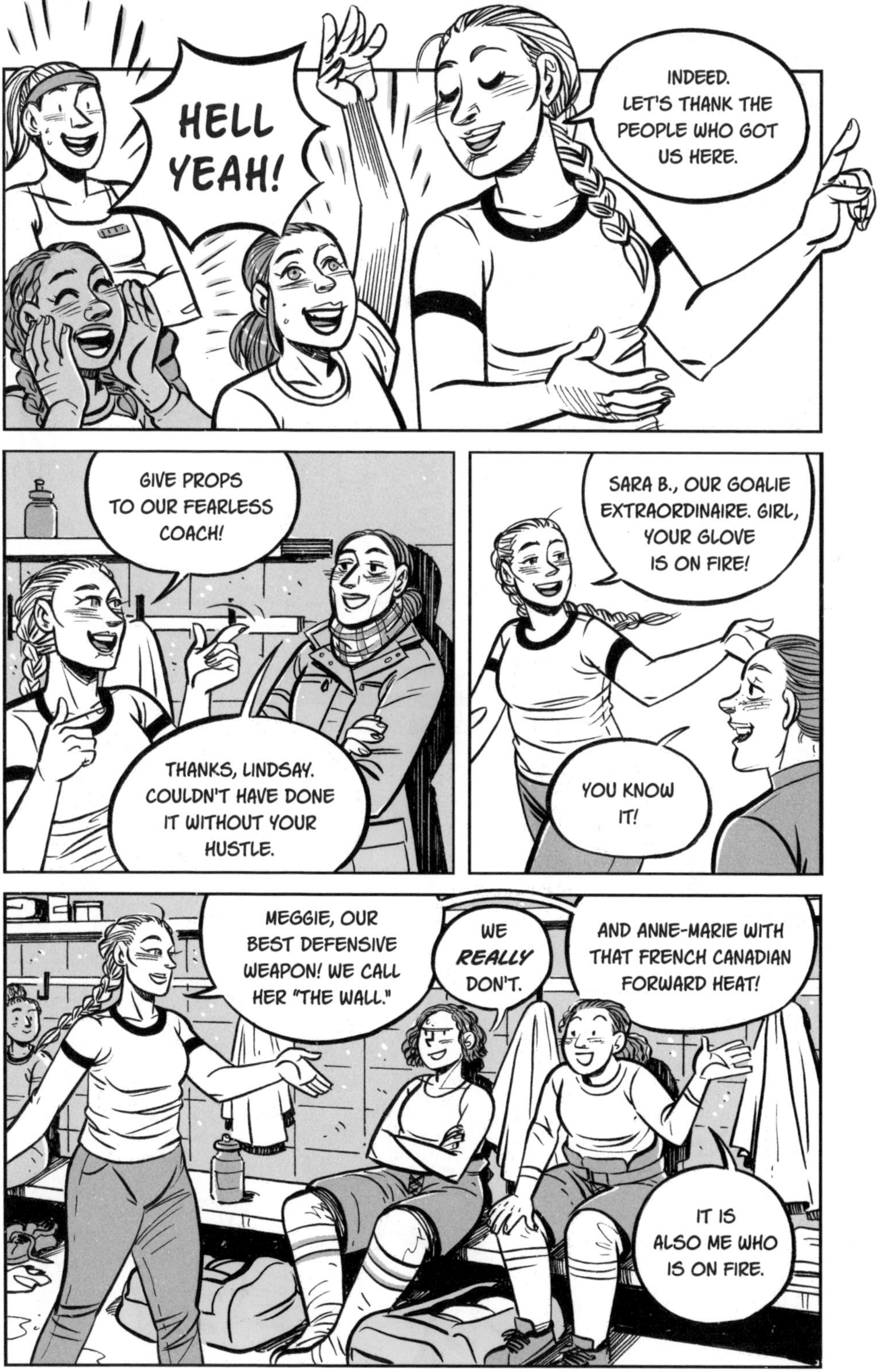
HELL YEAH!
INDEED. LET'S THANK THE PEOPLE WHO GOT US HERE.
GIVE PROPS TO OUR FEARLESS COACH!
THANKS, LINDSAY. COULDN'T HAVE DONE IT WITHOUT YOUR HUSTLE.
SARA B., OUR GOALIE EXTRAORDINAIRE. GIRL, YOUR GLOVE IS ON FIRE!
YOU KNOW IT!
MEGGIE, OUR BEST DEFENSIVE WEAPON! WE CALL HER "THE WALL."
WE *REALLY* DON'T.
AND ANNE-MARIE WITH THAT FRENCH CANADIAN FORWARD HEAT!
IT IS ALSO ME WHO IS ON FIRE.

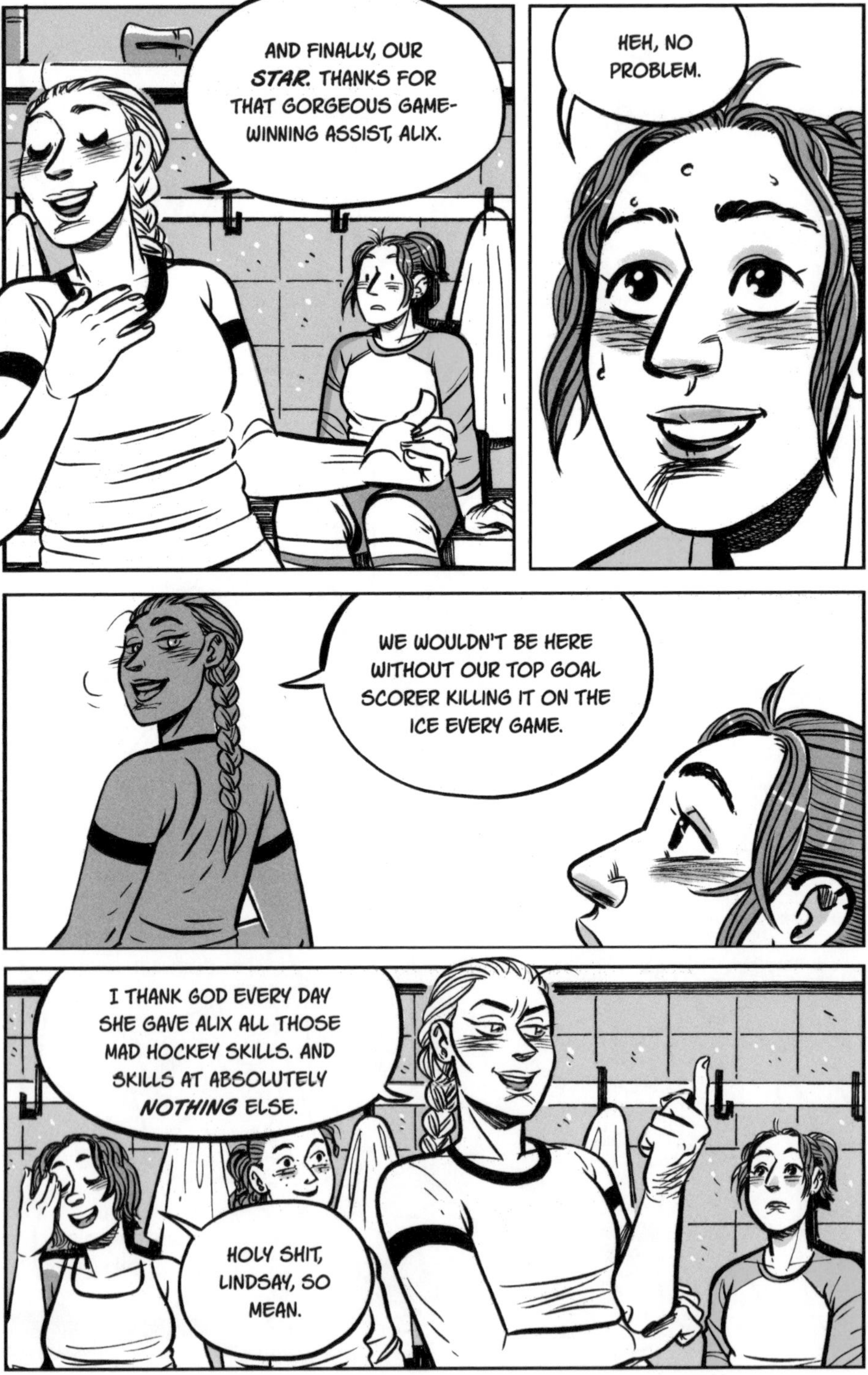
AND FINALLY, OUR *STAR.* THANKS FOR THAT GORGEOUS GAME-WINNING ASSIST, ALIX.
HEH, NO PROBLEM.
WE WOULDN'T BE HERE WITHOUT OUR TOP GOAL SCORER KILLING IT ON THE ICE EVERY GAME.
I THANK GOD EVERY DAY SHE GAVE ALIX ALL THOSE MAD HOCKEY SKILLS. AND SKILLS AT ABSOLUTELY *NOTHING* ELSE.
HOLY SHIT, LINDSAY, SO MEAN.

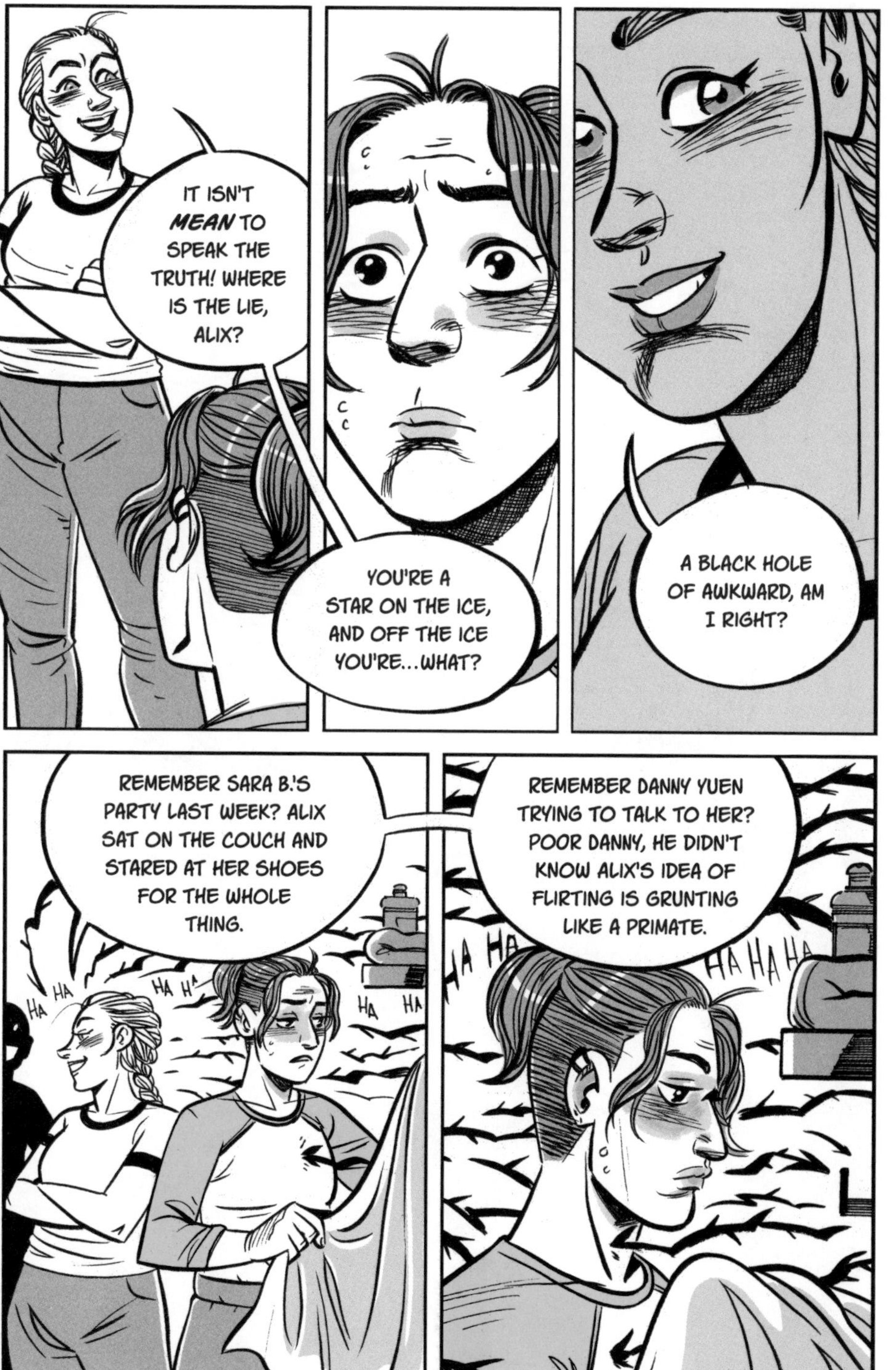
IT ISN'T *MEAN* TO SPEAK THE TRUTH! WHERE IS THE LIE, ALIX?
YOU'RE A STAR ON THE ICE, AND OFF THE ICE YOU'RE...WHAT?
A BLACK HOLE OF AWKWARD, AM I RIGHT?
REMEMBER SARA B.'S PARTY LAST WEEK? ALIX SAT ON THE COUCH AND STARED AT HER SHOES FOR THE WHOLE THING.
HA HA
HA HA
HA
HA
REMEMBER DANNY YUEN TRYING TO TALK TO HER? POOR DANNY, HE DIDN'T KNOW ALIX'S IDEA OF FLIRTING IS GRUNTING LIKE A PRIMATE.
HA HA
HA HA HA

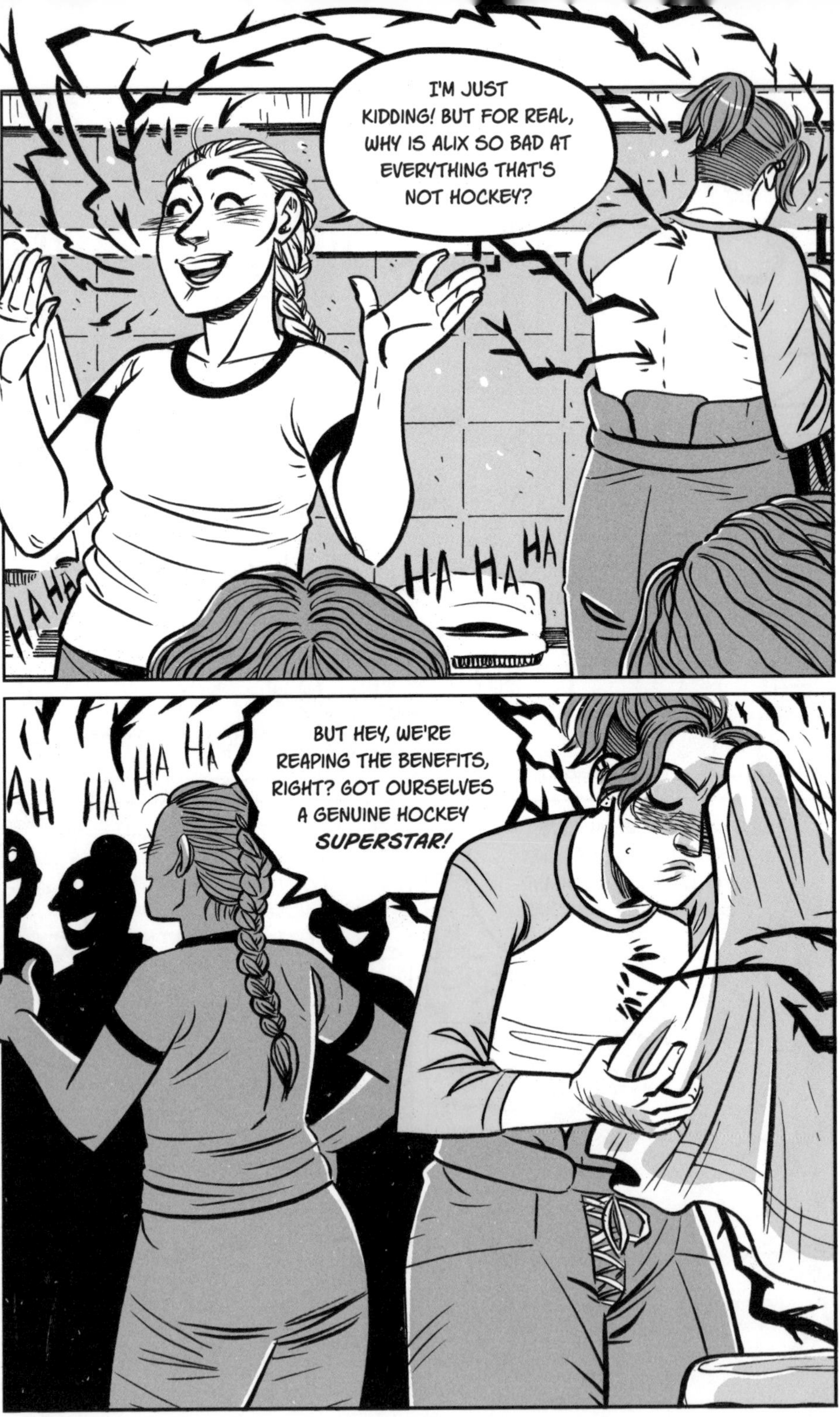
I'M JUST KIDDING! BUT FOR REAL, WHY IS ALIX SO BAD AT EVERYTHING THAT'S NOT HOCKEY?
HA HA HA
HA HA HA
AH HA HA HA
BUT HEY, WE'RE REAPING THE BENEFITS, RIGHT? GOT OURSELVES A GENUINE HOCKEY *SUPERSTAR!*

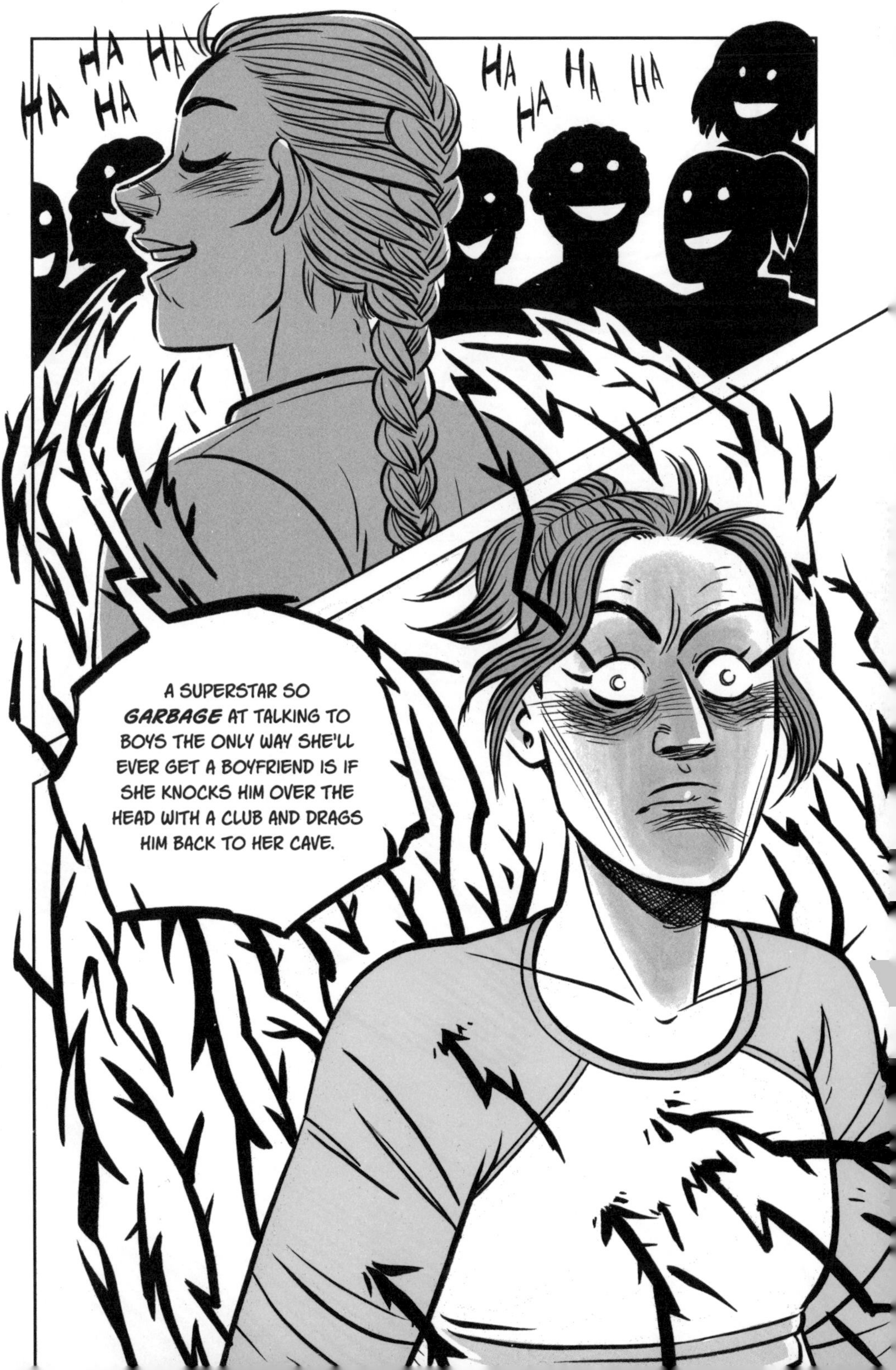
HA HA HA HA HA
HA HA HA HA
A SUPERSTAR SO *GARBAGE* AT TALKING TO BOYS THE ONLY WAY SHE'LL EVER GET A BOYFRIEND IS IF SHE KNOCKS HIM OVER THE HEAD WITH A CLUB AND DRAGS HIM BACK TO HER CAVE.

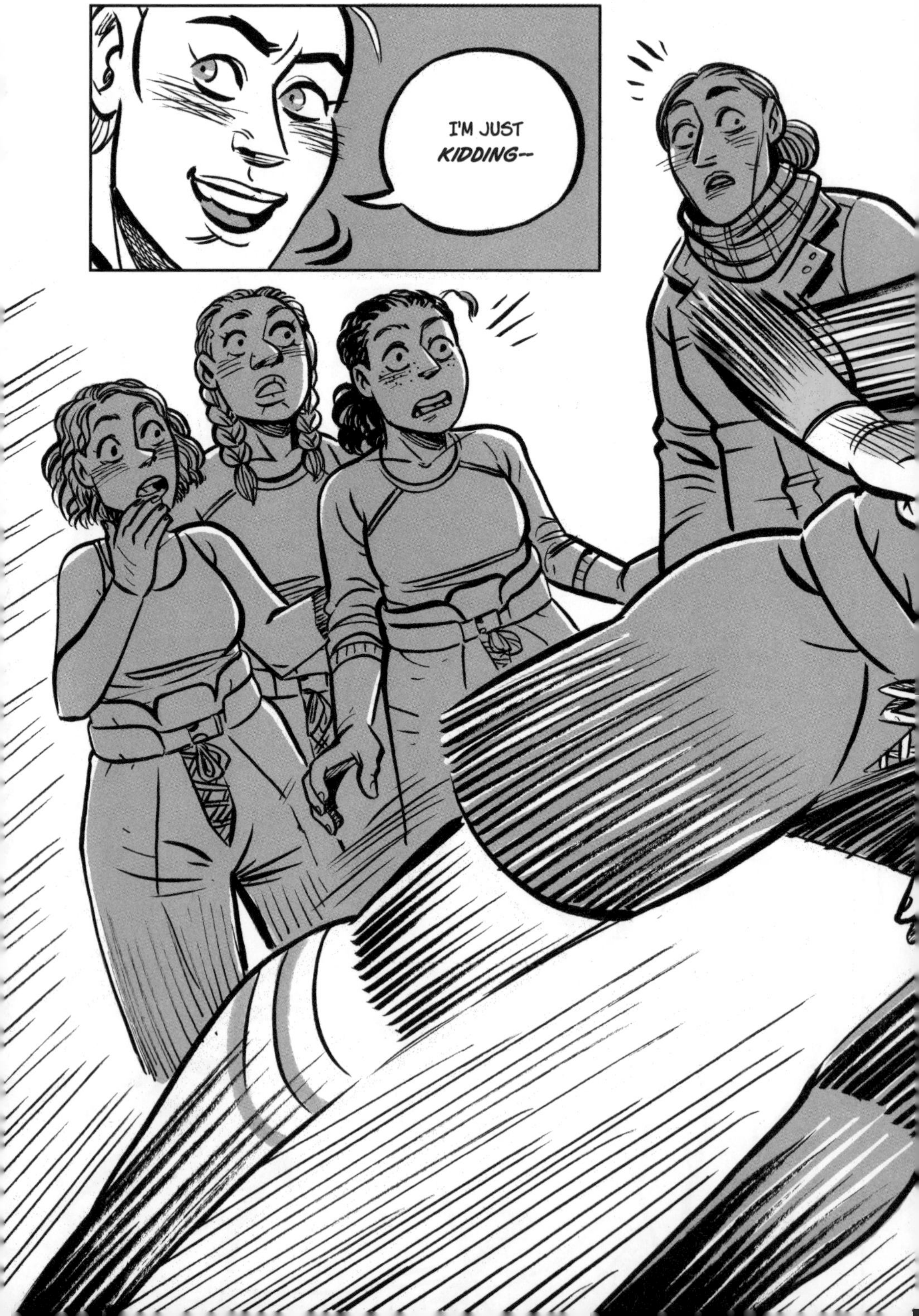
I'M JUST *KIDDING--*

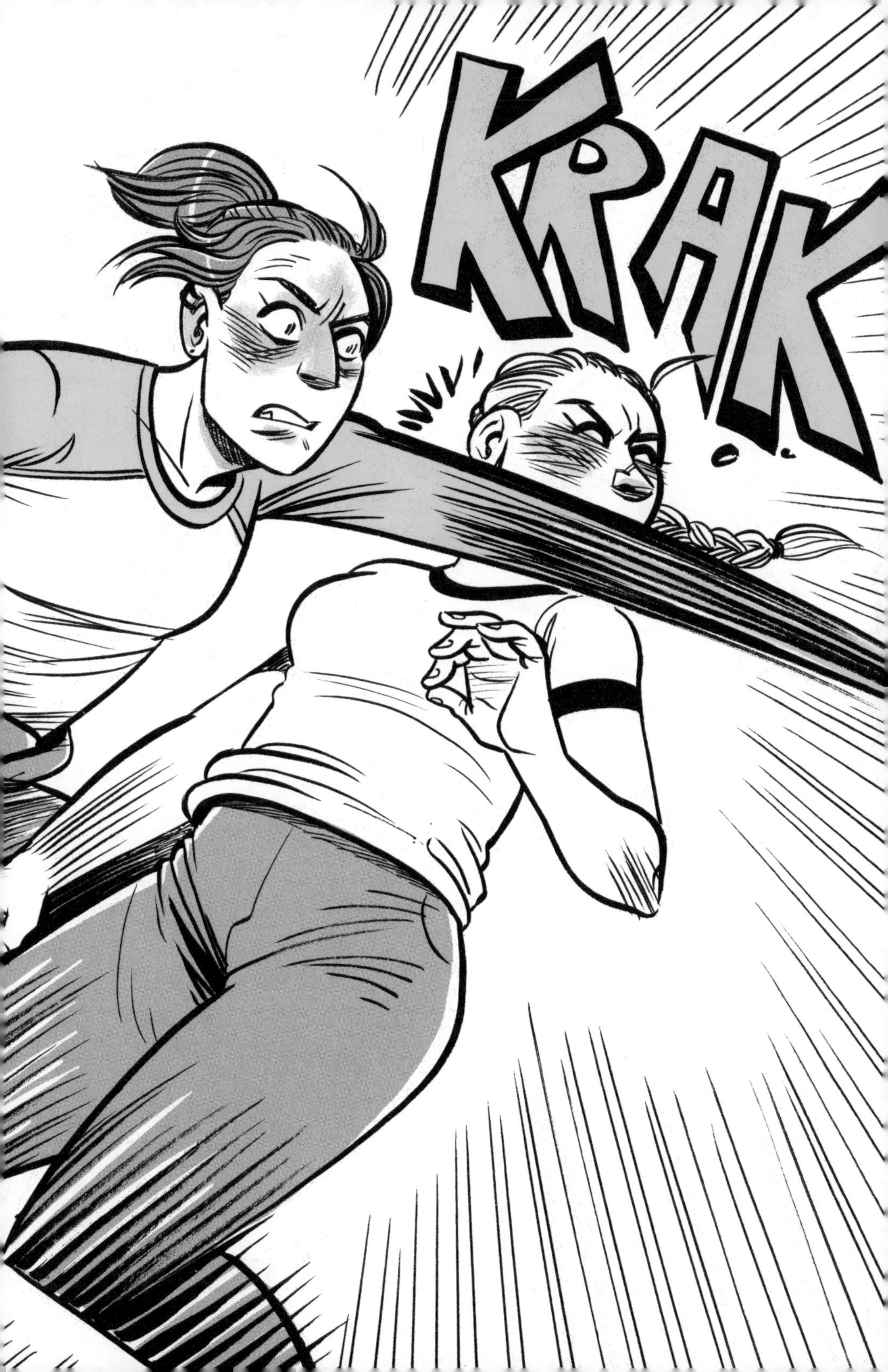
KRAK

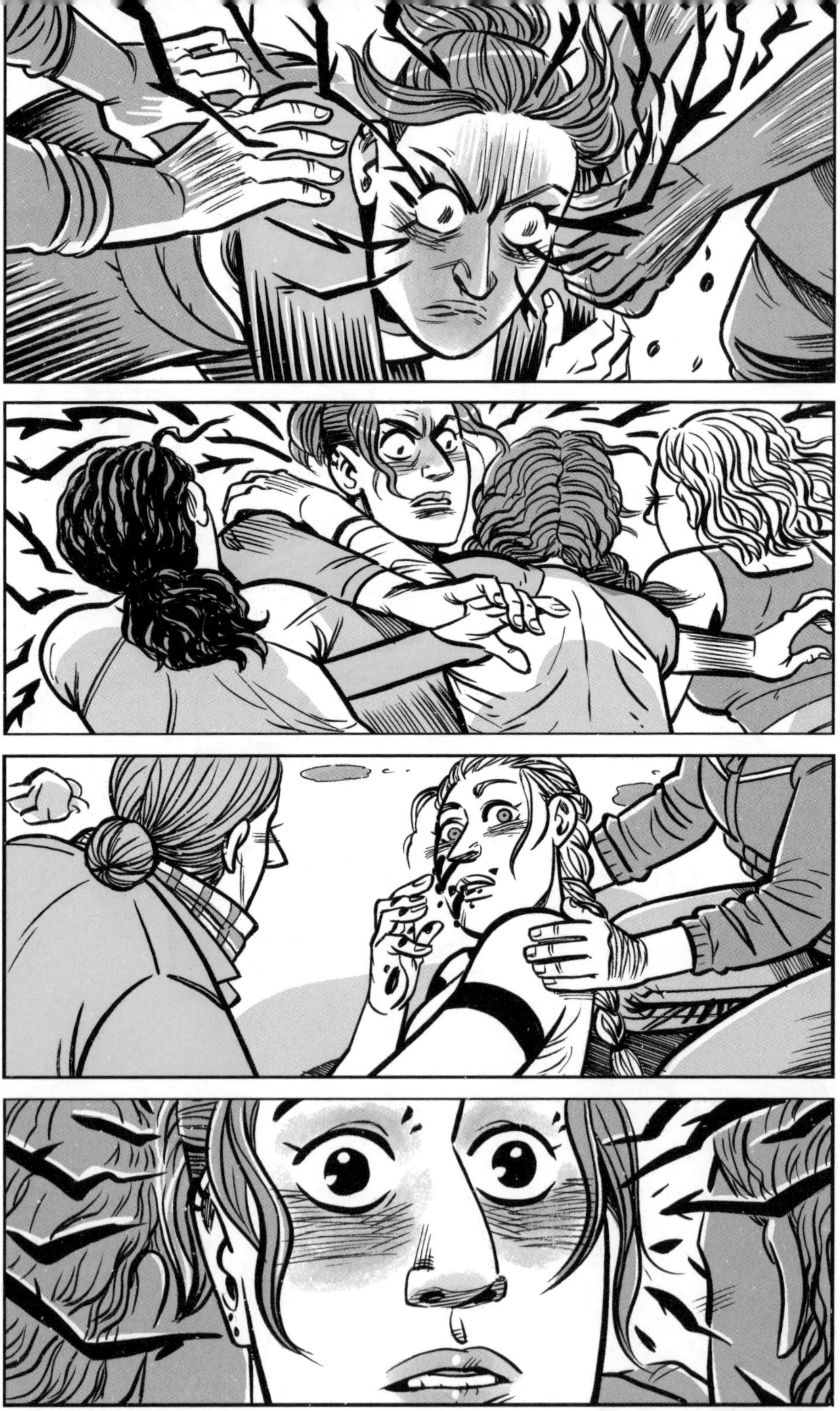

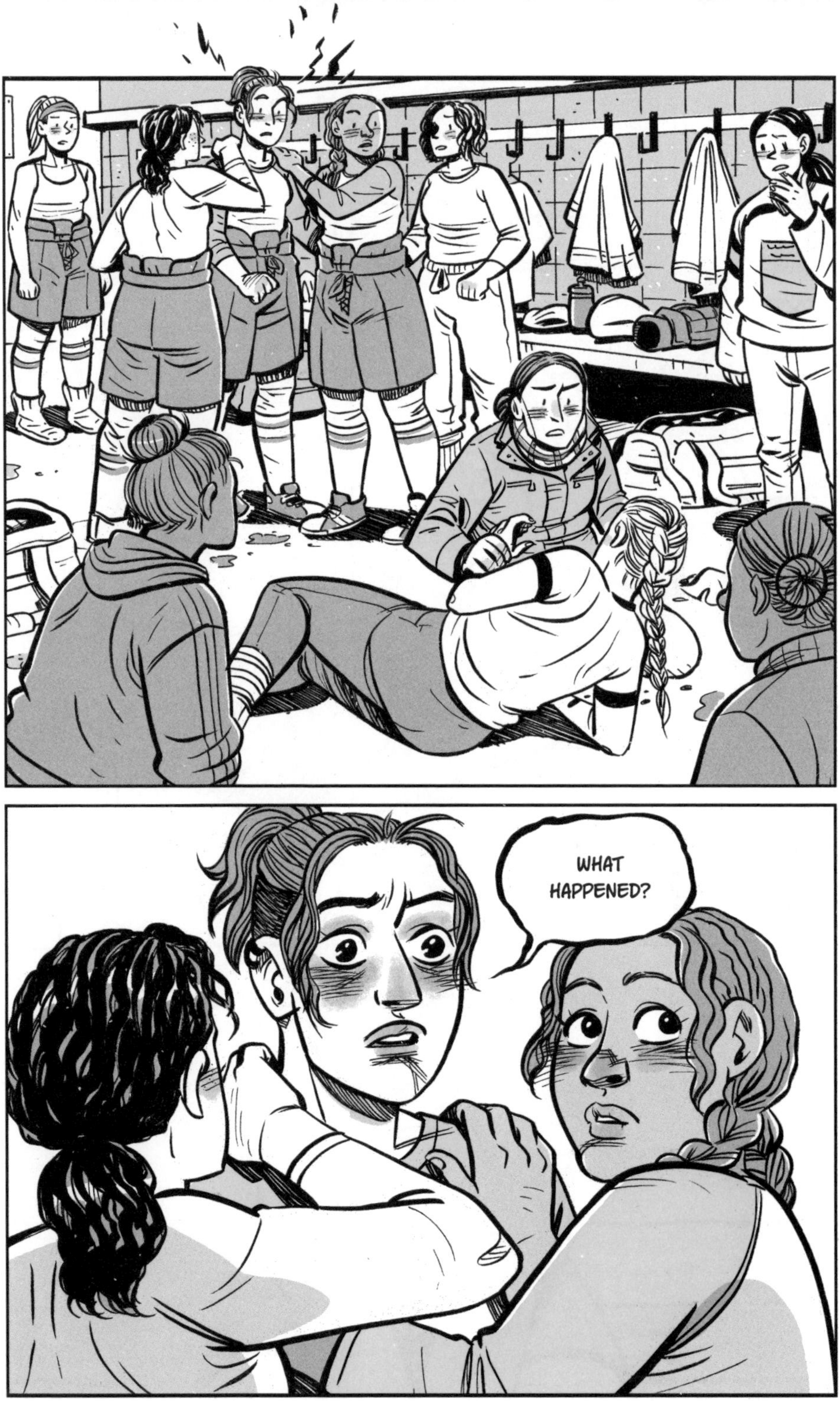
WHAT HAPPENED?

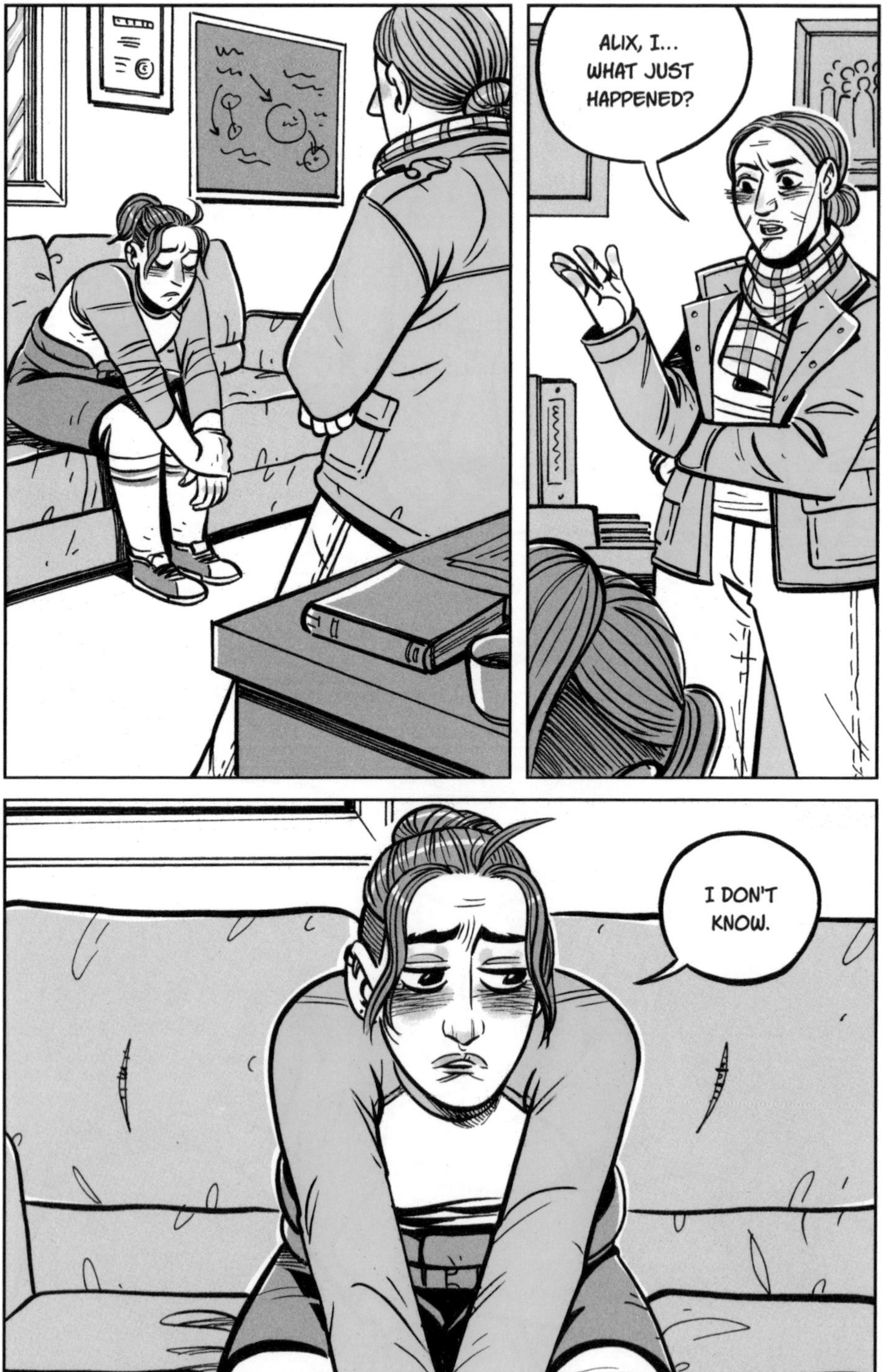
ALIX, I...
WHAT JUST
HAPPENED?
I DON'T
KNOW.

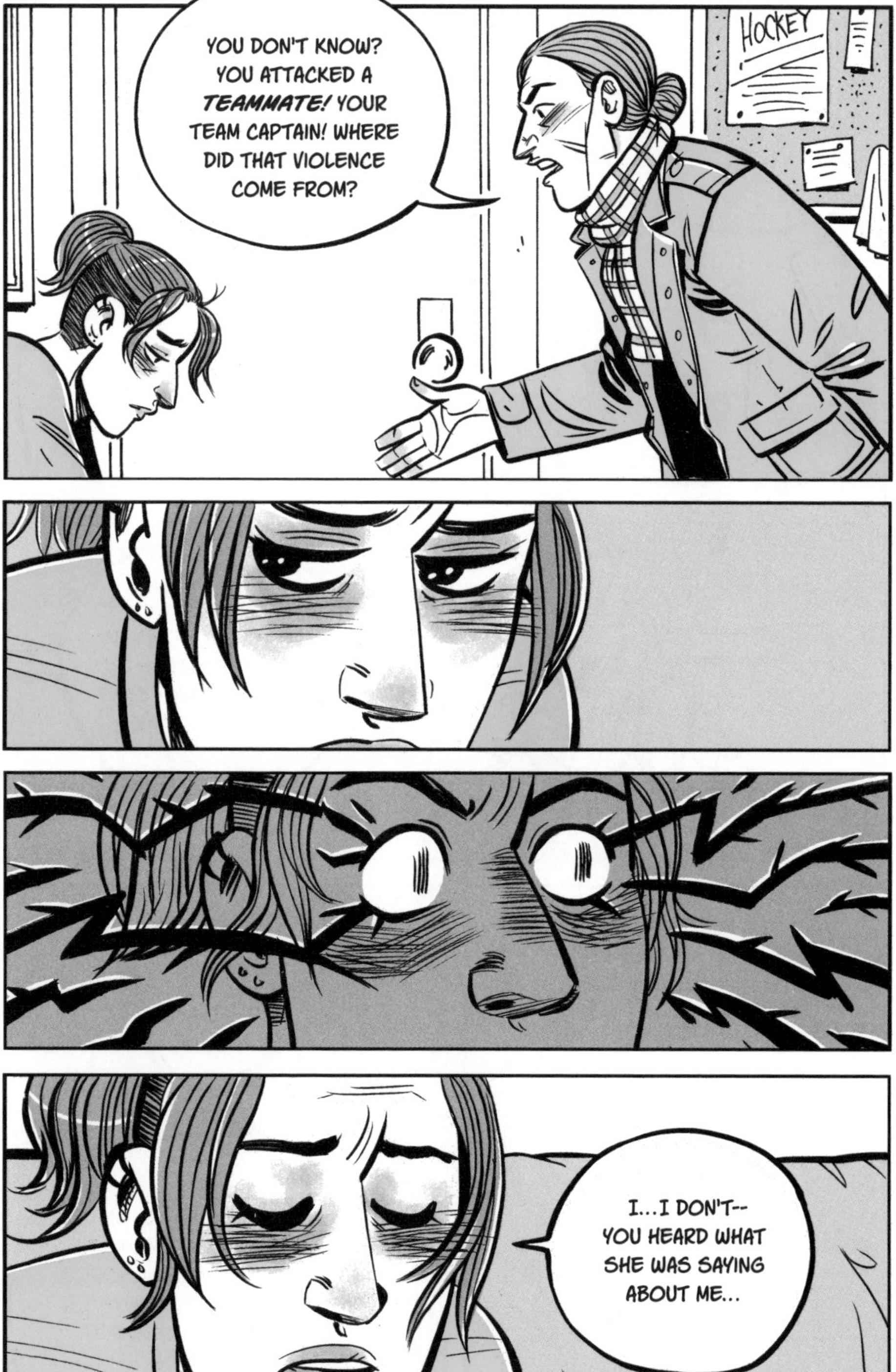
HOCKEY
YOU DON'T KNOW? YOU ATTACKED A *TEAMMATE!* YOUR TEAM CAPTAIN! WHERE DID THAT VIOLENCE COME FROM?
I...I DON'T-- YOU HEARD WHAT SHE WAS SAYING ABOUT ME...

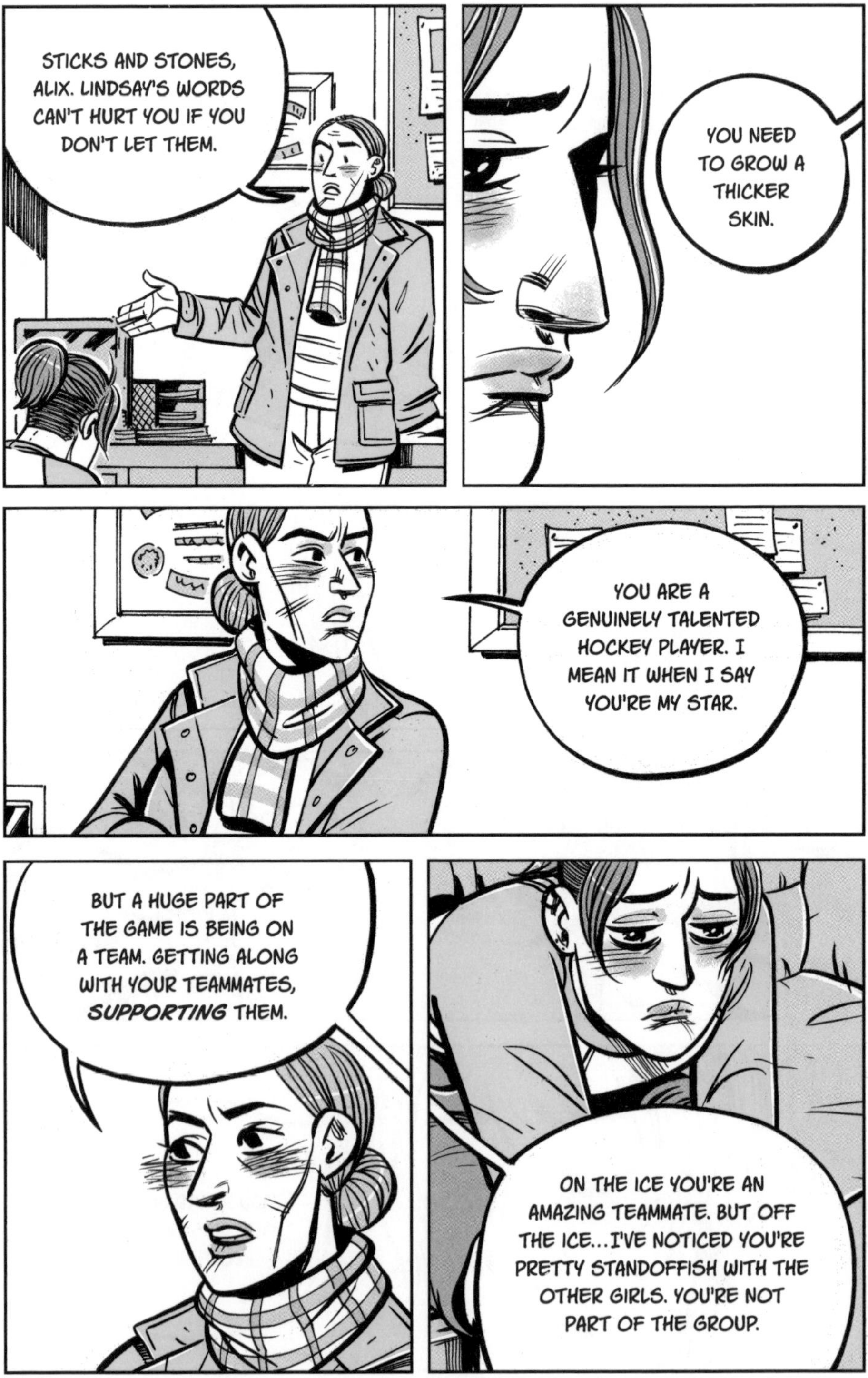
STICKS AND STONES, ALIX. LINDSAY'S WORDS CAN'T HURT YOU IF YOU DON'T LET THEM.
YOU NEED TO GROW A THICKER SKIN.
YOU ARE A GENUINELY TALENTED HOCKEY PLAYER. I MEAN IT WHEN I SAY YOU'RE MY STAR.
BUT A HUGE PART OF THE GAME IS BEING ON A TEAM. GETTING ALONG WITH YOUR TEAMMATES, *SUPPORTING* THEM.
ON THE ICE YOU'RE AN AMAZING TEAMMATE. BUT OFF THE ICE...I'VE NOTICED YOU'RE PRETTY STANDOFFISH WITH THE OTHER GIRLS. YOU'RE NOT PART OF THE GROUP.

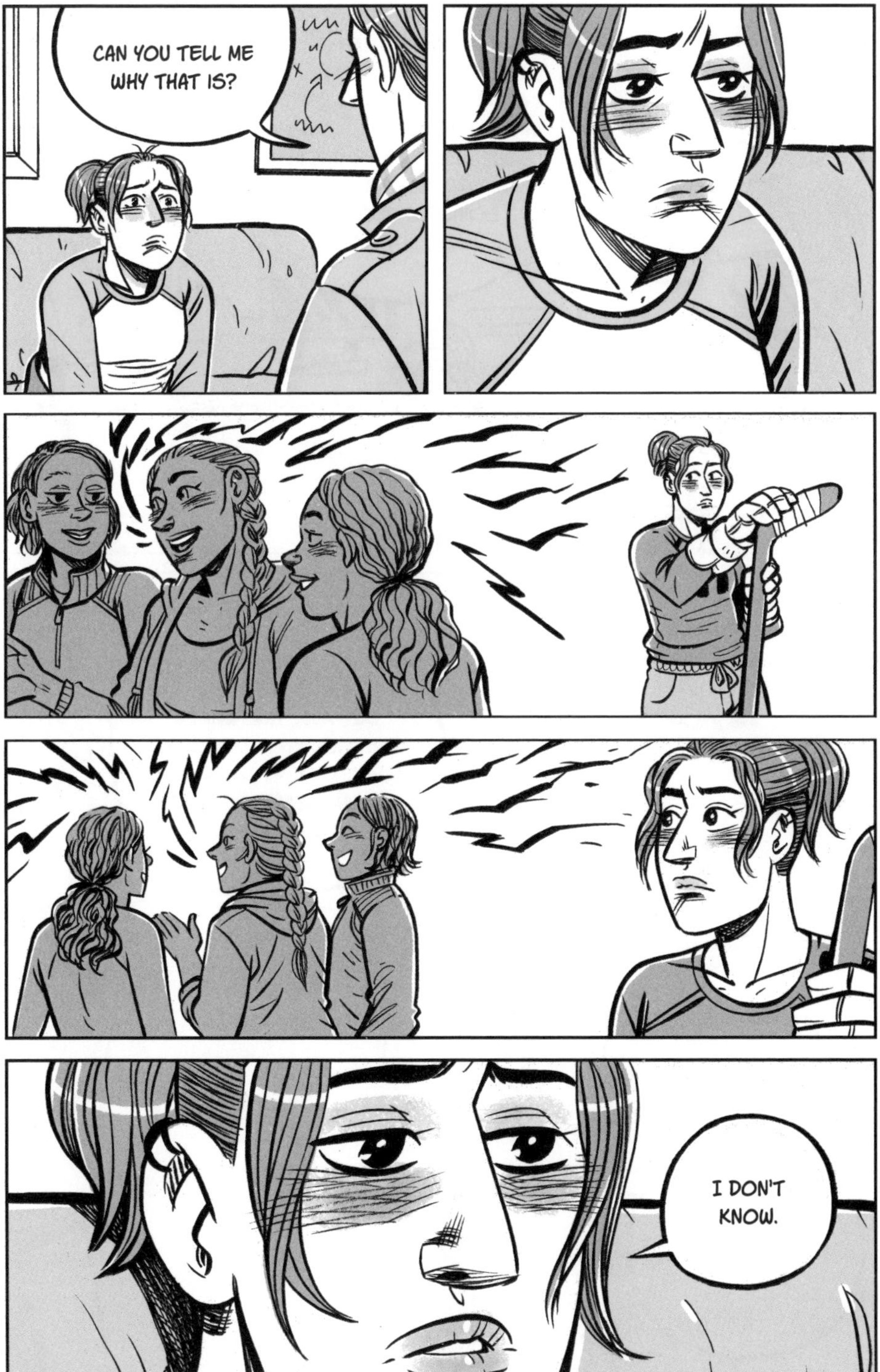
CAN YOU TELL ME WHY THAT IS?
I DON'T KNOW.

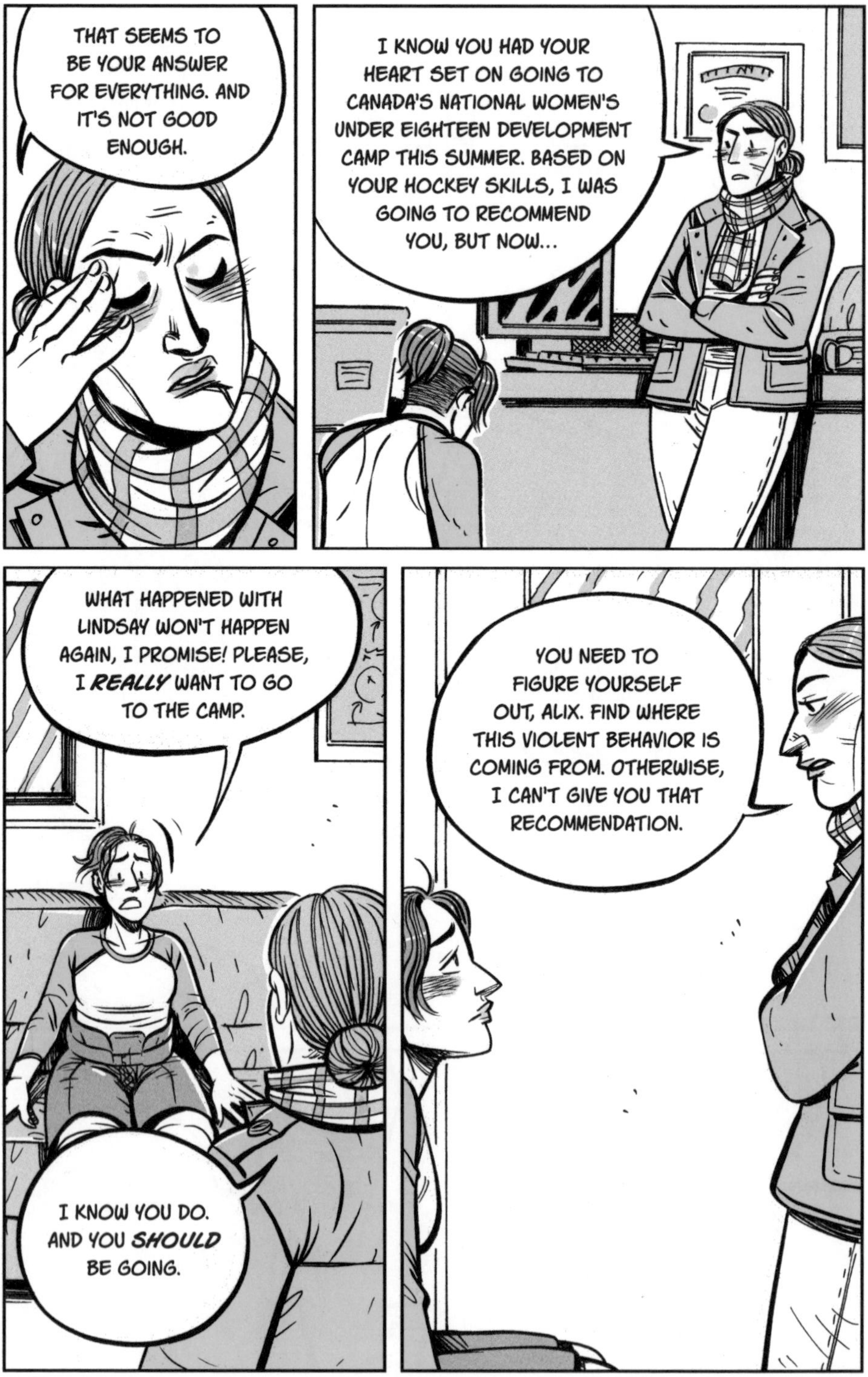
THAT SEEMS TO BE YOUR ANSWER FOR EVERYTHING. AND IT'S NOT GOOD ENOUGH.
I KNOW YOU HAD YOUR HEART SET ON GOING TO CANADA'S NATIONAL WOMEN'S UNDER EIGHTEEN DEVELOPMENT CAMP THIS SUMMER. BASED ON YOUR HOCKEY SKILLS, I WAS GOING TO RECOMMEND YOU, BUT NOW...
WHAT HAPPENED WITH LINDSAY WON'T HAPPEN AGAIN, I PROMISE! PLEASE, I *REALLY* WANT TO GO TO THE CAMP.
I KNOW YOU DO. AND YOU *SHOULD* BE GOING.
YOU NEED TO FIGURE YOURSELF OUT, ALIX. FIND WHERE THIS VIOLENT BEHAVIOR IS COMING FROM. OTHERWISE, I CAN'T GIVE YOU THAT RECOMMENDATION.

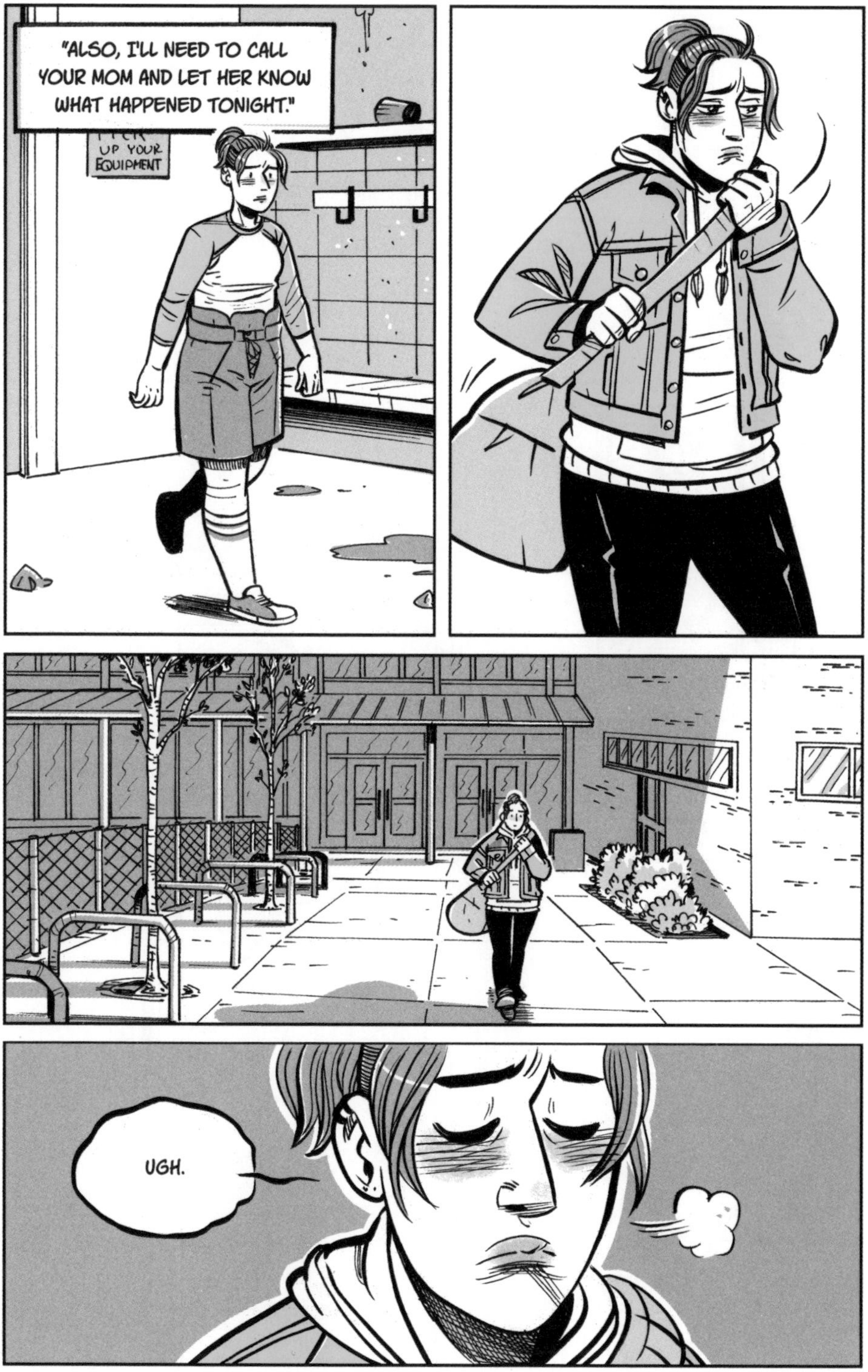
"ALSO, I'LL NEED TO CALL YOUR MOM AND LET HER KNOW WHAT HAPPENED TONIGHT."
UP YOUR EQUIPMENT
UGH.

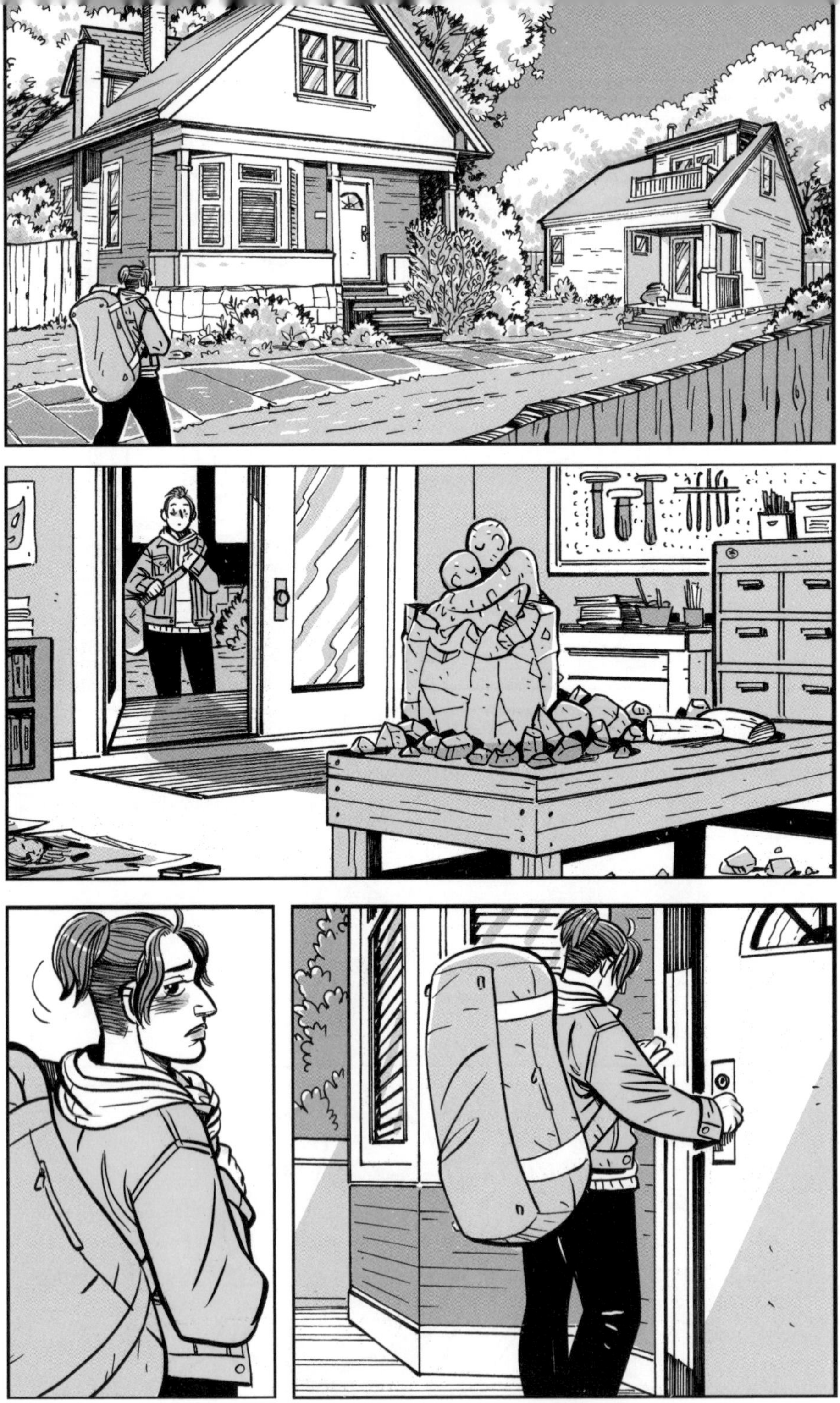

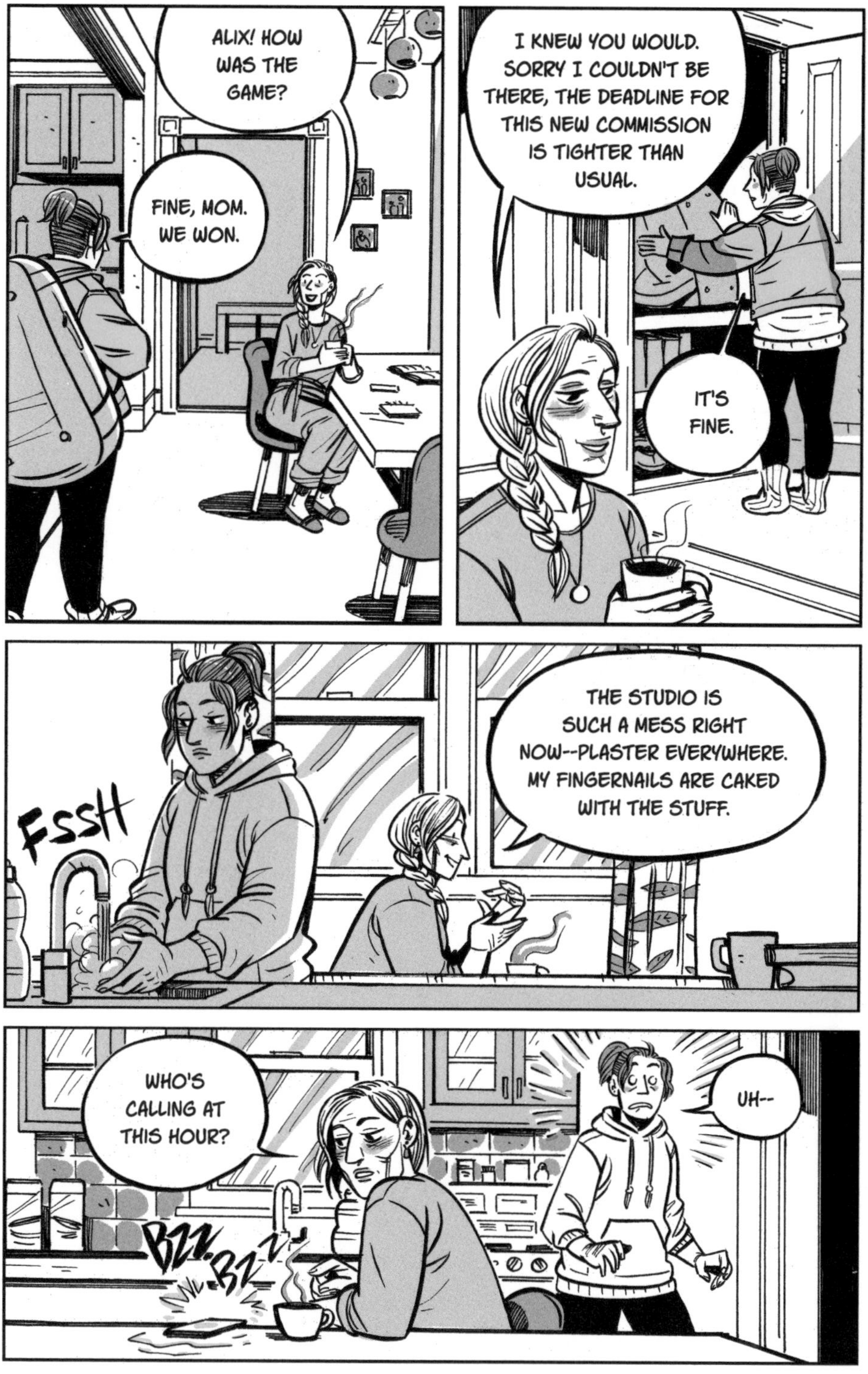
ALIX! HOW WAS THE GAME?
FINE, MOM. WE WON.
I KNEW YOU WOULD. SORRY I COULDN'T BE THERE, THE DEADLINE FOR THIS NEW COMMISSION IS TIGHTER THAN USUAL.
IT'S FINE.
FSSH
THE STUDIO IS SUCH A MESS RIGHT NOW--PLASTER EVERYWHERE. MY FINGERNAILS ARE CAKED WITH THE STUFF.
WHO'S CALLING AT THIS HOUR?
UH--
BZZ BZZ

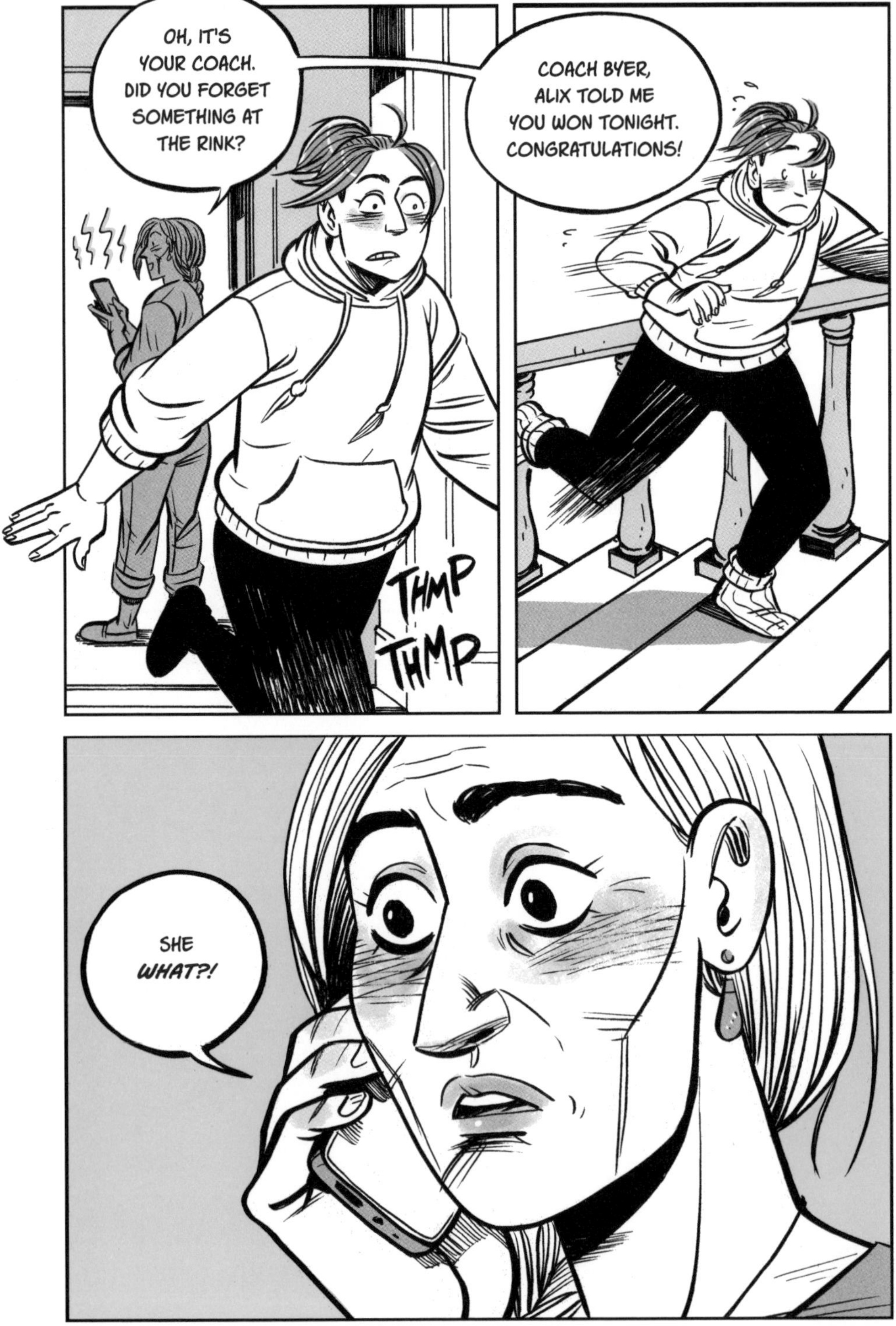
OH, IT'S YOUR COACH. DID YOU FORGET SOMETHING AT THE RINK?
COACH BYER, ALIX TOLD ME YOU WON TONIGHT. CONGRATULATIONS!
THMP THMP
SHE *WHAT?!*

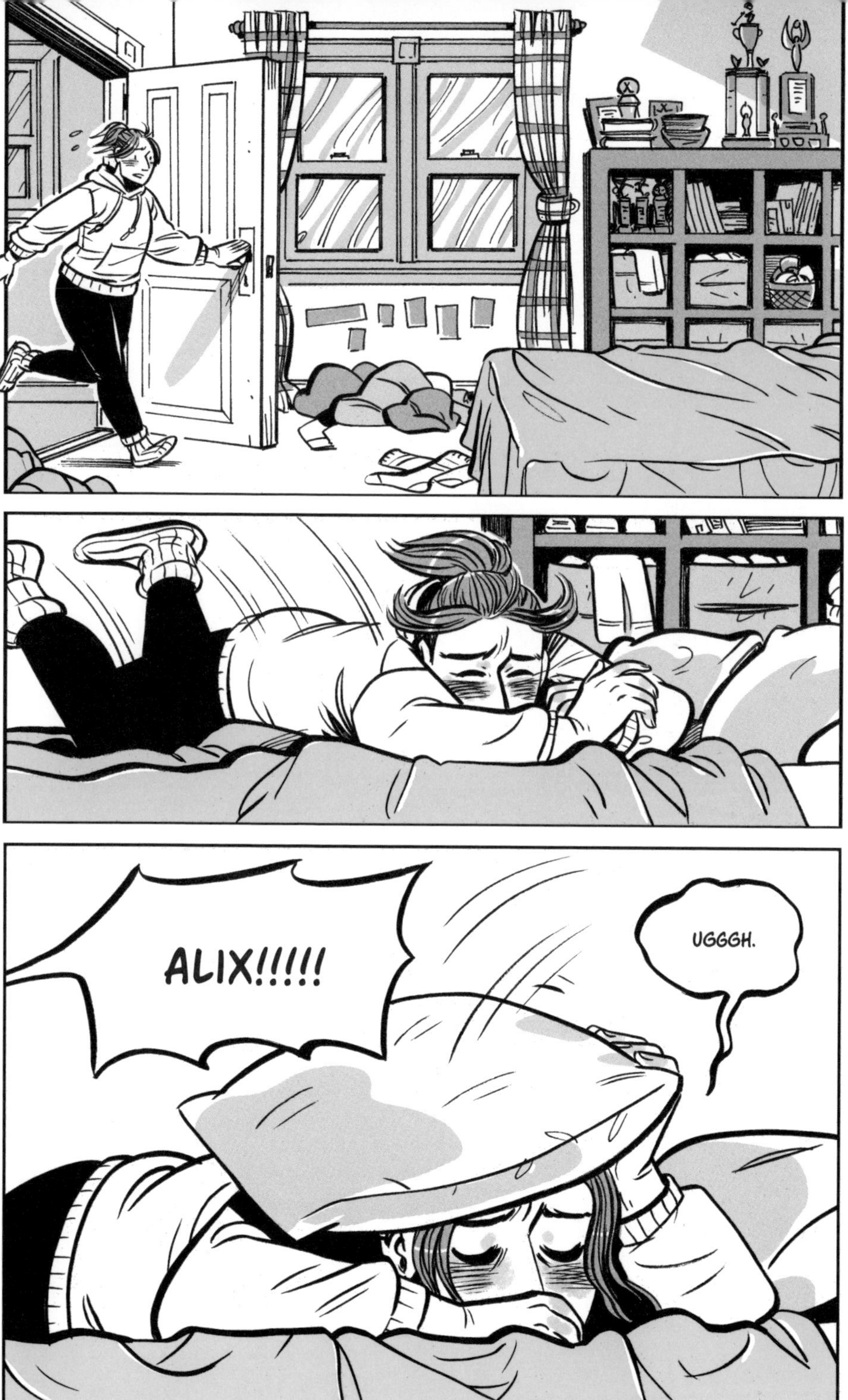
ALIX!!!!!
UGGGH.

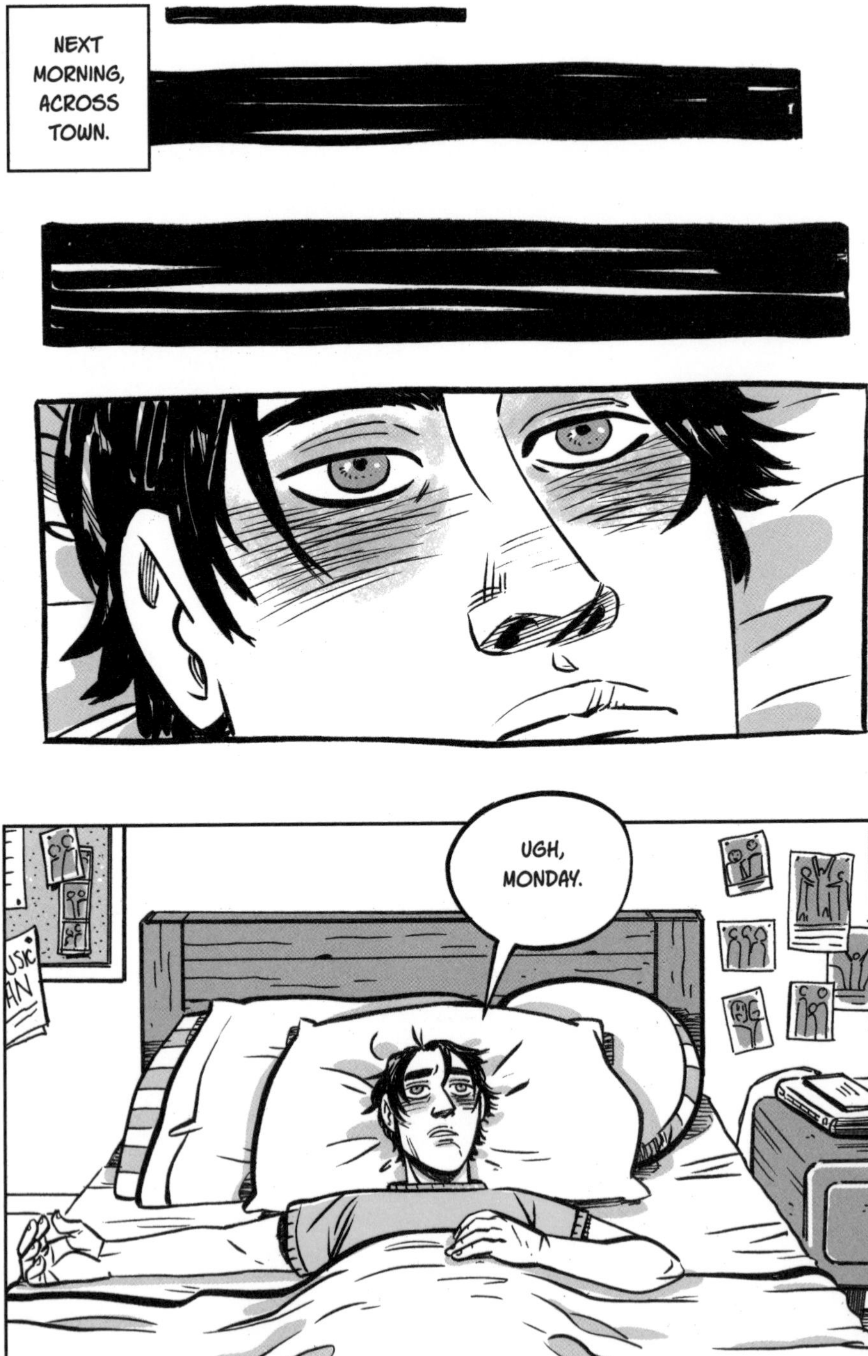
NEXT MORNING, ACROSS TOWN.
UGH, MONDAY.

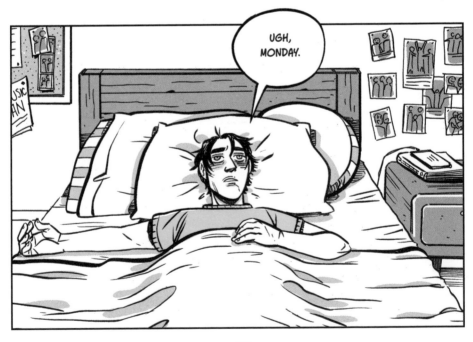

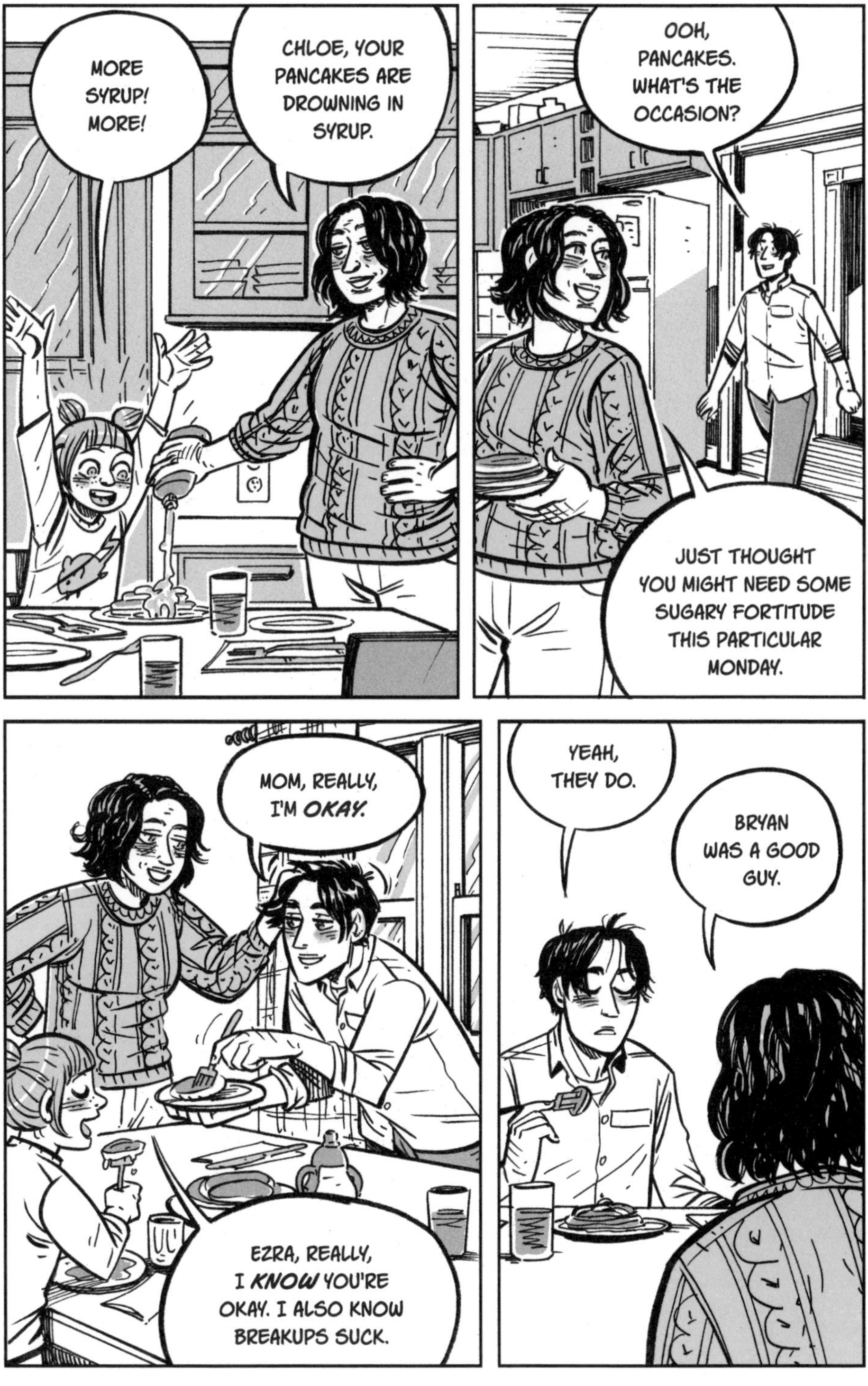
MORE SYRUP! MORE!
CHLOE, YOUR PANCAKES ARE DROWNING IN SYRUP.
OOH, PANCAKES. WHAT'S THE OCCASION?
JUST THOUGHT YOU MIGHT NEED SOME SUGARY FORTITUDE THIS PARTICULAR MONDAY.
MOM, REALLY, I'M *OKAY.*
EZRA, REALLY, I ***KNOW*** YOU'RE OKAY. I ALSO KNOW BREAKUPS SUCK.
YEAH, THEY DO.
BRYAN WAS A GOOD GUY.

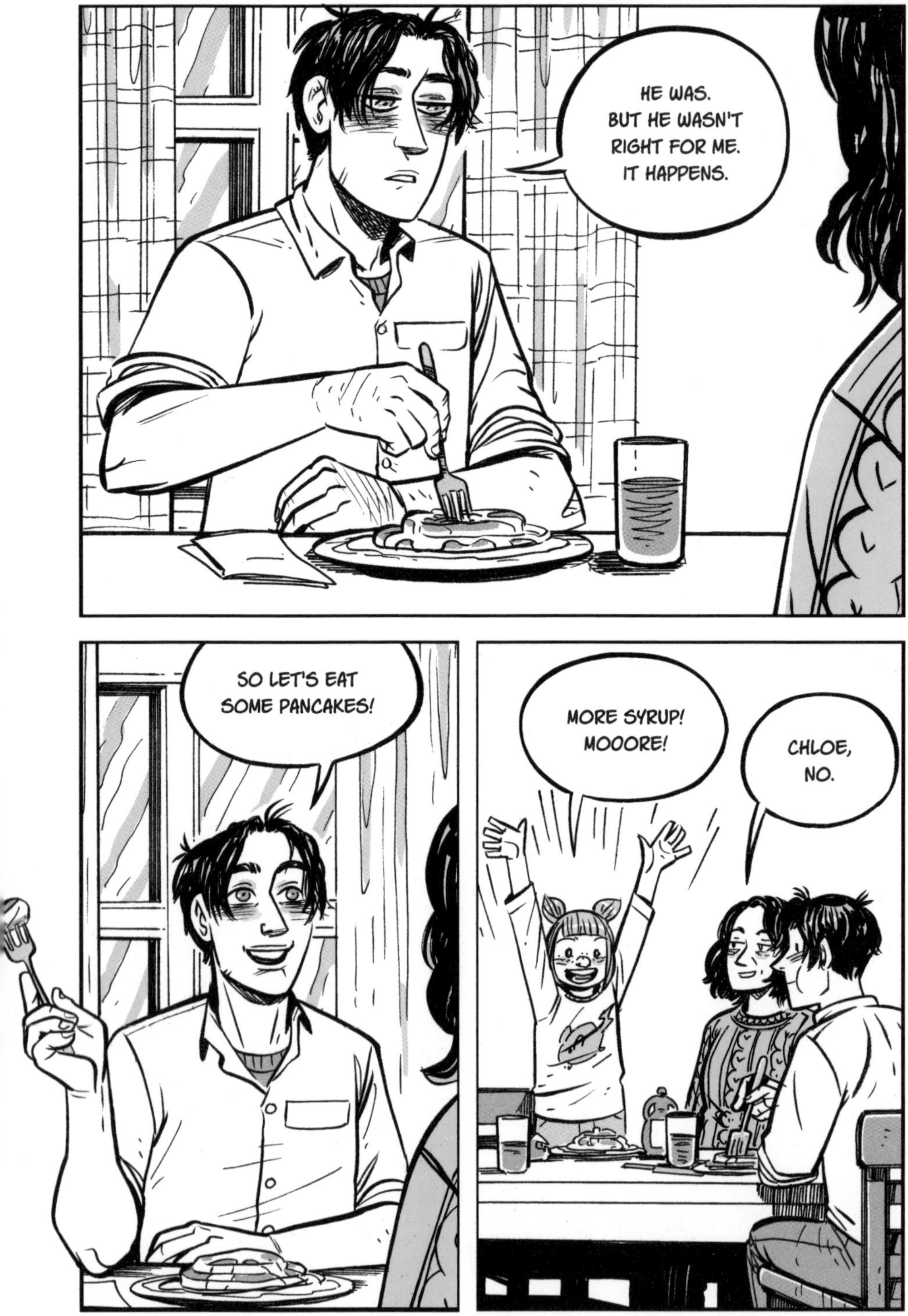
HE WAS. BUT HE WASN'T RIGHT FOR ME. IT HAPPENS.
SO LET'S EAT SOME PANCAKES!
MORE SYRUP! MOOORE!
CHLOE, NO.

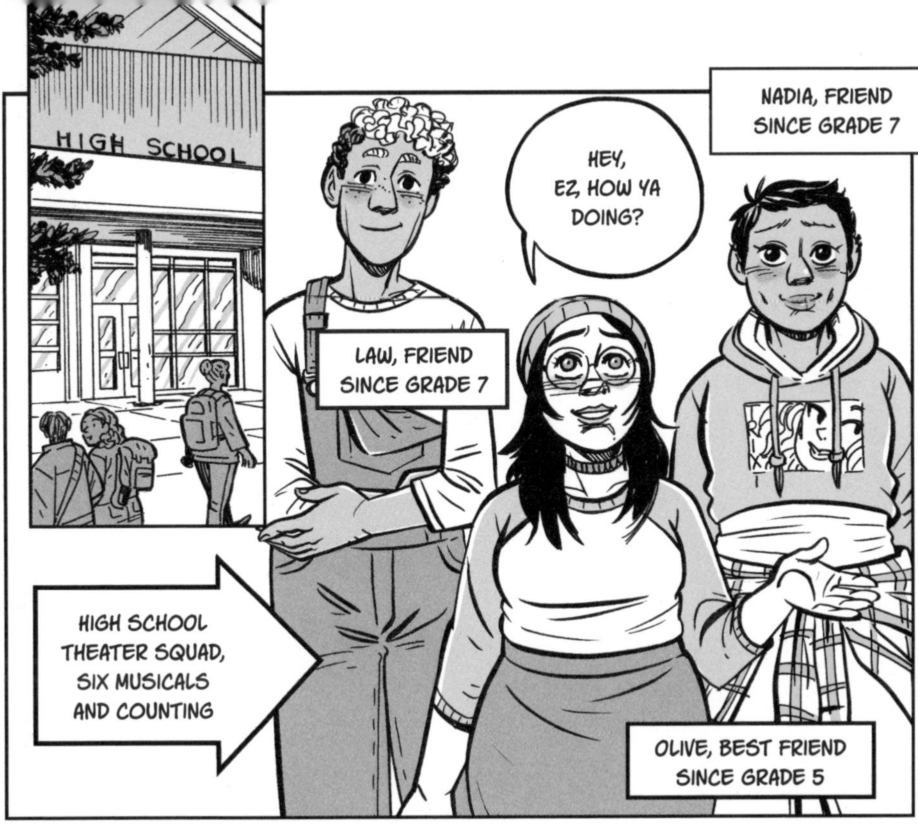
HIGH SCHOOL
NADIA, FRIEND SINCE GRADE 7
HEY, EZ, HOW YA DOING?
LAW, FRIEND SINCE GRADE 7
HIGH SCHOOL THEATER SQUAD, SIX MUSICALS AND COUNTING
OLIVE, BEST FRIEND SINCE GRADE 5

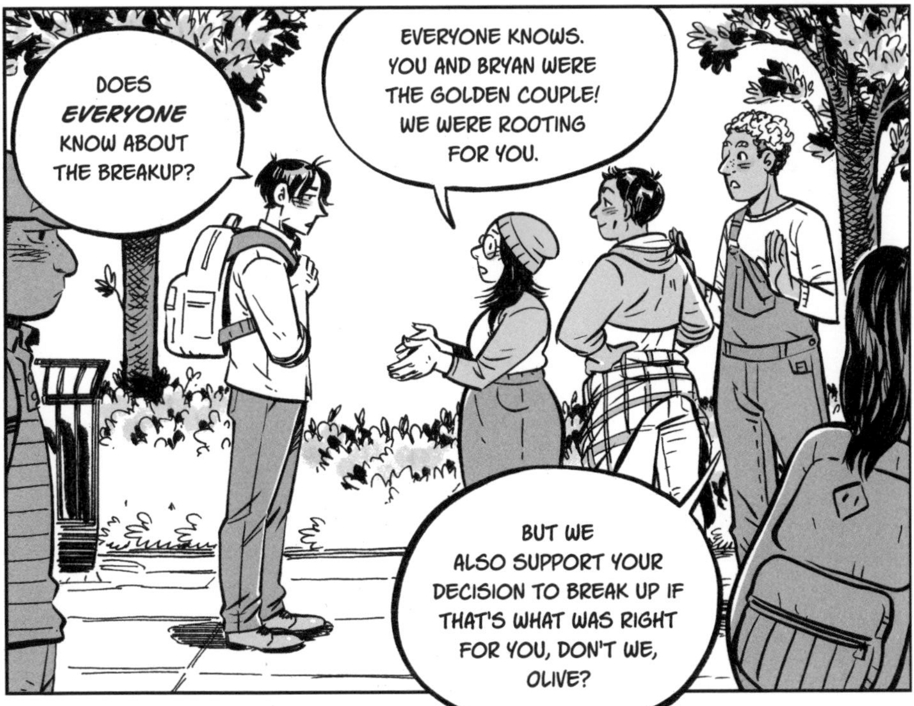
DOES *EVERYONE* KNOW ABOUT THE BREAKUP?
EVERYONE KNOWS. YOU AND BRYAN WERE THE GOLDEN COUPLE! WE WERE ROOTING FOR YOU.
BUT WE ALSO SUPPORT YOUR DECISION TO BREAK UP IF THAT'S WHAT WAS RIGHT FOR YOU, DON'T WE, OLIVE?

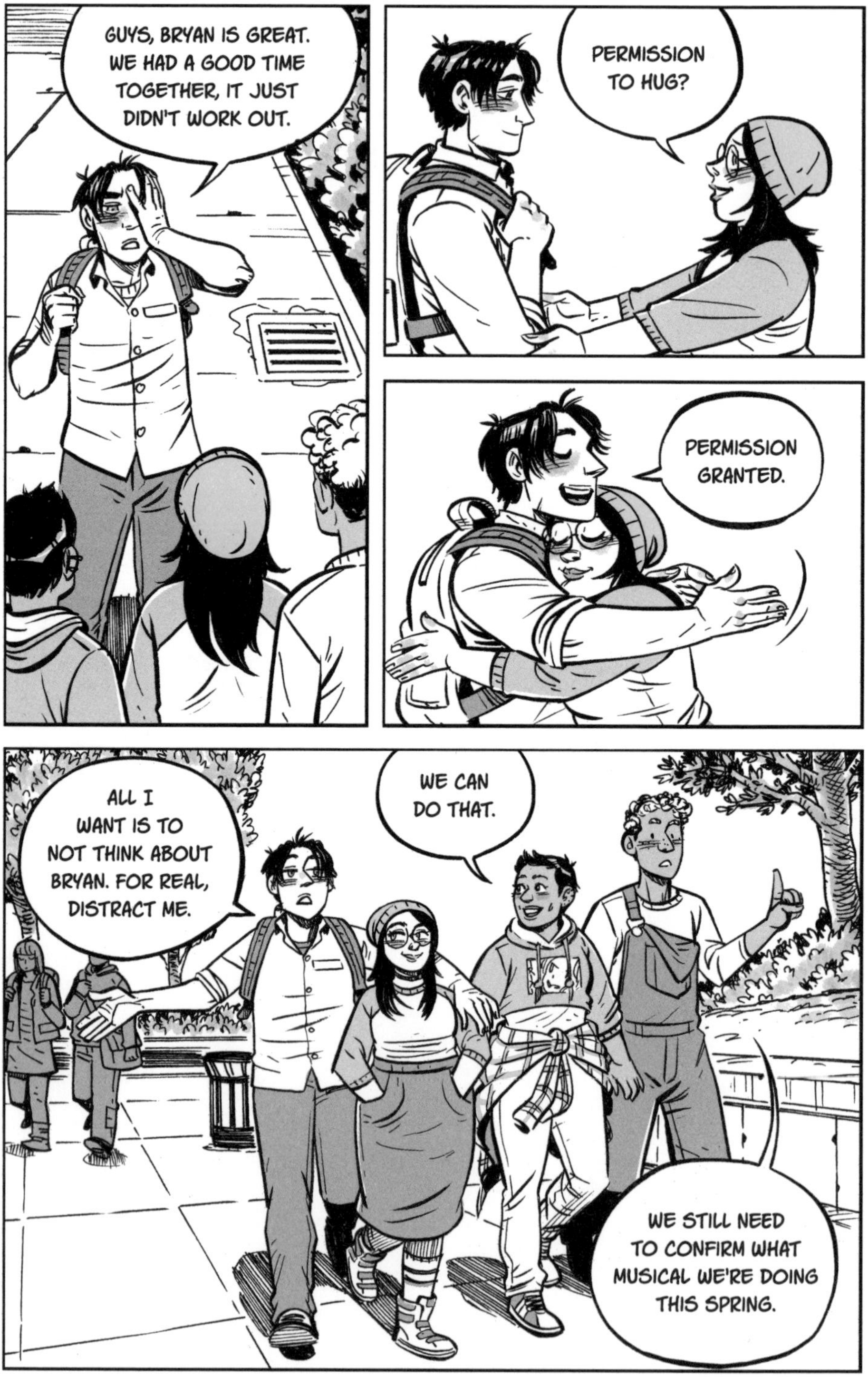
GUYS, BRYAN IS GREAT. WE HAD A GOOD TIME TOGETHER, IT JUST DIDN'T WORK OUT.
PERMISSION TO HUG?
PERMISSION GRANTED.
ALL I WANT IS TO NOT THINK ABOUT BRYAN. FOR REAL, DISTRACT ME.
WE CAN DO THAT.
WE STILL NEED TO CONFIRM WHAT MUSICAL WE'RE DOING THIS SPRING.

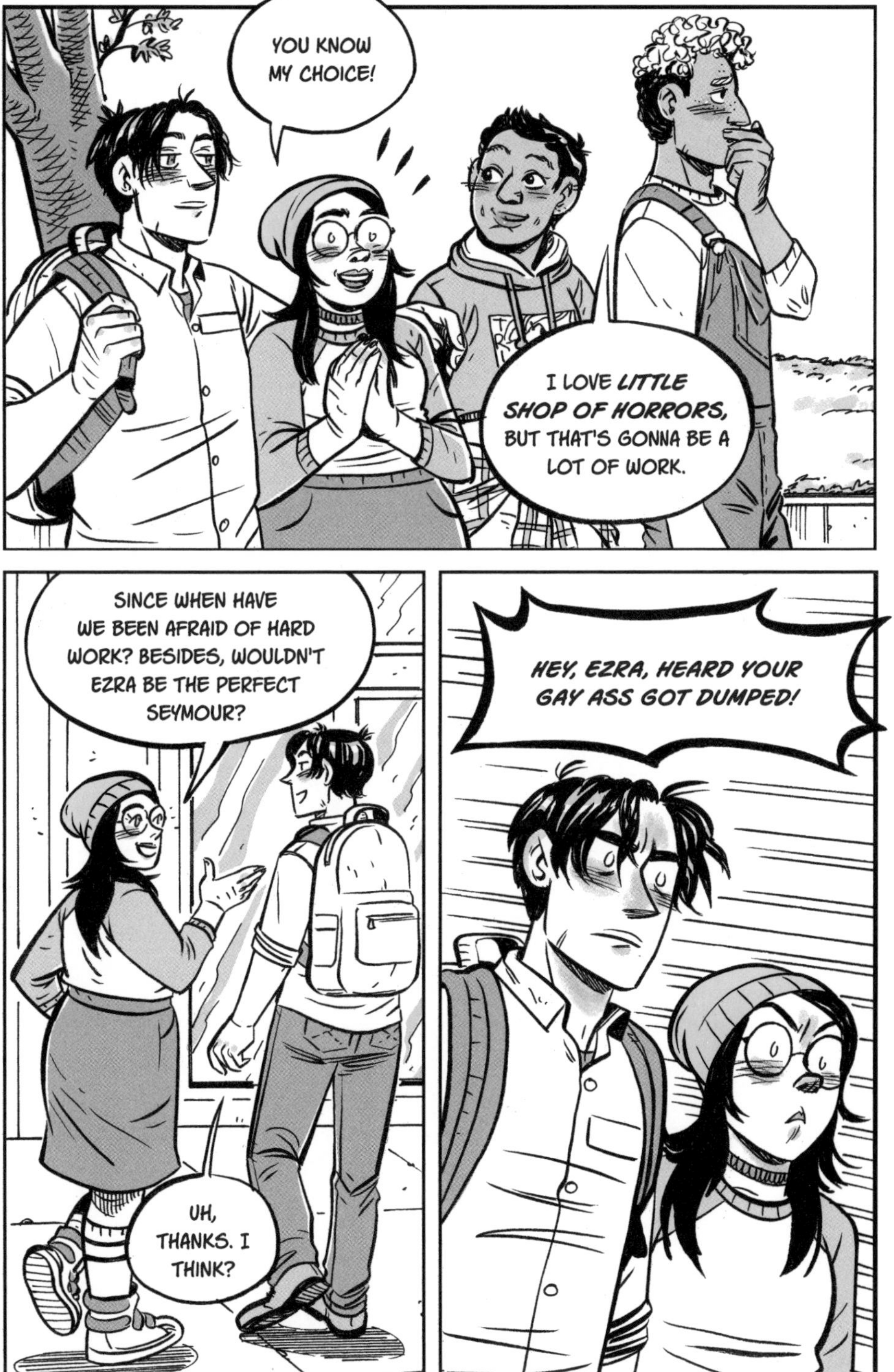
YOU KNOW MY CHOICE!
I LOVE *LITTLE SHOP OF HORRORS*, BUT THAT'S GONNA BE A LOT OF WORK.
SINCE WHEN HAVE WE BEEN AFRAID OF HARD WORK? BESIDES, WOULDN'T EZRA BE THE PERFECT SEYMOUR?
UH, THANKS. I THINK?
HEY, EZRA, HEARD YOUR GAY ASS GOT DUMPED!

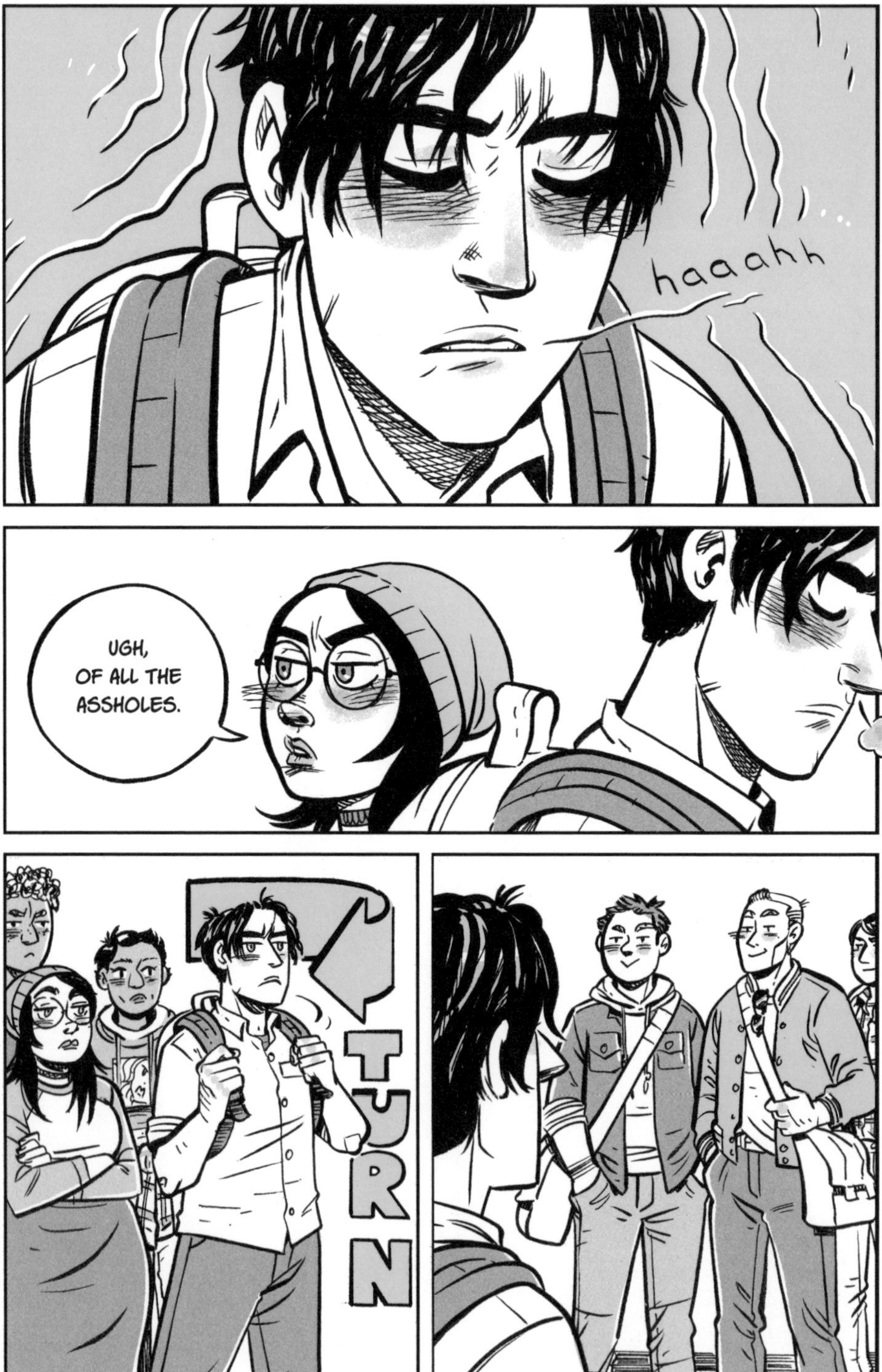
haaahh
UGH, OF ALL THE ASSHOLES.
TURN

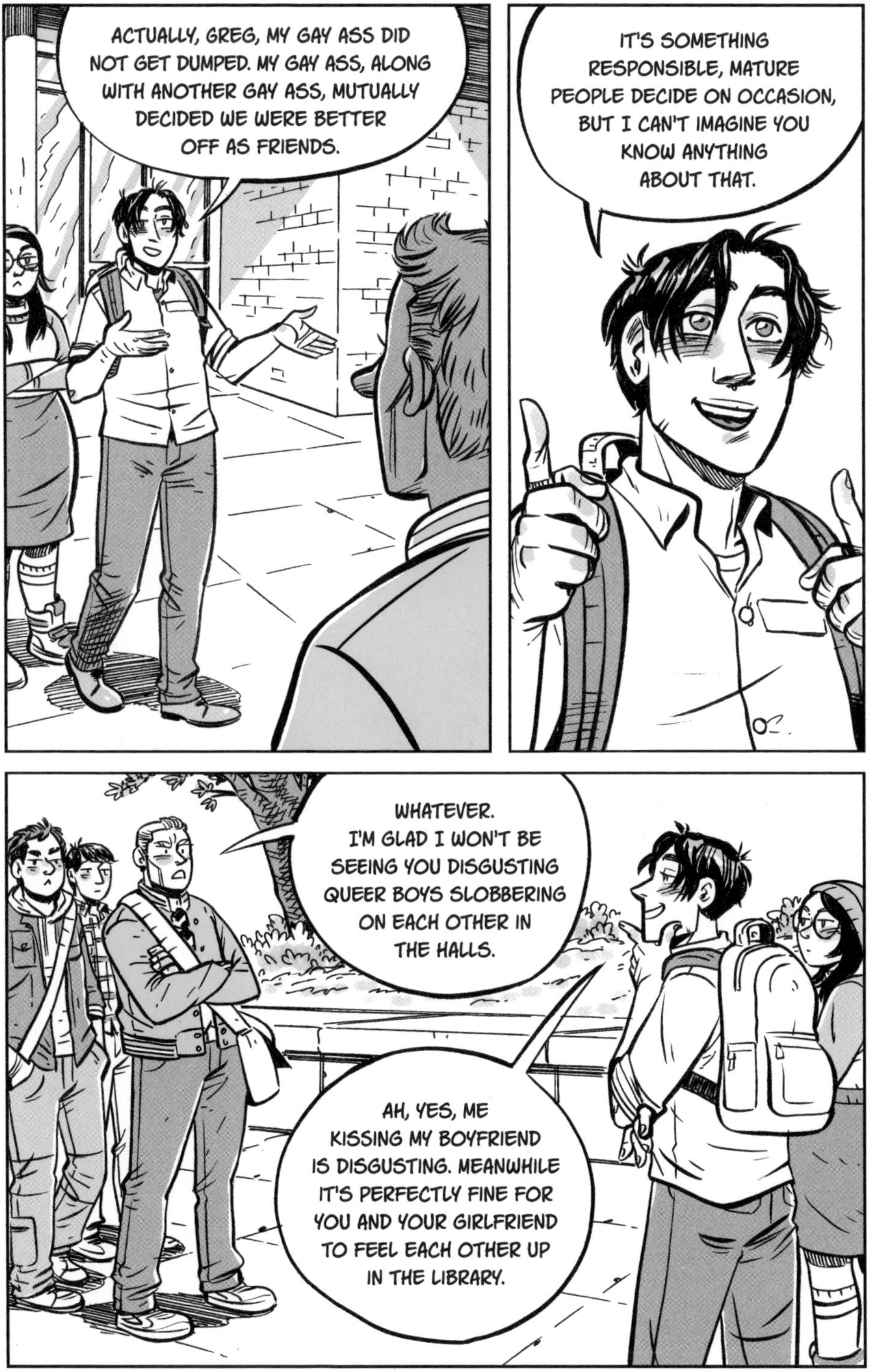
ACTUALLY, GREG, MY GAY ASS DID NOT GET DUMPED. MY GAY ASS, ALONG WITH ANOTHER GAY ASS, MUTUALLY DECIDED WE WERE BETTER OFF AS FRIENDS.
IT'S SOMETHING RESPONSIBLE, MATURE PEOPLE DECIDE ON OCCASION, BUT I CAN'T IMAGINE YOU KNOW ANYTHING ABOUT THAT.
WHATEVER. I'M GLAD I WON'T BE SEEING YOU DISGUSTING QUEER BOYS SLOBBERING ON EACH OTHER IN THE HALLS.
AH, YES, ME KISSING MY BOYFRIEND IS DISGUSTING. MEANWHILE IT'S PERFECTLY FINE FOR YOU AND YOUR GIRLFRIEND TO FEEL EACH OTHER UP IN THE LIBRARY.

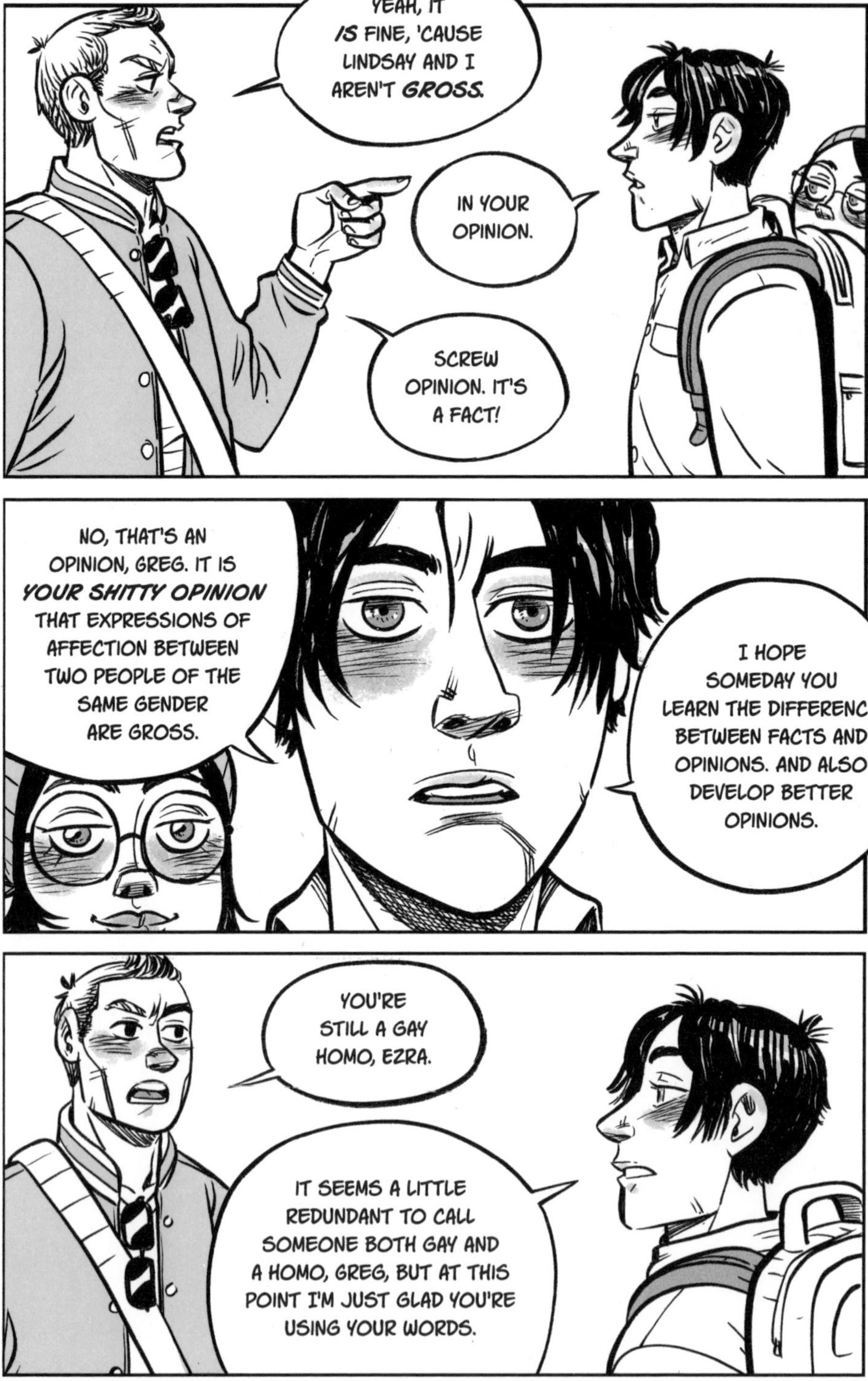

YEAH, IT *IS* FINE, 'CAUSE LINDSAY AND I AREN'T ***GROSS.***
IN YOUR OPINION.
SCREW OPINION. IT'S A FACT!
NO, THAT'S AN OPINION, GREG. IT IS ***YOUR SHITTY OPINION*** THAT EXPRESSIONS OF AFFECTION BETWEEN TWO PEOPLE OF THE SAME GENDER ARE GROSS.
I HOPE SOMEDAY YOU LEARN THE DIFFERENCE BETWEEN FACTS AND OPINIONS. AND ALSO DEVELOP BETTER OPINIONS.
YOU'RE STILL A GAY HOMO, EZRA.
IT SEEMS A LITTLE REDUNDANT TO CALL SOMEONE BOTH GAY AND A HOMO, GREG, BUT AT THIS POINT I'M JUST GLAD YOU'RE USING YOUR WORDS.

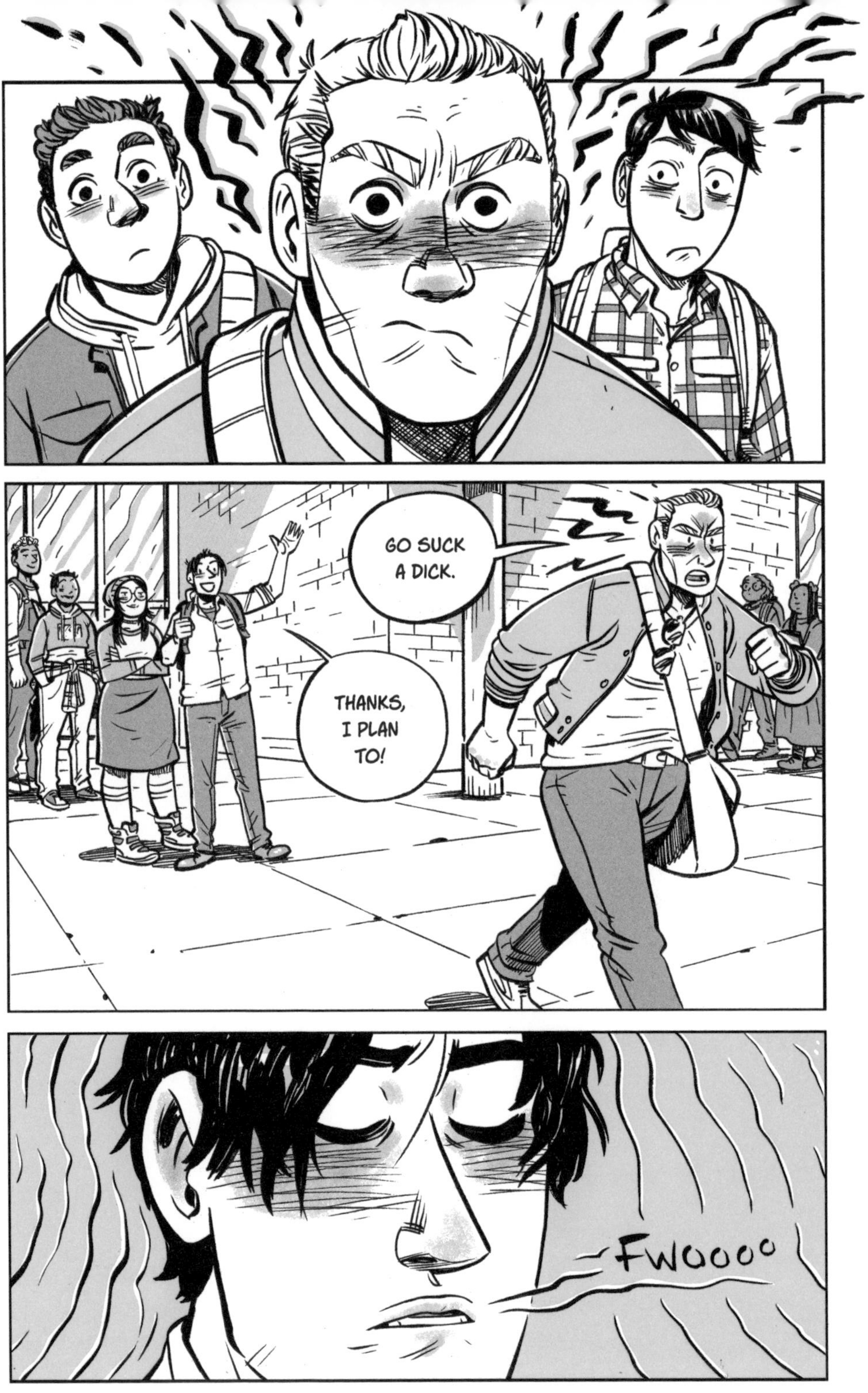

GO SUCK A DICK.
THANKS, I PLAN TO!
FWOOOO

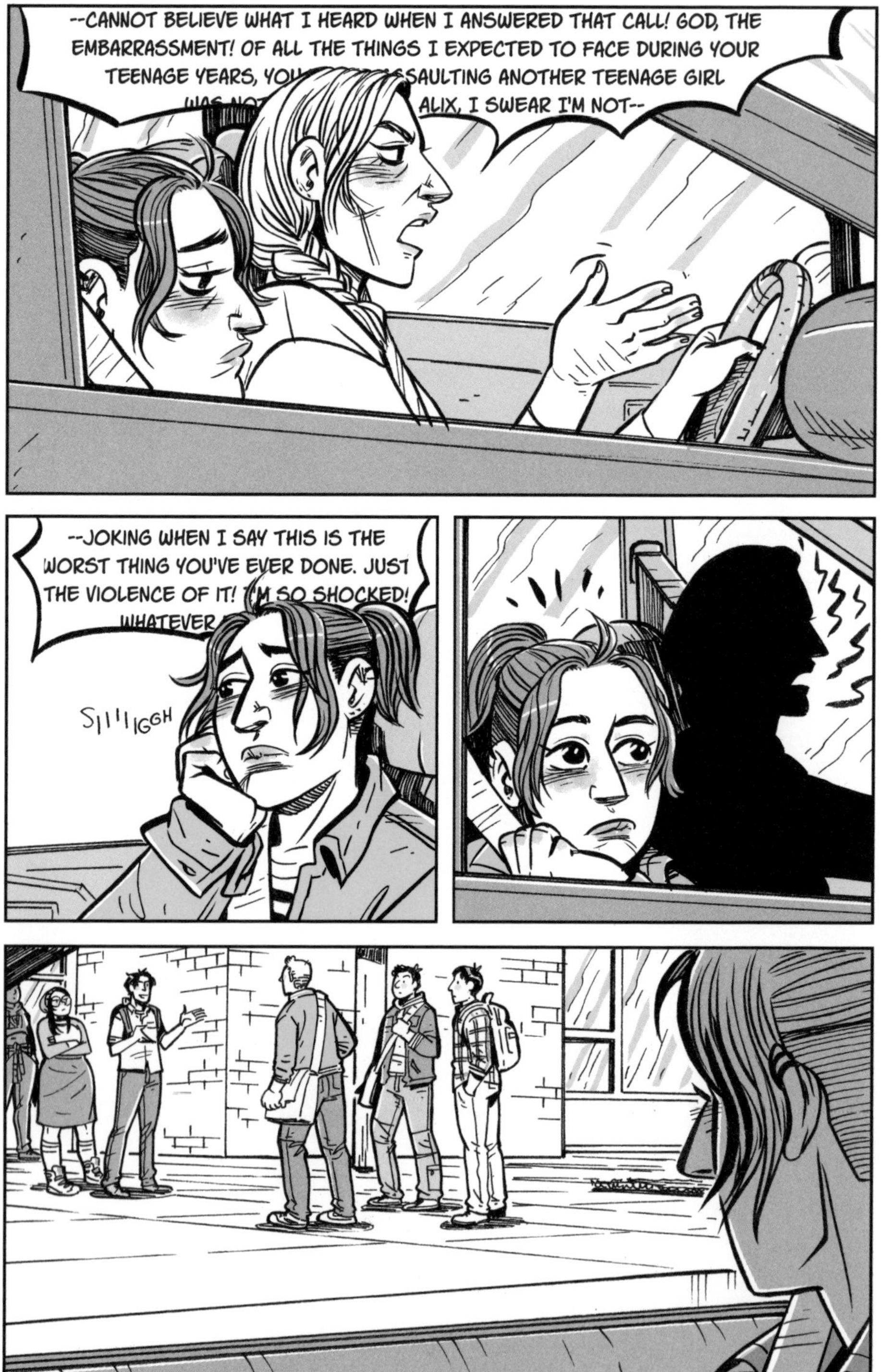
--CANNOT BELIEVE WHAT I HEARD WHEN I ANSWERED THAT CALL! GOD, THE EMBARRASSMENT! OF ALL THE THINGS I EXPECTED TO FACE DURING YOUR TEENAGE YEARS, YOU ASSAULTING ANOTHER TEENAGE GIRL
ALIX, I SWEAR I'M NOT--
--JOKING WHEN I SAY THIS IS THE WORST THING YOU'VE EVER DONE. JUST THE VIOLENCE OF IT! I'M SO SHOCKED! WHATEVER
SIIIIIGGH

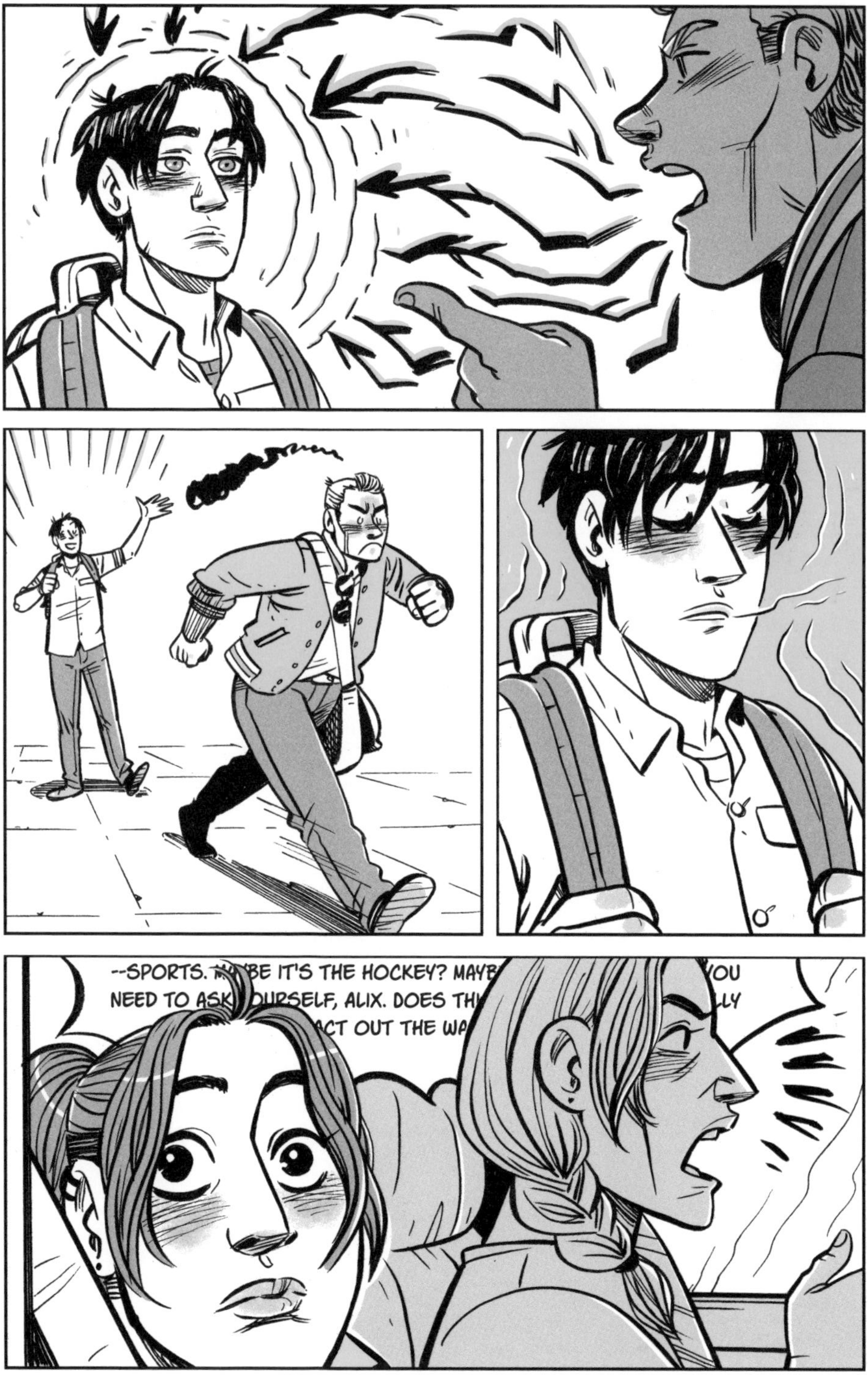
--SPORTS. MA BE IT'S THE HOCKEY? MAYB YOU
NEED TO ASK OURSELF, ALIX. DOES TH LLY
ACT OUT THE WA

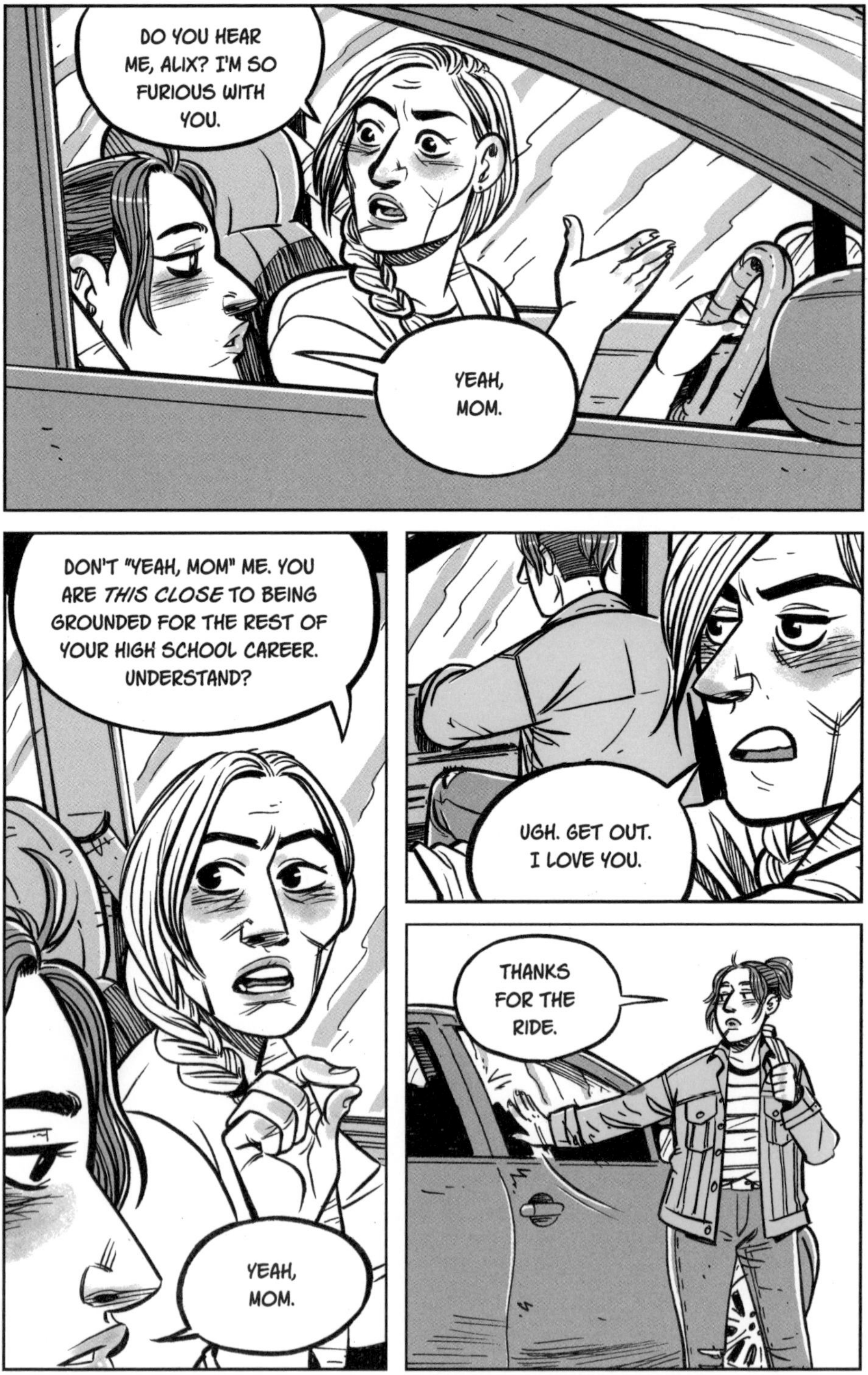
DO YOU HEAR ME, ALIX? I'M SO FURIOUS WITH YOU.
YEAH, MOM.
DON'T "YEAH, MOM" ME. YOU ARE *THIS CLOSE* TO BEING GROUNDED FOR THE REST OF YOUR HIGH SCHOOL CAREER. UNDERSTAND?
YEAH, MOM.
UGH. GET OUT. I LOVE YOU.
THANKS FOR THE RIDE.

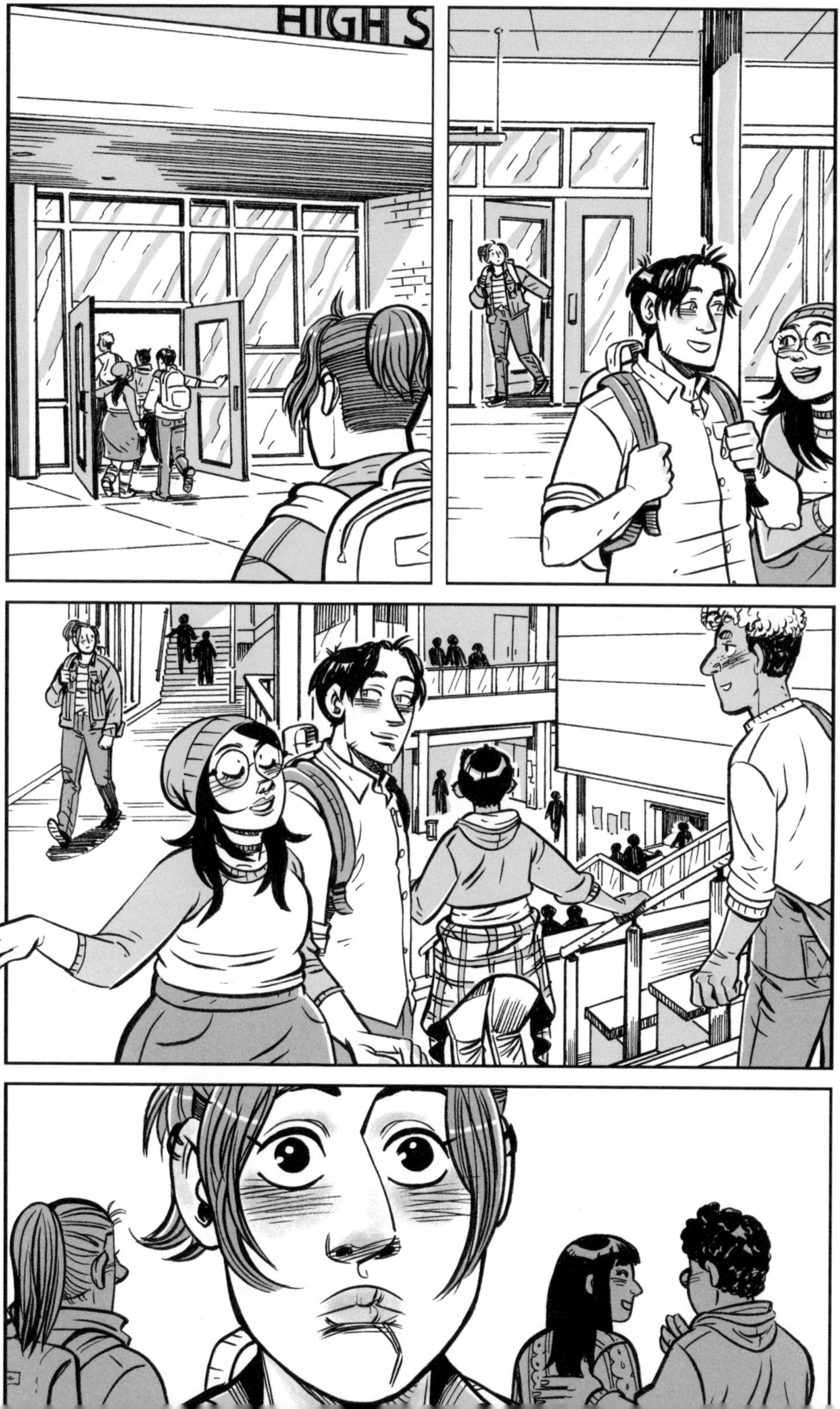
HIGH S

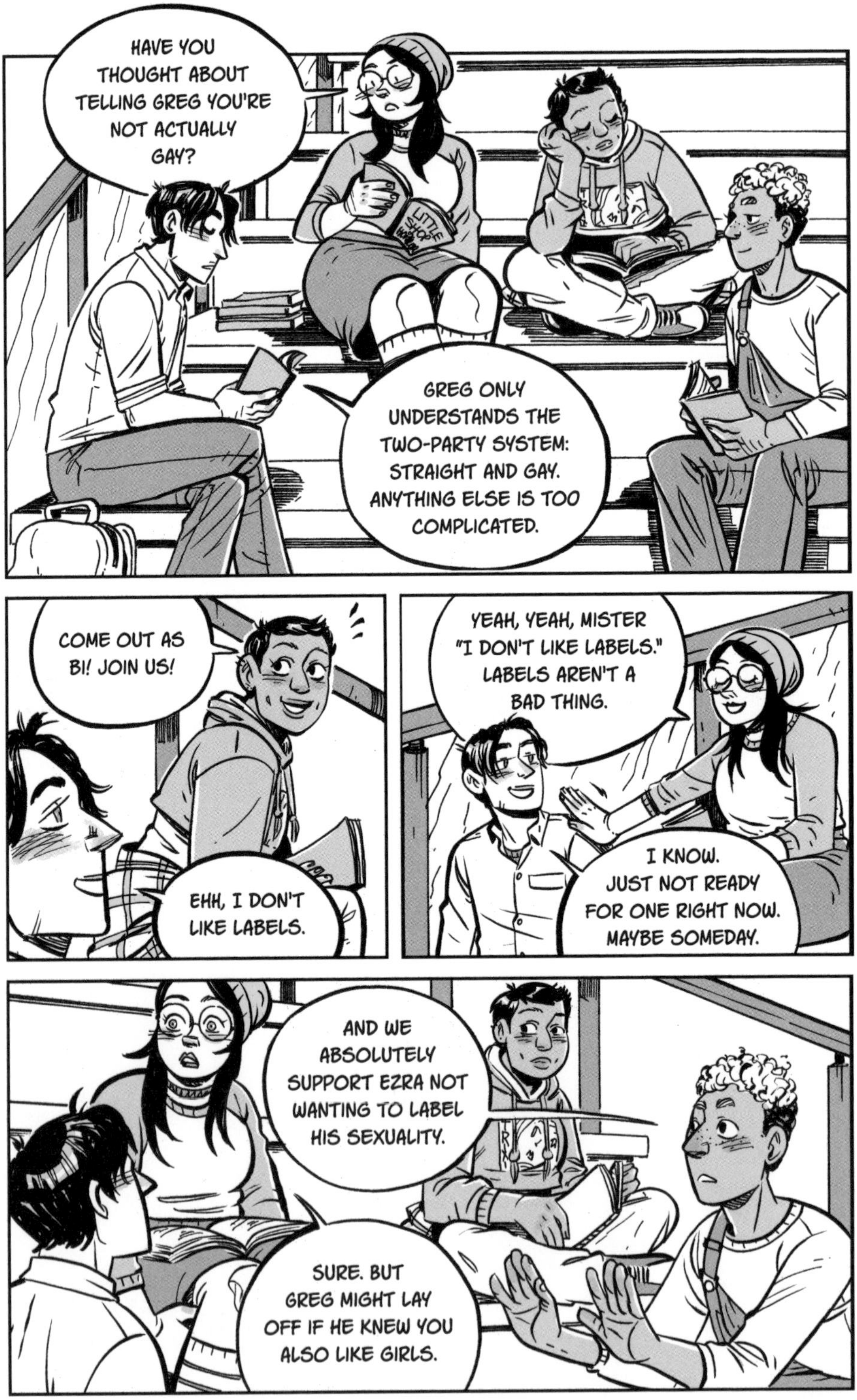
HAVE YOU THOUGHT ABOUT TELLING GREG YOU'RE NOT ACTUALLY GAY?
LITTLE SHOP OF HORRORS
GREG ONLY UNDERSTANDS THE TWO-PARTY SYSTEM: STRAIGHT AND GAY. ANYTHING ELSE IS TOO COMPLICATED.
COME OUT AS BI! JOIN US!
EHH, I DON'T LIKE LABELS.
YEAH, YEAH, MISTER "I DON'T LIKE LABELS." LABELS AREN'T A BAD THING.
I KNOW. JUST NOT READY FOR ONE RIGHT NOW. MAYBE SOMEDAY.
AND WE ABSOLUTELY SUPPORT EZRA NOT WANTING TO LABEL HIS SEXUALITY.
SURE. BUT GREG MIGHT LAY OFF IF HE KNEW YOU ALSO LIKE GIRLS.

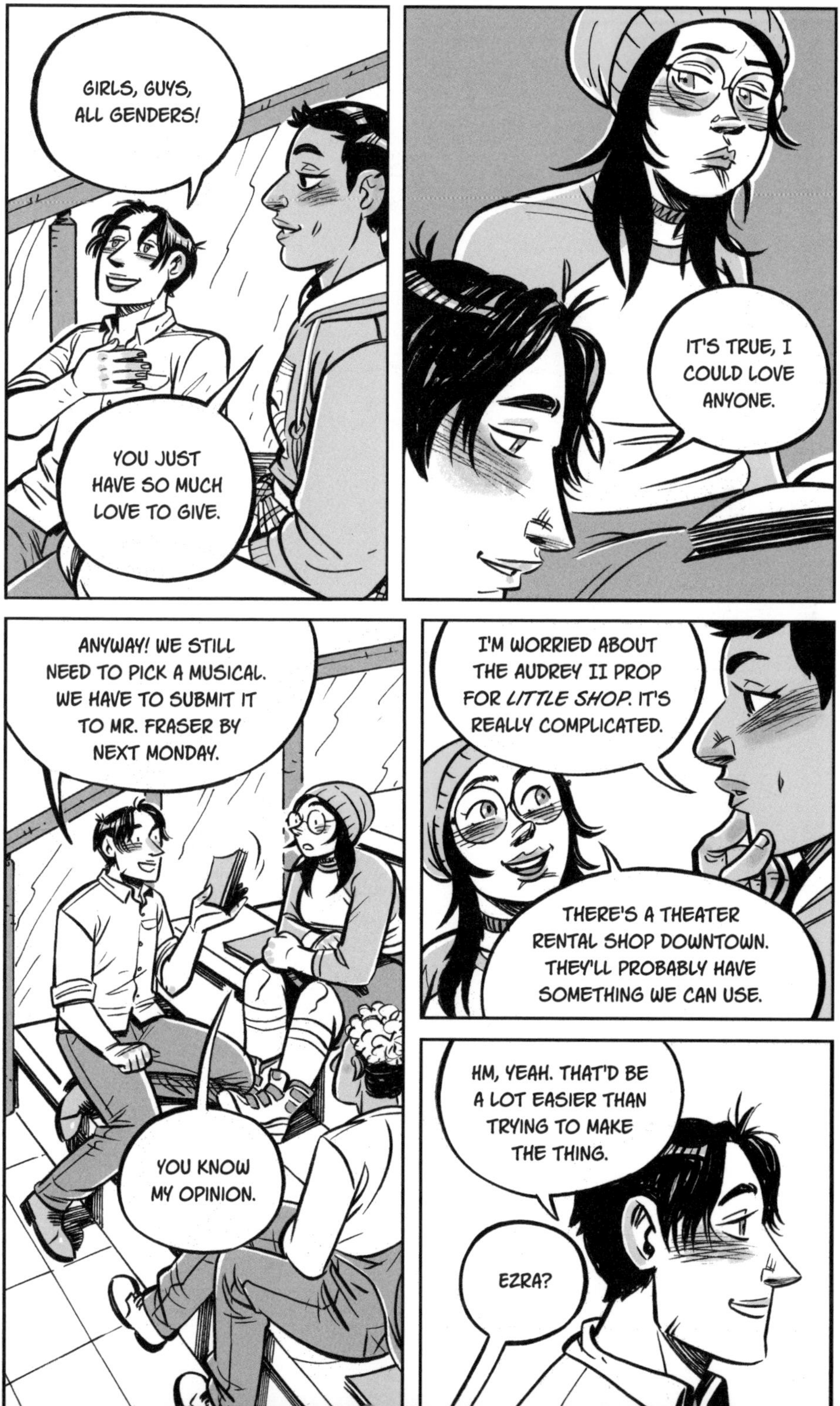
GIRLS, GUYS, ALL GENDERS!
YOU JUST HAVE SO MUCH LOVE TO GIVE.
IT'S TRUE, I COULD LOVE ANYONE.
ANYWAY! WE STILL NEED TO PICK A MUSICAL. WE HAVE TO SUBMIT IT TO MR. FRASER BY NEXT MONDAY.
YOU KNOW MY OPINION.
I'M WORRIED ABOUT THE AUDREY II PROP FOR *LITTLE SHOP*. IT'S REALLY COMPLICATED.
THERE'S A THEATER RENTAL SHOP DOWNTOWN. THEY'LL PROBABLY HAVE SOMETHING WE CAN USE.
HM, YEAH. THAT'D BE A LOT EASIER THAN TRYING TO MAKE THE THING.
EZRA?

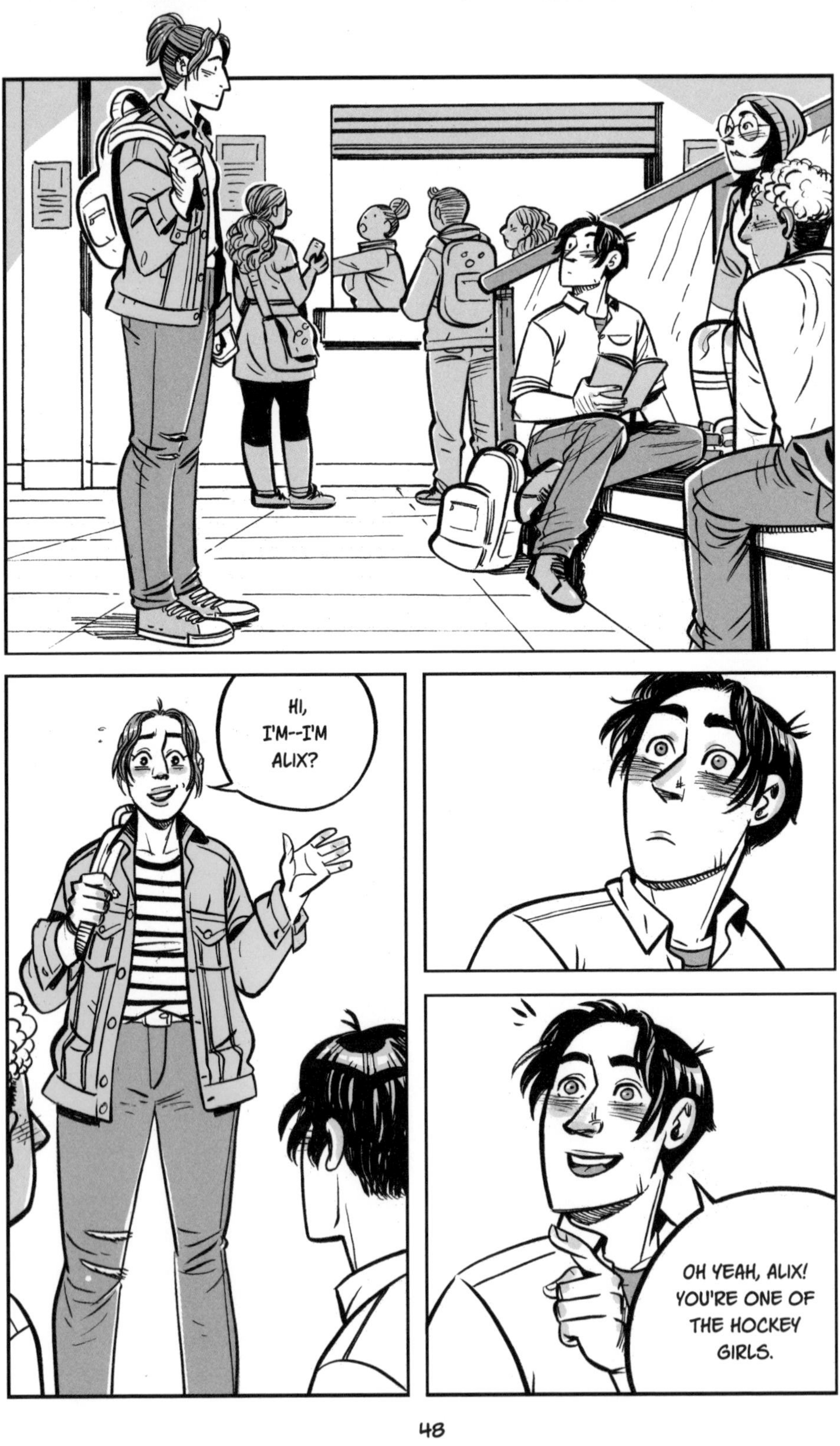
HI, I'M--I'M ALIX?
OH YEAH, ALIX! YOU'RE ONE OF THE HOCKEY GIRLS.

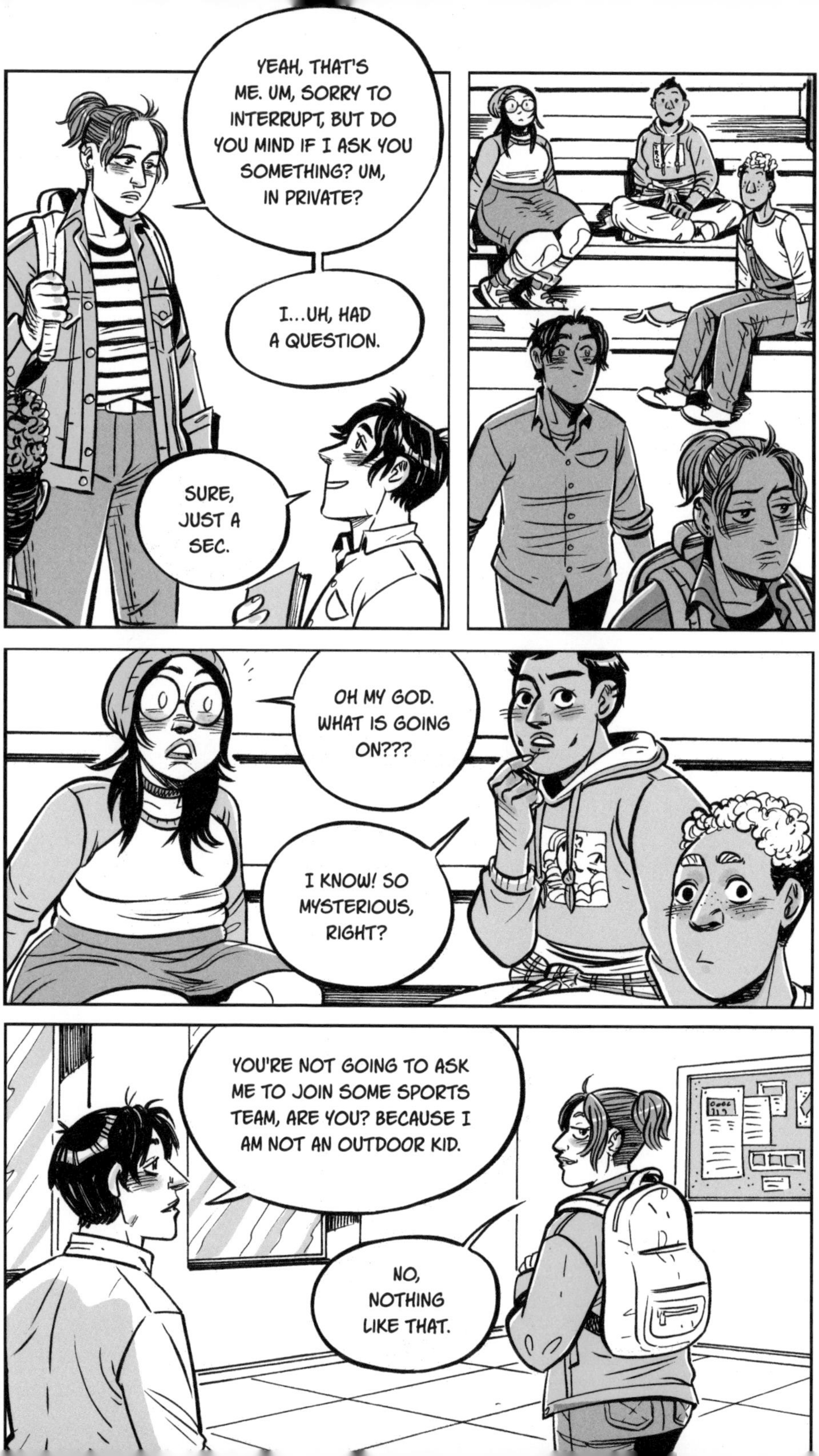
YEAH, THAT'S ME. UM, SORRY TO INTERRUPT, BUT DO YOU MIND IF I ASK YOU SOMETHING? UM, IN PRIVATE?
I...UH, HAD A QUESTION.
SURE, JUST A SEC.
OH MY GOD. WHAT IS GOING ON???
I KNOW! SO MYSTERIOUS, RIGHT?
YOU'RE NOT GOING TO ASK ME TO JOIN SOME SPORTS TEAM, ARE YOU? BECAUSE I AM NOT AN OUTDOOR KID.
NO, NOTHING LIKE THAT.

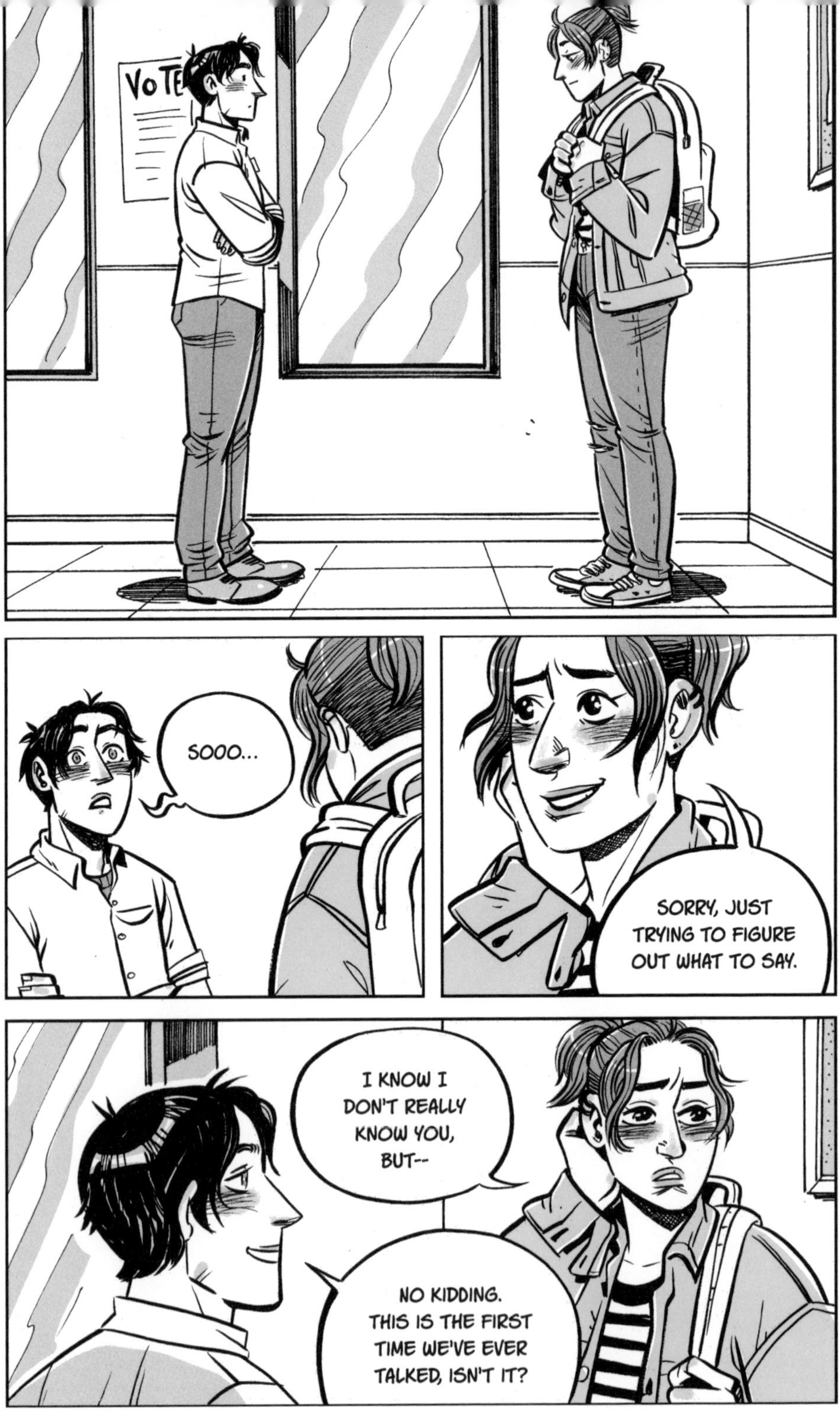
VOTE
SOOO...
SORRY, JUST TRYING TO FIGURE OUT WHAT TO SAY.
I KNOW I DON'T REALLY KNOW YOU, BUT--
NO KIDDING. THIS IS THE FIRST TIME WE'VE EVER TALKED, ISN'T IT?

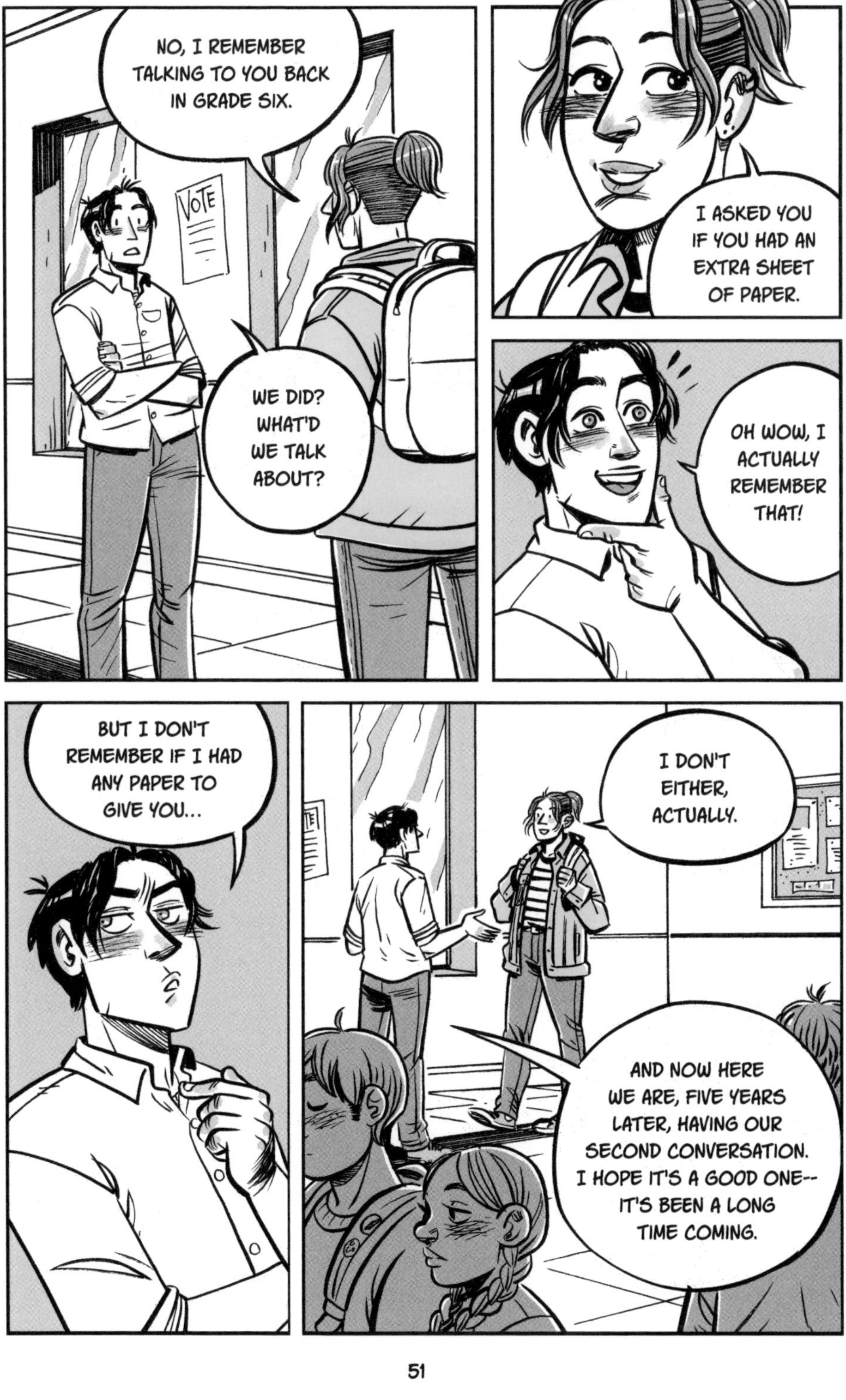
NO, I REMEMBER TALKING TO YOU BACK IN GRADE SIX.
WE DID? WHAT'D WE TALK ABOUT?
I ASKED YOU IF YOU HAD AN EXTRA SHEET OF PAPER.
OH WOW, I ACTUALLY REMEMBER THAT!
BUT I DON'T REMEMBER IF I HAD ANY PAPER TO GIVE YOU...
I DON'T EITHER, ACTUALLY.
AND NOW HERE WE ARE, FIVE YEARS LATER, HAVING OUR SECOND CONVERSATION. I HOPE IT'S A GOOD ONE-- IT'S BEEN A LONG TIME COMING.

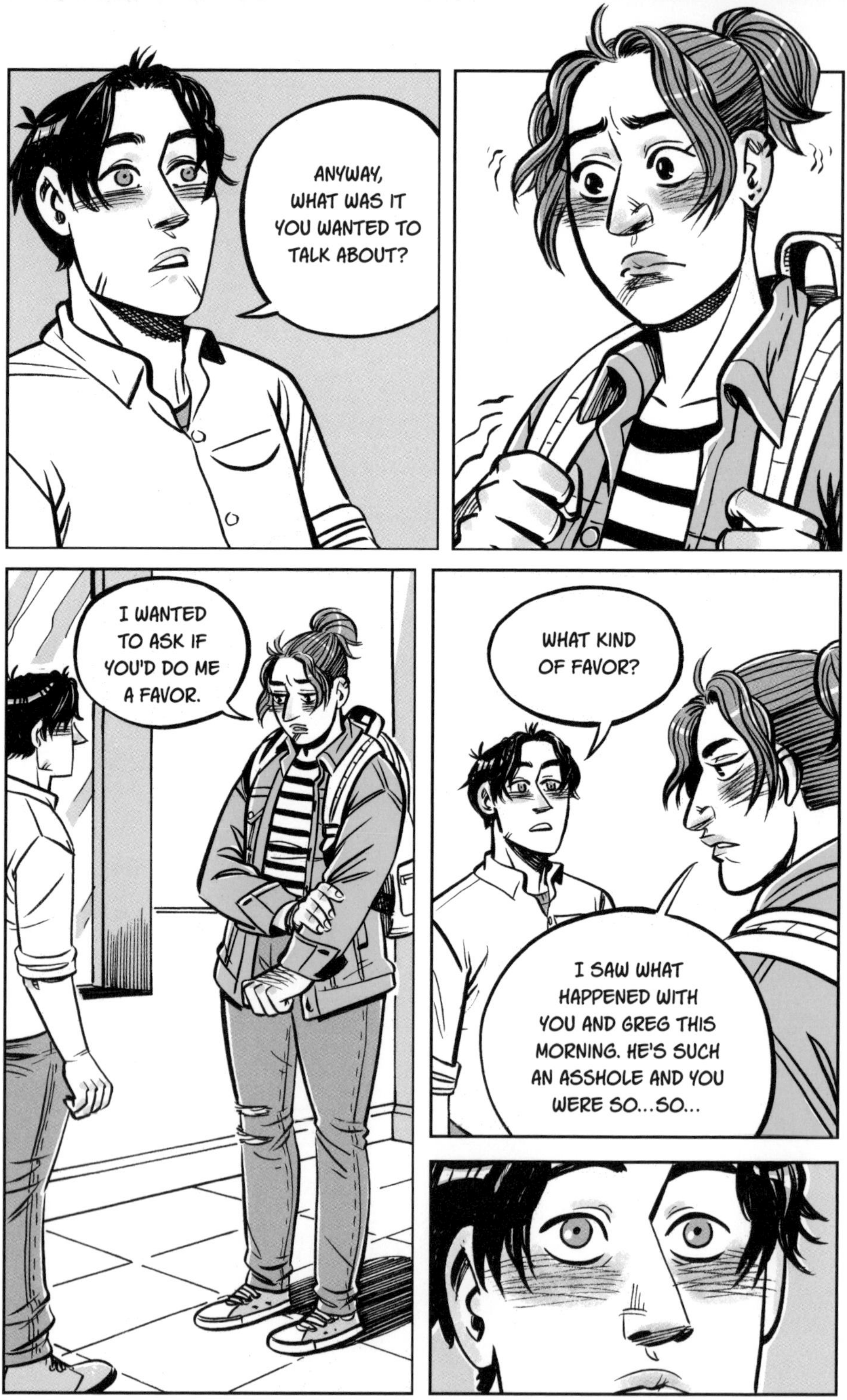
ANYWAY, WHAT WAS IT YOU WANTED TO TALK ABOUT?
I WANTED TO ASK IF YOU'D DO ME A FAVOR.
WHAT KIND OF FAVOR?
I SAW WHAT HAPPENED WITH YOU AND GREG THIS MORNING. HE'S SUCH AN ASSHOLE AND YOU WERE SO...SO...

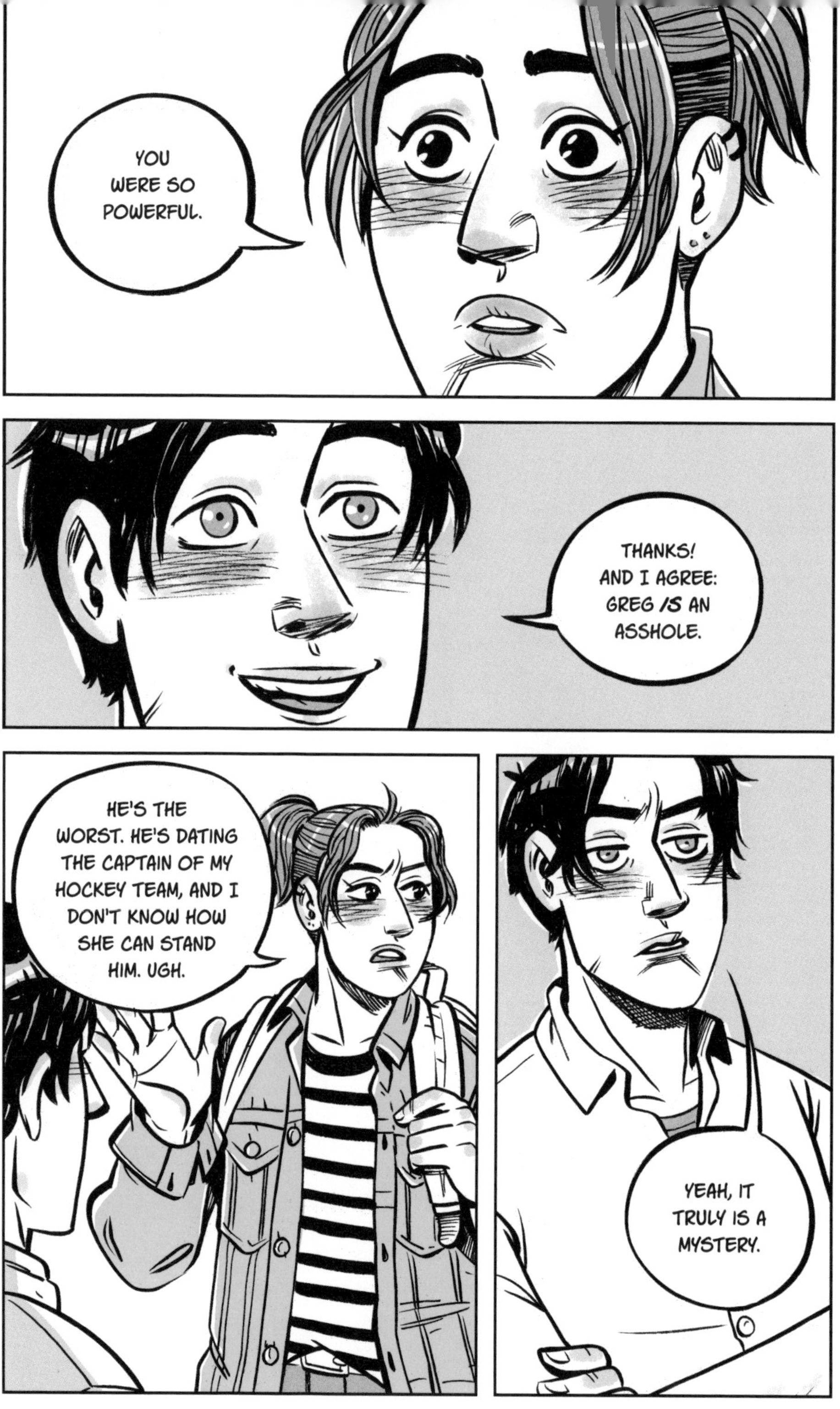
YOU WERE SO POWERFUL.
THANKS! AND I AGREE: GREG *IS* AN ASSHOLE.
HE'S THE WORST. HE'S DATING THE CAPTAIN OF MY HOCKEY TEAM, AND I DON'T KNOW HOW SHE CAN STAND HIM. UGH.
YEAH, IT TRULY IS A MYSTERY.

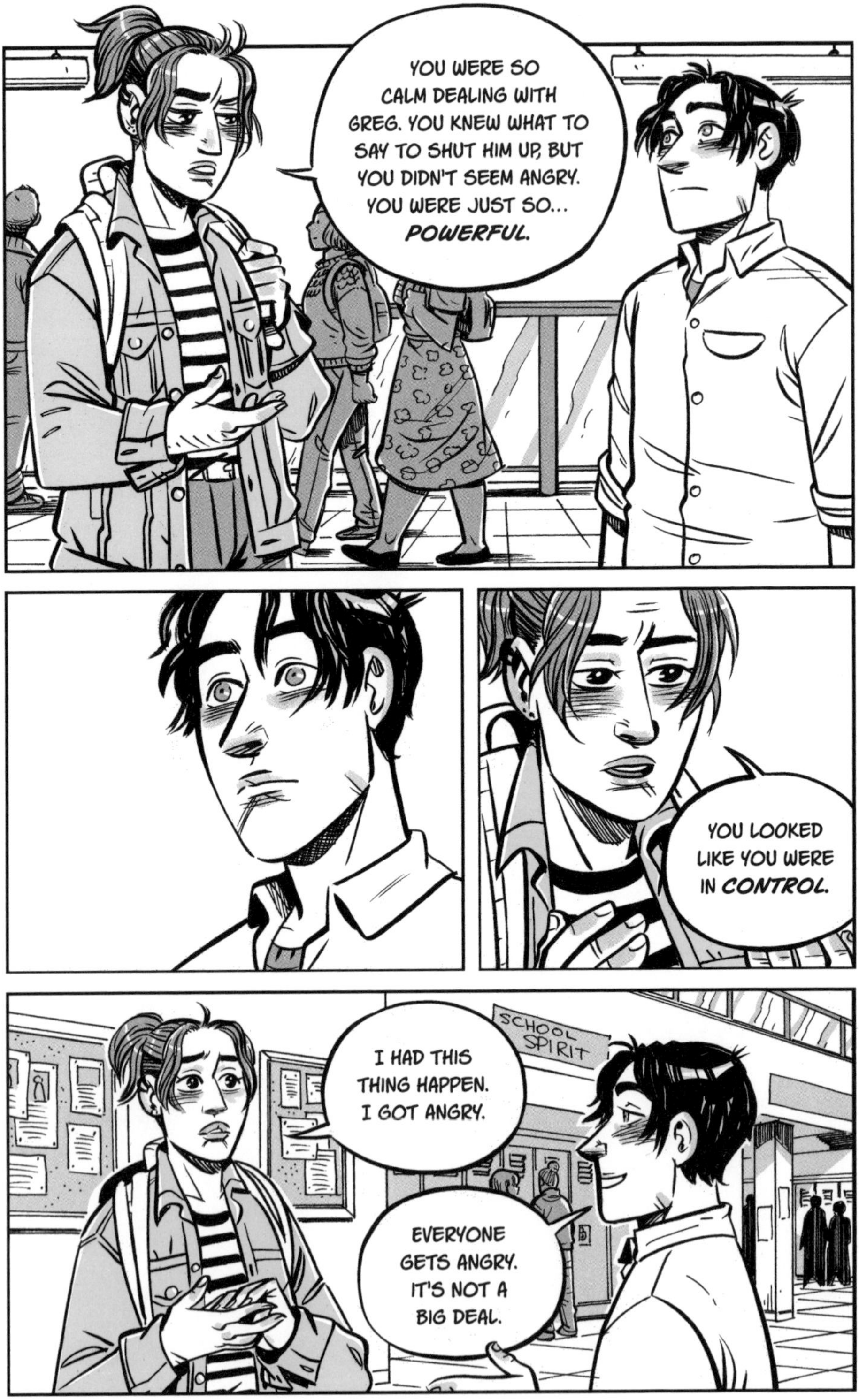
YOU WERE SO CALM DEALING WITH GREG. YOU KNEW WHAT TO SAY TO SHUT HIM UP, BUT YOU DIDN'T SEEM ANGRY. YOU WERE JUST SO... *POWERFUL.*
YOU LOOKED LIKE YOU WERE IN *CONTROL.*
SCHOOL SPIRIT
I HAD THIS THING HAPPEN. I GOT ANGRY.
EVERYONE GETS ANGRY. IT'S NOT A BIG DEAL.

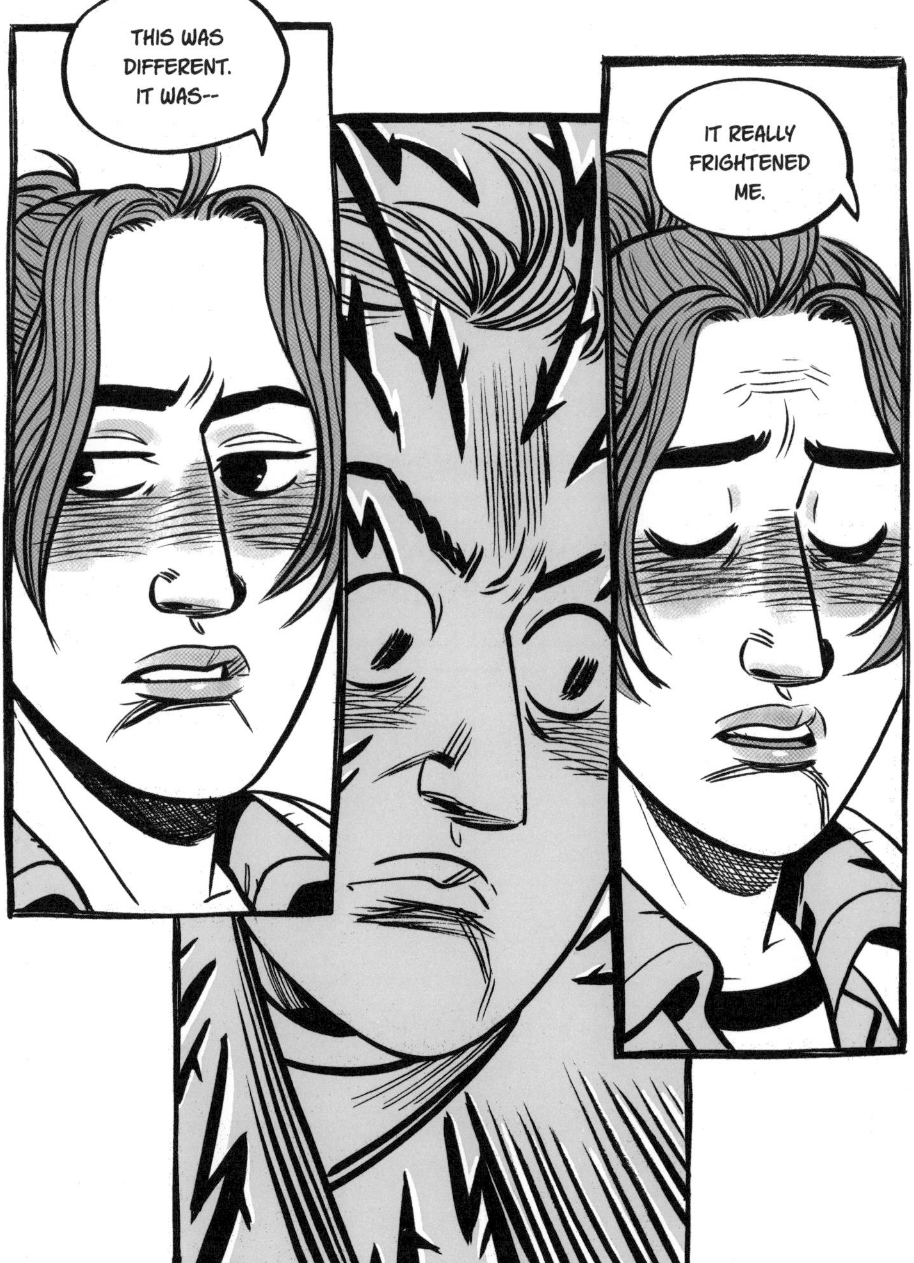
THIS WAS DIFFERENT. IT WAS--
IT REALLY FRIGHTENED ME.

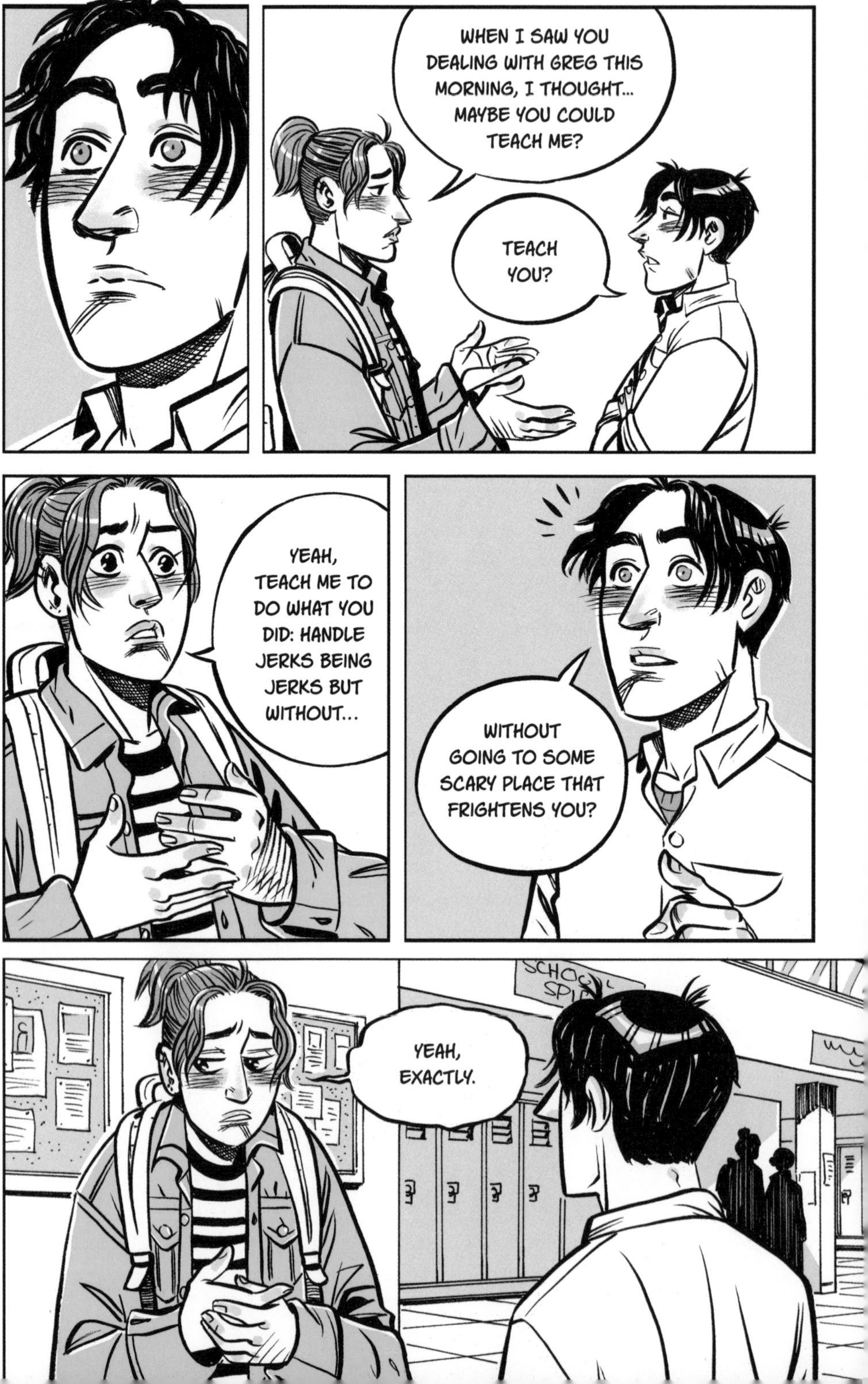
WHEN I SAW YOU DEALING WITH GREG THIS MORNING, I THOUGHT... MAYBE YOU COULD TEACH ME?
TEACH YOU?
YEAH, TEACH ME TO DO WHAT YOU DID: HANDLE JERKS BEING JERKS BUT WITHOUT...
WITHOUT GOING TO SOME SCARY PLACE THAT FRIGHTENS YOU?
YEAH, EXACTLY.

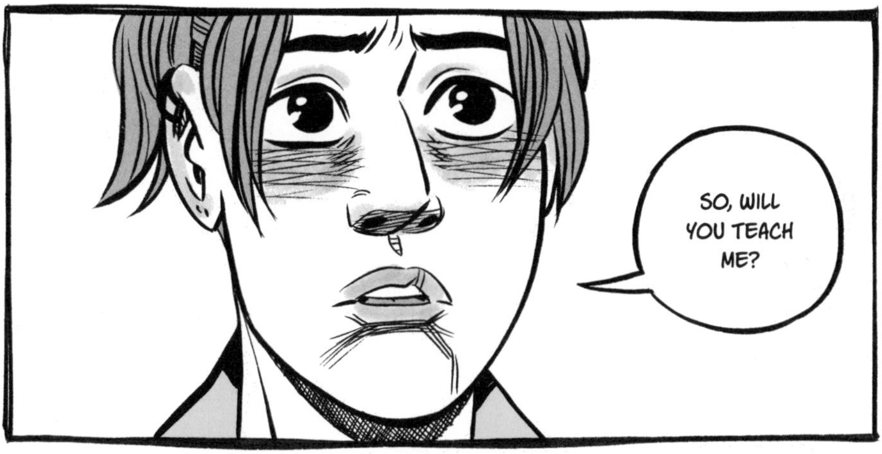
SO, WILL YOU TEACH ME?
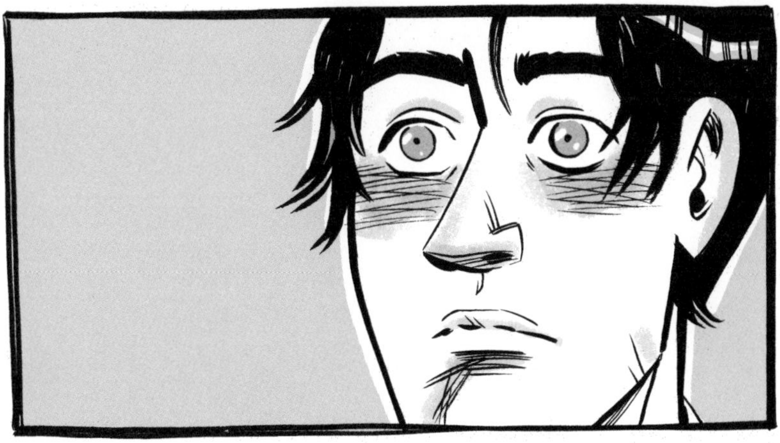

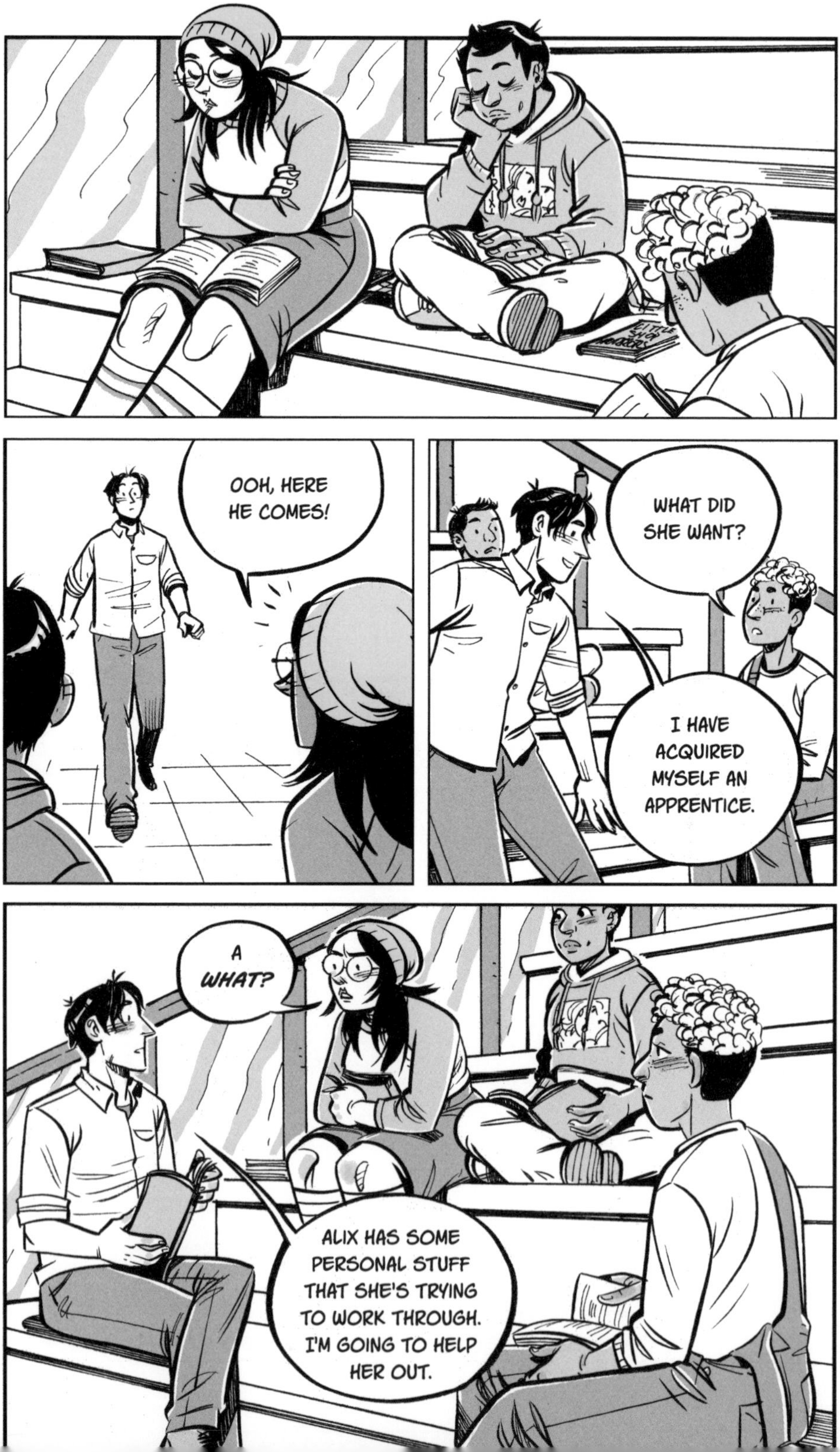
OOH, HERE HE COMES!
WHAT DID SHE WANT?
I HAVE ACQUIRED MYSELF AN APPRENTICE.
A *WHAT?*
ALIX HAS SOME PERSONAL STUFF THAT SHE'S TRYING TO WORK THROUGH. I'M GOING TO HELP HER OUT.

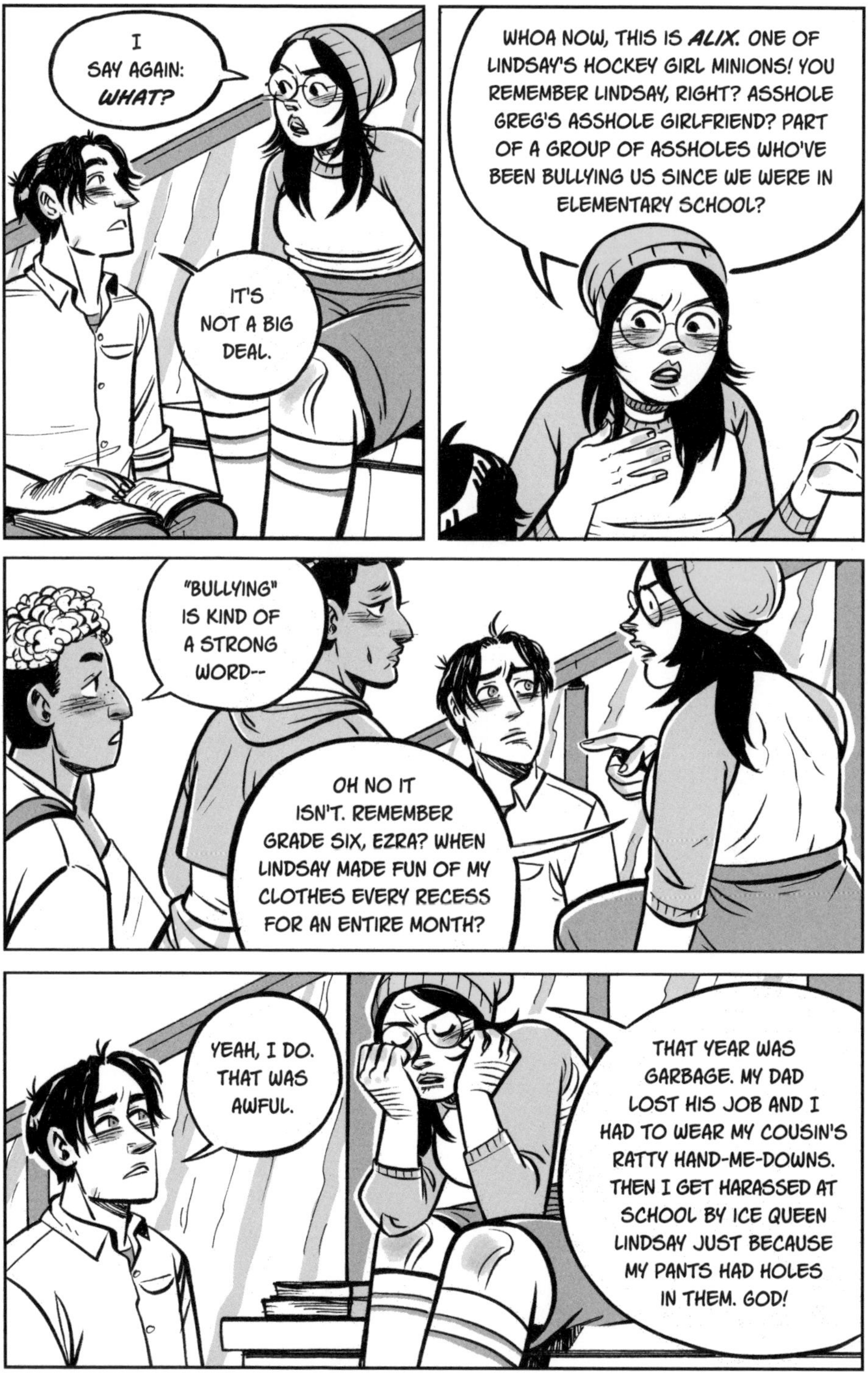
I SAY AGAIN: *WHAT?*
IT'S NOT A BIG DEAL.
WHOA NOW, THIS IS *ALIX*. ONE OF LINDSAY'S HOCKEY GIRL MINIONS! YOU REMEMBER LINDSAY, RIGHT? ASSHOLE GREG'S ASSHOLE GIRLFRIEND? PART OF A GROUP OF ASSHOLES WHO'VE BEEN BULLYING US SINCE WE WERE IN ELEMENTARY SCHOOL?
"BULLYING" IS KIND OF A STRONG WORD--
OH NO IT ISN'T. REMEMBER GRADE SIX, EZRA? WHEN LINDSAY MADE FUN OF MY CLOTHES EVERY RECESS FOR AN ENTIRE MONTH?
YEAH, I DO. THAT WAS AWFUL.
THAT YEAR WAS GARBAGE. MY DAD LOST HIS JOB AND I HAD TO WEAR MY COUSIN'S RATTY HAND-ME-DOWNS. THEN I GET HARASSED AT SCHOOL BY ICE QUEEN LINDSAY JUST BECAUSE MY PANTS HAD HOLES IN THEM. GOD!

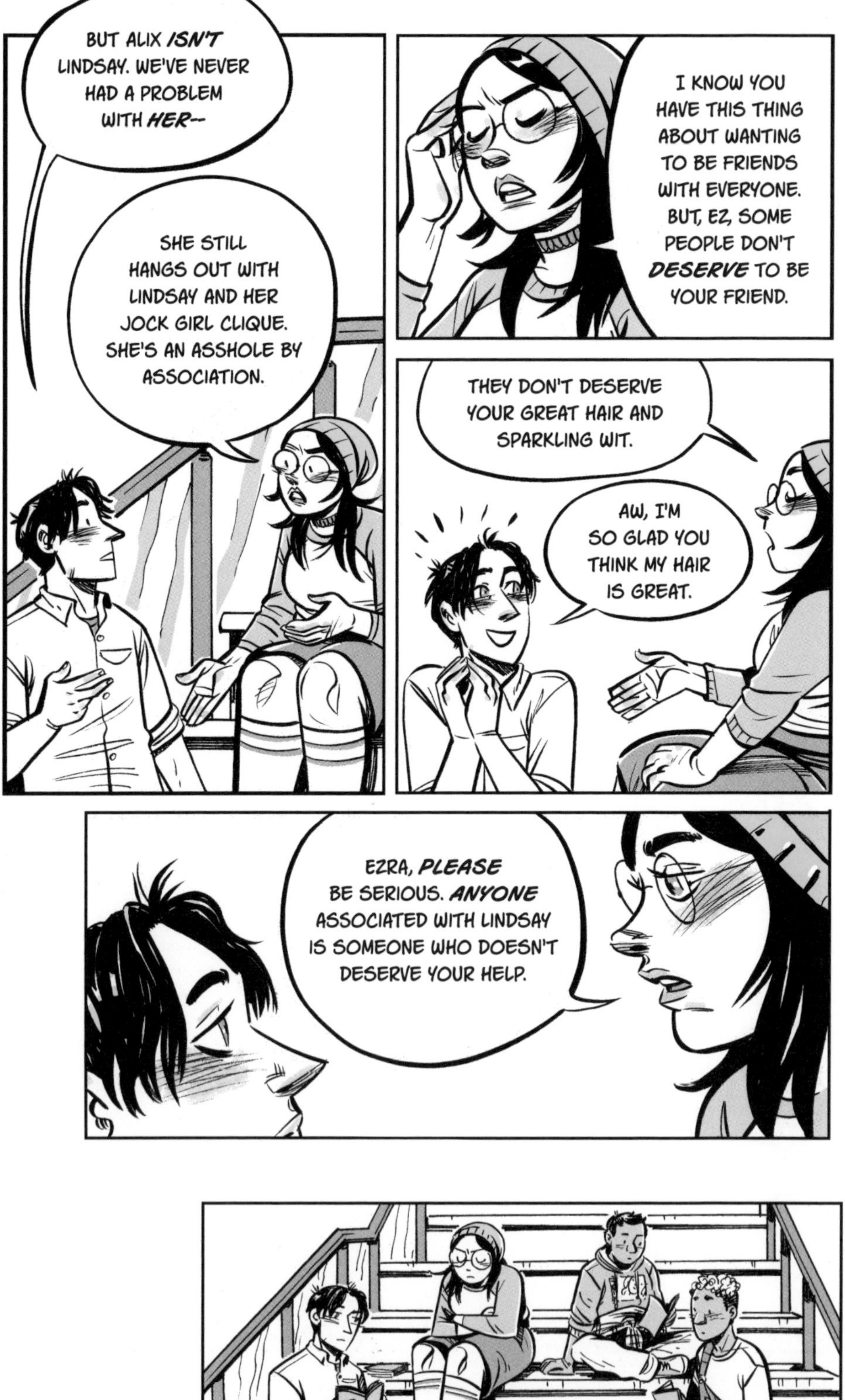
BUT ALIX ISN'T LINDSAY. WE'VE NEVER HAD A PROBLEM WITH HER--
SHE STILL HANGS OUT WITH LINDSAY AND HER JOCK GIRL CLIQUE. SHE'S AN ASSHOLE BY ASSOCIATION.
I KNOW YOU HAVE THIS THING ABOUT WANTING TO BE FRIENDS WITH EVERYONE. BUT, EZ, SOME PEOPLE DON'T DESERVE TO BE YOUR FRIEND.
THEY DON'T DESERVE YOUR GREAT HAIR AND SPARKLING WIT.
AW, I'M SO GLAD YOU THINK MY HAIR IS GREAT.
EZRA, PLEASE BE SERIOUS. ANYONE ASSOCIATED WITH LINDSAY IS SOMEONE WHO DOESN'T DESERVE YOUR HELP.

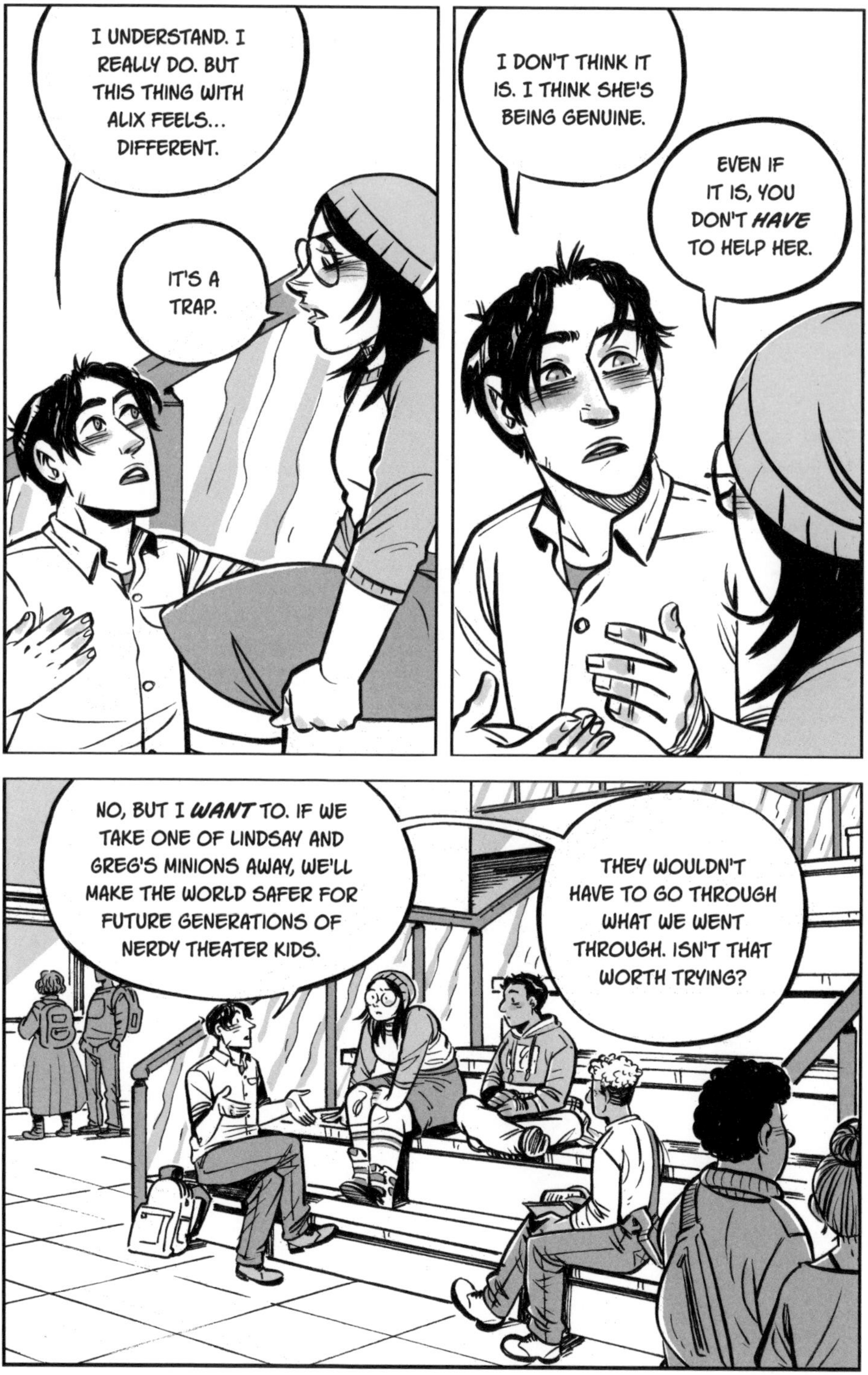
I UNDERSTAND. I REALLY DO. BUT THIS THING WITH ALIX FEELS... DIFFERENT.
IT'S A TRAP.
I DON'T THINK IT IS. I THINK SHE'S BEING GENUINE.
EVEN IF IT IS, YOU DON'T ***HAVE*** TO HELP HER.
NO, BUT I ***WANT*** TO. IF WE TAKE ONE OF LINDSAY AND GREG'S MINIONS AWAY, WE'LL MAKE THE WORLD SAFER FOR FUTURE GENERATIONS OF NERDY THEATER KIDS.
THEY WOULDN'T HAVE TO GO THROUGH WHAT WE WENT THROUGH. ISN'T THAT WORTH TRYING?

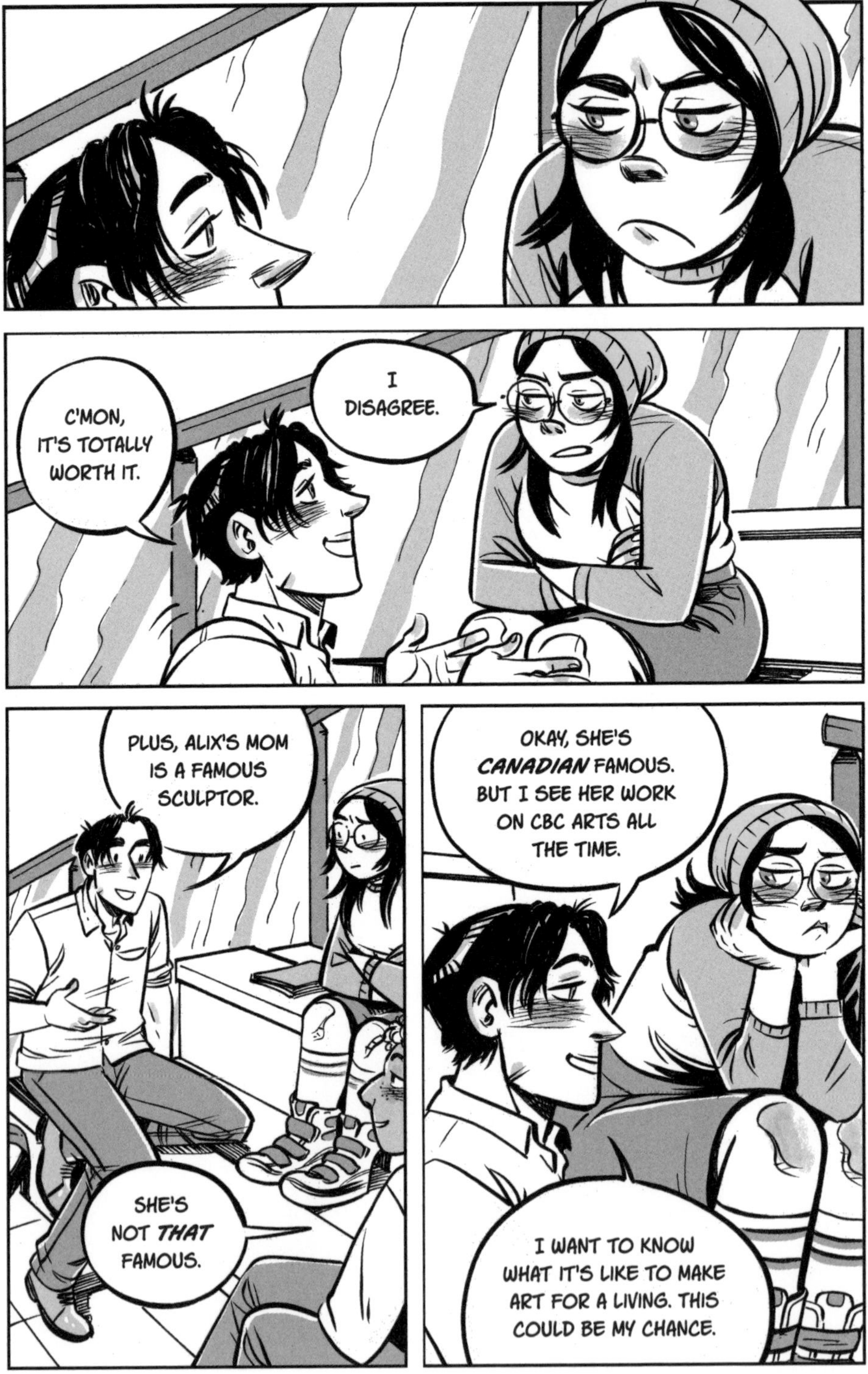
C'MON, IT'S TOTALLY WORTH IT.
I DISAGREE.
PLUS, ALIX'S MOM IS A FAMOUS SCULPTOR.
SHE'S NOT *THAT* FAMOUS.
OKAY, SHE'S *CANADIAN* FAMOUS. BUT I SEE HER WORK ON CBC ARTS ALL THE TIME.
I WANT TO KNOW WHAT IT'S LIKE TO MAKE ART FOR A LIVING. THIS COULD BE MY CHANCE.

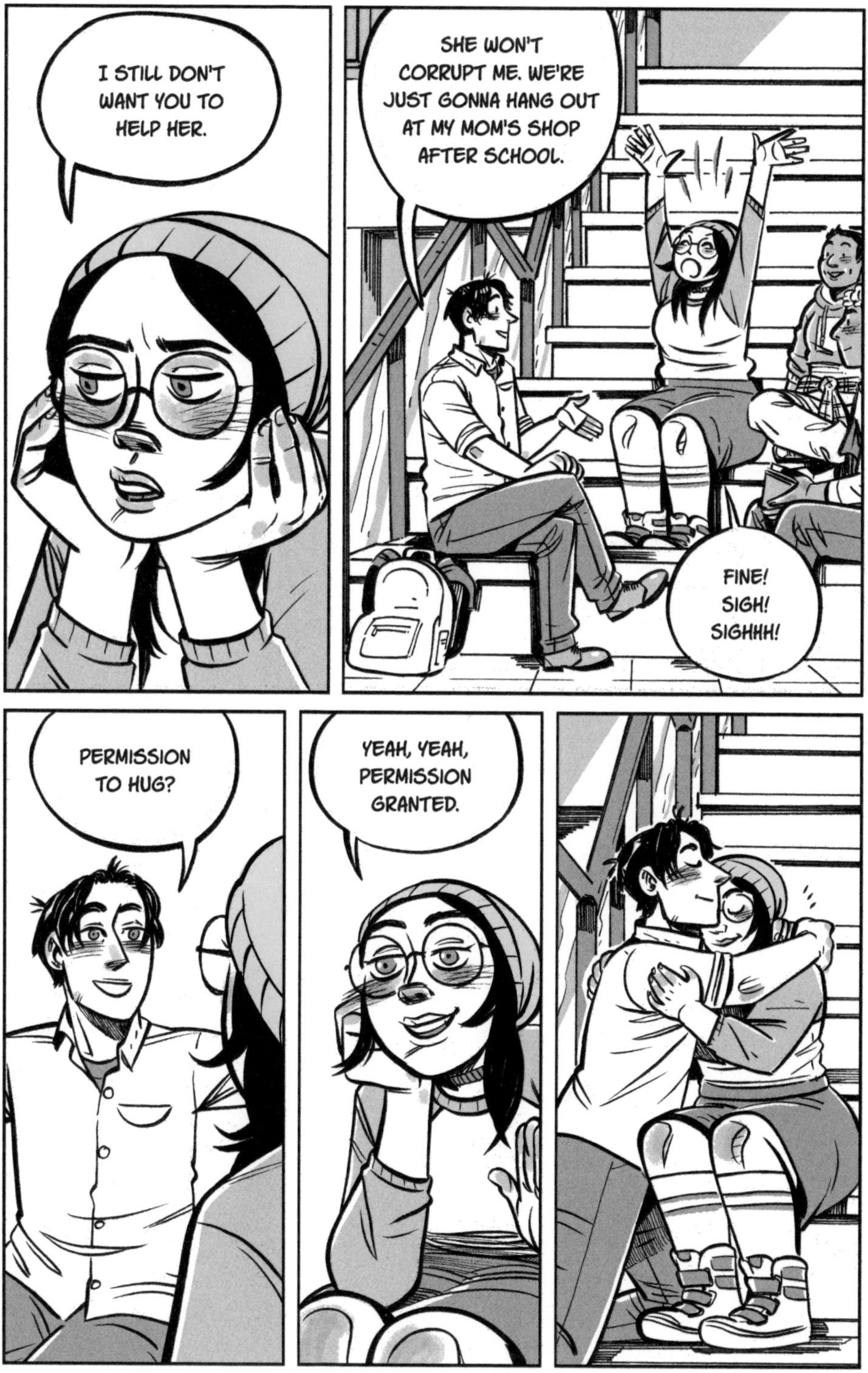
I STILL DON'T WANT YOU TO HELP HER.
SHE WON'T CORRUPT ME. WE'RE JUST GONNA HANG OUT AT MY MOM'S SHOP AFTER SCHOOL.
FINE! SIGH! SIGHHH!
PERMISSION TO HUG?
YEAH, YEAH, PERMISSION GRANTED.

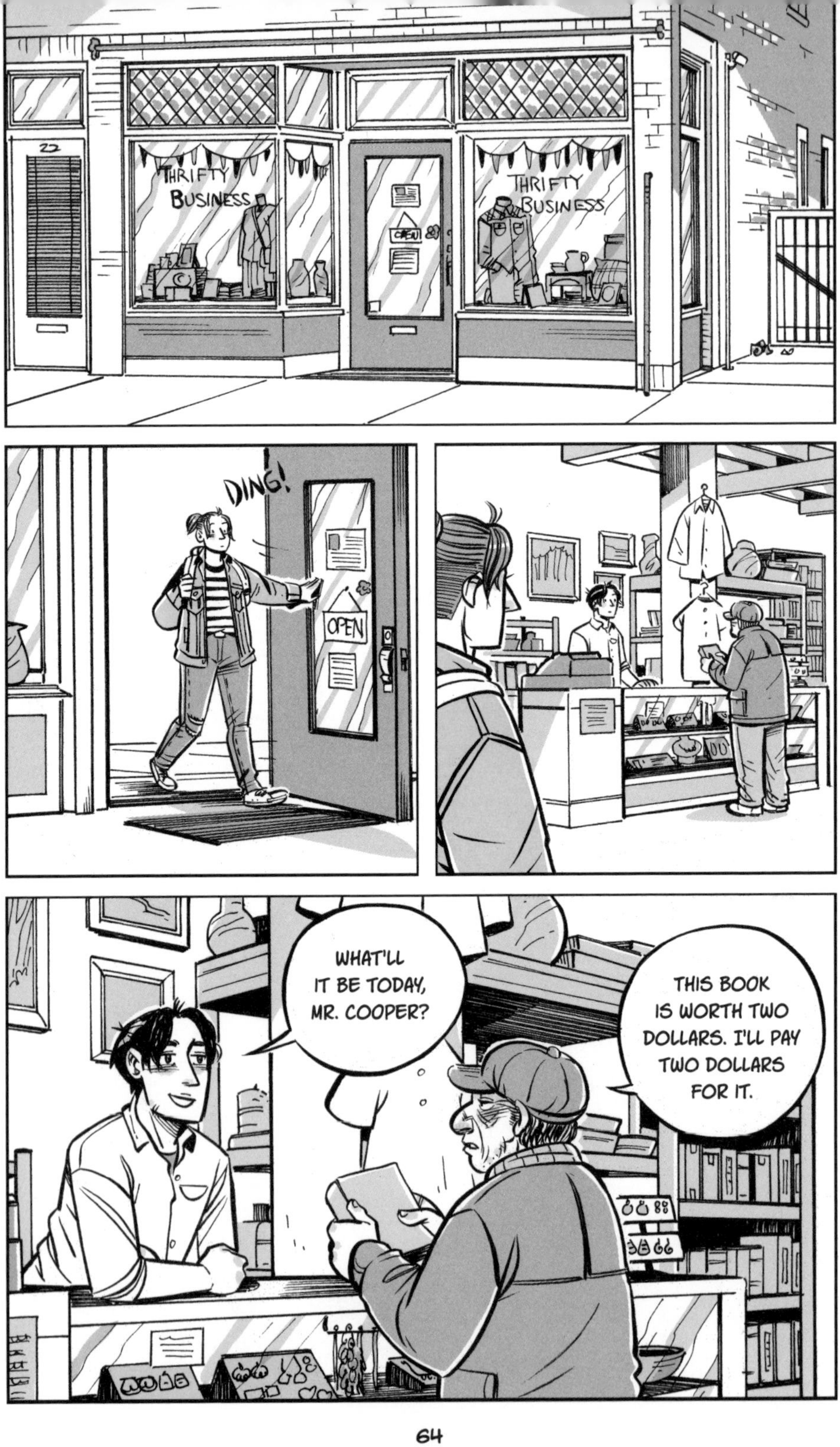
THRIFTY BUSINESS
THRIFTY BUSINESS
OPEN
DING!
OPEN
WHAT'LL IT BE TODAY, MR. COOPER?
THIS BOOK IS WORTH TWO DOLLARS. I'LL PAY TWO DOLLARS FOR IT.

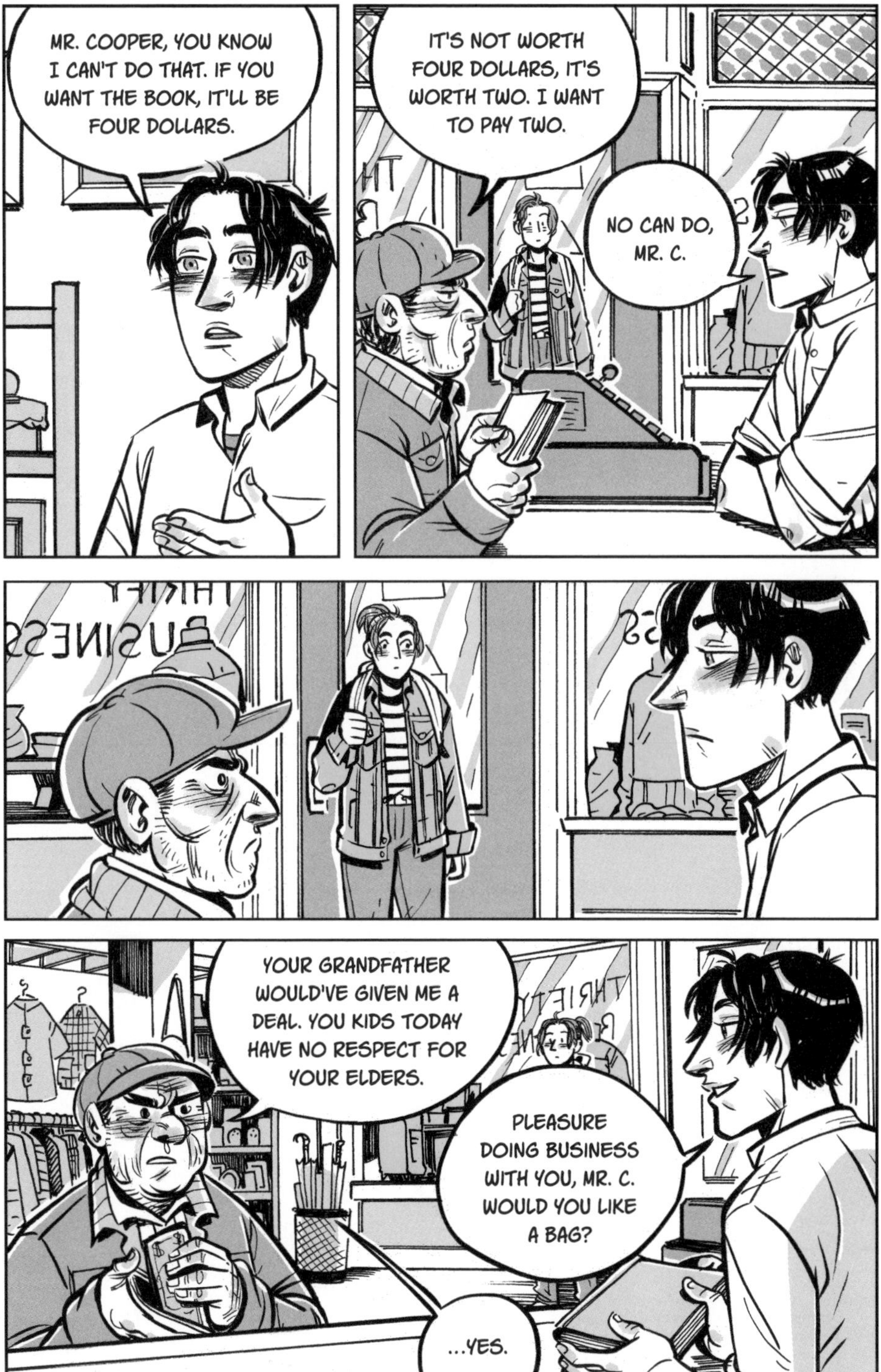
MR. COOPER, YOU KNOW I CAN'T DO THAT. IF YOU WANT THE BOOK, IT'LL BE FOUR DOLLARS.
IT'S NOT WORTH FOUR DOLLARS, IT'S WORTH TWO. I WANT TO PAY TWO.
NO CAN DO, MR. C.
YOUR GRANDFATHER WOULD'VE GIVEN ME A DEAL. YOU KIDS TODAY HAVE NO RESPECT FOR YOUR ELDERS.
PLEASURE DOING BUSINESS WITH YOU, MR. C. WOULD YOU LIKE A BAG?
...YES.

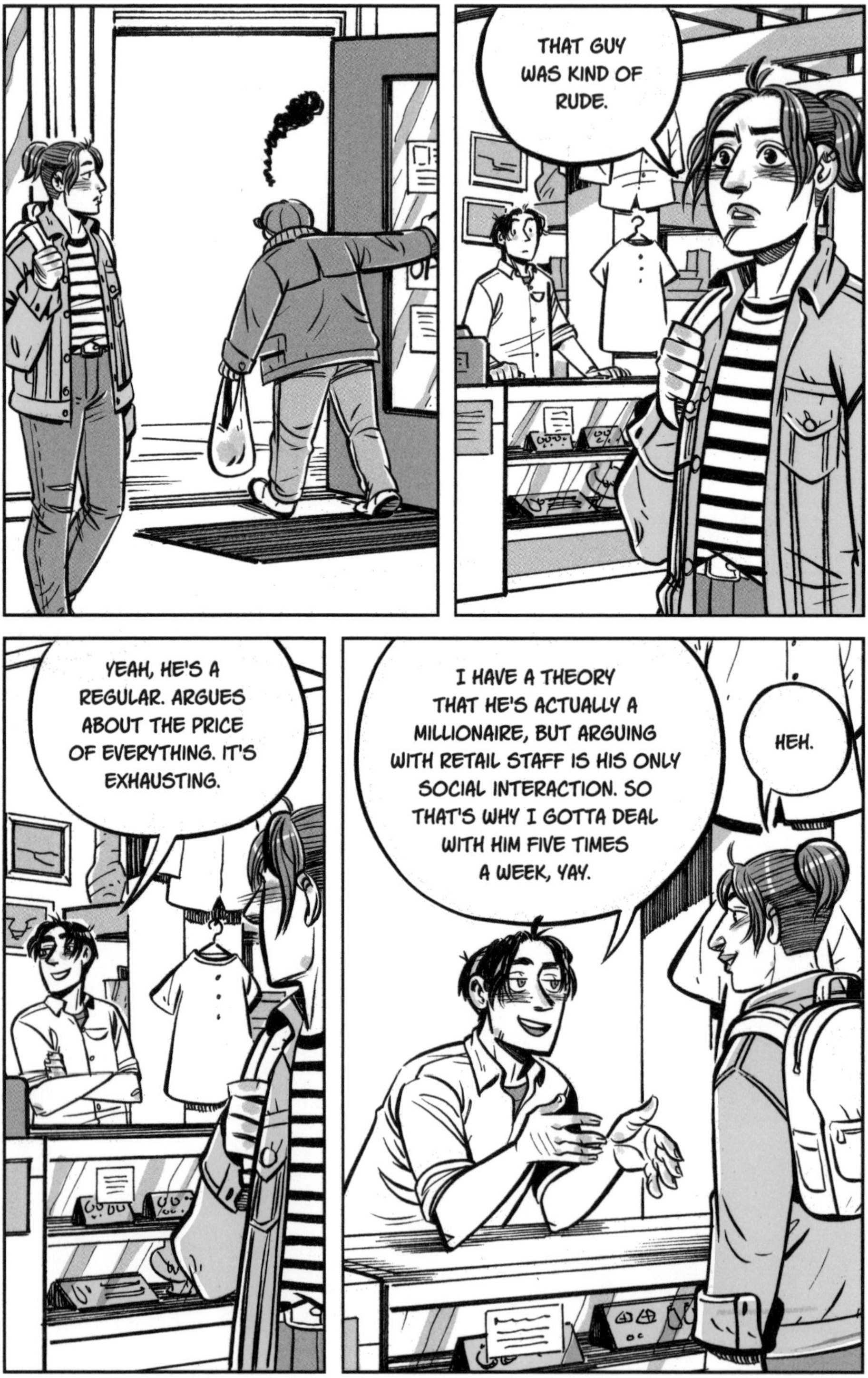
THAT GUY WAS KIND OF RUDE.
YEAH, HE'S A REGULAR. ARGUES ABOUT THE PRICE OF EVERYTHING. IT'S EXHAUSTING.
I HAVE A THEORY THAT HE'S ACTUALLY A MILLIONAIRE, BUT ARGUING WITH RETAIL STAFF IS HIS ONLY SOCIAL INTERACTION. SO THAT'S WHY I GOTTA DEAL WITH HIM FIVE TIMES A WEEK, YAY.
HEH.

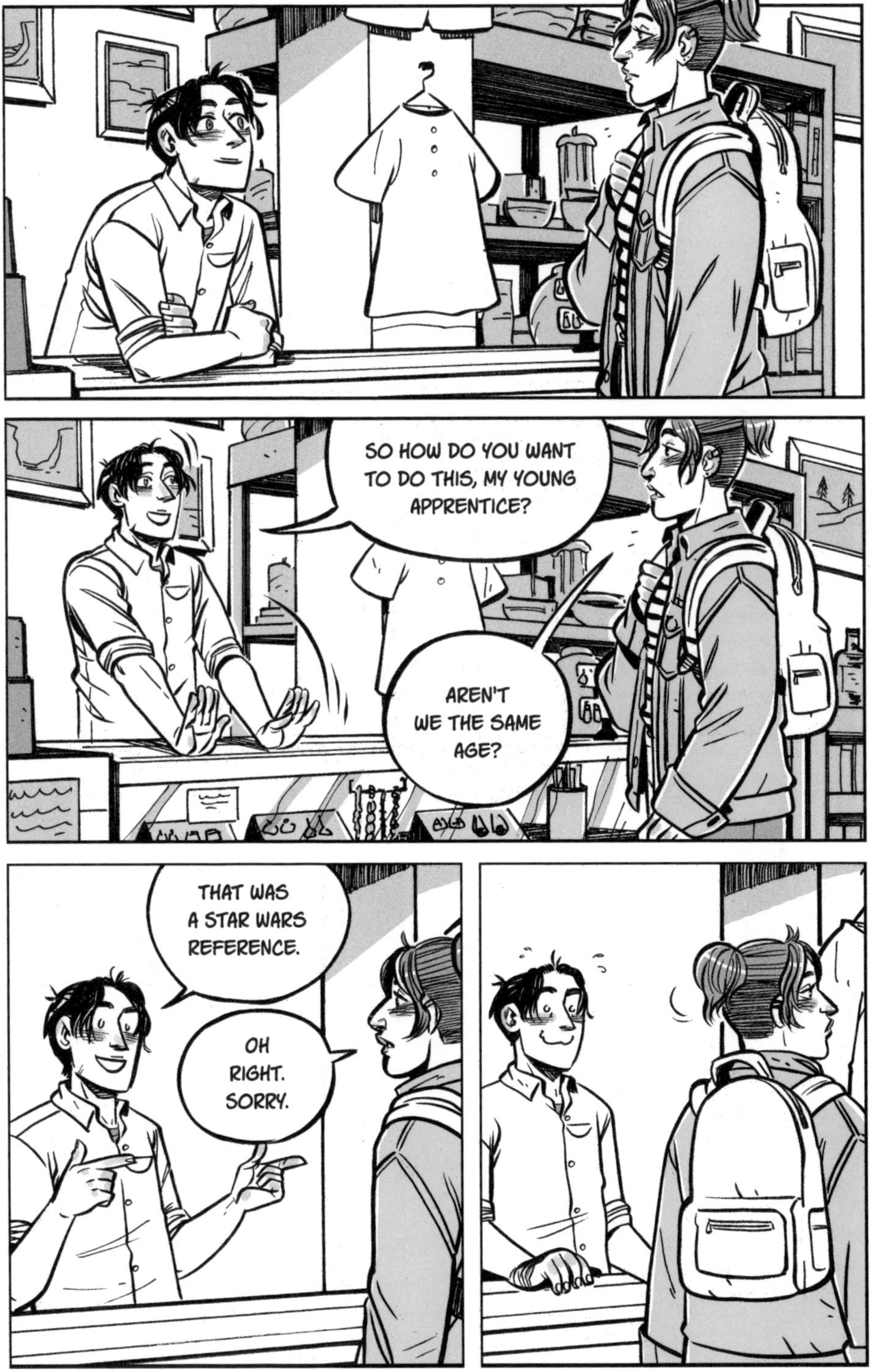
SO HOW DO YOU WANT TO DO THIS, MY YOUNG APPRENTICE?
AREN'T WE THE SAME AGE?
THAT WAS A STAR WARS REFERENCE.
OH RIGHT. SORRY.

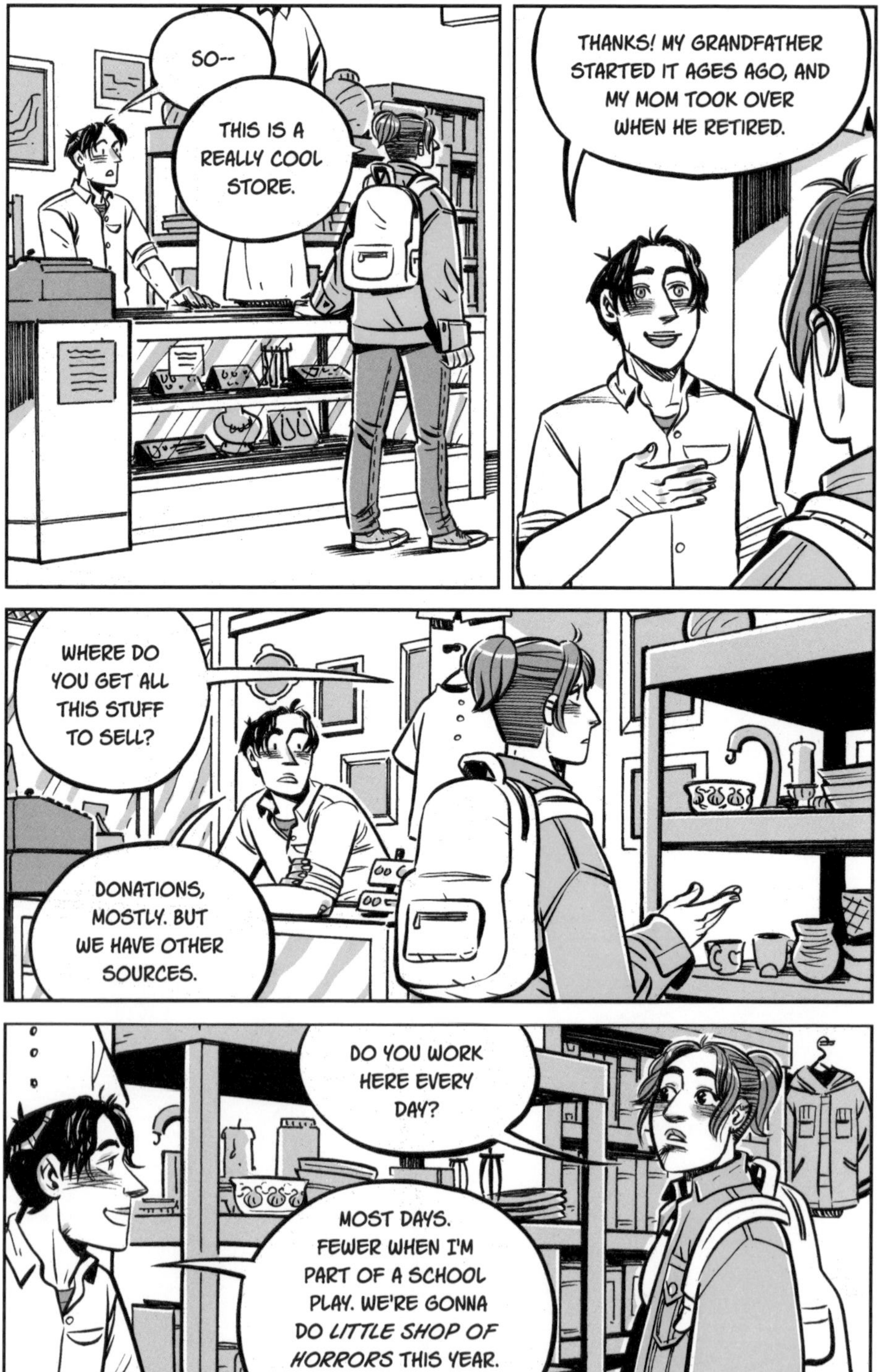
SO--
THIS IS A REALLY COOL STORE.
THANKS! MY GRANDFATHER STARTED IT AGES AGO, AND MY MOM TOOK OVER WHEN HE RETIRED.
WHERE DO YOU GET ALL THIS STUFF TO SELL?
DONATIONS, MOSTLY. BUT WE HAVE OTHER SOURCES.
. . .
DO YOU WORK HERE EVERY DAY?
MOST DAYS. FEWER WHEN I'M PART OF A SCHOOL PLAY. WE'RE GONNA DO *LITTLE SHOP OF HORRORS* THIS YEAR.

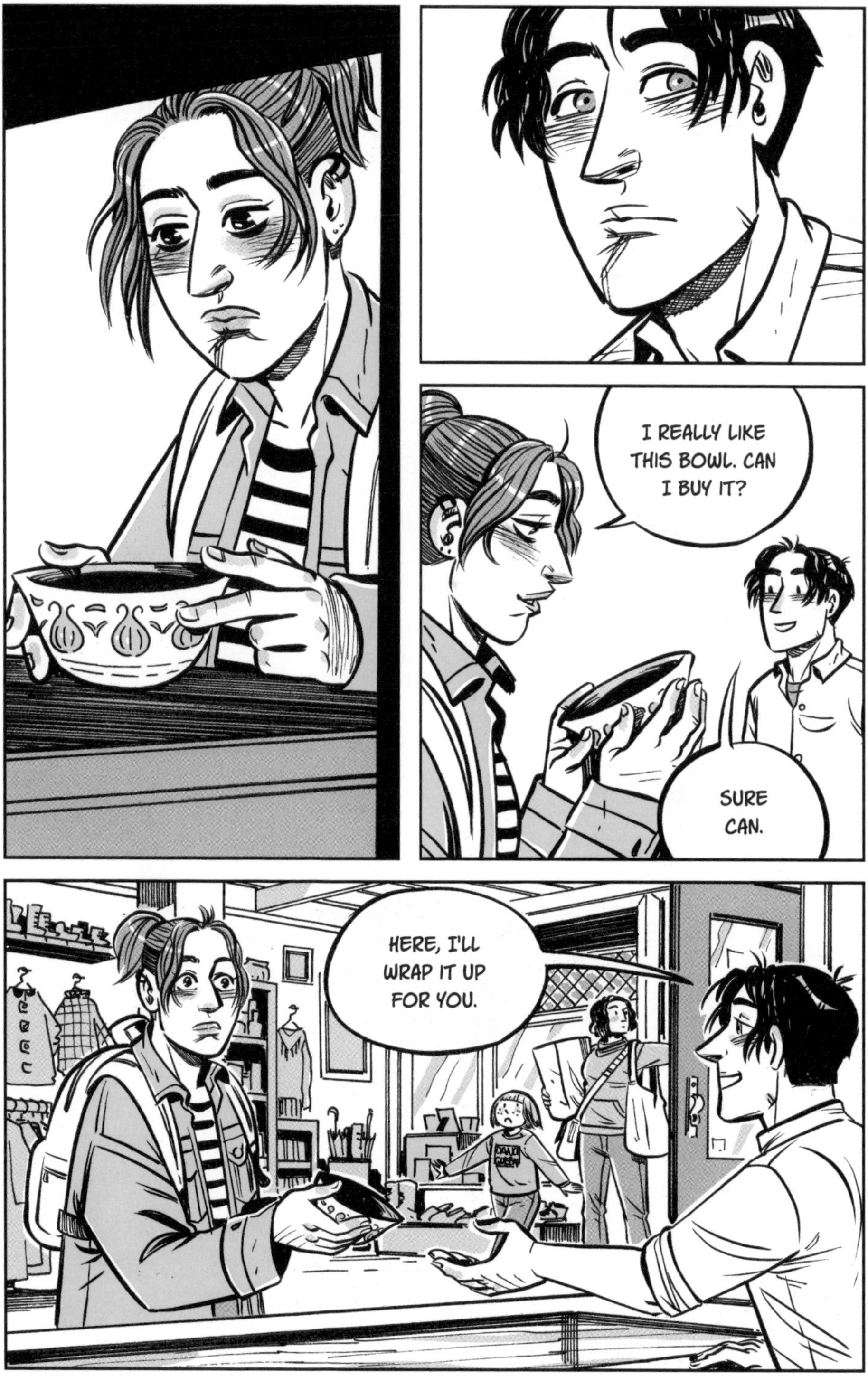
I REALLY LIKE THIS BOWL. CAN I BUY IT?
SURE CAN.
HERE, I'LL WRAP IT UP FOR YOU.

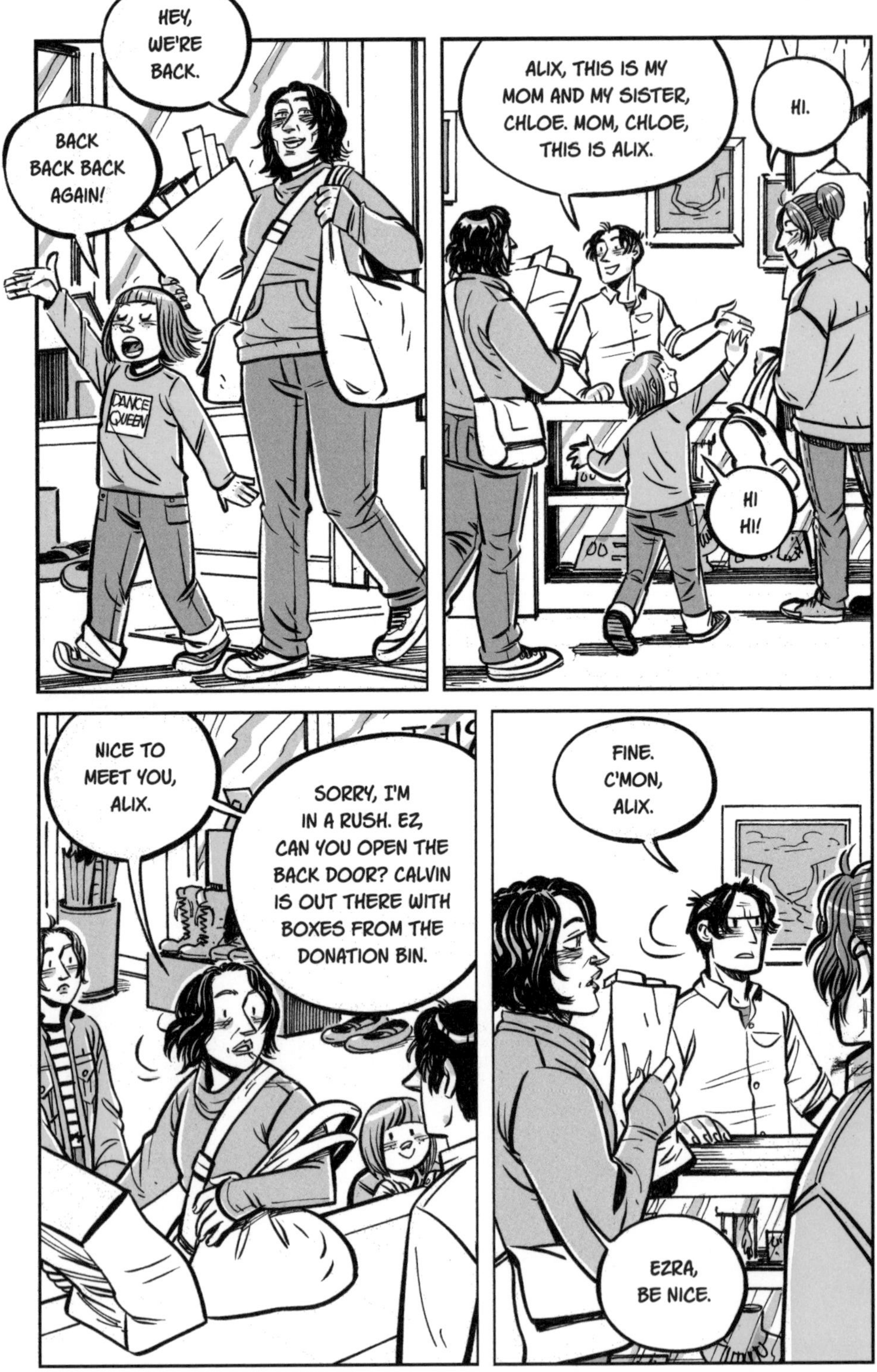
HEY, WE'RE BACK.
BACK BACK BACK AGAIN!
DANCE QUEEN
ALIX, THIS IS MY MOM AND MY SISTER, CHLOE. MOM, CHLOE, THIS IS ALIX.
HI.
HI HI!
NICE TO MEET YOU, ALIX.
SORRY, I'M IN A RUSH. EZ, CAN YOU OPEN THE BACK DOOR? CALVIN IS OUT THERE WITH BOXES FROM THE DONATION BIN.
FINE. C'MON, ALIX.
EZRA, BE NICE.

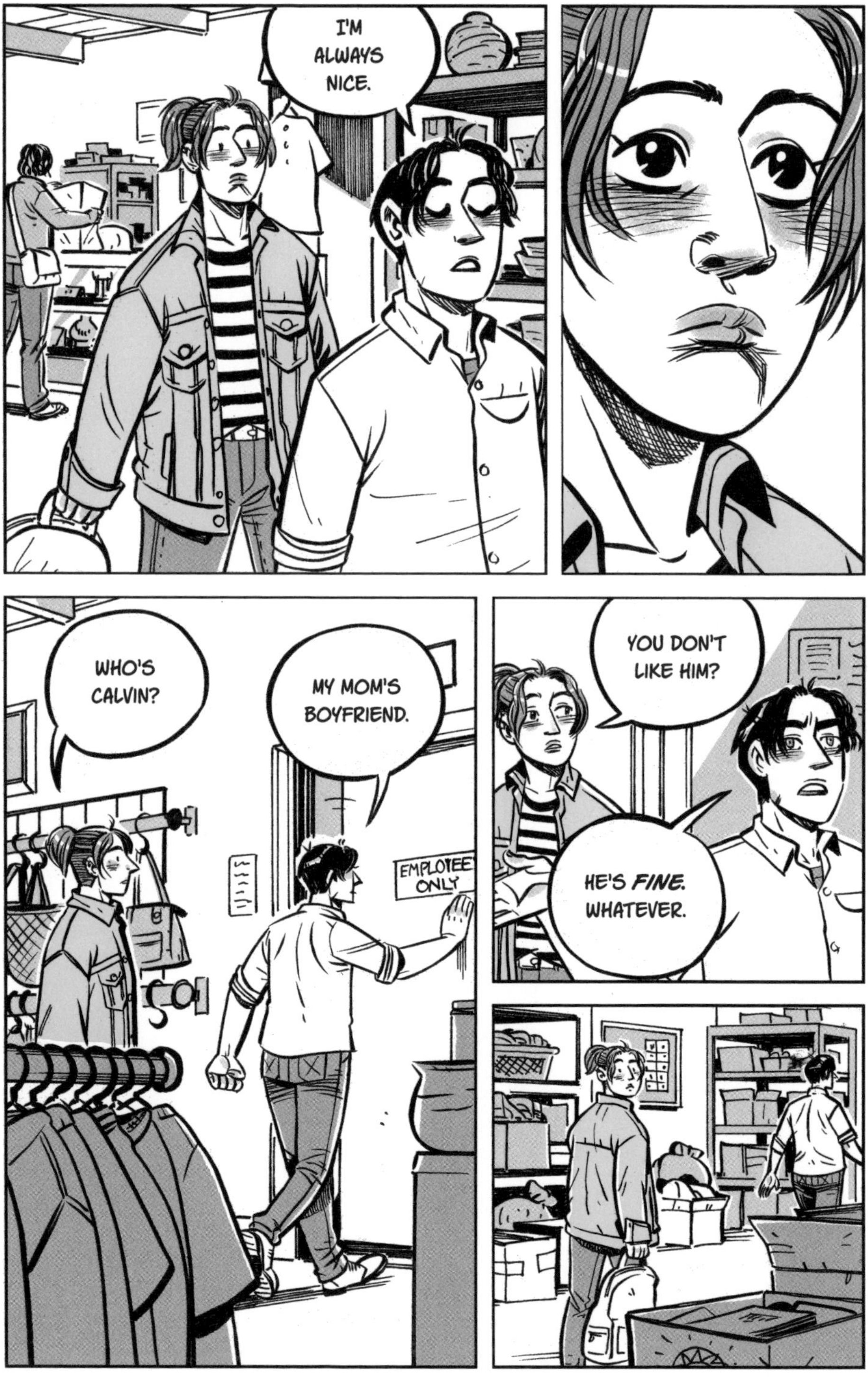
I'M ALWAYS NICE.
WHO'S CALVIN?
MY MOM'S BOYFRIEND.
EMPLOYEE ONLY
YOU DON'T LIKE HIM?
HE'S *FINE.* WHATEVER.

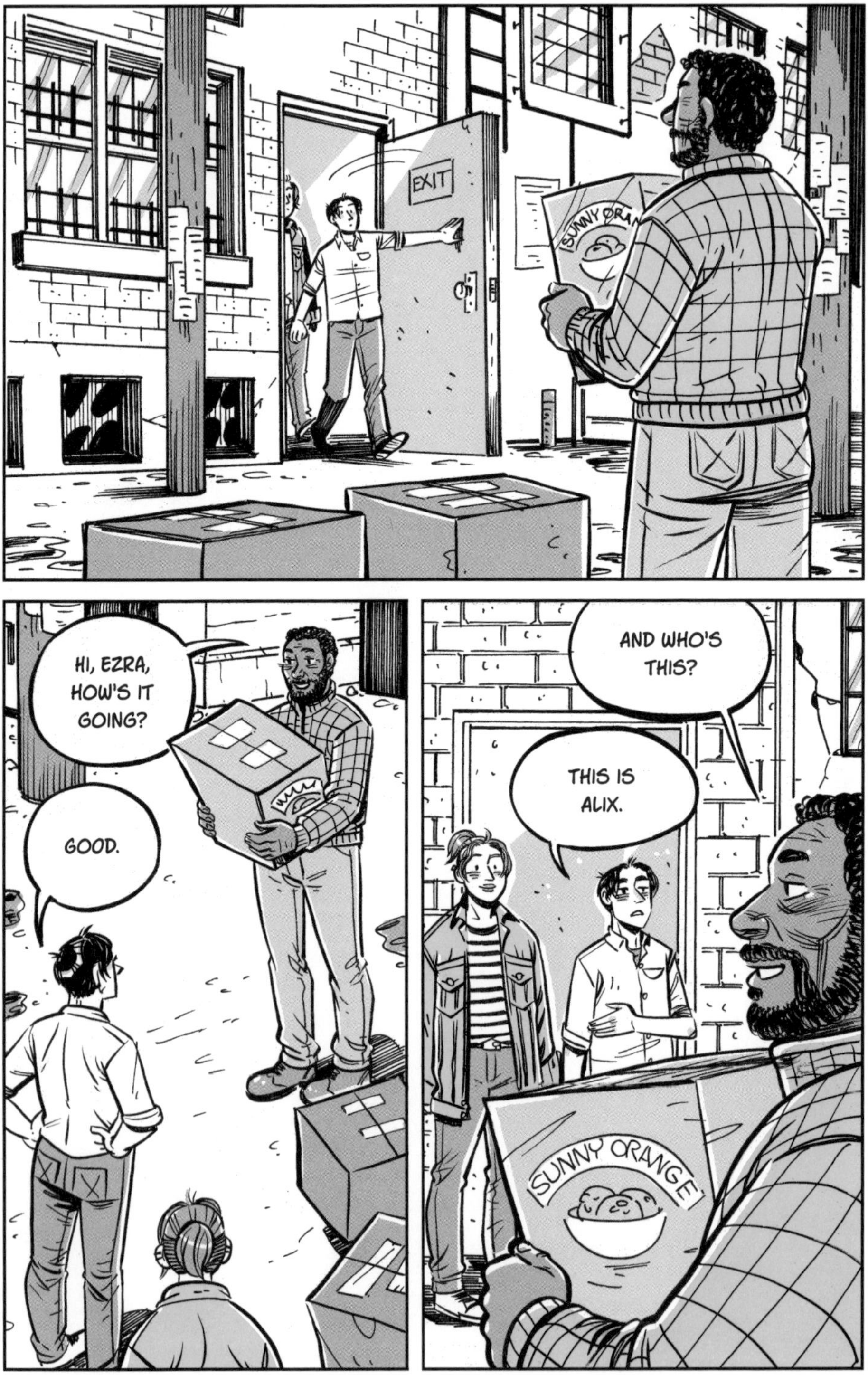
EXIT
SUNNY ORAN
HI, EZRA, HOW'S IT GOING?
GOOD.
AND WHO'S THIS?
THIS IS ALIX.
SUNNY ORANGE

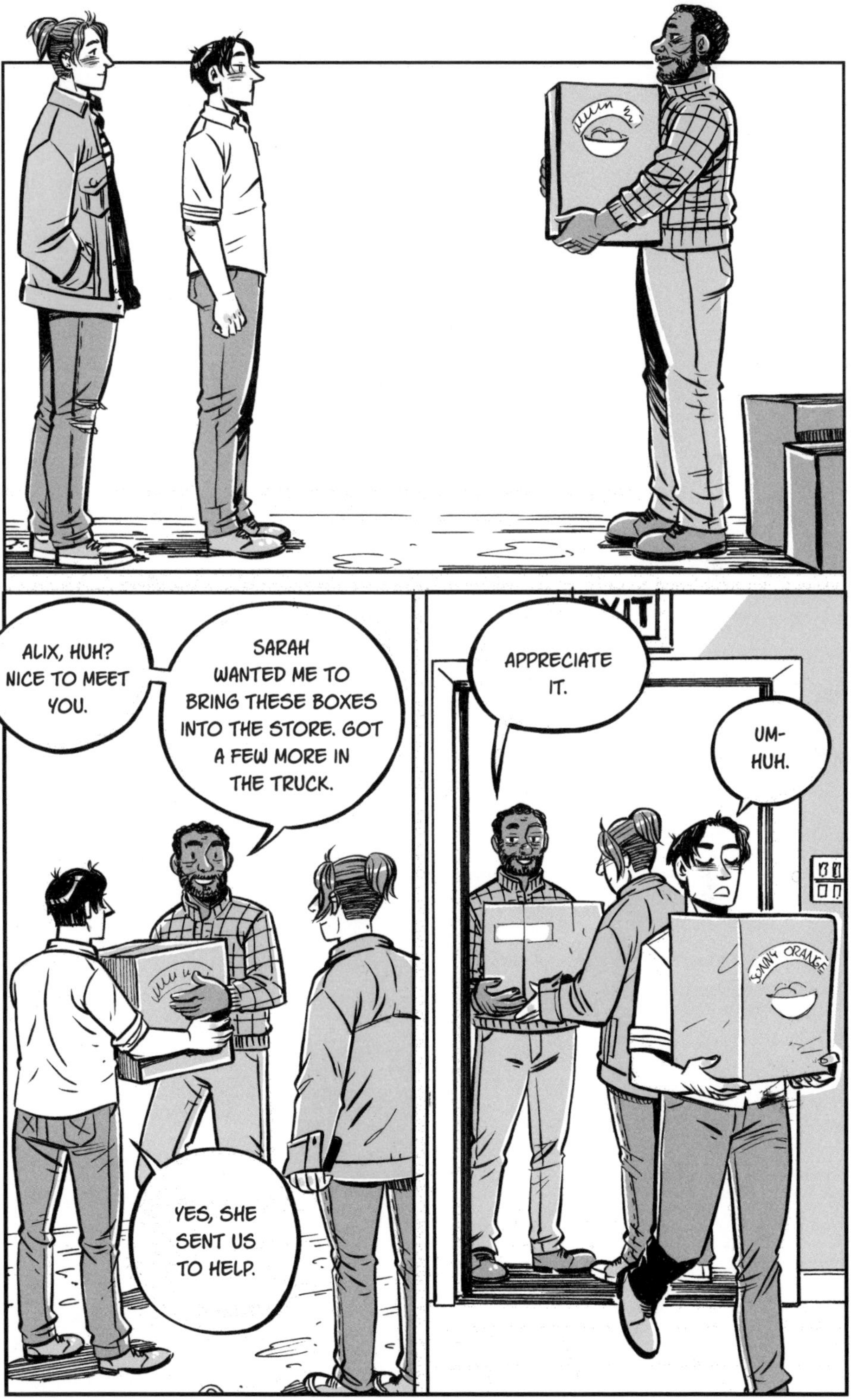
ALIX, HUH? NICE TO MEET YOU.
SARAH WANTED ME TO BRING THESE BOXES INTO THE STORE. GOT A FEW MORE IN THE TRUCK.
YES, SHE SENT US TO HELP.
APPRECIATE IT.
UM-HUH.

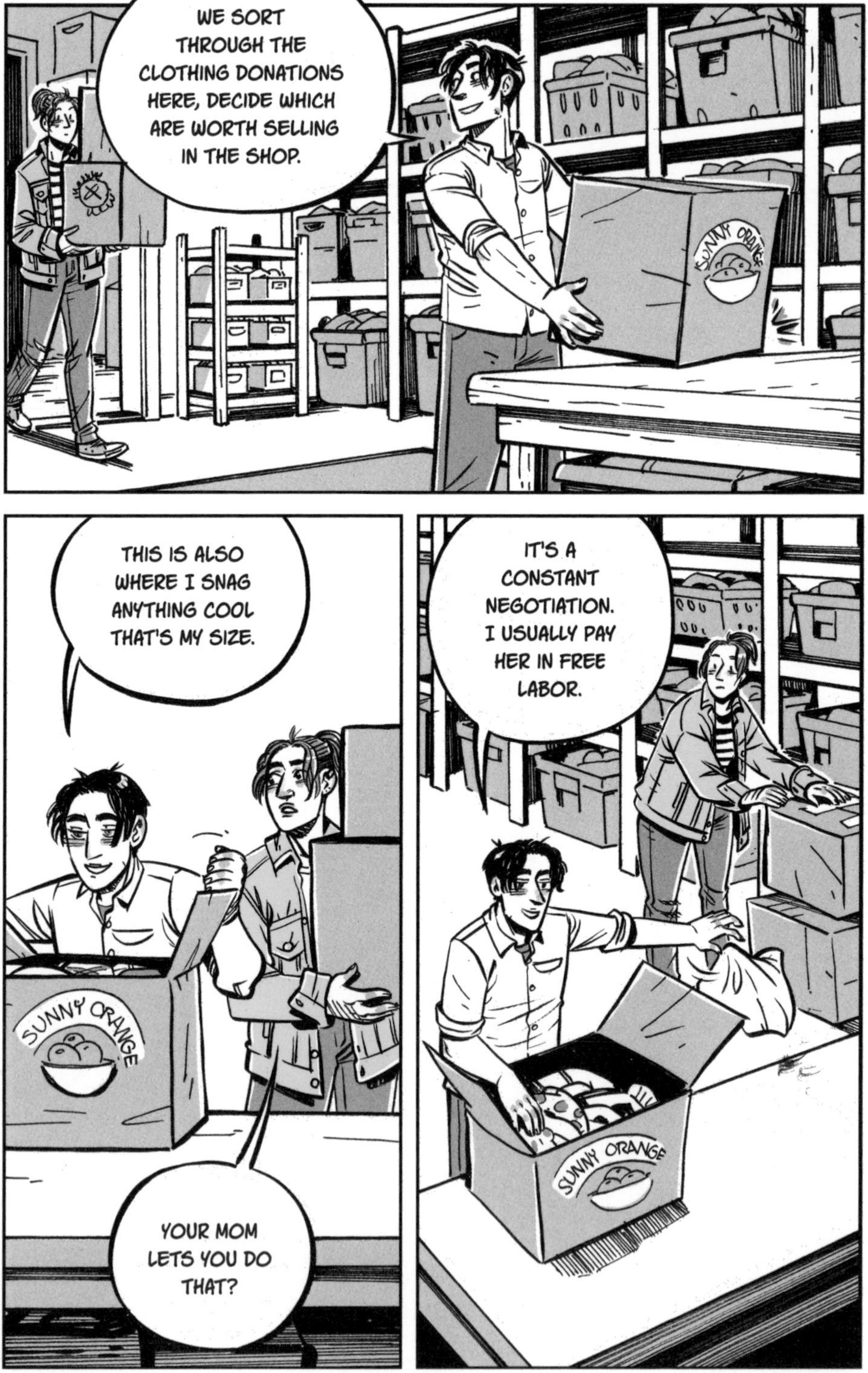
WE SORT THROUGH THE CLOTHING DONATIONS HERE, DECIDE WHICH ARE WORTH SELLING IN THE SHOP.
SUNNY ORANGE
THIS IS ALSO WHERE I SNAG ANYTHING COOL THAT'S MY SIZE.
SUNNY ORANGE
YOUR MOM LETS YOU DO THAT?
IT'S A CONSTANT NEGOTIATION. I USUALLY PAY HER IN FREE LABOR.
SUNNY ORANGE

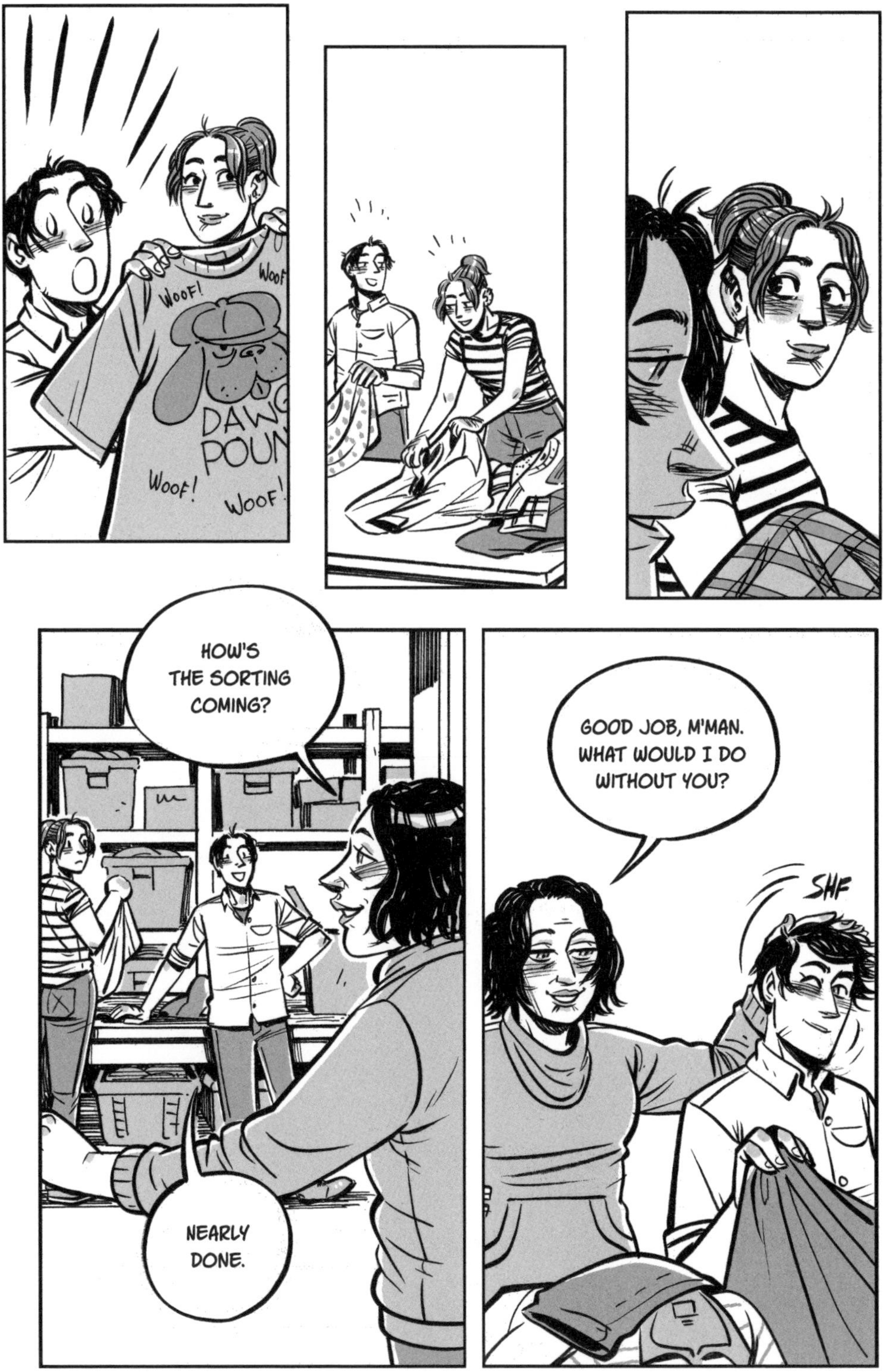
WOOF!
WOOF
DAWG
POUN
WOOF!
WOOF!
HOW'S THE SORTING COMING?
NEARLY DONE.
GOOD JOB, M'MAN. WHAT WOULD I DO WITHOUT YOU?
SHF

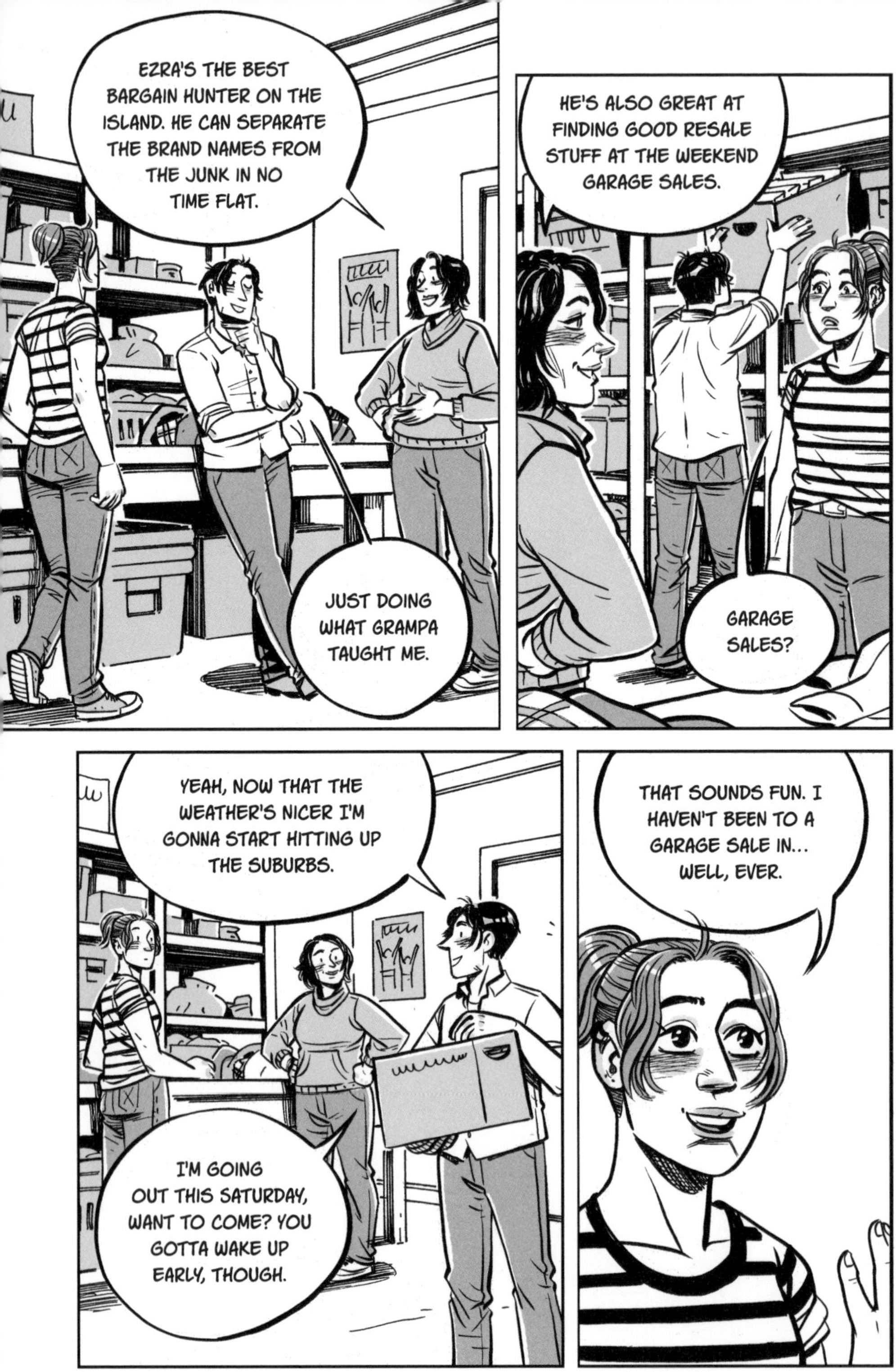
EZRA'S THE BEST BARGAIN HUNTER ON THE ISLAND. HE CAN SEPARATE THE BRAND NAMES FROM THE JUNK IN NO TIME FLAT.
JUST DOING WHAT GRAMPA TAUGHT ME.
HE'S ALSO GREAT AT FINDING GOOD RESALE STUFF AT THE WEEKEND GARAGE SALES.
GARAGE SALES?
YEAH, NOW THAT THE WEATHER'S NICER I'M GONNA START HITTING UP THE SUBURBS.
I'M GOING OUT THIS SATURDAY, WANT TO COME? YOU GOTTA WAKE UP EARLY, THOUGH.
THAT SOUNDS FUN. I HAVEN'T BEEN TO A GARAGE SALE IN... WELL, EVER.

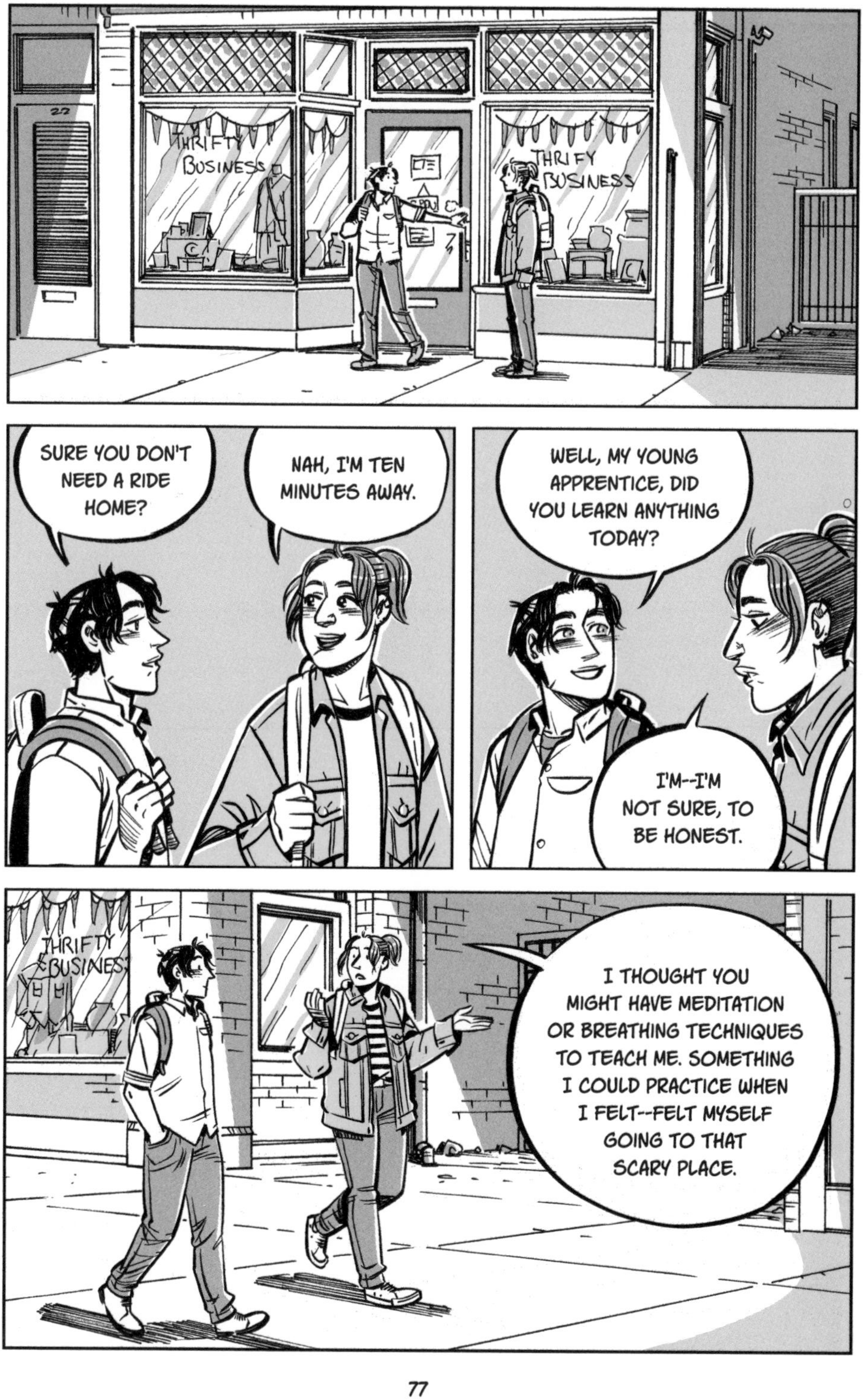
THRIFTY BUSINESS
THRIFY BUSINESS
SURE YOU DON'T NEED A RIDE HOME?
NAH, I'M TEN MINUTES AWAY.
WELL, MY YOUNG APPRENTICE, DID YOU LEARN ANYTHING TODAY?
I'M--I'M NOT SURE, TO BE HONEST.
I THOUGHT YOU MIGHT HAVE MEDITATION OR BREATHING TECHNIQUES TO TEACH ME. SOMETHING I COULD PRACTICE WHEN I FELT--FELT MYSELF GOING TO THAT SCARY PLACE.

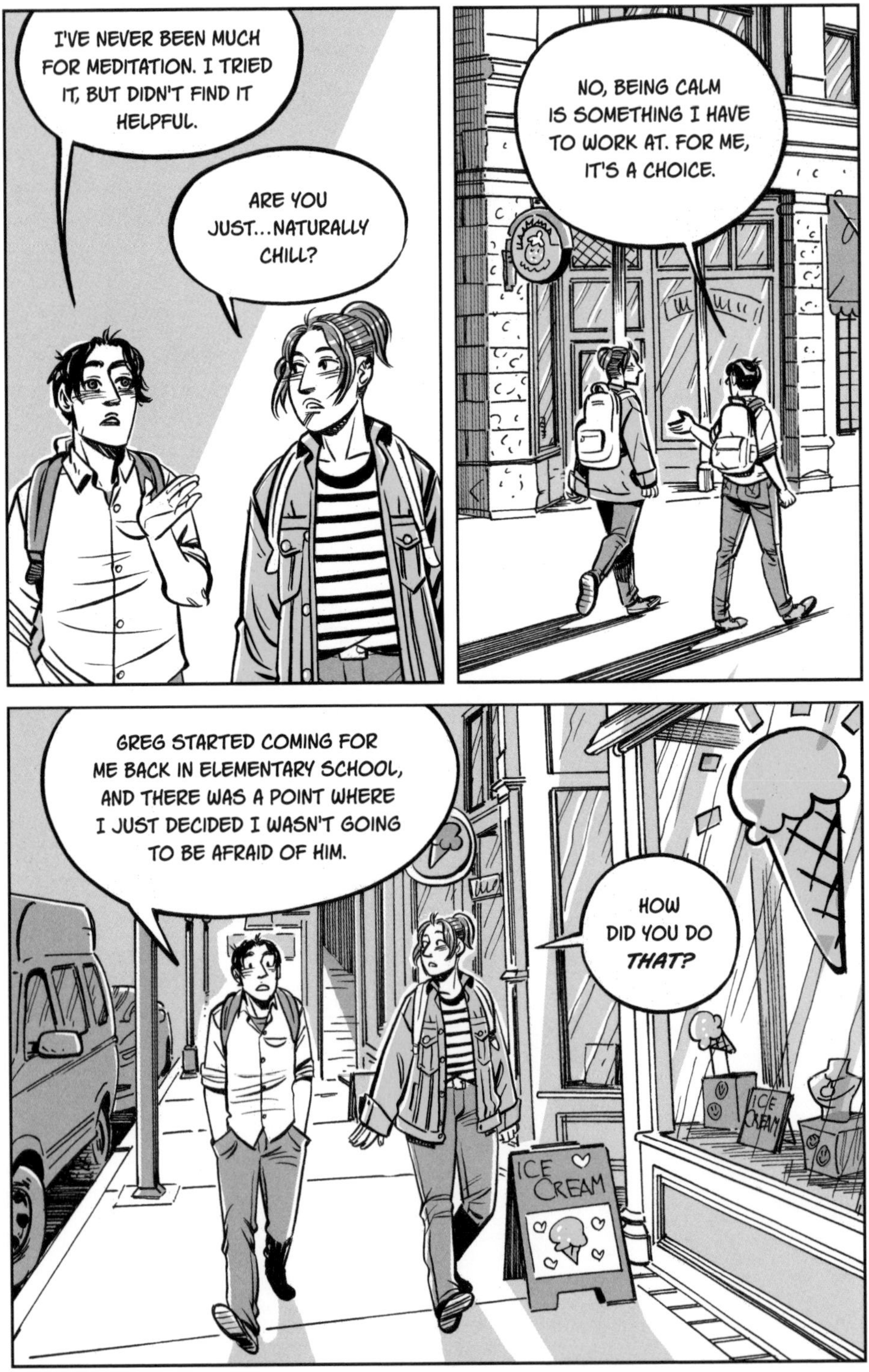
I'VE NEVER BEEN MUCH FOR MEDITATION. I TRIED IT, BUT DIDN'T FIND IT HELPFUL.
ARE YOU JUST...NATURALLY CHILL?
NO, BEING CALM IS SOMETHING I HAVE TO WORK AT. FOR ME, IT'S A CHOICE.
GREG STARTED COMING FOR ME BACK IN ELEMENTARY SCHOOL, AND THERE WAS A POINT WHERE I JUST DECIDED I WASN'T GOING TO BE AFRAID OF HIM.
HOW DID YOU DO *THAT?*
ICE CREAM
ICE CREAM

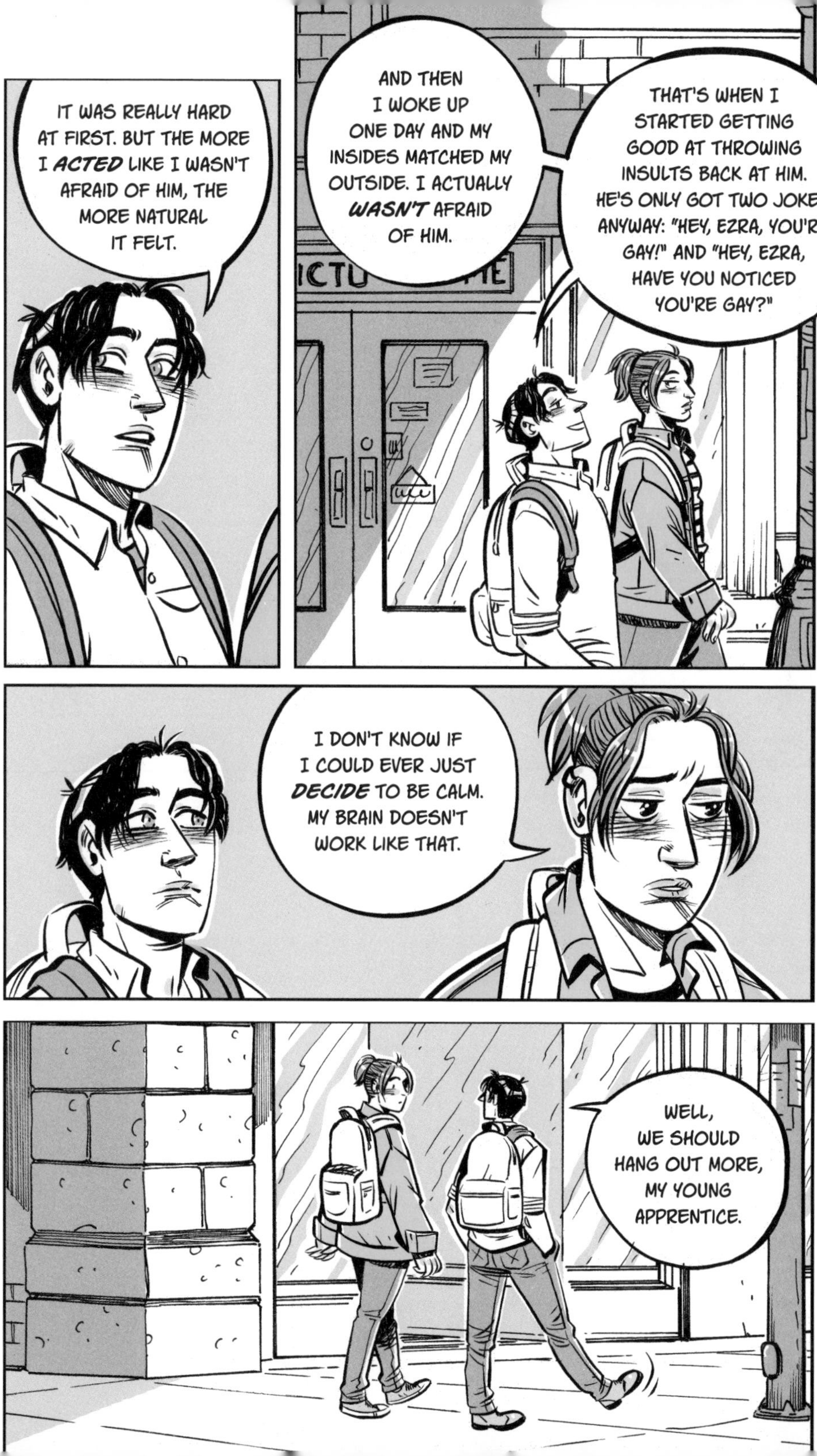
IT WAS REALLY HARD AT FIRST. BUT THE MORE I ACTED LIKE I WASN'T AFRAID OF HIM, THE MORE NATURAL IT FELT.
AND THEN I WOKE UP ONE DAY AND MY INSIDES MATCHED MY OUTSIDE. I ACTUALLY WASN'T AFRAID OF HIM.
THAT'S WHEN I STARTED GETTING GOOD AT THROWING INSULTS BACK AT HIM. HE'S ONLY GOT TWO JOKES ANYWAY: "HEY, EZRA, YOU'RE GAY!" AND "HEY, EZRA, HAVE YOU NOTICED YOU'RE GAY?"
I DON'T KNOW IF I COULD EVER JUST DECIDE TO BE CALM. MY BRAIN DOESN'T WORK LIKE THAT.
WELL, WE SHOULD HANG OUT MORE, MY YOUNG APPRENTICE.

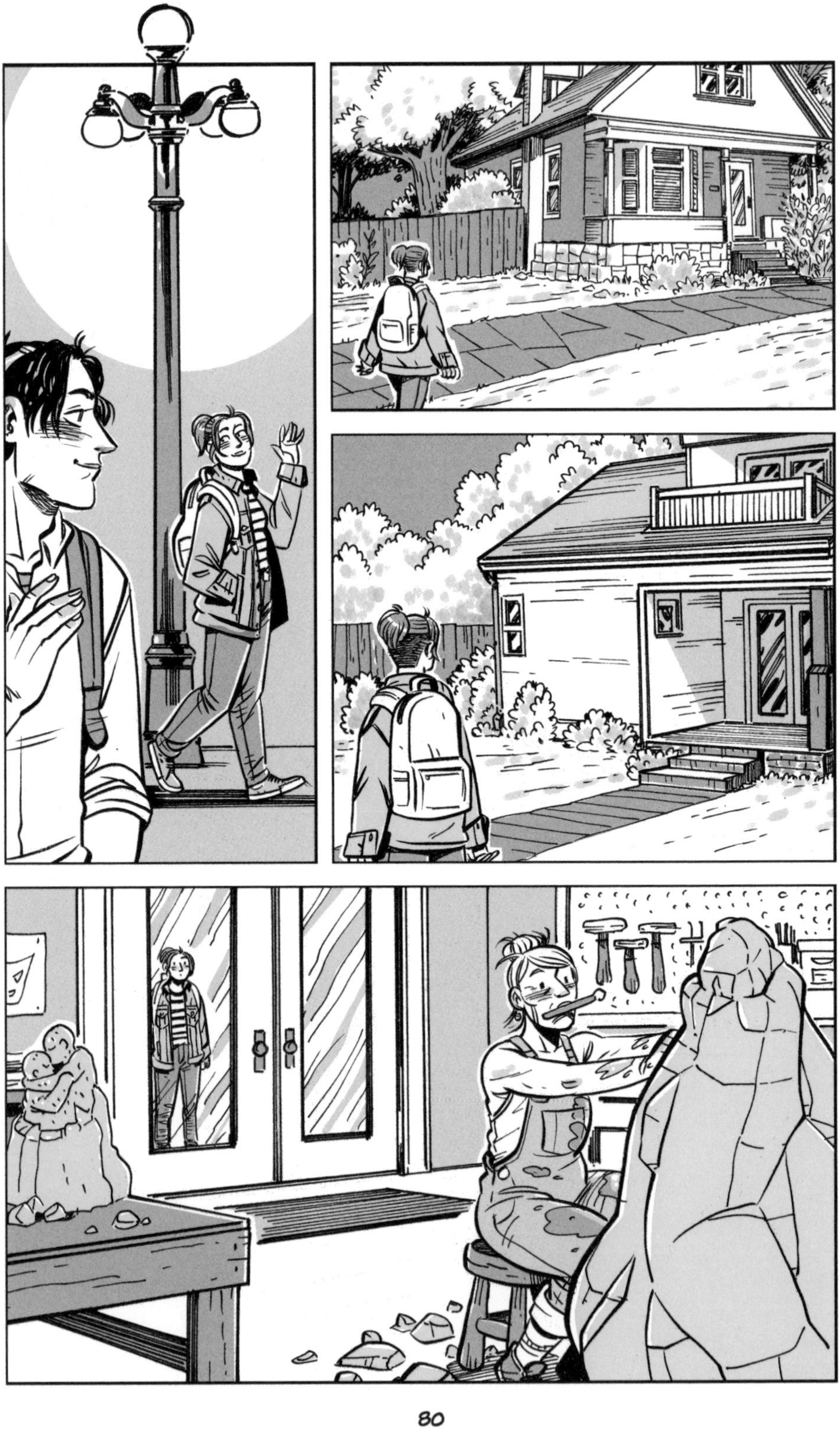

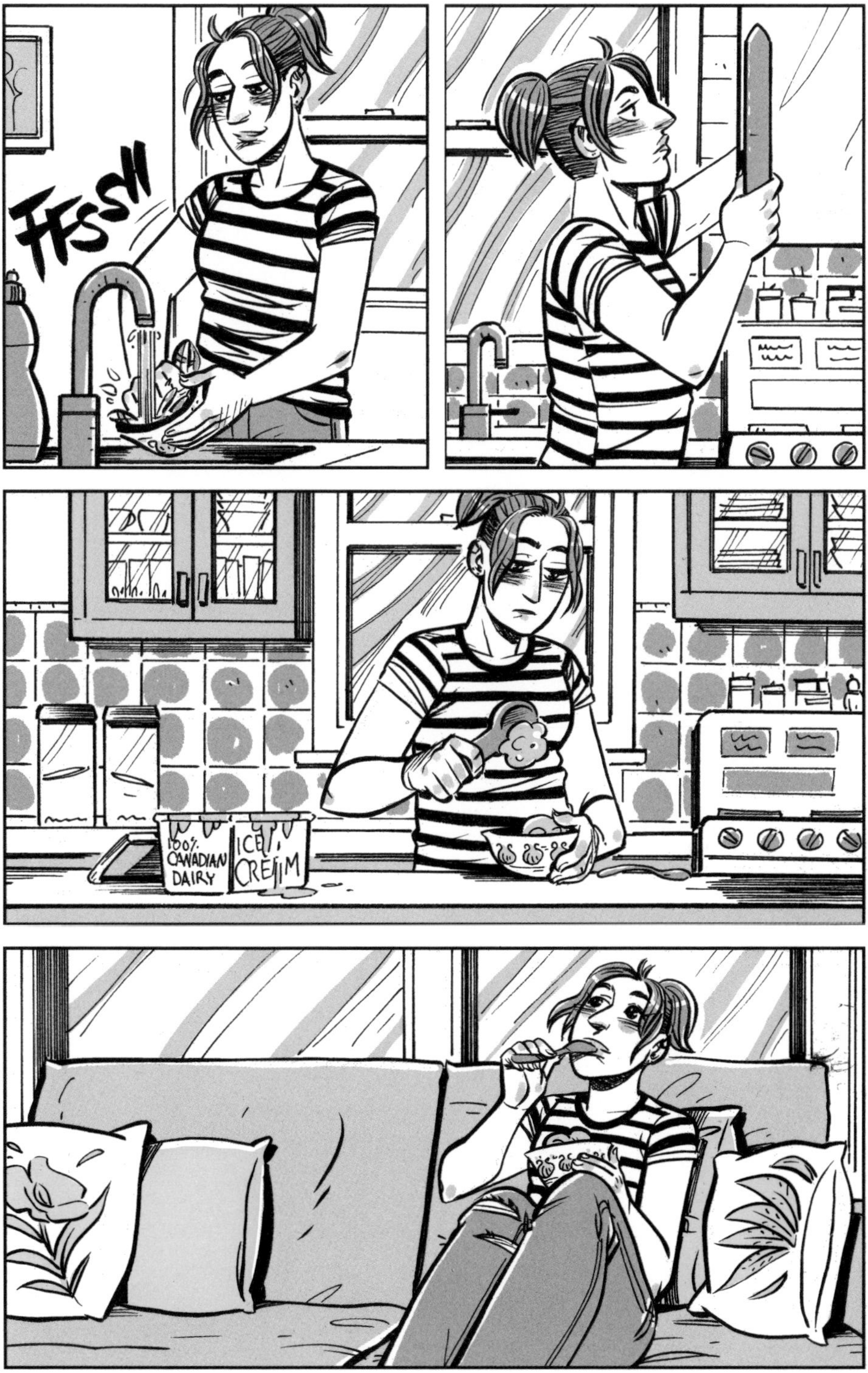
FFSSH
100% CANADIAN DAIRY
ICE CREAM

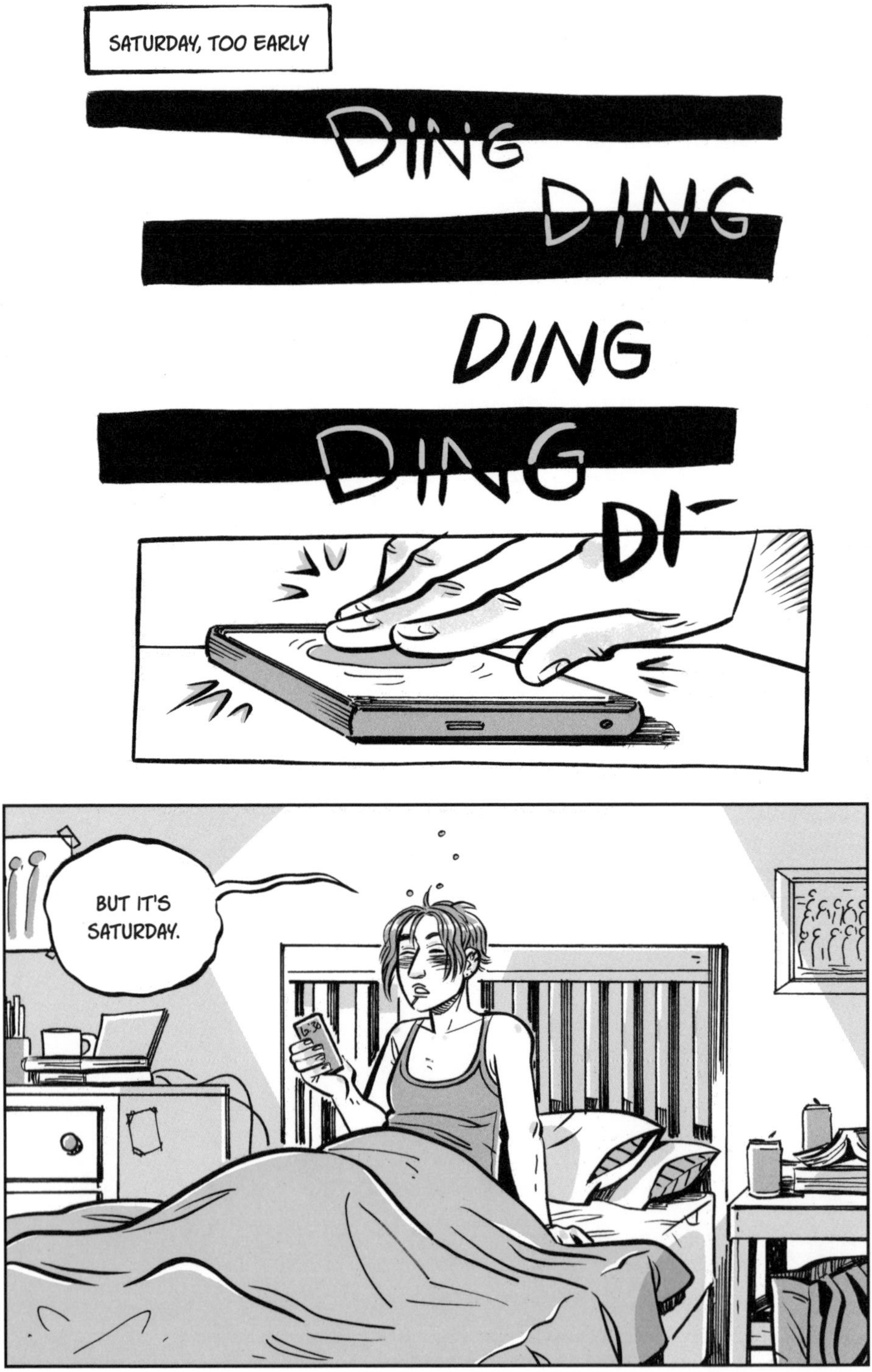
SATURDAY, TOO EARLY
DING
DING
DING
DING
DI-
BUT IT'S SATURDAY.

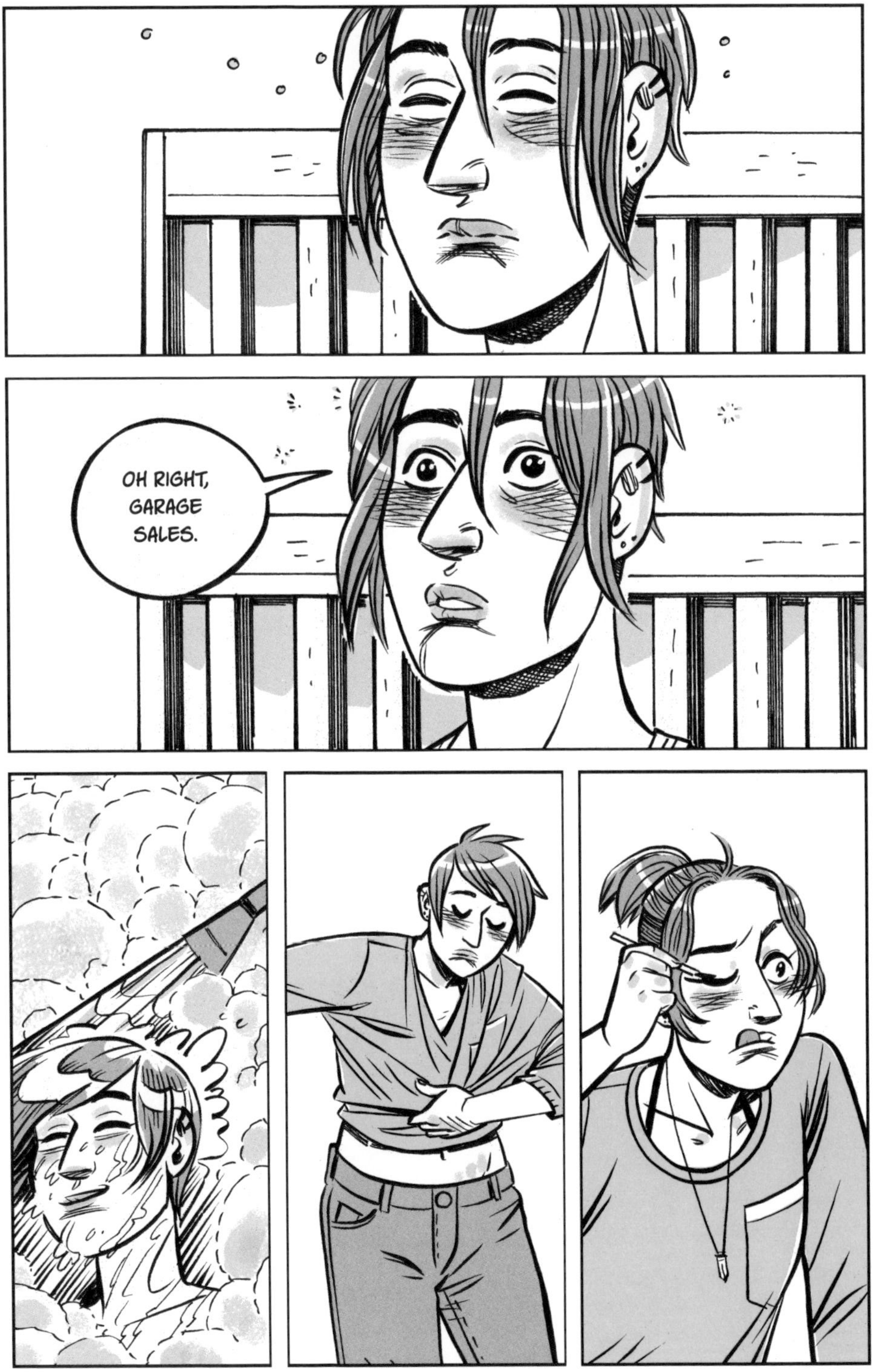
OH RIGHT, GARAGE SALES.

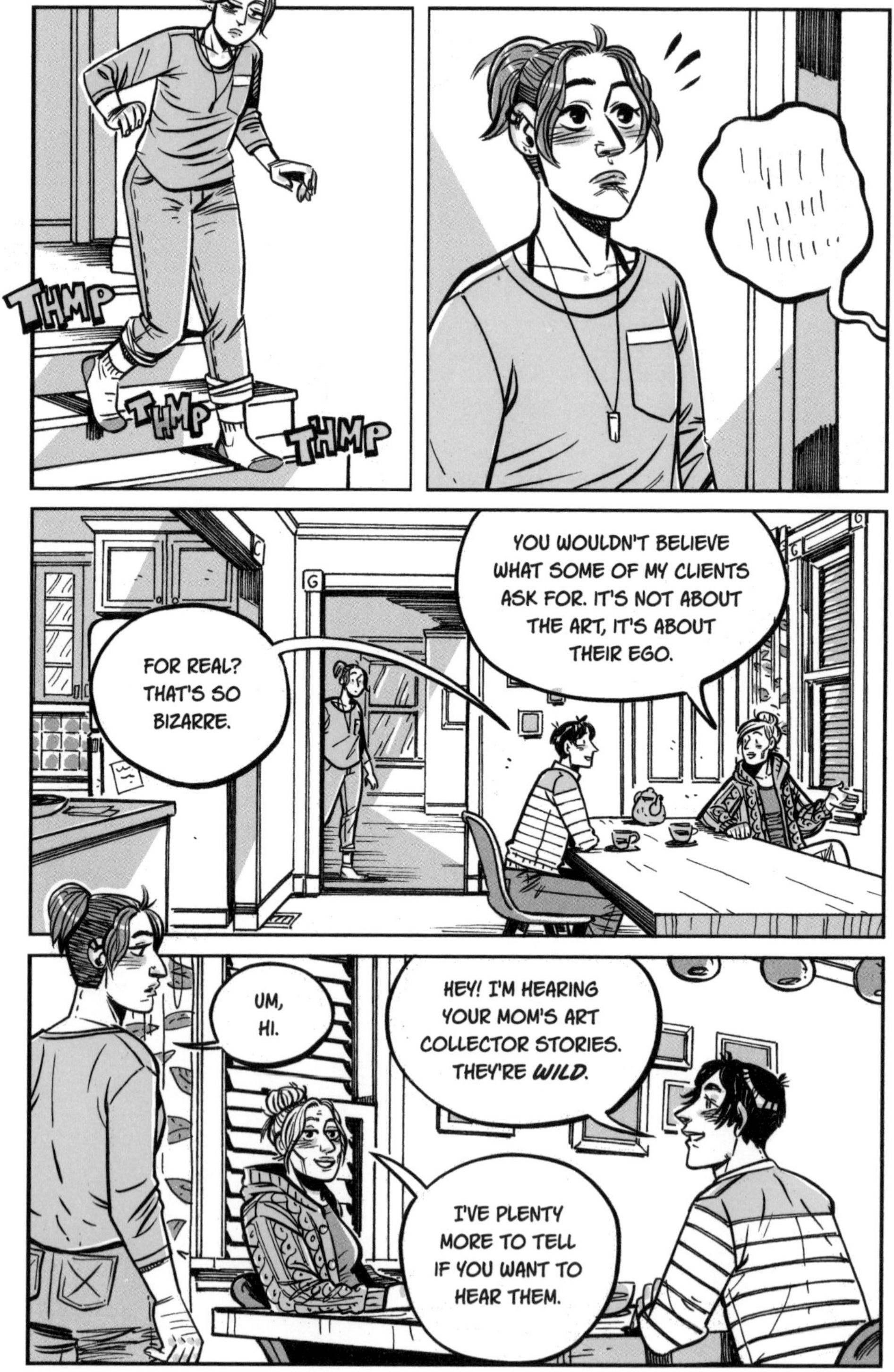
THMP
THMP
THMP
YOU WOULDN'T BELIEVE WHAT SOME OF MY CLIENTS ASK FOR. IT'S NOT ABOUT THE ART, IT'S ABOUT THEIR EGO.
FOR REAL? THAT'S SO BIZARRE.
UM, HI.
HEY! I'M HEARING YOUR MOM'S ART COLLECTOR STORIES. THEY'RE *WILD*.
I'VE PLENTY MORE TO TELL IF YOU WANT TO HEAR THEM.

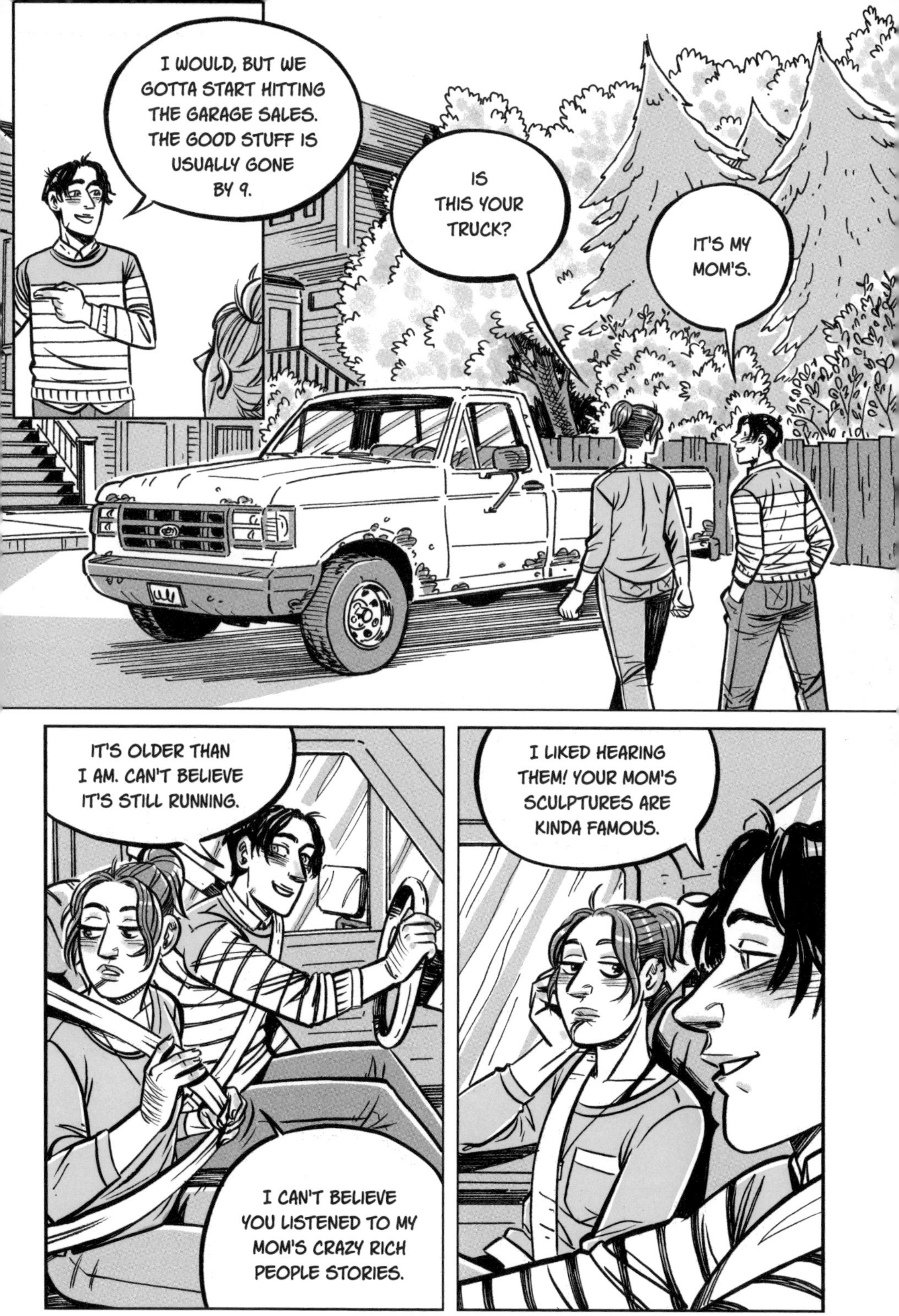
I WOULD, BUT WE GOTTA START HITTING THE GARAGE SALES. THE GOOD STUFF IS USUALLY GONE BY 9.
IS THIS YOUR TRUCK?
IT'S MY MOM'S.
IT'S OLDER THAN I AM. CAN'T BELIEVE IT'S STILL RUNNING.
I CAN'T BELIEVE YOU LISTENED TO MY MOM'S CRAZY RICH PEOPLE STORIES.
I LIKED HEARING THEM! YOUR MOM'S SCULPTURES ARE KINDA FAMOUS.

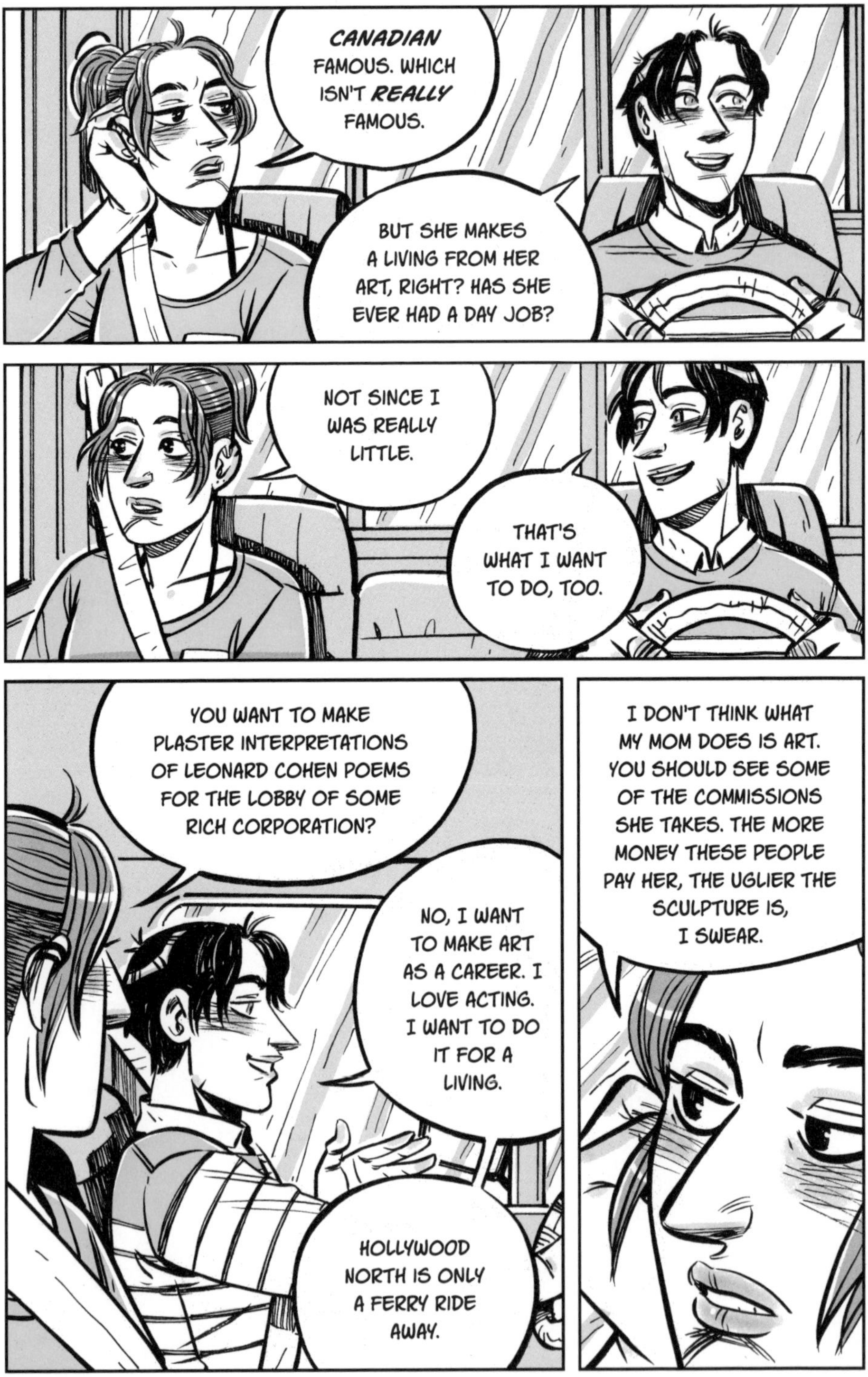

CANADIAN FAMOUS. WHICH ISN'T ***REALLY*** FAMOUS.
BUT SHE MAKES A LIVING FROM HER ART, RIGHT? HAS SHE EVER HAD A DAY JOB?
NOT SINCE I WAS REALLY LITTLE.
THAT'S WHAT I WANT TO DO, TOO.
YOU WANT TO MAKE PLASTER INTERPRETATIONS OF LEONARD COHEN POEMS FOR THE LOBBY OF SOME RICH CORPORATION?
NO, I WANT TO MAKE ART AS A CAREER. I LOVE ACTING. I WANT TO DO IT FOR A LIVING.
HOLLYWOOD NORTH IS ONLY A FERRY RIDE AWAY.
I DON'T THINK WHAT MY MOM DOES IS ART. YOU SHOULD SEE SOME OF THE COMMISSIONS SHE TAKES. THE MORE MONEY THESE PEOPLE PAY HER, THE UGLIER THE SCULPTURE IS, I SWEAR.

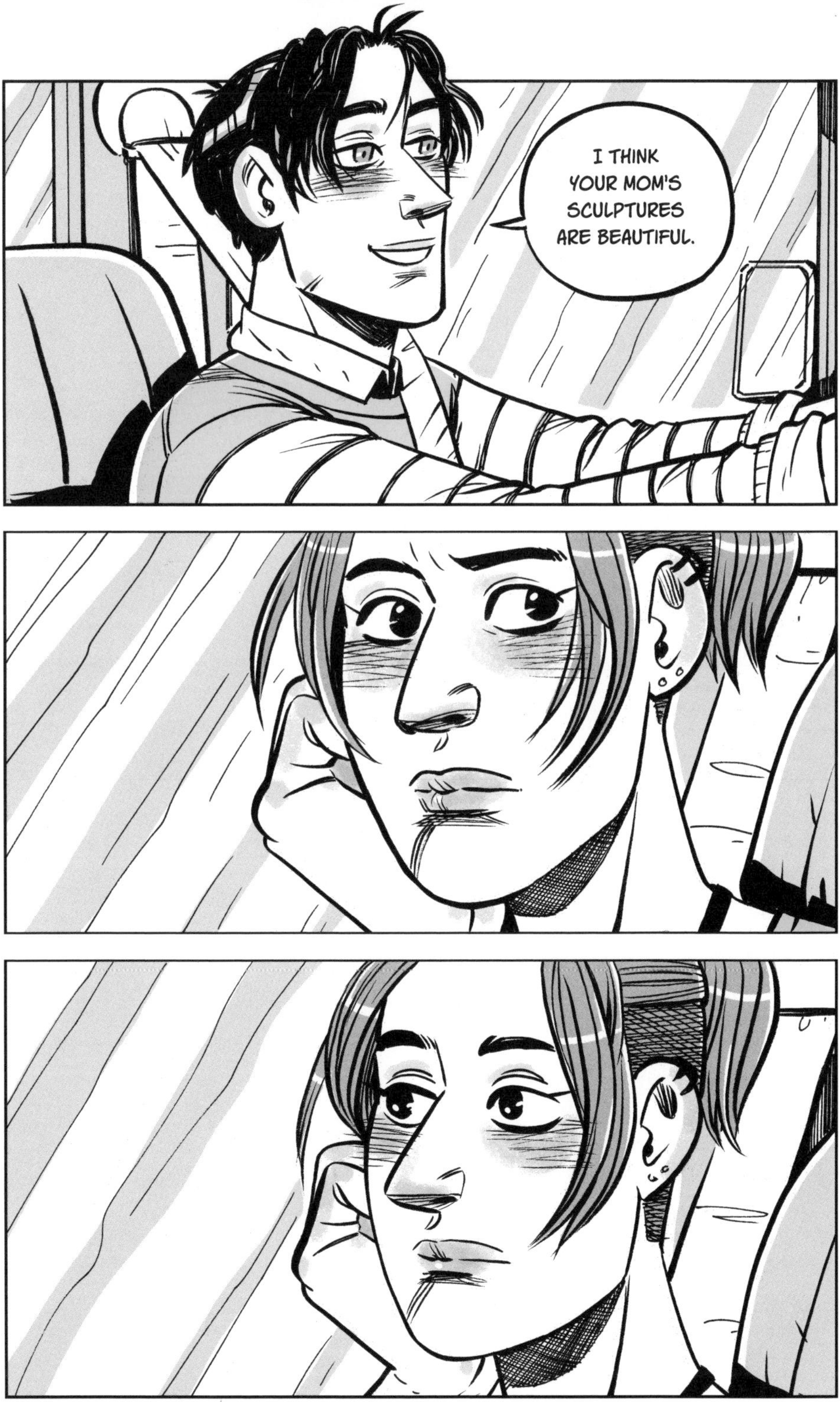
I THINK YOUR MOM'S SCULPTURES ARE BEAUTIFUL.

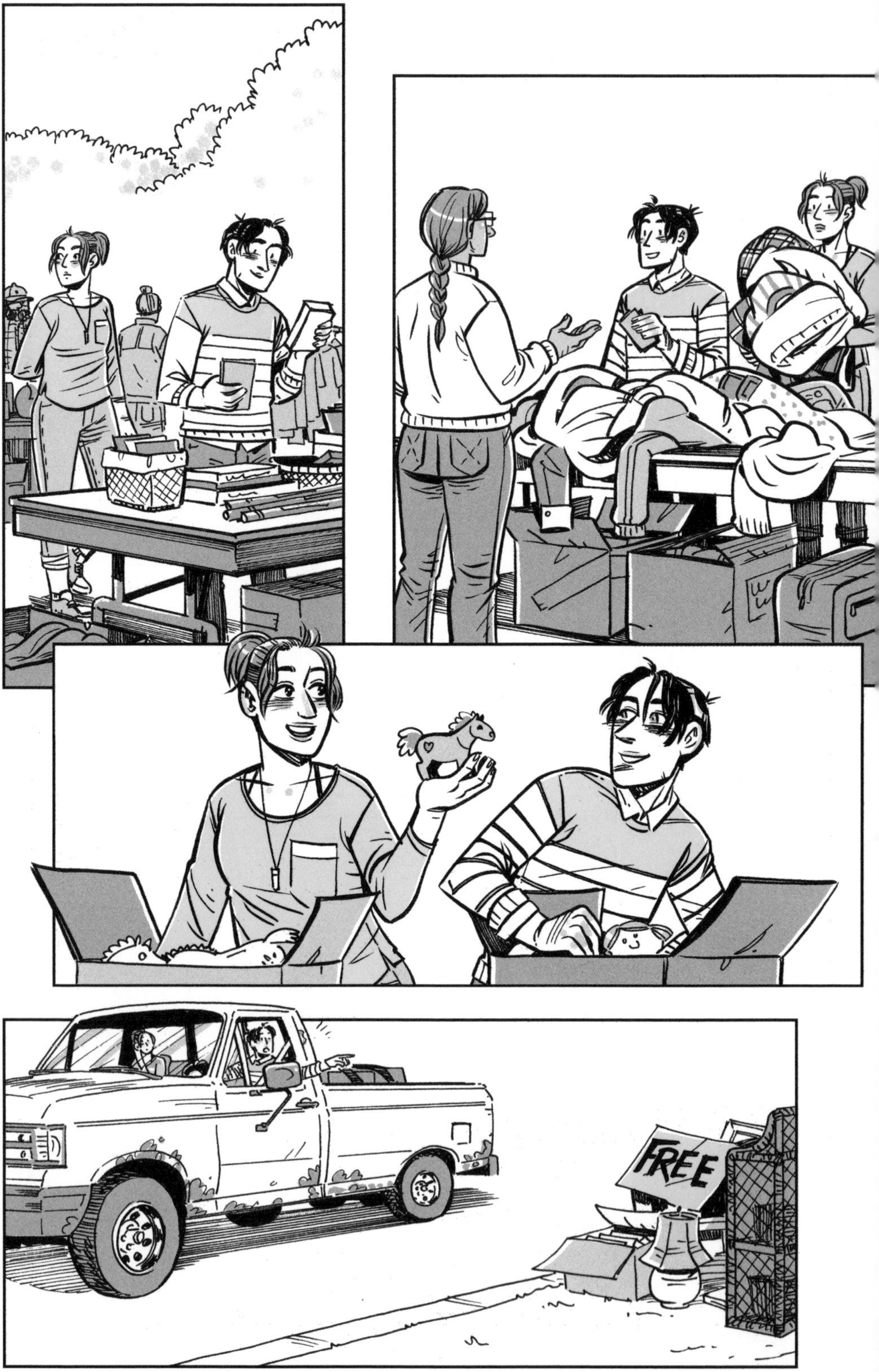
FREE

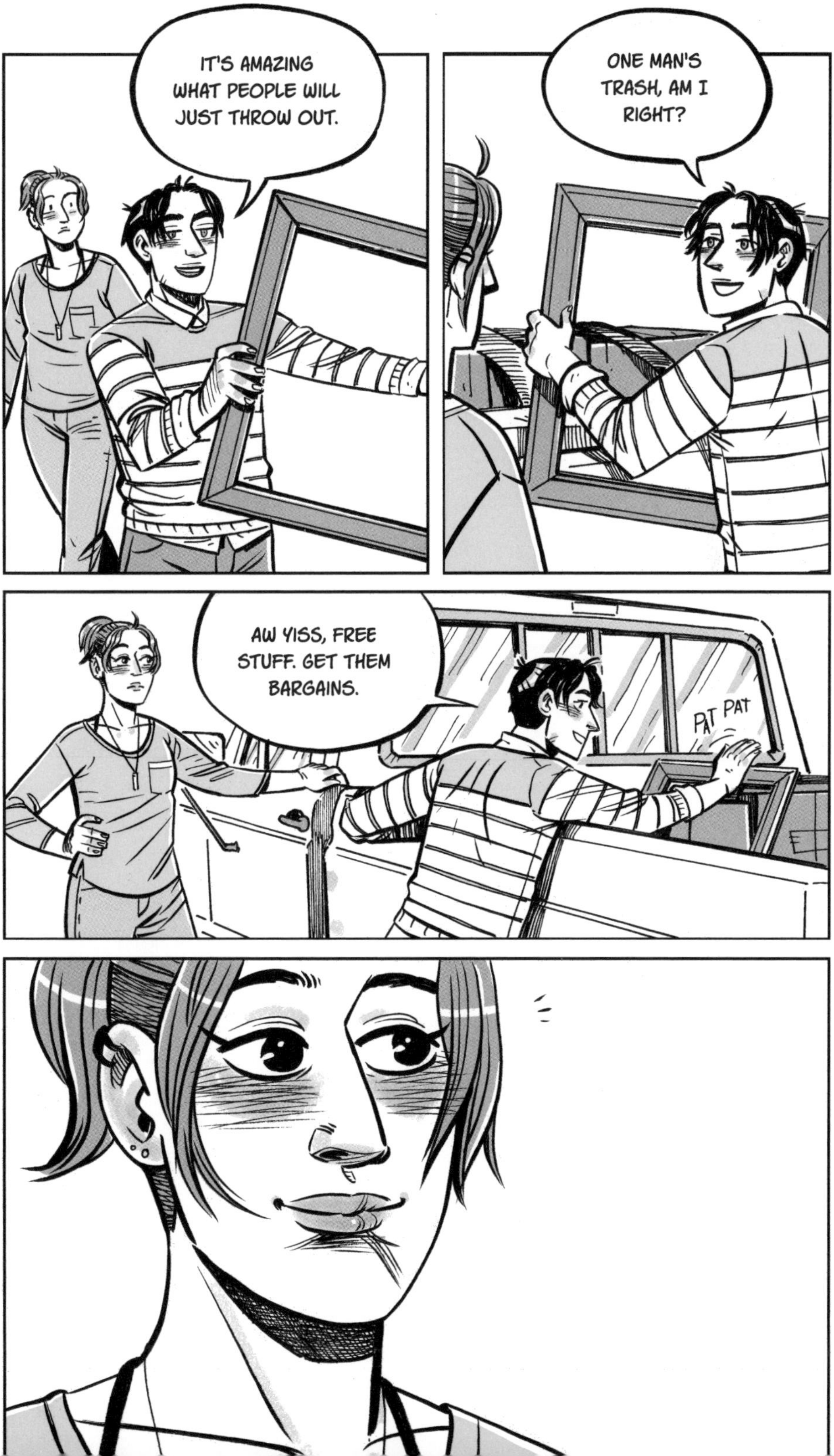
IT'S AMAZING WHAT PEOPLE WILL JUST THROW OUT.
ONE MAN'S TRASH, AM I RIGHT?
AW YISS, FREE STUFF. GET THEM BARGAINS.
PAT PAT

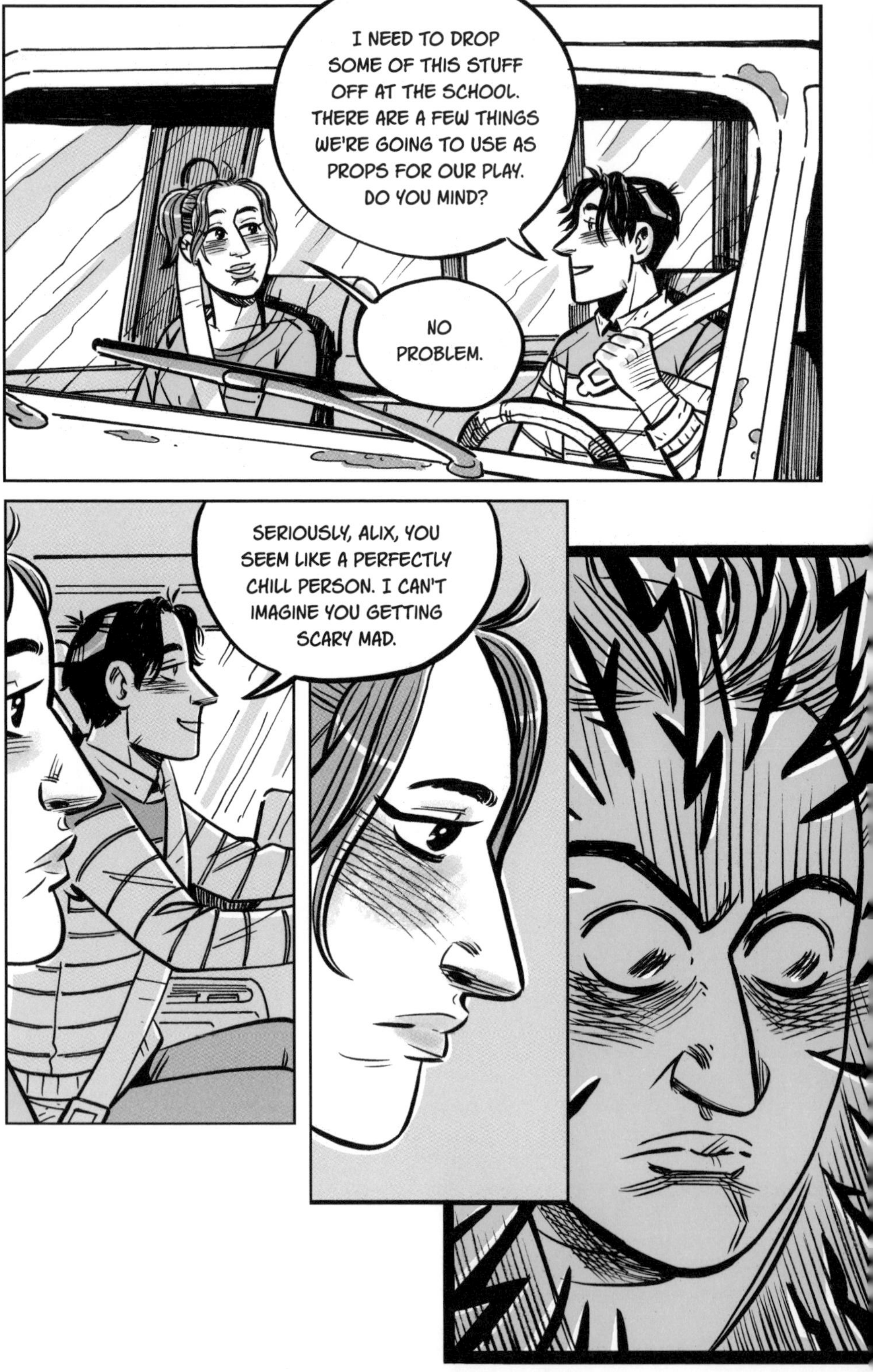
I NEED TO DROP SOME OF THIS STUFF OFF AT THE SCHOOL. THERE ARE A FEW THINGS WE'RE GOING TO USE AS PROPS FOR OUR PLAY. DO YOU MIND?
NO PROBLEM.
SERIOUSLY, ALIX, YOU SEEM LIKE A PERFECTLY CHILL PERSON. I CAN'T IMAGINE YOU GETTING SCARY MAD.

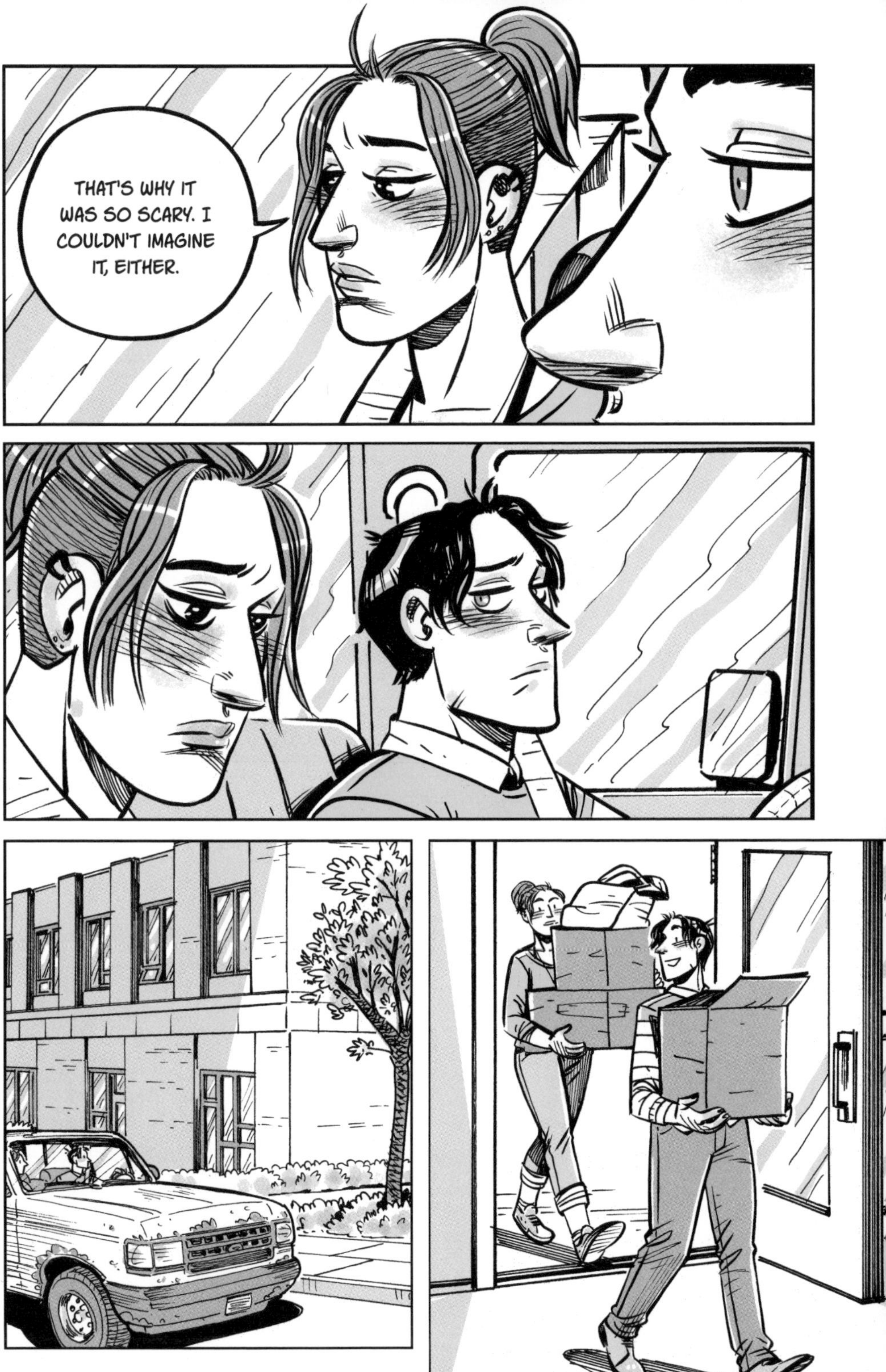
THAT'S WHY IT WAS SO SCARY. I COULDN'T IMAGINE IT, EITHER.

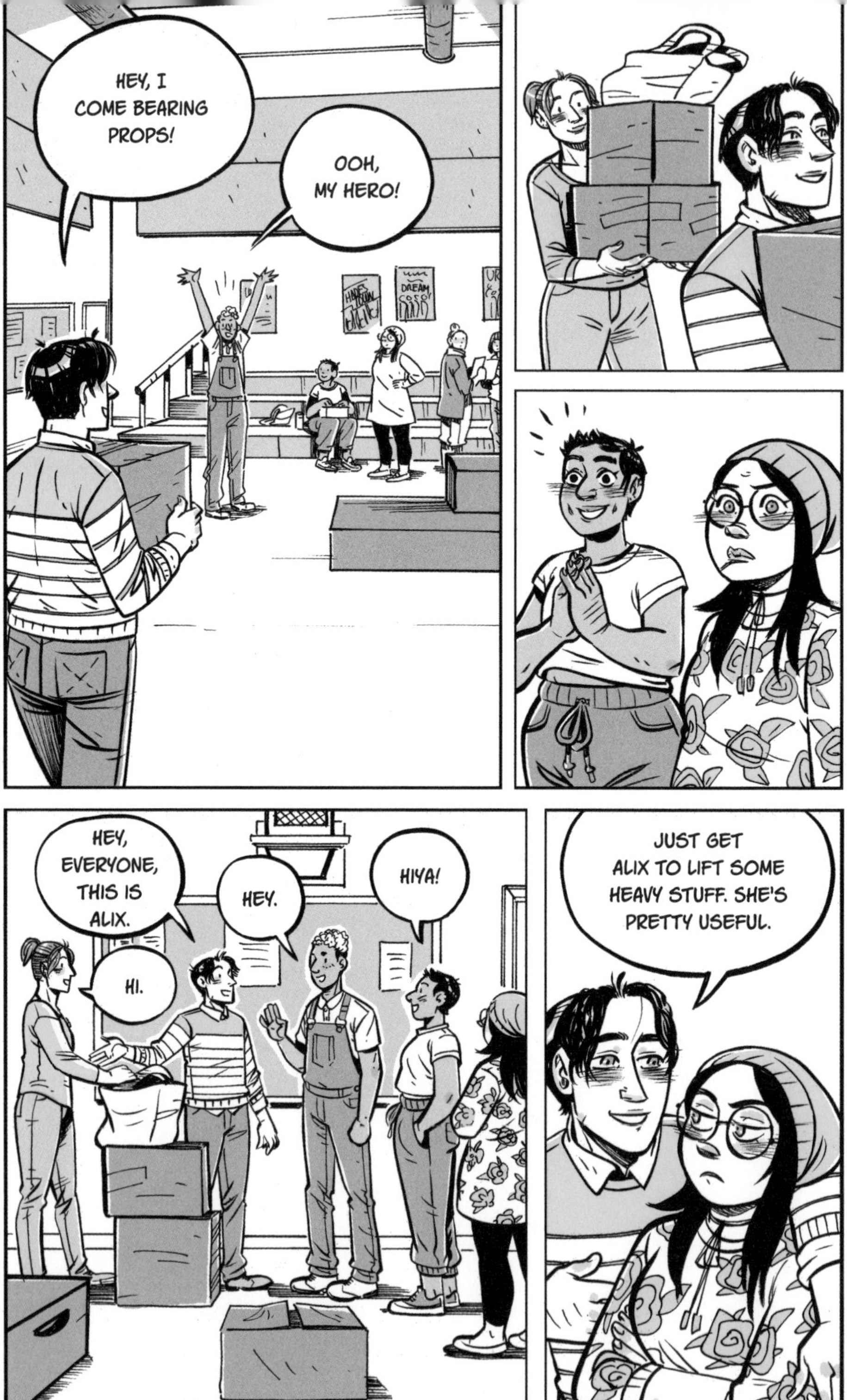
HEY, I COME BEARING PROPS!
OOH, MY HERO!
HEY, EVERYONE, THIS IS ALIX.
HEY.
HIYA!
HI.
JUST GET ALIX TO LIFT SOME HEAVY STUFF. SHE'S PRETTY USEFUL.

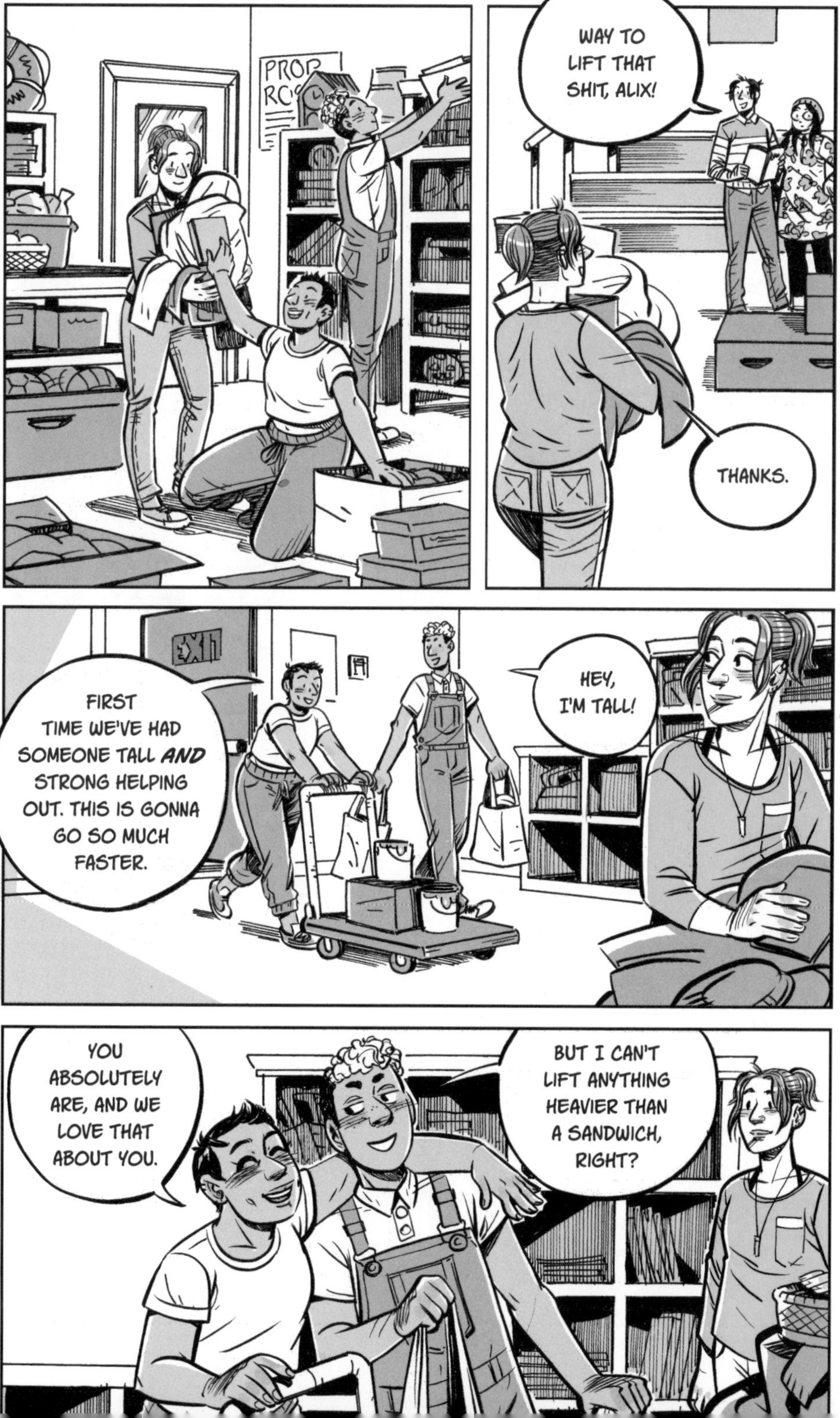
PROP RO
WAY TO LIFT THAT SHIT, ALIX!
THANKS.
EXIT
FIRST TIME WE'VE HAD SOMEONE TALL *AND* STRONG HELPING OUT. THIS IS GONNA GO SO MUCH FASTER.
HEY, I'M TALL!
YOU ABSOLUTELY ARE, AND WE LOVE THAT ABOUT YOU.
BUT I CAN'T LIFT ANYTHING HEAVIER THAN A SANDWICH, RIGHT?

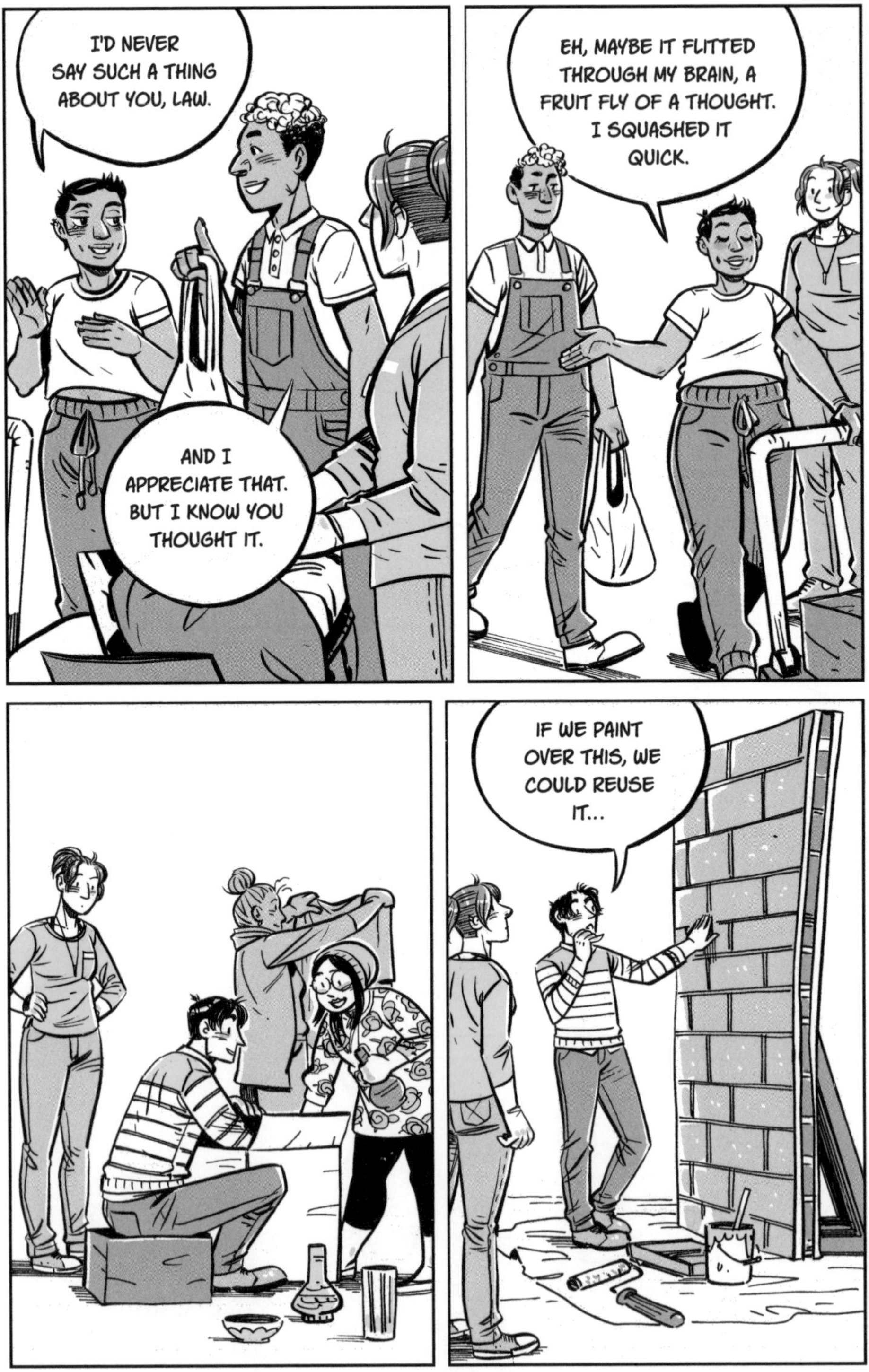
I'D NEVER SAY SUCH A THING ABOUT YOU, LAW.
AND I APPRECIATE THAT. BUT I KNOW YOU THOUGHT IT.
EH, MAYBE IT FLITTED THROUGH MY BRAIN, A FRUIT FLY OF A THOUGHT. I SQUASHED IT QUICK.
IF WE PAINT OVER THIS, WE COULD REUSE IT...

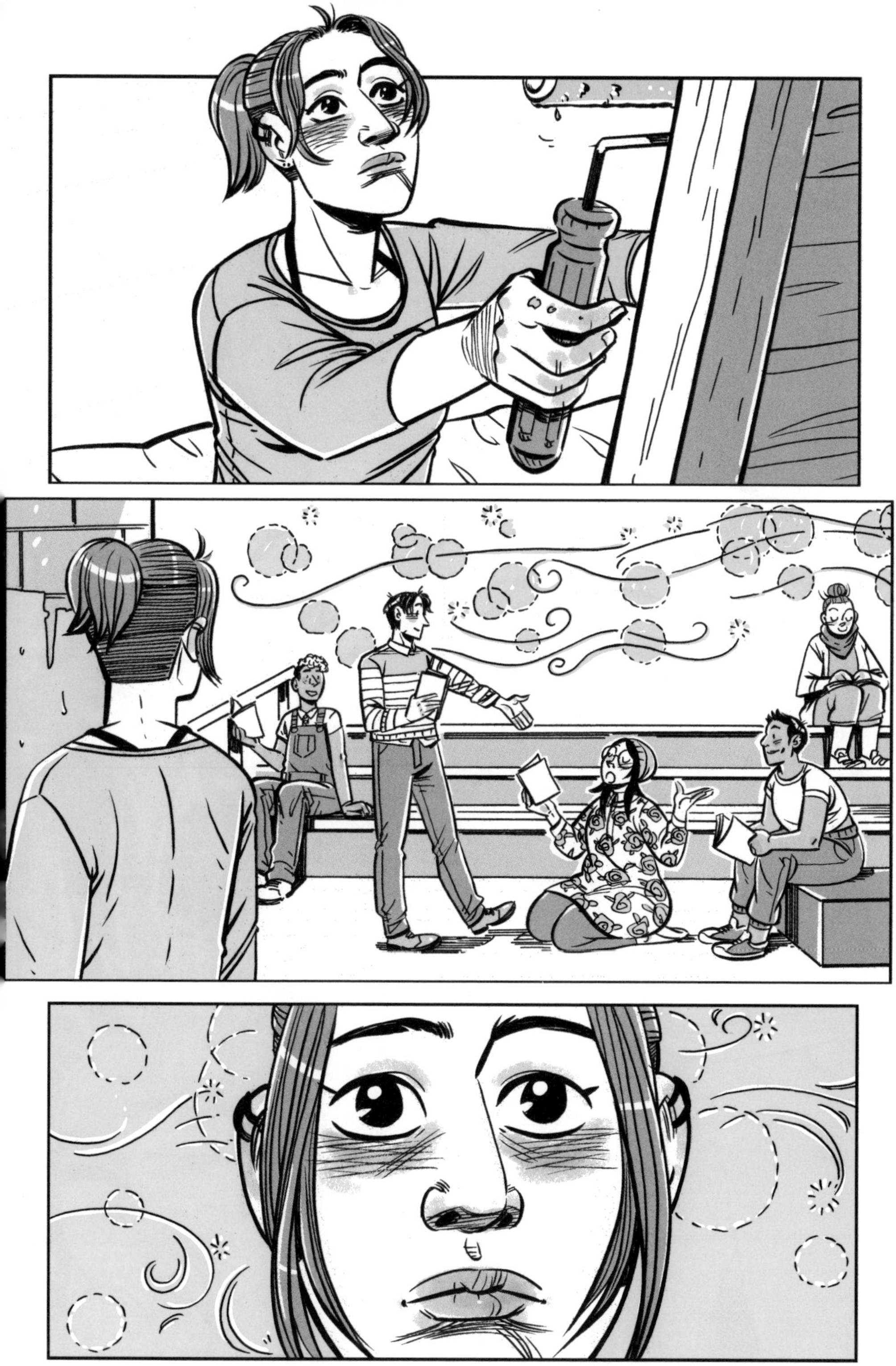

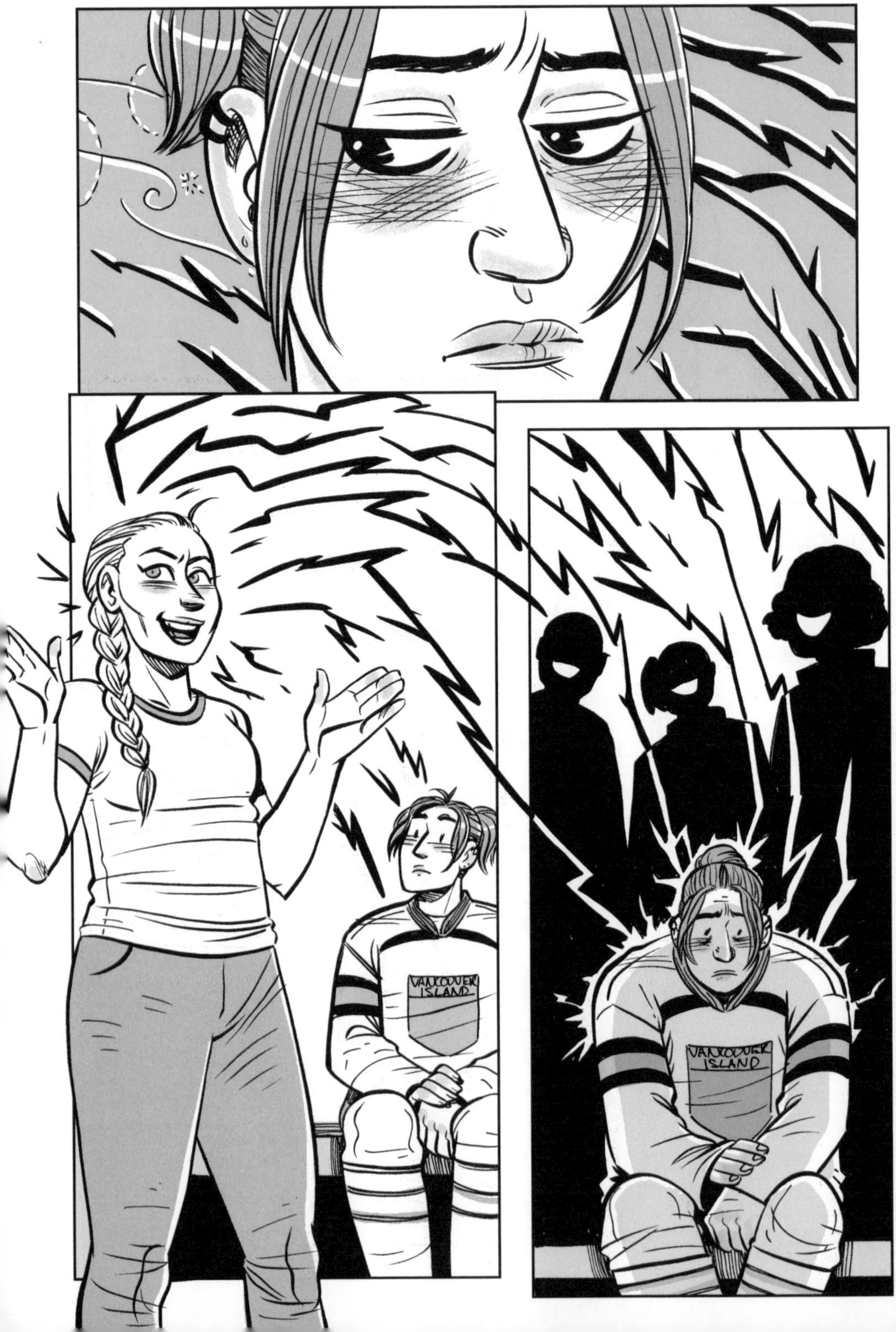
VANCOUVER ISLAND
VANCOUVER ISLAND

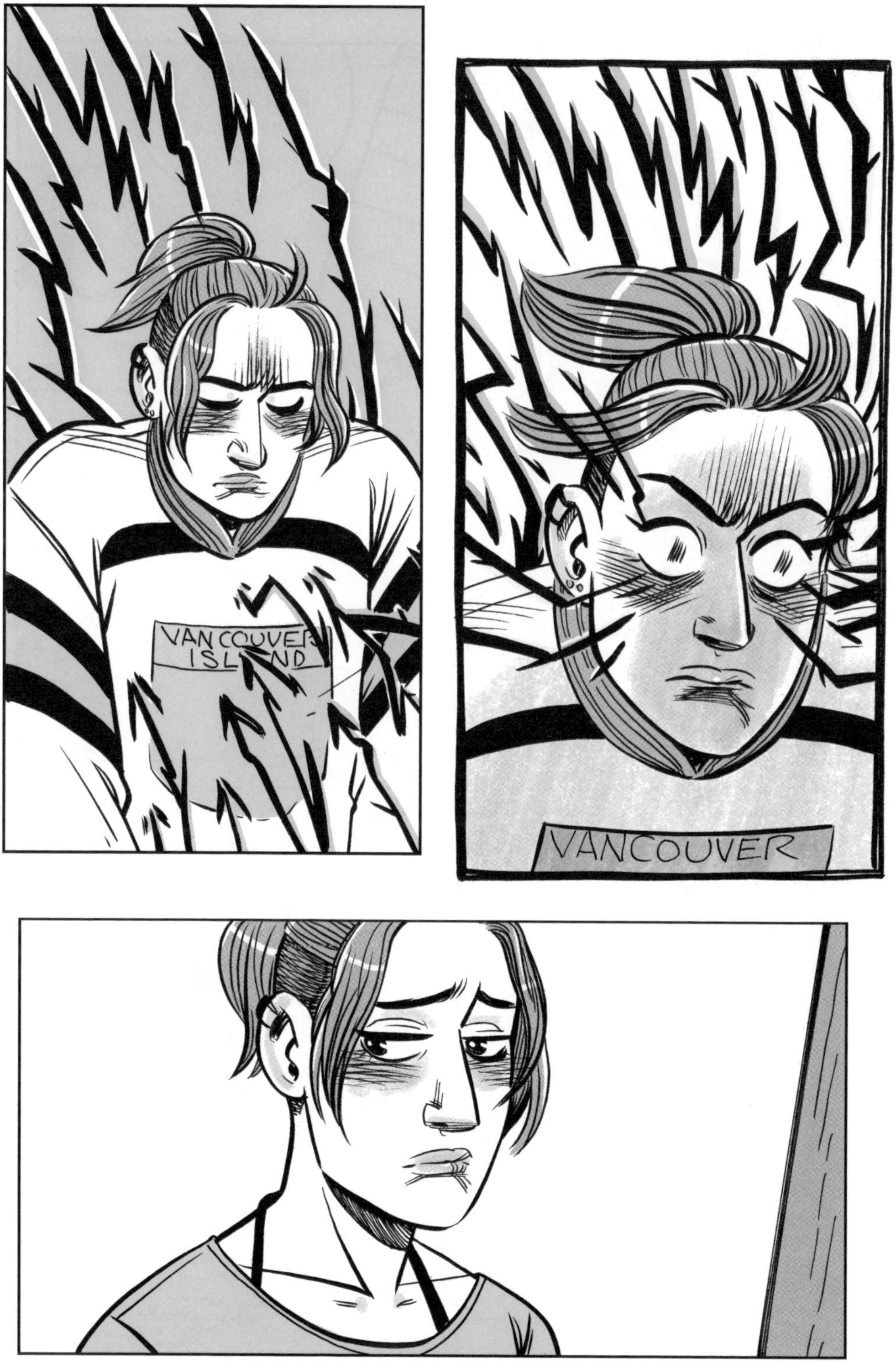
VANCOUVER ISLAND
VANCOUVER

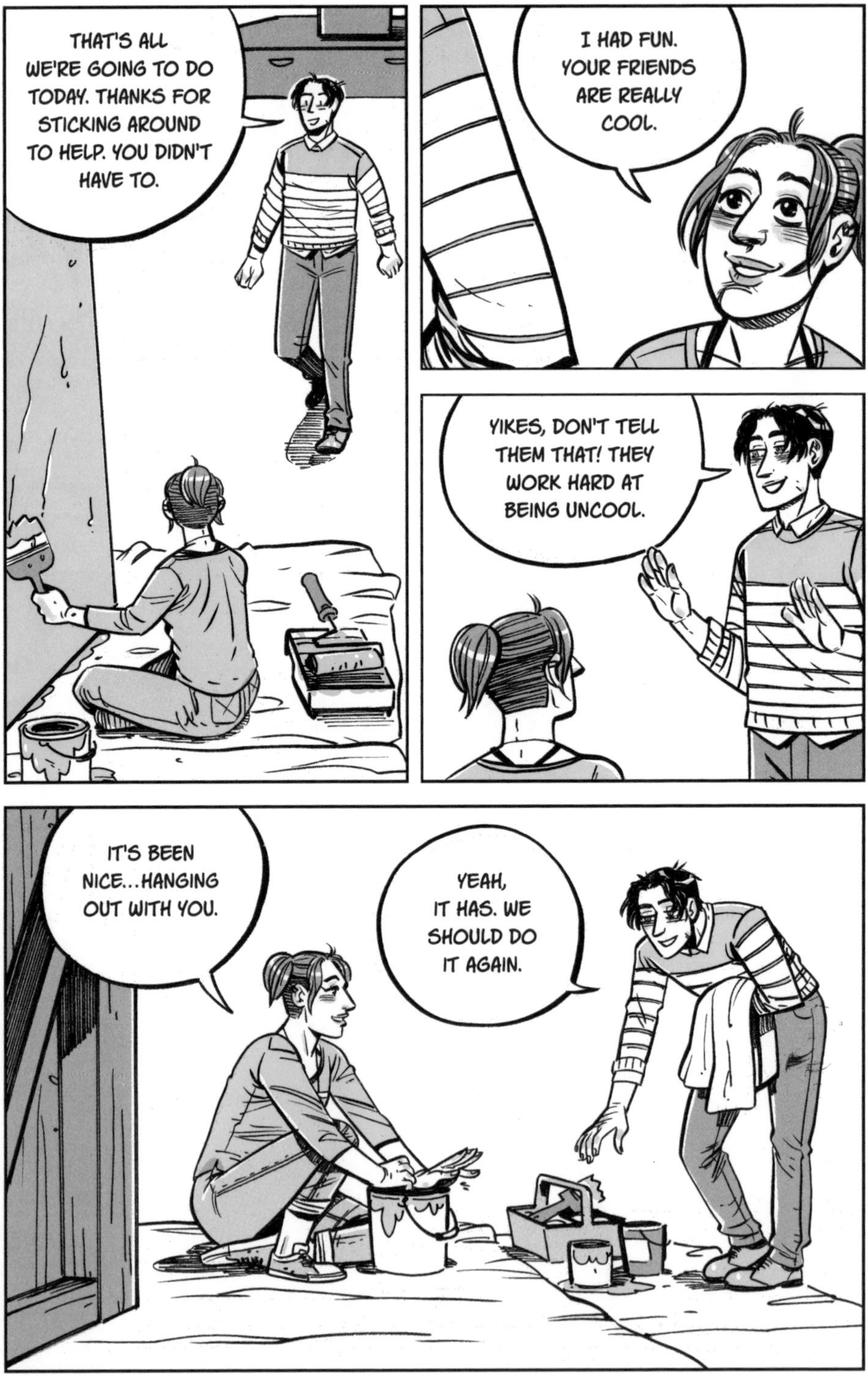
THAT'S ALL WE'RE GOING TO DO TODAY. THANKS FOR STICKING AROUND TO HELP. YOU DIDN'T HAVE TO.
I HAD FUN. YOUR FRIENDS ARE REALLY COOL.
YIKES, DON'T TELL THEM THAT! THEY WORK HARD AT BEING UNCOOL.
IT'S BEEN NICE...HANGING OUT WITH YOU.
YEAH, IT HAS. WE SHOULD DO IT AGAIN.

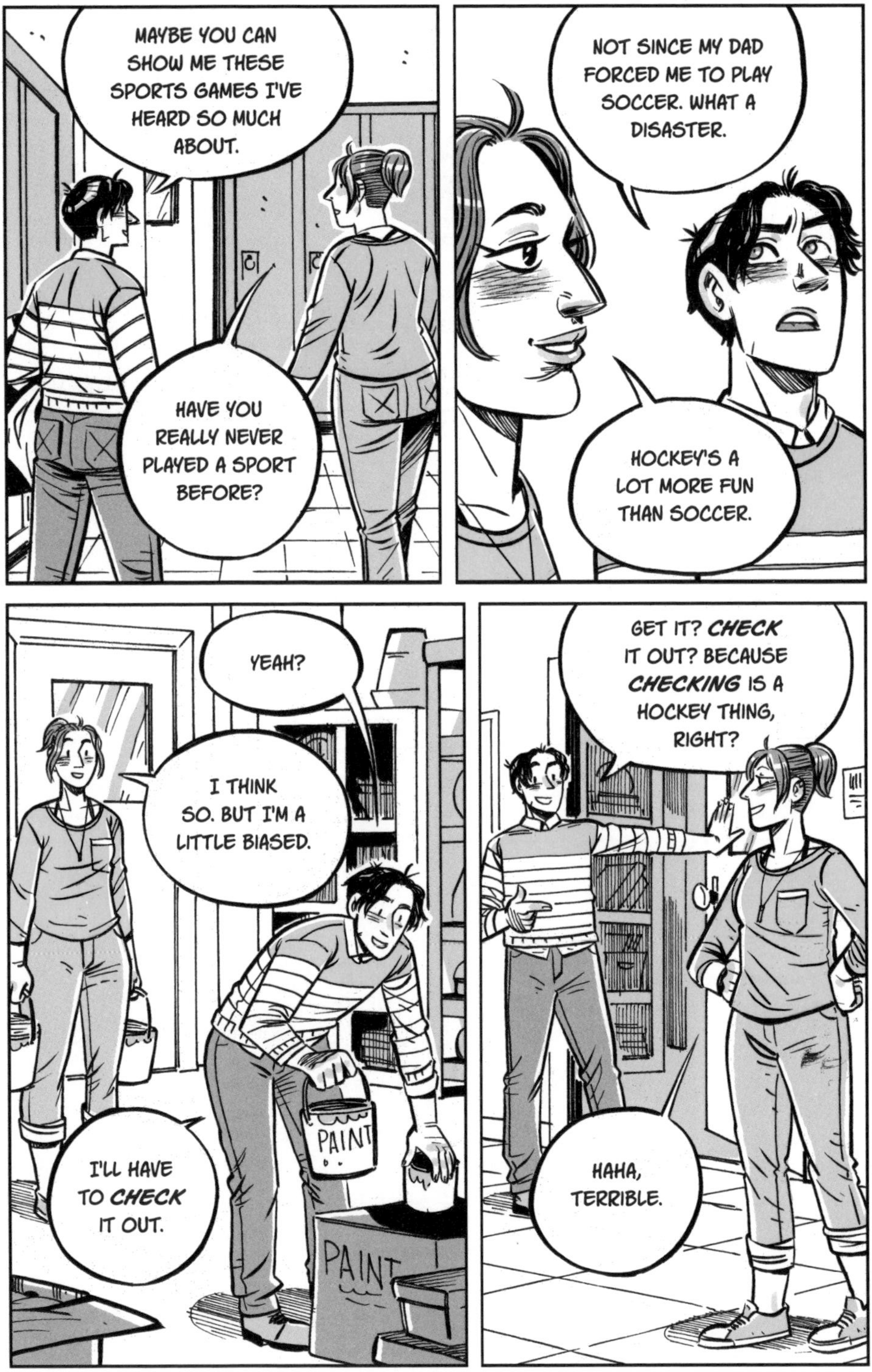
MAYBE YOU CAN SHOW ME THESE SPORTS GAMES I'VE HEARD SO MUCH ABOUT.
HAVE YOU REALLY NEVER PLAYED A SPORT BEFORE?
NOT SINCE MY DAD FORCED ME TO PLAY SOCCER. WHAT A DISASTER.
HOCKEY'S A LOT MORE FUN THAN SOCCER.
YEAH?
I THINK SO. BUT I'M A LITTLE BIASED.
I'LL HAVE TO ***CHECK*** IT OUT.
PAINT
PAINT
GET IT? ***CHECK*** IT OUT? BECAUSE ***CHECKING*** IS A HOCKEY THING, RIGHT?
HAHA, TERRIBLE.

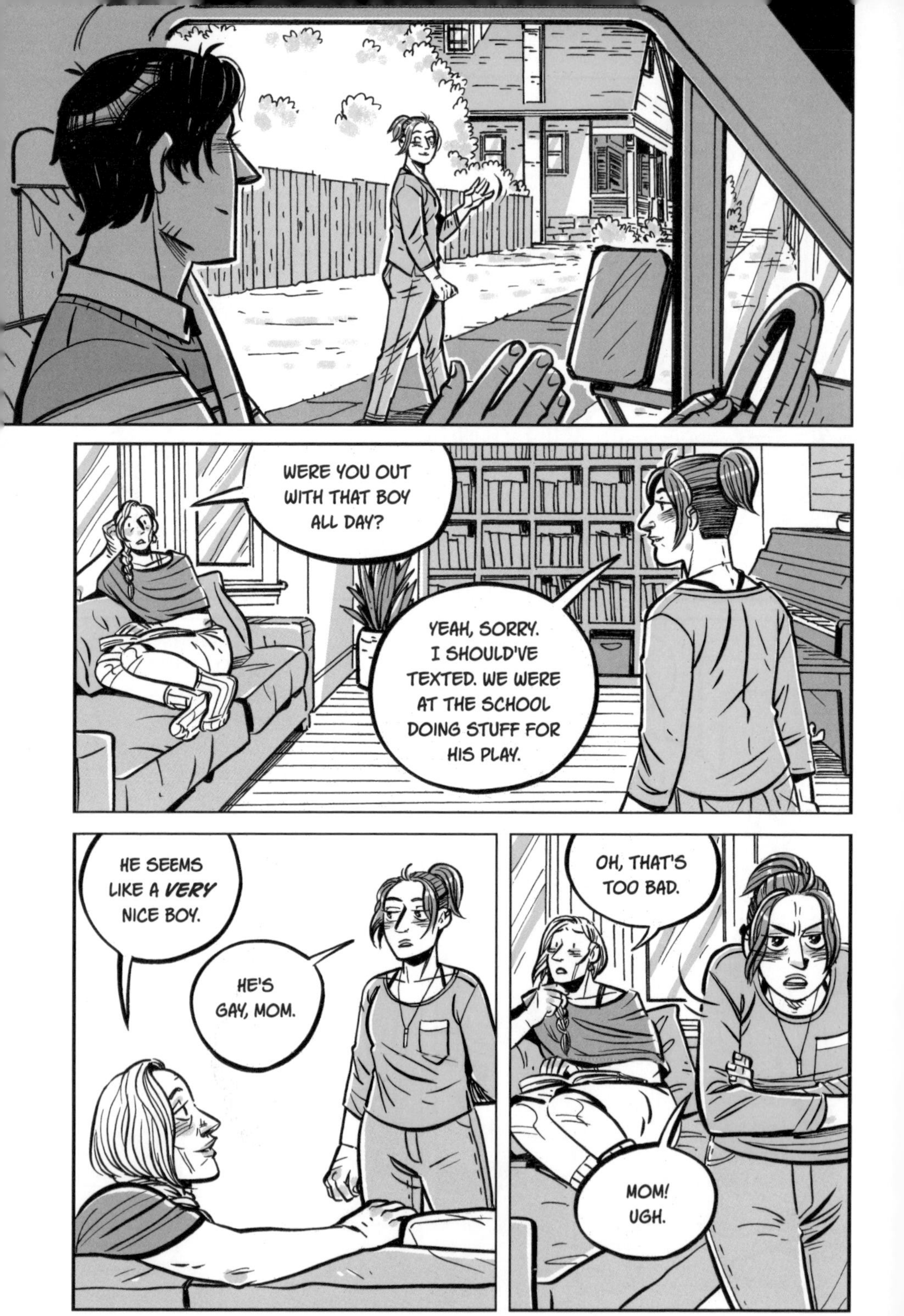
WERE YOU OUT WITH THAT BOY ALL DAY?
YEAH, SORRY. I SHOULD'VE TEXTED. WE WERE AT THE SCHOOL DOING STUFF FOR HIS PLAY.
HE SEEMS LIKE A *VERY* NICE BOY.
HE'S GAY, MOM.
OH, THAT'S TOO BAD.
MOM! UGH.

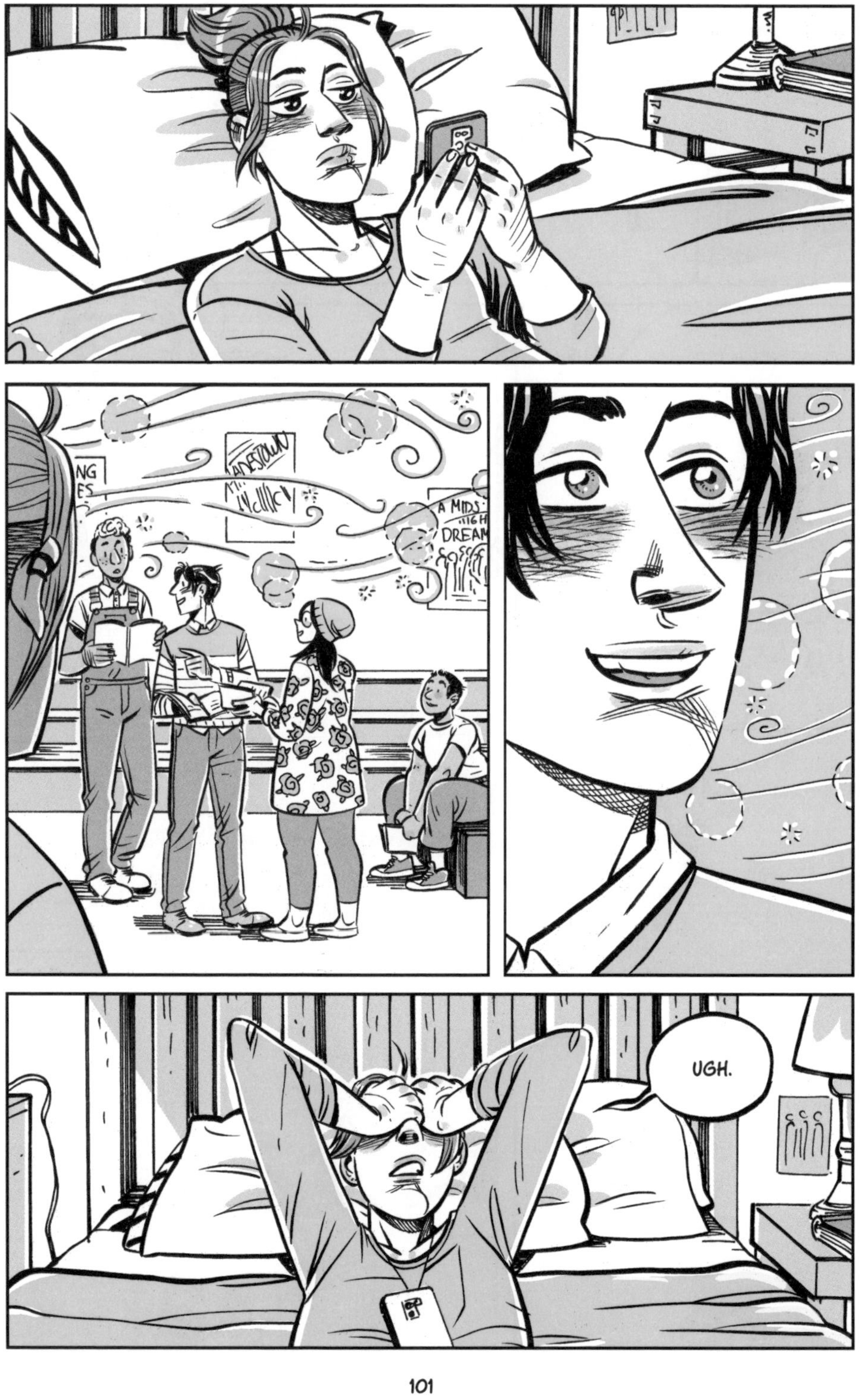
UGH.

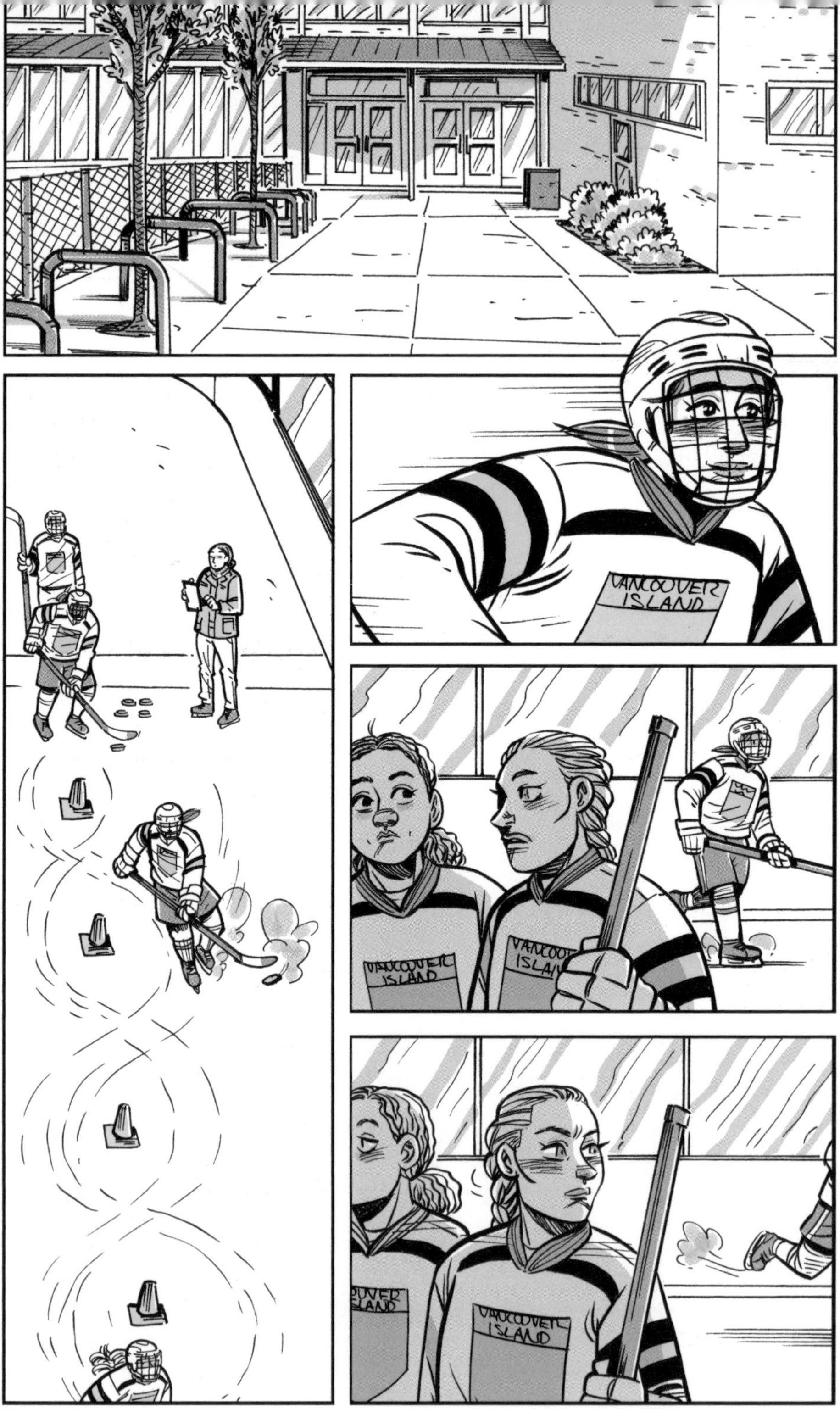
VANCOOVER ISLAND
VANCOOVER ISLAND
VANCOOVER ISLAND
VANCOOVER ISLAND

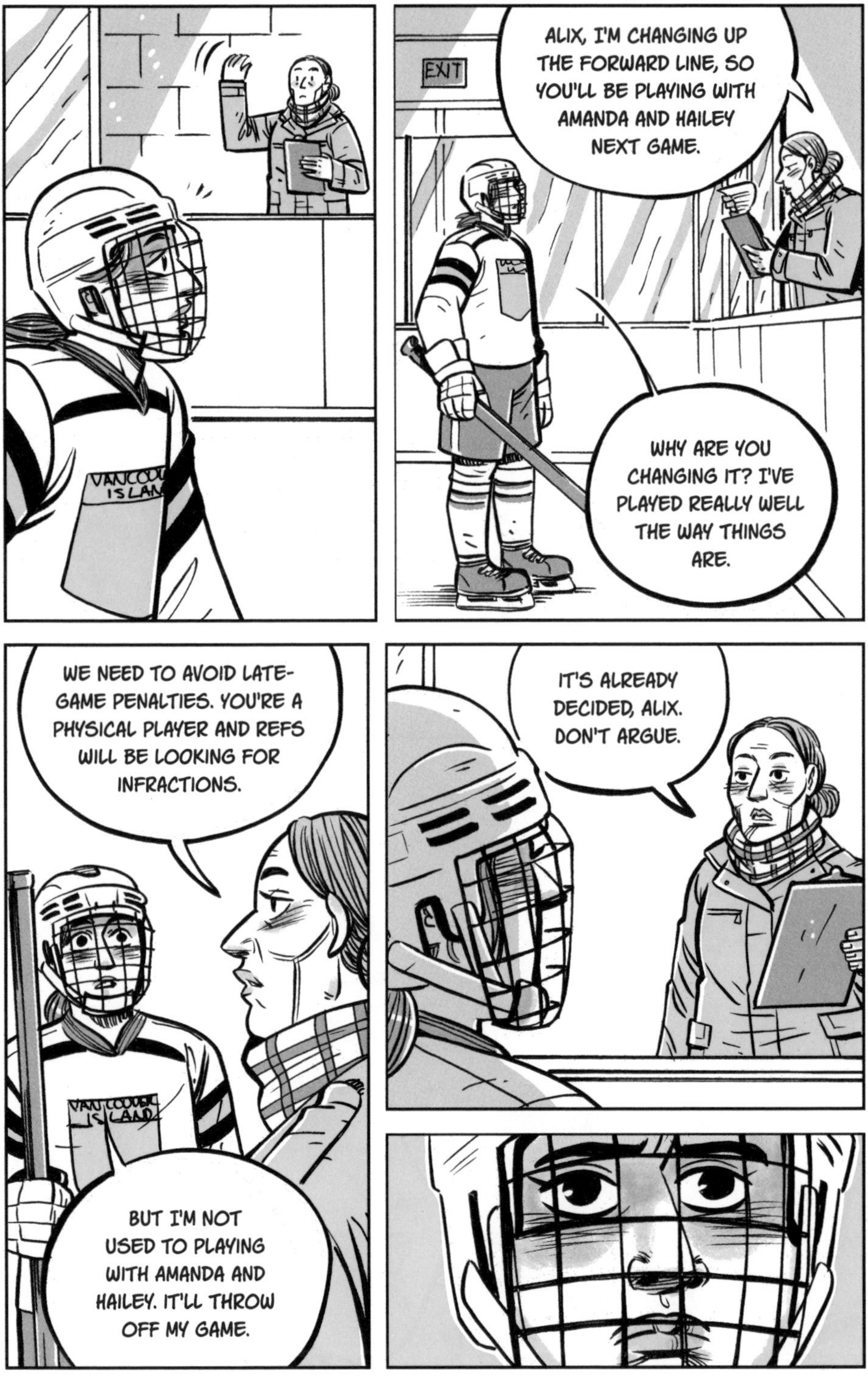
EXIT
ALIX, I'M CHANGING UP THE FORWARD LINE, SO YOU'LL BE PLAYING WITH AMANDA AND HAILEY NEXT GAME.
WHY ARE YOU CHANGING IT? I'VE PLAYED REALLY WELL THE WAY THINGS ARE.
WE NEED TO AVOID LATE-GAME PENALTIES. YOU'RE A PHYSICAL PLAYER AND REFS WILL BE LOOKING FOR INFRACTIONS.
BUT I'M NOT USED TO PLAYING WITH AMANDA AND HAILEY. IT'LL THROW OFF MY GAME.
IT'S ALREADY DECIDED, ALIX. DON'T ARGUE.

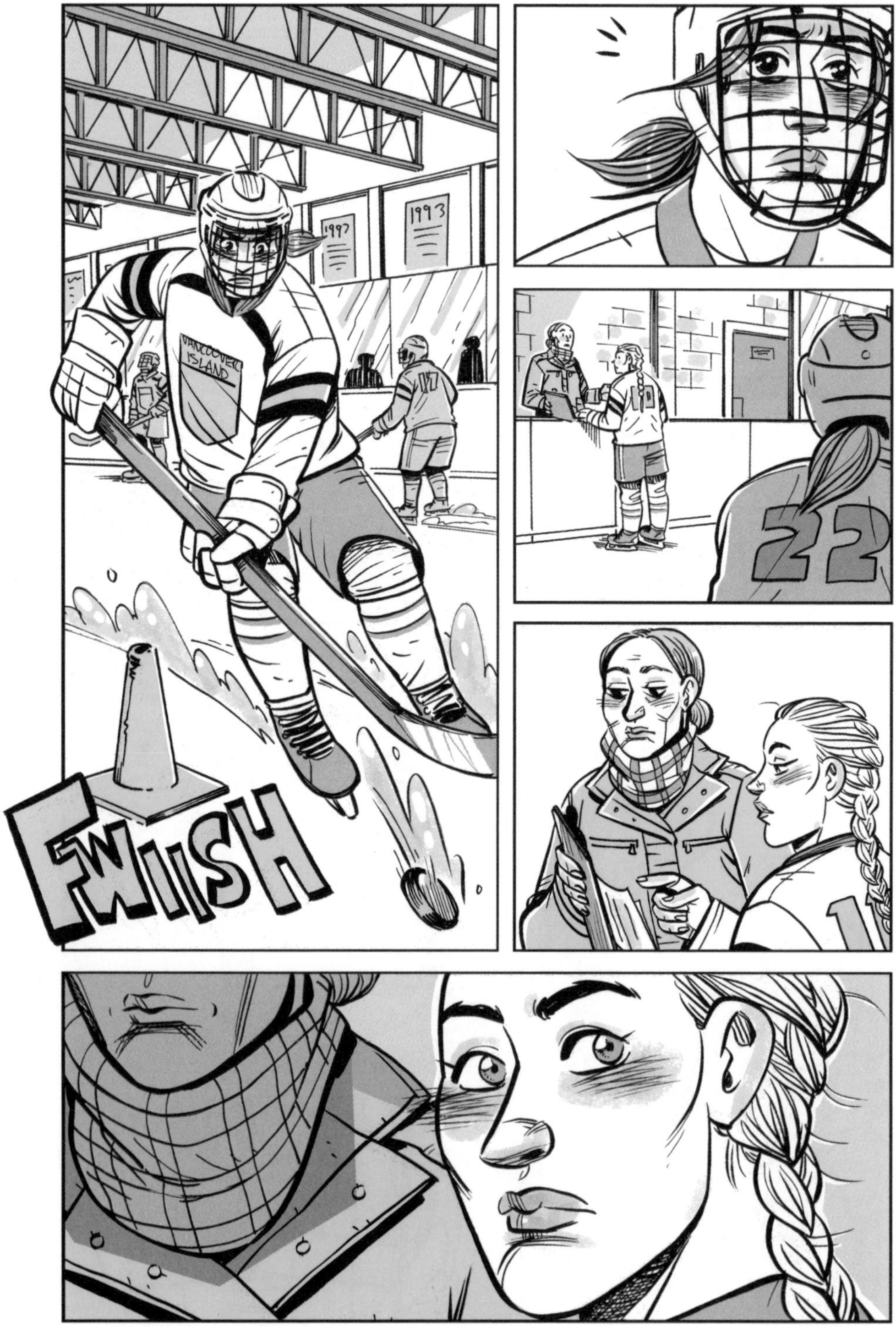
1997
1993
VANCOUVER ISLAND
FWISH
22

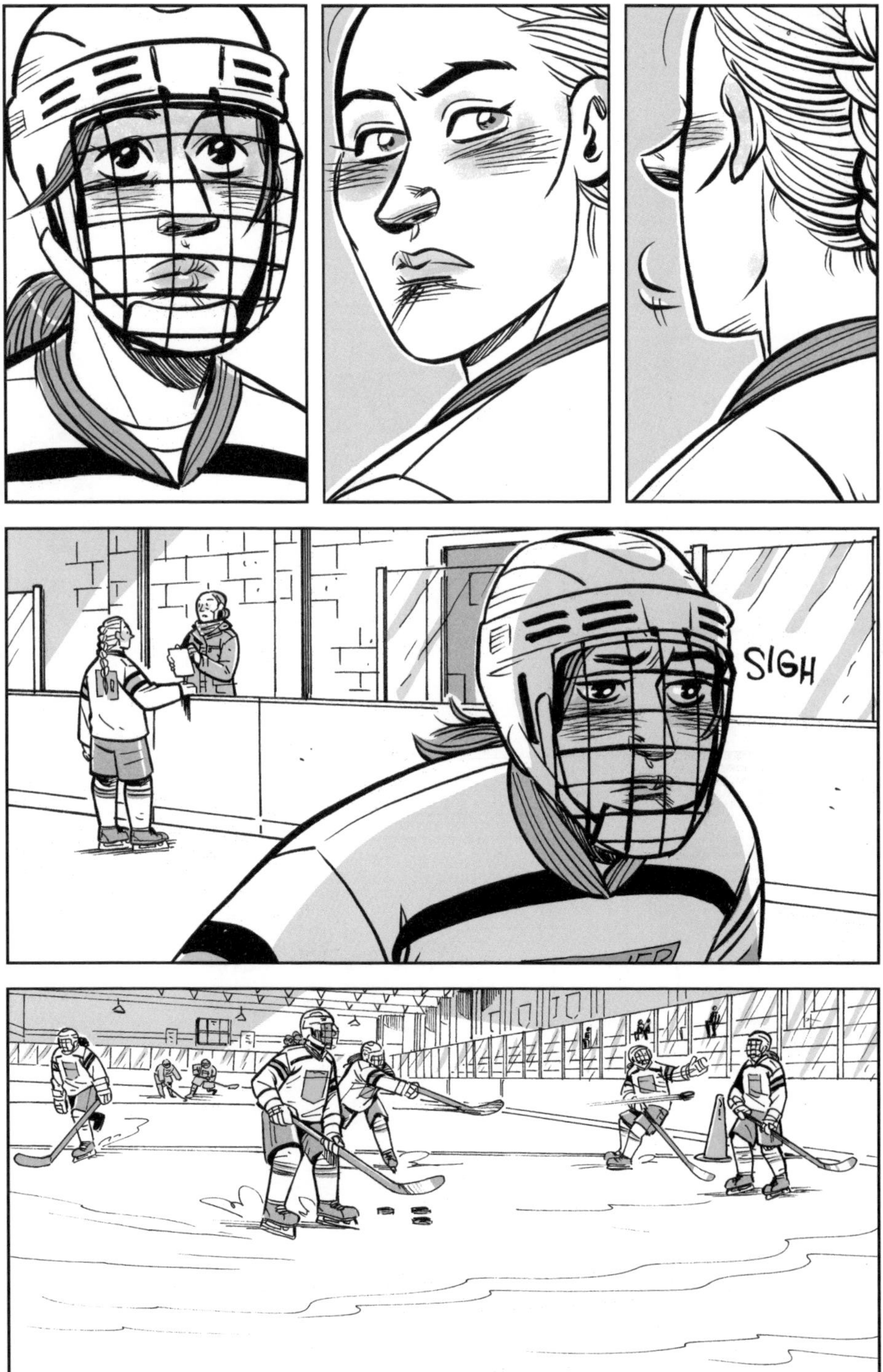
SIGH

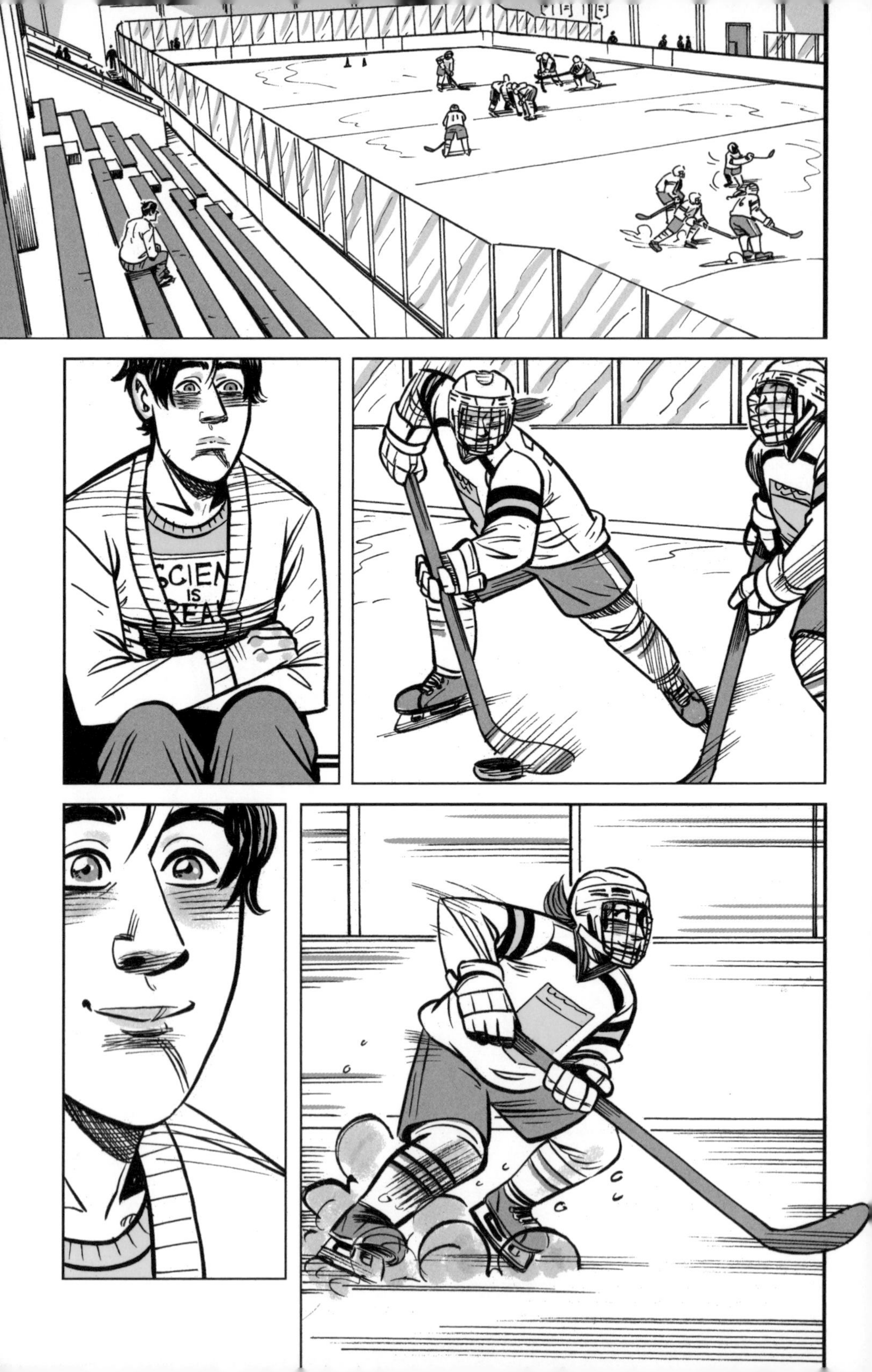
SCIEN
IS
REAL

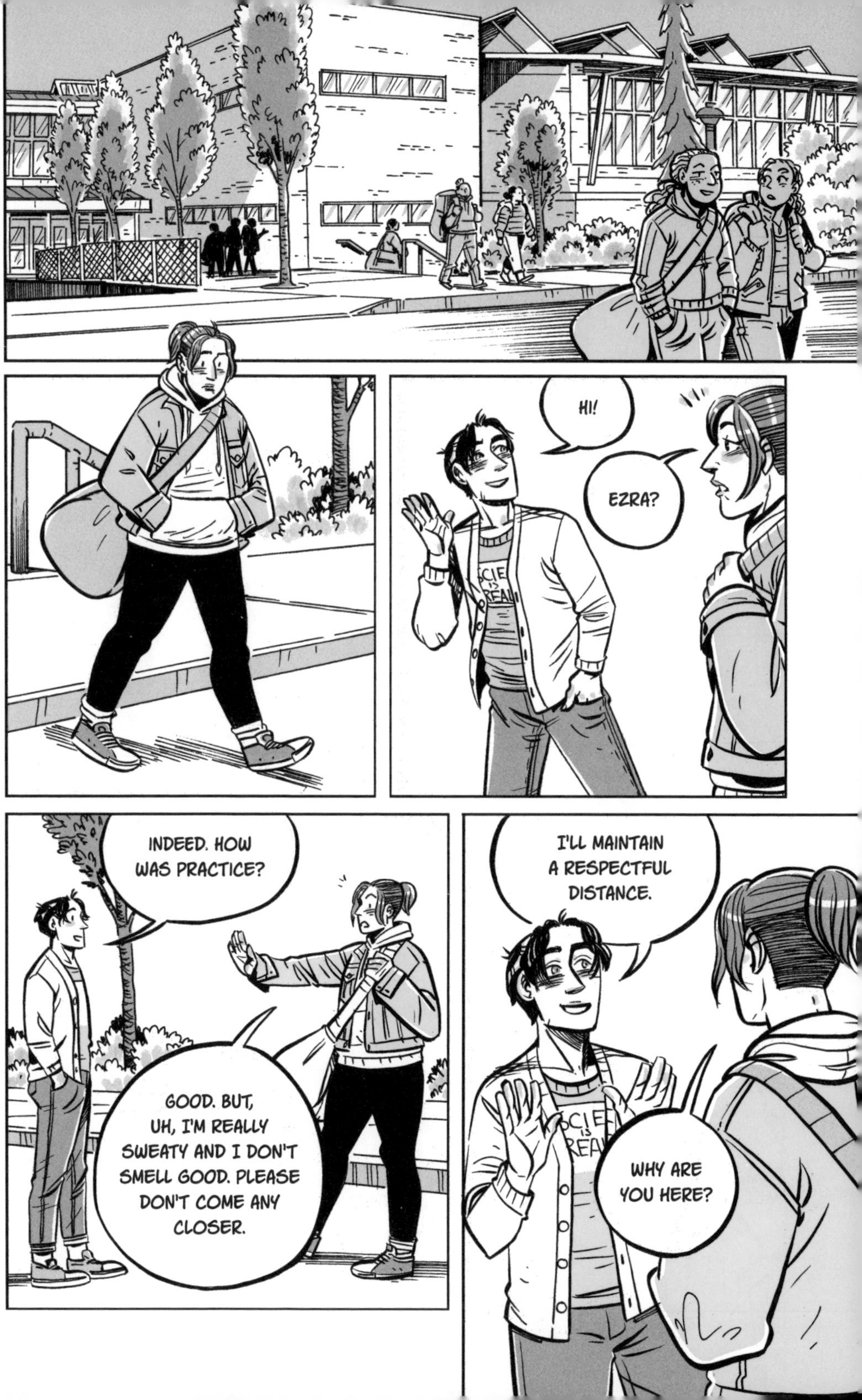
HI!
EZRA?
INDEED. HOW WAS PRACTICE?
GOOD. BUT, UH, I'M REALLY SWEATY AND I DON'T SMELL GOOD. PLEASE DON'T COME ANY CLOSER.
I'LL MAINTAIN A RESPECTFUL DISTANCE.
WHY ARE YOU HERE?
SCIENCE IS REAL

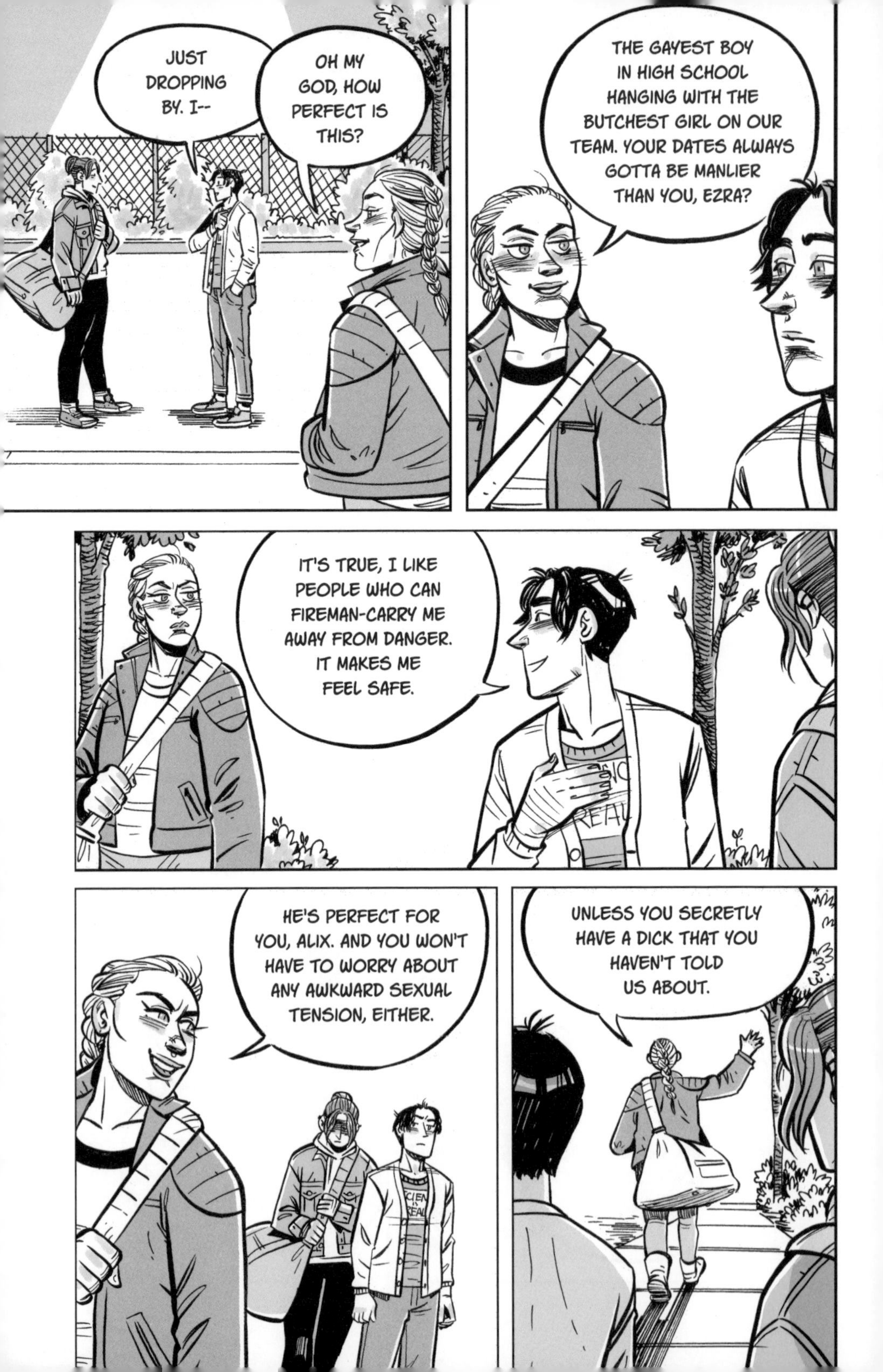
JUST DROPPING BY. I--
OH MY GOD, HOW PERFECT IS THIS?
THE GAYEST BOY IN HIGH SCHOOL HANGING WITH THE BUTCHEST GIRL ON OUR TEAM. YOUR DATES ALWAYS GOTTA BE MANLIER THAN YOU, EZRA?
IT'S TRUE, I LIKE PEOPLE WHO CAN FIREMAN-CARRY ME AWAY FROM DANGER. IT MAKES ME FEEL SAFE.
HE'S PERFECT FOR YOU, ALIX. AND YOU WON'T HAVE TO WORRY ABOUT ANY AWKWARD SEXUAL TENSION, EITHER.
UNLESS YOU SECRETLY HAVE A DICK THAT YOU HAVEN'T TOLD US ABOUT.

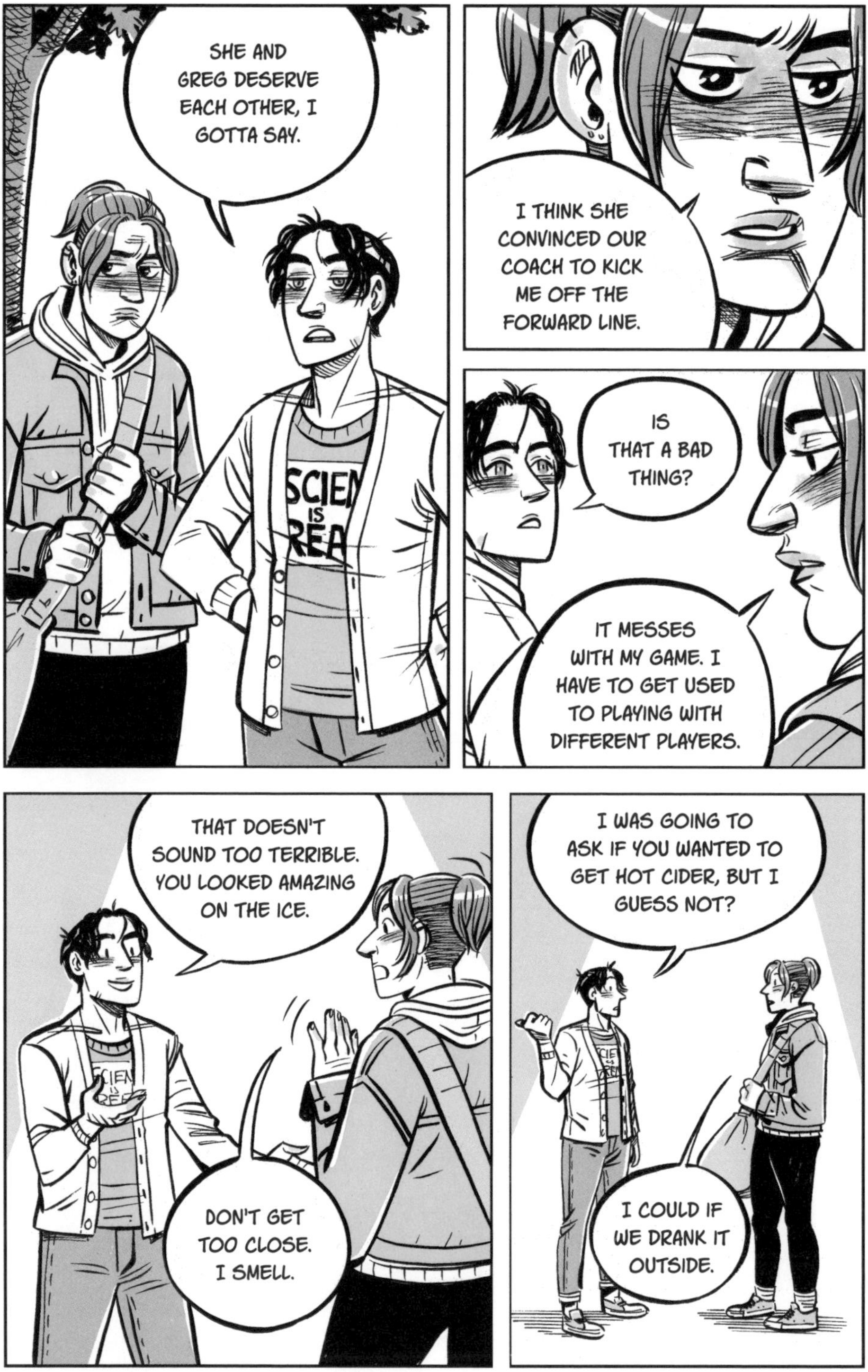
SHE AND GREG DESERVE EACH OTHER, I GOTTA SAY.
I THINK SHE CONVINCED OUR COACH TO KICK ME OFF THE FORWARD LINE.
IS THAT A BAD THING?
IT MESSES WITH MY GAME. I HAVE TO GET USED TO PLAYING WITH DIFFERENT PLAYERS.
THAT DOESN'T SOUND TOO TERRIBLE. YOU LOOKED AMAZING ON THE ICE.
DON'T GET TOO CLOSE. I SMELL.
I WAS GOING TO ASK IF YOU WANTED TO GET HOT CIDER, BUT I GUESS NOT?
I COULD IF WE DRANK IT OUTSIDE.

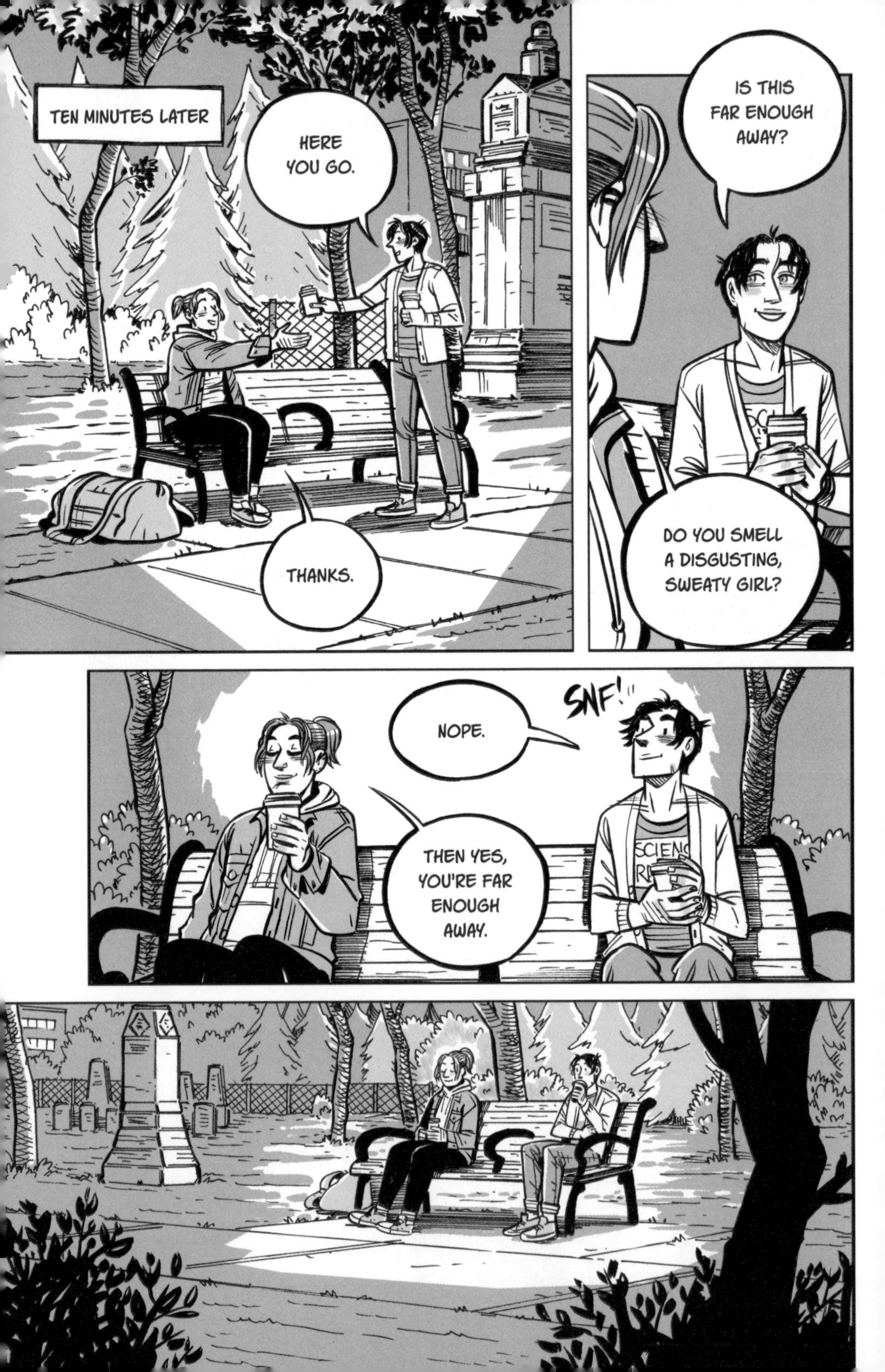
TEN MINUTES LATER
HERE YOU GO.
THANKS.
IS THIS FAR ENOUGH AWAY?
DO YOU SMELL A DISGUSTING, SWEATY GIRL?
SNF!
NOPE.
THEN YES, YOU'RE FAR ENOUGH AWAY.

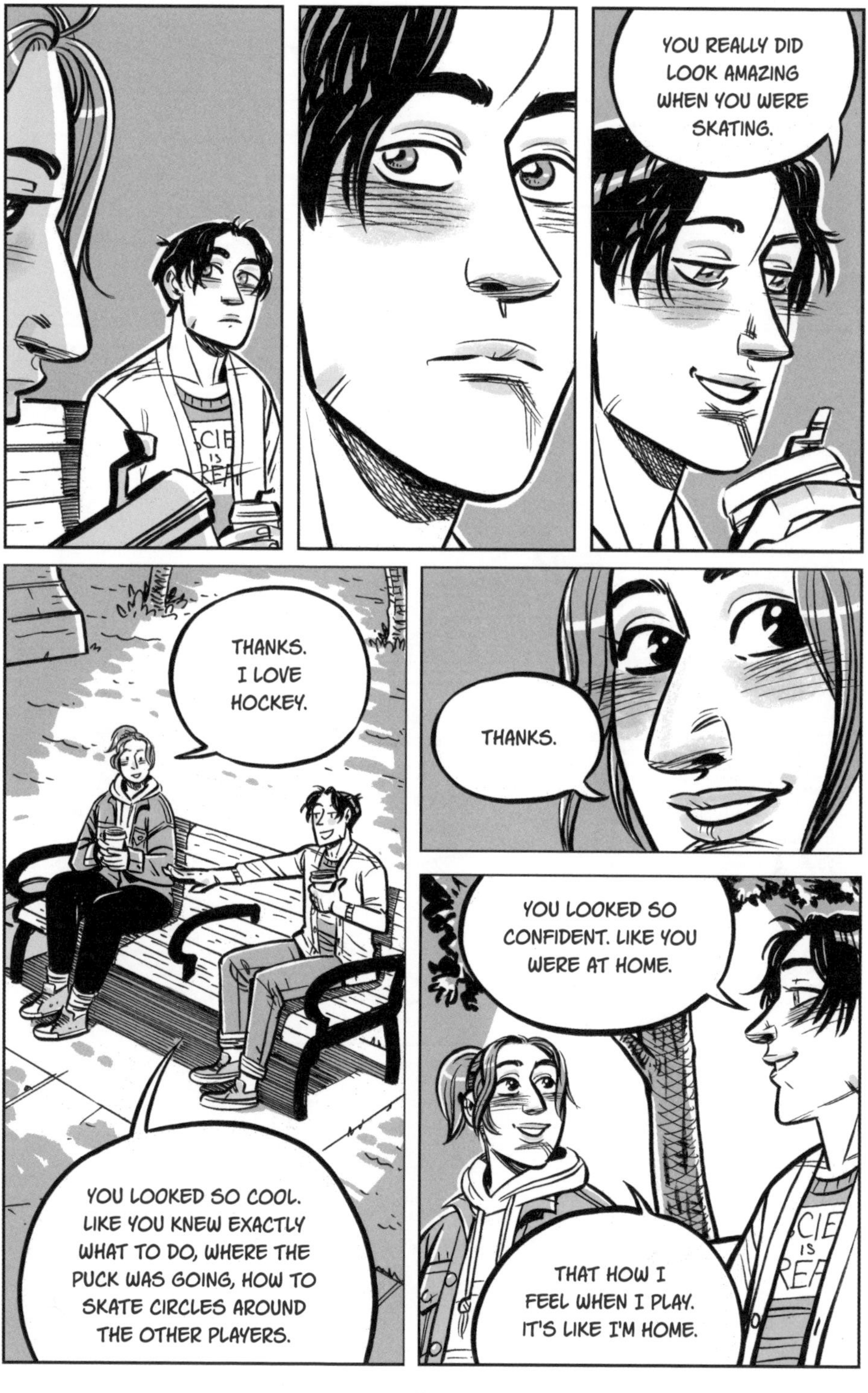
YOU REALLY DID LOOK AMAZING WHEN YOU WERE SKATING.
THANKS. I LOVE HOCKEY.
YOU LOOKED SO COOL. LIKE YOU KNEW EXACTLY WHAT TO DO, WHERE THE PUCK WAS GOING, HOW TO SKATE CIRCLES AROUND THE OTHER PLAYERS.
THANKS.
YOU LOOKED SO CONFIDENT. LIKE YOU WERE AT HOME.
THAT HOW I FEEL WHEN I PLAY. IT'S LIKE I'M HOME.

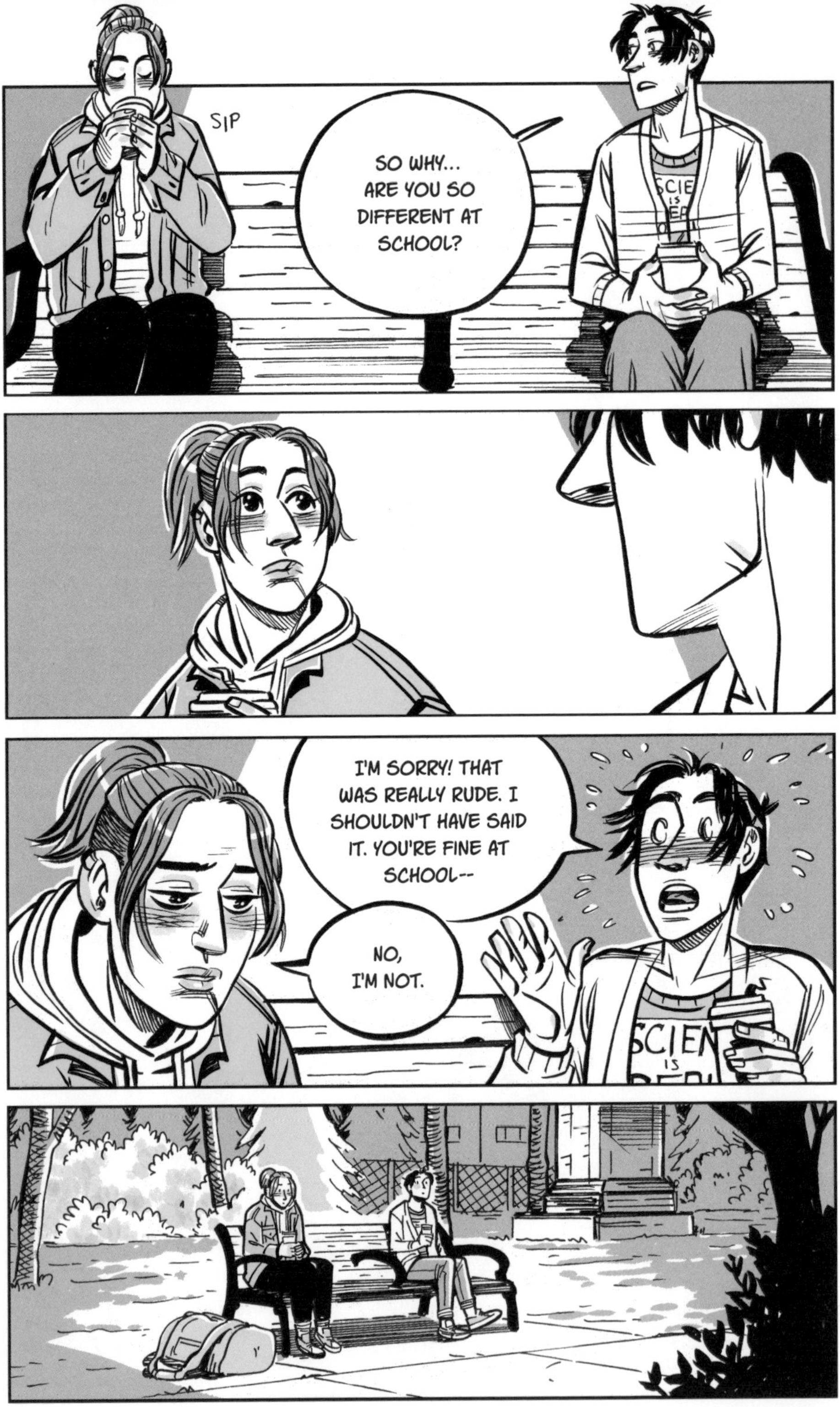
SIP
SO WHY... ARE YOU SO DIFFERENT AT SCHOOL?
I'M SORRY! THAT WAS REALLY RUDE. I SHOULDN'T HAVE SAID IT. YOU'RE FINE AT SCHOOL--
NO, I'M NOT.

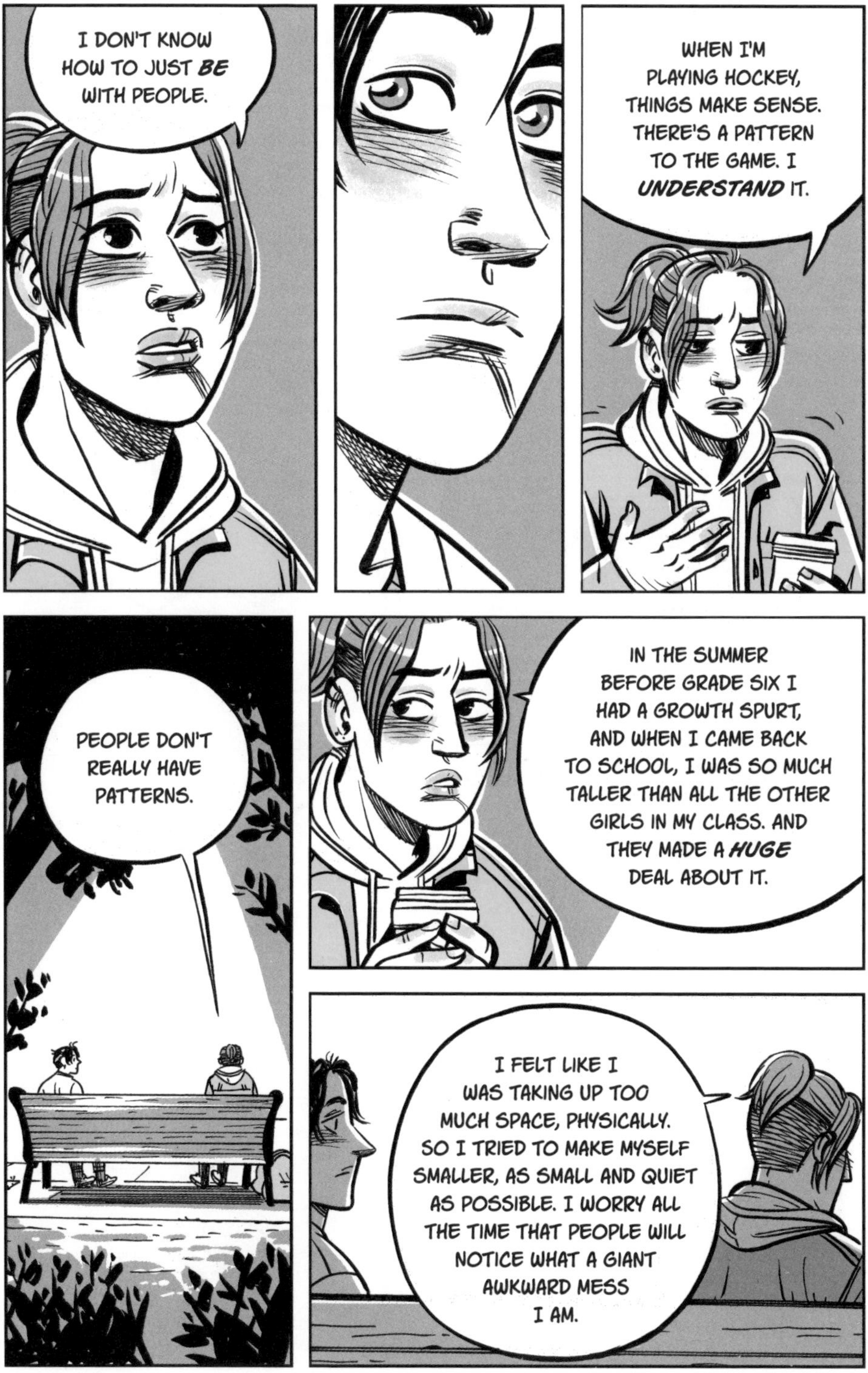
I DON'T KNOW HOW TO JUST *BE* WITH PEOPLE.
WHEN I'M PLAYING HOCKEY, THINGS MAKE SENSE. THERE'S A PATTERN TO THE GAME. I ***UNDERSTAND*** IT.
PEOPLE DON'T REALLY HAVE PATTERNS.
IN THE SUMMER BEFORE GRADE SIX I HAD A GROWTH SPURT, AND WHEN I CAME BACK TO SCHOOL, I WAS SO MUCH TALLER THAN ALL THE OTHER GIRLS IN MY CLASS. AND THEY MADE A ***HUGE*** DEAL ABOUT IT.
I FELT LIKE I WAS TAKING UP TOO MUCH SPACE, PHYSICALLY. SO I TRIED TO MAKE MYSELF SMALLER, AS SMALL AND QUIET AS POSSIBLE. I WORRY ALL THE TIME THAT PEOPLE WILL NOTICE WHAT A GIANT AWKWARD MESS I AM.

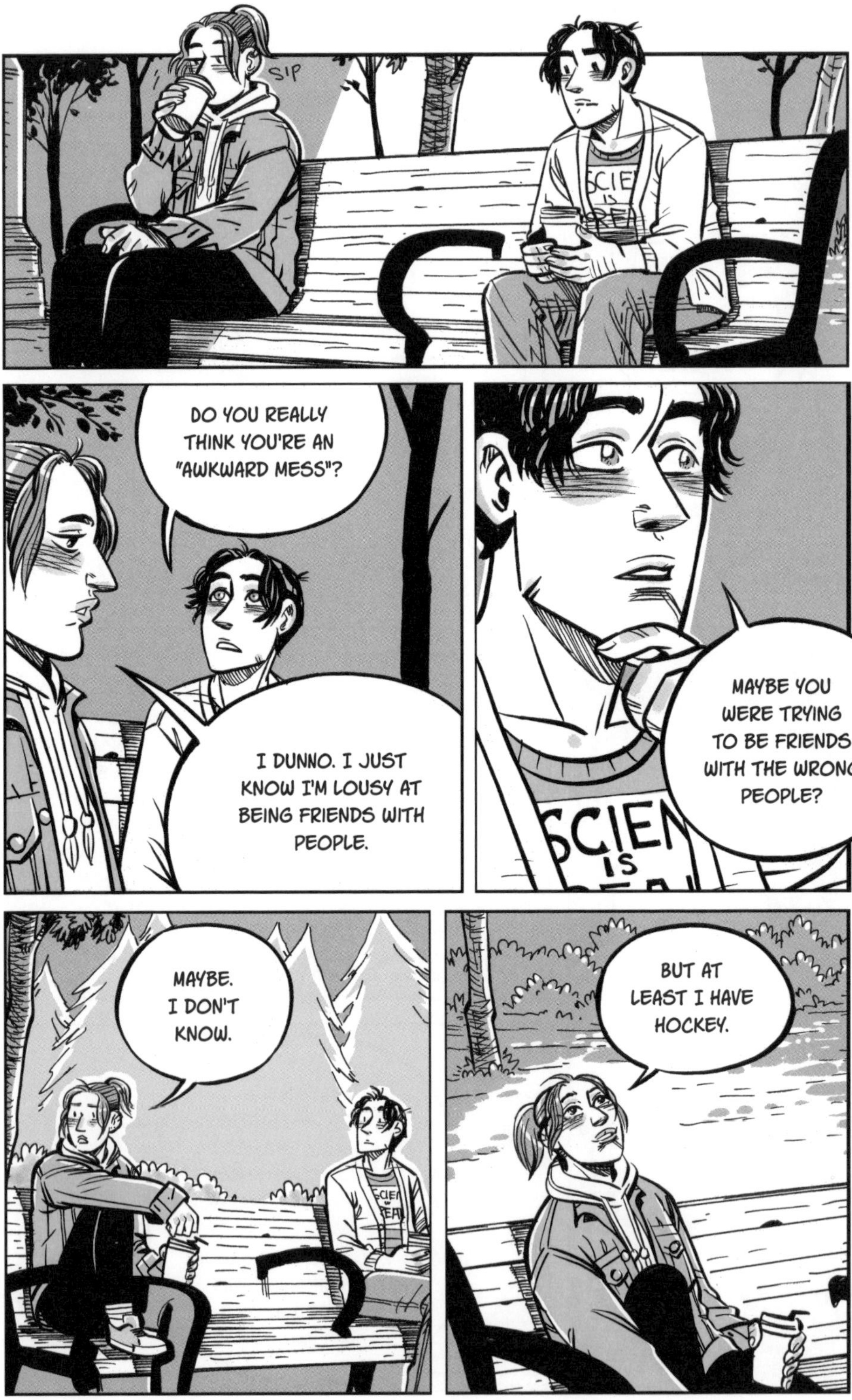
SIP
DO YOU REALLY THINK YOU'RE AN "AWKWARD MESS"?
I DUNNO. I JUST KNOW I'M LOUSY AT BEING FRIENDS WITH PEOPLE.
SCIEN IS
MAYBE YOU WERE TRYING TO BE FRIENDS WITH THE WRONG PEOPLE?
MAYBE. I DON'T KNOW.
BUT AT LEAST I HAVE HOCKEY.

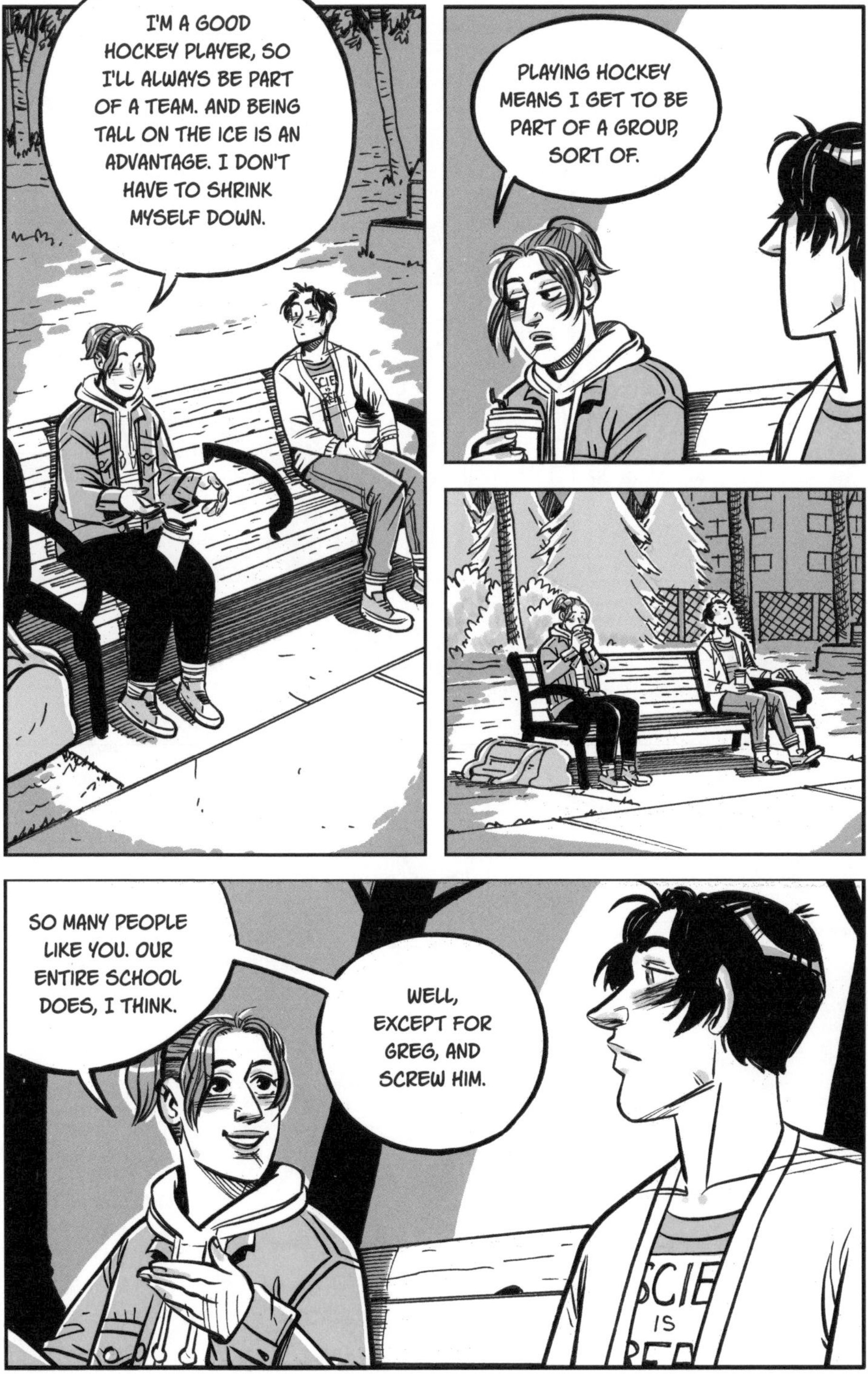
I'M A GOOD HOCKEY PLAYER, SO I'LL ALWAYS BE PART OF A TEAM. AND BEING TALL ON THE ICE IS AN ADVANTAGE. I DON'T HAVE TO SHRINK MYSELF DOWN.
PLAYING HOCKEY MEANS I GET TO BE PART OF A GROUP, SORT OF.
SO MANY PEOPLE LIKE YOU. OUR ENTIRE SCHOOL DOES, I THINK.
WELL, EXCEPT FOR GREG, AND SCREW HIM.

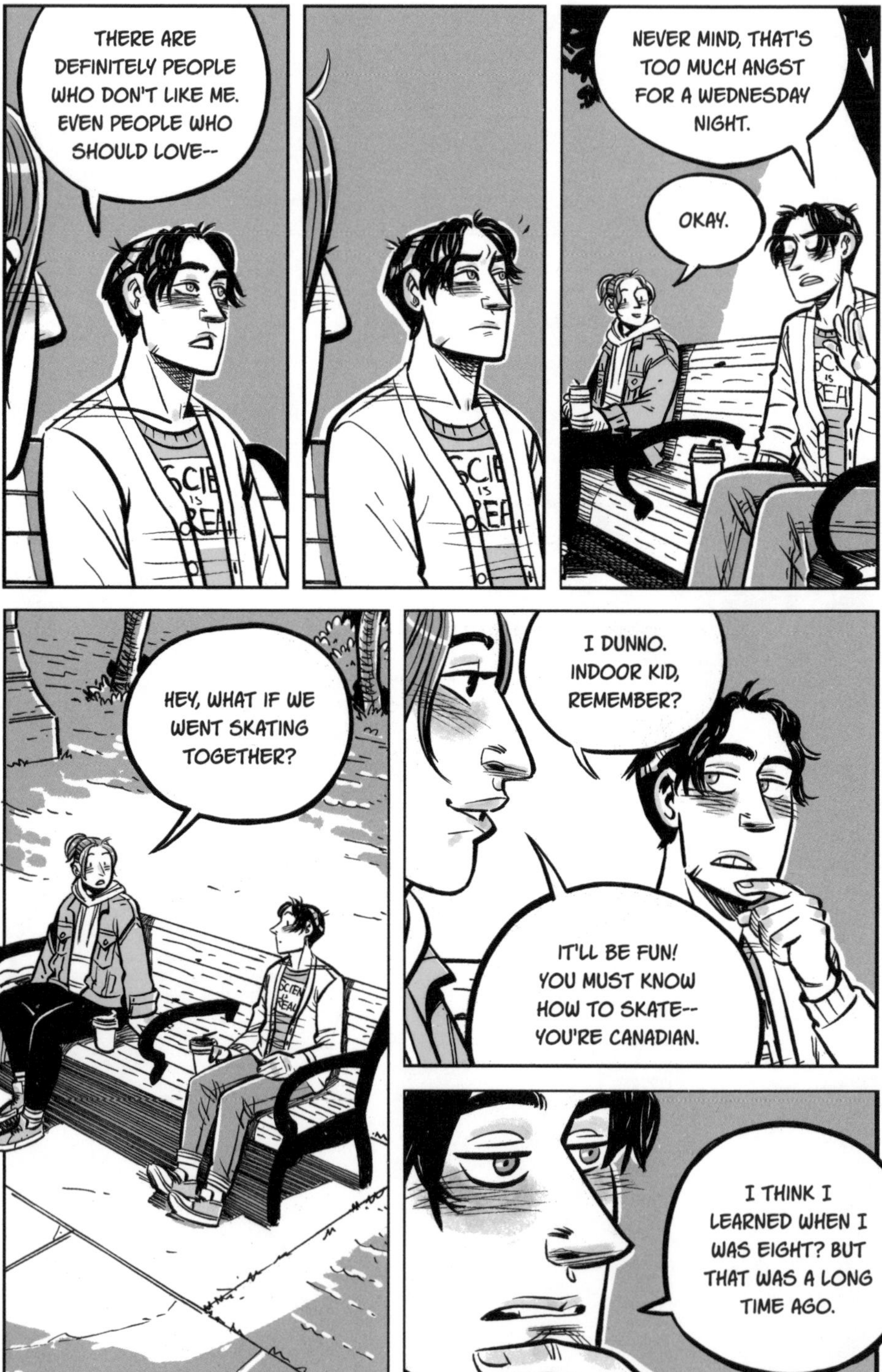
THERE ARE DEFINITELY PEOPLE WHO DON'T LIKE ME. EVEN PEOPLE WHO SHOULD LOVE--
NEVER MIND, THAT'S TOO MUCH ANGST FOR A WEDNESDAY NIGHT.
OKAY.
HEY, WHAT IF WE WENT SKATING TOGETHER?
I DUNNO. INDOOR KID, REMEMBER?
IT'LL BE FUN! YOU MUST KNOW HOW TO SKATE-- YOU'RE CANADIAN.
I THINK I LEARNED WHEN I WAS EIGHT? BUT THAT WAS A LONG TIME AGO.

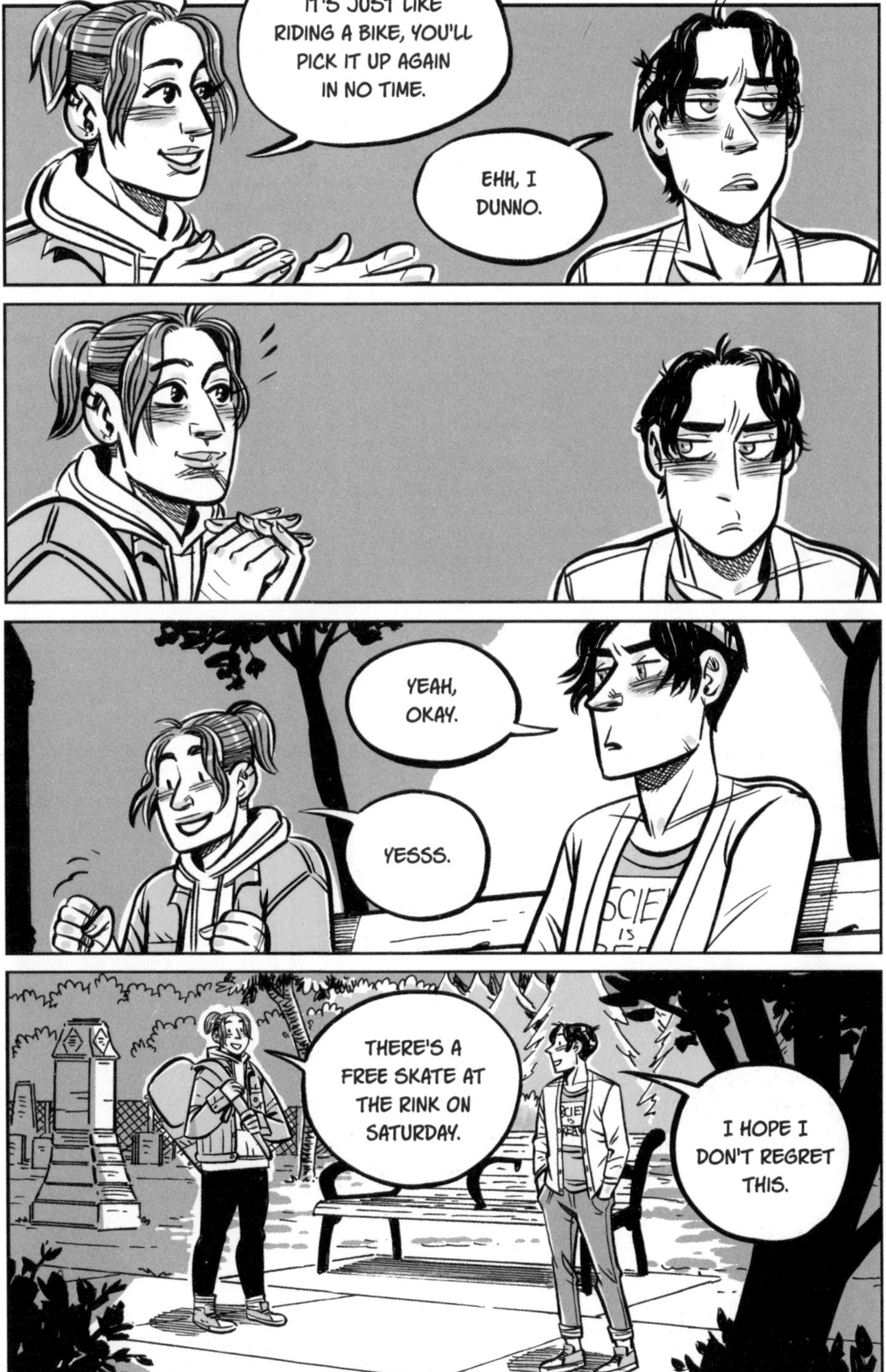
IT'S JUST LIKE RIDING A BIKE, YOU'LL PICK IT UP AGAIN IN NO TIME.
EHH, I DUNNO.
YEAH, OKAY.
YESSS.
SCIE IS
THERE'S A FREE SKATE AT THE RINK ON SATURDAY.
I HOPE I DON'T REGRET THIS.

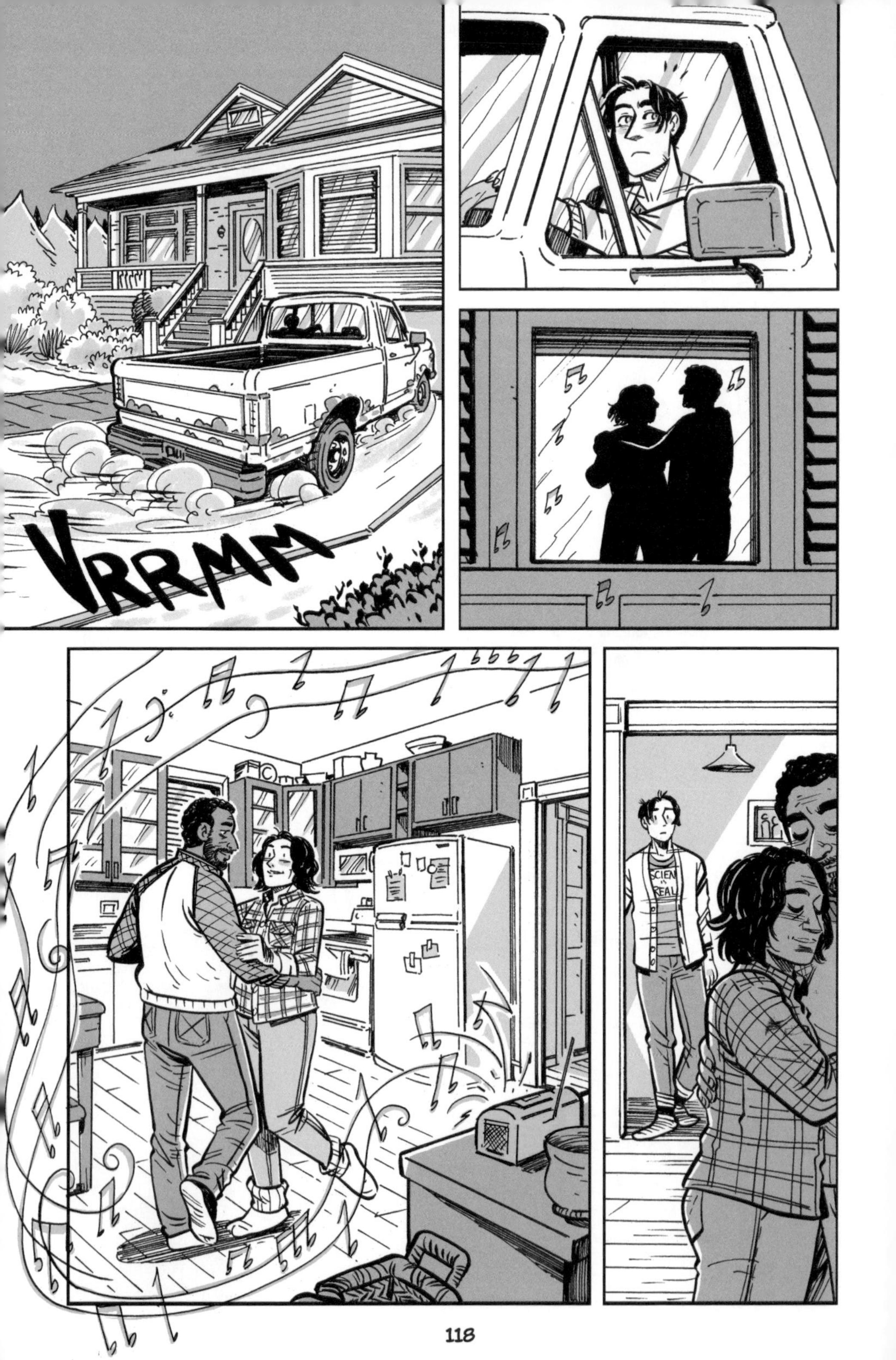
VRRMM

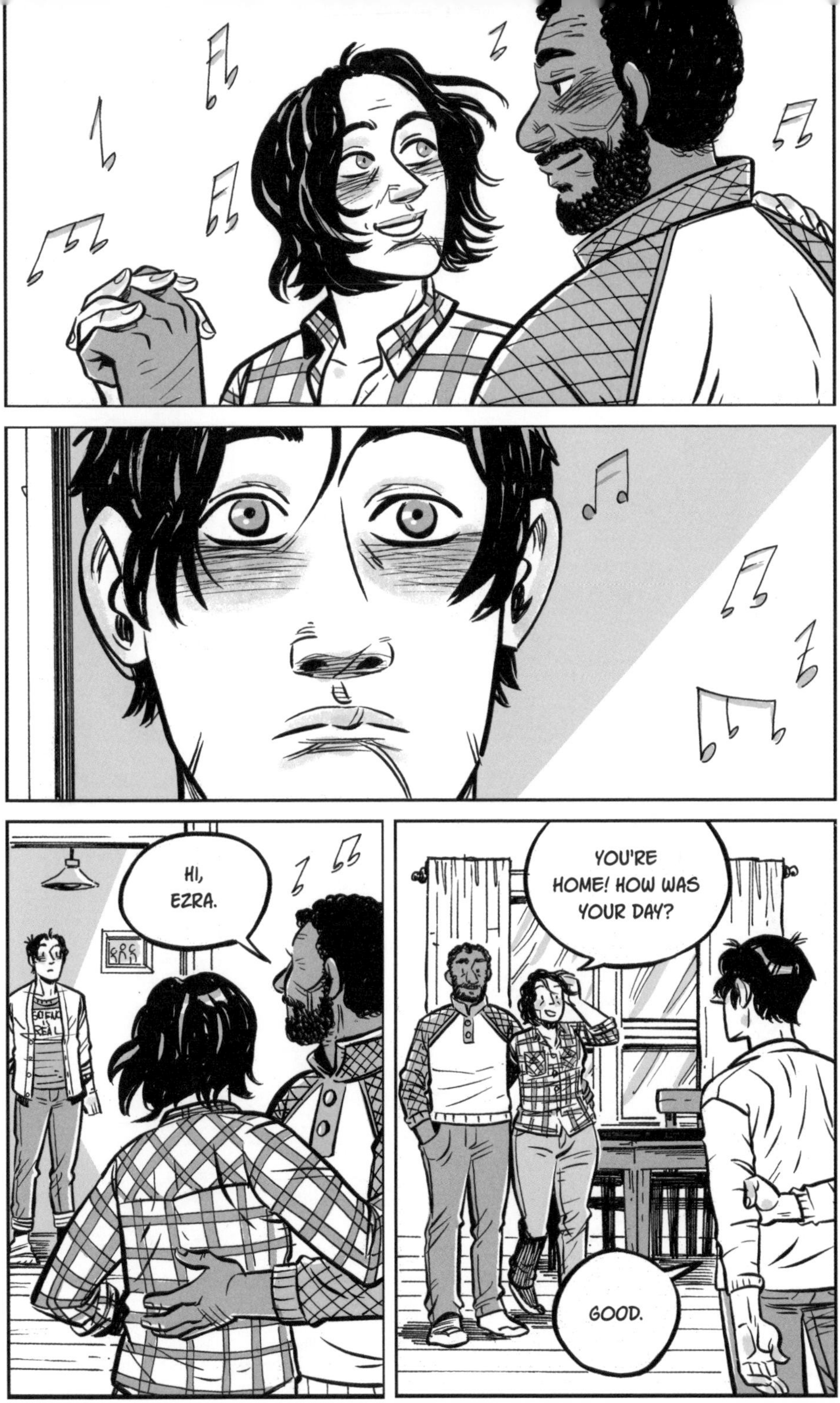
HI, EZRA.
YOU'RE HOME! HOW WAS YOUR DAY?
GOOD.

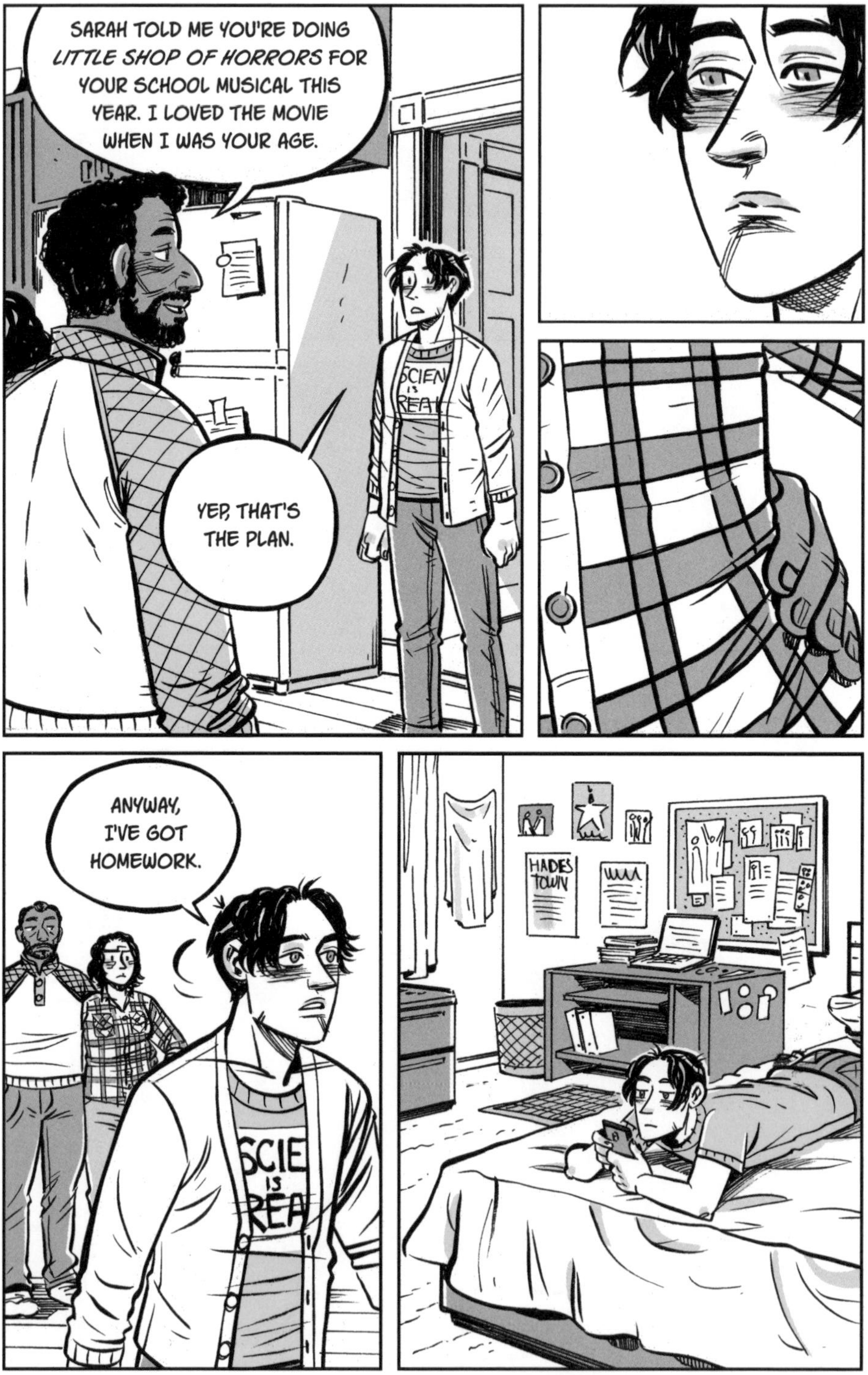
SARAH TOLD ME YOU'RE DOING *LITTLE SHOP OF HORRORS* FOR YOUR SCHOOL MUSICAL THIS YEAR. I LOVED THE MOVIE WHEN I WAS YOUR AGE.
YEP, THAT'S THE PLAN.
SCIEN IS REA
ANYWAY, I'VE GOT HOMEWORK.
SCIE IS REA
HADES TOWN

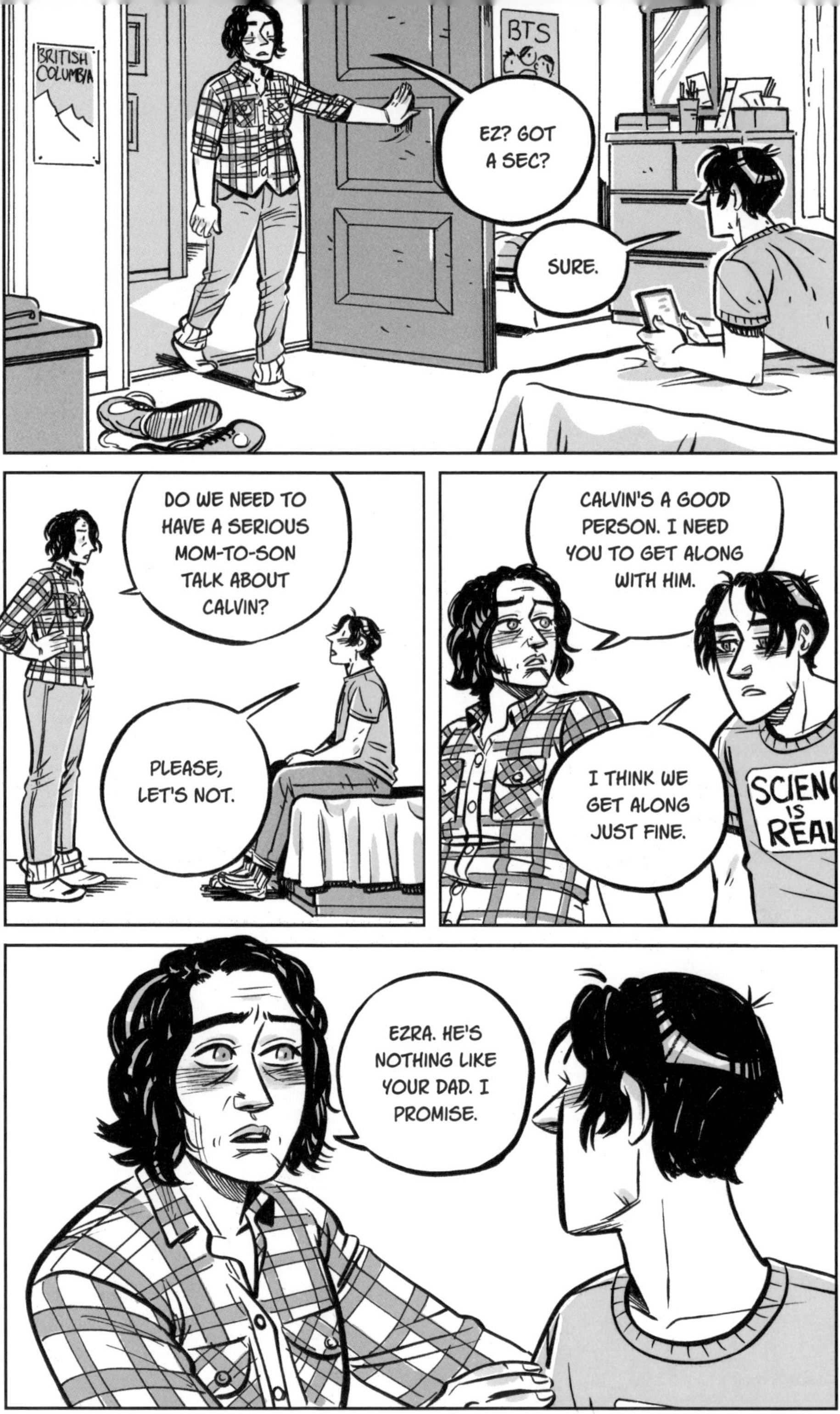
BRITISH COLUMBIA
BTS
EZ? GOT A SEC?
SURE.
DO WE NEED TO HAVE A SERIOUS MOM-TO-SON TALK ABOUT CALVIN?
PLEASE, LET'S NOT.
CALVIN'S A GOOD PERSON. I NEED YOU TO GET ALONG WITH HIM.
I THINK WE GET ALONG JUST FINE.
EZRA. HE'S NOTHING LIKE YOUR DAD. I PROMISE.

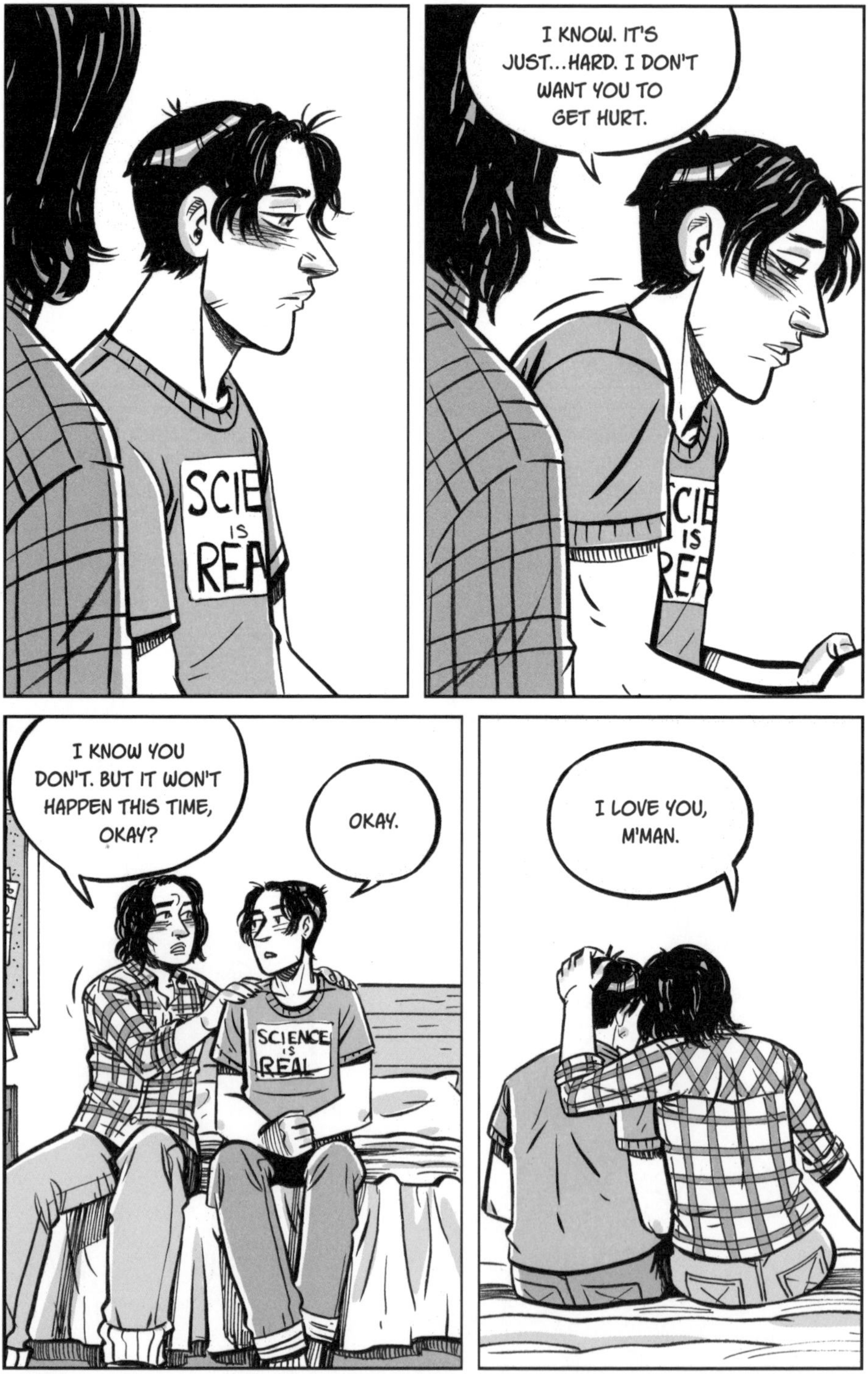

SCIE IS REA
I KNOW. IT'S JUST...HARD. I DON'T WANT YOU TO GET HURT.
I KNOW YOU DON'T. BUT IT WON'T HAPPEN THIS TIME, OKAY?
OKAY.
SCIENCE IS REAL
I LOVE YOU, M'MAN.

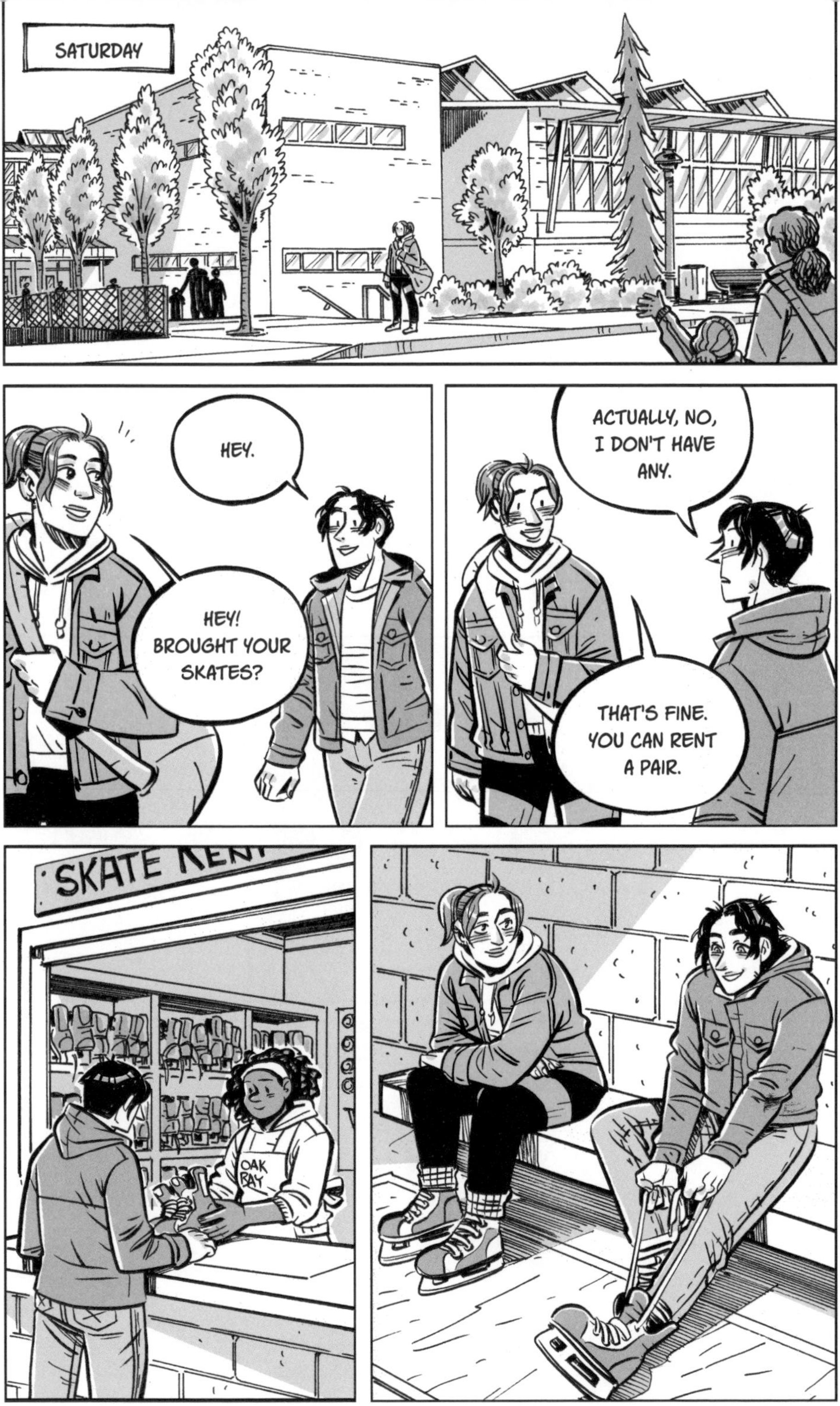
SATURDAY
HEY.
HEY!
BROUGHT YOUR
SKATES?
ACTUALLY, NO,
I DON'T HAVE
ANY.
THAT'S FINE.
YOU CAN RENT
A PAIR.
SKATE RENT
OAK
BAY

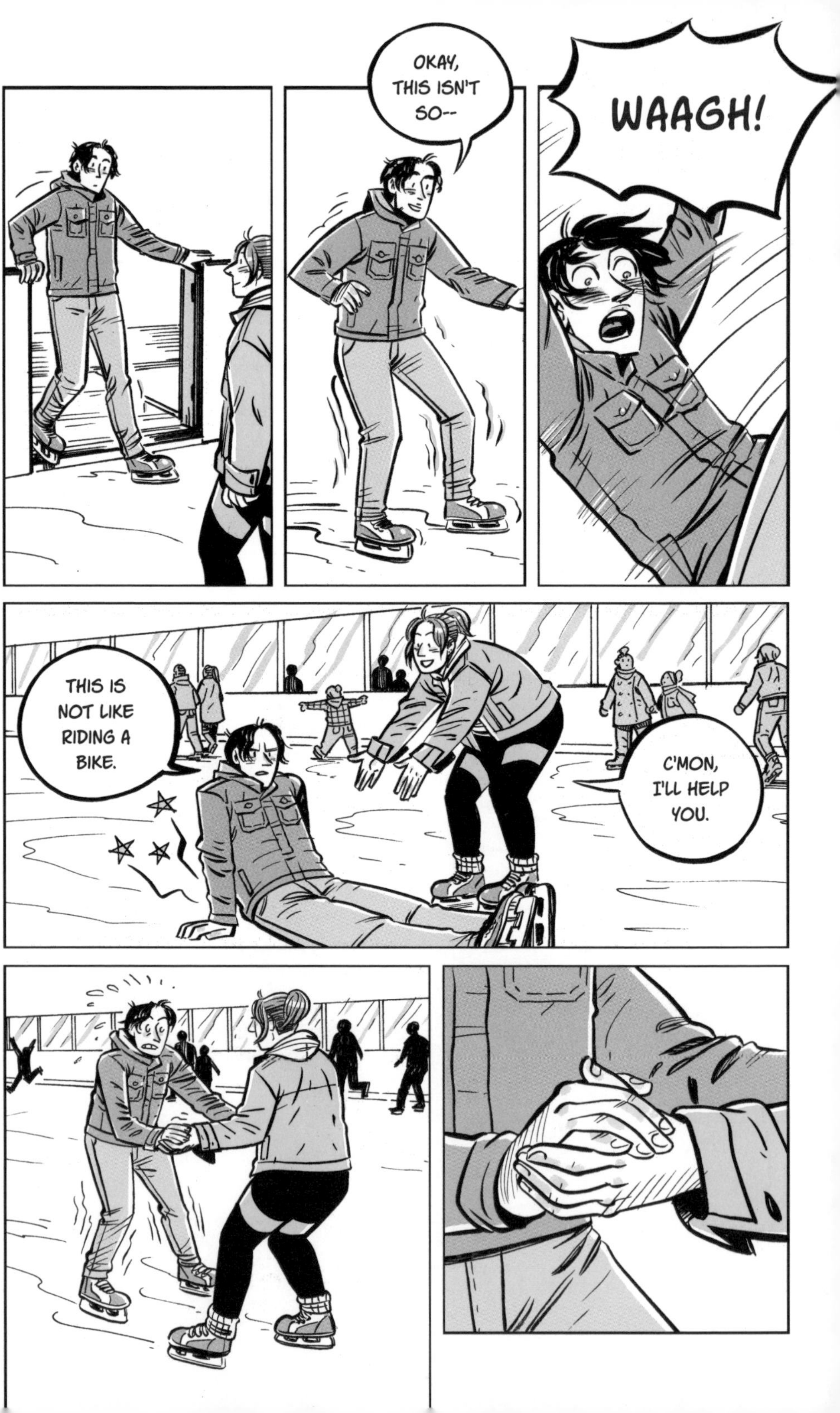
OKAY, THIS ISN'T SO--
WAAGH!
THIS IS NOT LIKE RIDING A BIKE.
C'MON, I'LL HELP YOU.

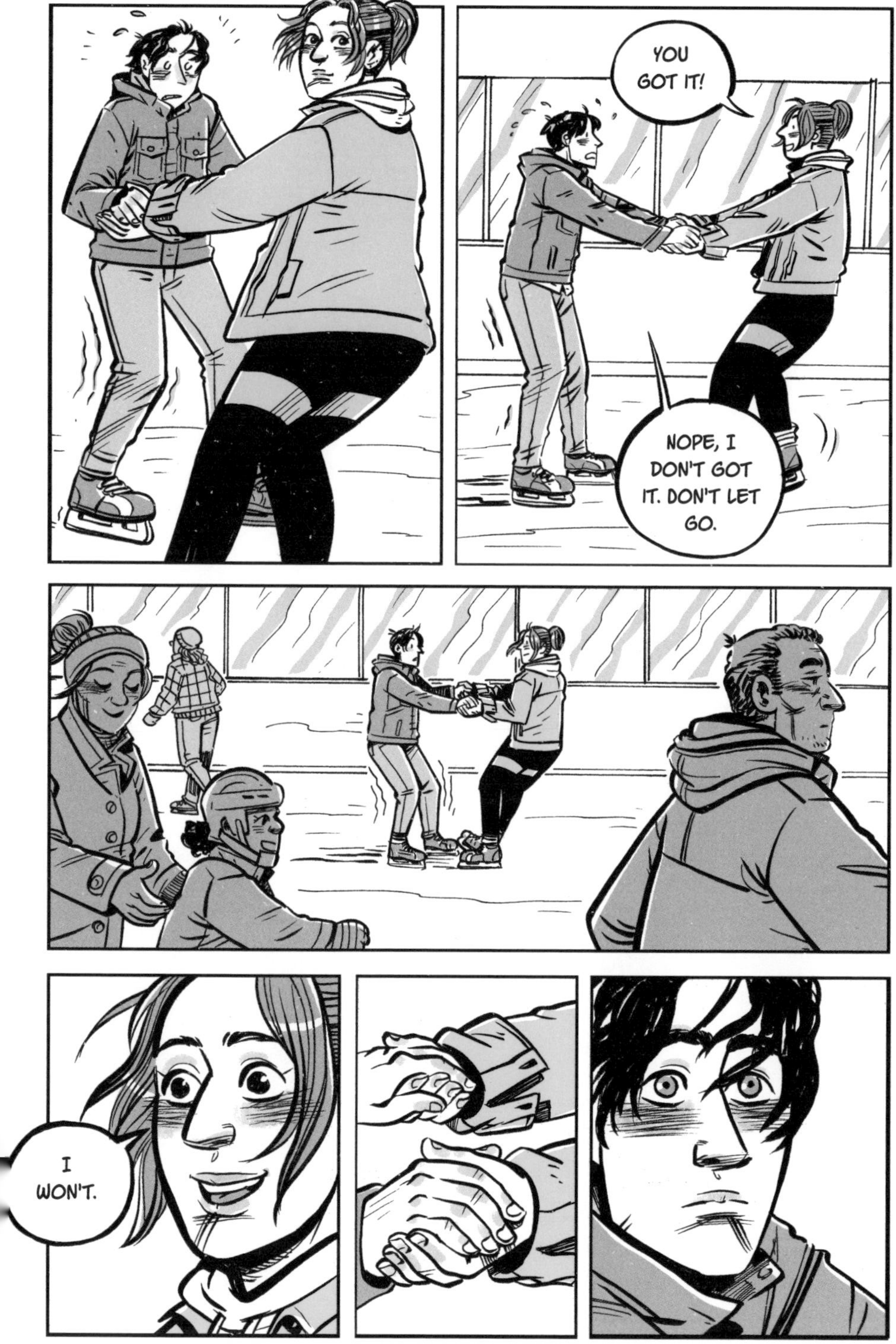
YOU GOT IT!
NOPE, I DON'T GOT IT. DON'T LET GO.
I WON'T.

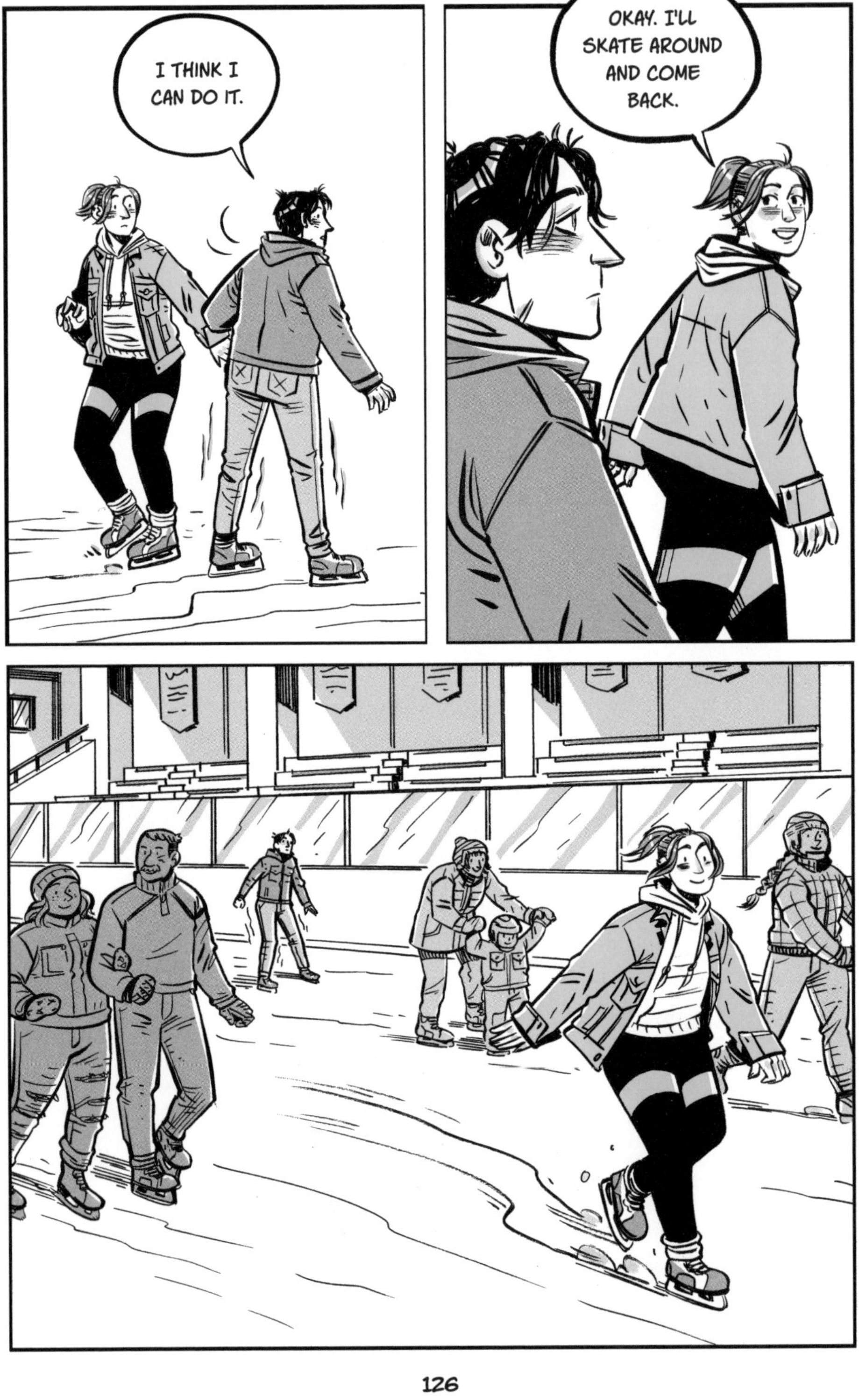
I THINK I CAN DO IT.
OKAY. I'LL SKATE AROUND AND COME BACK.

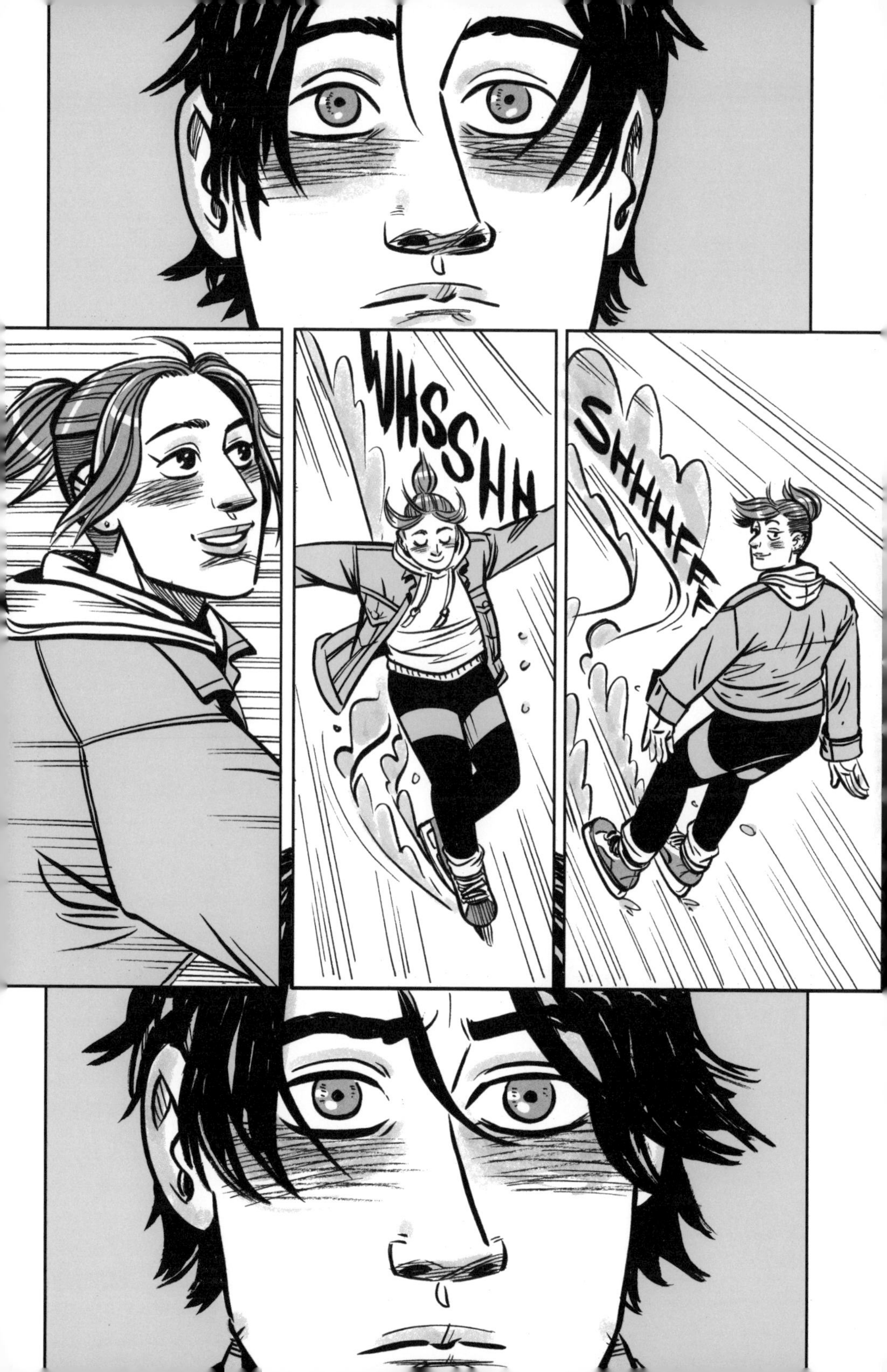
WHSSHH
SHHHFFF

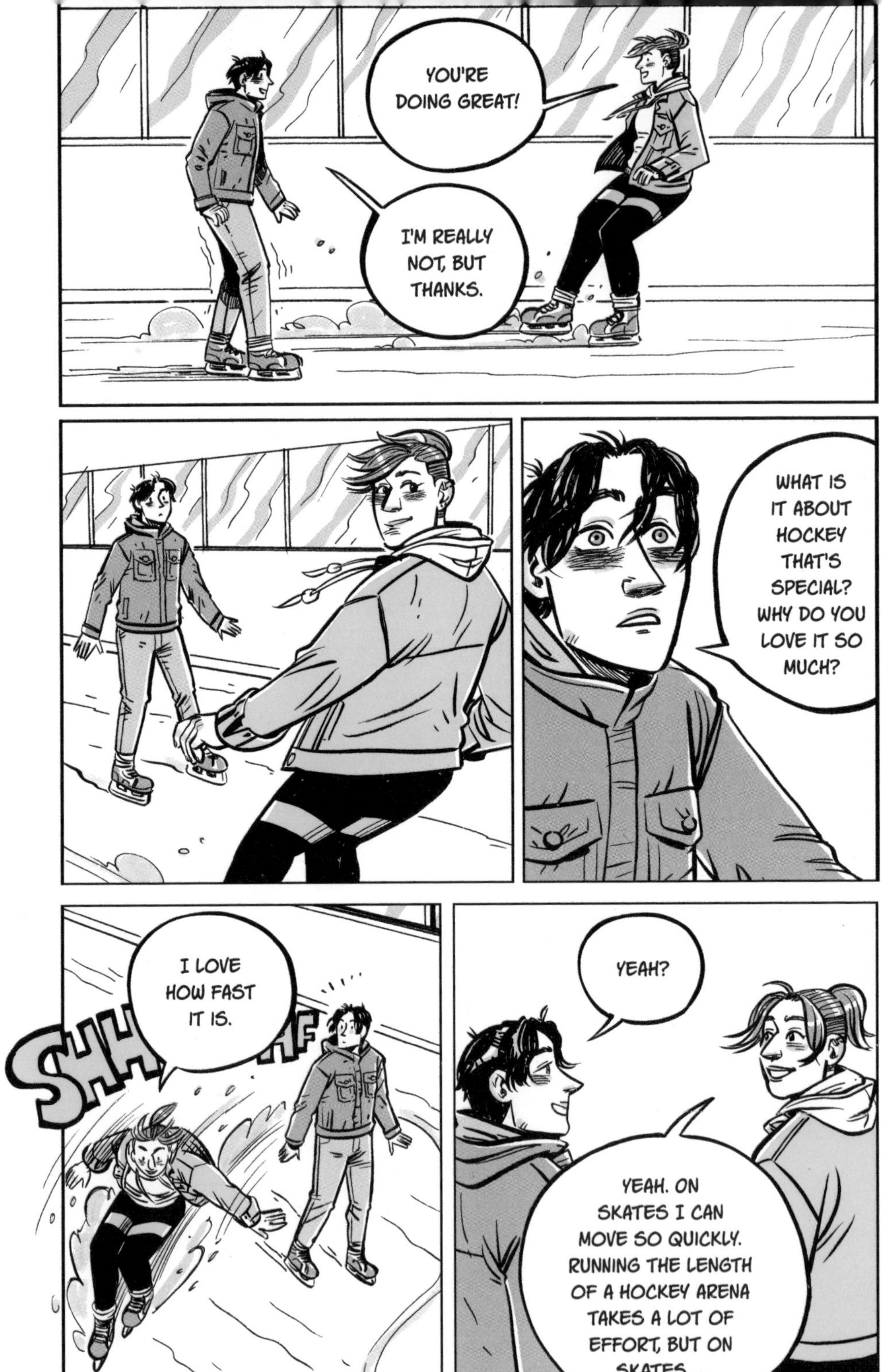
YOU'RE DOING GREAT!
I'M REALLY NOT, BUT THANKS.
WHAT IS IT ABOUT HOCKEY THAT'S SPECIAL? WHY DO YOU LOVE IT SO MUCH?
I LOVE HOW FAST IT IS.
YEAH?
YEAH. ON SKATES I CAN MOVE SO QUICKLY. RUNNING THE LENGTH OF A HOCKEY ARENA TAKES A LOT OF EFFORT, BUT ON SKATES...

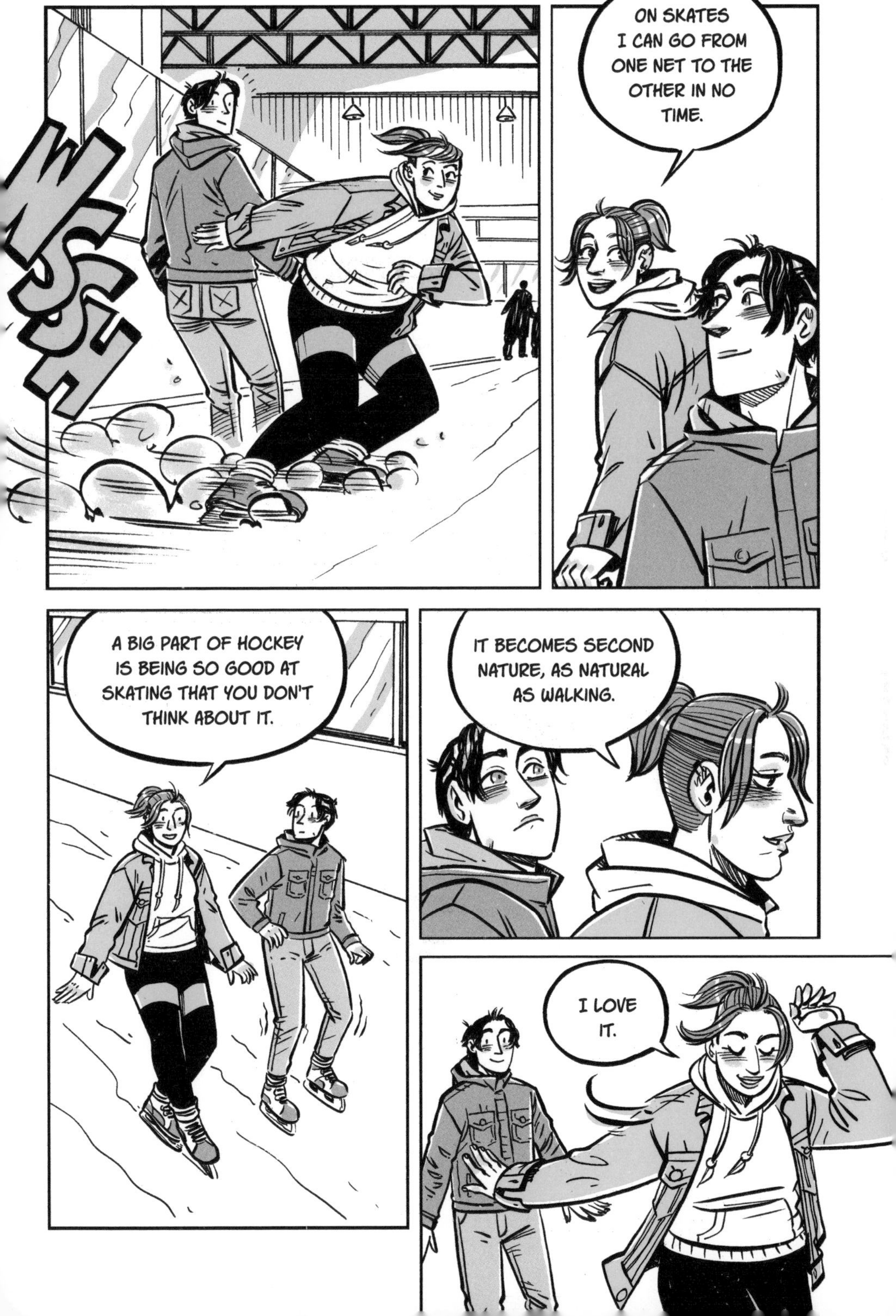
WSSH
ON SKATES I CAN GO FROM ONE NET TO THE OTHER IN NO TIME.
A BIG PART OF HOCKEY IS BEING SO GOOD AT SKATING THAT YOU DON'T THINK ABOUT IT.
IT BECOMES SECOND NATURE, AS NATURAL AS WALKING.
I LOVE IT.

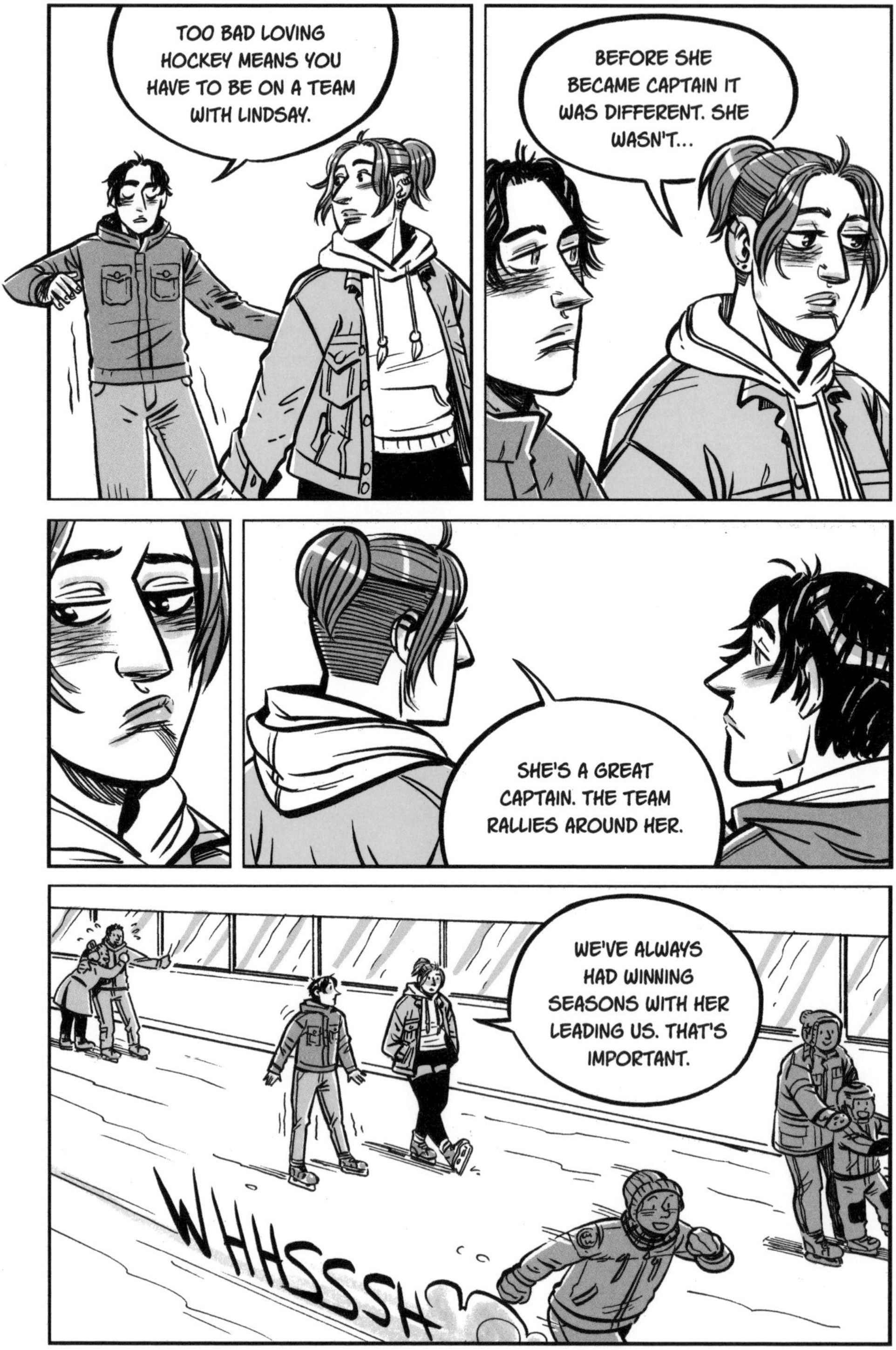
TOO BAD LOVING HOCKEY MEANS YOU HAVE TO BE ON A TEAM WITH LINDSAY.
BEFORE SHE BECAME CAPTAIN IT WAS DIFFERENT. SHE WASN'T...
SHE'S A GREAT CAPTAIN. THE TEAM RALLIES AROUND HER.
WE'VE ALWAYS HAD WINNING SEASONS WITH HER LEADING US. THAT'S IMPORTANT.
WHHSSSSH

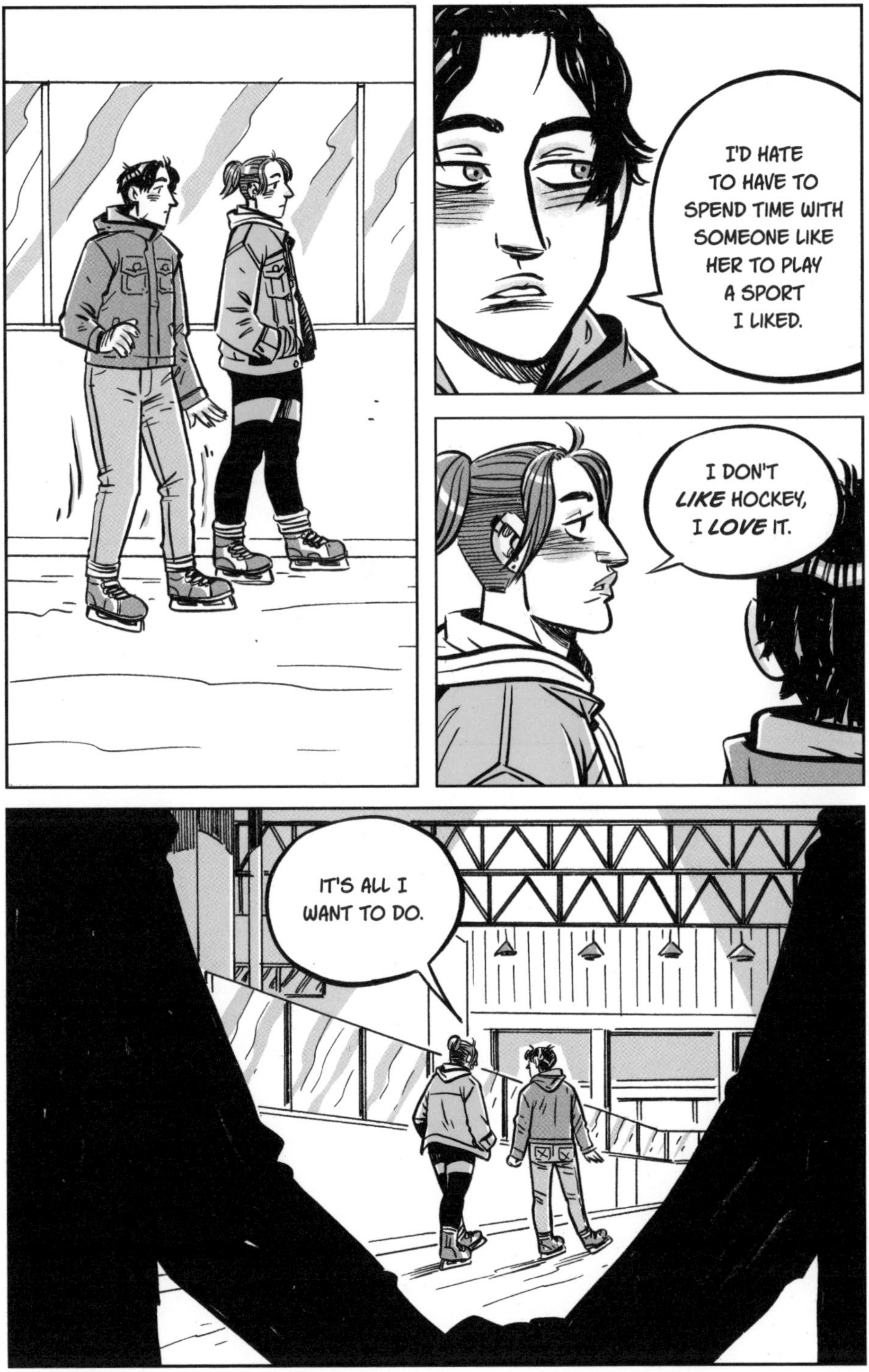
I'D HATE TO HAVE TO SPEND TIME WITH SOMEONE LIKE HER TO PLAY A SPORT I LIKED.
I DON'T *LIKE* HOCKEY, I *LOVE* IT.
IT'S ALL I WANT TO DO.

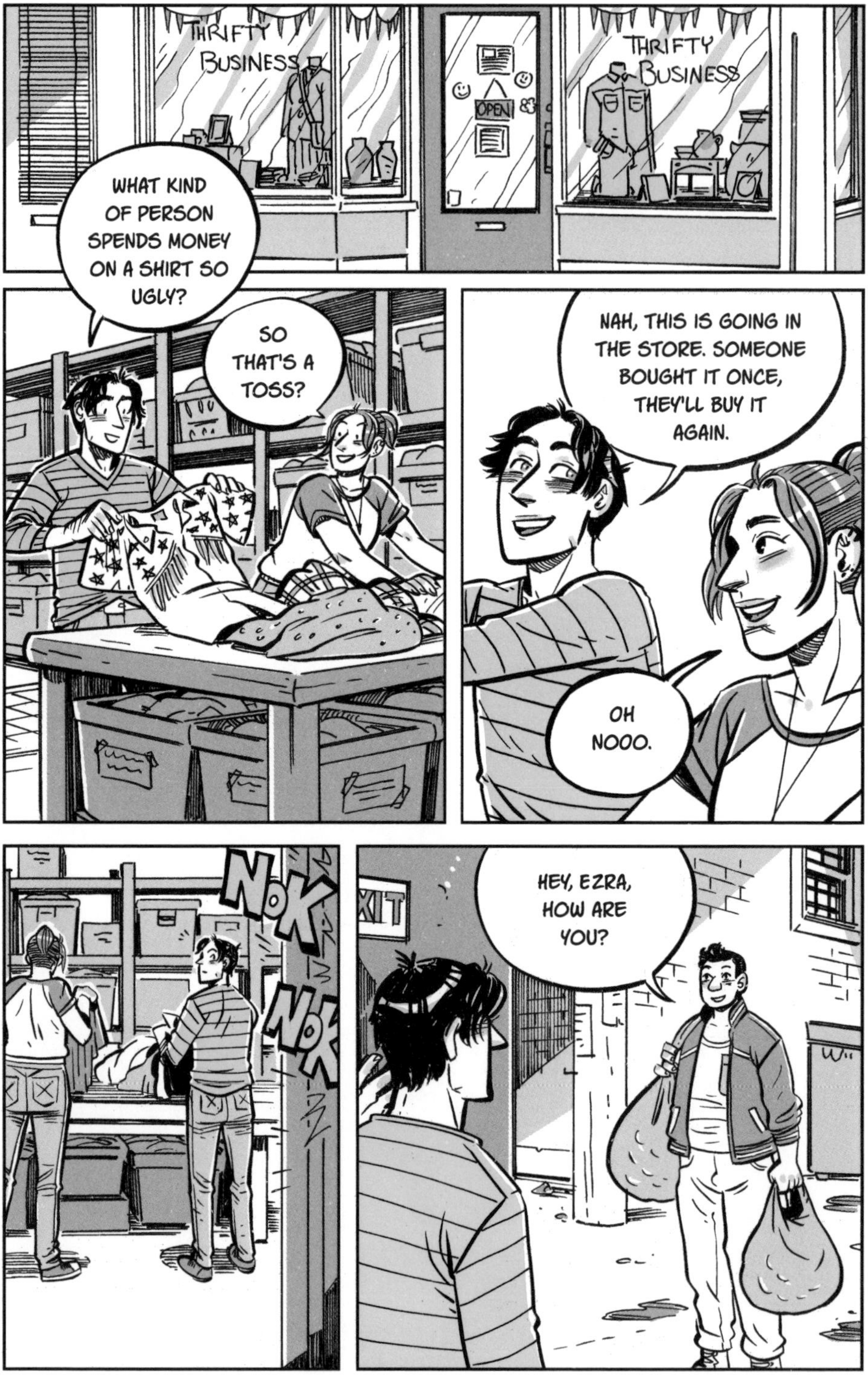

THRIFTY BUSINESS
OPEN
THRIFTY BUSINESS
WHAT KIND OF PERSON SPENDS MONEY ON A SHIRT SO UGLY?
SO THAT'S A TOSS?
NAH, THIS IS GOING IN THE STORE. SOMEONE BOUGHT IT ONCE, THEY'LL BUY IT AGAIN.
OH NOOO.
NOK
NOK
EXIT
HEY, EZRA, HOW ARE YOU?

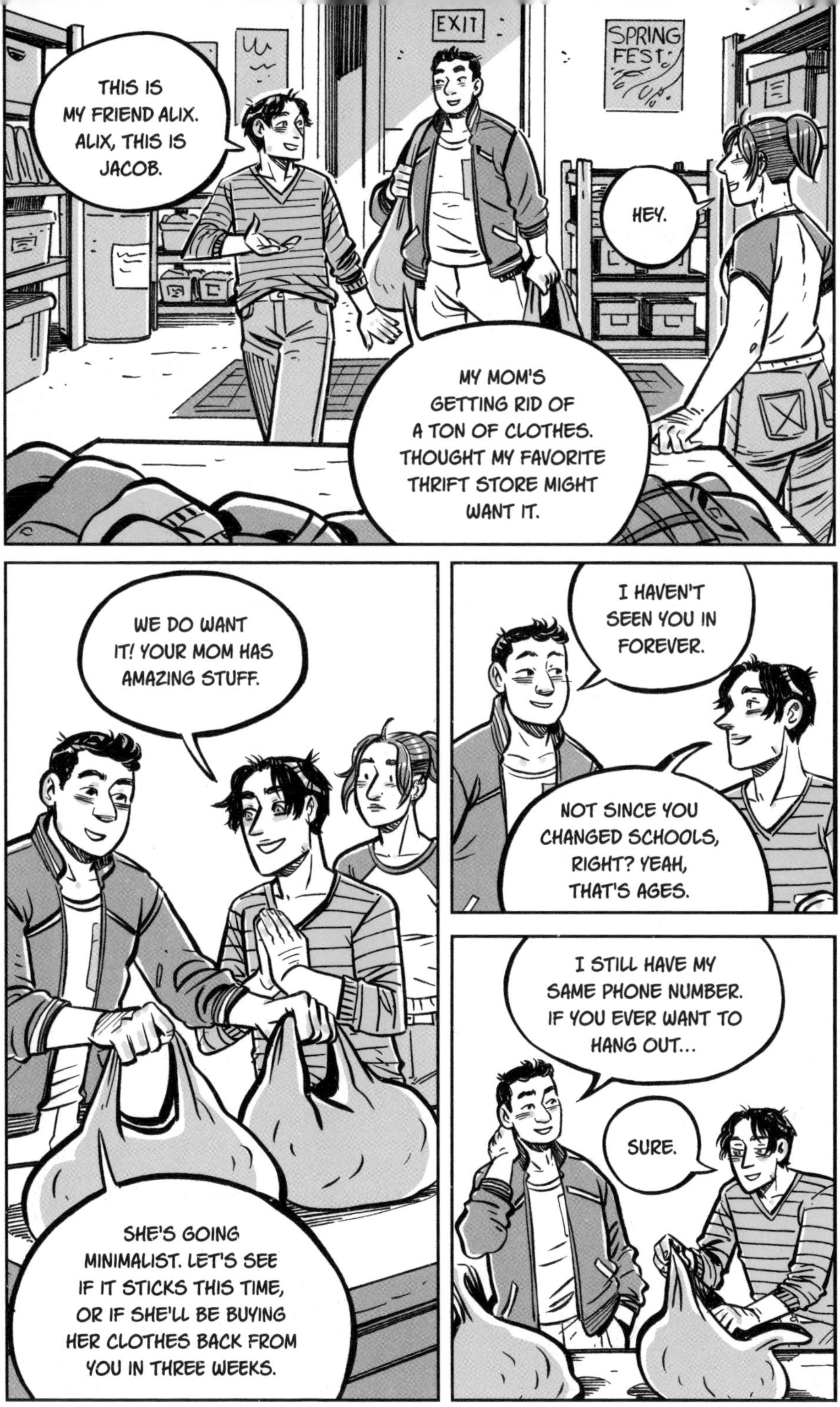
EXIT
SPRING FEST
THIS IS MY FRIEND ALIX. ALIX, THIS IS JACOB.
HEY.
MY MOM'S GETTING RID OF A TON OF CLOTHES. THOUGHT MY FAVORITE THRIFT STORE MIGHT WANT IT.
WE DO WANT IT! YOUR MOM HAS AMAZING STUFF.
SHE'S GOING MINIMALIST. LET'S SEE IF IT STICKS THIS TIME, OR IF SHE'LL BE BUYING HER CLOTHES BACK FROM YOU IN THREE WEEKS.
I HAVEN'T SEEN YOU IN FOREVER.
NOT SINCE YOU CHANGED SCHOOLS, RIGHT? YEAH, THAT'S AGES.
I STILL HAVE MY SAME PHONE NUMBER. IF YOU EVER WANT TO HANG OUT...
SURE.

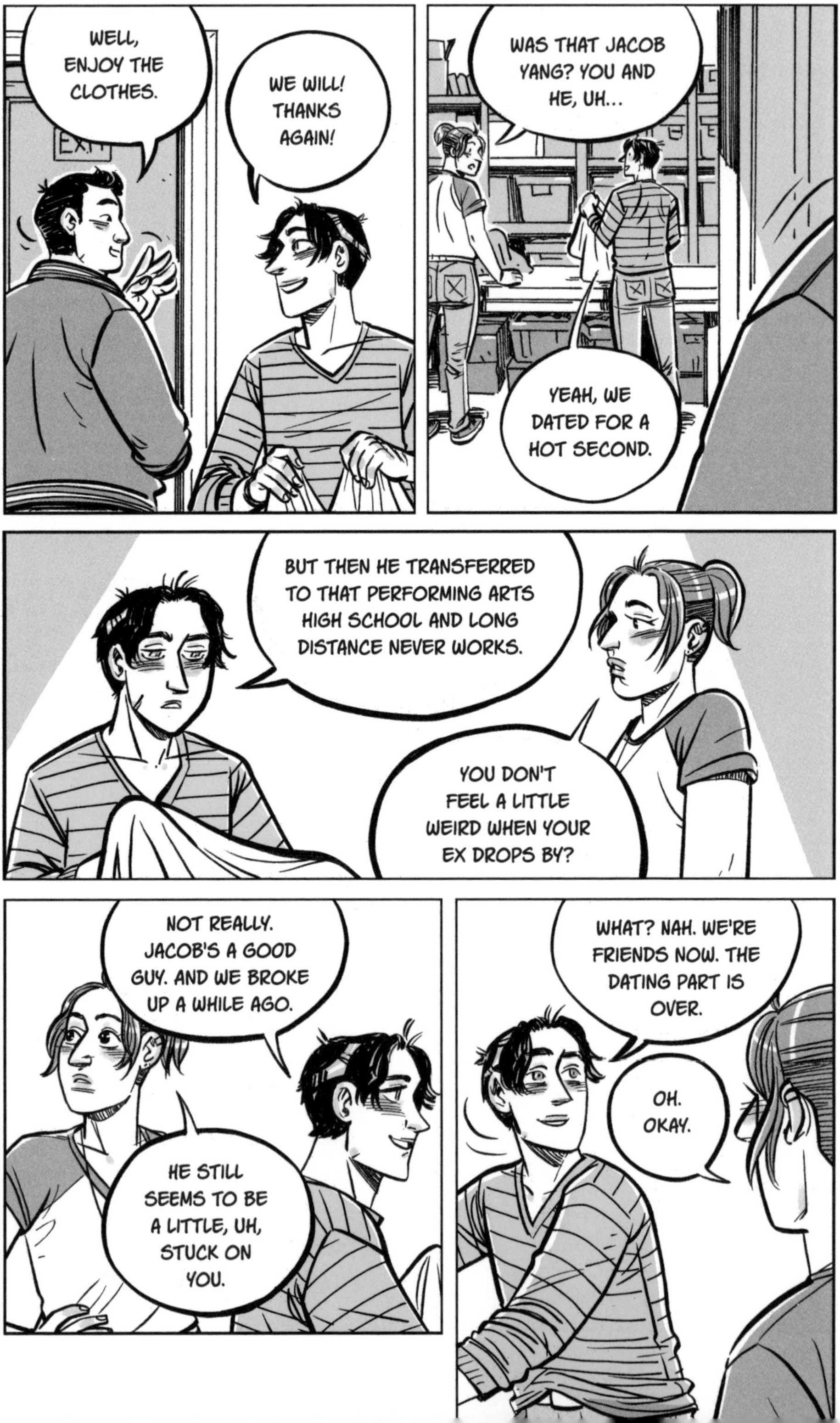
WELL, ENJOY THE CLOTHES.
WE WILL! THANKS AGAIN!
WAS THAT JACOB YANG? YOU AND HE, UH...
YEAH, WE DATED FOR A HOT SECOND.
BUT THEN HE TRANSFERRED TO THAT PERFORMING ARTS HIGH SCHOOL AND LONG DISTANCE NEVER WORKS.
YOU DON'T FEEL A LITTLE WEIRD WHEN YOUR EX DROPS BY?
NOT REALLY. JACOB'S A GOOD GUY. AND WE BROKE UP A WHILE AGO.
HE STILL SEEMS TO BE A LITTLE, UH, STUCK ON YOU.
WHAT? NAH. WE'RE FRIENDS NOW. THE DATING PART IS OVER.
OH. OKAY.

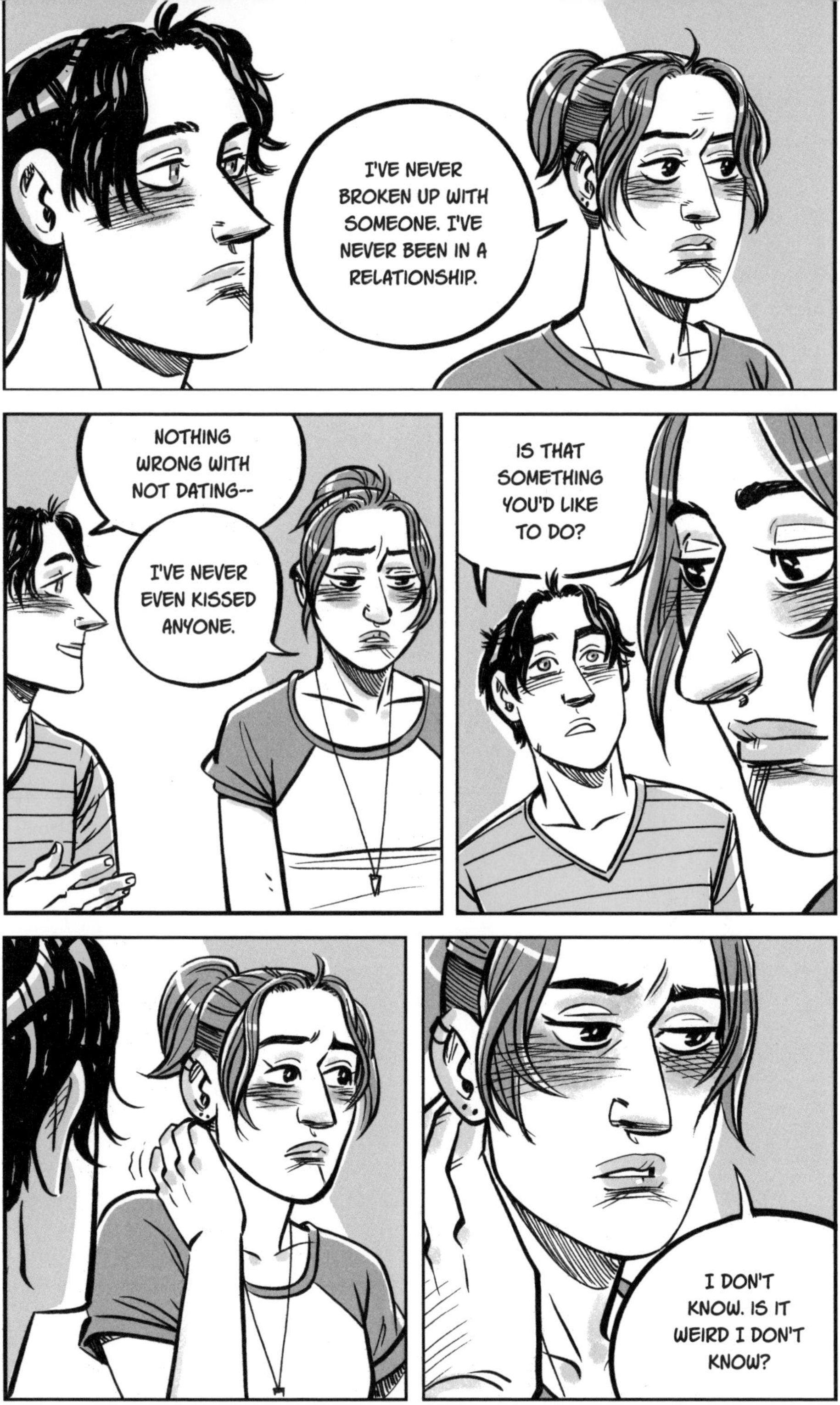
I'VE NEVER BROKEN UP WITH SOMEONE. I'VE NEVER BEEN IN A RELATIONSHIP.
NOTHING WRONG WITH NOT DATING--
I'VE NEVER EVEN KISSED ANYONE.
IS THAT SOMETHING YOU'D LIKE TO DO?
I DON'T KNOW. IS IT WEIRD I DON'T KNOW?

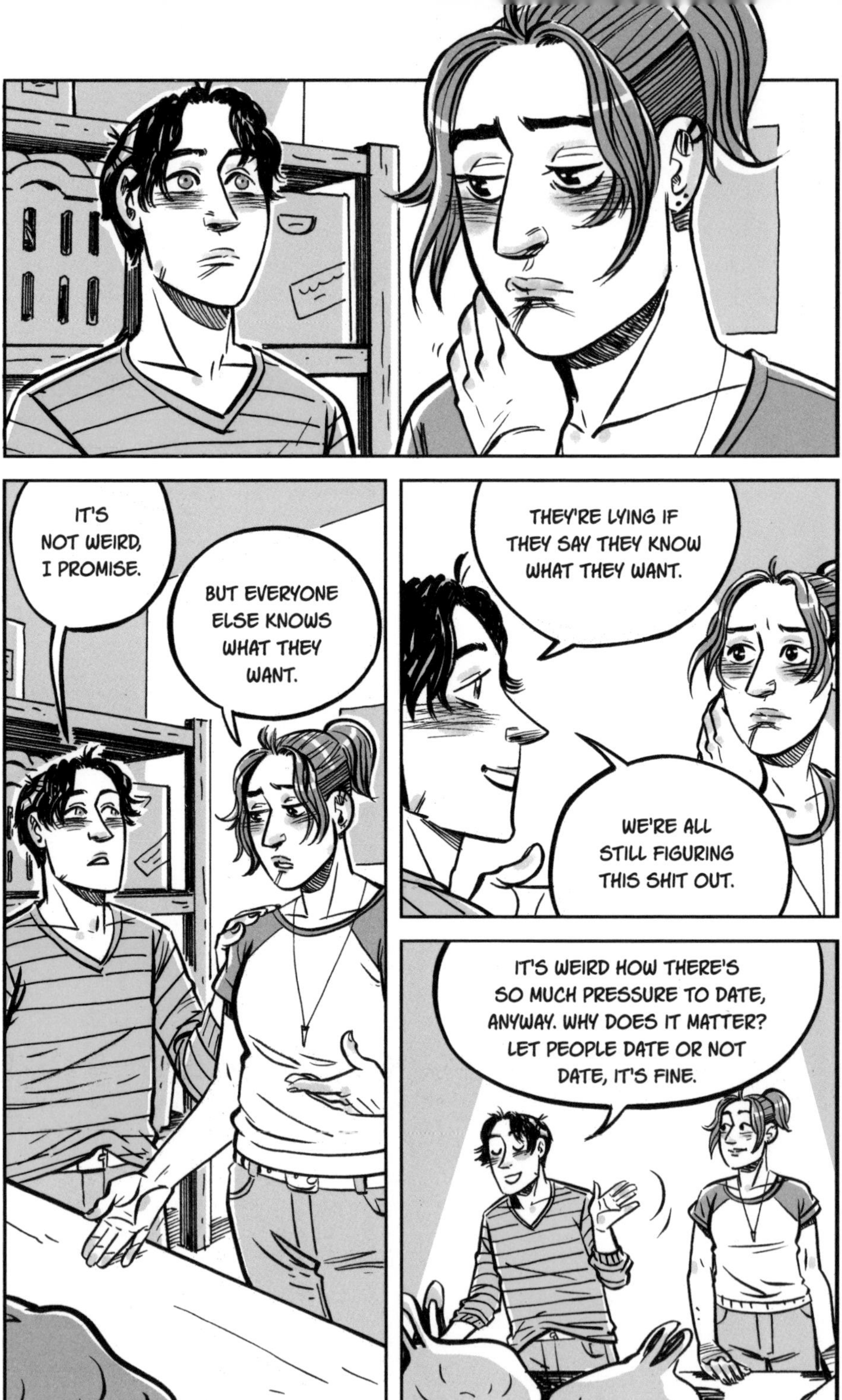
IT'S NOT WEIRD, I PROMISE.
BUT EVERYONE ELSE KNOWS WHAT THEY WANT.
THEY'RE LYING IF THEY SAY THEY KNOW WHAT THEY WANT.
WE'RE ALL STILL FIGURING THIS SHIT OUT.
IT'S WEIRD HOW THERE'S SO MUCH PRESSURE TO DATE, ANYWAY. WHY DOES IT MATTER? LET PEOPLE DATE OR NOT DATE, IT'S FINE.

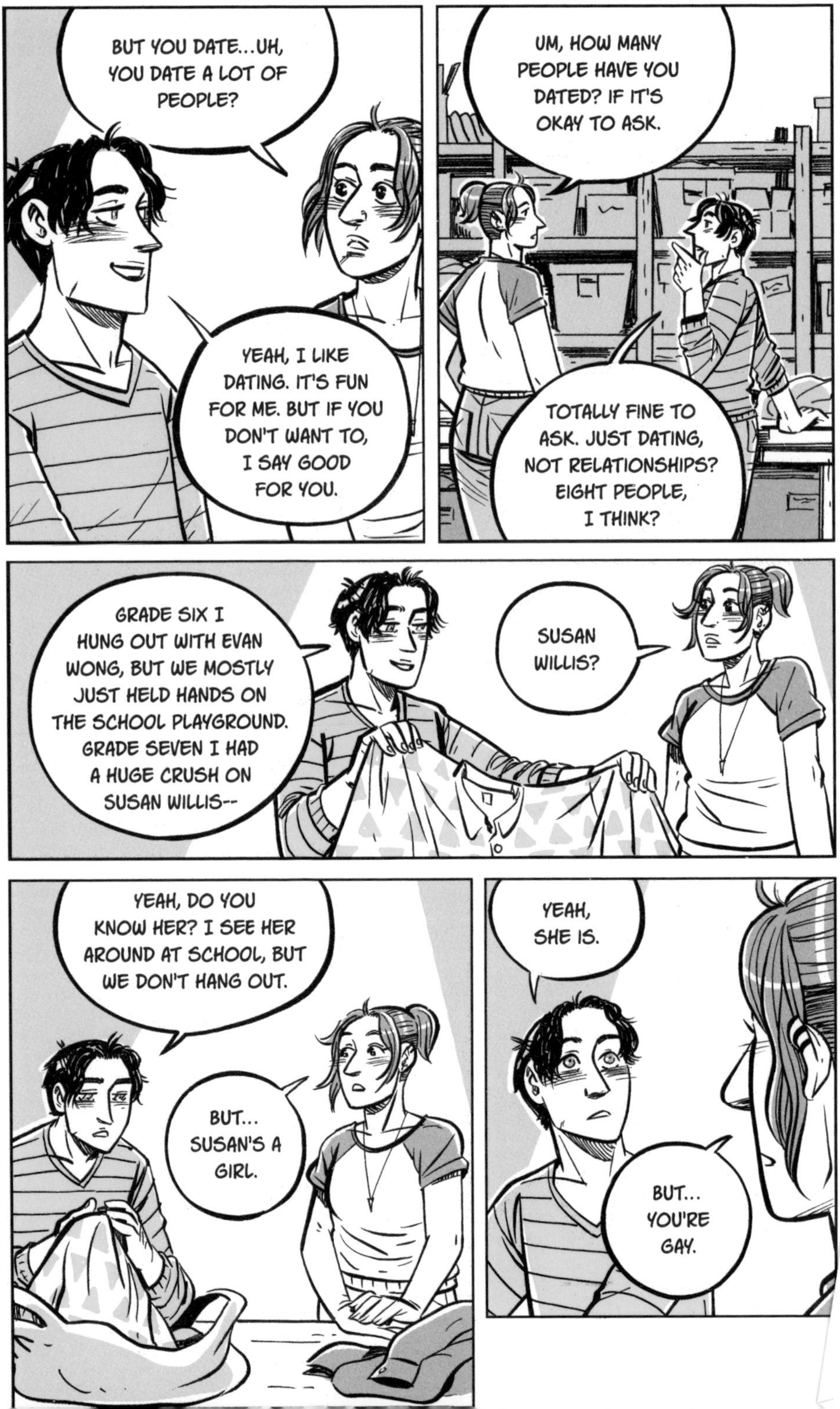
BUT YOU DATE...UH, YOU DATE A LOT OF PEOPLE?
YEAH, I LIKE DATING. IT'S FUN FOR ME. BUT IF YOU DON'T WANT TO, I SAY GOOD FOR YOU.
UM, HOW MANY PEOPLE HAVE YOU DATED? IF IT'S OKAY TO ASK.
TOTALLY FINE TO ASK. JUST DATING, NOT RELATIONSHIPS? EIGHT PEOPLE, I THINK?
GRADE SIX I HUNG OUT WITH EVAN WONG, BUT WE MOSTLY JUST HELD HANDS ON THE SCHOOL PLAYGROUND. GRADE SEVEN I HAD A HUGE CRUSH ON SUSAN WILLIS--
SUSAN WILLIS?
YEAH, DO YOU KNOW HER? I SEE HER AROUND AT SCHOOL, BUT WE DON'T HANG OUT.
BUT... SUSAN'S A GIRL.
YEAH, SHE IS.
BUT... YOU'RE GAY.

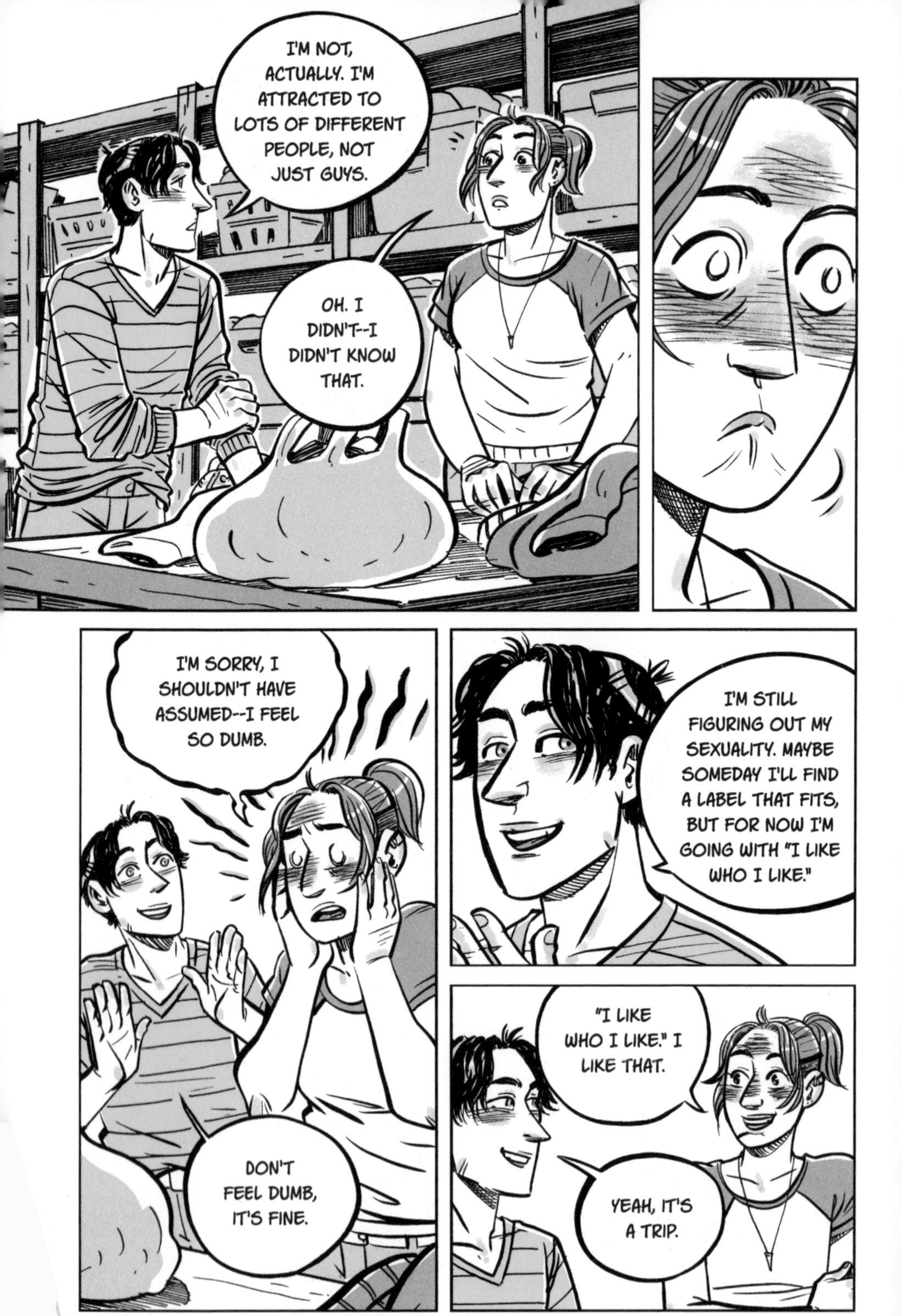
I'M NOT, ACTUALLY. I'M ATTRACTED TO LOTS OF DIFFERENT PEOPLE, NOT JUST GUYS.
OH. I DIDN'T--I DIDN'T KNOW THAT.
I'M SORRY, I SHOULDN'T HAVE ASSUMED--I FEEL SO DUMB.
DON'T FEEL DUMB, IT'S FINE.
I'M STILL FIGURING OUT MY SEXUALITY. MAYBE SOMEDAY I'LL FIND A LABEL THAT FITS, BUT FOR NOW I'M GOING WITH "I LIKE WHO I LIKE."
"I LIKE WHO I LIKE." I LIKE THAT.
YEAH, IT'S A TRIP.

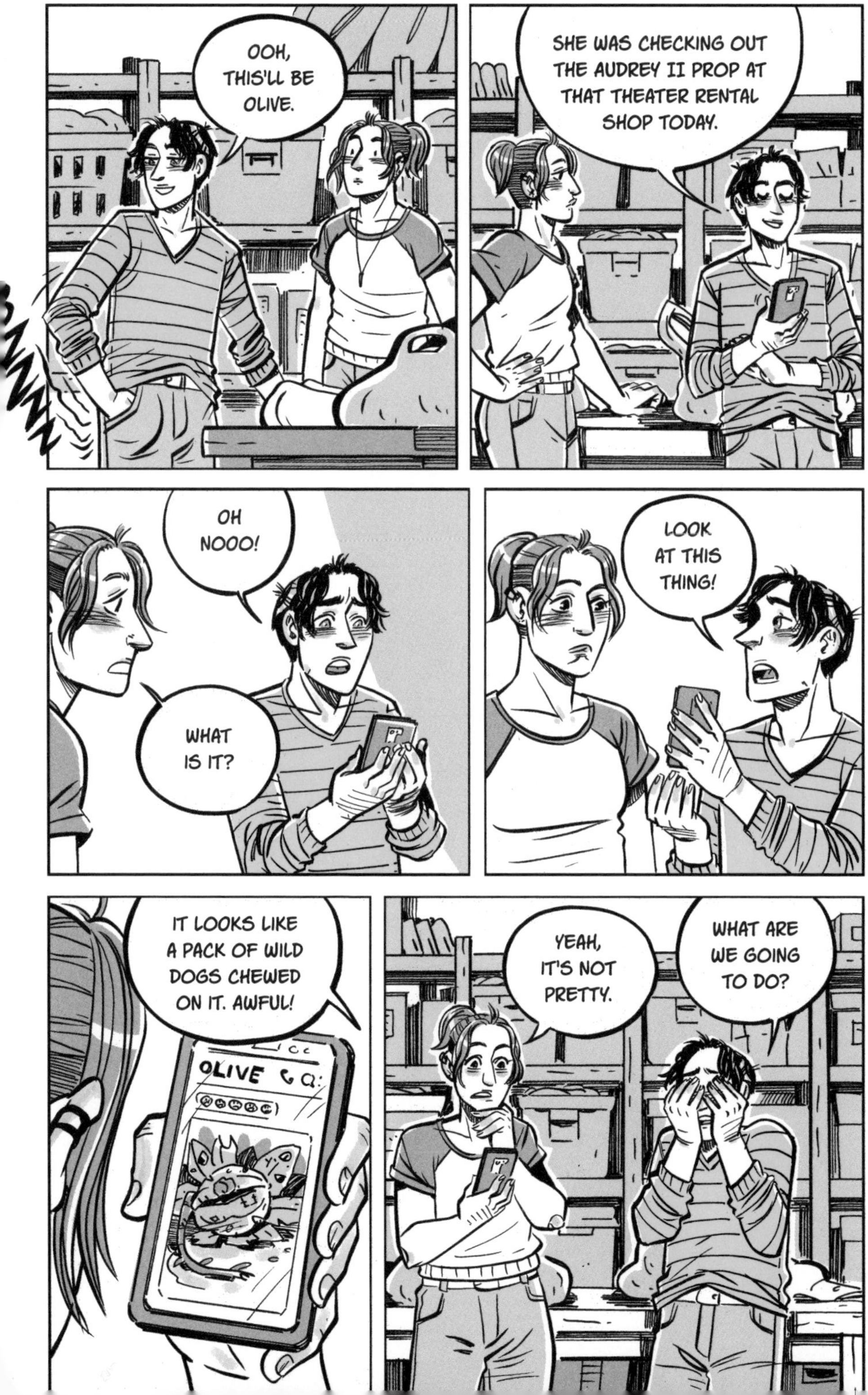
OOH, THIS'LL BE OLIVE.
SHE WAS CHECKING OUT THE AUDREY II PROP AT THAT THEATER RENTAL SHOP TODAY.
OH NOOO!
WHAT IS IT?
LOOK AT THIS THING!
IT LOOKS LIKE A PACK OF WILD DOGS CHEWED ON IT. AWFUL!
OLIVE
YEAH, IT'S NOT PRETTY.
WHAT ARE WE GOING TO DO?

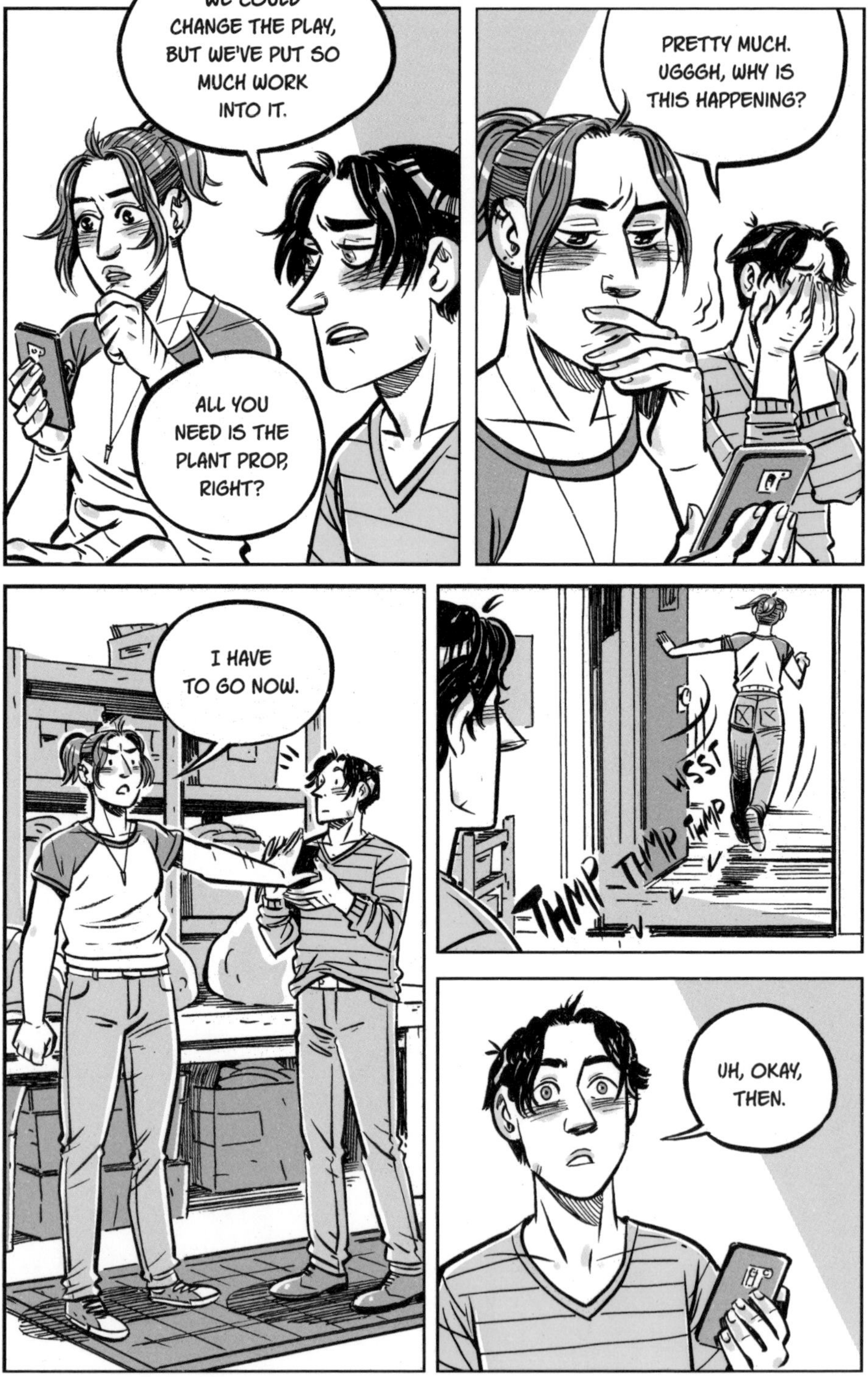
WE COULD CHANGE THE PLAY, BUT WE'VE PUT SO MUCH WORK INTO IT.
ALL YOU NEED IS THE PLANT PROP, RIGHT?
PRETTY MUCH. UGGGH, WHY IS THIS HAPPENING?
I HAVE TO GO NOW.
WSST
THMP THMP THMP
UH, OKAY, THEN.

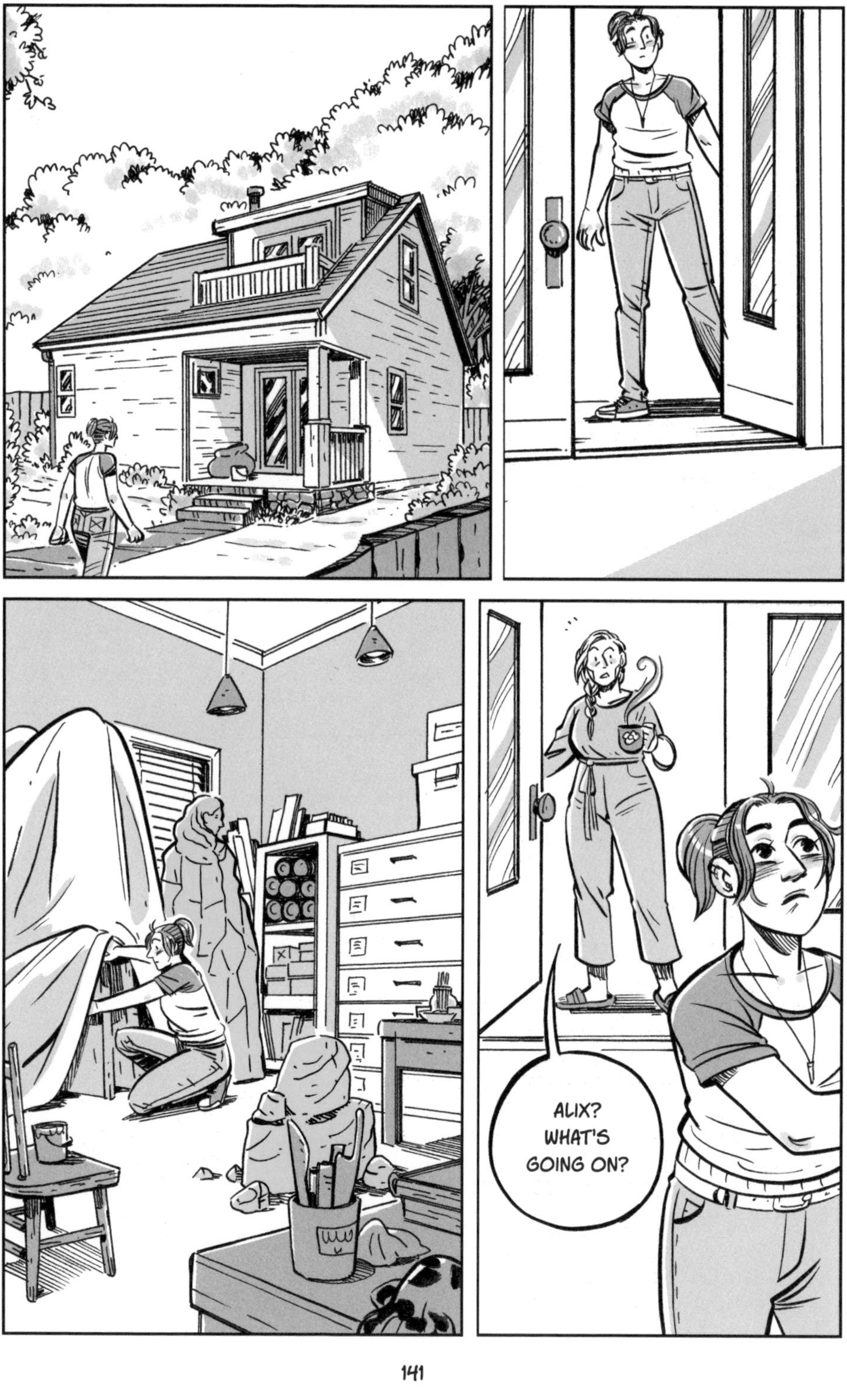
ALIX? WHAT'S GOING ON?

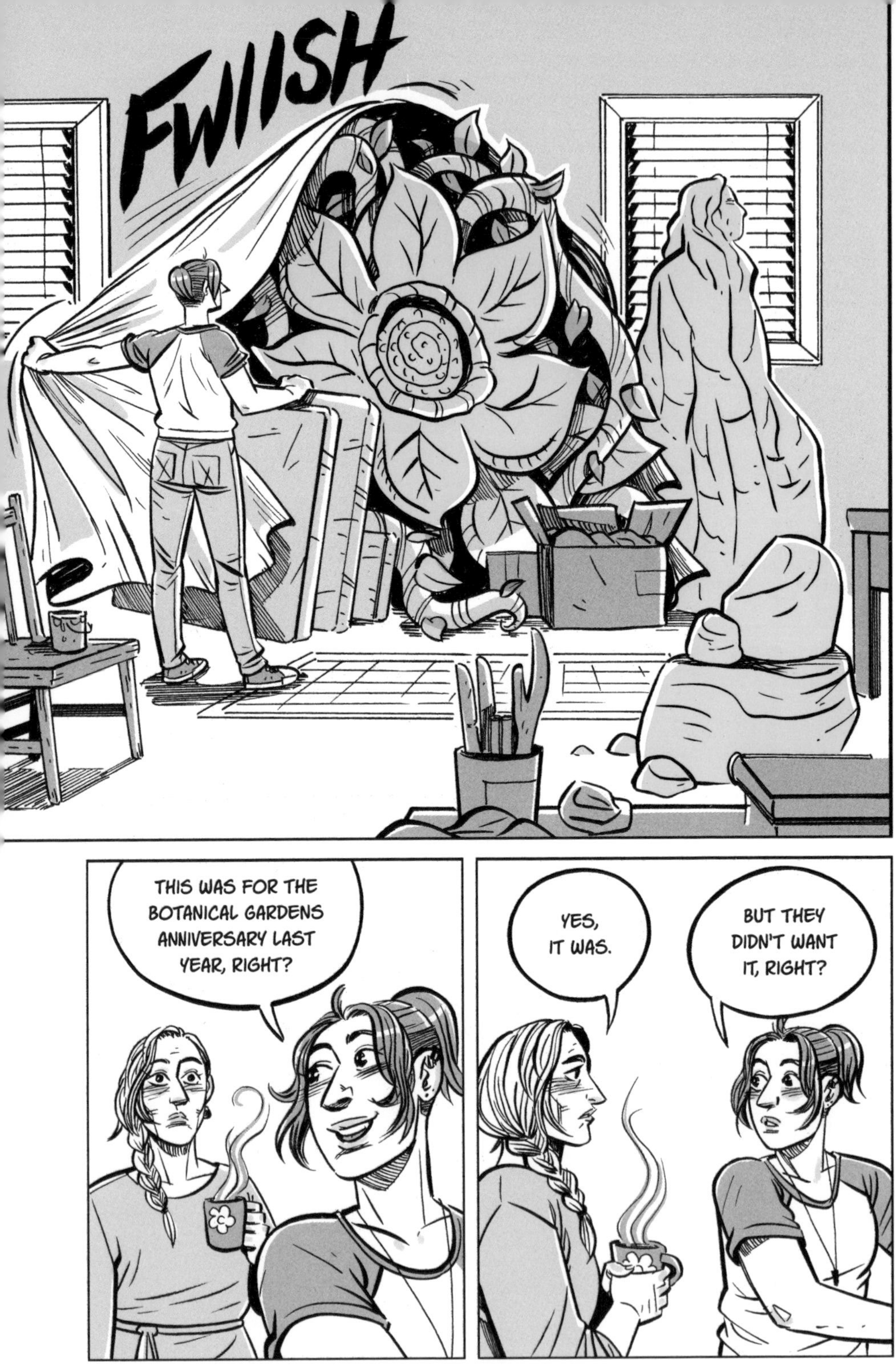
FWIISH
THIS WAS FOR THE BOTANICAL GARDENS ANNIVERSARY LAST YEAR, RIGHT?
YES, IT WAS.
BUT THEY DIDN'T WANT IT, RIGHT?

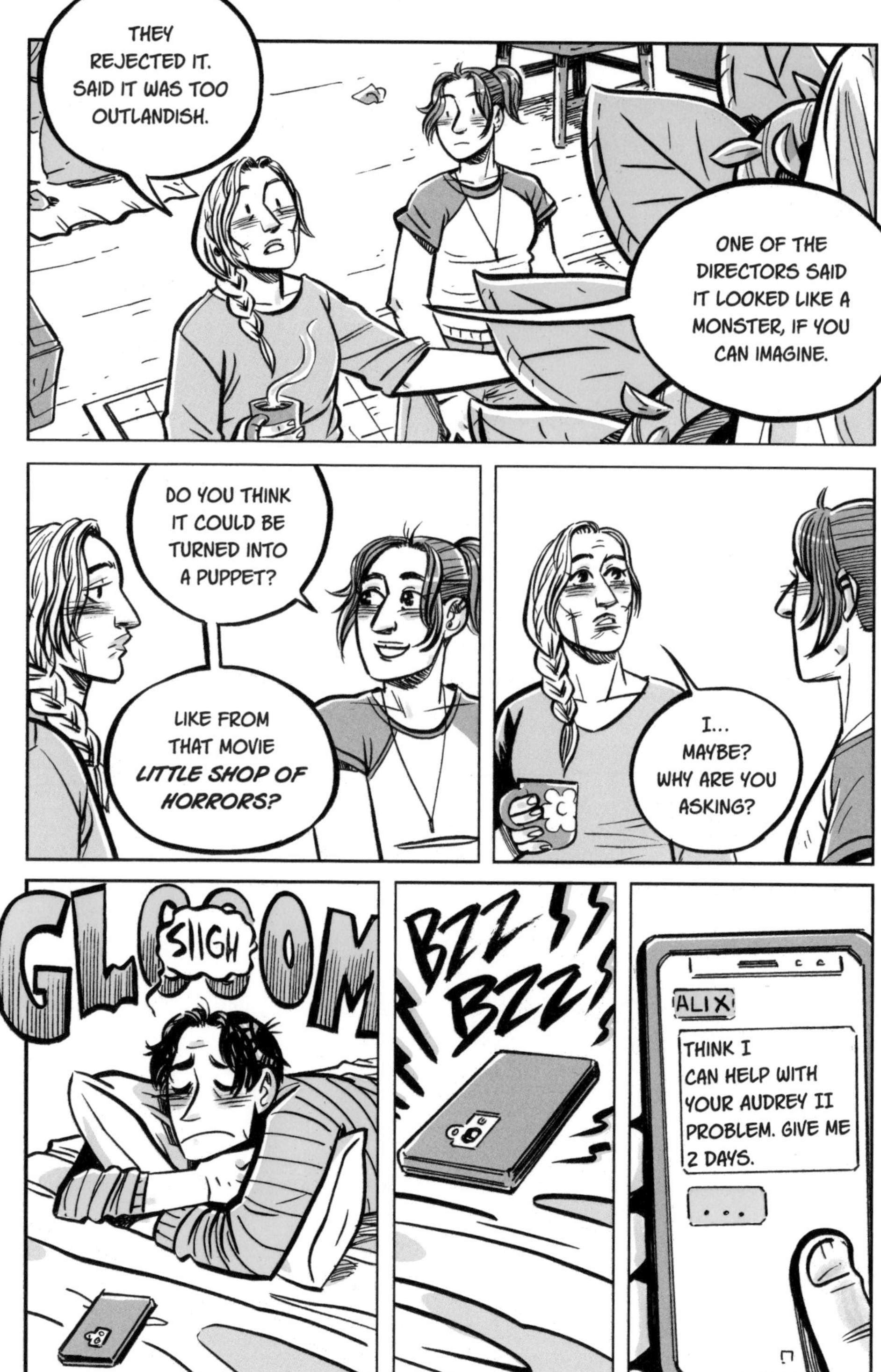
THEY REJECTED IT. SAID IT WAS TOO OUTLANDISH.
ONE OF THE DIRECTORS SAID IT LOOKED LIKE A MONSTER, IF YOU CAN IMAGINE.
DO YOU THINK IT COULD BE TURNED INTO A PUPPET?
LIKE FROM THAT MOVIE *LITTLE SHOP OF HORRORS?*
I... MAYBE? WHY ARE YOU ASKING?
GLOOOM
SIIGH
BZZ BZZ
ALIX
THINK I CAN HELP WITH YOUR AUDREY II PROBLEM. GIVE ME 2 DAYS.
...

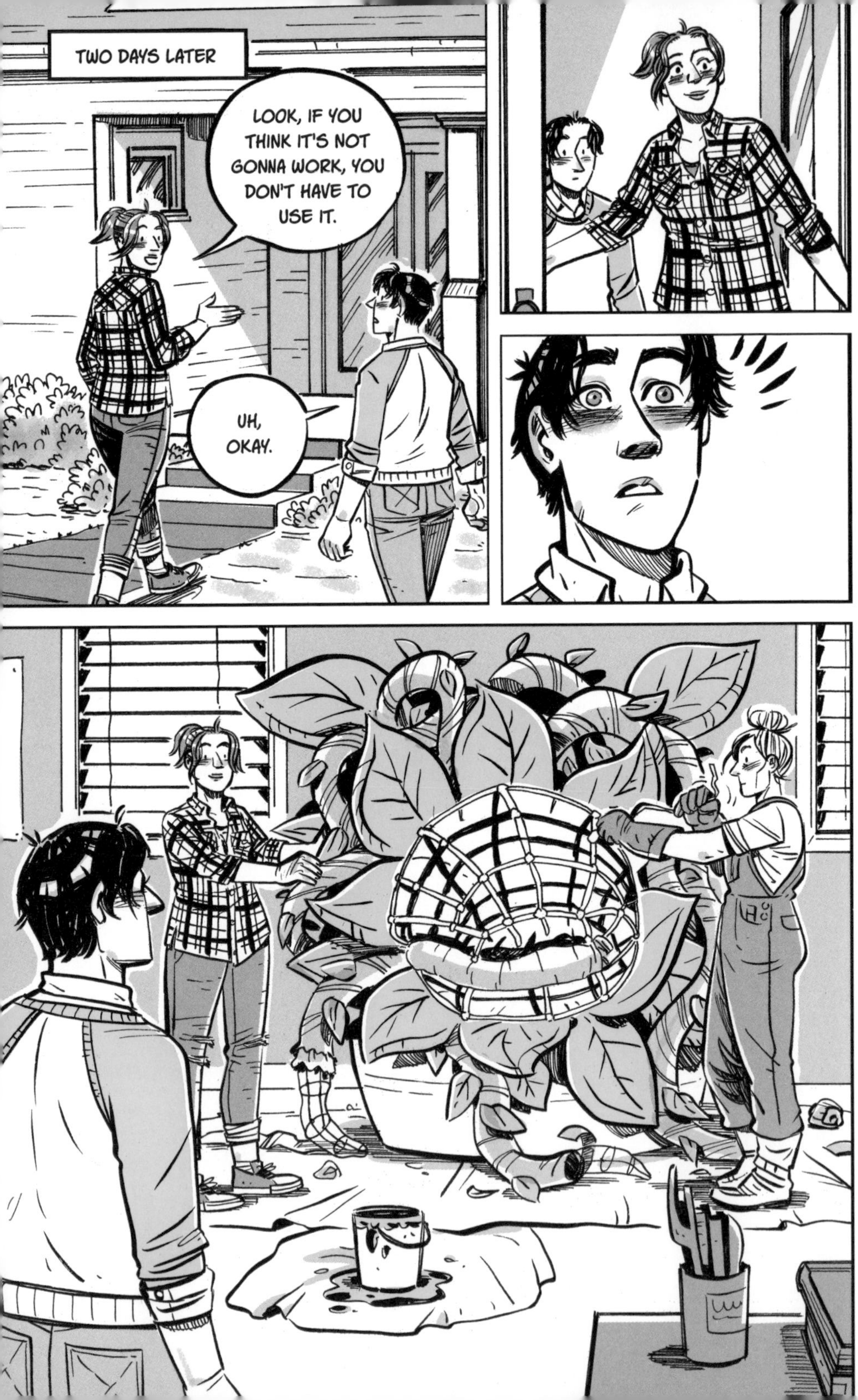
TWO DAYS LATER
LOOK, IF YOU THINK IT'S NOT GONNA WORK, YOU DON'T HAVE TO USE IT.
UH, OKAY.

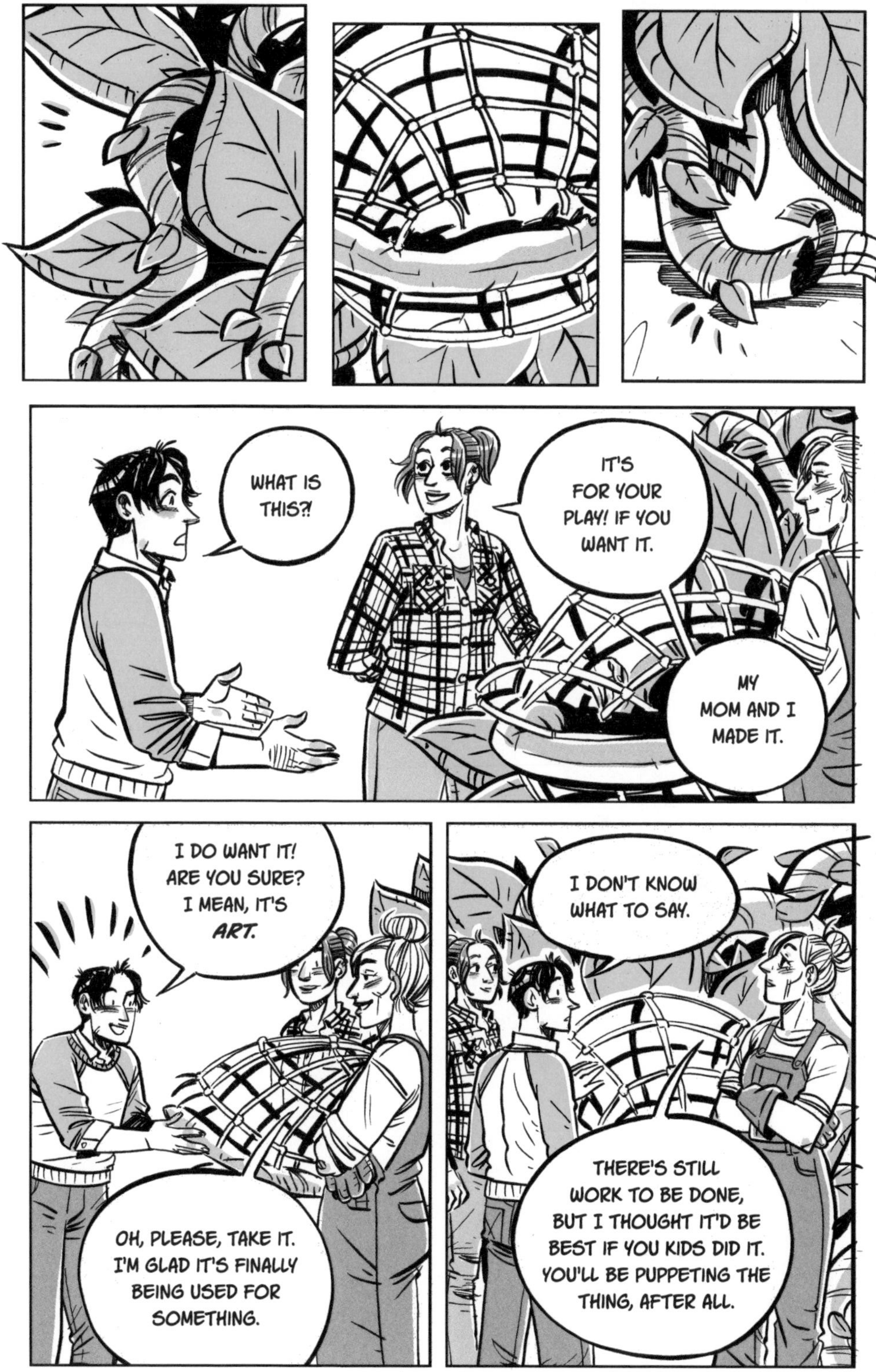
WHAT IS THIS?!
IT'S FOR YOUR PLAY! IF YOU WANT IT.
MY MOM AND I MADE IT.
I DO WANT IT! ARE YOU SURE? I MEAN, IT'S *ART.*
OH, PLEASE, TAKE IT. I'M GLAD IT'S FINALLY BEING USED FOR SOMETHING.
I DON'T KNOW WHAT TO SAY.
THERE'S STILL WORK TO BE DONE, BUT I THOUGHT IT'D BE BEST IF YOU KIDS DID IT. YOU'LL BE PUPPETING THE THING, AFTER ALL.

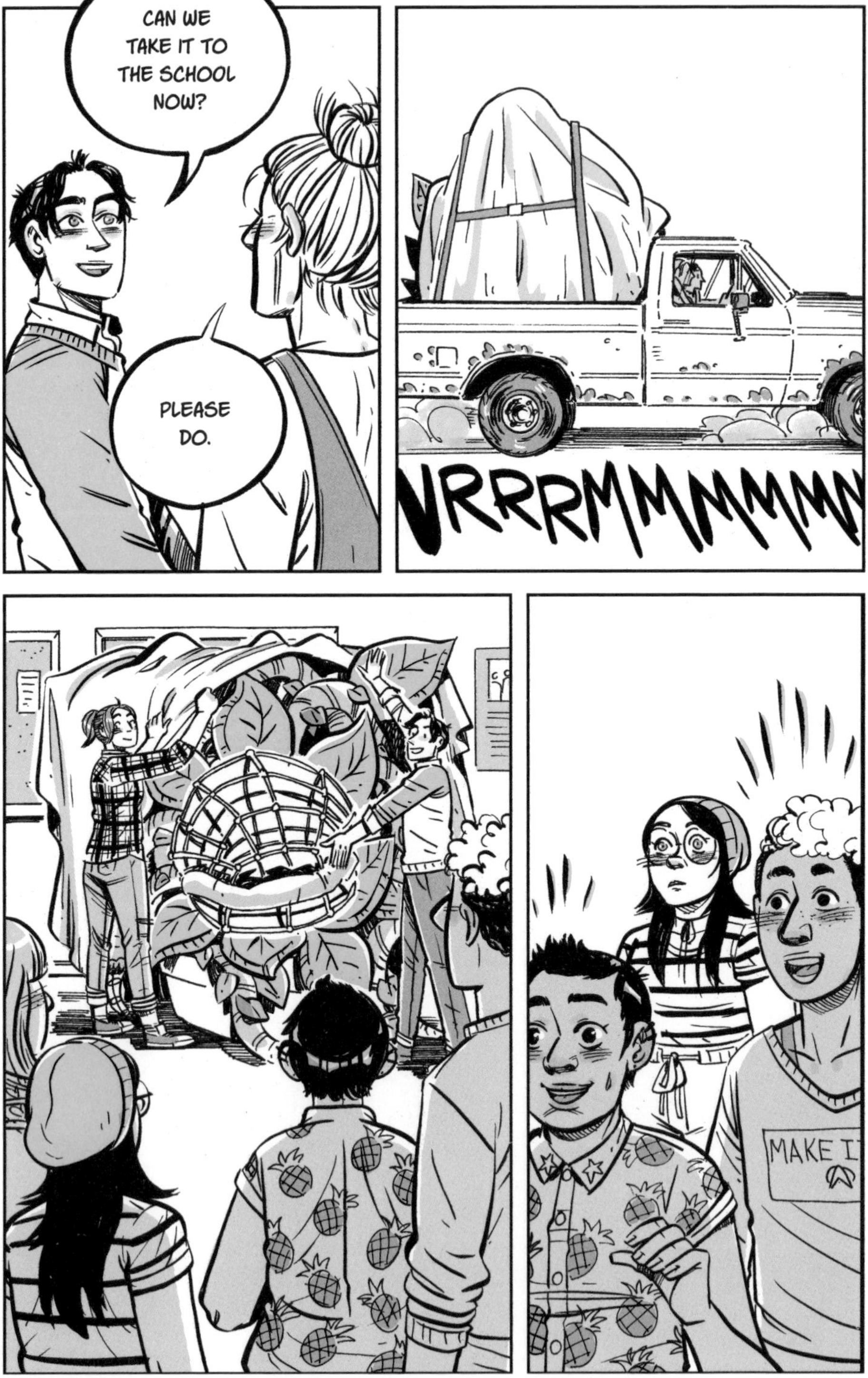

CAN WE TAKE IT TO THE SCHOOL NOW?
PLEASE DO.
VRRRMMMMM

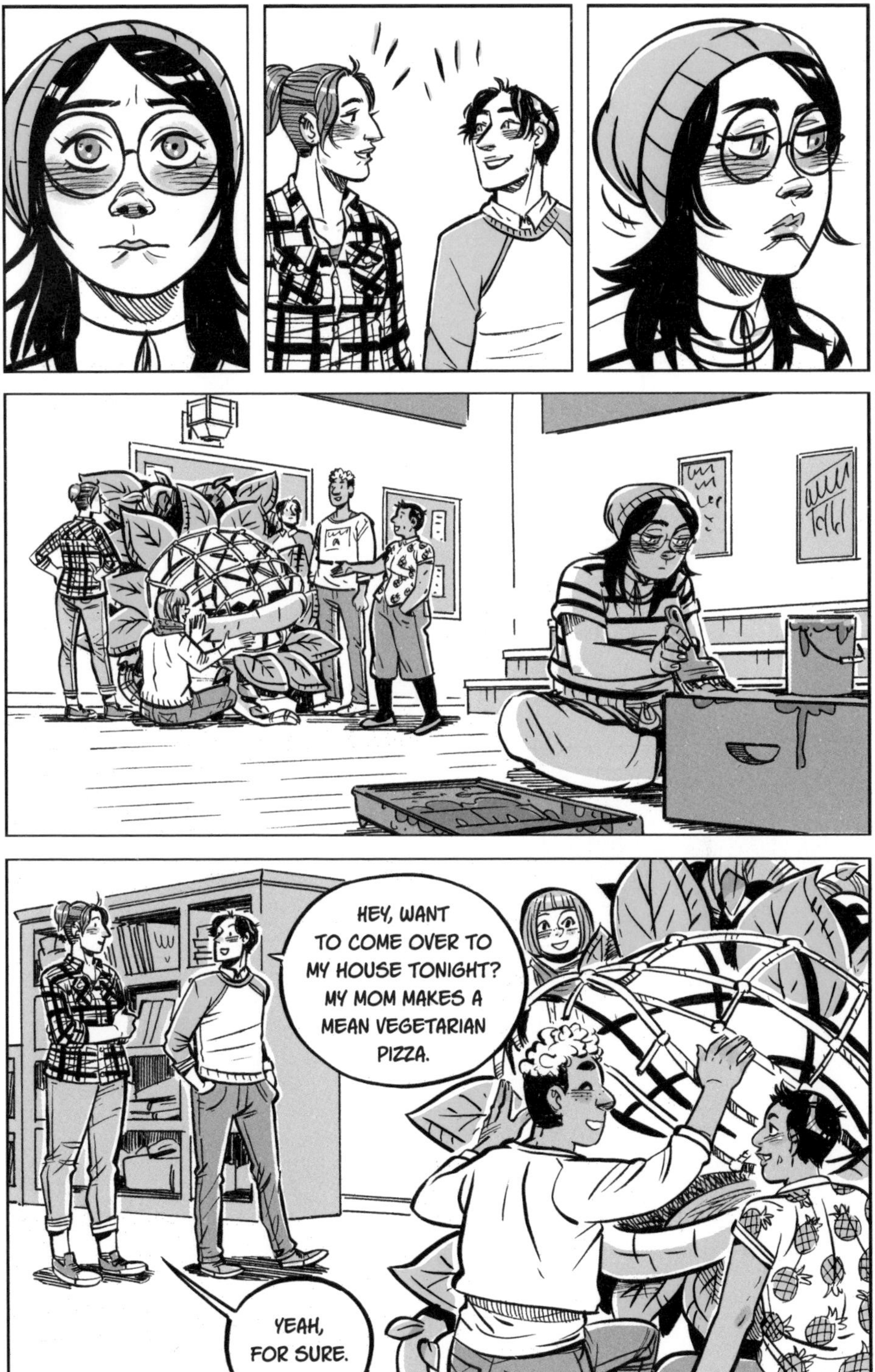
HEY, WANT TO COME OVER TO MY HOUSE TONIGHT? MY MOM MAKES A MEAN VEGETARIAN PIZZA.
YEAH, FOR SURE.

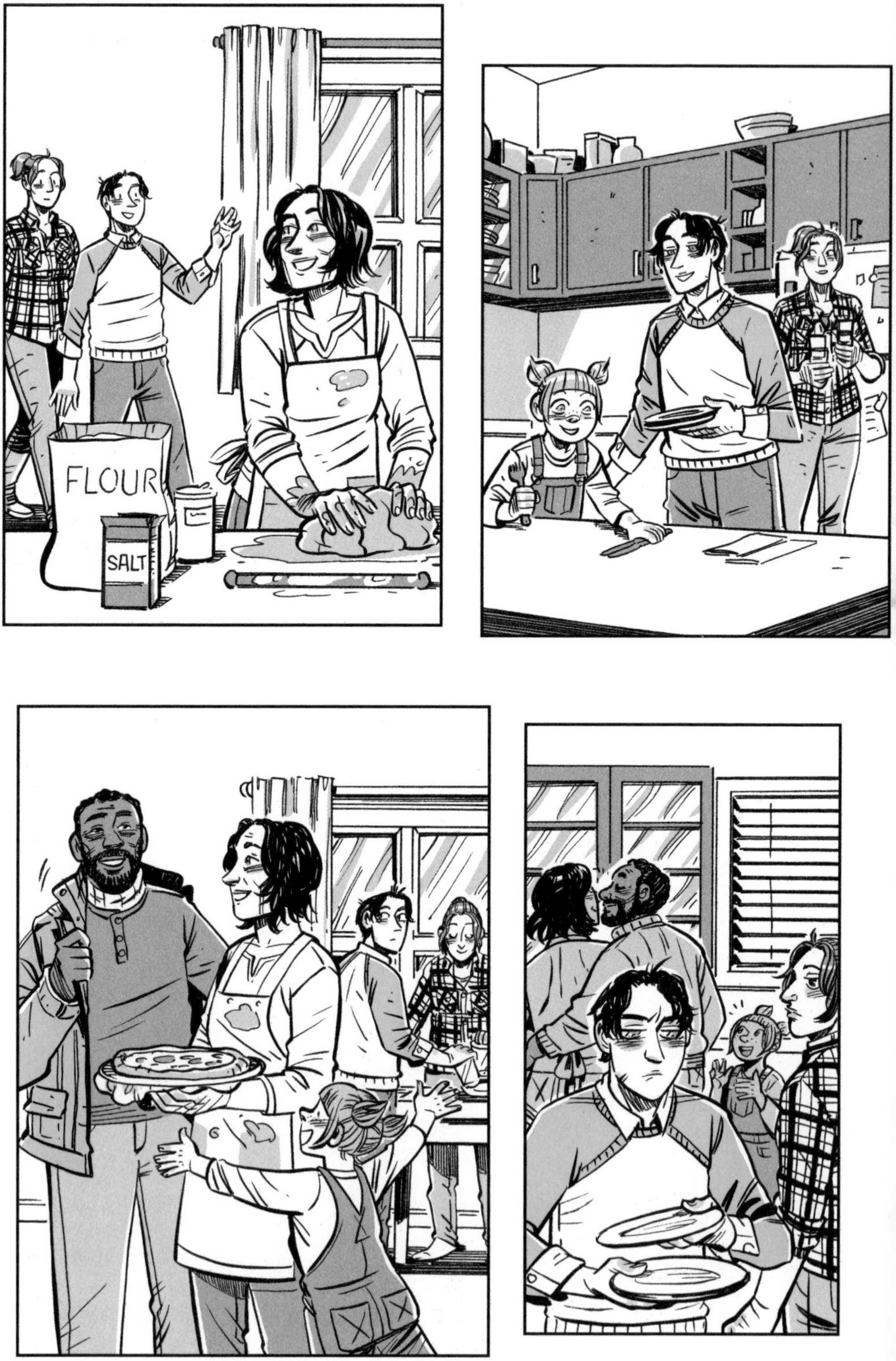
FLOUR
SALT

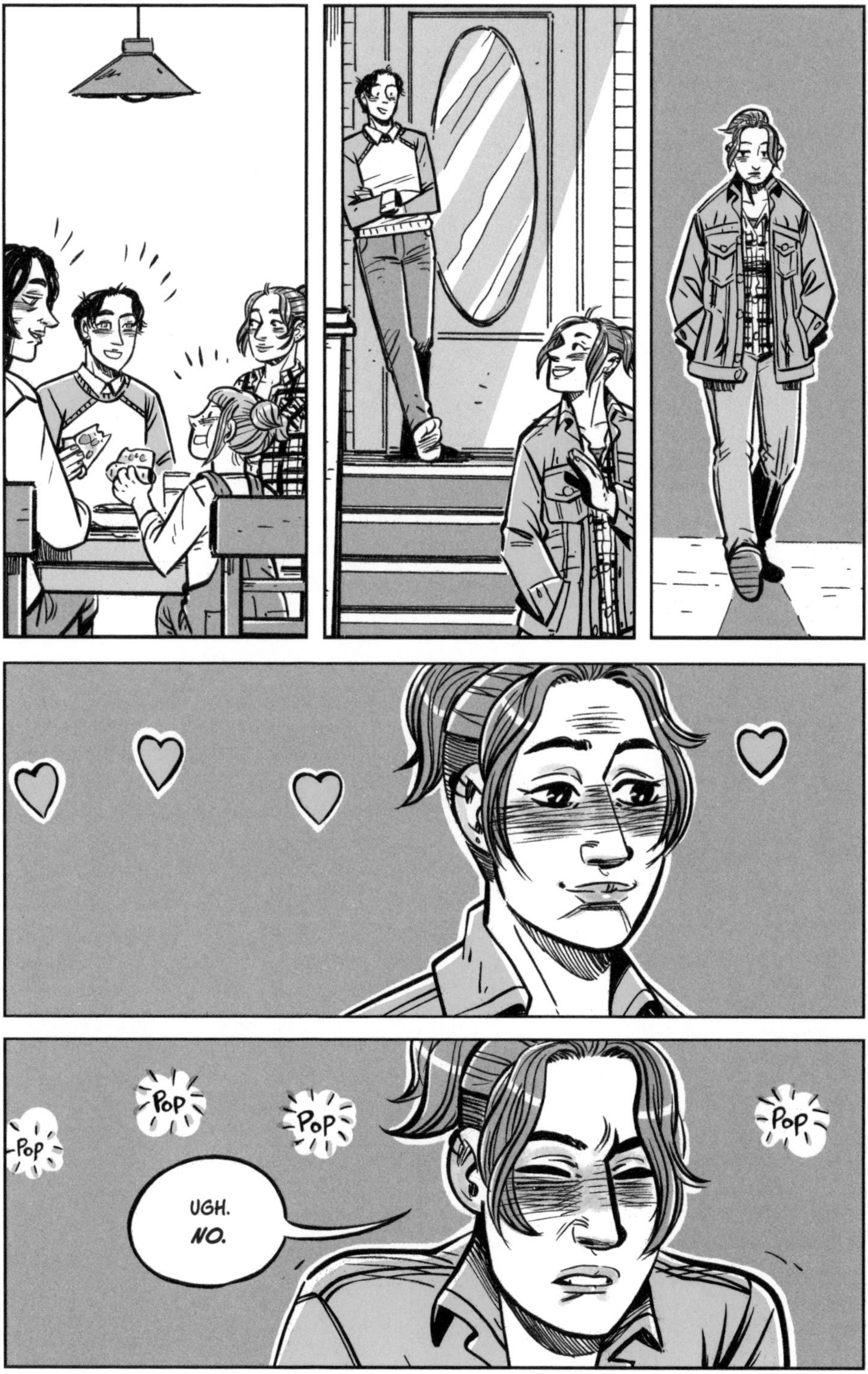
POP
POP
POP
POP
UGH.
NO.

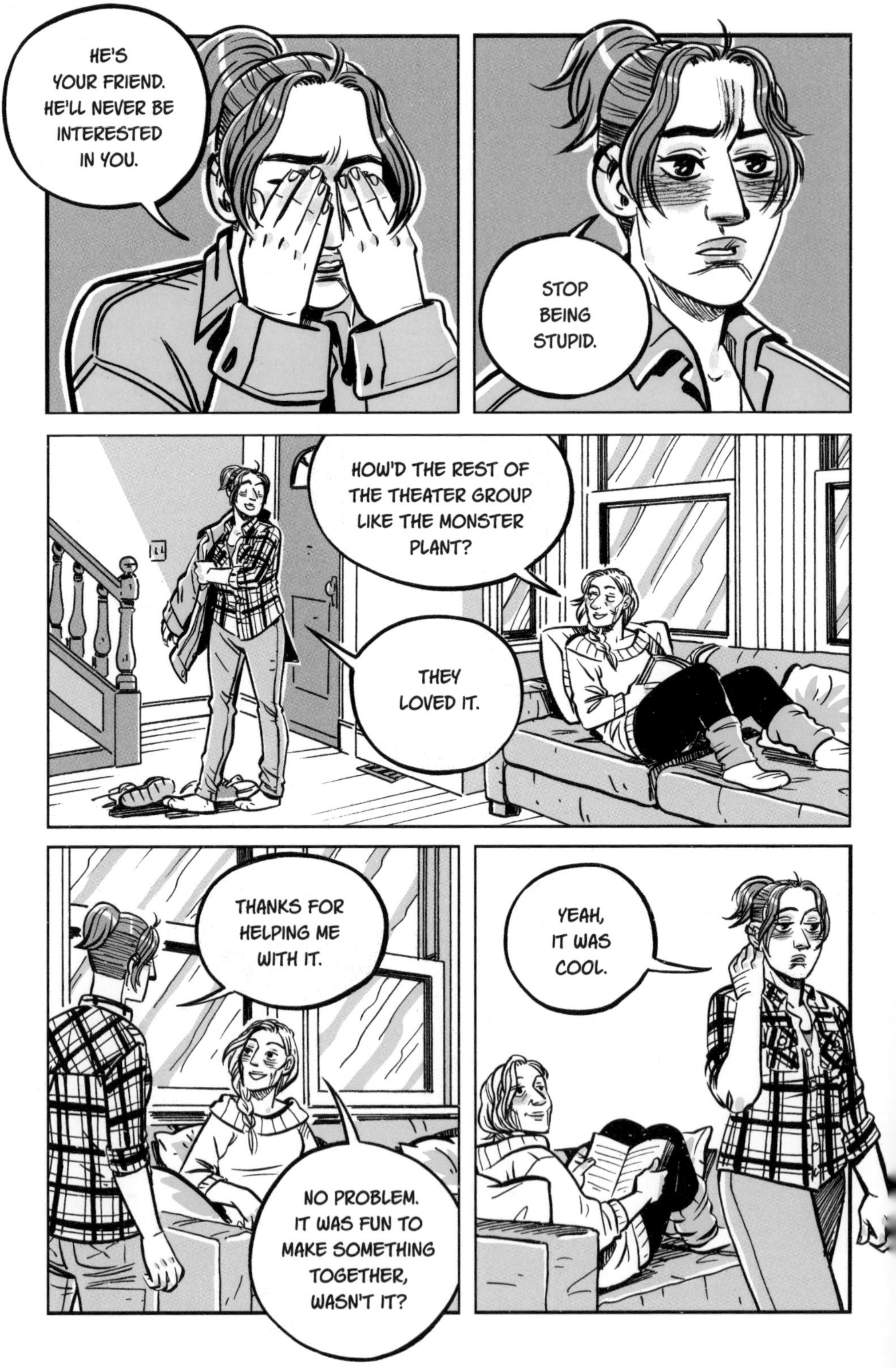
HE'S YOUR FRIEND. HE'LL NEVER BE INTERESTED IN YOU.
STOP BEING STUPID.
HOW'D THE REST OF THE THEATER GROUP LIKE THE MONSTER PLANT?
THEY LOVED IT.
THANKS FOR HELPING ME WITH IT.
NO PROBLEM. IT WAS FUN TO MAKE SOMETHING TOGETHER, WASN'T IT?
YEAH, IT WAS COOL.

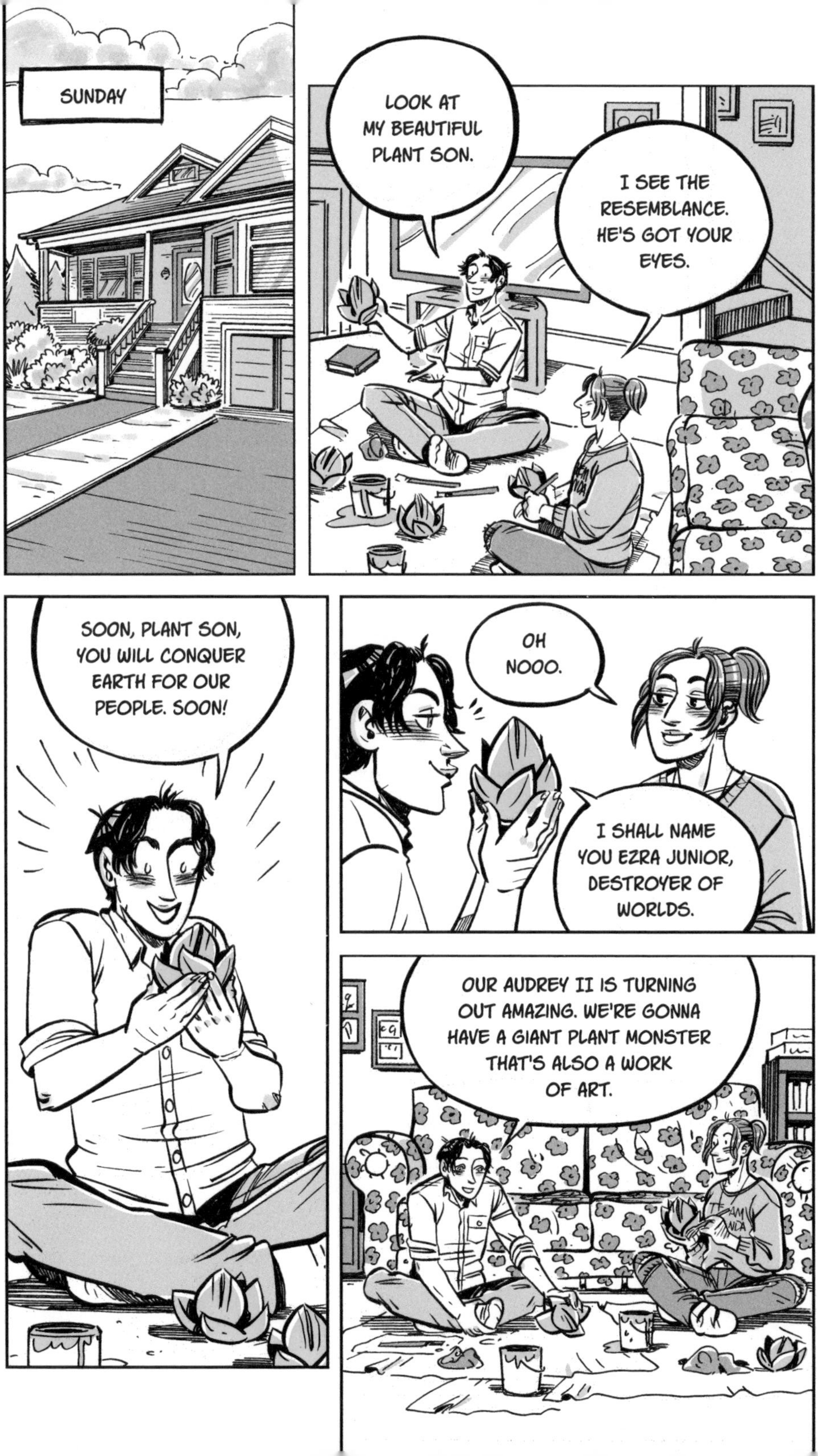
SUNDAY
LOOK AT MY BEAUTIFUL PLANT SON.
I SEE THE RESEMBLANCE. HE'S GOT YOUR EYES.
SOON, PLANT SON, YOU WILL CONQUER EARTH FOR OUR PEOPLE. SOON!
OH NOOO.
I SHALL NAME YOU EZRA JUNIOR, DESTROYER OF WORLDS.
OUR AUDREY II IS TURNING OUT AMAZING. WE'RE GONNA HAVE A GIANT PLANT MONSTER THAT'S ALSO A WORK OF ART.

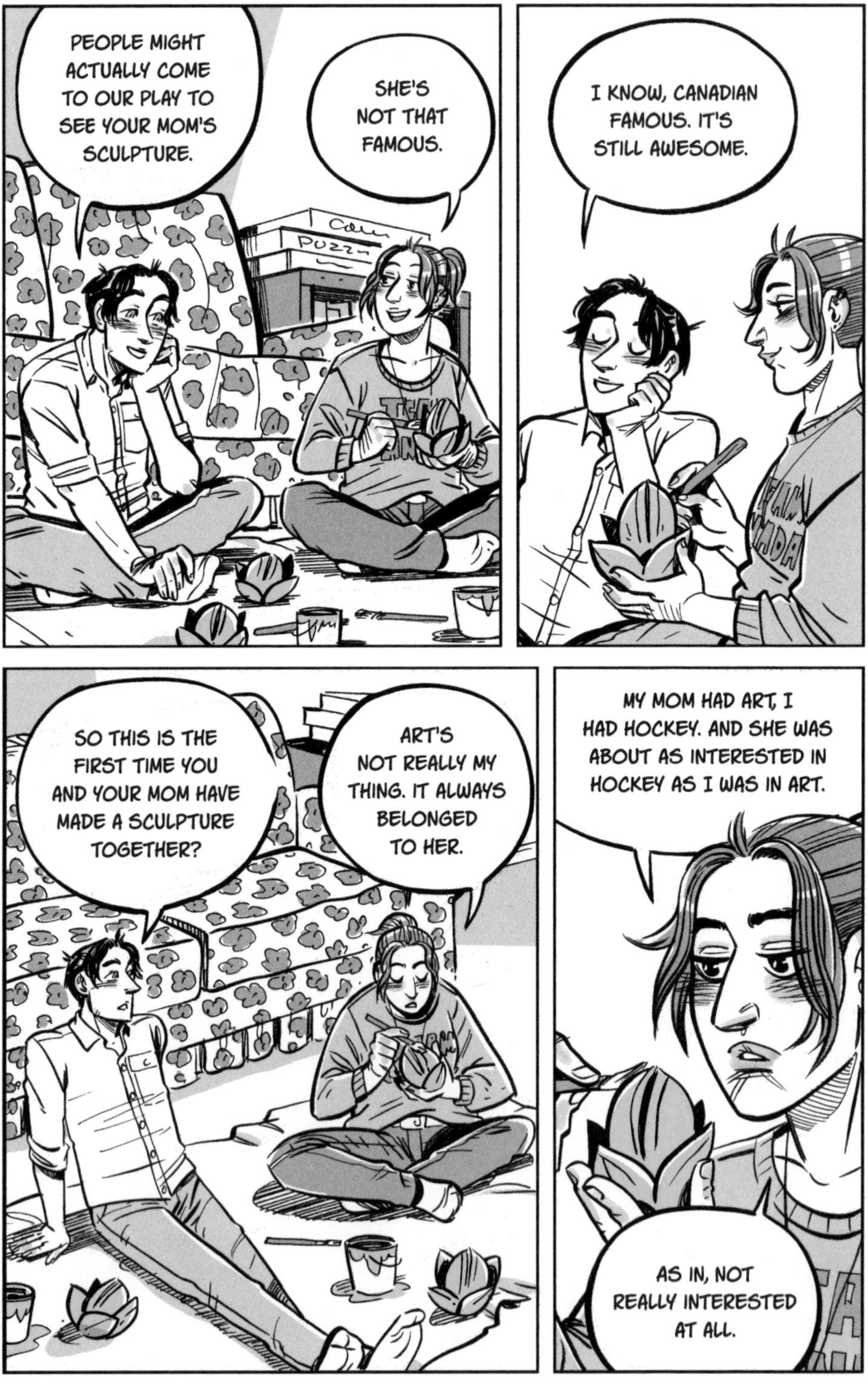
PEOPLE MIGHT ACTUALLY COME TO OUR PLAY TO SEE YOUR MOM'S SCULPTURE.
SHE'S NOT THAT FAMOUS.
I KNOW, CANADIAN FAMOUS. IT'S STILL AWESOME.
SO THIS IS THE FIRST TIME YOU AND YOUR MOM HAVE MADE A SCULPTURE TOGETHER?
ART'S NOT REALLY MY THING. IT ALWAYS BELONGED TO HER.
MY MOM HAD ART, I HAD HOCKEY. AND SHE WAS ABOUT AS INTERESTED IN HOCKEY AS I WAS IN ART.
AS IN, NOT REALLY INTERESTED AT ALL.

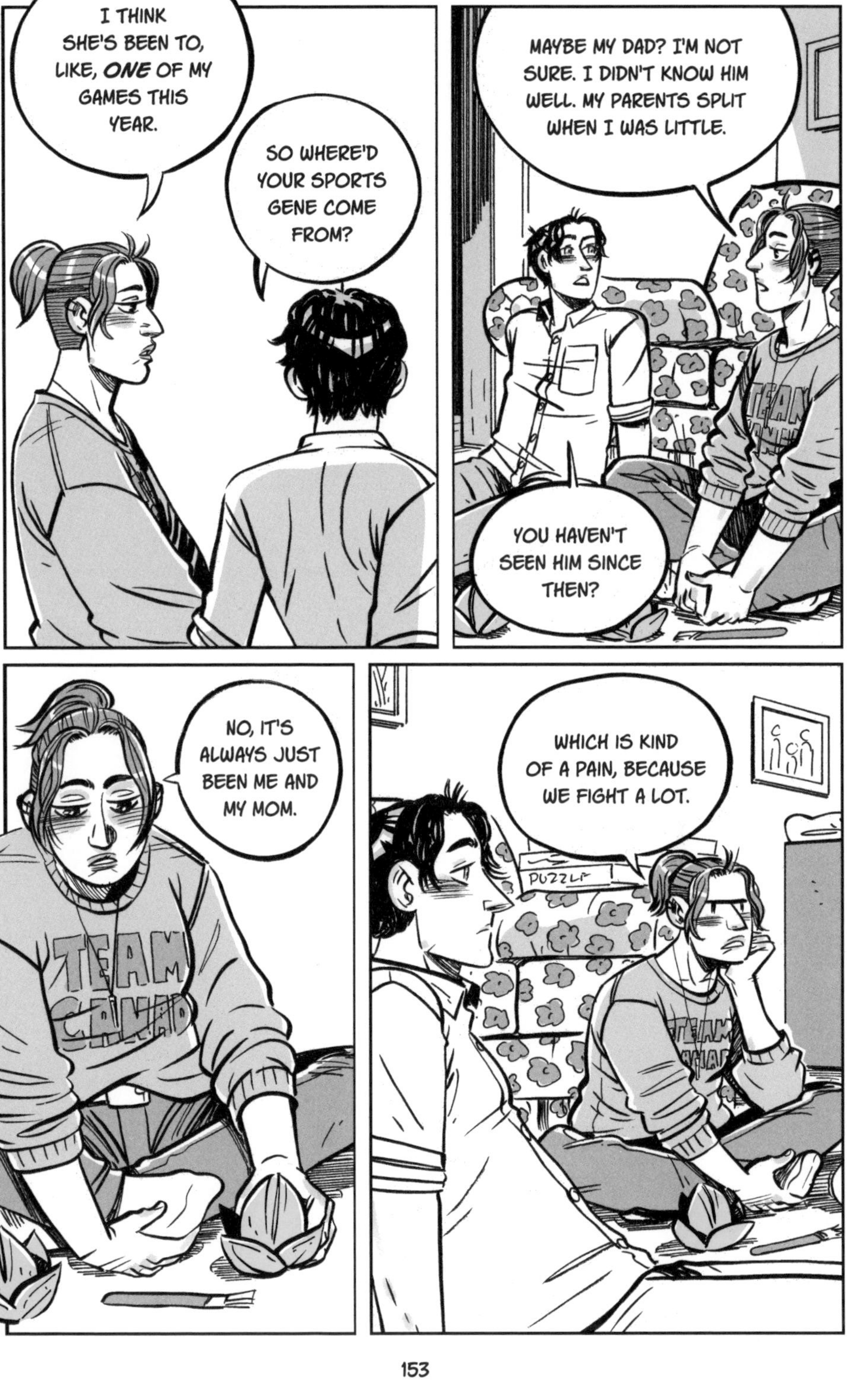
I THINK SHE'S BEEN TO, LIKE, *ONE* OF MY GAMES THIS YEAR.
SO WHERE'D YOUR SPORTS GENE COME FROM?
MAYBE MY DAD? I'M NOT SURE. I DIDN'T KNOW HIM WELL. MY PARENTS SPLIT WHEN I WAS LITTLE.
YOU HAVEN'T SEEN HIM SINCE THEN?
NO, IT'S ALWAYS JUST BEEN ME AND MY MOM.
WHICH IS KIND OF A PAIN, BECAUSE WE FIGHT A LOT.
PUZZLE

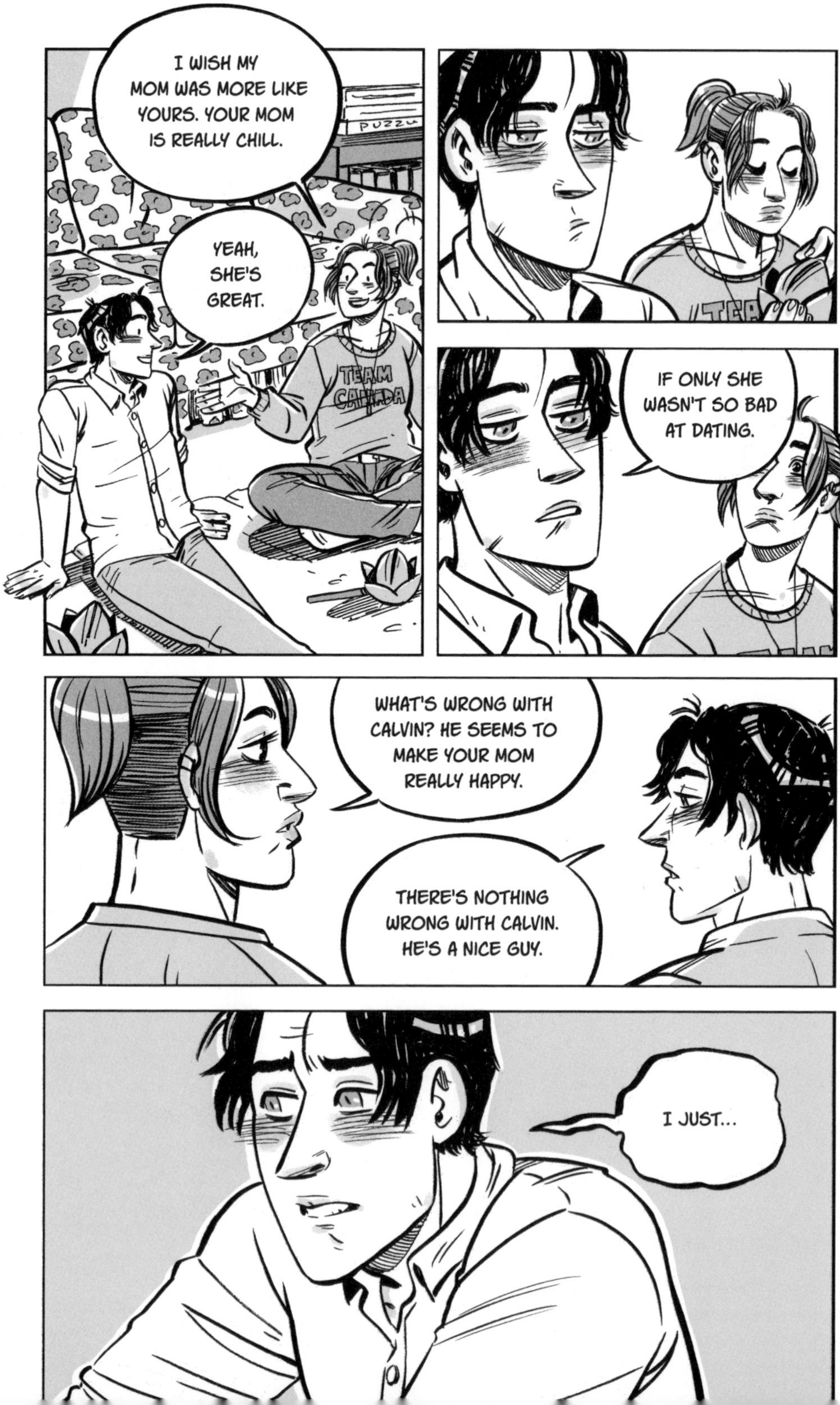
I WISH MY MOM WAS MORE LIKE YOURS. YOUR MOM IS REALLY CHILL.
YEAH, SHE'S GREAT.
TEAM CANADA
IF ONLY SHE WASN'T SO BAD AT DATING.
WHAT'S WRONG WITH CALVIN? HE SEEMS TO MAKE YOUR MOM REALLY HAPPY.
THERE'S NOTHING WRONG WITH CALVIN. HE'S A NICE GUY.
I JUST...

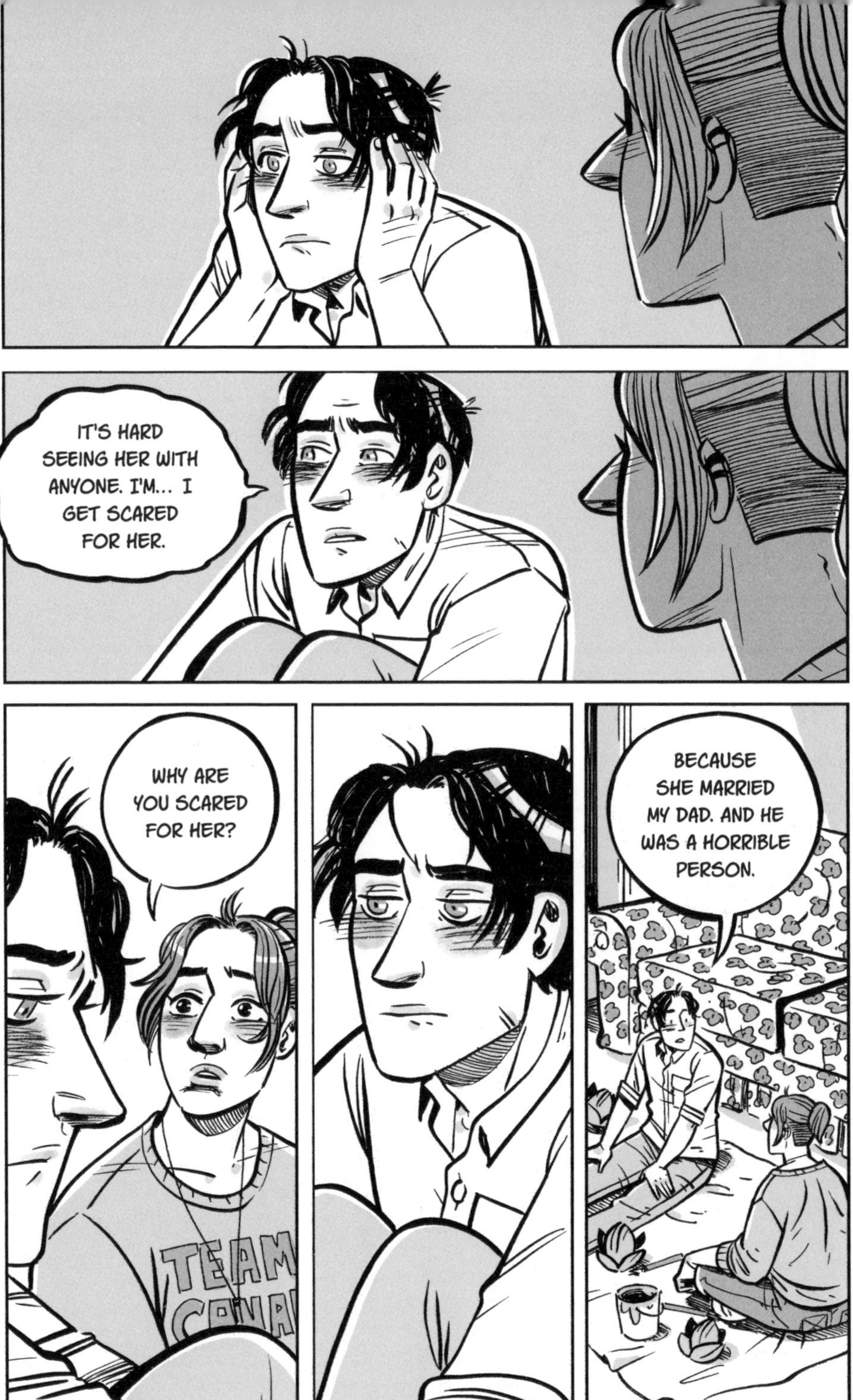
IT'S HARD SEEING HER WITH ANYONE. I'M... I GET SCARED FOR HER.
WHY ARE YOU SCARED FOR HER?
TEAM
BECAUSE SHE MARRIED MY DAD. AND HE WAS A HORRIBLE PERSON.

HE WAS ALWAYS A JERK. HE WAS CRUEL. HE'D PUT ME DOWN.

I DIDN'T KNOW THAT WASN'T HOW DADS WERE SUPPOSED TO ACT. I THOUGHT IT WAS NORMAL.

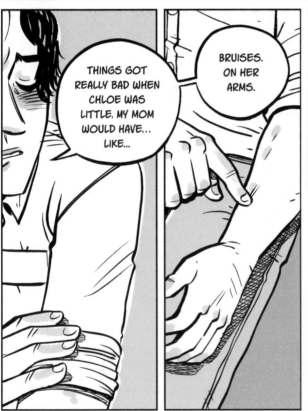

THINGS GOT REALLY BAD WHEN CHLOE WAS LITTLE. MY MOM WOULD HAVE... LIKE...

BRUISES. ON HER ARMS.

I DIDN'T KNOW. I WAS TEN. HE WAS THE ONLY DAD I'D EVER HAD.

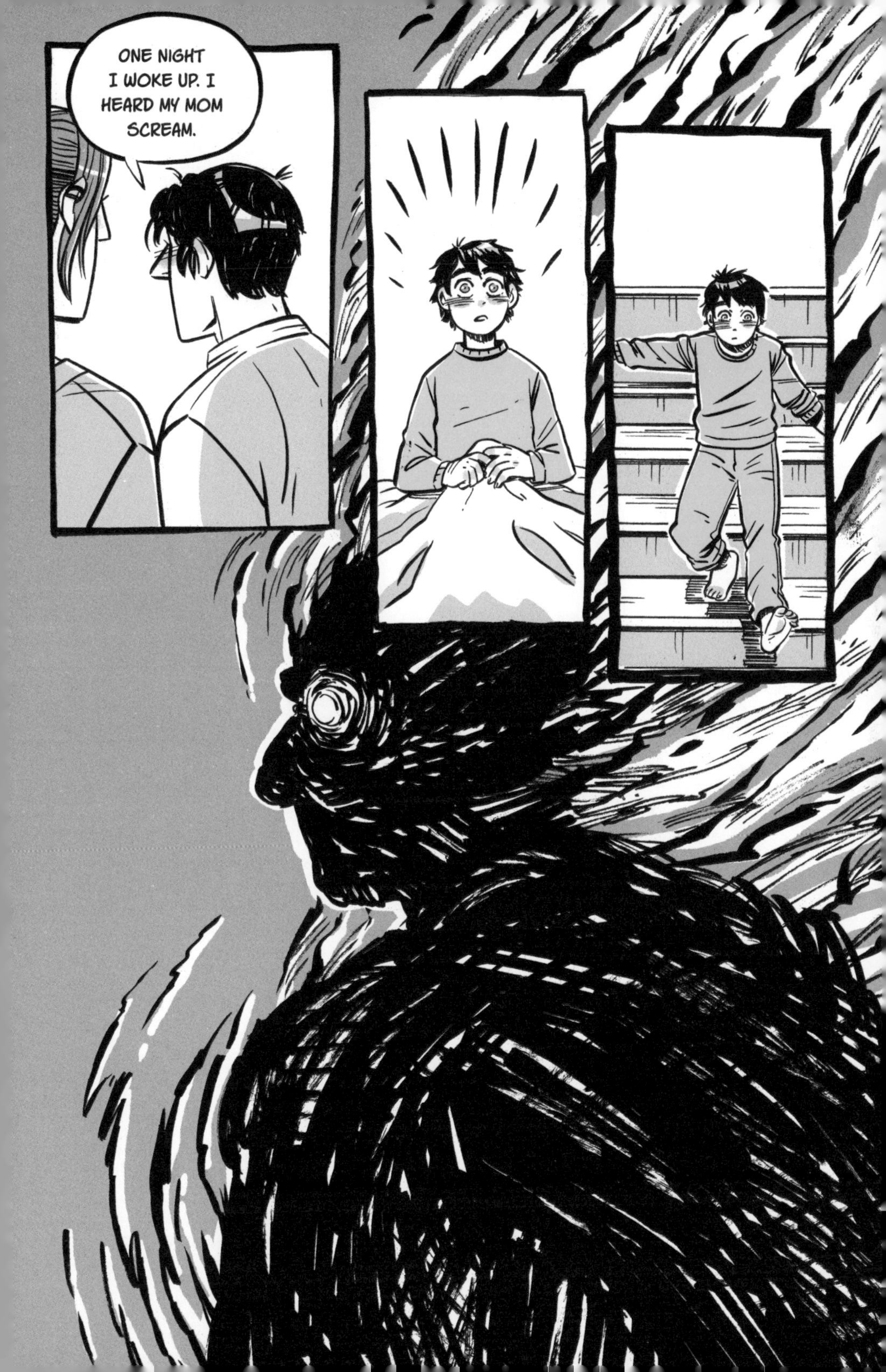
ONE NIGHT I WOKE UP. I HEARD MY MOM SCREAM.

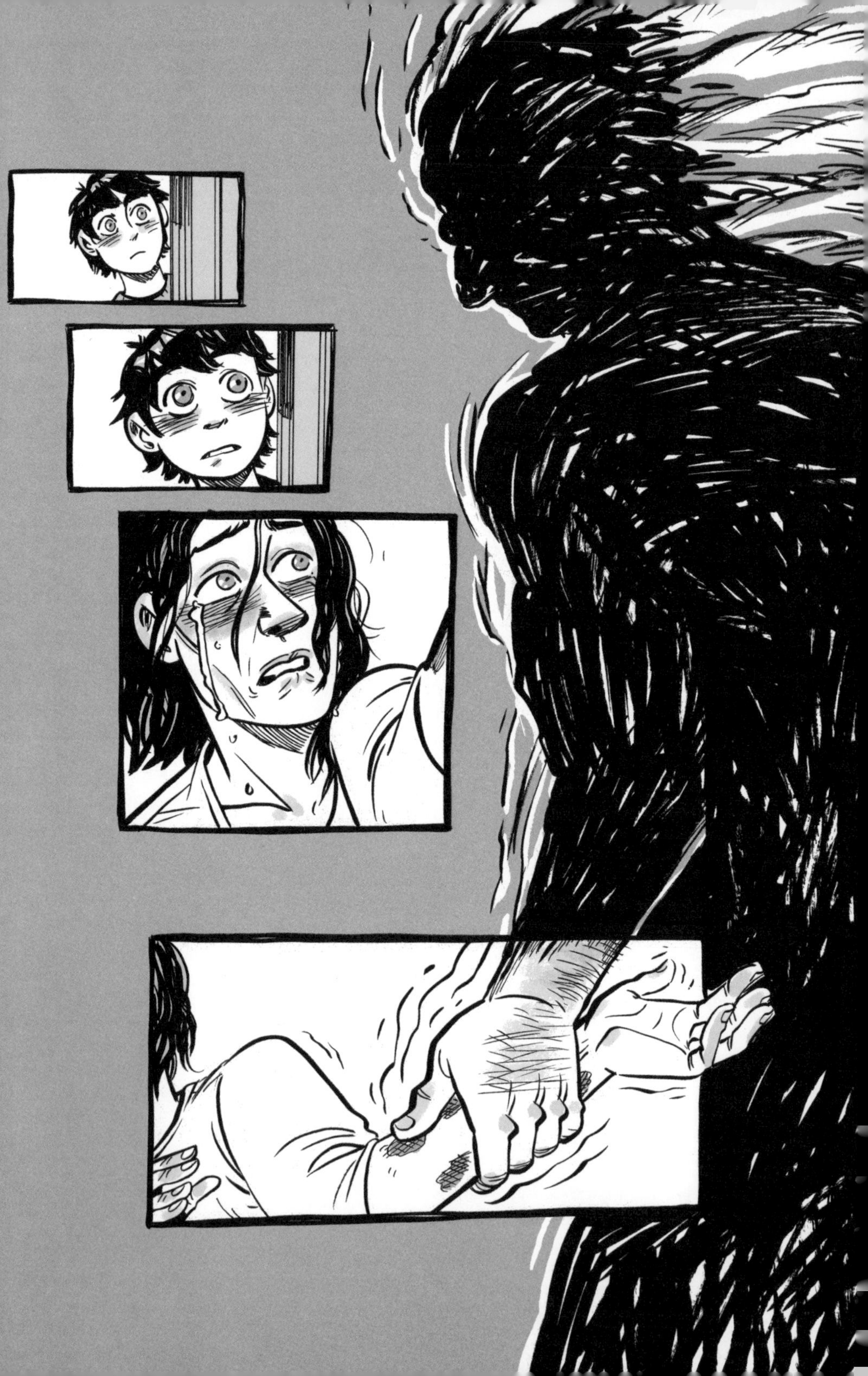

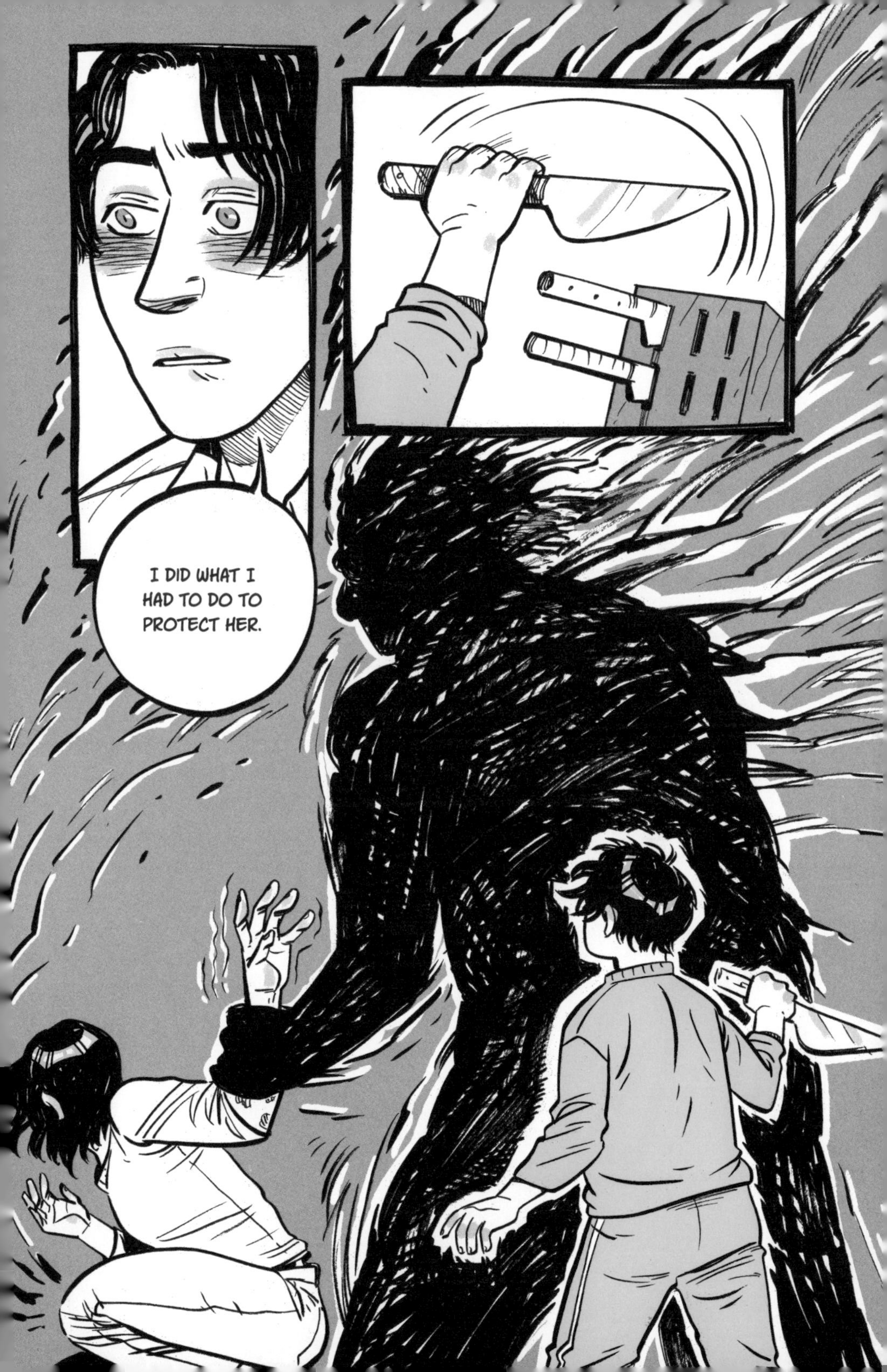
I DID WHAT I HAD TO DO TO PROTECT HER.

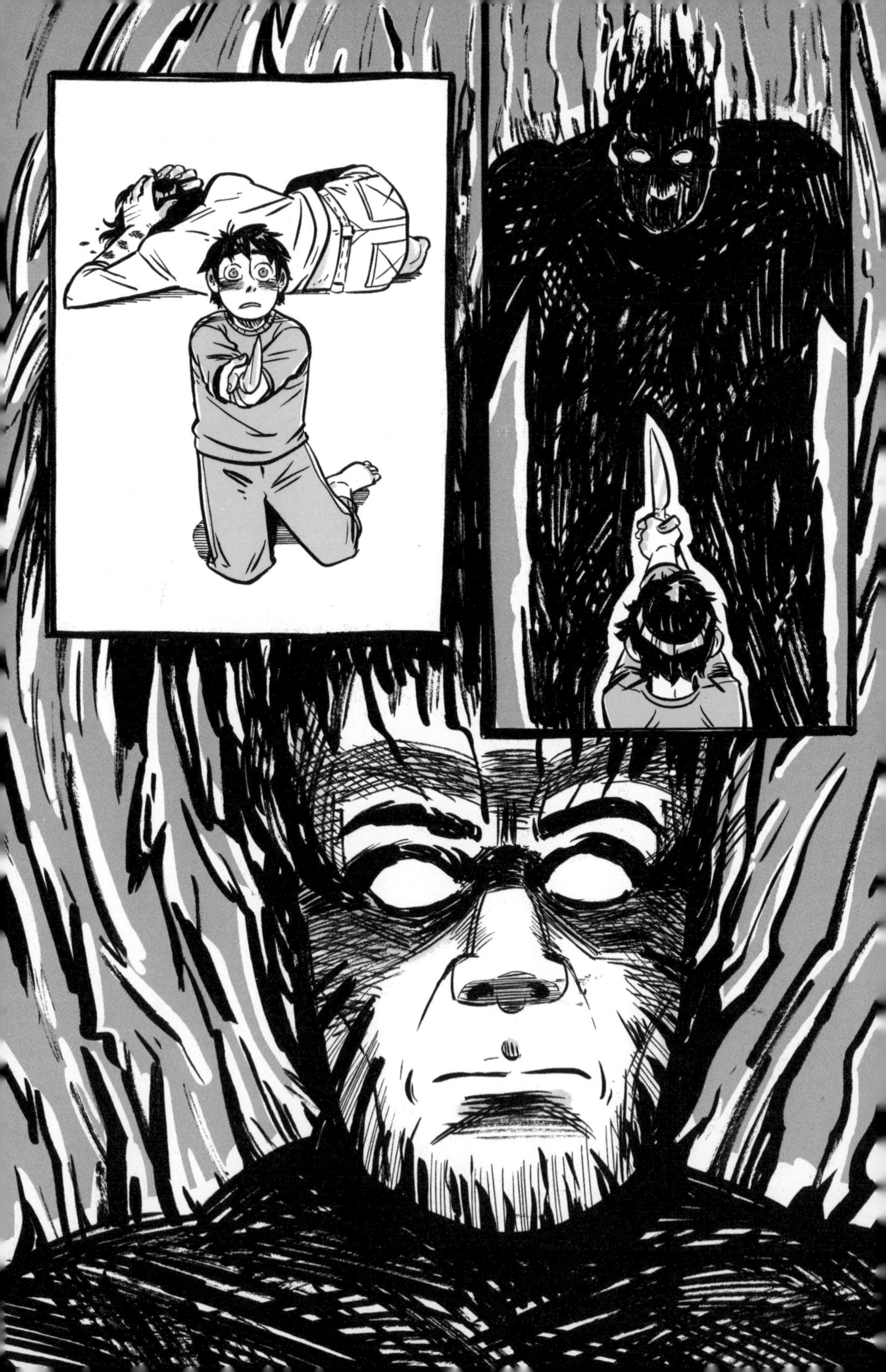

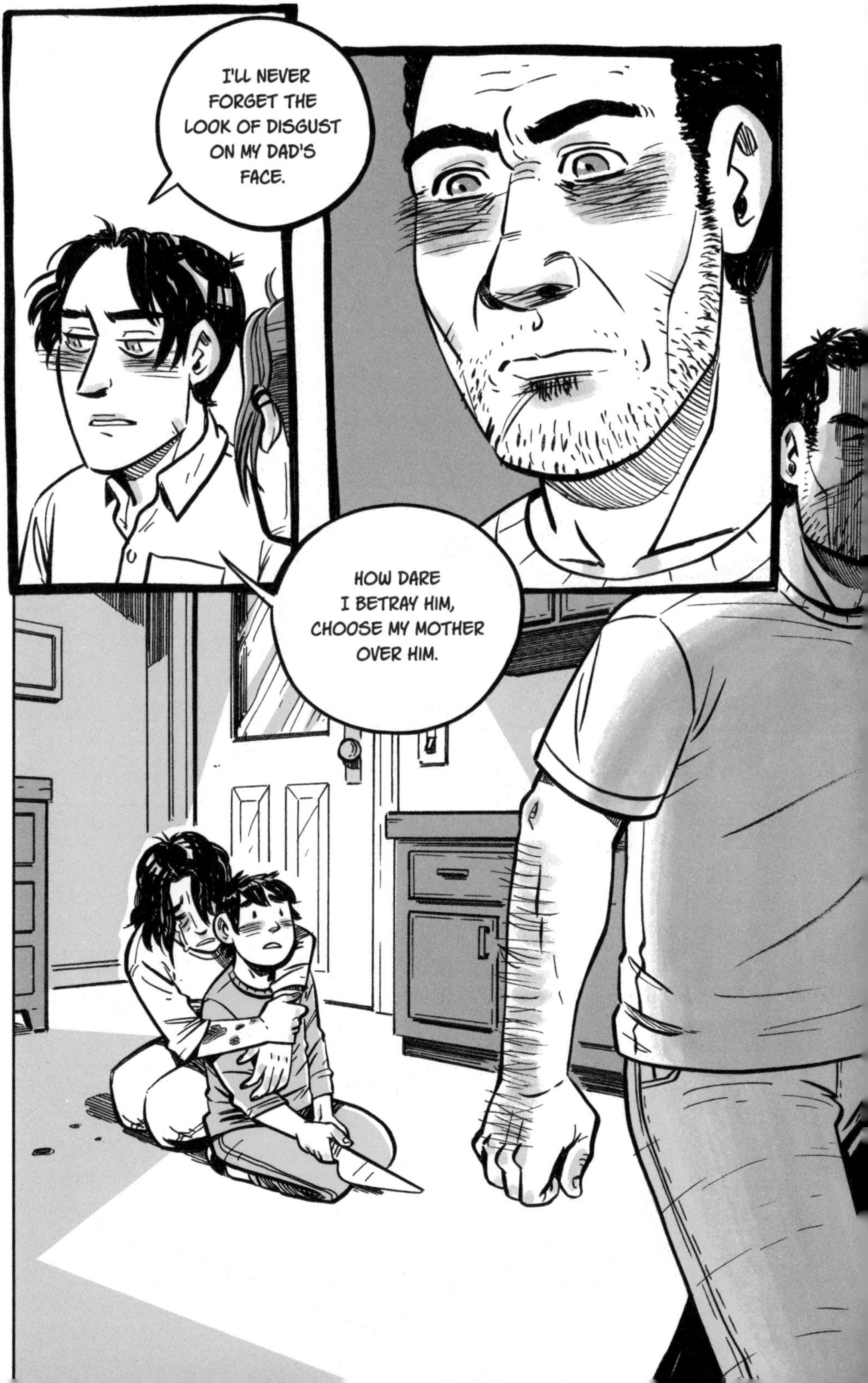
I'LL NEVER FORGET THE LOOK OF DISGUST ON MY DAD'S FACE.
HOW DARE I BETRAY HIM, CHOOSE MY MOTHER OVER HIM.

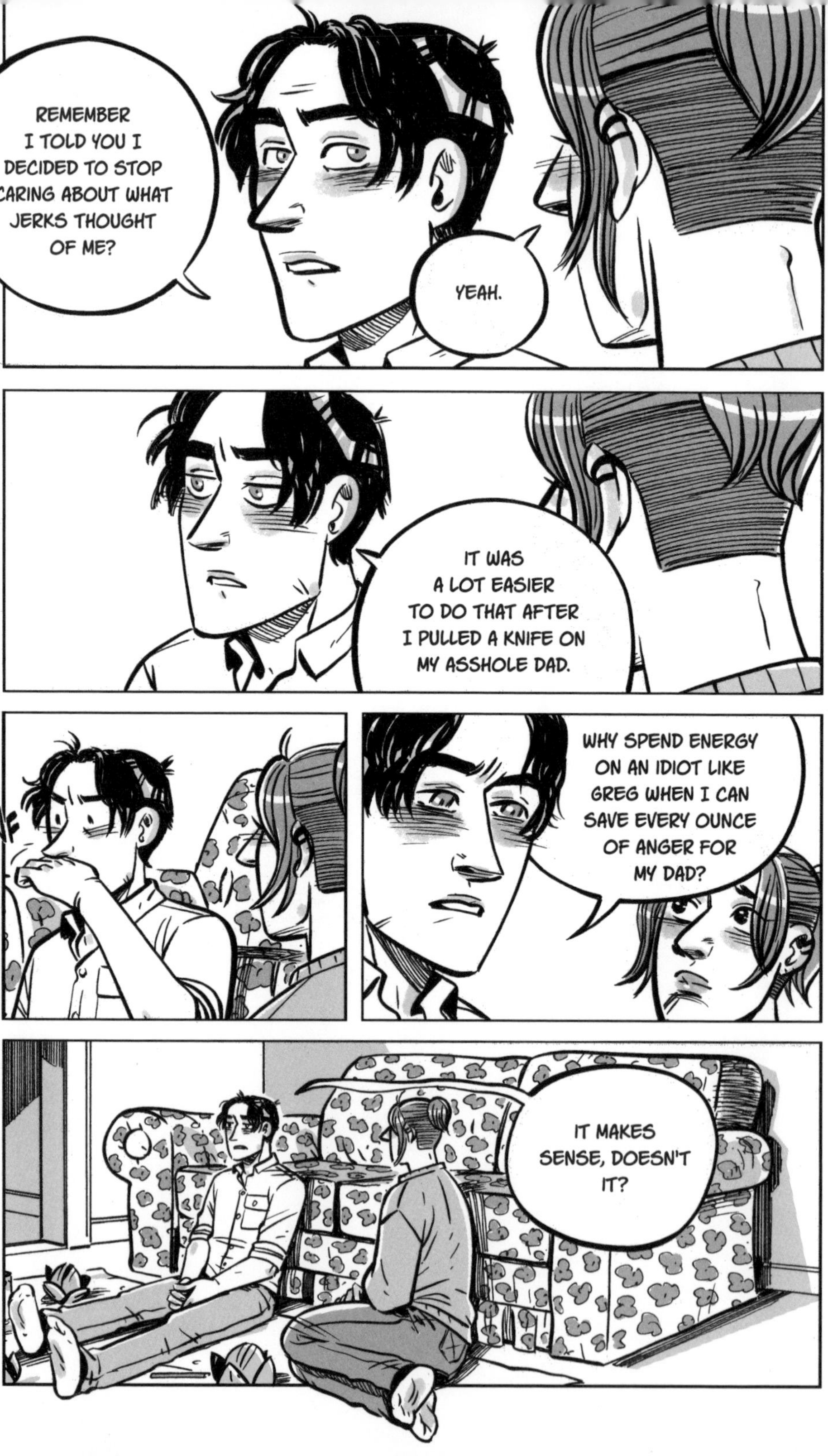
REMEMBER I TOLD YOU I DECIDED TO STOP CARING ABOUT WHAT JERKS THOUGHT OF ME?
YEAH.
IT WAS A LOT EASIER TO DO THAT AFTER I PULLED A KNIFE ON MY ASSHOLE DAD.
SNF
WHY SPEND ENERGY ON AN IDIOT LIKE GREG WHEN I CAN SAVE EVERY OUNCE OF ANGER FOR MY DAD?
IT MAKES SENSE, DOESN'T IT?

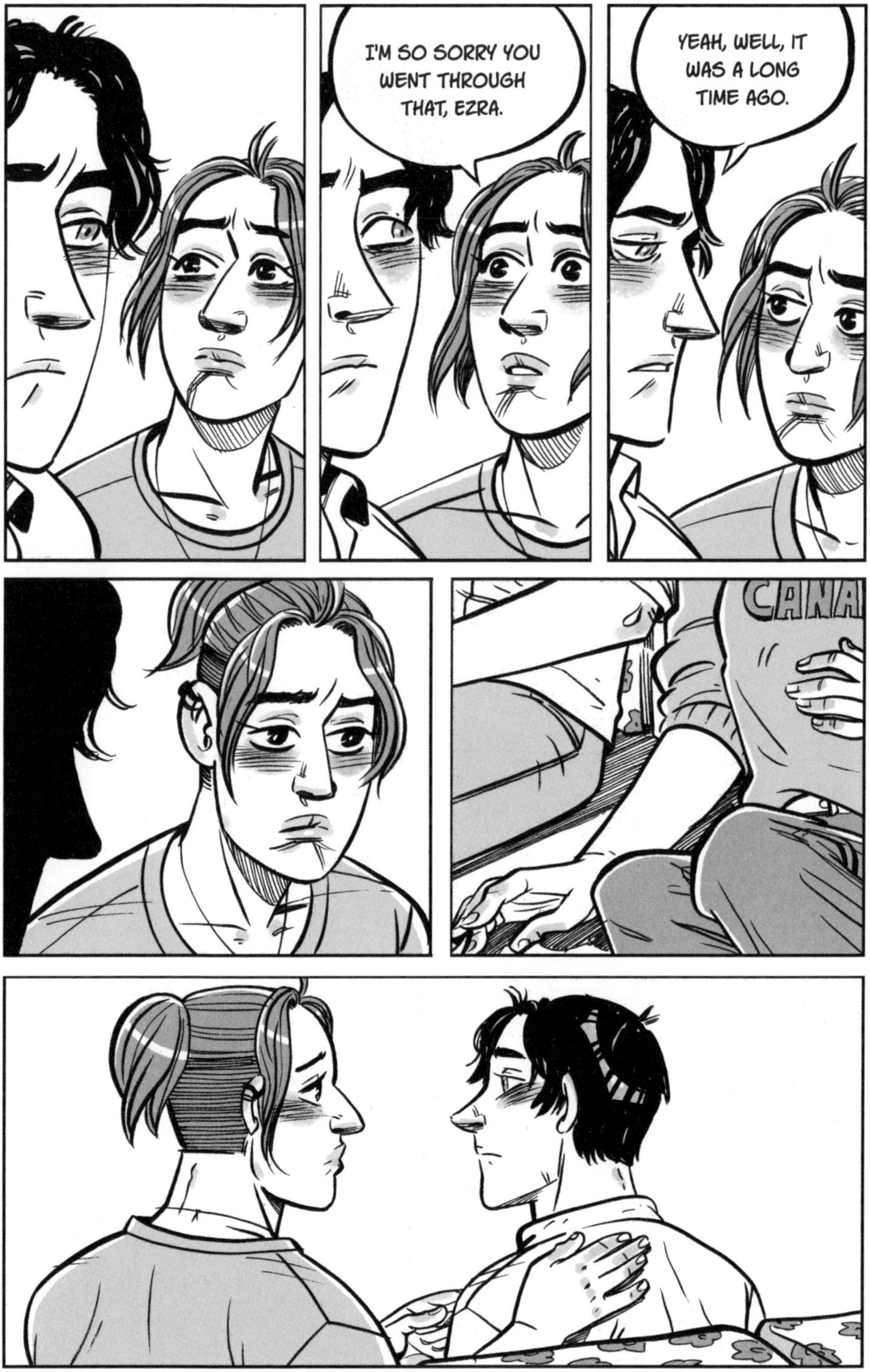
I'M SO SORRY YOU WENT THROUGH THAT, EZRA.
YEAH, WELL, IT WAS A LONG TIME AGO.
CANA

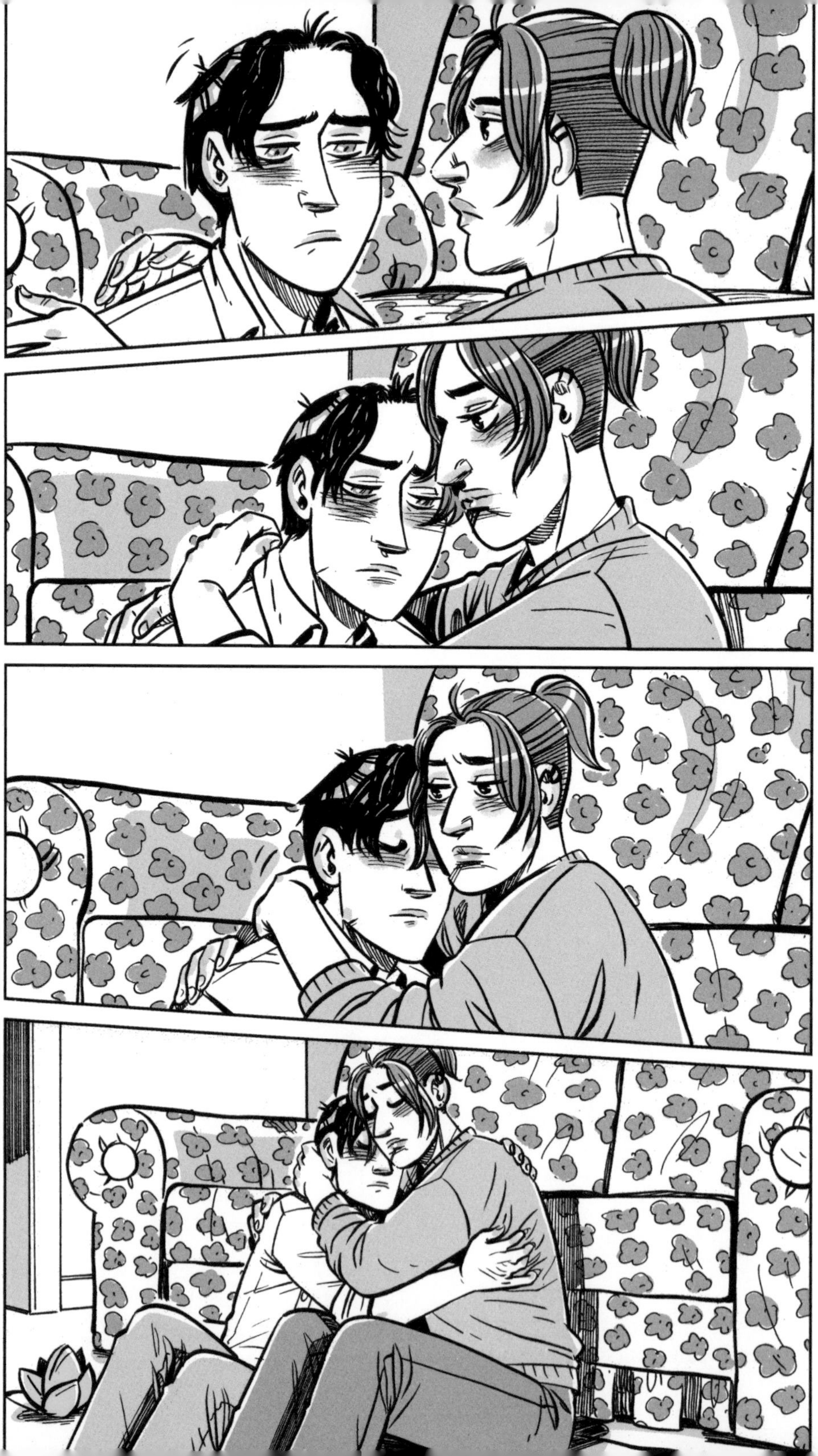

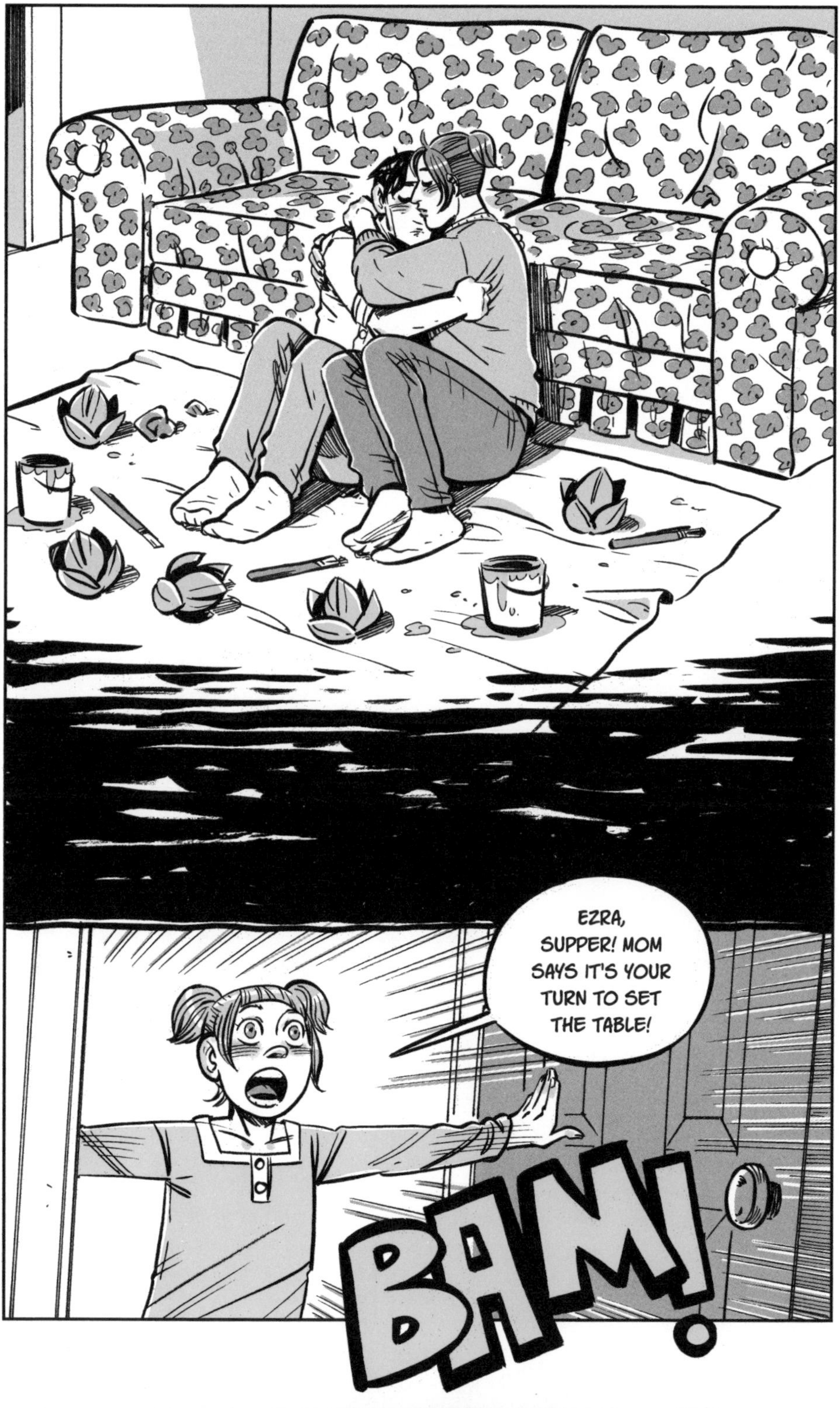
EZRA, SUPPER! MOM SAYS IT'S YOUR TURN TO SET THE TABLE!
BAM!

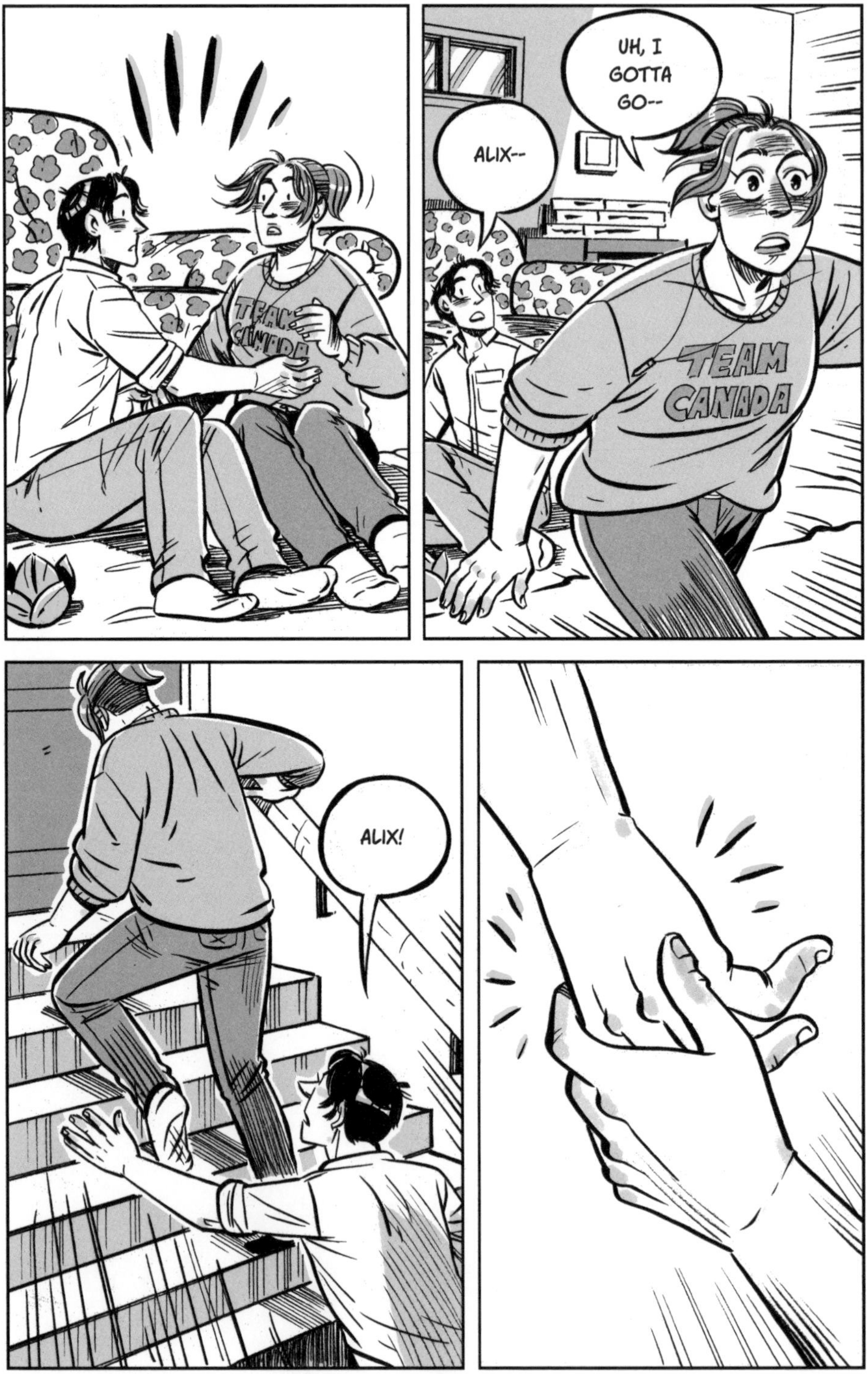
TEAM CANADA
ALIX--
UH, I GOTTA GO--
TEAM CANADA
ALIX!

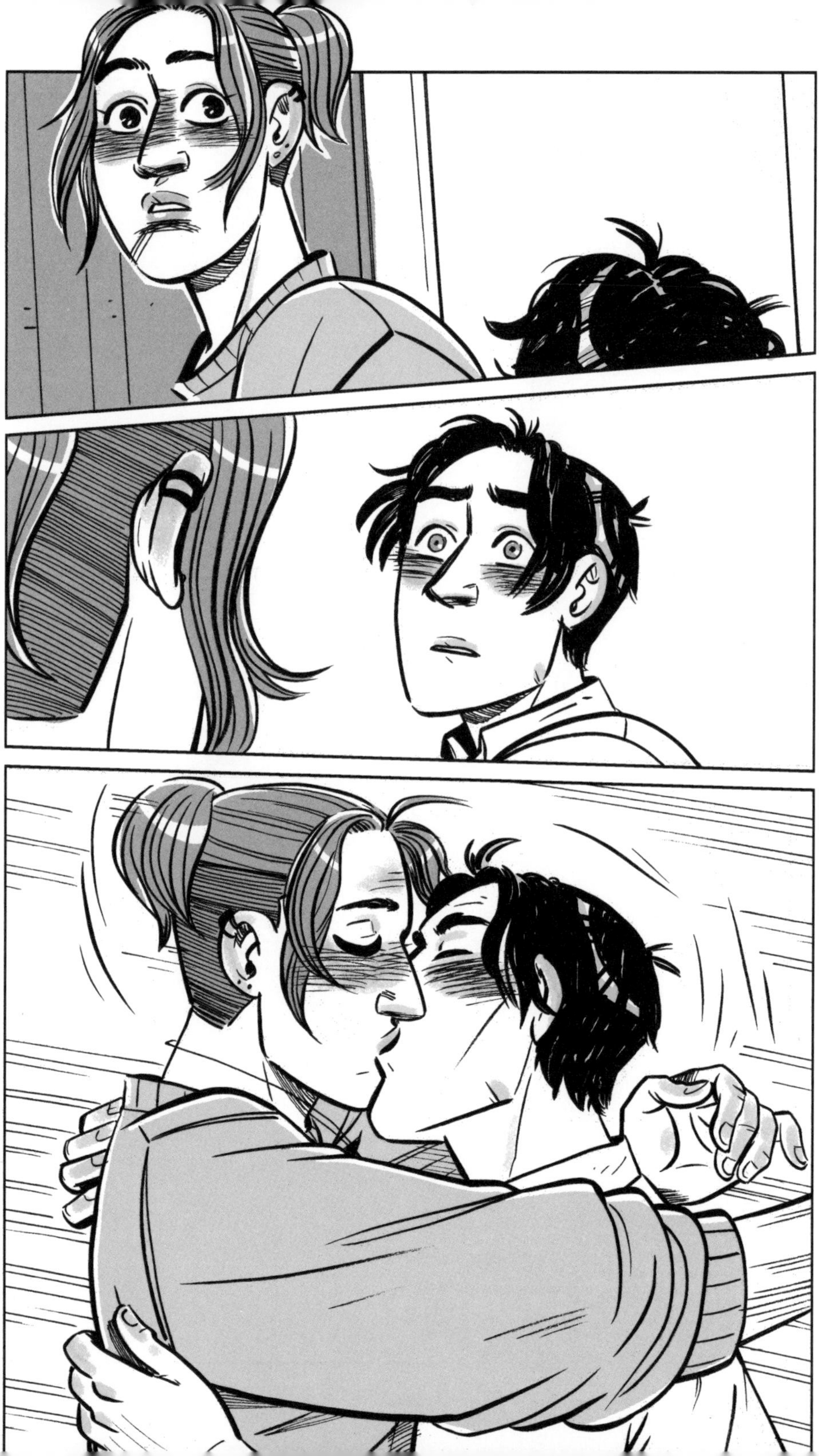

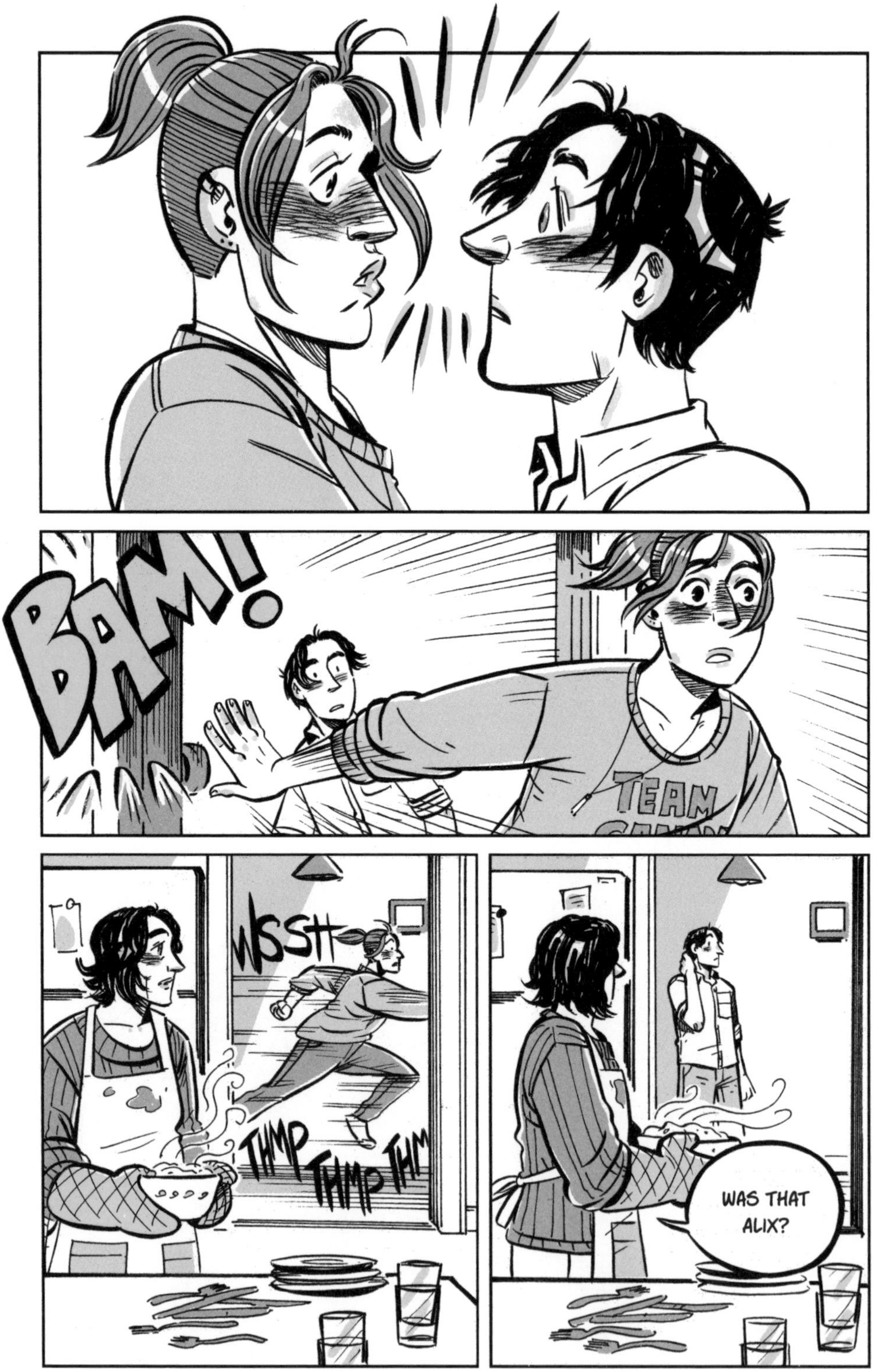
BAM!
TEAM
WSSH
THMP THMP THM
WAS THAT ALIX?

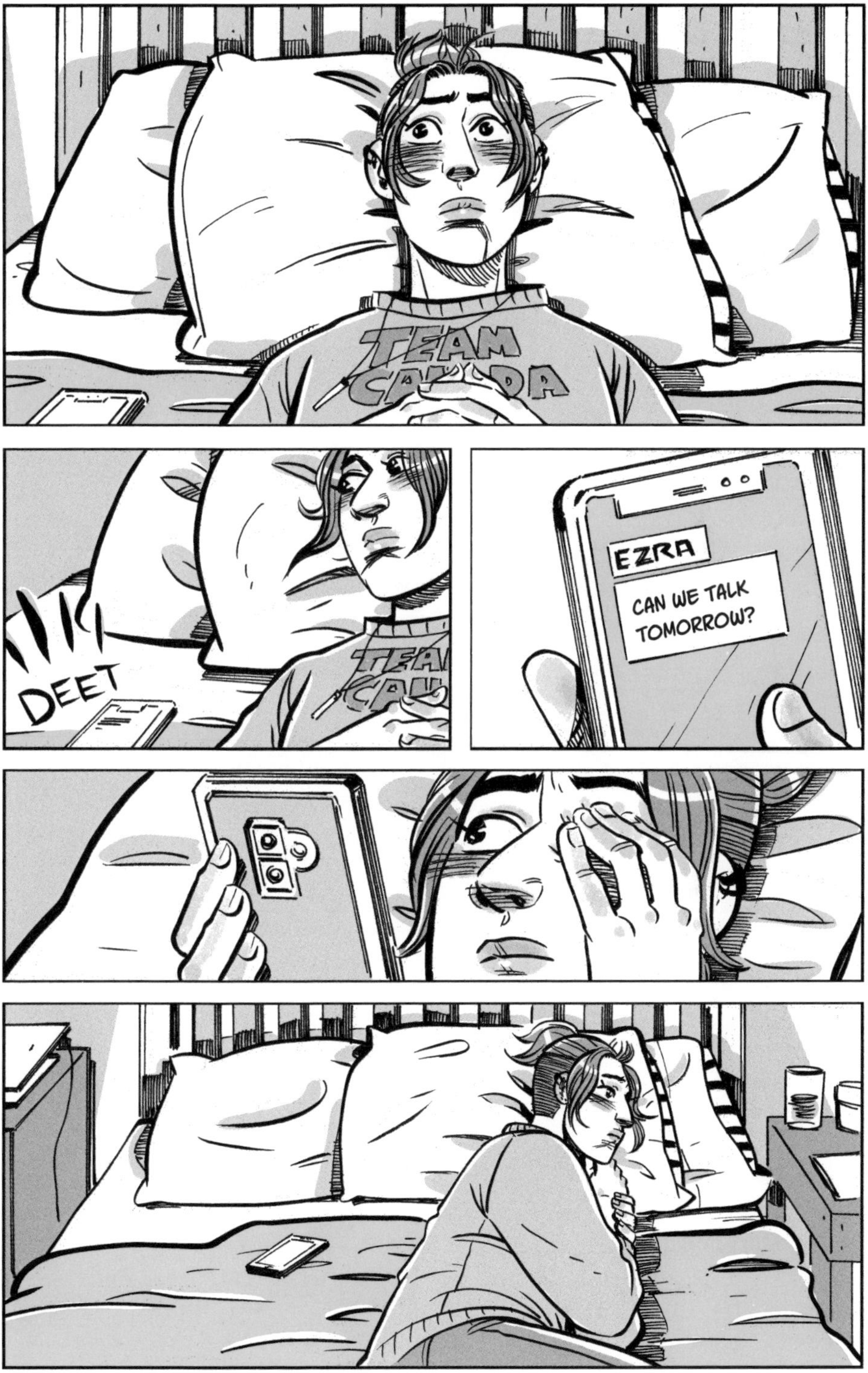
TEAM CAL DA
DEET
EZRA
CAN WE TALK TOMORROW?

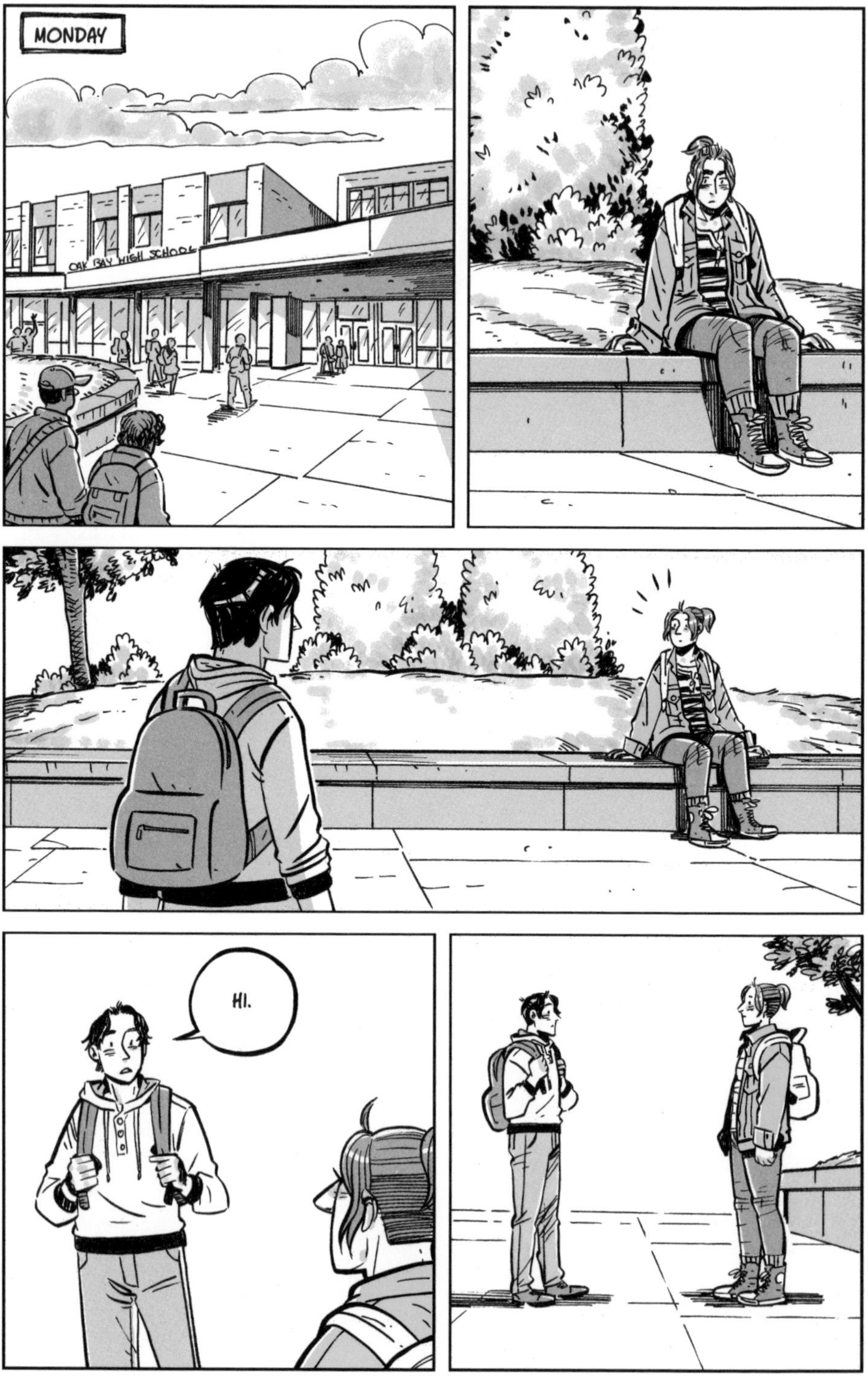
MONDAY
OAK BAY HIGH SCHOOL
HI.

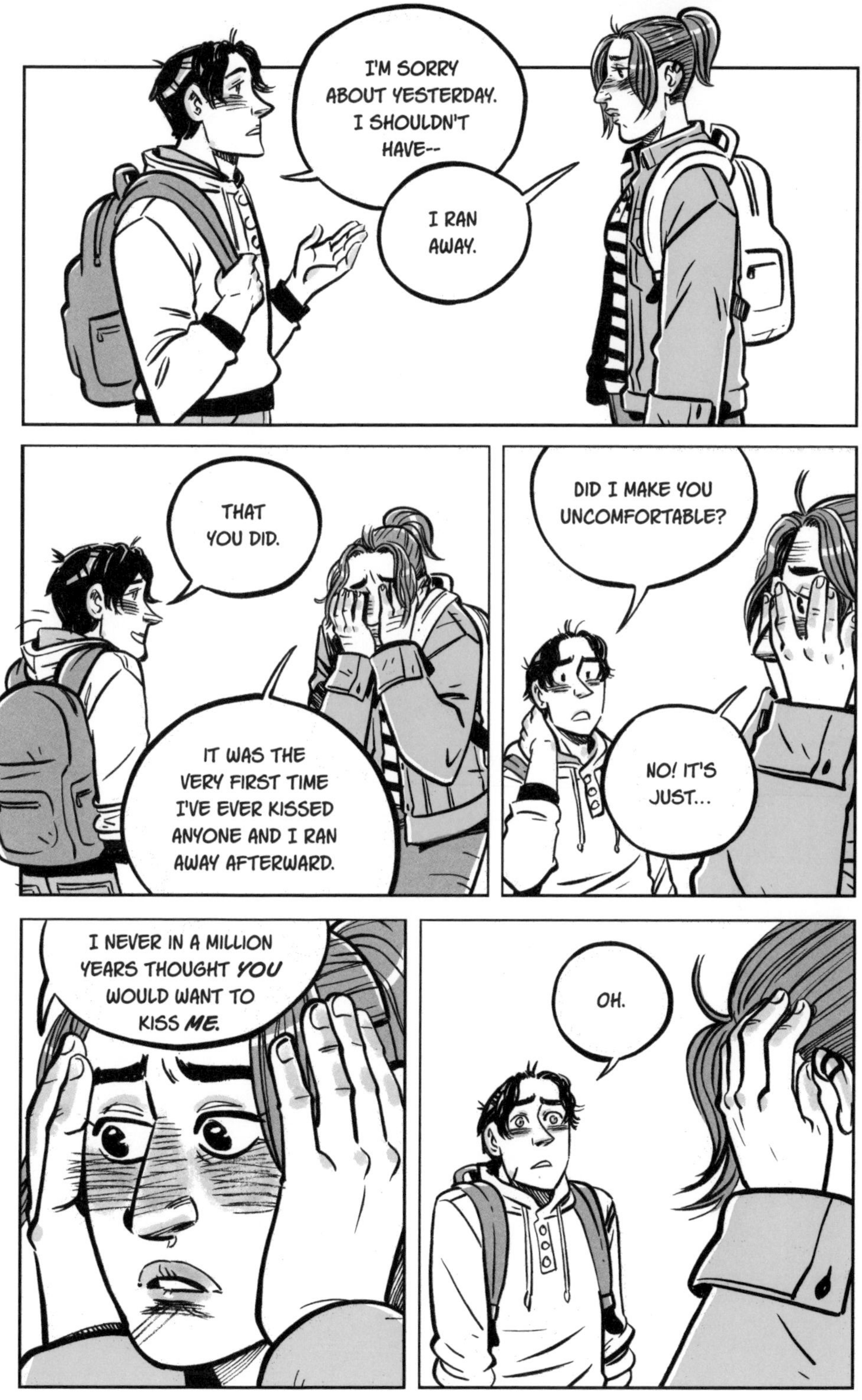
I'M SORRY ABOUT YESTERDAY. I SHOULDN'T HAVE--
I RAN AWAY.
THAT YOU DID.
IT WAS THE VERY FIRST TIME I'VE EVER KISSED ANYONE AND I RAN AWAY AFTERWARD.
DID I MAKE YOU UNCOMFORTABLE?
NO! IT'S JUST...
I NEVER IN A MILLION YEARS THOUGHT *YOU* WOULD WANT TO KISS *ME*.
OH.

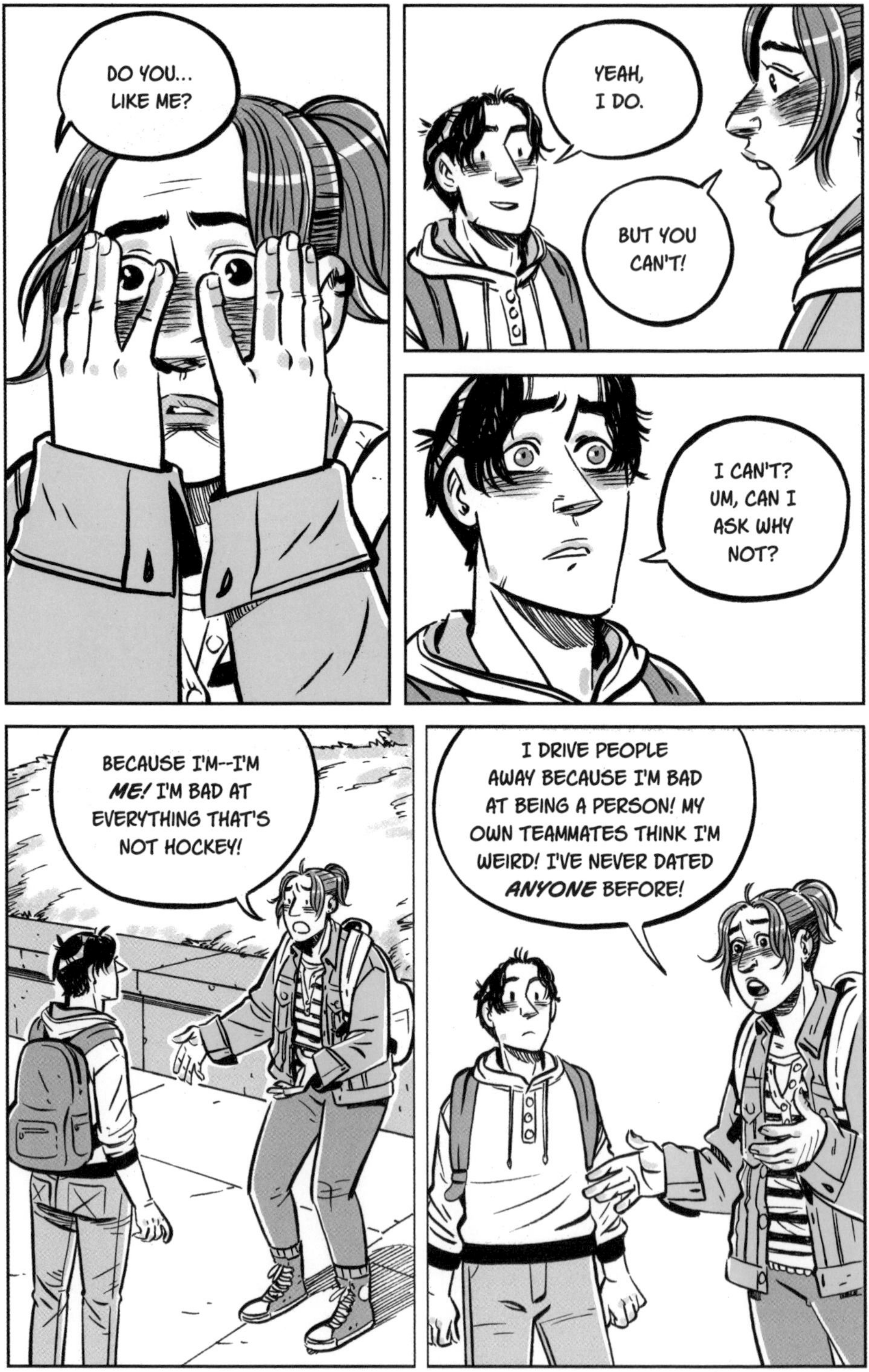
DO YOU... LIKE ME?
YEAH, I DO.
BUT YOU CAN'T!
I CAN'T? UM, CAN I ASK WHY NOT?
BECAUSE I'M--I'M *ME!* I'M BAD AT EVERYTHING THAT'S NOT HOCKEY!
I DRIVE PEOPLE AWAY BECAUSE I'M BAD AT BEING A PERSON! MY OWN TEAMMATES THINK I'M WEIRD! I'VE NEVER DATED *ANYONE* BEFORE!

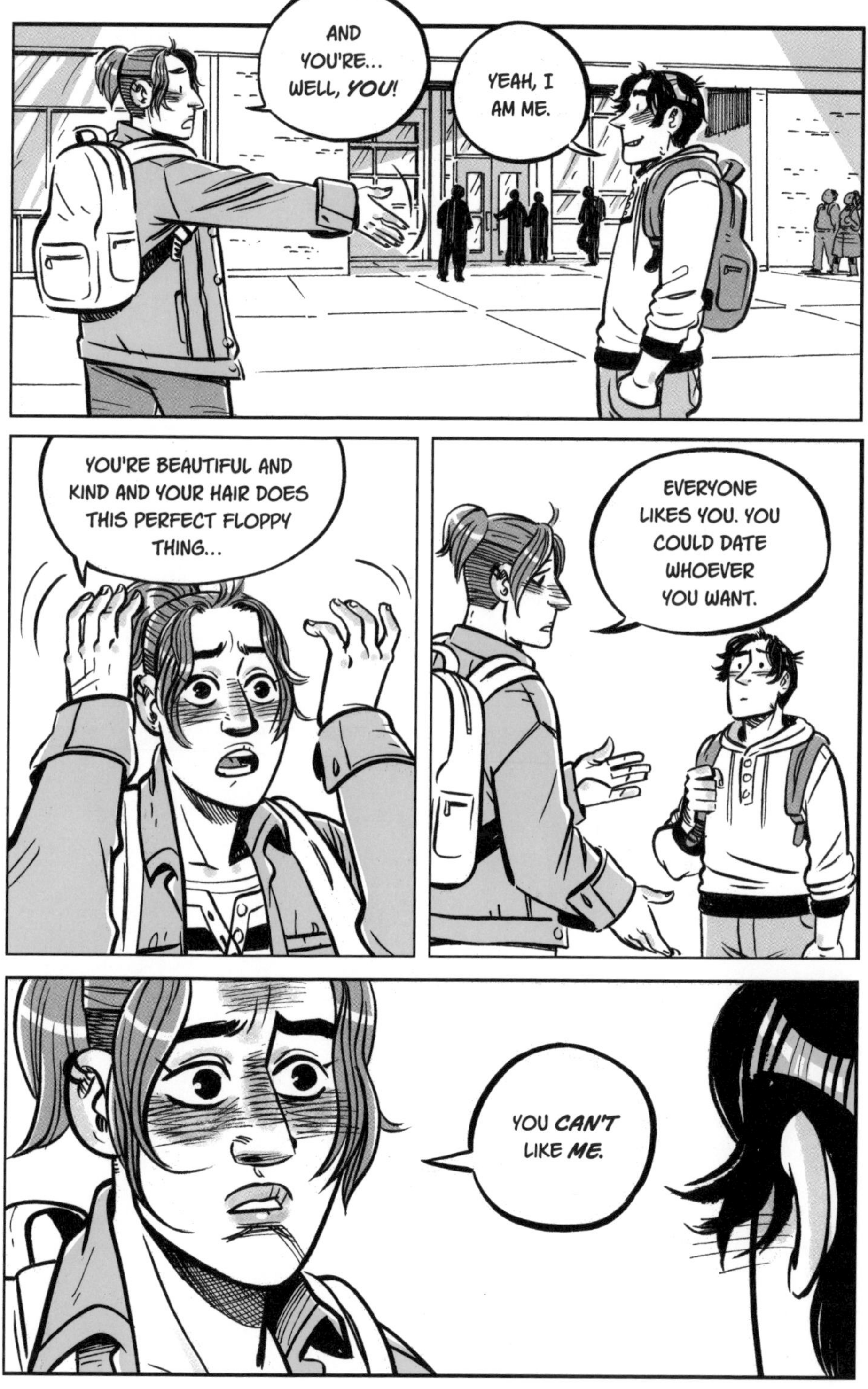
AND YOU'RE... WELL, *YOU!*
YEAH, I AM ME.
YOU'RE BEAUTIFUL AND KIND AND YOUR HAIR DOES THIS PERFECT FLOPPY THING...
EVERYONE LIKES YOU. YOU COULD DATE WHOEVER YOU WANT.
YOU *CAN'T* LIKE *ME.*

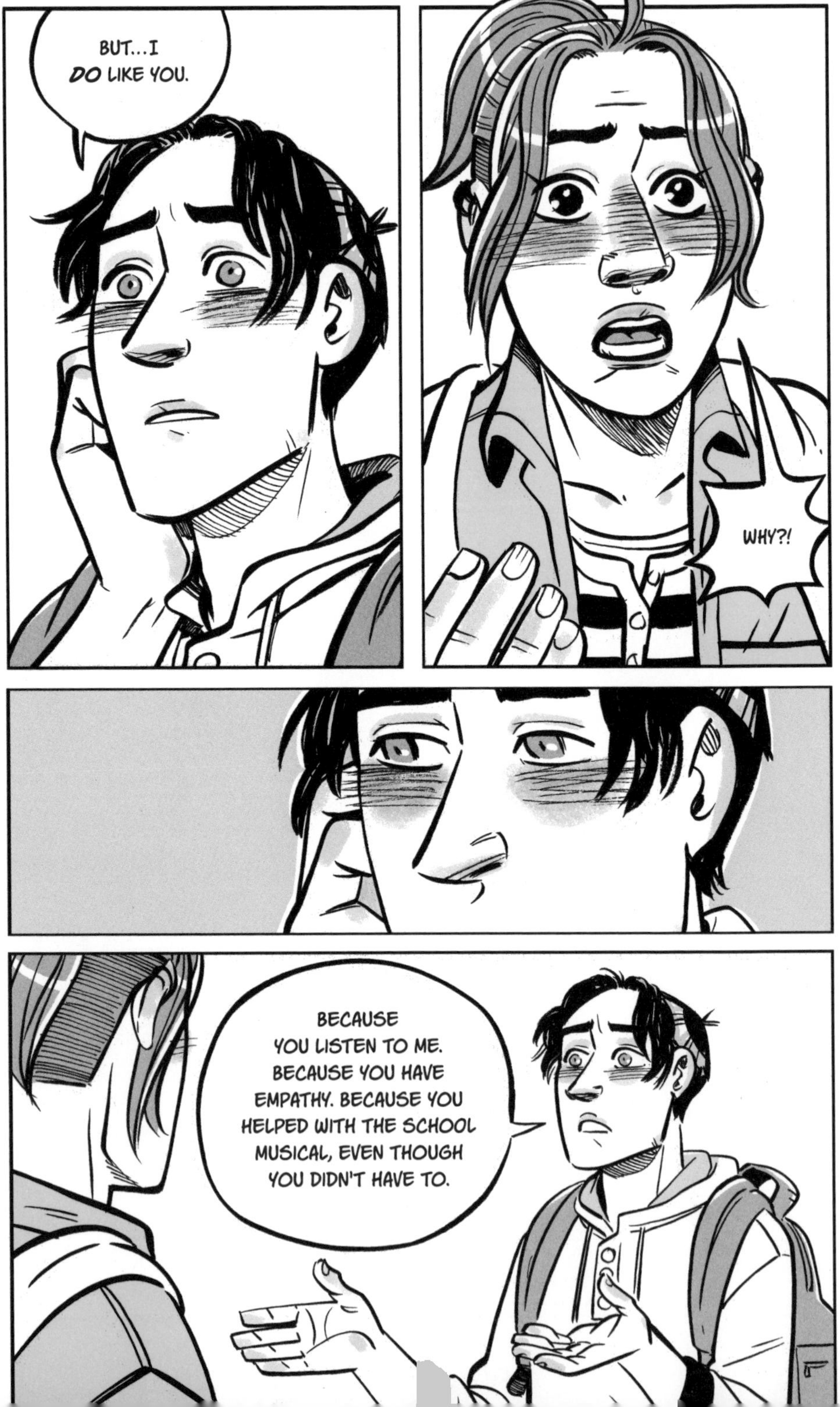
BUT...I DO LIKE YOU.
WHY?!
BECAUSE YOU LISTEN TO ME. BECAUSE YOU HAVE EMPATHY. BECAUSE YOU HELPED WITH THE SCHOOL MUSICAL, EVEN THOUGH YOU DIDN'T HAVE TO.

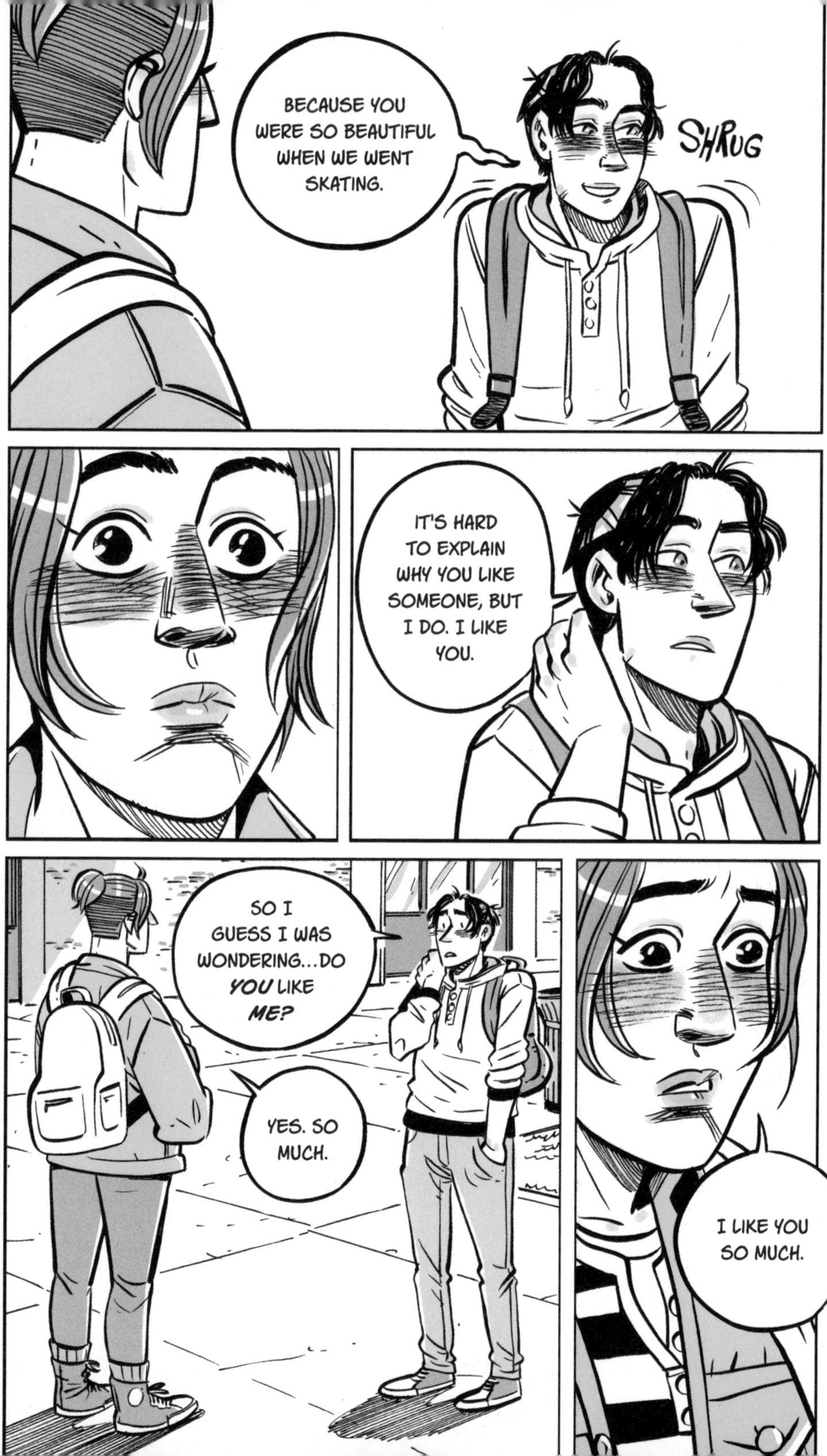
BECAUSE YOU WERE SO BEAUTIFUL WHEN WE WENT SKATING.
SHRUG
IT'S HARD TO EXPLAIN WHY YOU LIKE SOMEONE, BUT I DO. I LIKE YOU.
SO I GUESS I WAS WONDERING...DO *YOU* LIKE *ME?*
YES. SO MUCH.
I LIKE YOU SO MUCH.

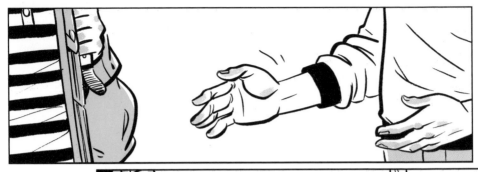

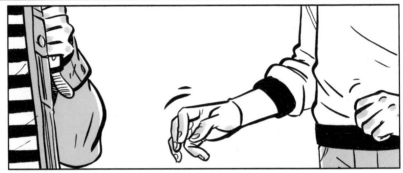

CAN I?

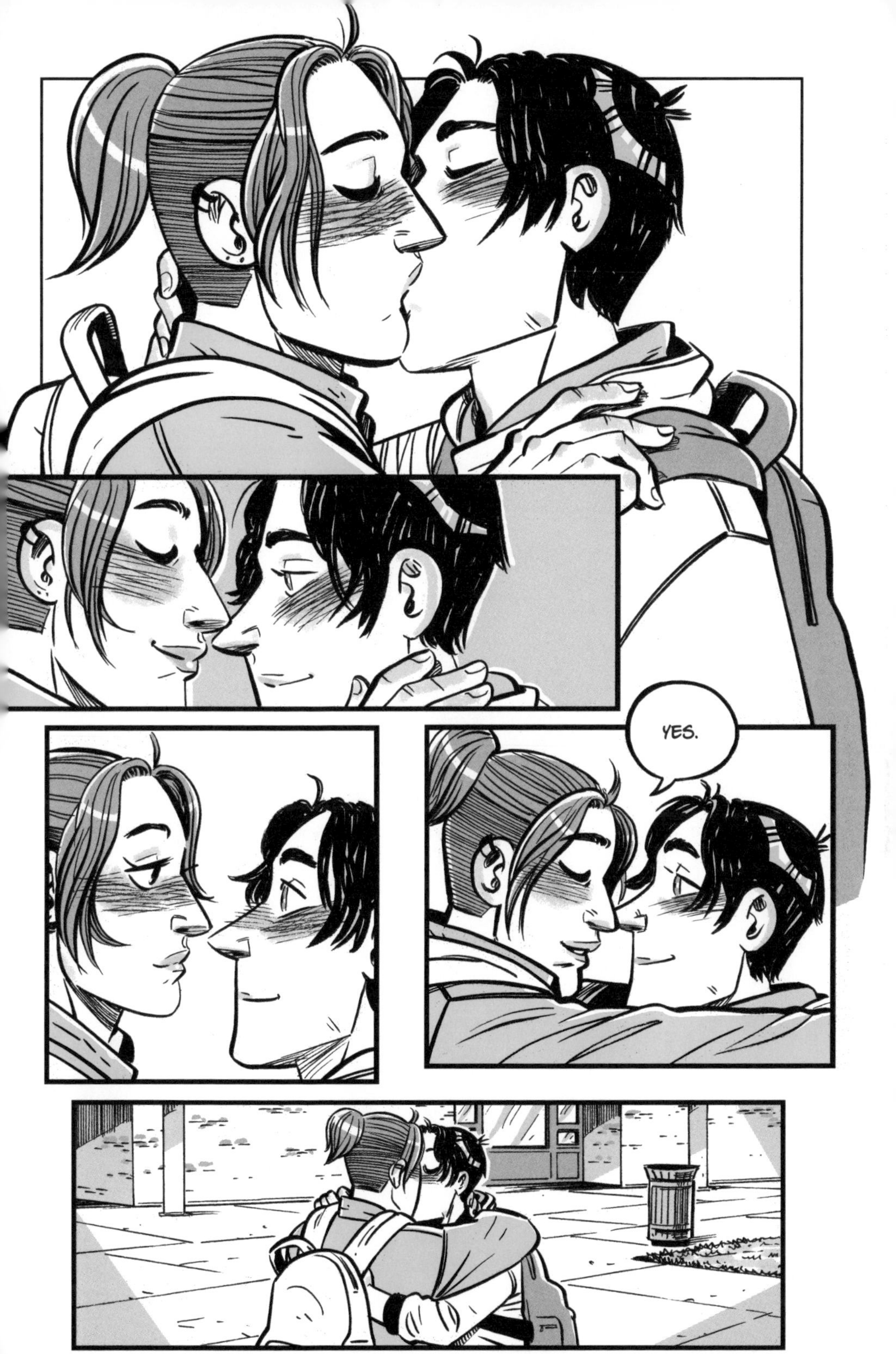
YES.

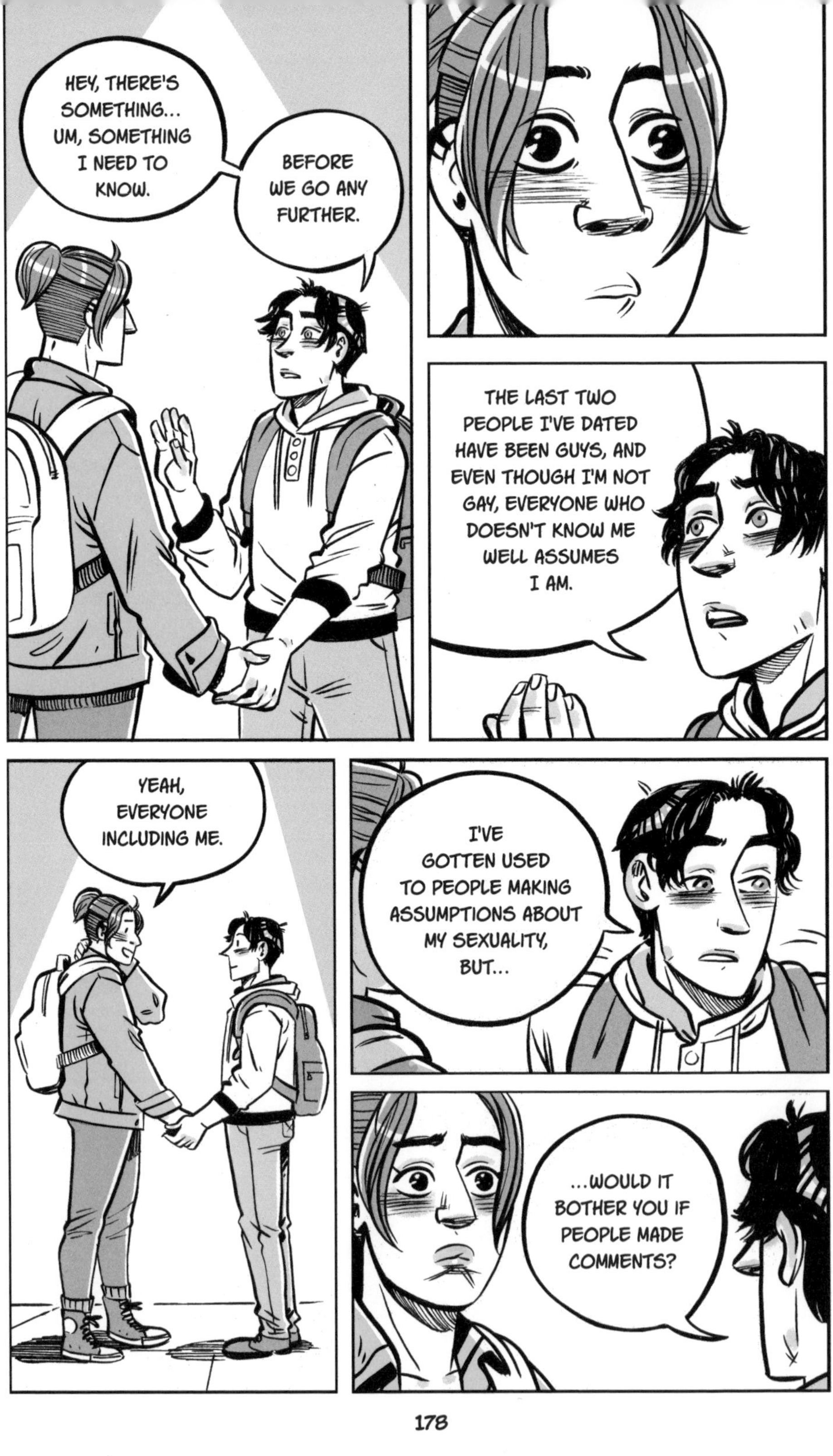
HEY, THERE'S SOMETHING... UM, SOMETHING I NEED TO KNOW.
BEFORE WE GO ANY FURTHER.
THE LAST TWO PEOPLE I'VE DATED HAVE BEEN GUYS, AND EVEN THOUGH I'M NOT GAY, EVERYONE WHO DOESN'T KNOW ME WELL ASSUMES I AM.
YEAH, EVERYONE INCLUDING ME.
I'VE GOTTEN USED TO PEOPLE MAKING ASSUMPTIONS ABOUT MY SEXUALITY, BUT...
...WOULD IT BOTHER YOU IF PEOPLE MADE COMMENTS?

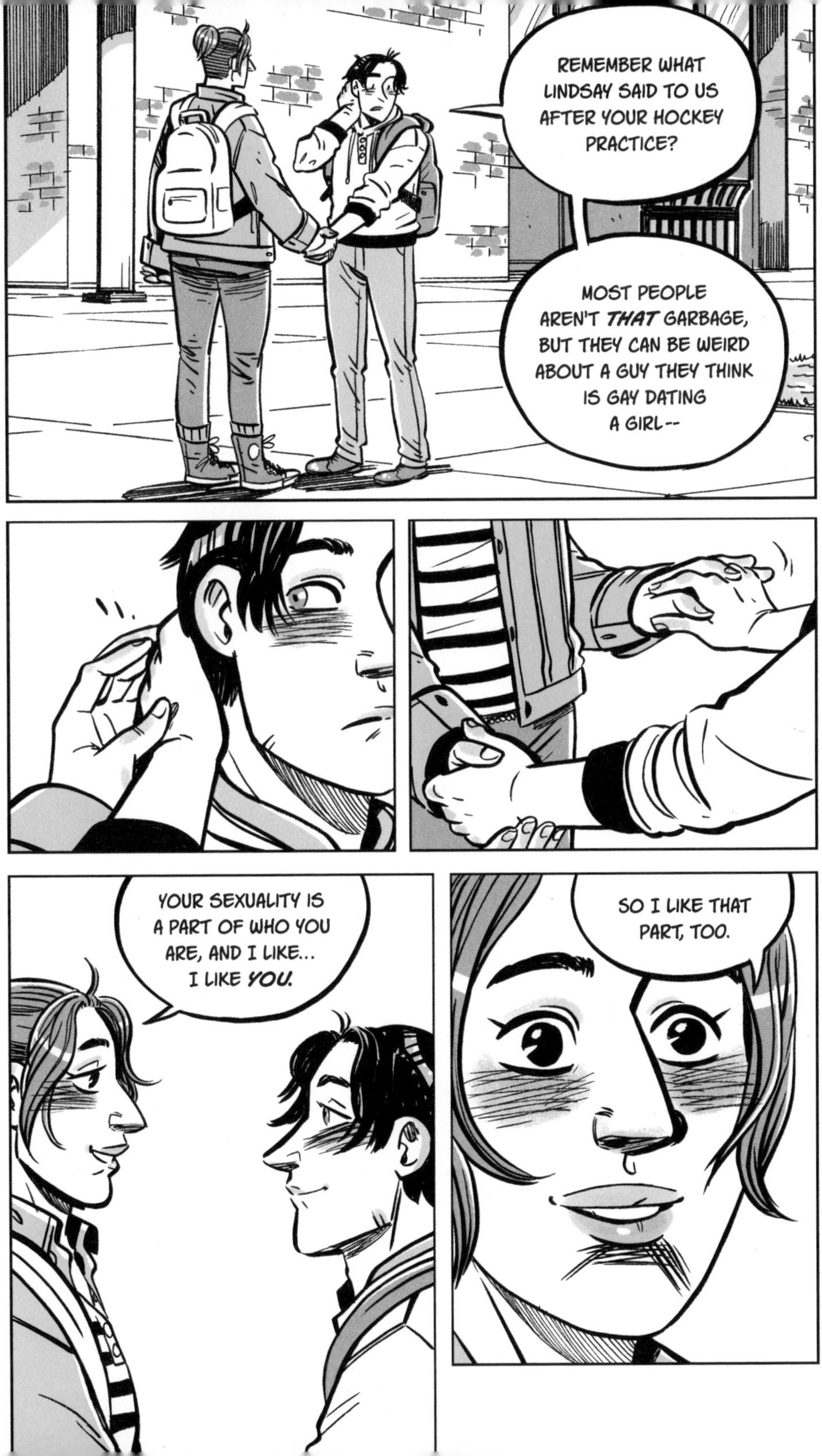
REMEMBER WHAT LINDSAY SAID TO US AFTER YOUR HOCKEY PRACTICE?
MOST PEOPLE AREN'T *THAT* GARBAGE, BUT THEY CAN BE WEIRD ABOUT A GUY THEY THINK IS GAY DATING A GIRL--
YOUR SEXUALITY IS A PART OF WHO YOU ARE, AND I LIKE... I LIKE *YOU*.
SO I LIKE THAT PART, TOO.

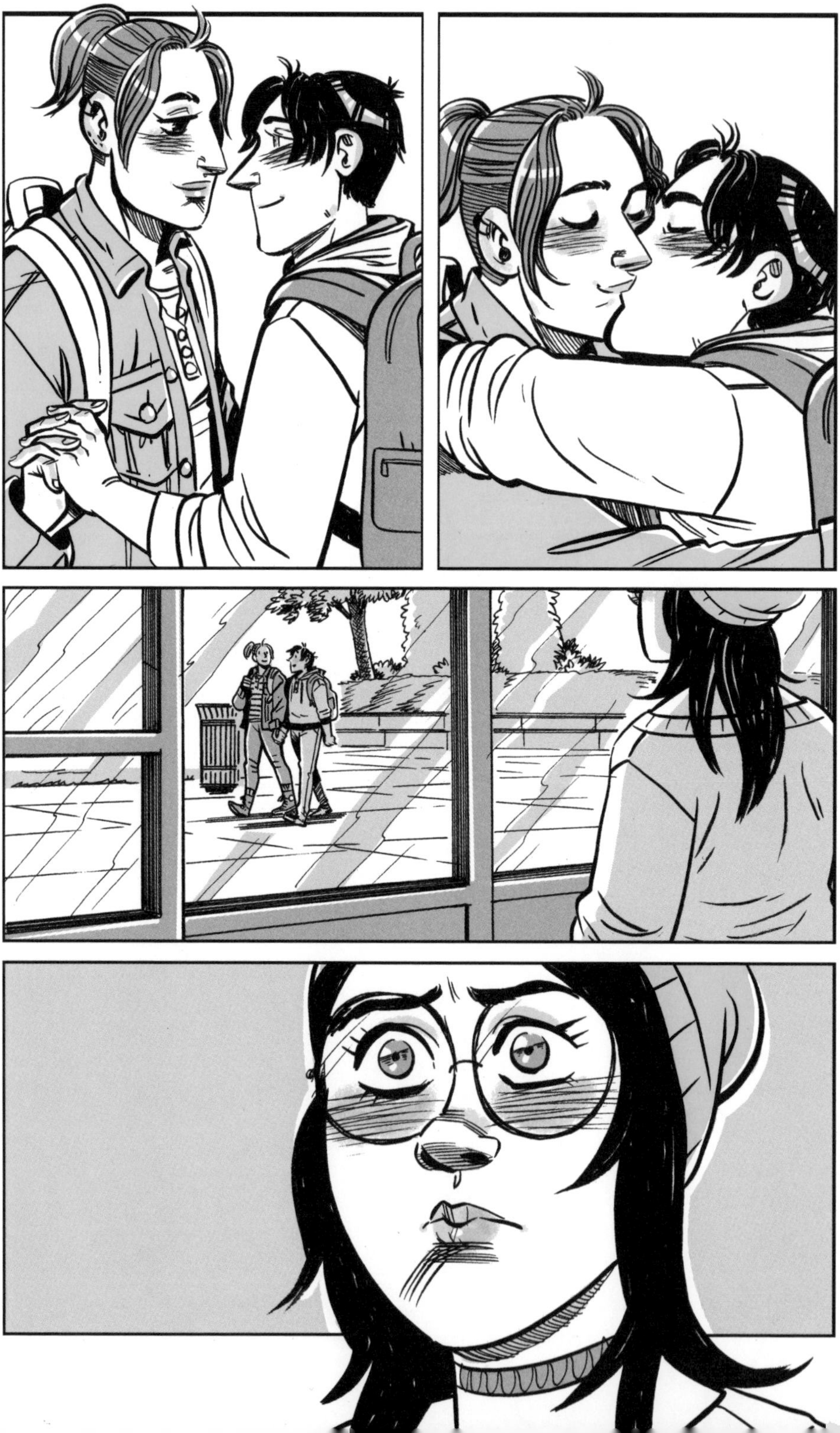

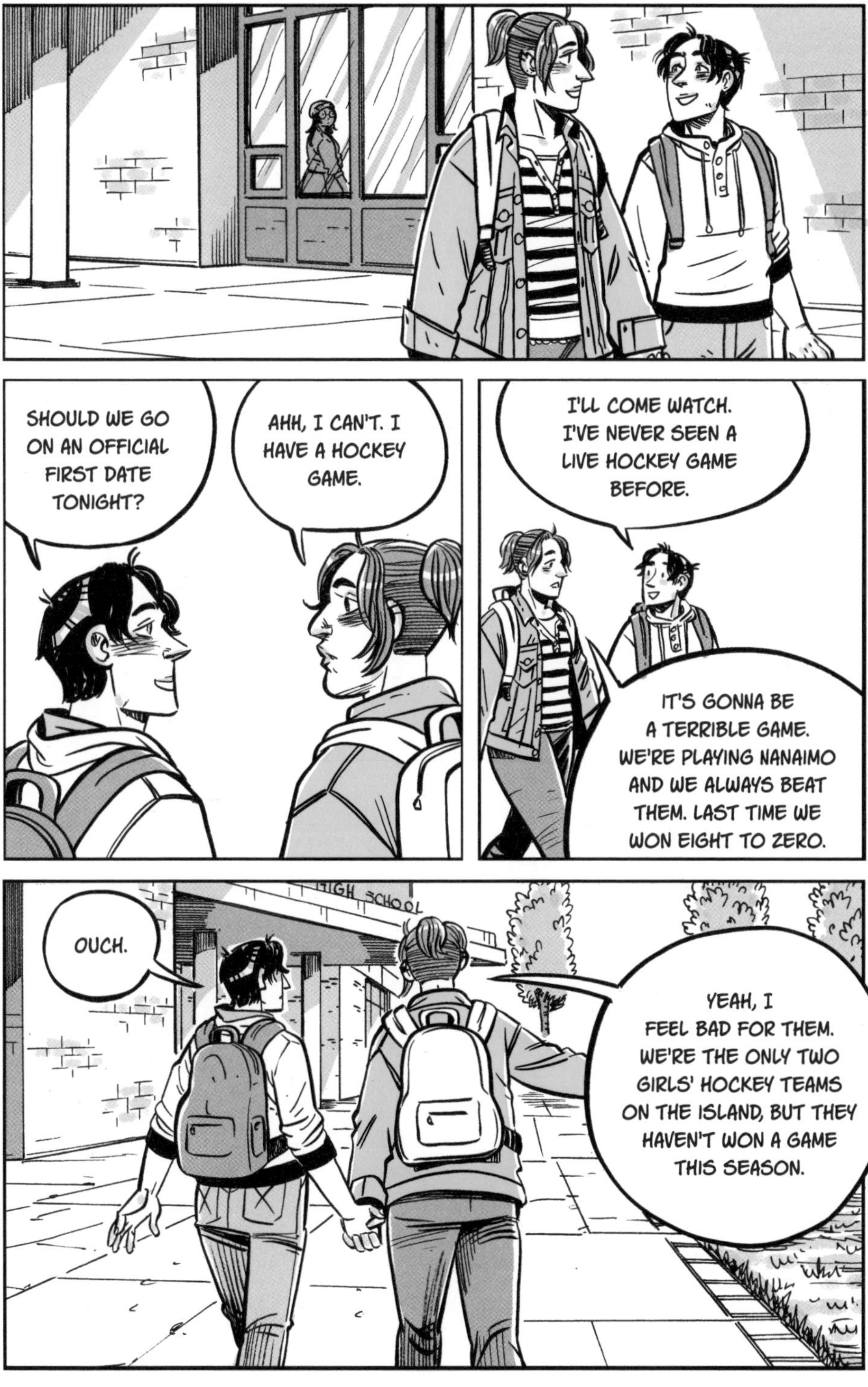
SHOULD WE GO ON AN OFFICIAL FIRST DATE TONIGHT?
AHH, I CAN'T. I HAVE A HOCKEY GAME.
I'LL COME WATCH. I'VE NEVER SEEN A LIVE HOCKEY GAME BEFORE.
IT'S GONNA BE A TERRIBLE GAME. WE'RE PLAYING NANAIMO AND WE ALWAYS BEAT THEM. LAST TIME WE WON EIGHT TO ZERO.
HIGH SCHOOL
OUCH.
YEAH, I FEEL BAD FOR THEM. WE'RE THE ONLY TWO GIRLS' HOCKEY TEAMS ON THE ISLAND, BUT THEY HAVEN'T WON A GAME THIS SEASON.

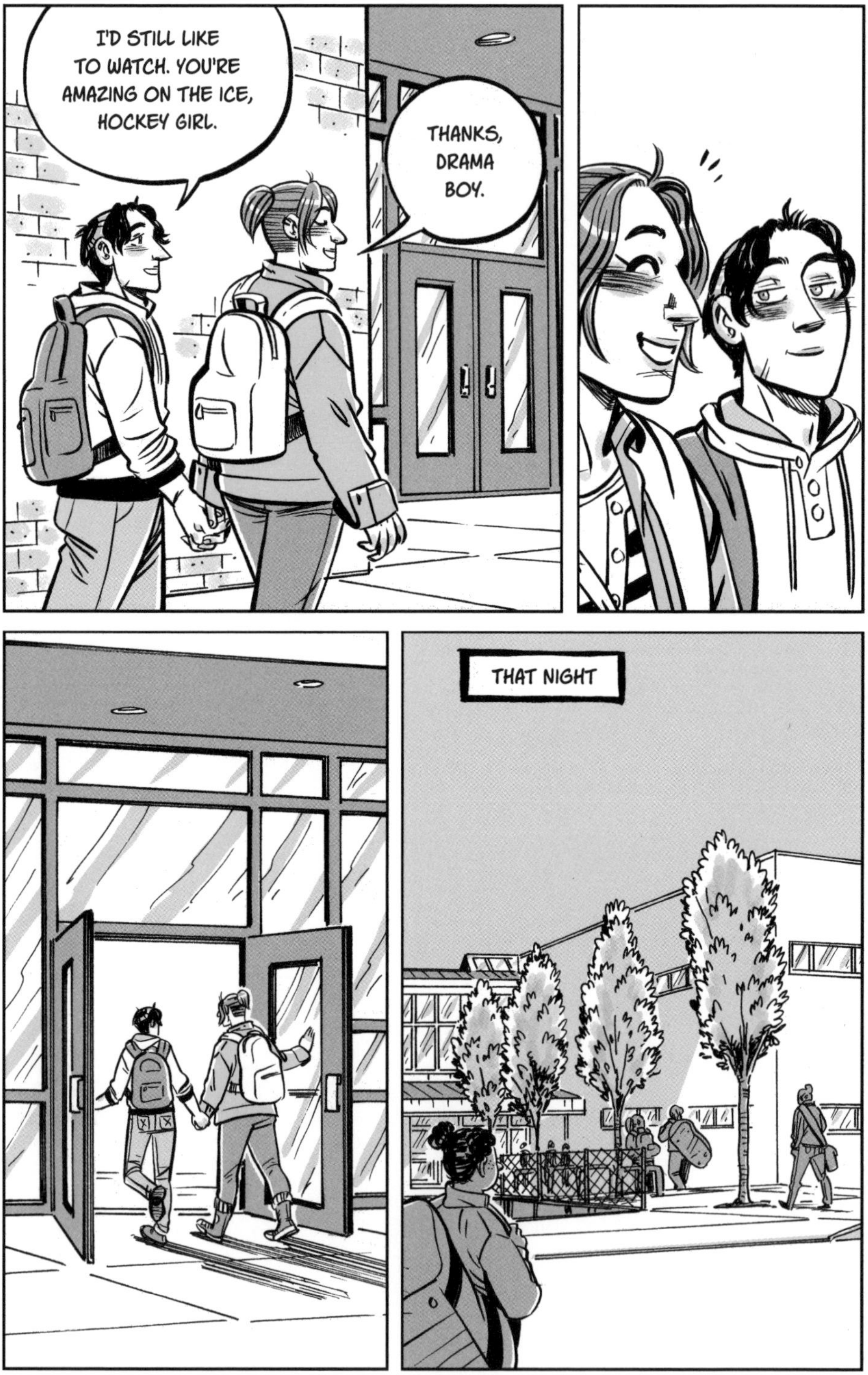
I'D STILL LIKE TO WATCH. YOU'RE AMAZING ON THE ICE, HOCKEY GIRL.
THANKS, DRAMA BOY.
THAT NIGHT

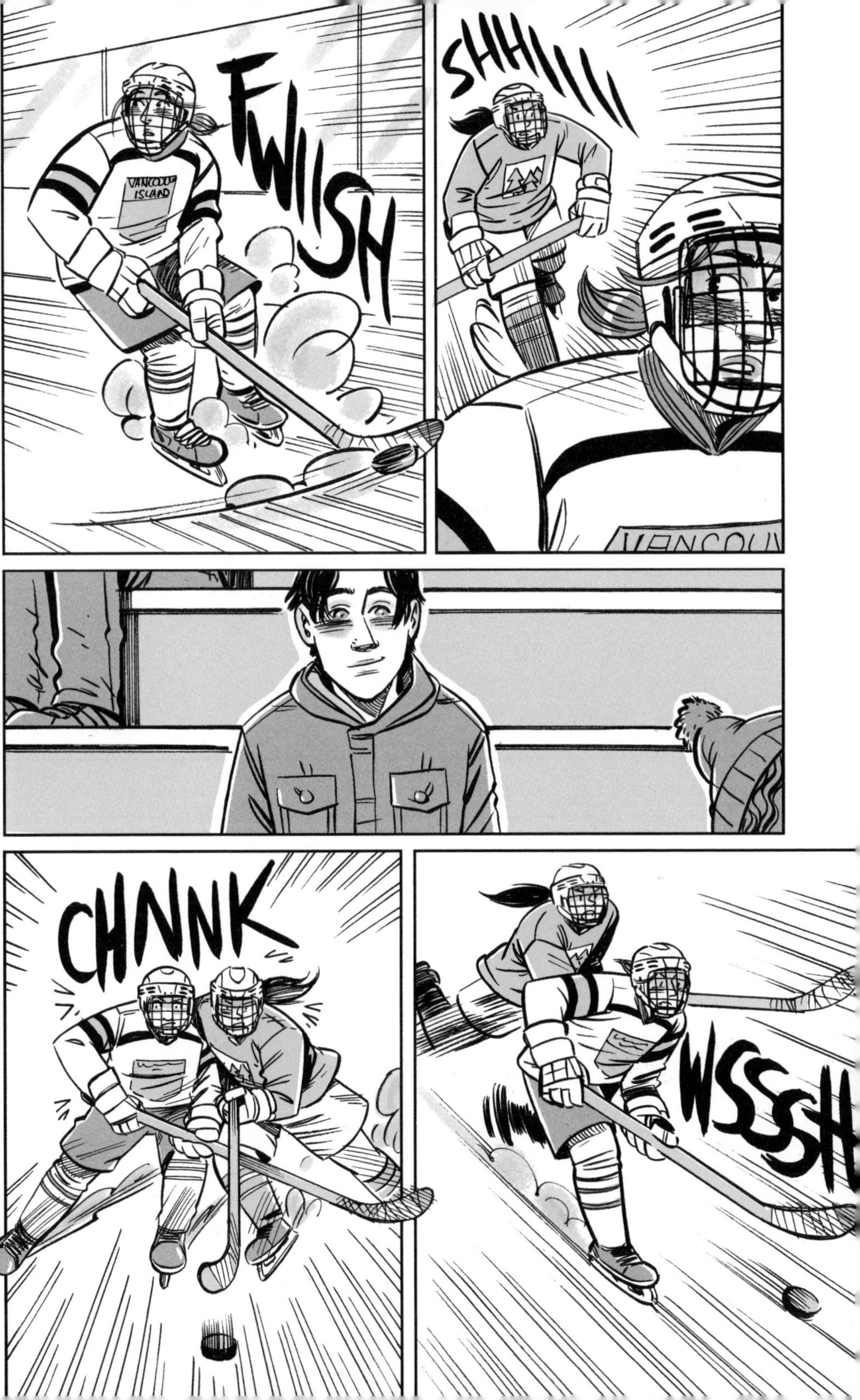
FWIISH
VANCOUVER ISLAND
SHHIIIII
VANCOU
CHNNK
WSSSH

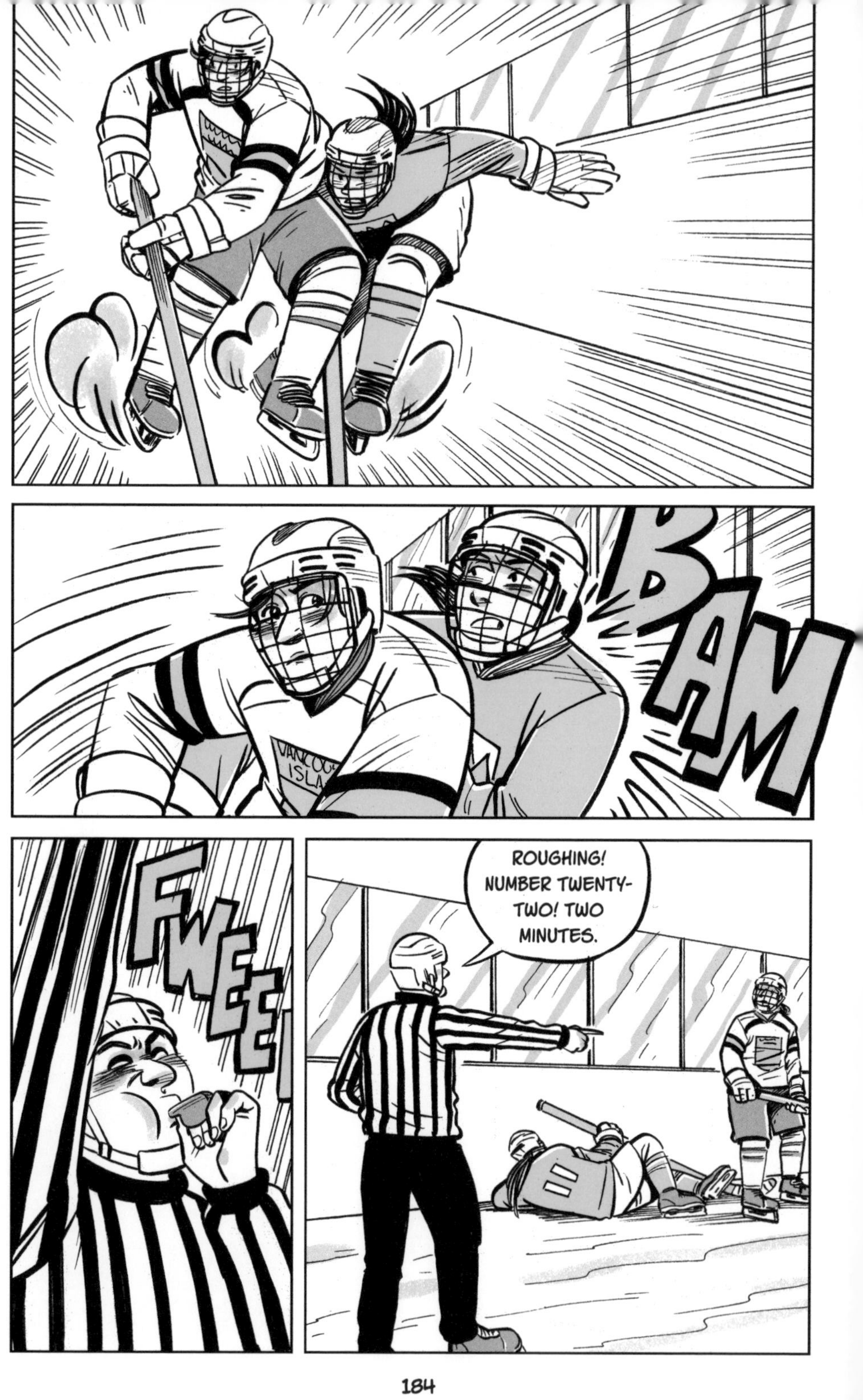
BAM
FWEE
ROUGHING! NUMBER TWENTY-TWO! TWO MINUTES.

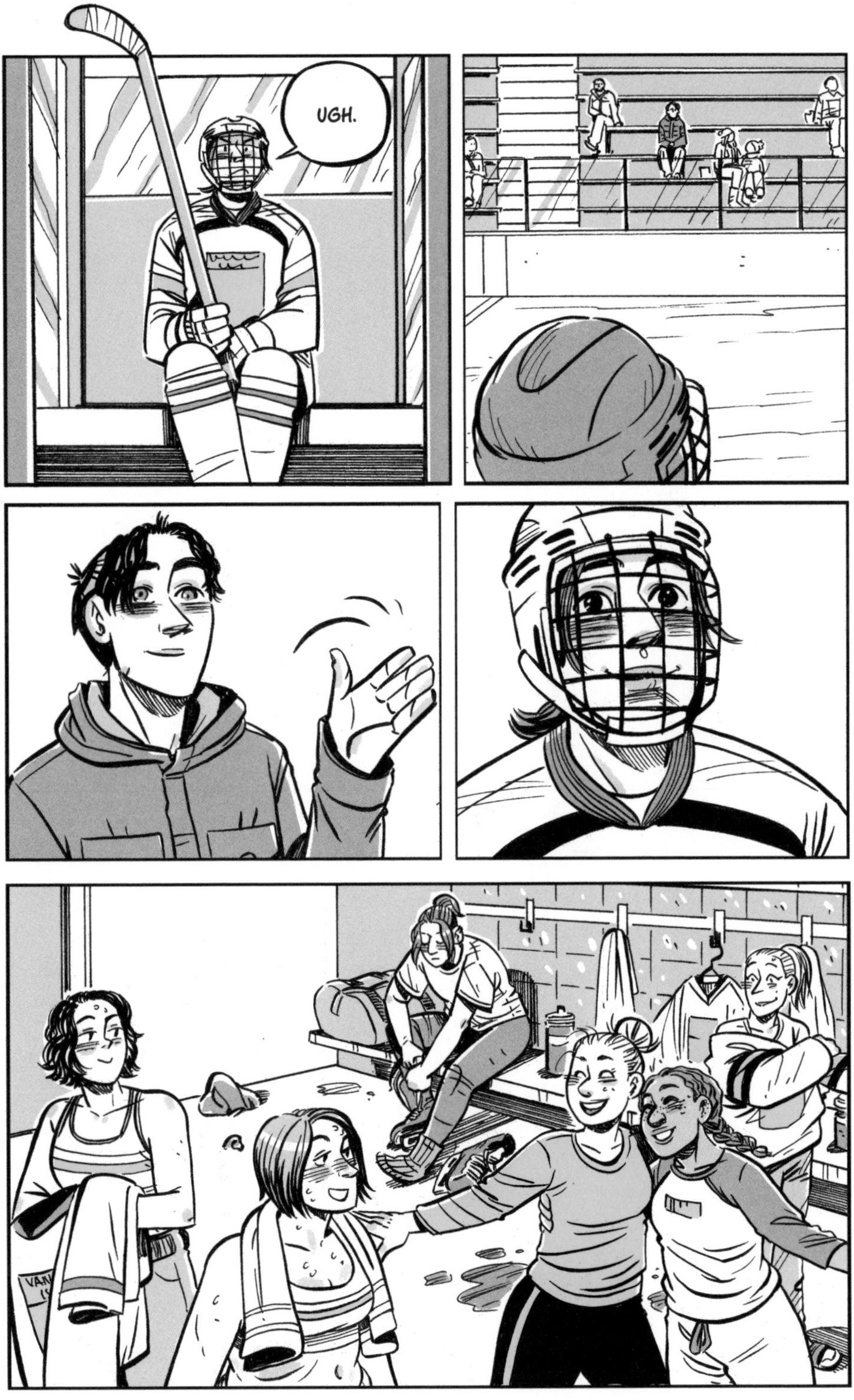
UGH.

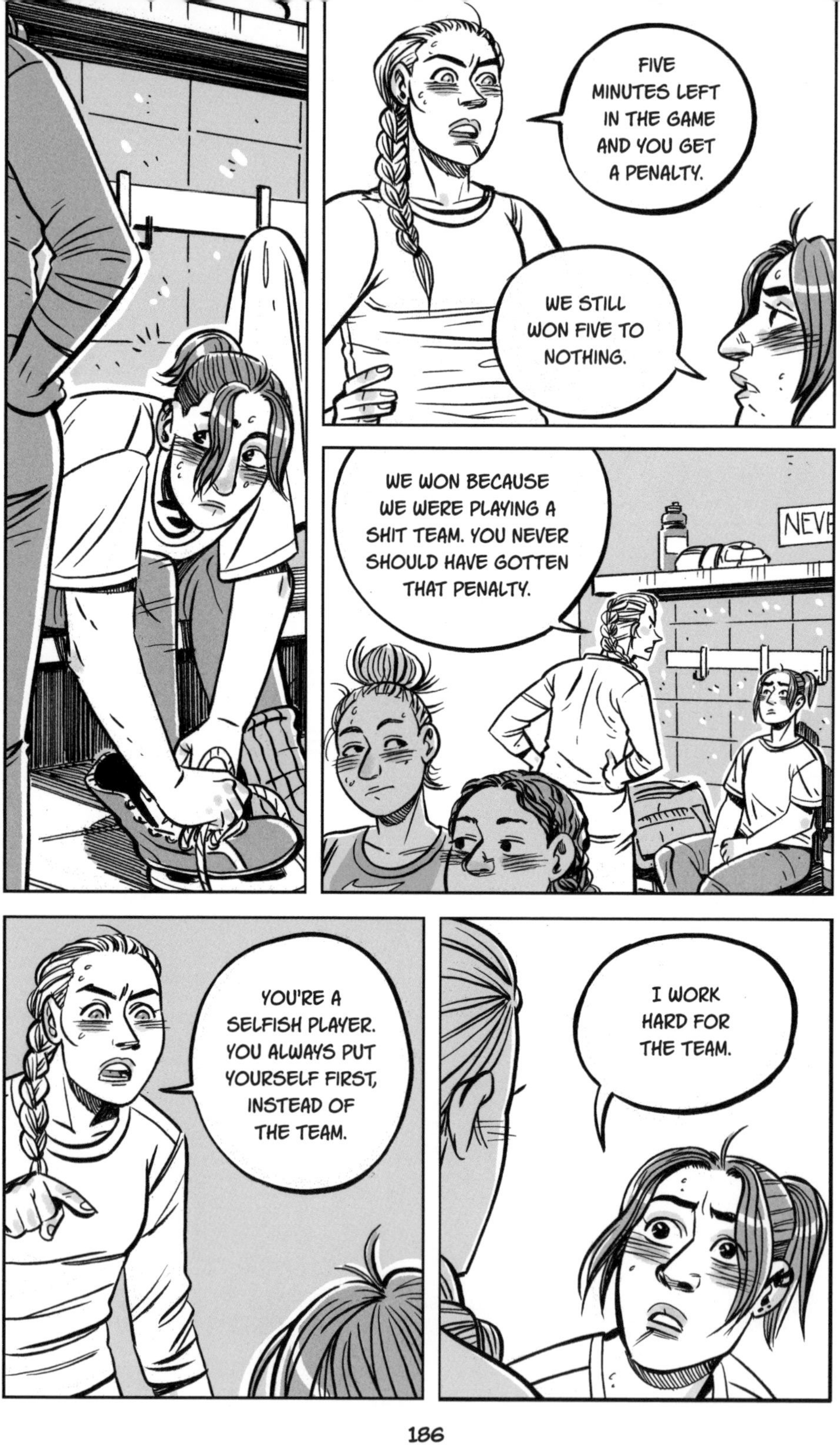
FIVE MINUTES LEFT IN THE GAME AND YOU GET A PENALTY.
WE STILL WON FIVE TO NOTHING.
WE WON BECAUSE WE WERE PLAYING A SHIT TEAM. YOU NEVER SHOULD HAVE GOTTEN THAT PENALTY.
NEV
YOU'RE A SELFISH PLAYER. YOU ALWAYS PUT YOURSELF FIRST, INSTEAD OF THE TEAM.
I WORK HARD FOR THE TEAM.

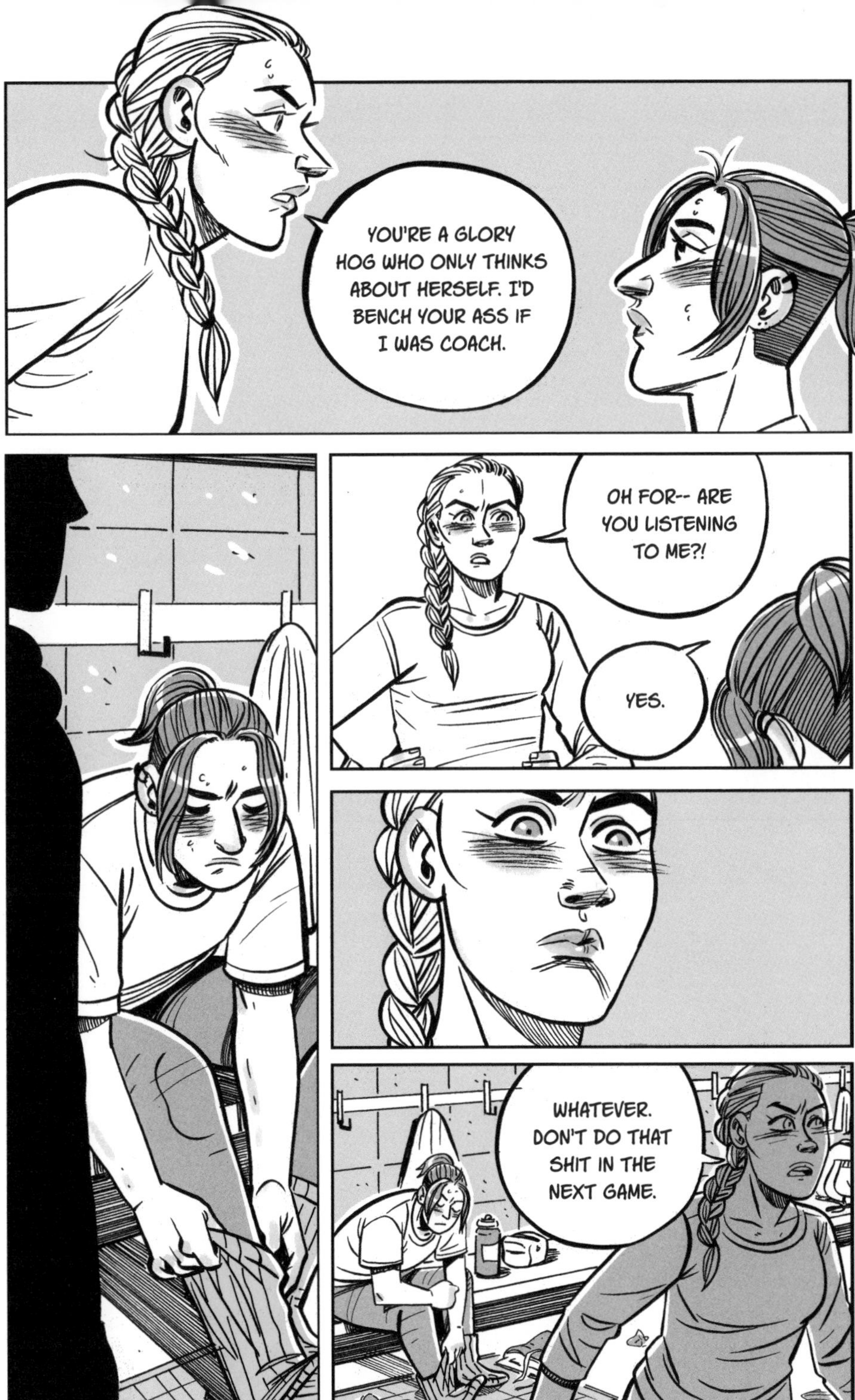
YOU'RE A GLORY HOG WHO ONLY THINKS ABOUT HERSELF. I'D BENCH YOUR ASS IF I WAS COACH.
OH FOR-- ARE YOU LISTENING TO ME?!
YES.
WHATEVER. DON'T DO THAT SHIT IN THE NEXT GAME.

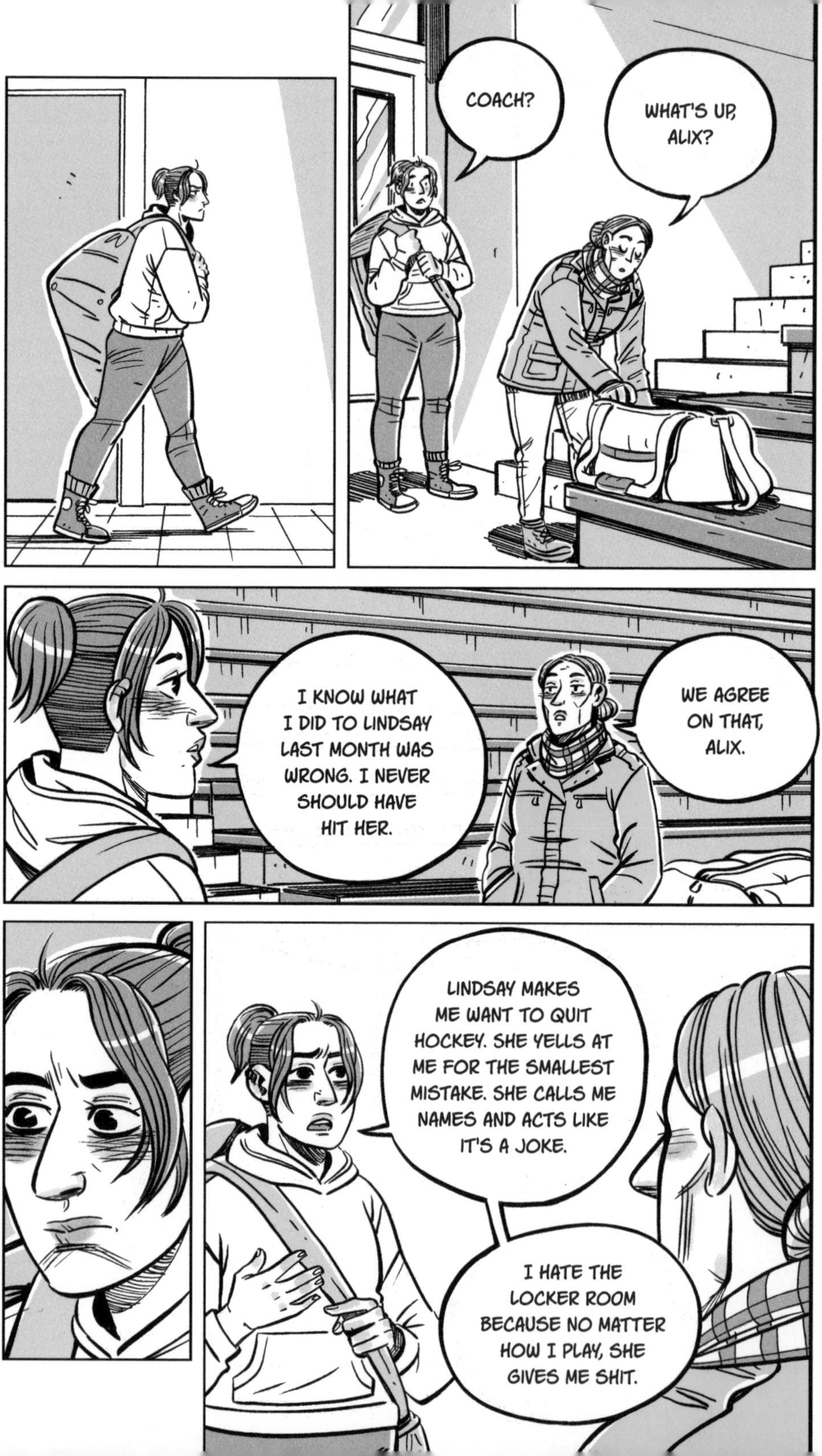
COACH?
WHAT'S UP, ALIX?
I KNOW WHAT I DID TO LINDSAY LAST MONTH WAS WRONG. I NEVER SHOULD HAVE HIT HER.
WE AGREE ON THAT, ALIX.
LINDSAY MAKES ME WANT TO QUIT HOCKEY. SHE YELLS AT ME FOR THE SMALLEST MISTAKE. SHE CALLS ME NAMES AND ACTS LIKE IT'S A JOKE.
I HATE THE LOCKER ROOM BECAUSE NO MATTER HOW I PLAY, SHE GIVES ME SHIT.

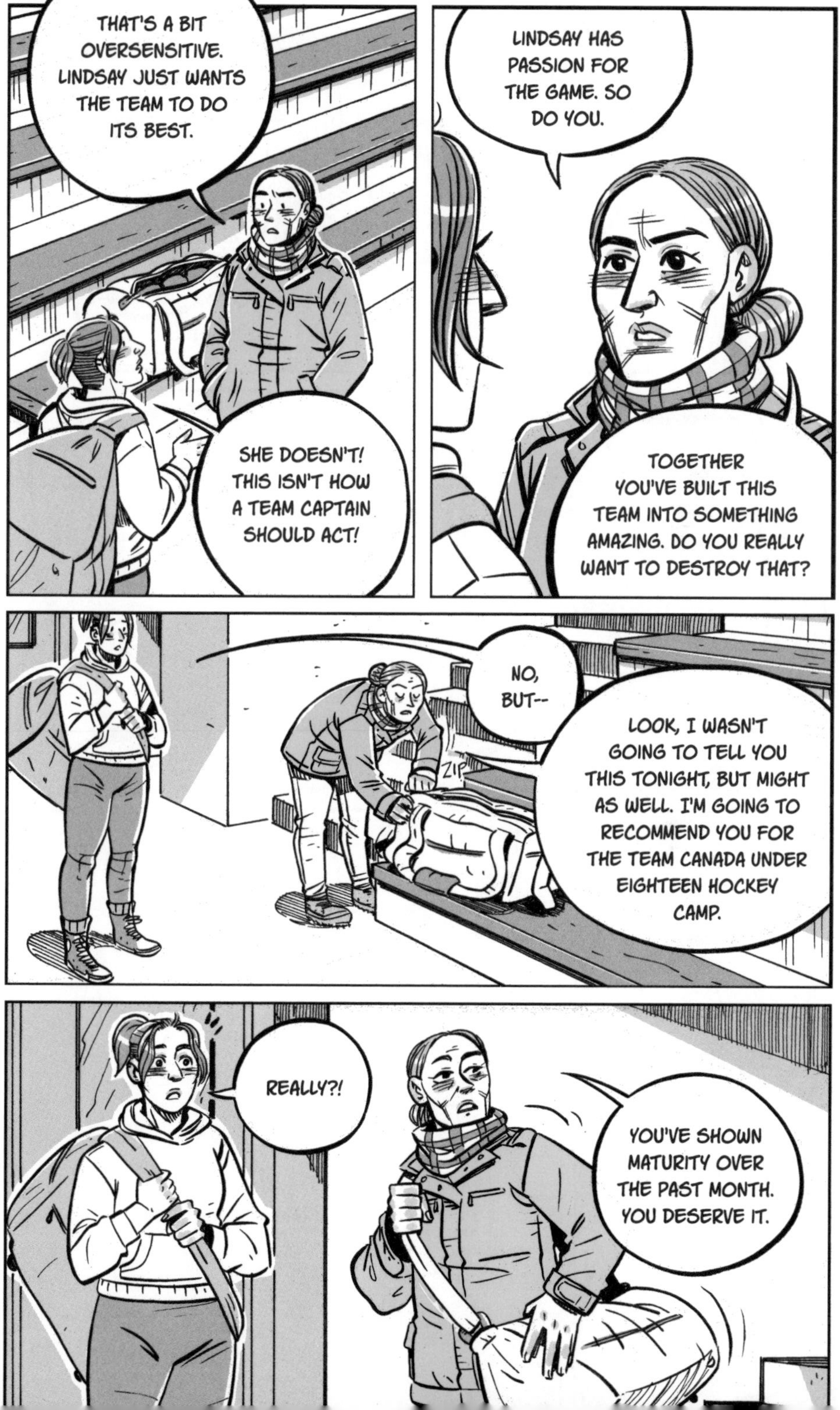
THAT'S A BIT OVERSENSITIVE. LINDSAY JUST WANTS THE TEAM TO DO ITS BEST.
SHE DOESN'T! THIS ISN'T HOW A TEAM CAPTAIN SHOULD ACT!
LINDSAY HAS PASSION FOR THE GAME. SO DO YOU.
TOGETHER YOU'VE BUILT THIS TEAM INTO SOMETHING AMAZING. DO YOU REALLY WANT TO DESTROY THAT?
NO, BUT--
ZIP
LOOK, I WASN'T GOING TO TELL YOU THIS TONIGHT, BUT MIGHT AS WELL. I'M GOING TO RECOMMEND YOU FOR THE TEAM CANADA UNDER EIGHTEEN HOCKEY CAMP.
REALLY?!
YOU'VE SHOWN MATURITY OVER THE PAST MONTH. YOU DESERVE IT.

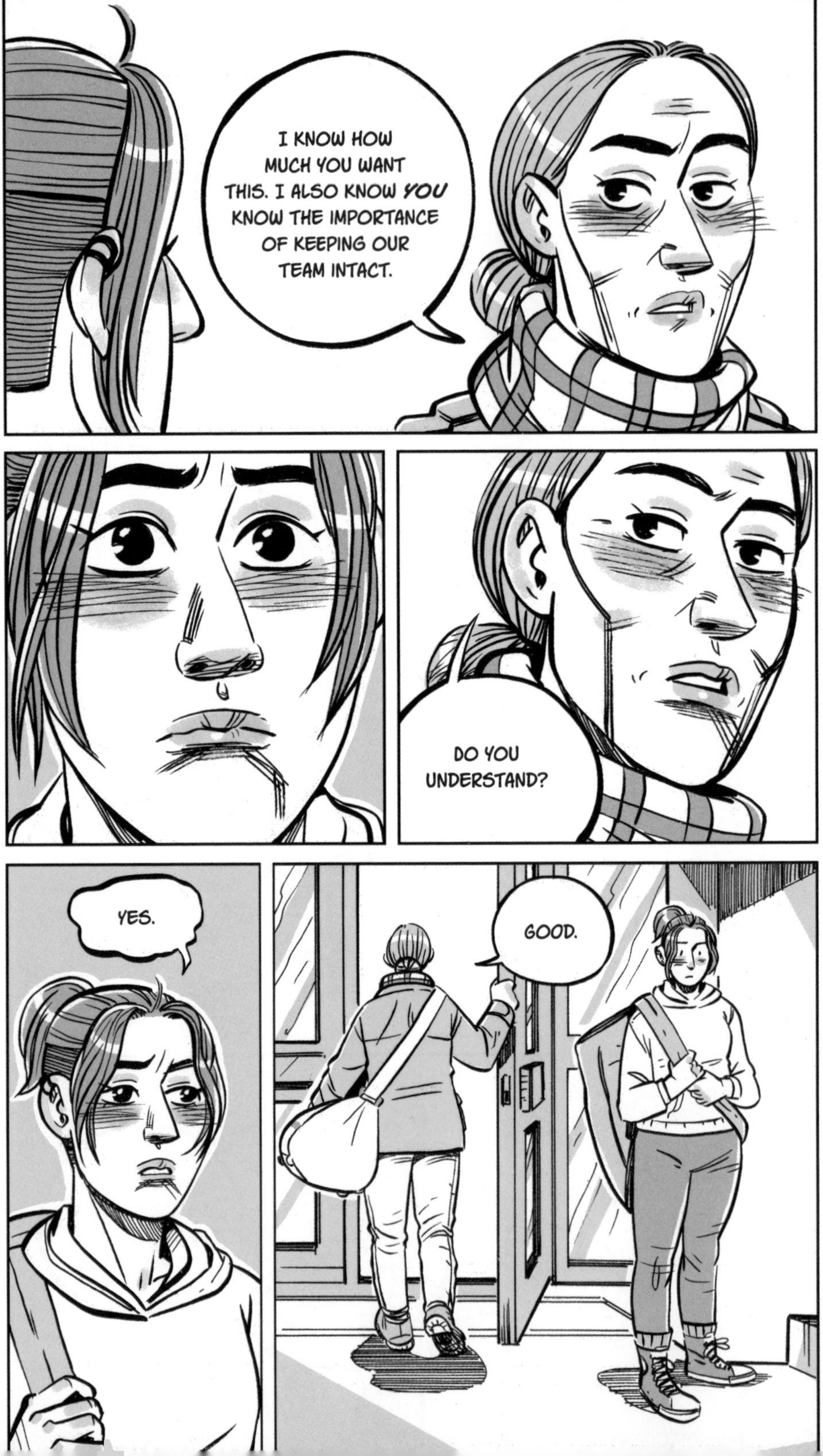
I KNOW HOW MUCH YOU WANT THIS. I ALSO KNOW *YOU* KNOW THE IMPORTANCE OF KEEPING OUR TEAM INTACT.
DO YOU UNDERSTAND?
YES.
GOOD.

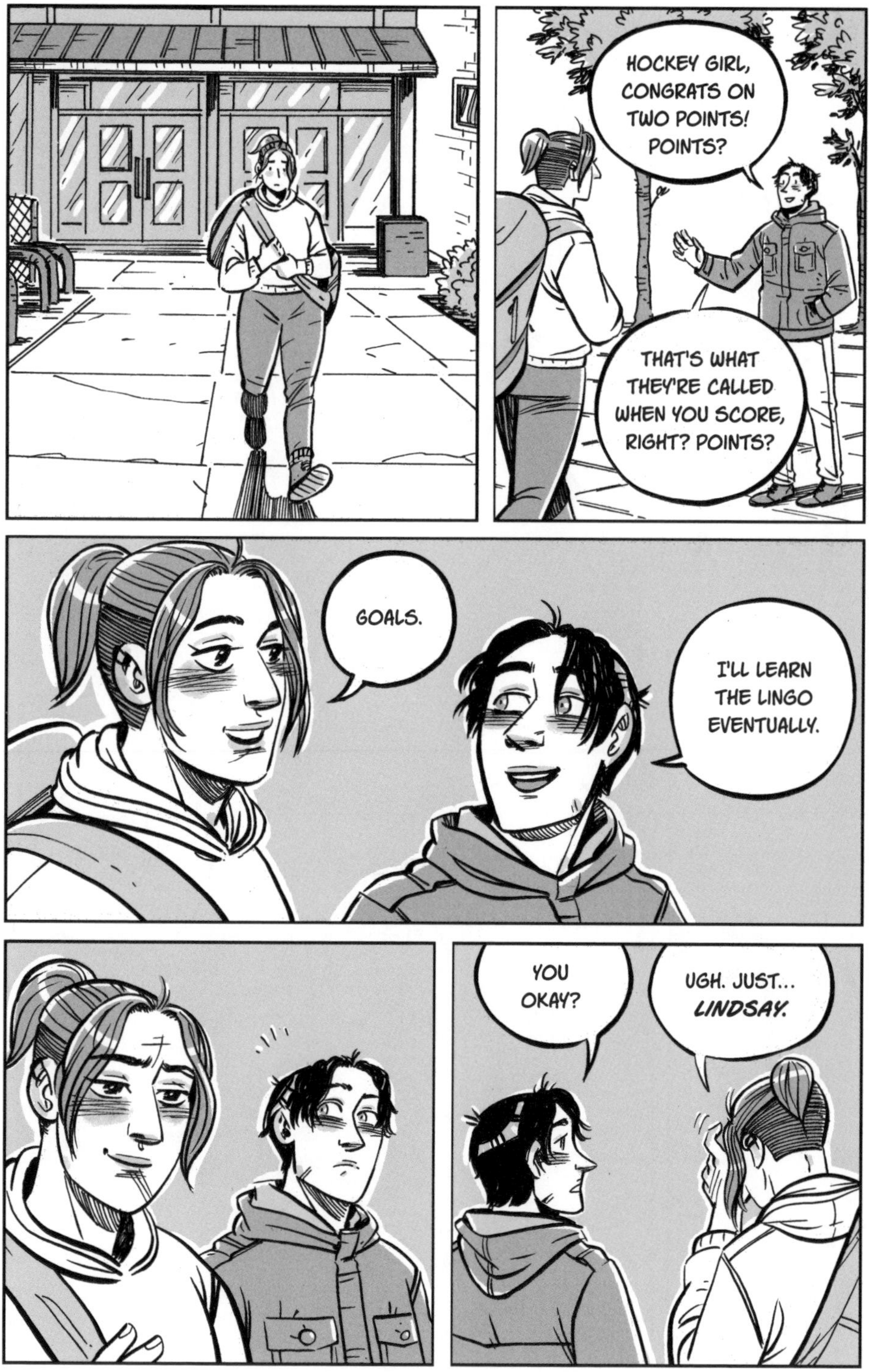
HOCKEY GIRL, CONGRATS ON TWO POINTS! POINTS?
THAT'S WHAT THEY'RE CALLED WHEN YOU SCORE, RIGHT? POINTS?
GOALS.
I'LL LEARN THE LINGO EVENTUALLY.
YOU OKAY?
UGH. JUST... *LINDSAY.*

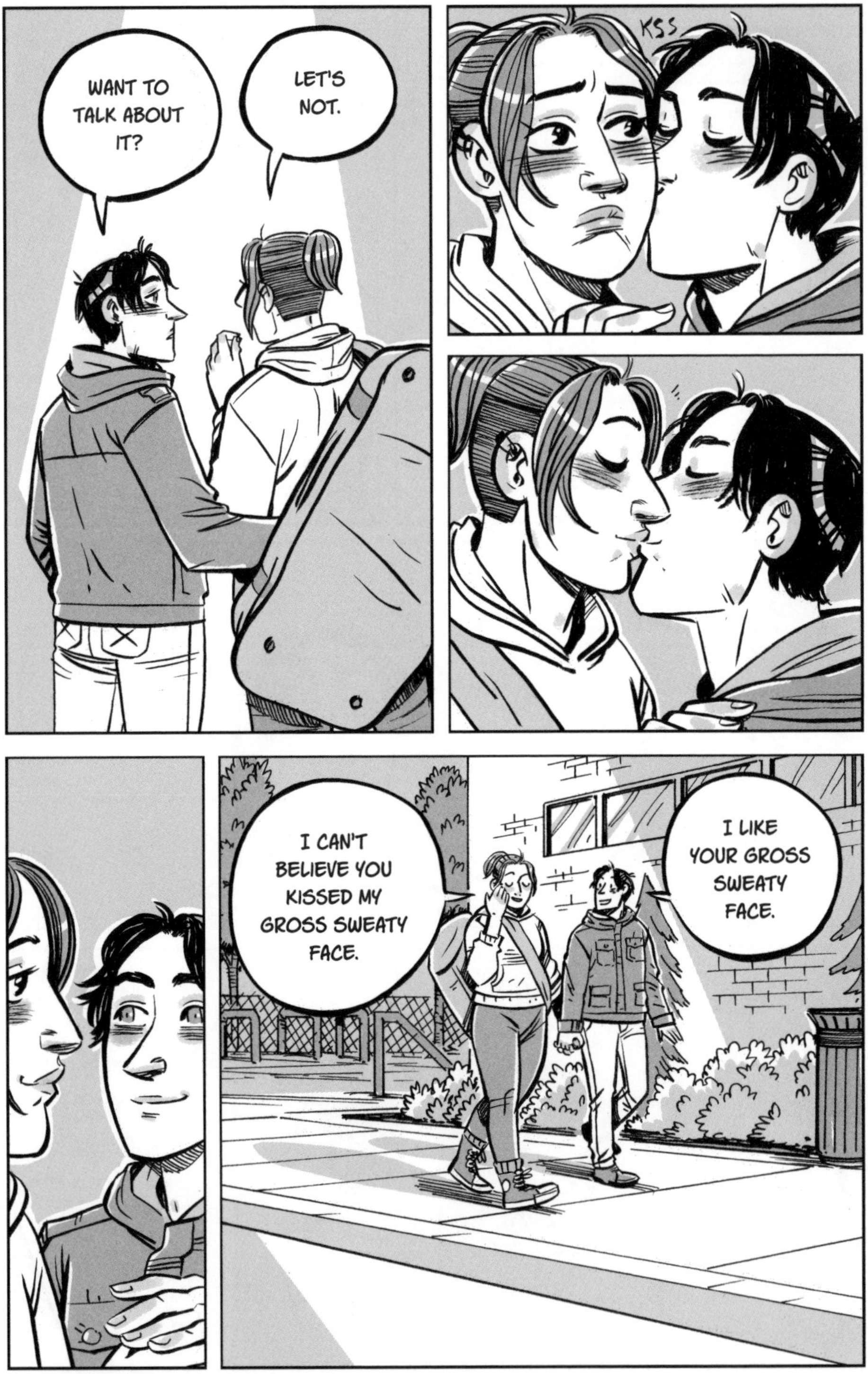
WANT TO TALK ABOUT IT?
LET'S NOT.
KSS
I CAN'T BELIEVE YOU KISSED MY GROSS SWEATY FACE.
I LIKE YOUR GROSS SWEATY FACE.

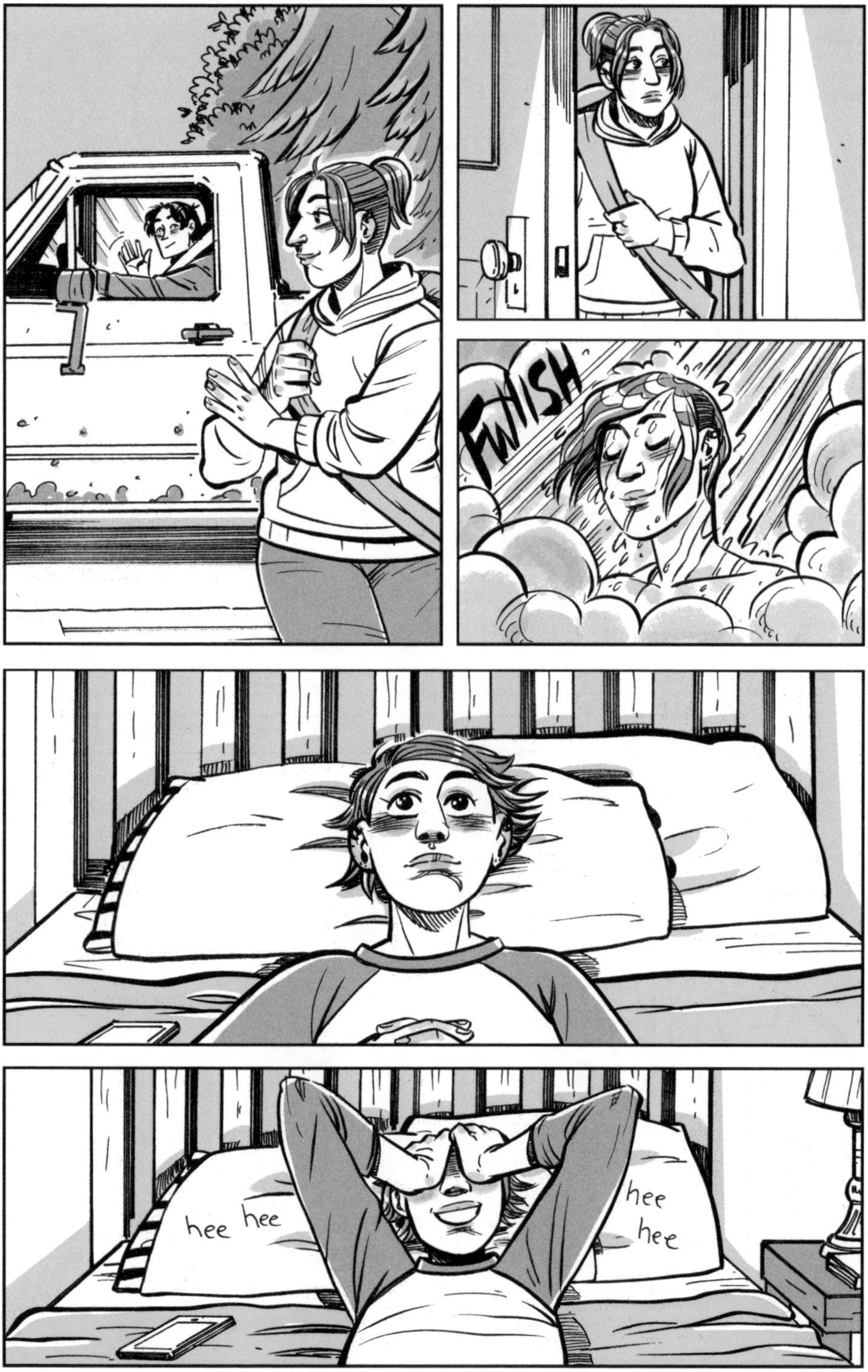
FWISH
hee hee
hee hee

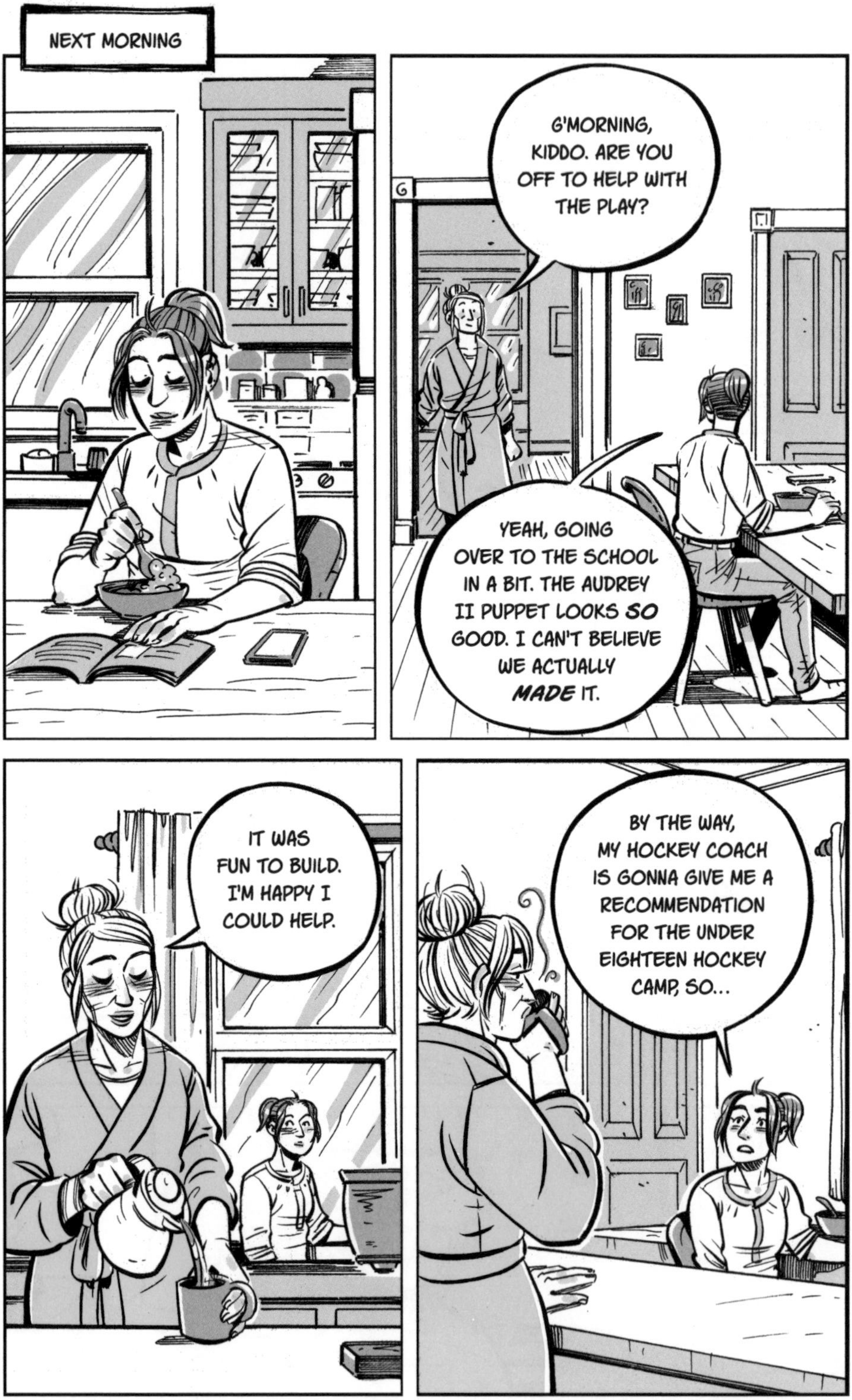
NEXT MORNING
G'MORNING, KIDDO. ARE YOU OFF TO HELP WITH THE PLAY?
YEAH, GOING OVER TO THE SCHOOL IN A BIT. THE AUDREY II PUPPET LOOKS SO GOOD. I CAN'T BELIEVE WE ACTUALLY MADE IT.
IT WAS FUN TO BUILD. I'M HAPPY I COULD HELP.
BY THE WAY, MY HOCKEY COACH IS GONNA GIVE ME A RECOMMENDATION FOR THE UNDER EIGHTEEN HOCKEY CAMP, SO...

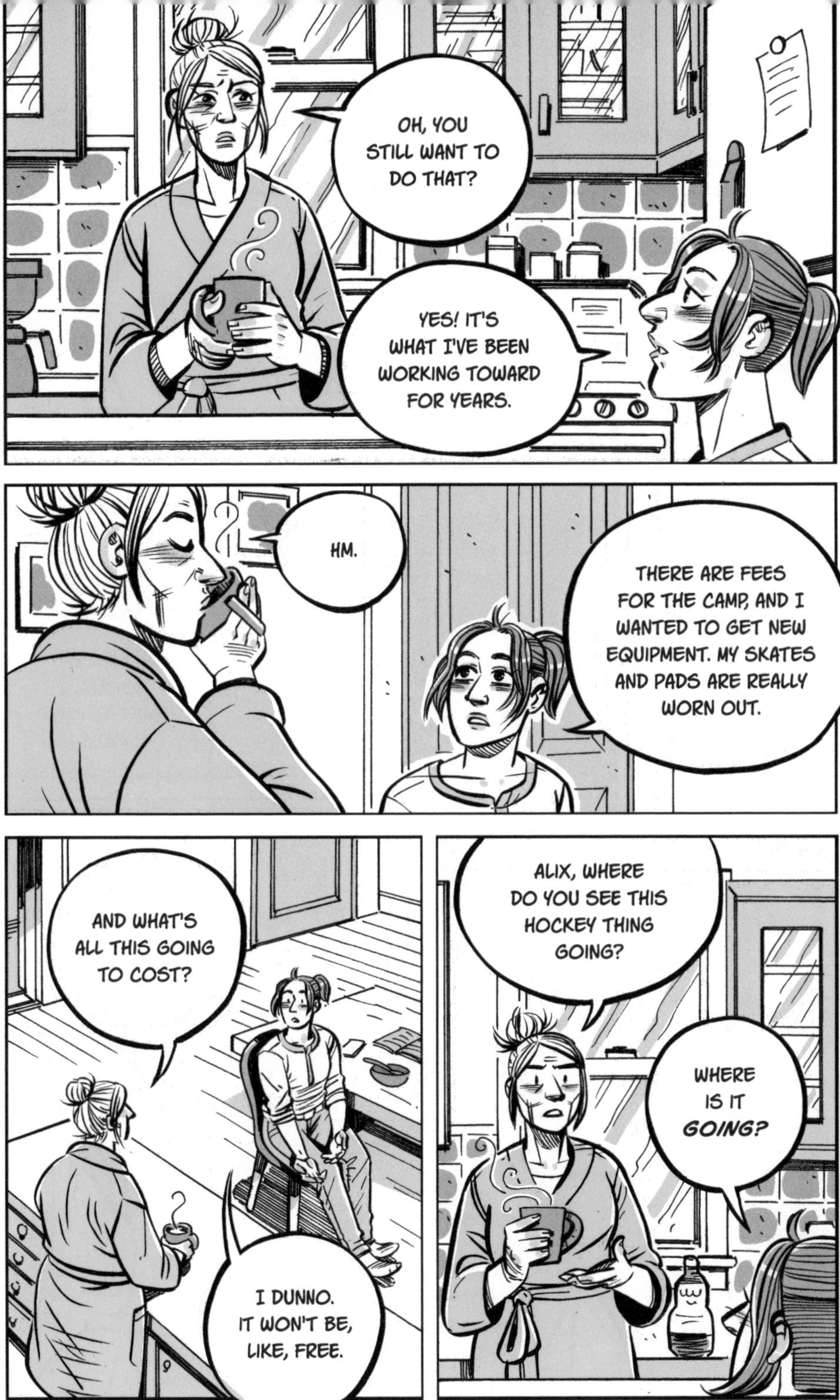
OH, YOU STILL WANT TO DO THAT?
YES! IT'S WHAT I'VE BEEN WORKING TOWARD FOR YEARS.
HM.
THERE ARE FEES FOR THE CAMP, AND I WANTED TO GET NEW EQUIPMENT. MY SKATES AND PADS ARE REALLY WORN OUT.
AND WHAT'S ALL THIS GOING TO COST?
I DUNNO. IT WON'T BE, LIKE, FREE.
ALIX, WHERE DO YOU SEE THIS HOCKEY THING GOING?
WHERE IS IT *GOING?*

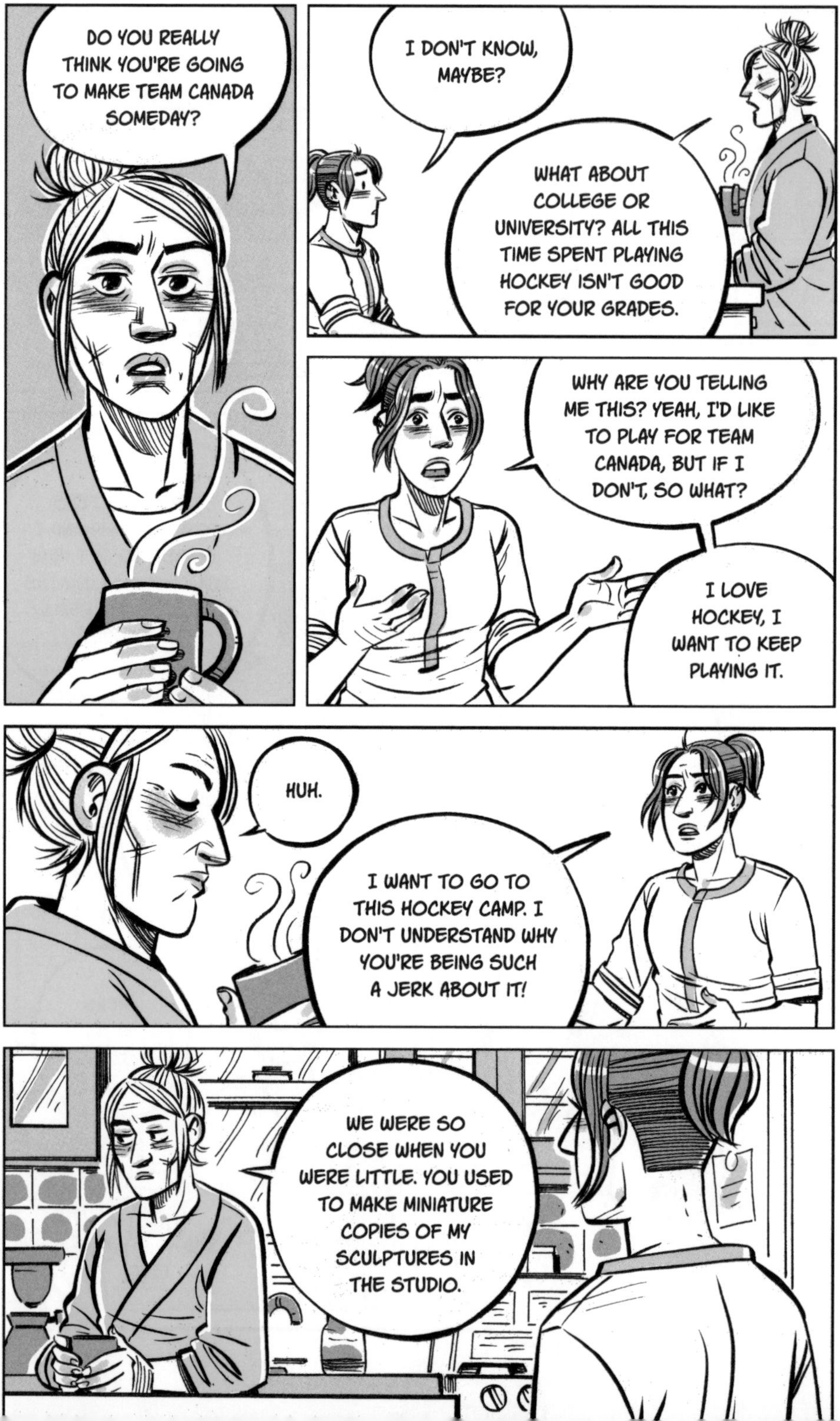
DO YOU REALLY THINK YOU'RE GOING TO MAKE TEAM CANADA SOMEDAY?
I DON'T KNOW, MAYBE?
WHAT ABOUT COLLEGE OR UNIVERSITY? ALL THIS TIME SPENT PLAYING HOCKEY ISN'T GOOD FOR YOUR GRADES.
WHY ARE YOU TELLING ME THIS? YEAH, I'D LIKE TO PLAY FOR TEAM CANADA, BUT IF I DON'T, SO WHAT?
I LOVE HOCKEY, I WANT TO KEEP PLAYING IT.
HUH.
I WANT TO GO TO THIS HOCKEY CAMP. I DON'T UNDERSTAND WHY YOU'RE BEING SUCH A JERK ABOUT IT!
WE WERE SO CLOSE WHEN YOU WERE LITTLE. YOU USED TO MAKE MINIATURE COPIES OF MY SCULPTURES IN THE STUDIO.

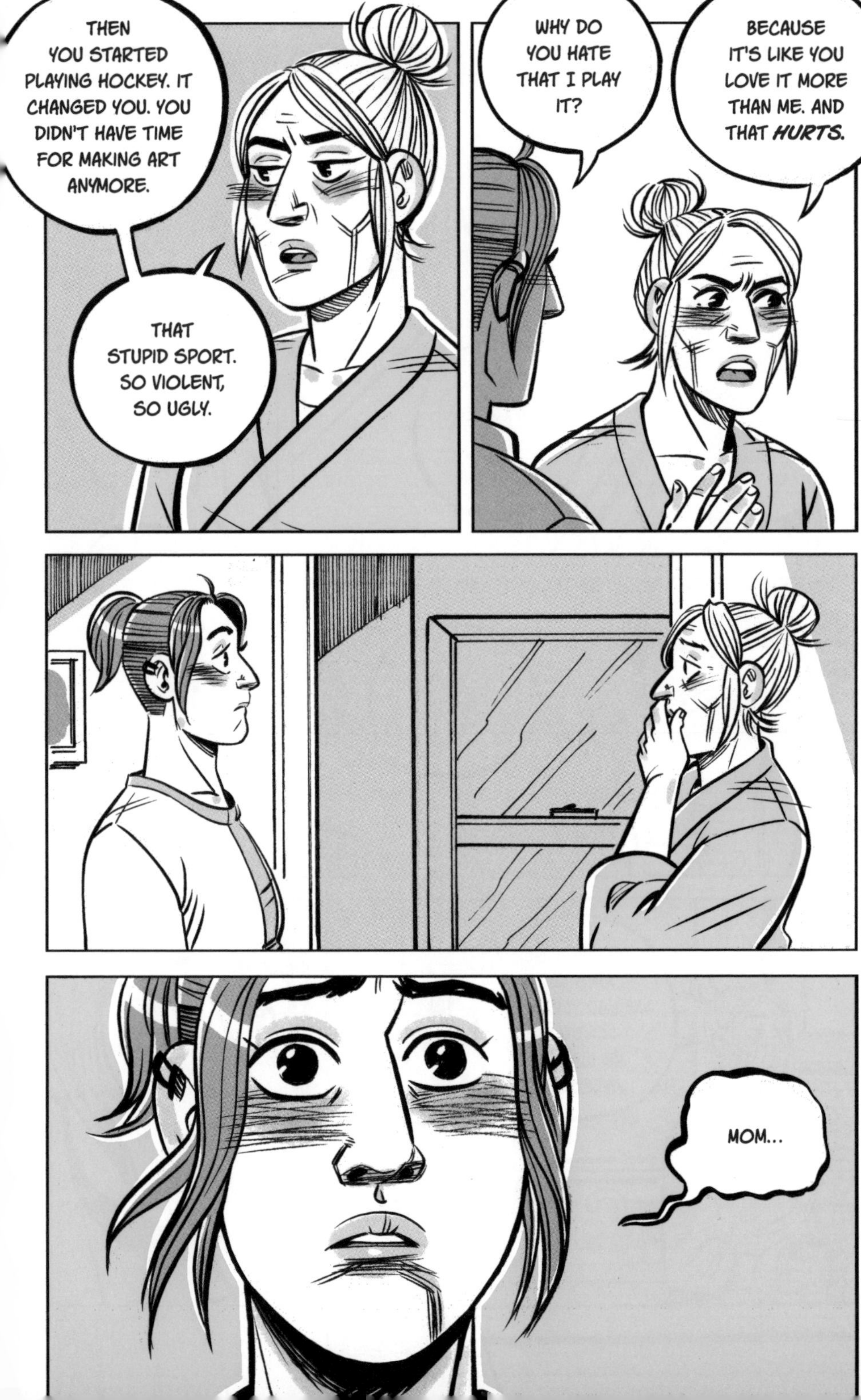
THEN YOU STARTED PLAYING HOCKEY. IT CHANGED YOU. YOU DIDN'T HAVE TIME FOR MAKING ART ANYMORE.
THAT STUPID SPORT. SO VIOLENT, SO UGLY.
WHY DO YOU HATE THAT I PLAY IT?
BECAUSE IT'S LIKE YOU LOVE IT MORE THAN ME. AND THAT *HURTS*.
MOM...

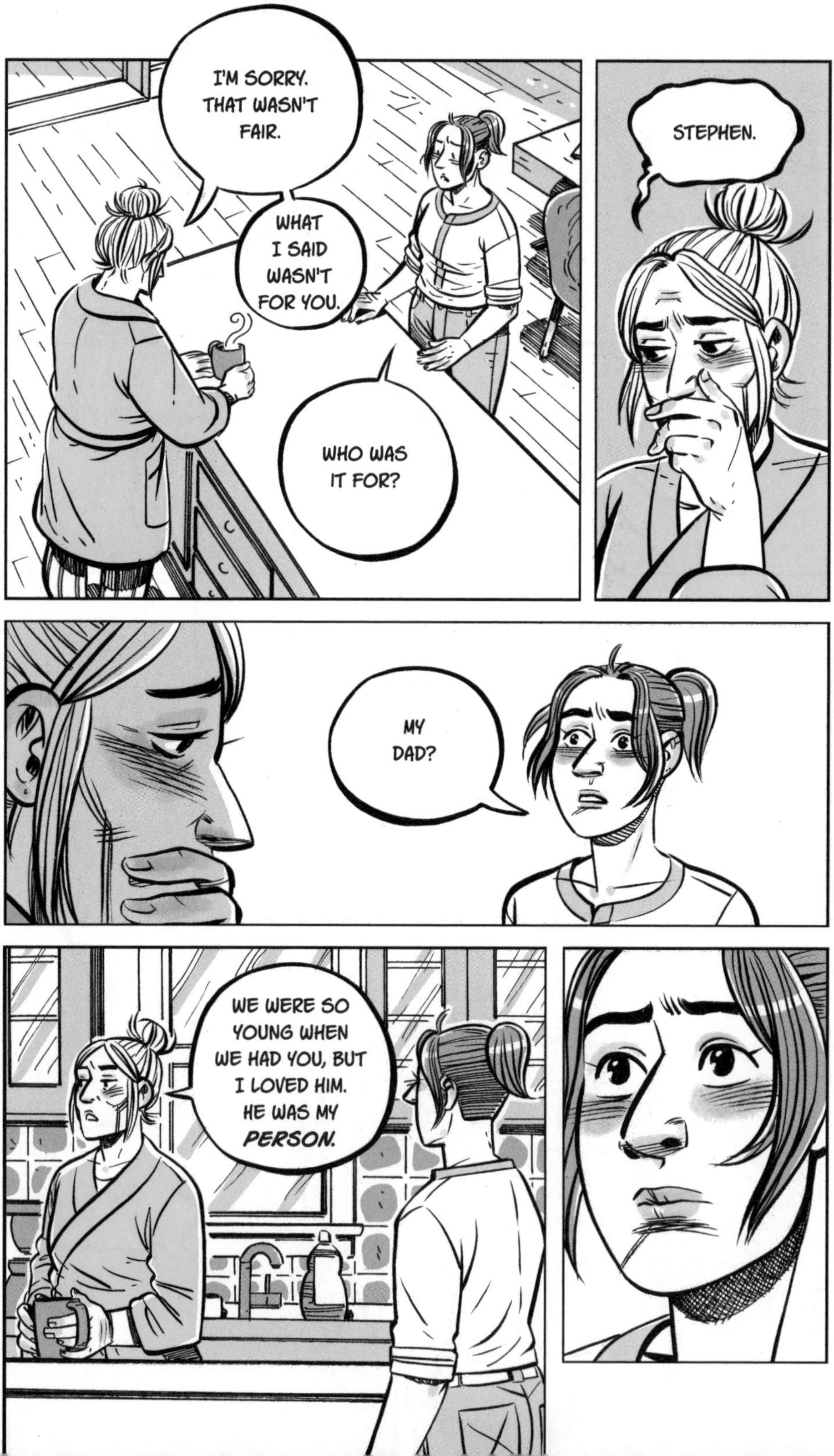
I'M SORRY. THAT WASN'T FAIR.
WHAT I SAID WASN'T FOR YOU.
WHO WAS IT FOR?
STEPHEN.
MY DAD?
WE WERE SO YOUNG WHEN WE HAD YOU, BUT I LOVED HIM. HE WAS MY *PERSON*.

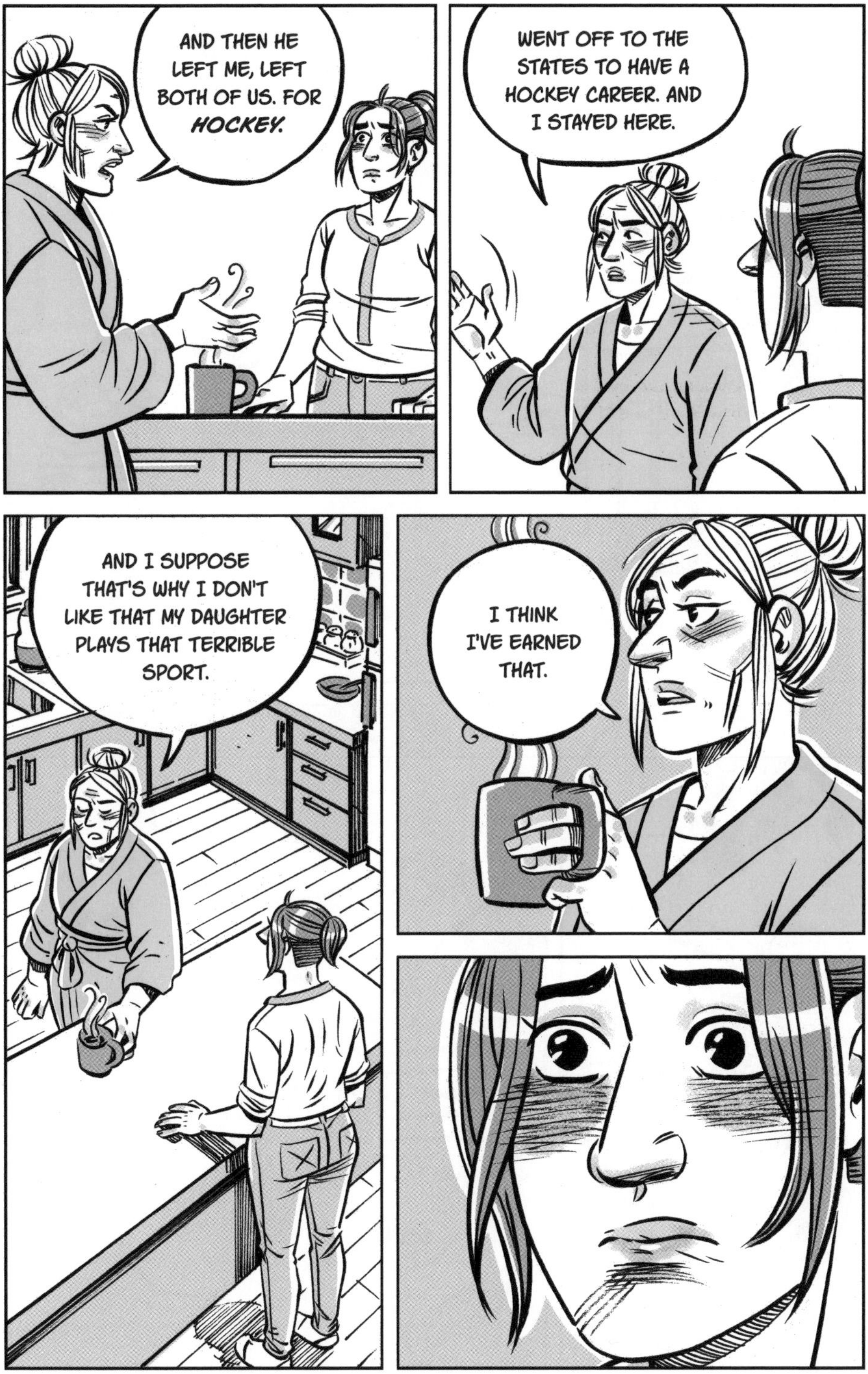
AND THEN HE LEFT ME, LEFT BOTH OF US. FOR *HOCKEY.*
WENT OFF TO THE STATES TO HAVE A HOCKEY CAREER. AND I STAYED HERE.
AND I SUPPOSE THAT'S WHY I DON'T LIKE THAT MY DAUGHTER PLAYS THAT TERRIBLE SPORT.
I THINK I'VE EARNED THAT.

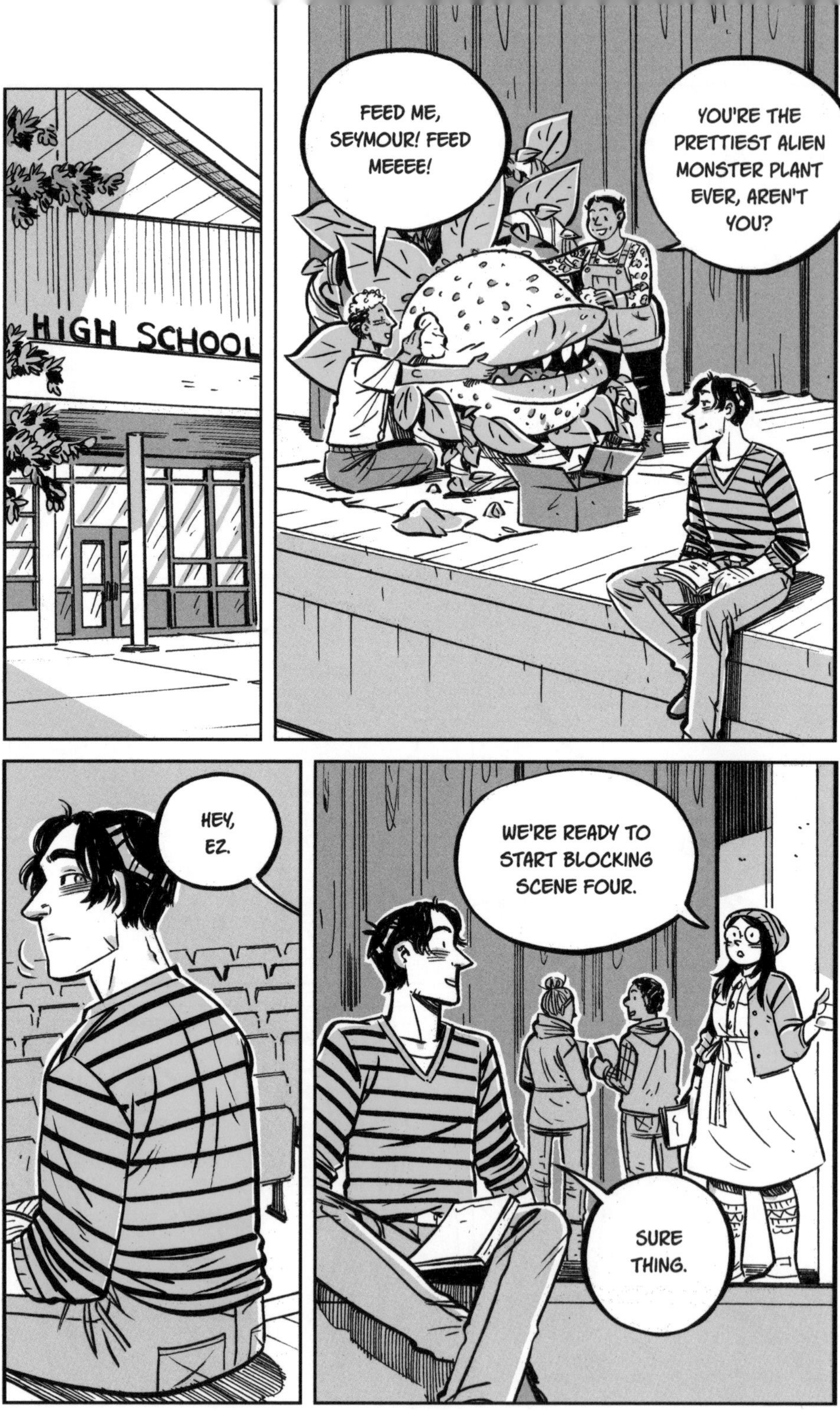
HIGH SCHOOL
FEED ME, SEYMOUR! FEED MEEEE!
YOU'RE THE PRETTIEST ALIEN MONSTER PLANT EVER, AREN'T YOU?
HEY, EZ.
WE'RE READY TO START BLOCKING SCENE FOUR.
SURE THING.

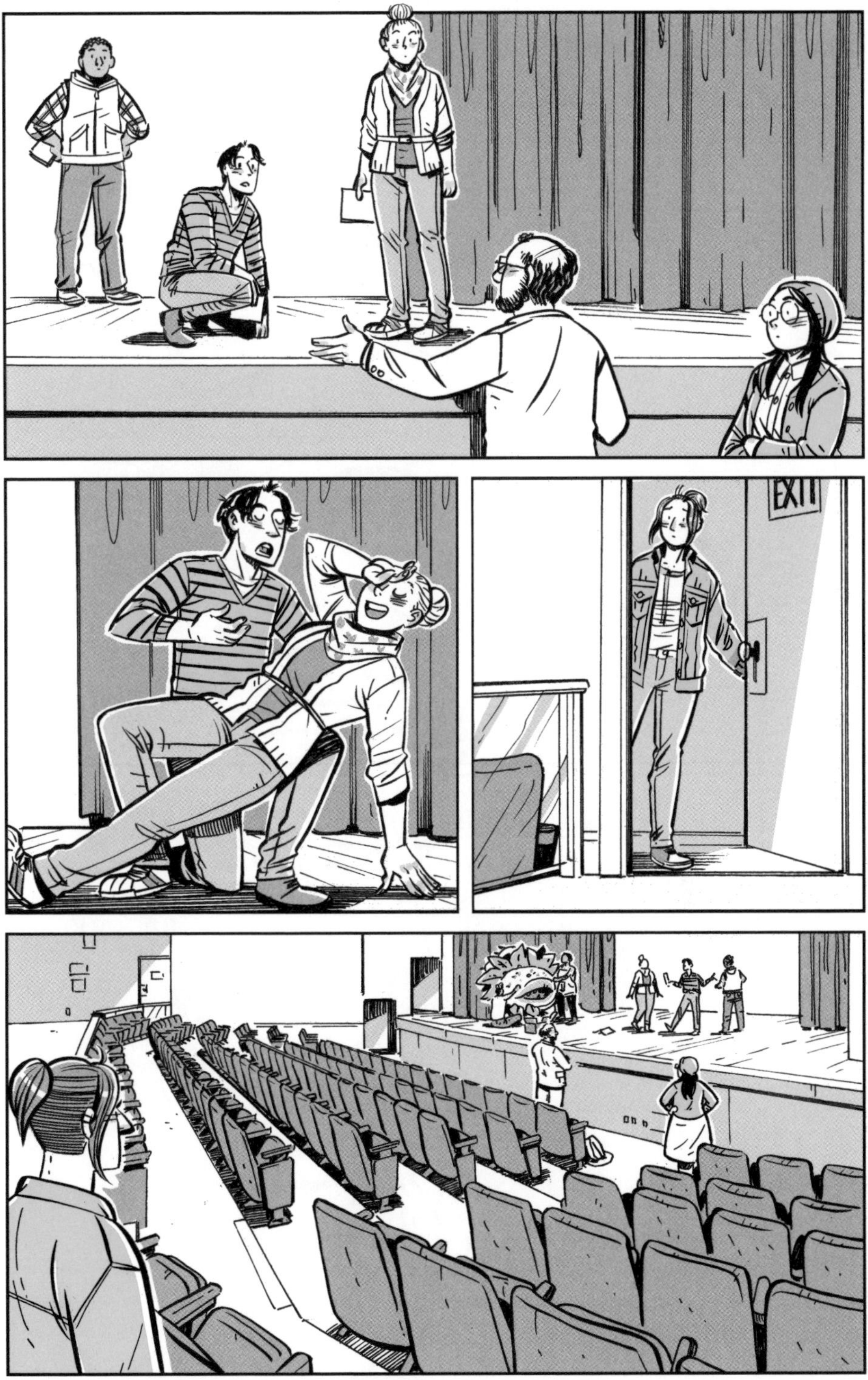
EXIT

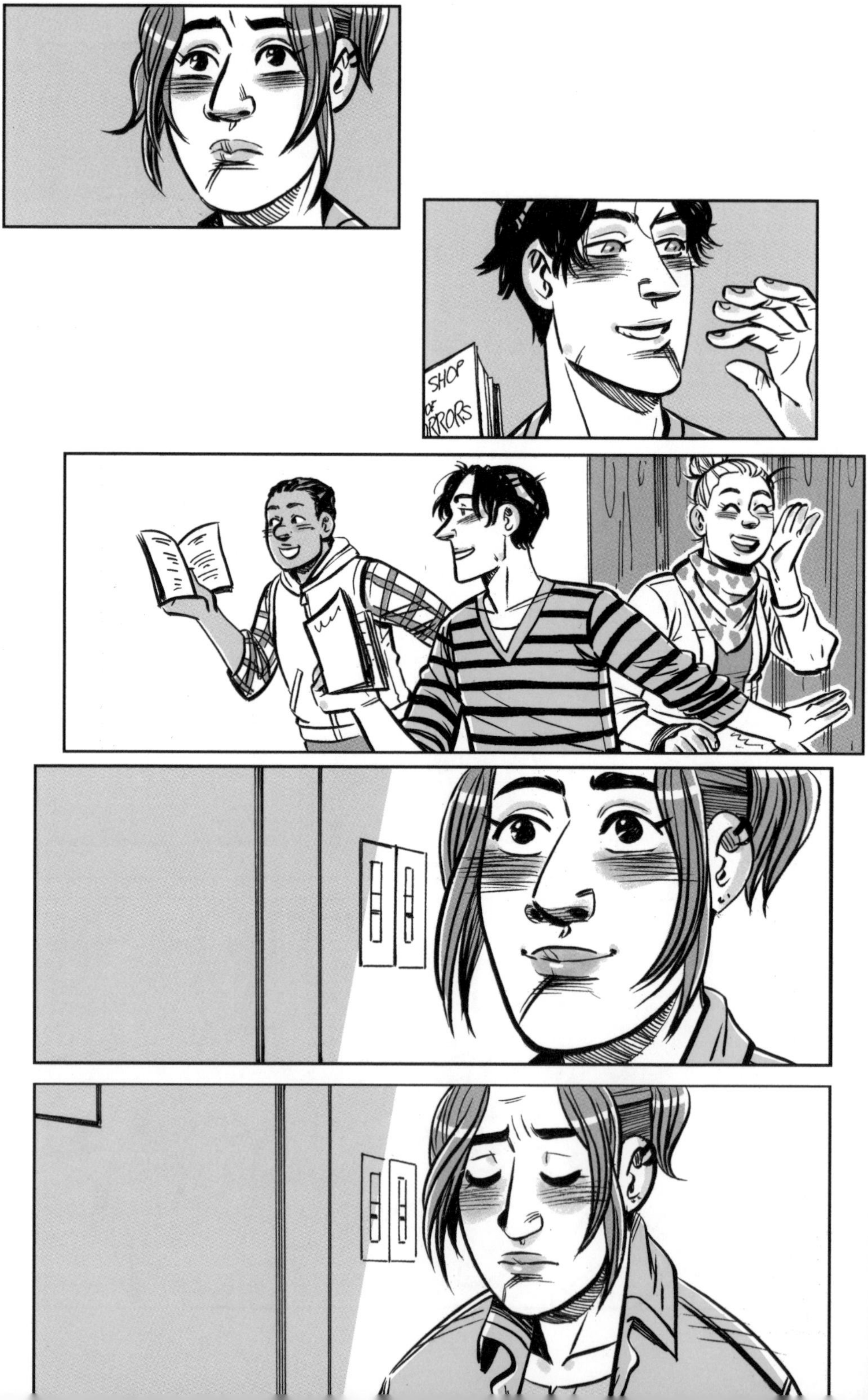
SHOP
OF
RRORS

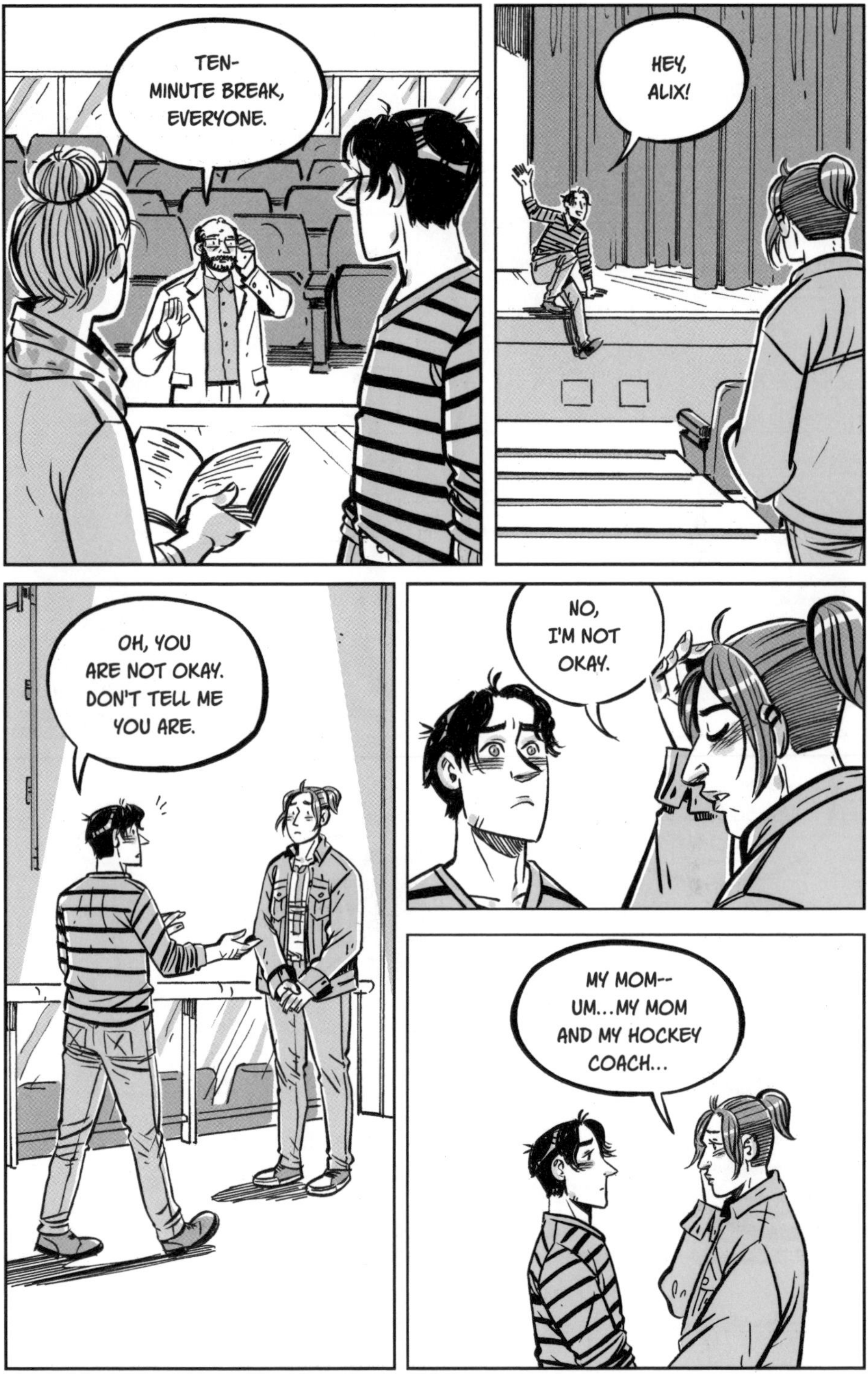
TEN-
MINUTE BREAK,
EVERYONE.
HEY,
ALIX!
OH, YOU
ARE NOT OKAY.
DON'T TELL ME
YOU ARE.
NO,
I'M NOT
OKAY.
MY MOM--
UM...MY MOM
AND MY HOCKEY
COACH...

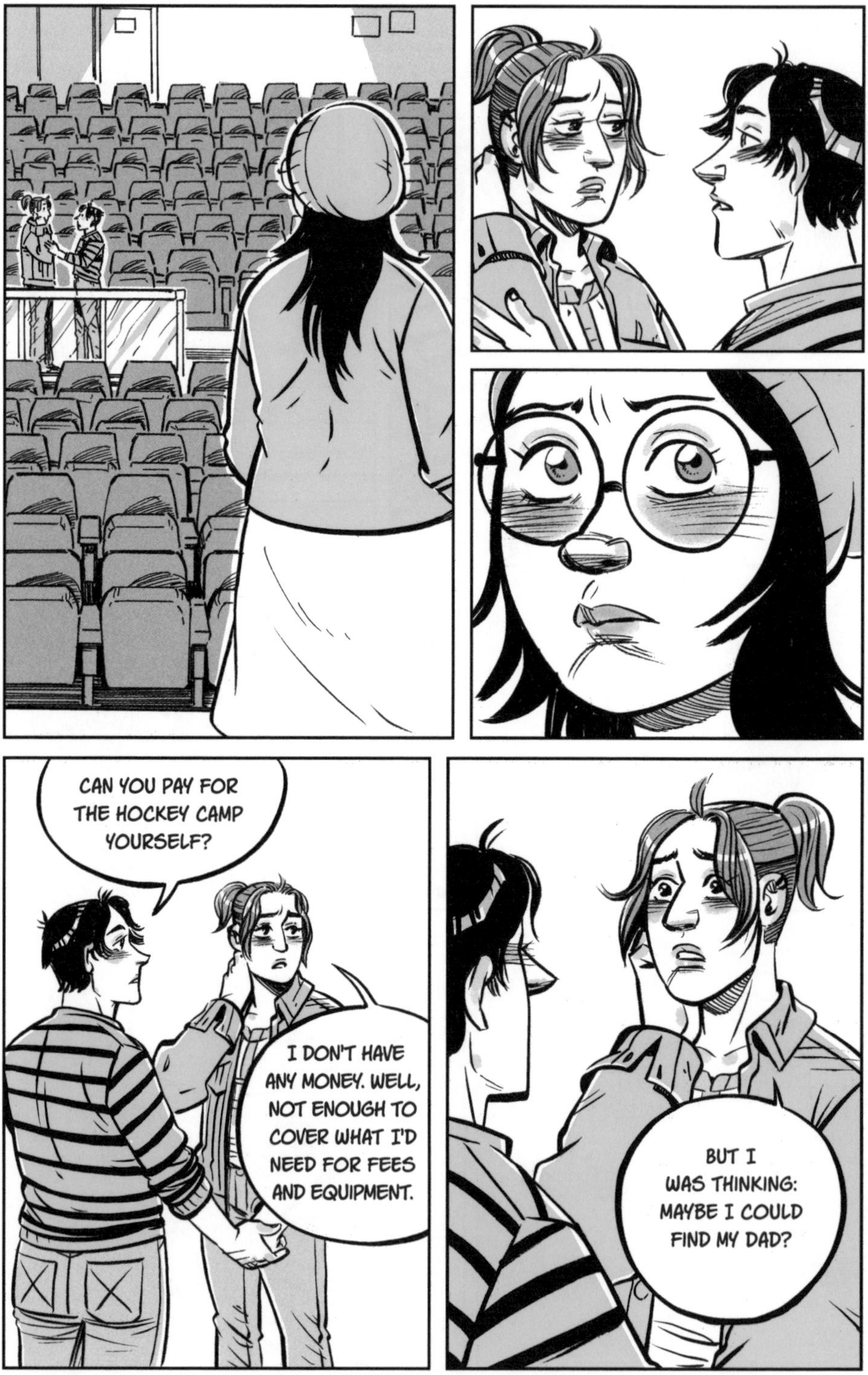
CAN YOU PAY FOR THE HOCKEY CAMP YOURSELF?
I DON'T HAVE ANY MONEY. WELL, NOT ENOUGH TO COVER WHAT I'D NEED FOR FEES AND EQUIPMENT.
BUT I WAS THINKING: MAYBE I COULD FIND MY DAD?

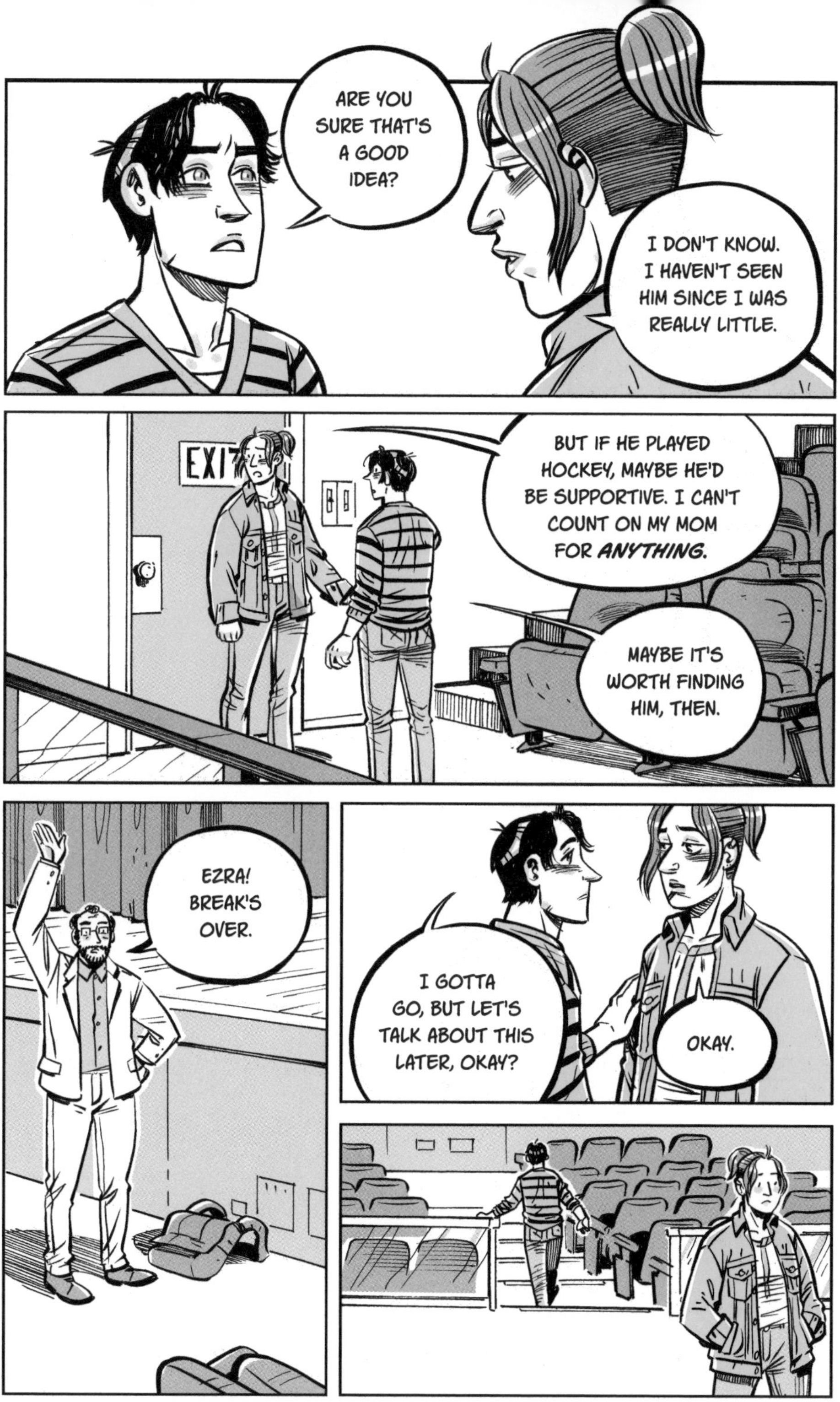
ARE YOU SURE THAT'S A GOOD IDEA?
I DON'T KNOW. I HAVEN'T SEEN HIM SINCE I WAS REALLY LITTLE.
EXIT
BUT IF HE PLAYED HOCKEY, MAYBE HE'D BE SUPPORTIVE. I CAN'T COUNT ON MY MOM FOR ***ANYTHING***.
MAYBE IT'S WORTH FINDING HIM, THEN.
EZRA! BREAK'S OVER.
I GOTTA GO, BUT LET'S TALK ABOUT THIS LATER, OKAY?
OKAY.

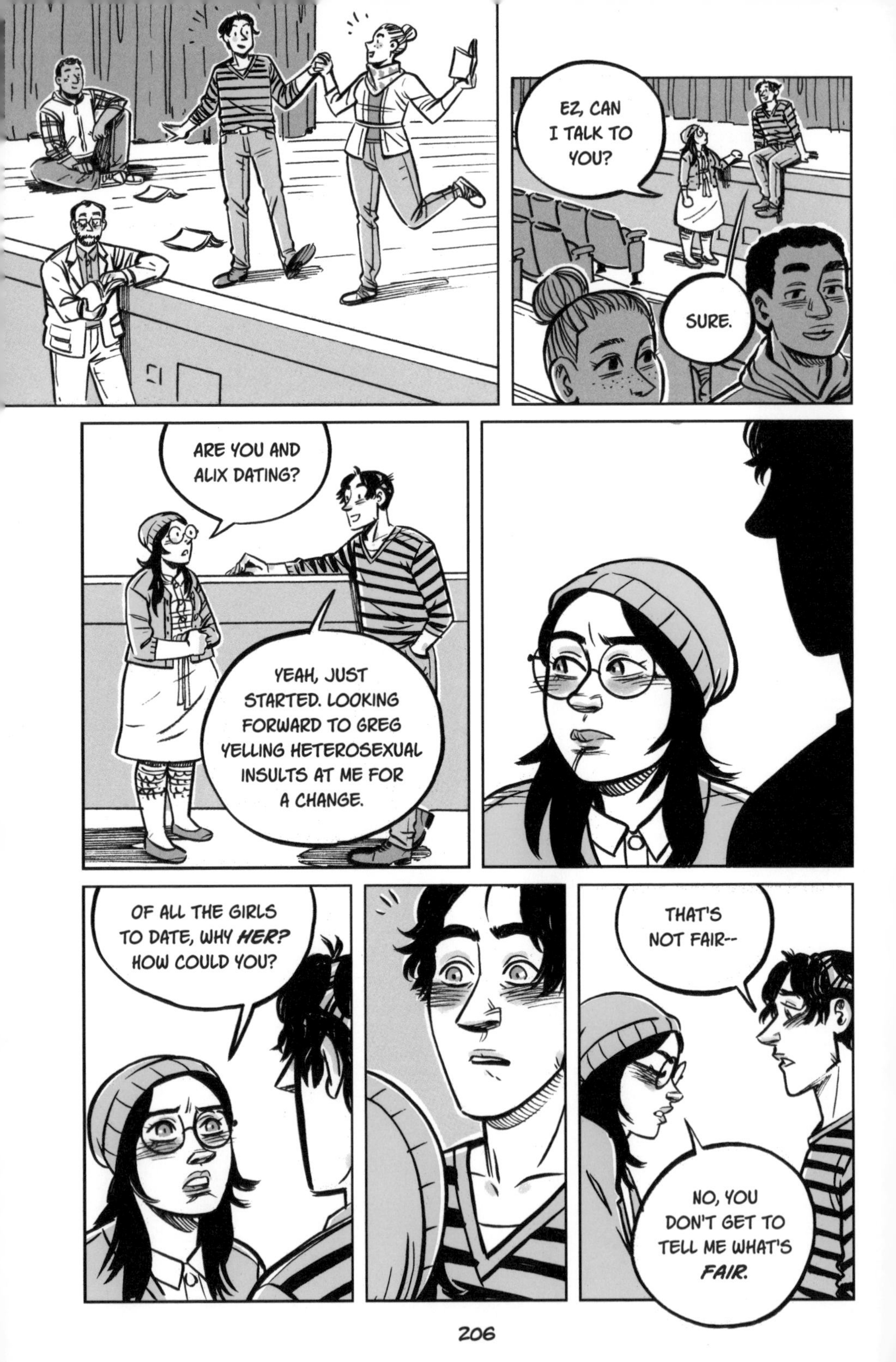
EZ, CAN I TALK TO YOU?
SURE.
ARE YOU AND ALIX DATING?
YEAH, JUST STARTED. LOOKING FORWARD TO GREG YELLING HETEROSEXUAL INSULTS AT ME FOR A CHANGE.
OF ALL THE GIRLS TO DATE, WHY *HER*? HOW COULD YOU?
THAT'S NOT FAIR--
NO, YOU DON'T GET TO TELL ME WHAT'S ***FAIR***.

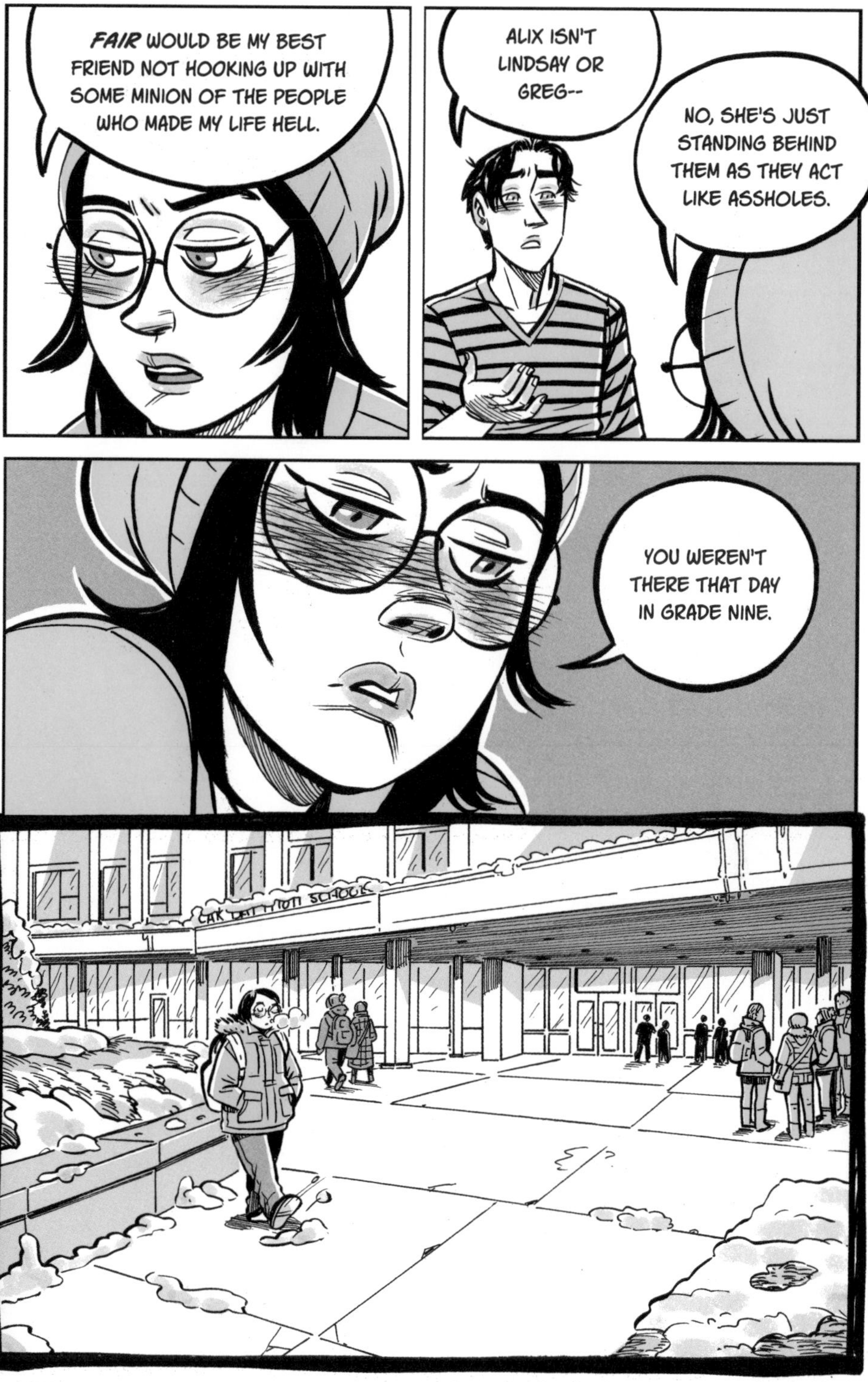
FAIR WOULD BE MY BEST FRIEND NOT HOOKING UP WITH SOME MINION OF THE PEOPLE WHO MADE MY LIFE HELL.
ALIX ISN'T LINDSAY OR GREG--
NO, SHE'S JUST STANDING BEHIND THEM AS THEY ACT LIKE ASSHOLES.
YOU WEREN'T THERE THAT DAY IN GRADE NINE.

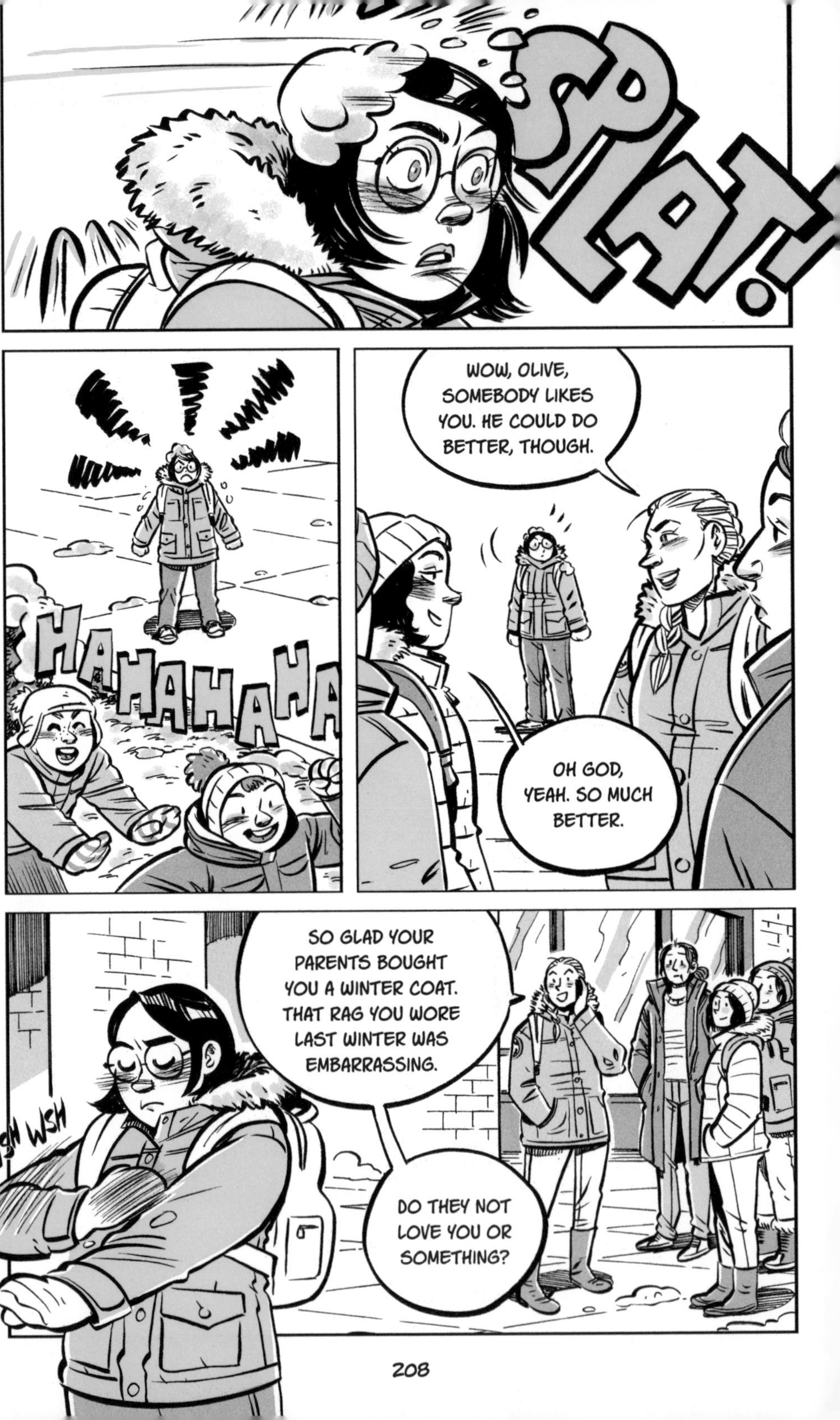
SPLAT!
HAHAHAHAHA
WOW, OLIVE, SOMEBODY LIKES YOU. HE COULD DO BETTER, THOUGH.
OH GOD, YEAH. SO MUCH BETTER.
SO GLAD YOUR PARENTS BOUGHT YOU A WINTER COAT. THAT RAG YOU WORE LAST WINTER WAS EMBARRASSING.
DO THEY NOT LOVE YOU OR SOMETHING?
WSH WSH

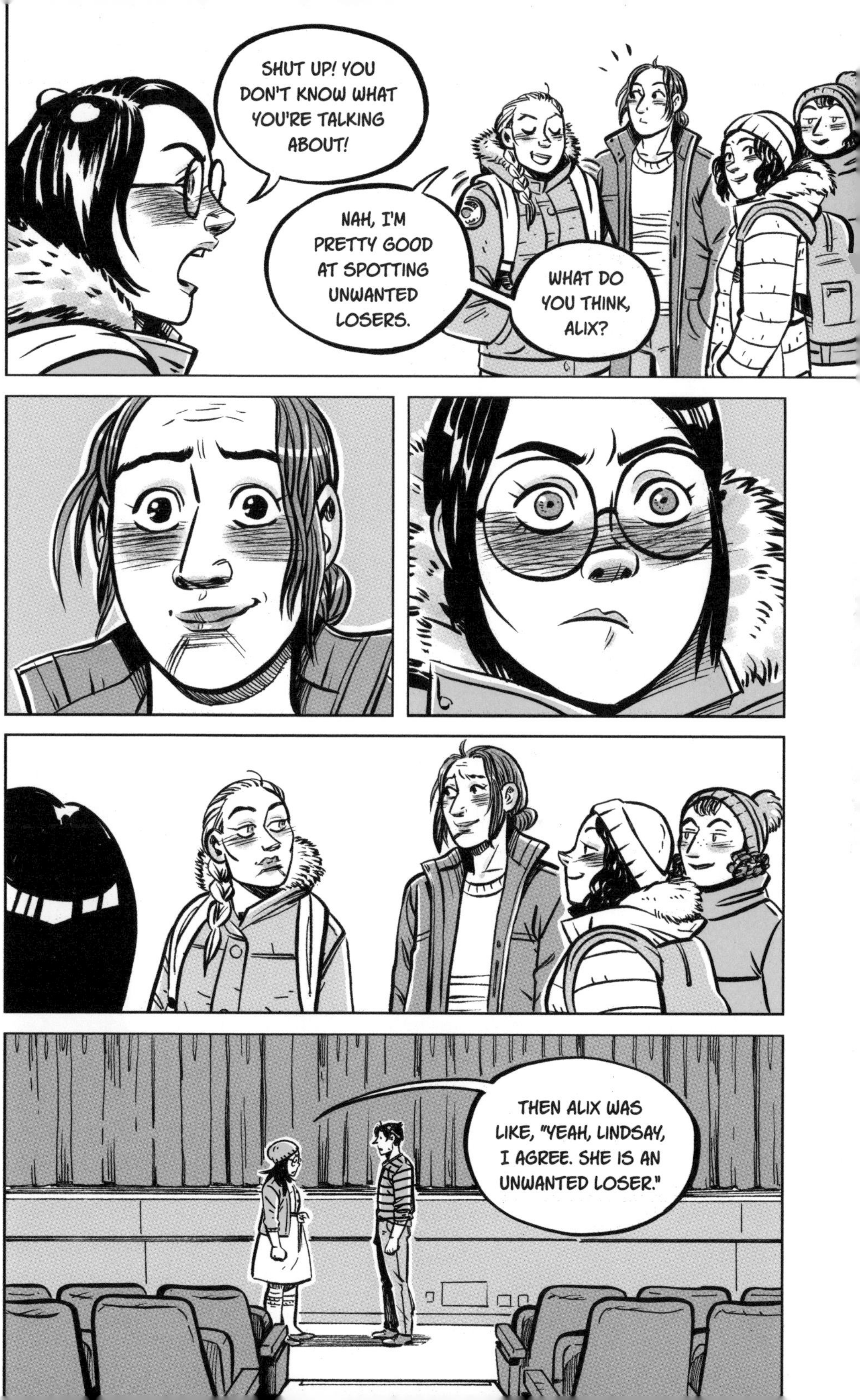
SHUT UP! YOU DON'T KNOW WHAT YOU'RE TALKING ABOUT!
NAH, I'M PRETTY GOOD AT SPOTTING UNWANTED LOSERS.
WHAT DO YOU THINK, ALIX?
THEN ALIX WAS LIKE, "YEAH, LINDSAY, I AGREE. SHE IS AN UNWANTED LOSER."

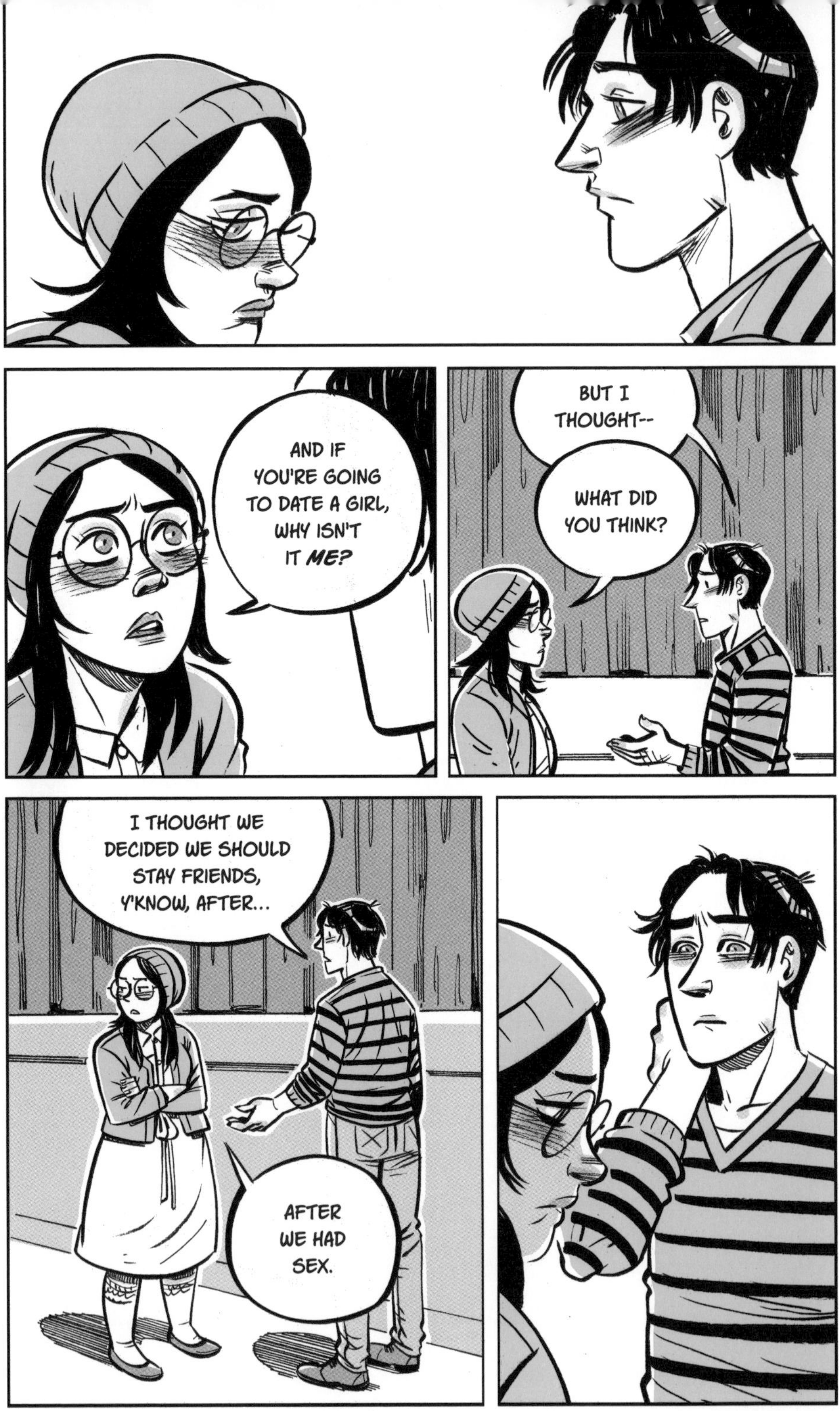
AND IF YOU'RE GOING TO DATE A GIRL, WHY ISN'T IT *ME?*
BUT I THOUGHT--
WHAT DID YOU THINK?
I THOUGHT WE DECIDED WE SHOULD STAY FRIENDS, Y'KNOW, AFTER...
AFTER WE HAD SEX.

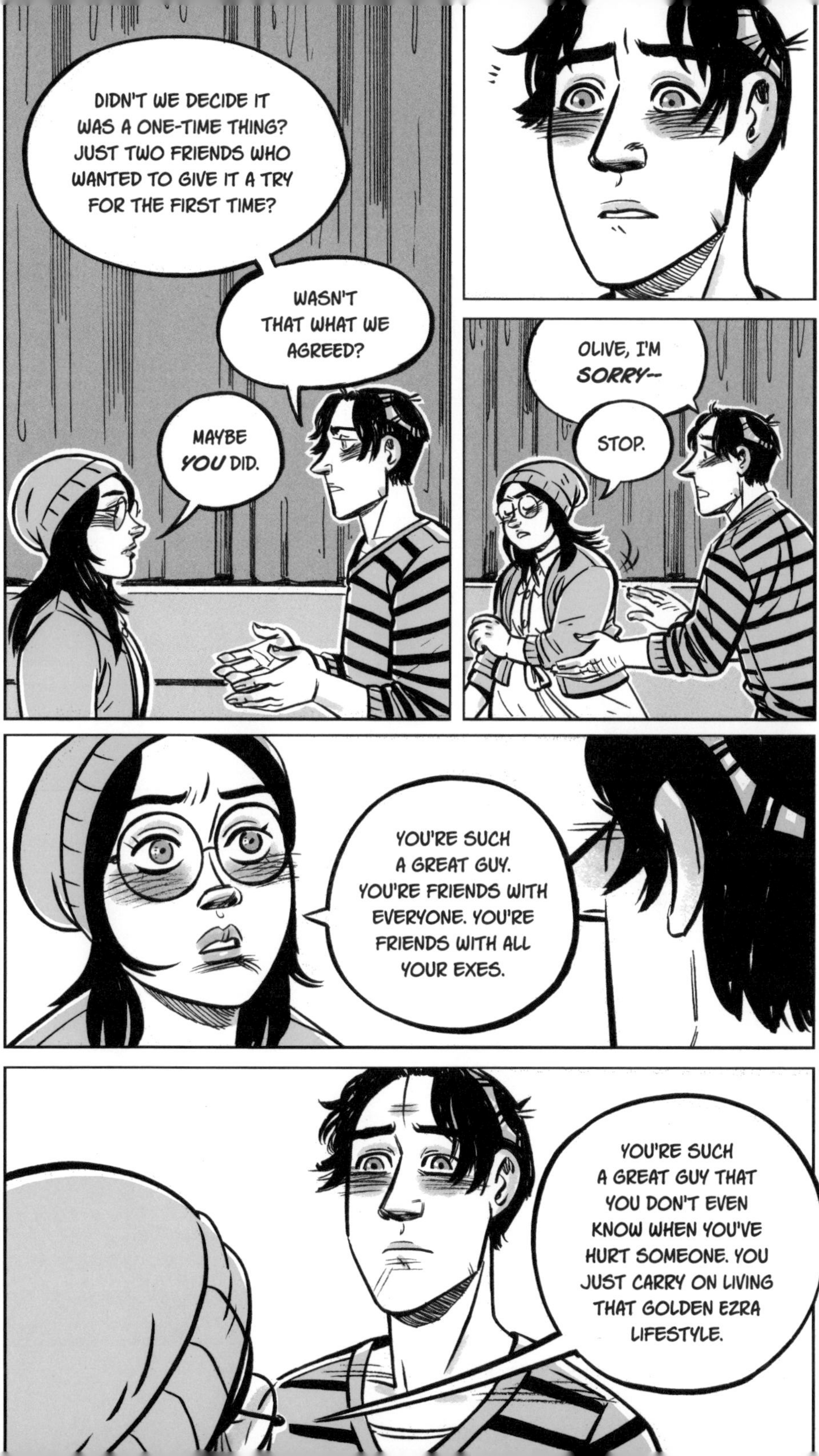
DIDN'T WE DECIDE IT WAS A ONE-TIME THING? JUST TWO FRIENDS WHO WANTED TO GIVE IT A TRY FOR THE FIRST TIME?
WASN'T THAT WHAT WE AGREED?
MAYBE YOU DID.
OLIVE, I'M SORRY--
STOP.
YOU'RE SUCH A GREAT GUY. YOU'RE FRIENDS WITH EVERYONE. YOU'RE FRIENDS WITH ALL YOUR EXES.
YOU'RE SUCH A GREAT GUY THAT YOU DON'T EVEN KNOW WHEN YOU'VE HURT SOMEONE. YOU JUST CARRY ON LIVING THAT GOLDEN EZRA LIFESTYLE.

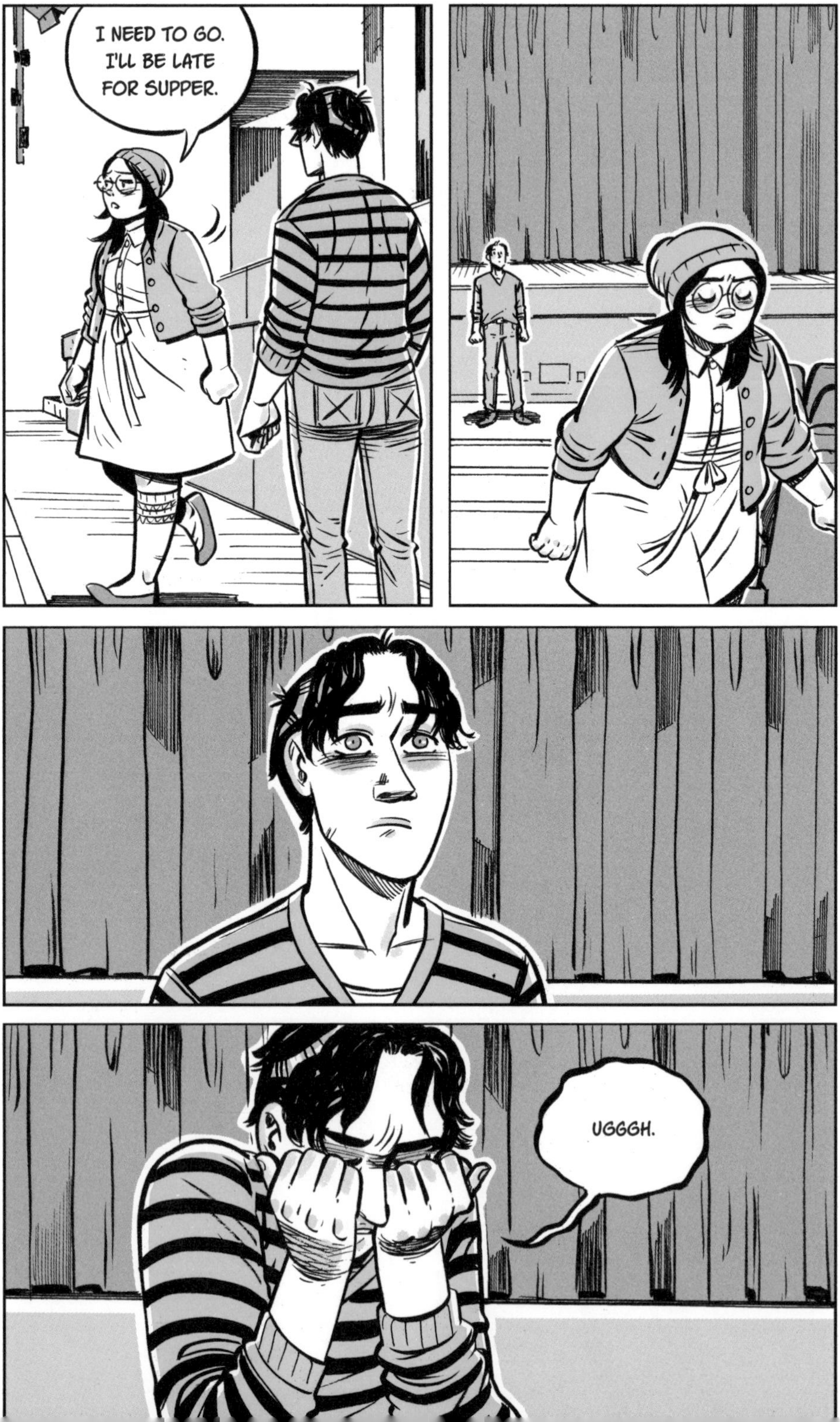
I NEED TO GO. I'LL BE LATE FOR SUPPER.
UGGGH.

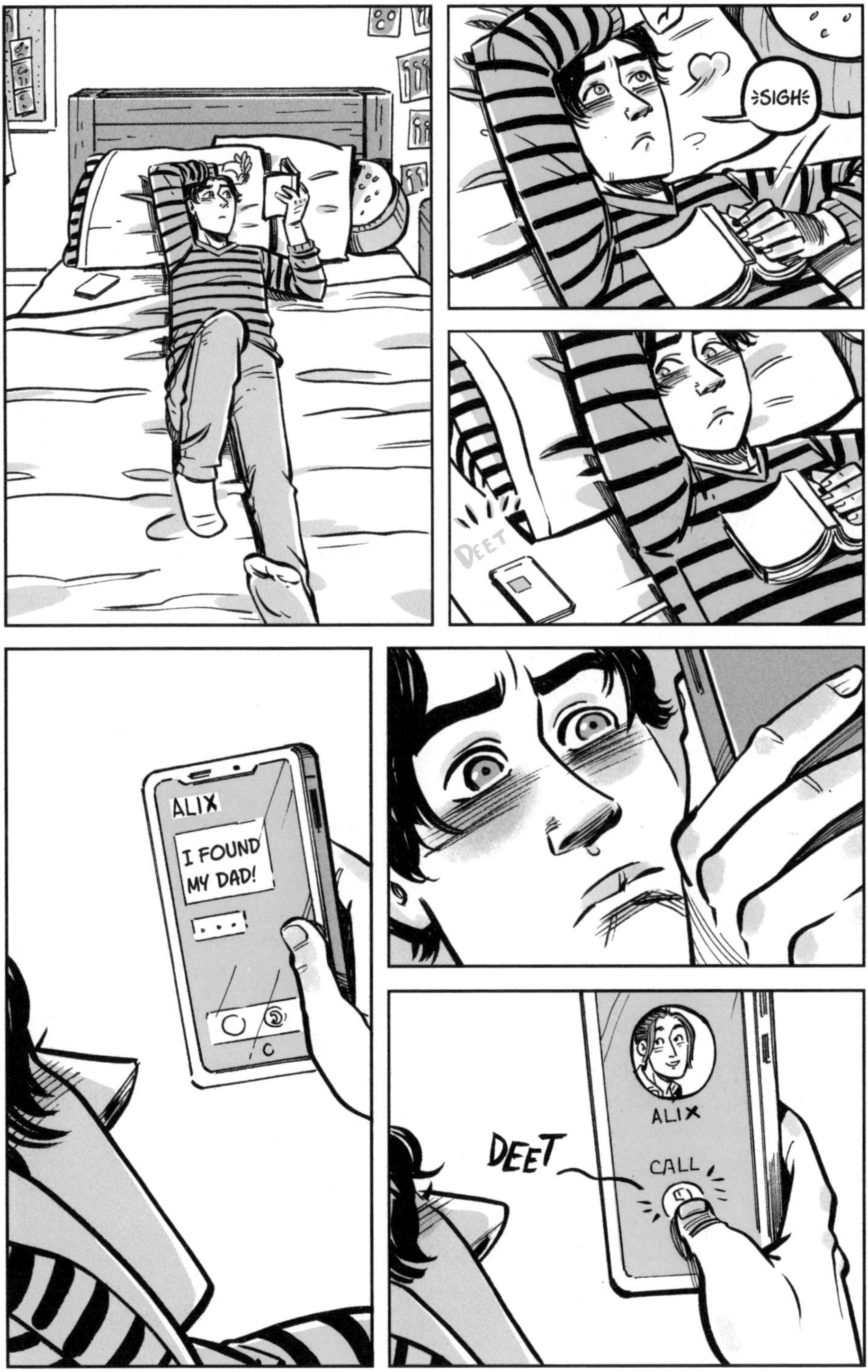
SIGH
DEET
ALIX
I FOUND MY DAD!
ALIX
DEET
CALL

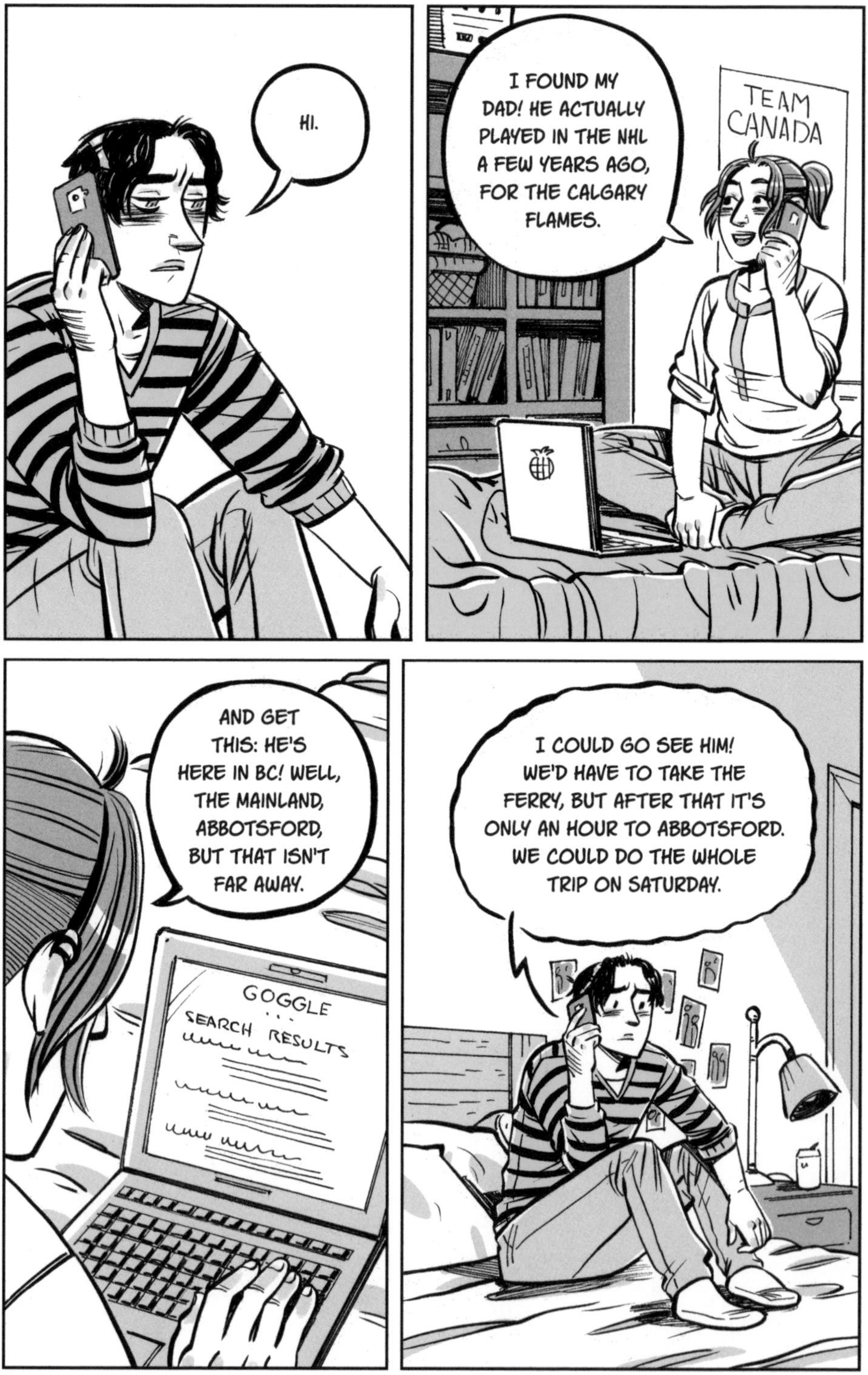
HI.
TEAM CANADA
I FOUND MY DAD! HE ACTUALLY PLAYED IN THE NHL A FEW YEARS AGO, FOR THE CALGARY FLAMES.
AND GET THIS: HE'S HERE IN BC! WELL, THE MAINLAND, ABBOTSFORD, BUT THAT ISN'T FAR AWAY.
GOGGLE
SEARCH RESULTS
I COULD GO SEE HIM! WE'D HAVE TO TAKE THE FERRY, BUT AFTER THAT IT'S ONLY AN HOUR TO ABBOTSFORD. WE COULD DO THE WHOLE TRIP ON SATURDAY.

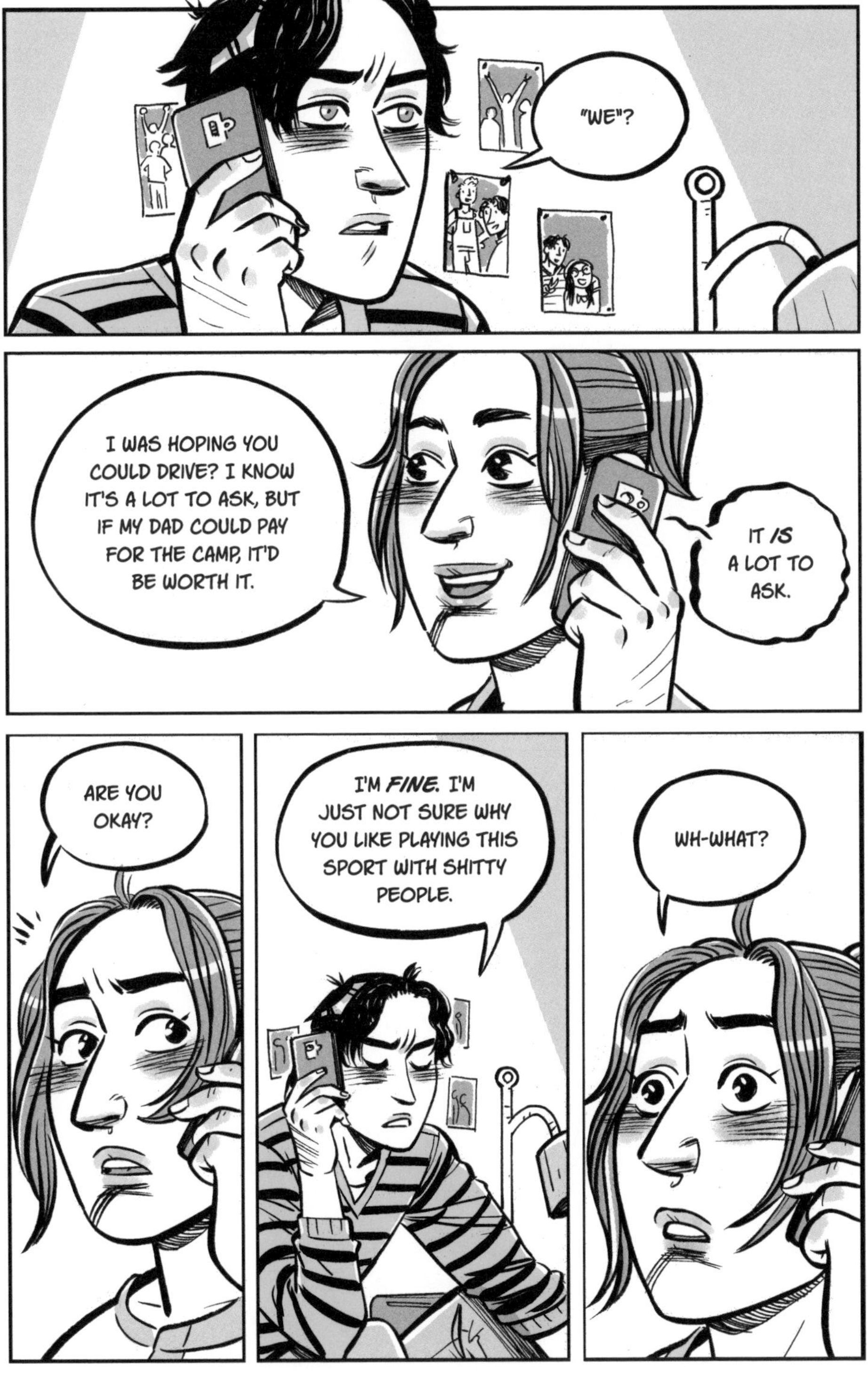
"WE"?
I WAS HOPING YOU COULD DRIVE? I KNOW IT'S A LOT TO ASK, BUT IF MY DAD COULD PAY FOR THE CAMP, IT'D BE WORTH IT.
IT *IS* A LOT TO ASK.
ARE YOU OKAY?
I'M *FINE*. I'M JUST NOT SURE WHY YOU LIKE PLAYING THIS SPORT WITH SHITTY PEOPLE.
WH-WHAT?

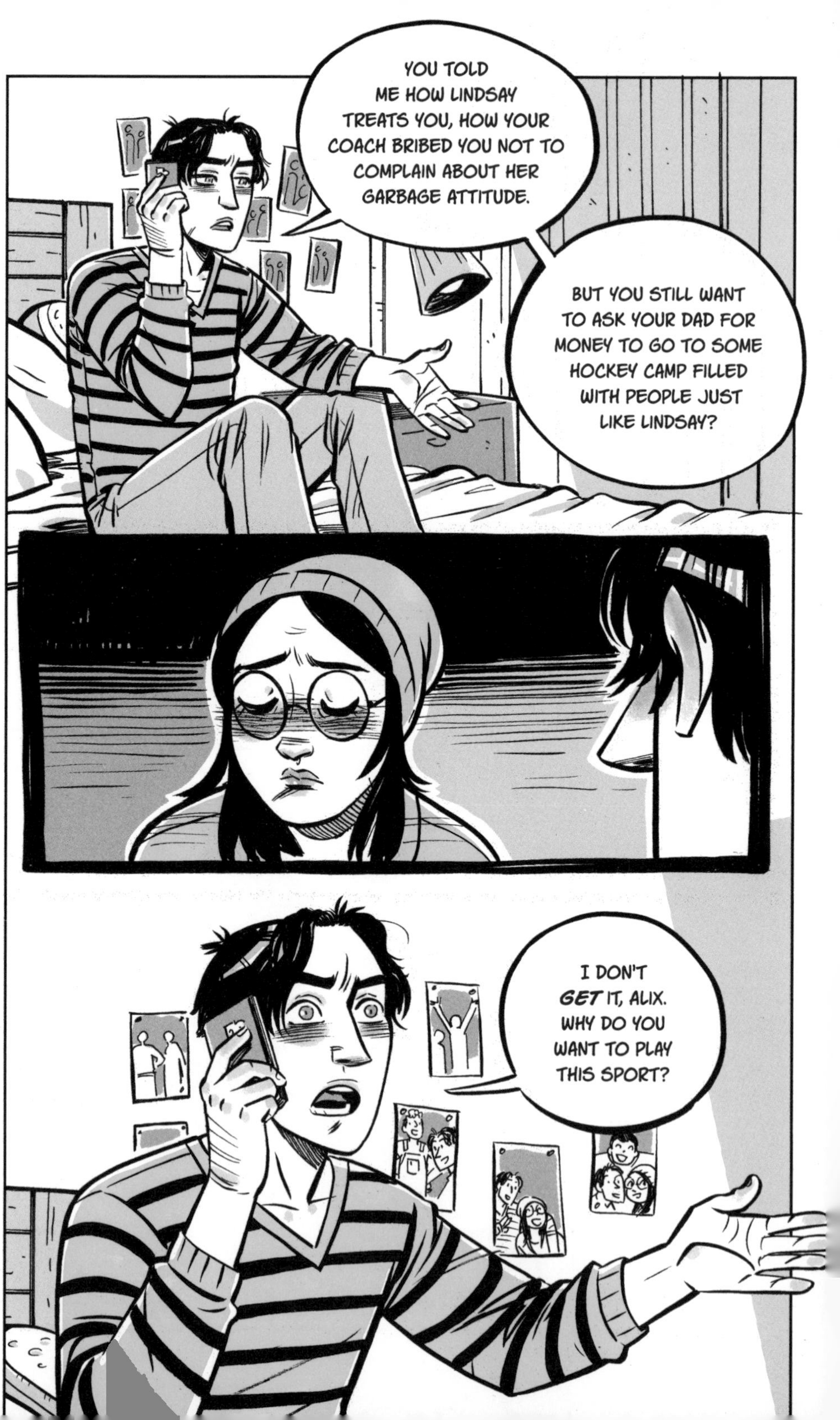
YOU TOLD ME HOW LINDSAY TREATS YOU, HOW YOUR COACH BRIBED YOU NOT TO COMPLAIN ABOUT HER GARBAGE ATTITUDE.
BUT YOU STILL WANT TO ASK YOUR DAD FOR MONEY TO GO TO SOME HOCKEY CAMP FILLED WITH PEOPLE JUST LIKE LINDSAY?
I DON'T ***GET*** IT, ALIX. WHY DO YOU WANT TO PLAY THIS SPORT?

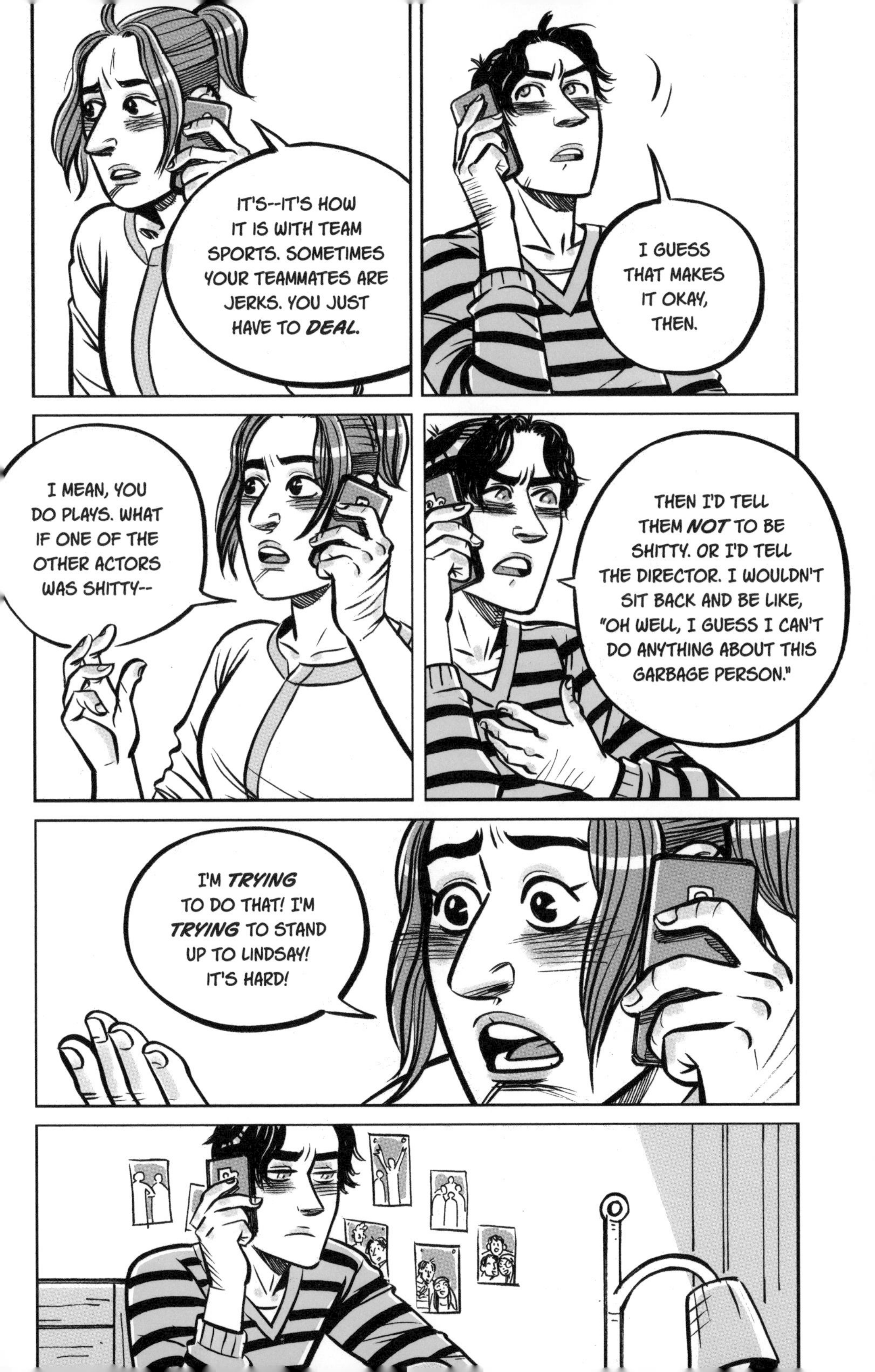
IT'S--IT'S HOW IT IS WITH TEAM SPORTS. SOMETIMES YOUR TEAMMATES ARE JERKS. YOU JUST HAVE TO DEAL.
I GUESS THAT MAKES IT OKAY, THEN.
I MEAN, YOU DO PLAYS. WHAT IF ONE OF THE OTHER ACTORS WAS SHITTY--
THEN I'D TELL THEM NOT TO BE SHITTY. OR I'D TELL THE DIRECTOR. I WOULDN'T SIT BACK AND BE LIKE, "OH WELL, I GUESS I CAN'T DO ANYTHING ABOUT THIS GARBAGE PERSON."
I'M TRYING TO DO THAT! I'M TRYING TO STAND UP TO LINDSAY! IT'S HARD!

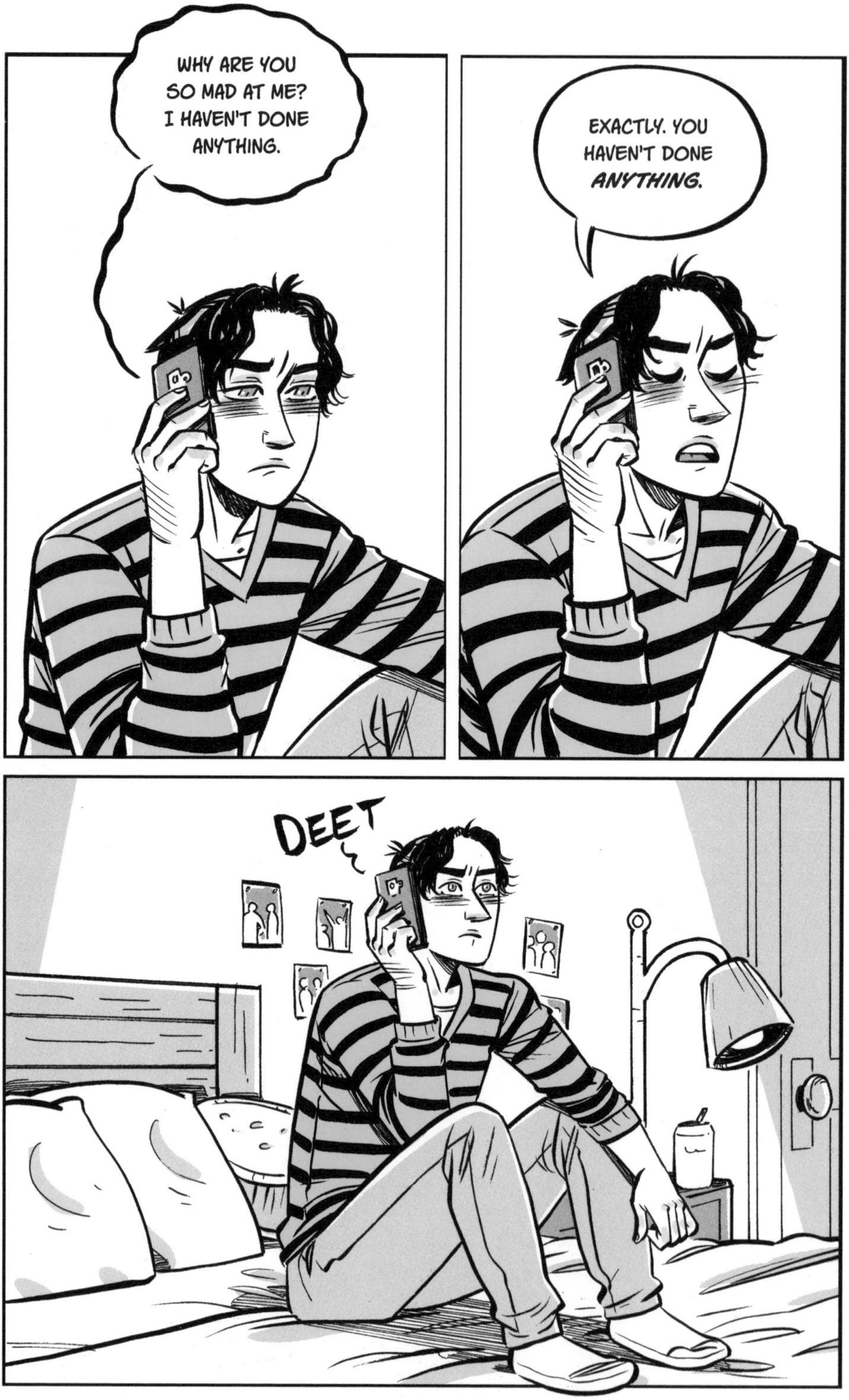
WHY ARE YOU SO MAD AT ME? I HAVEN'T DONE ANYTHING.
EXACTLY. YOU HAVEN'T DONE *ANYTHING.*
DEET

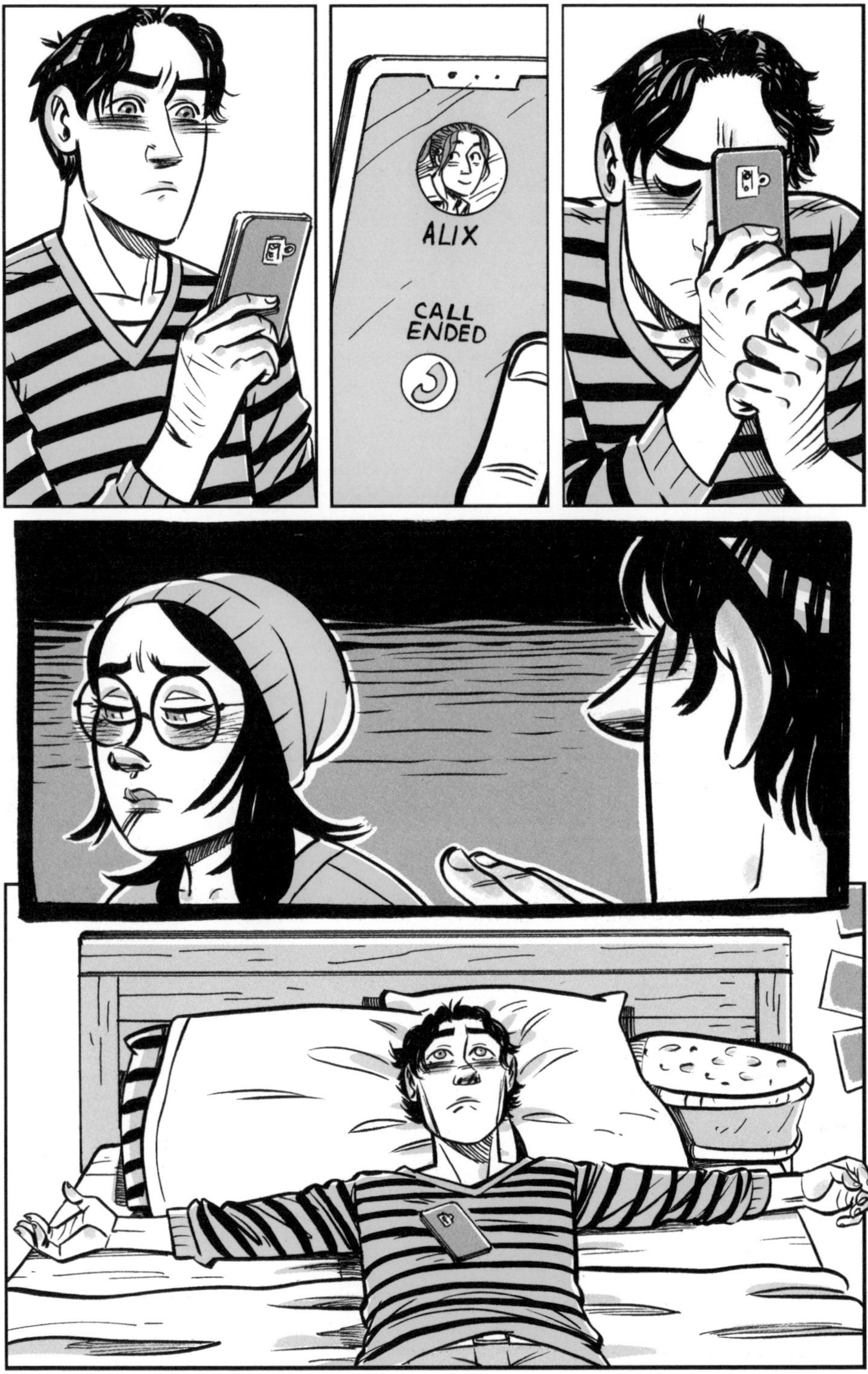
ALIX
CALL ENDED

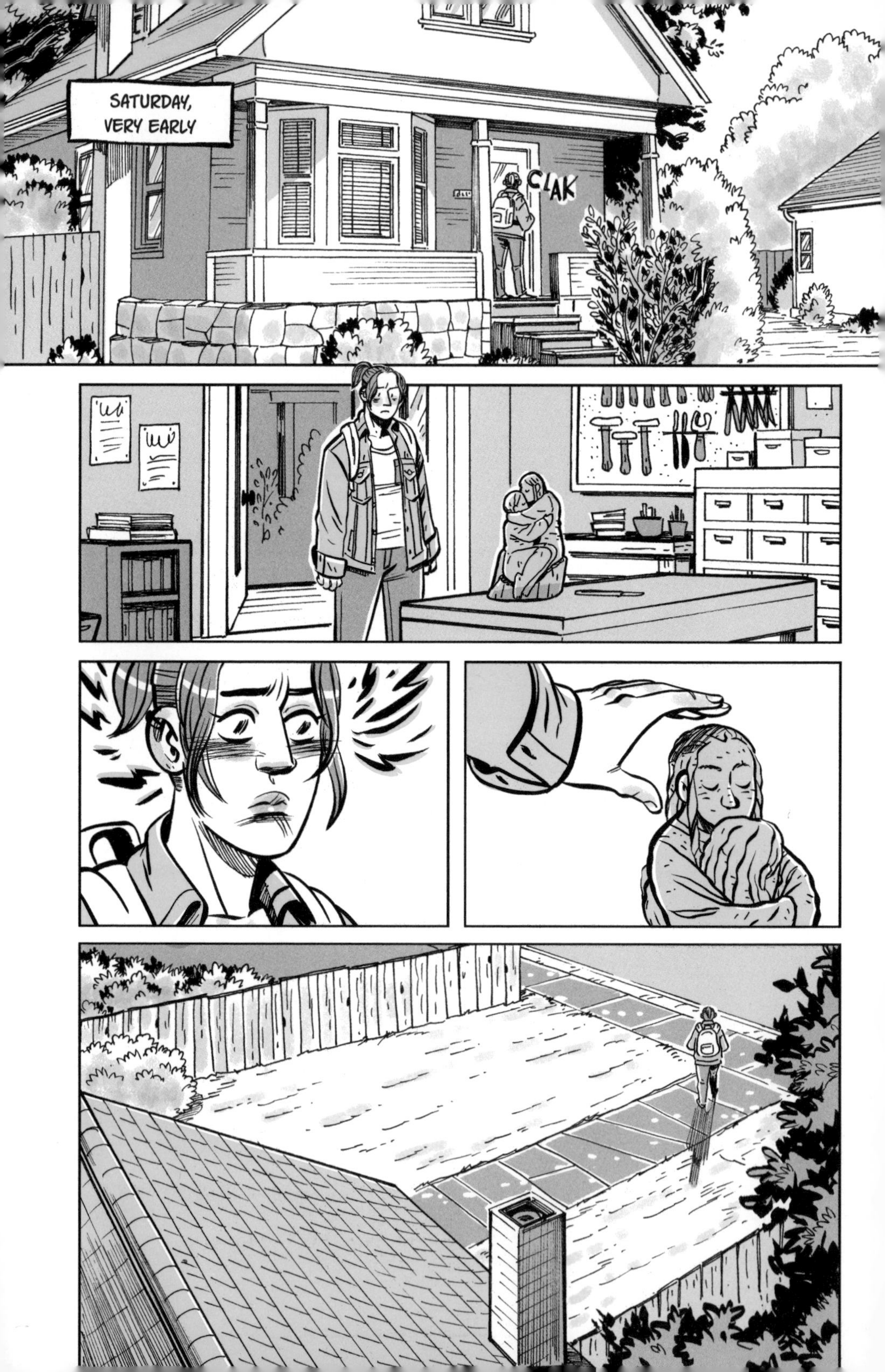
SATURDAY, VERY EARLY
CLAK

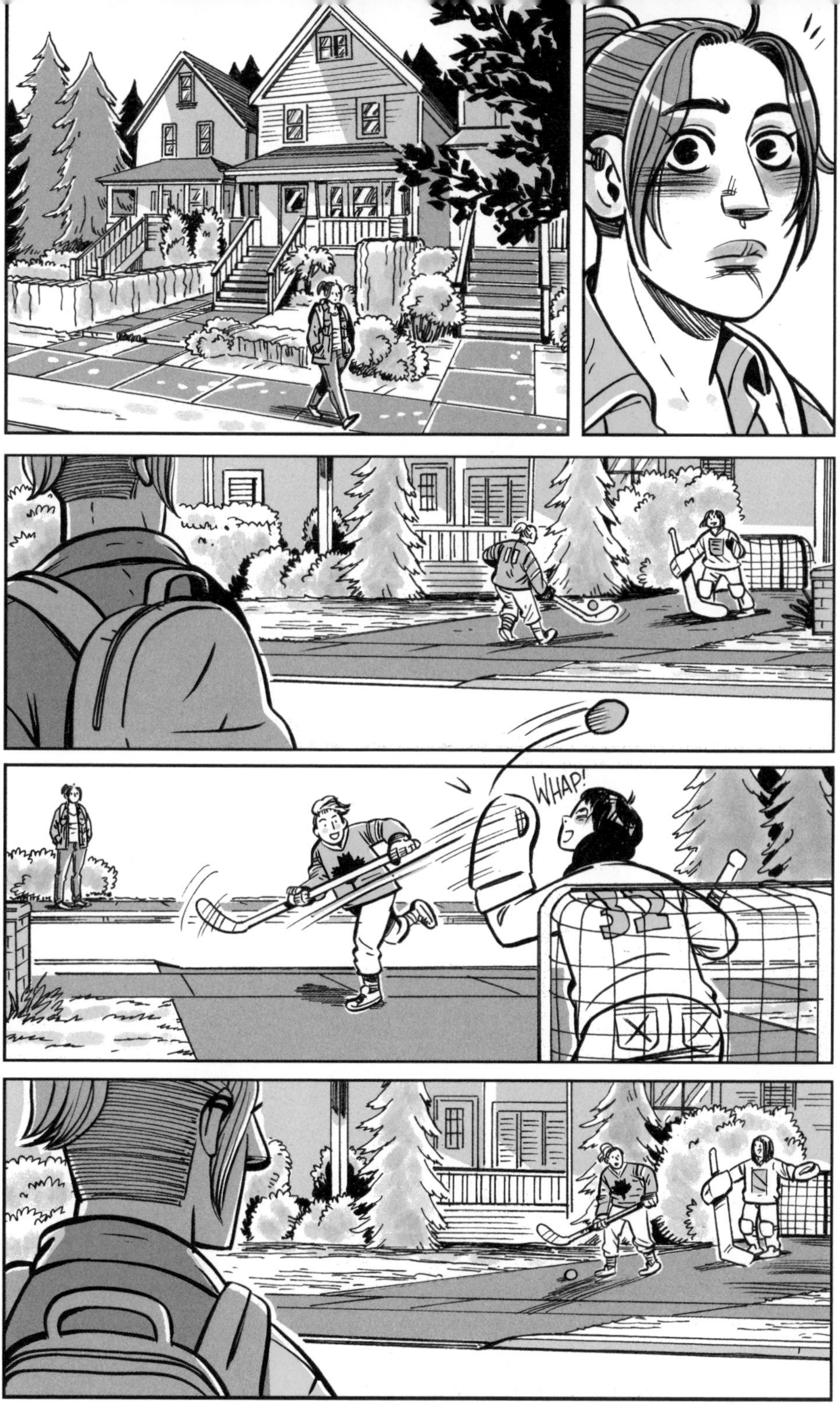
WHAP!

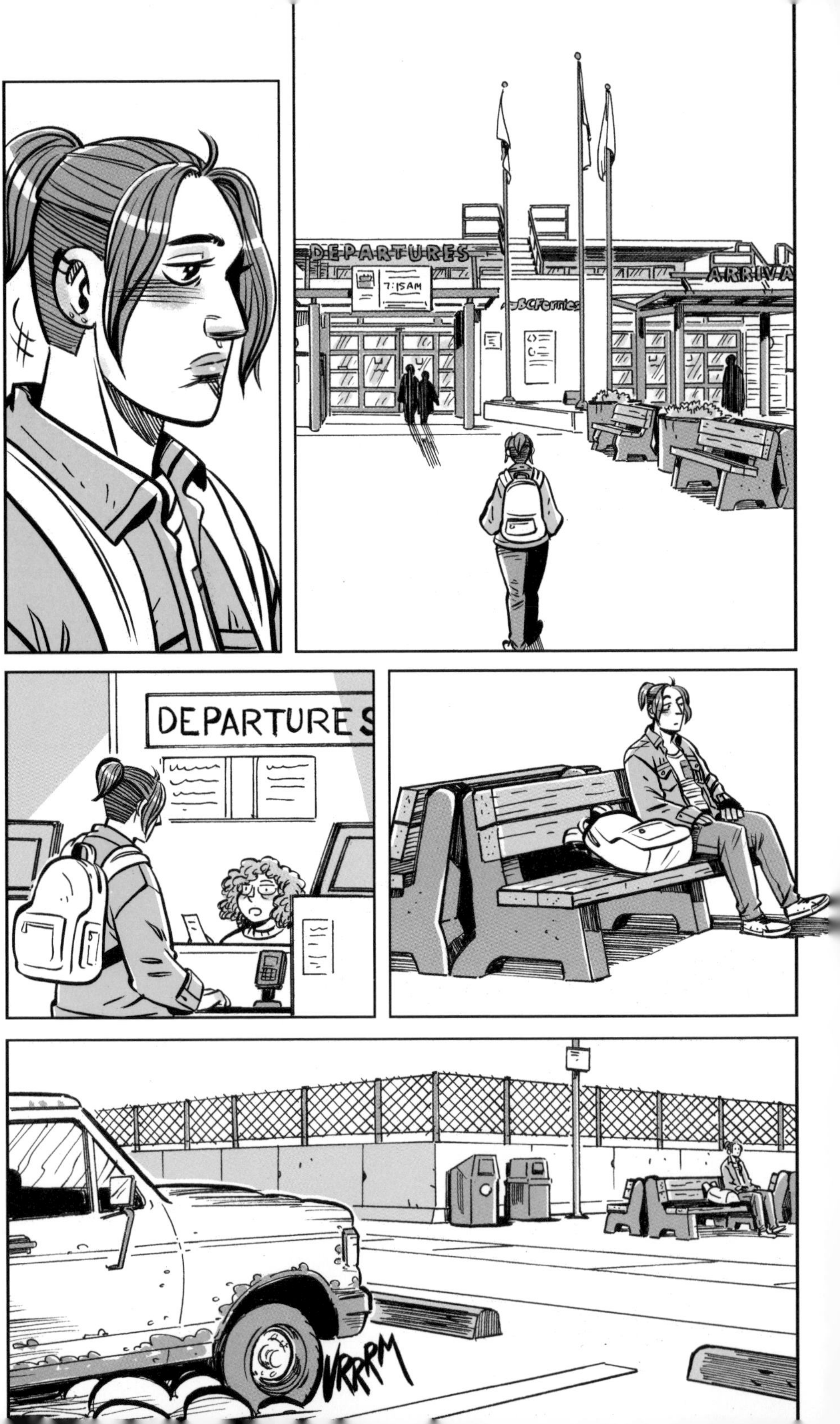
DEPARTURES
7:15AM
BC Ferries
ARRIVA
DEPARTURES
VRRRPM

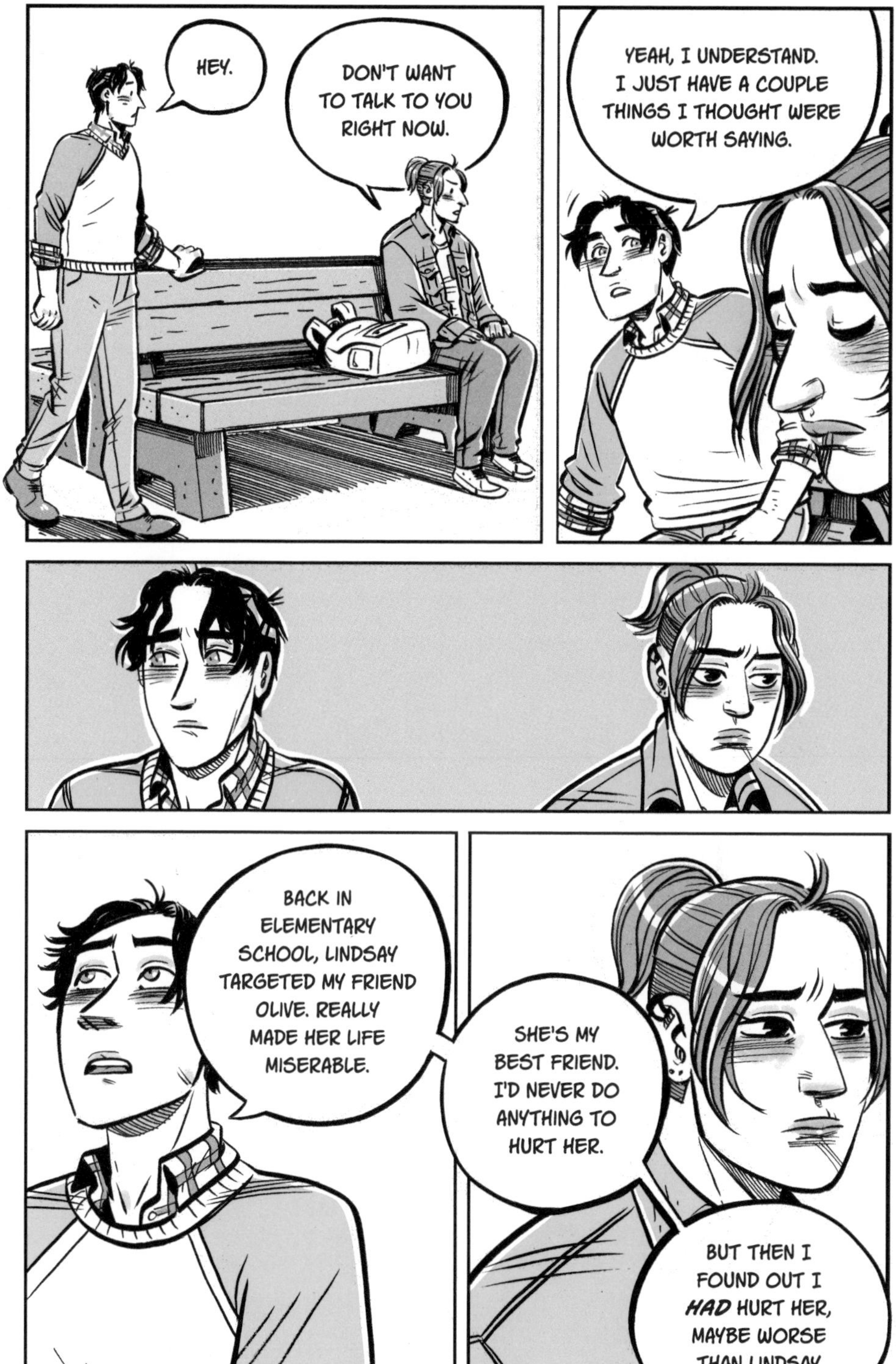
HEY.
DON'T WANT TO TALK TO YOU RIGHT NOW.
YEAH, I UNDERSTAND. I JUST HAVE A COUPLE THINGS I THOUGHT WERE WORTH SAYING.
BACK IN ELEMENTARY SCHOOL, LINDSAY TARGETED MY FRIEND OLIVE. REALLY MADE HER LIFE MISERABLE.
SHE'S MY BEST FRIEND. I'D NEVER DO ANYTHING TO HURT HER.
BUT THEN I FOUND OUT I ***HAD*** HURT HER, MAYBE WORSE THAN LINDSAY DID.

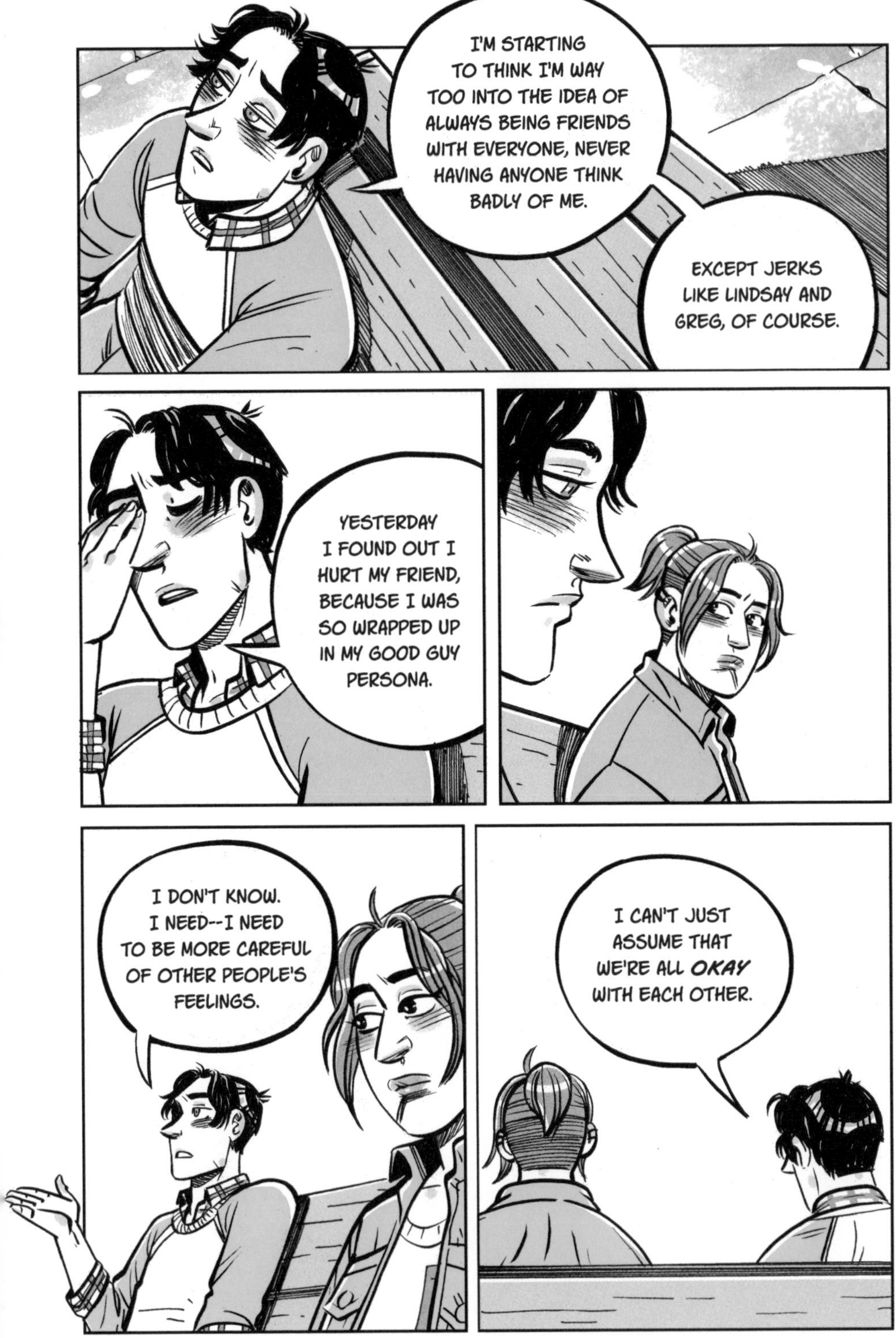
I'M STARTING TO THINK I'M WAY TOO INTO THE IDEA OF ALWAYS BEING FRIENDS WITH EVERYONE, NEVER HAVING ANYONE THINK BADLY OF ME.
EXCEPT JERKS LIKE LINDSAY AND GREG, OF COURSE.
YESTERDAY I FOUND OUT I HURT MY FRIEND, BECAUSE I WAS SO WRAPPED UP IN MY GOOD GUY PERSONA.
I DON'T KNOW. I NEED--I NEED TO BE MORE CAREFUL OF OTHER PEOPLE'S FEELINGS.
I CAN'T JUST ASSUME THAT WE'RE ALL *OKAY* WITH EACH OTHER.

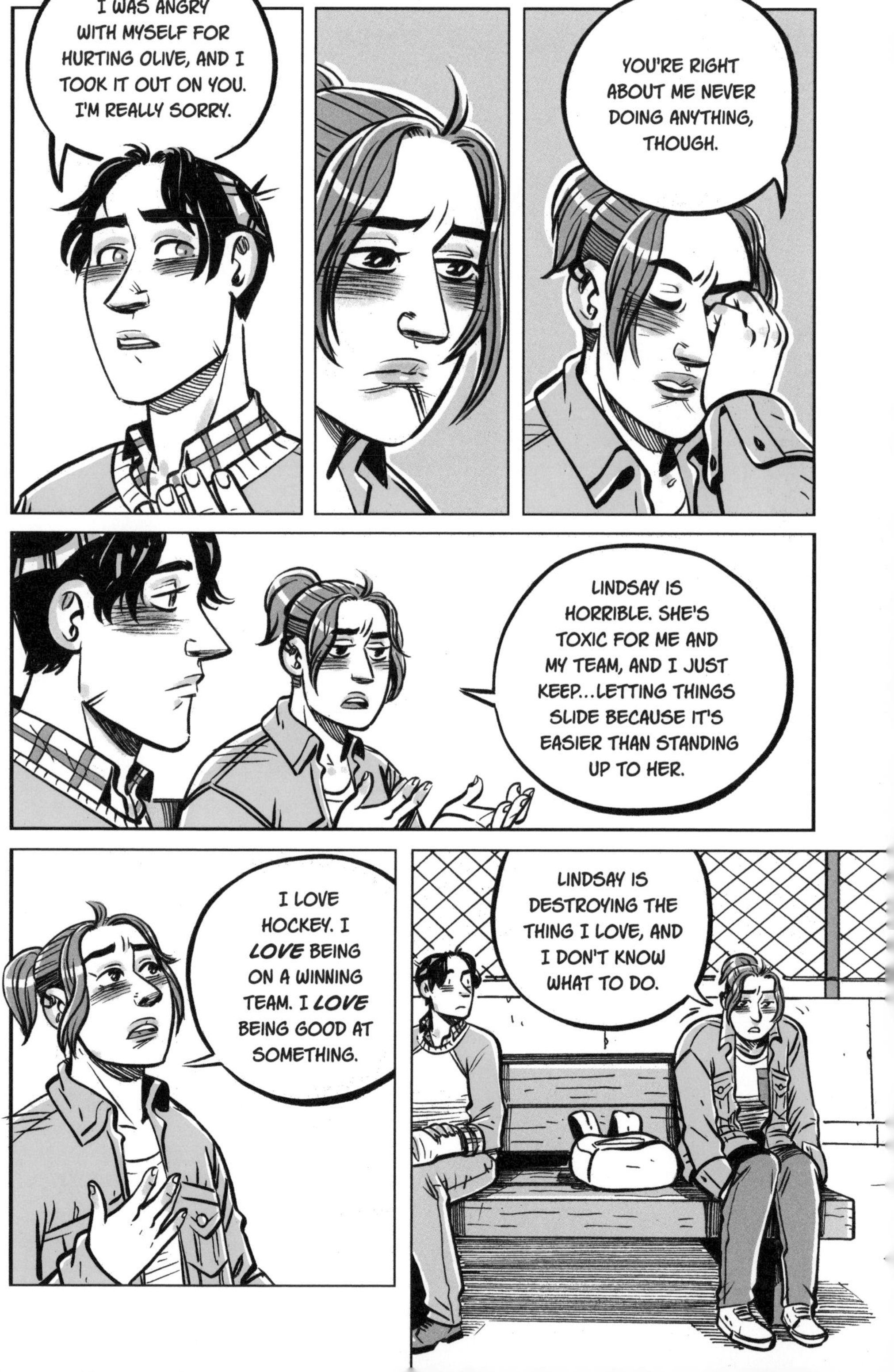
I WAS ANGRY WITH MYSELF FOR HURTING OLIVE, AND I TOOK IT OUT ON YOU. I'M REALLY SORRY.
YOU'RE RIGHT ABOUT ME NEVER DOING ANYTHING, THOUGH.
LINDSAY IS HORRIBLE. SHE'S TOXIC FOR ME AND MY TEAM, AND I JUST KEEP...LETTING THINGS SLIDE BECAUSE IT'S EASIER THAN STANDING UP TO HER.
I LOVE HOCKEY. I ***LOVE*** BEING ON A WINNING TEAM. I ***LOVE*** BEING GOOD AT SOMETHING.
LINDSAY IS DESTROYING THE THING I LOVE, AND I DON'T KNOW WHAT TO DO.

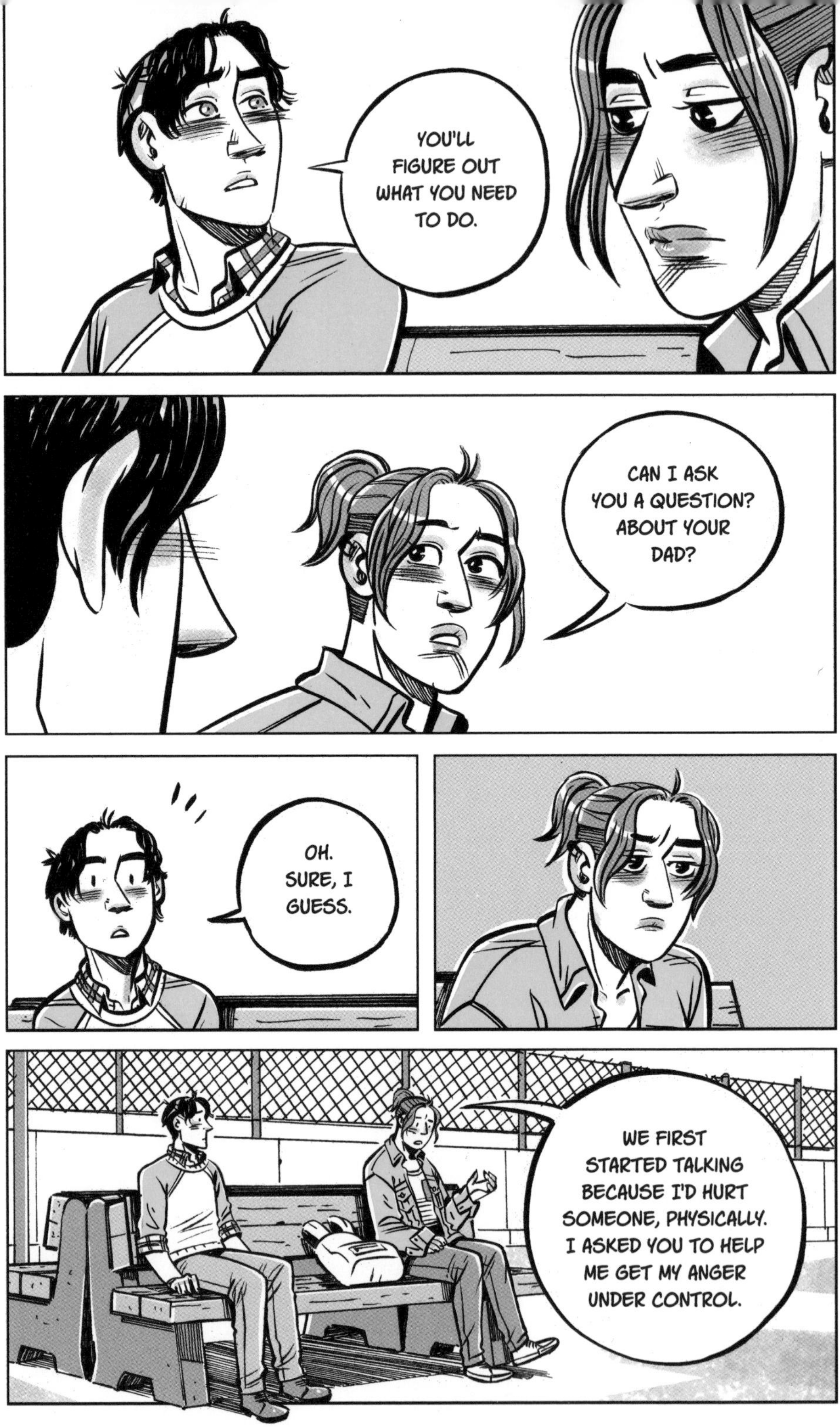
YOU'LL FIGURE OUT WHAT YOU NEED TO DO.
CAN I ASK YOU A QUESTION? ABOUT YOUR DAD?
OH. SURE, I GUESS.
WE FIRST STARTED TALKING BECAUSE I'D HURT SOMEONE, PHYSICALLY. I ASKED YOU TO HELP ME GET MY ANGER UNDER CONTROL.

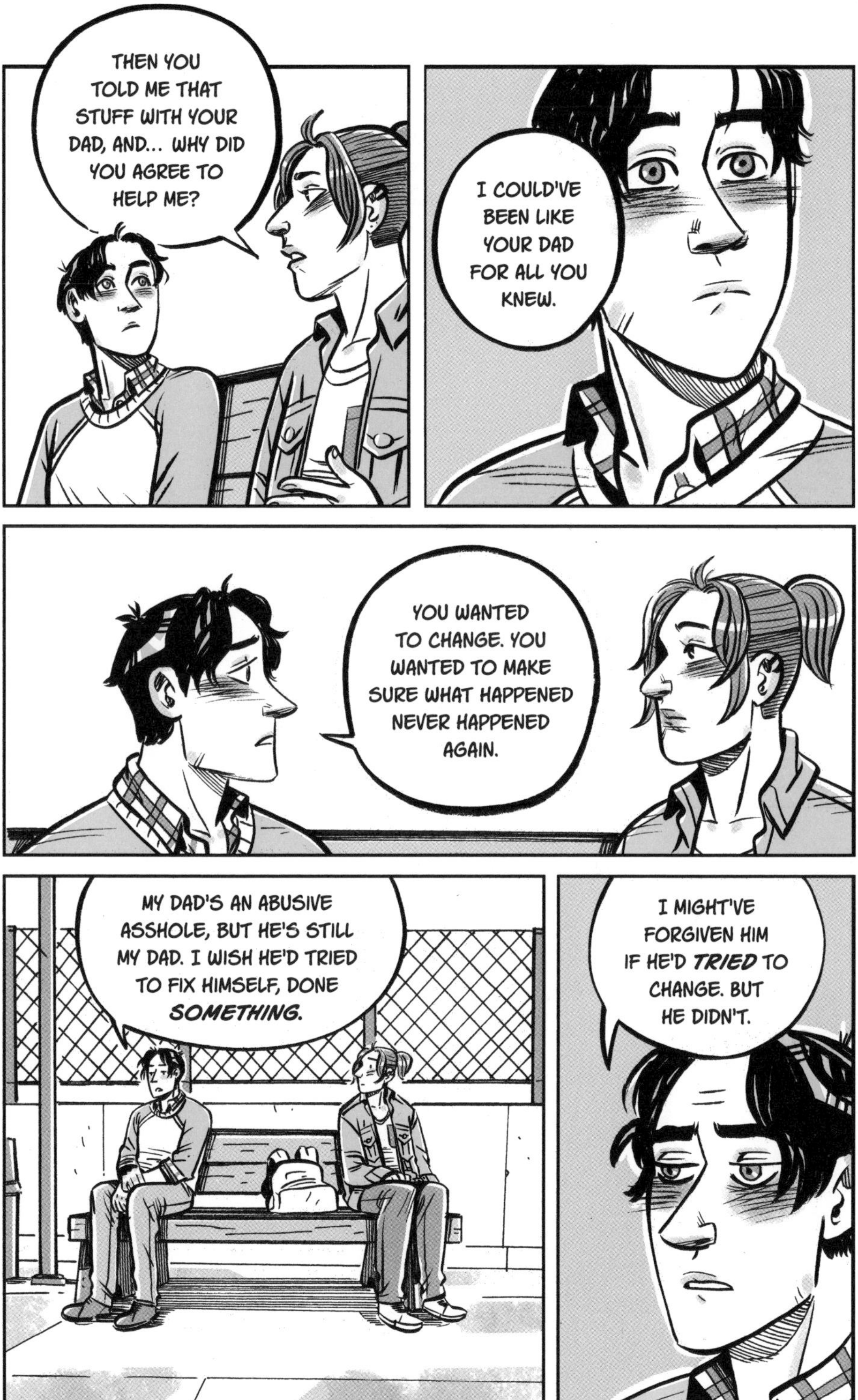
THEN YOU TOLD ME THAT STUFF WITH YOUR DAD, AND... WHY DID YOU AGREE TO HELP ME?
I COULD'VE BEEN LIKE YOUR DAD FOR ALL YOU KNEW.
YOU WANTED TO CHANGE. YOU WANTED TO MAKE SURE WHAT HAPPENED NEVER HAPPENED AGAIN.
MY DAD'S AN ABUSIVE ASSHOLE, BUT HE'S STILL MY DAD. I WISH HE'D TRIED TO FIX HIMSELF, DONE *SOMETHING*.
I MIGHT'VE FORGIVEN HIM IF HE'D *TRIED* TO CHANGE. BUT HE DIDN'T.

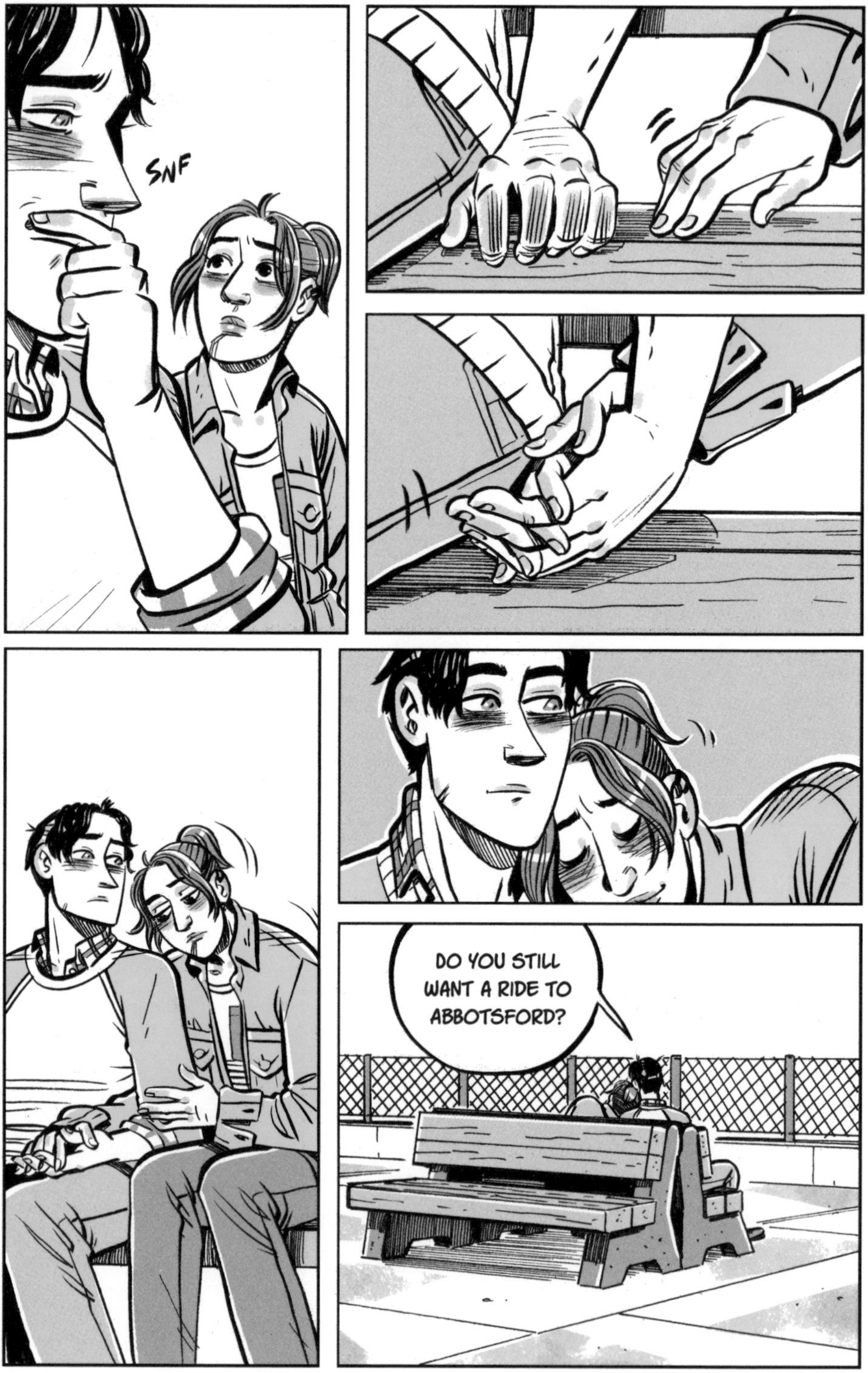
SNF
DO YOU STILL WANT A RIDE TO ABBOTSFORD?

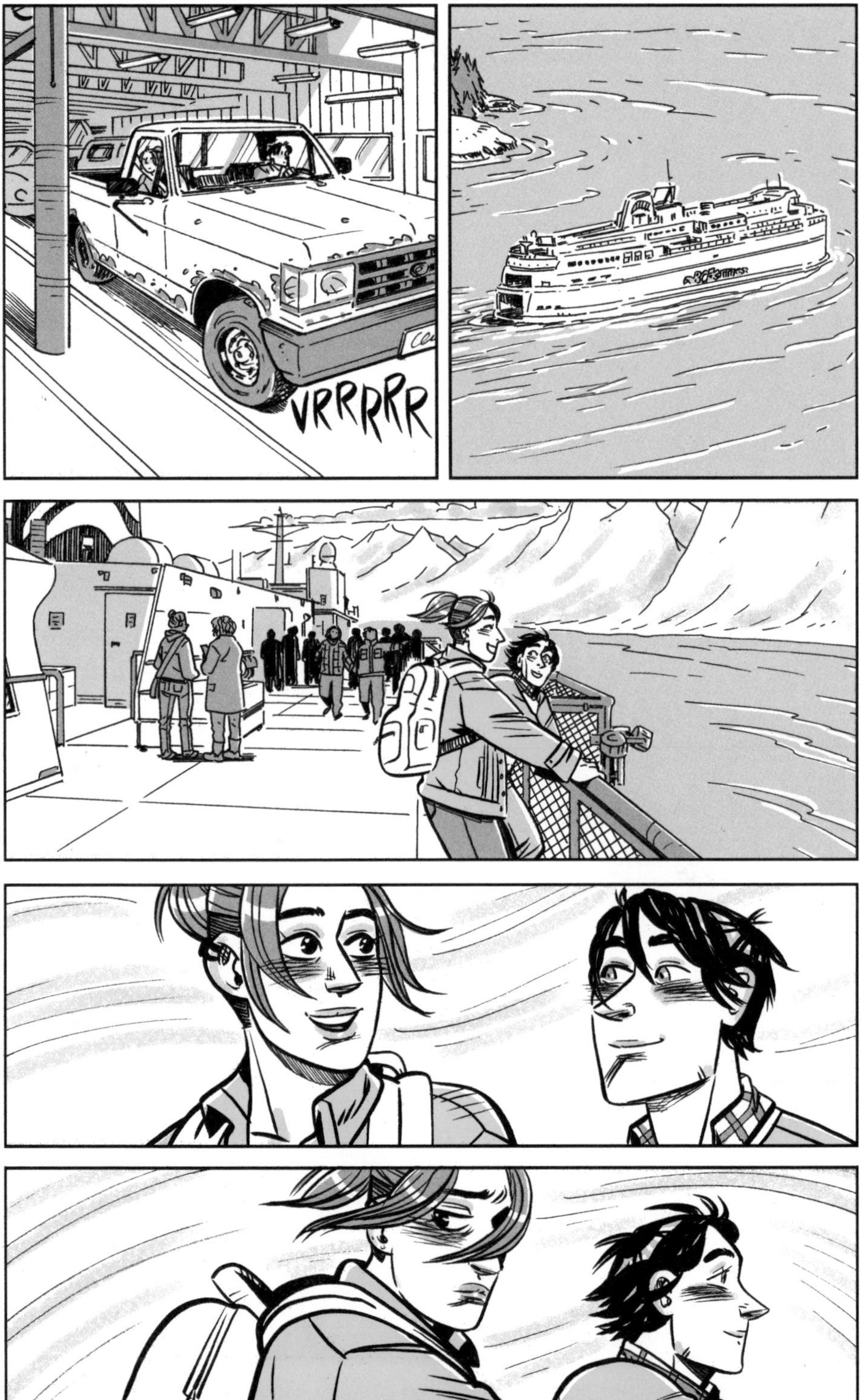
VRRRRR

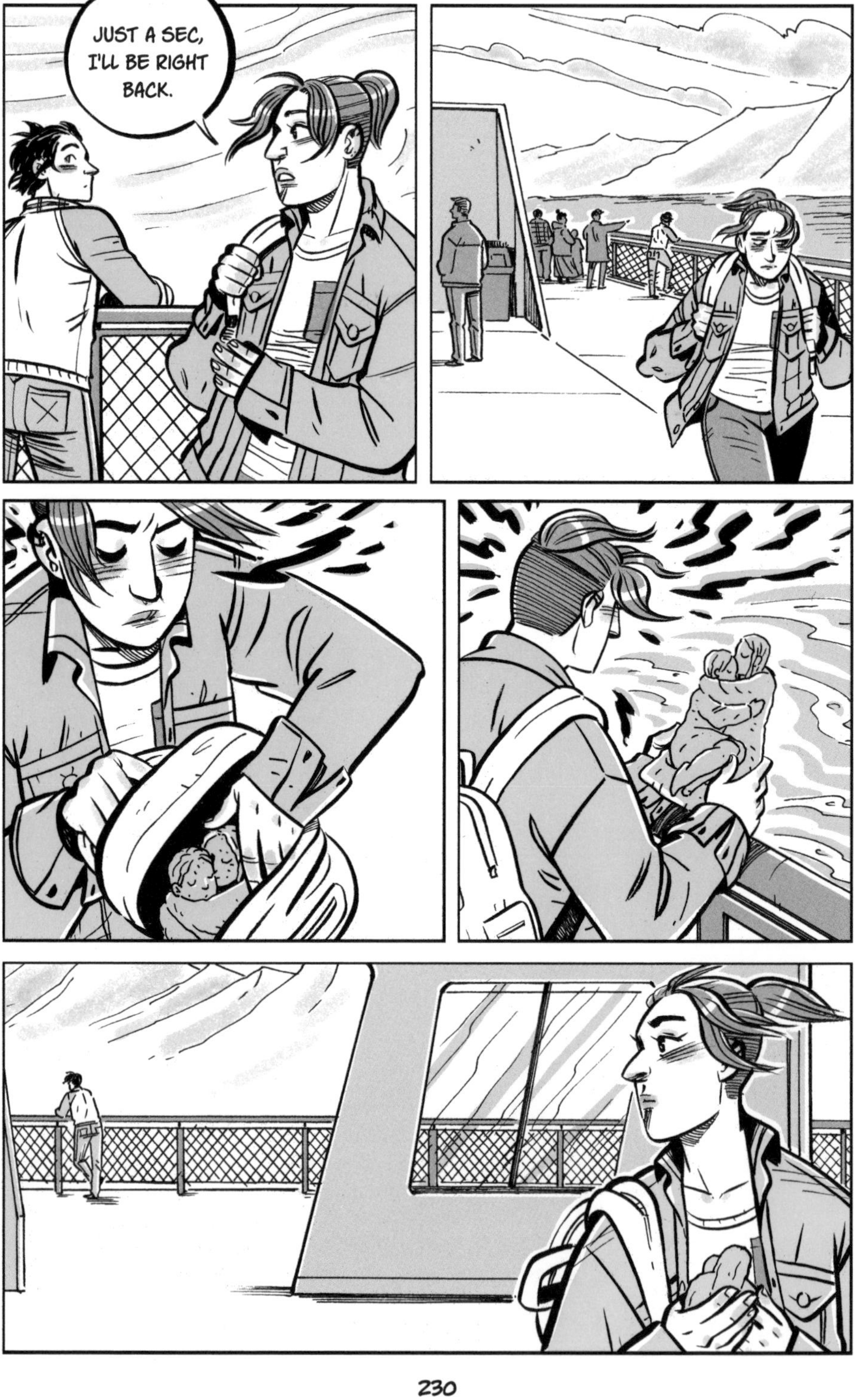
JUST A SEC, I'LL BE RIGHT BACK.

RRRRM

VRRMM

VRRRRM

ABBOTSFO
VANCOUVI

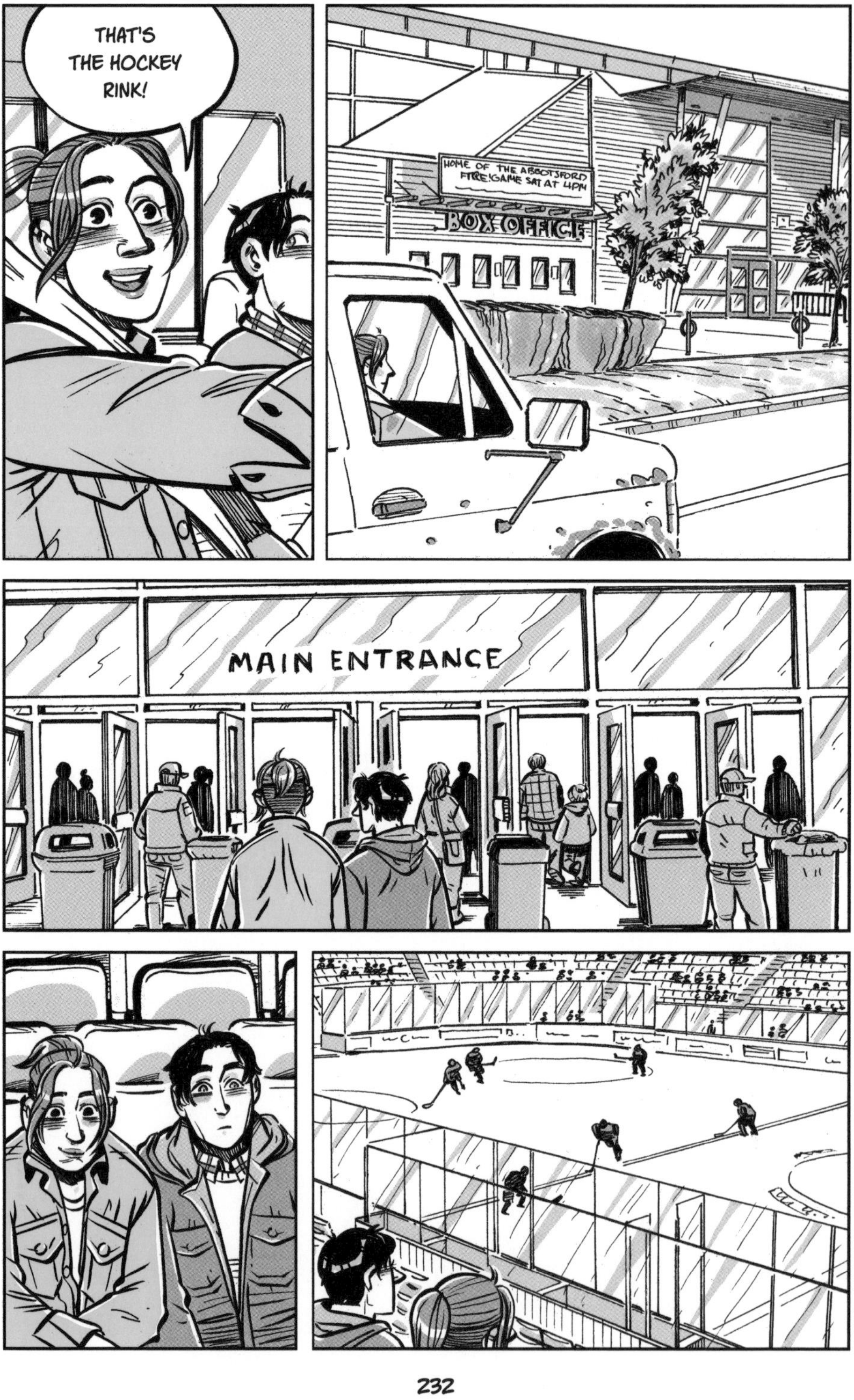
THAT'S THE HOCKEY RINK!
HOME OF THE ABBOTSFORD FIRE! GAME SAT AT 4PM
BOX OFFICE
MAIN ENTRANCE

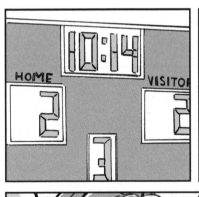

THAT'S HIM! THAT'S MY DAD.

YOU SURE?

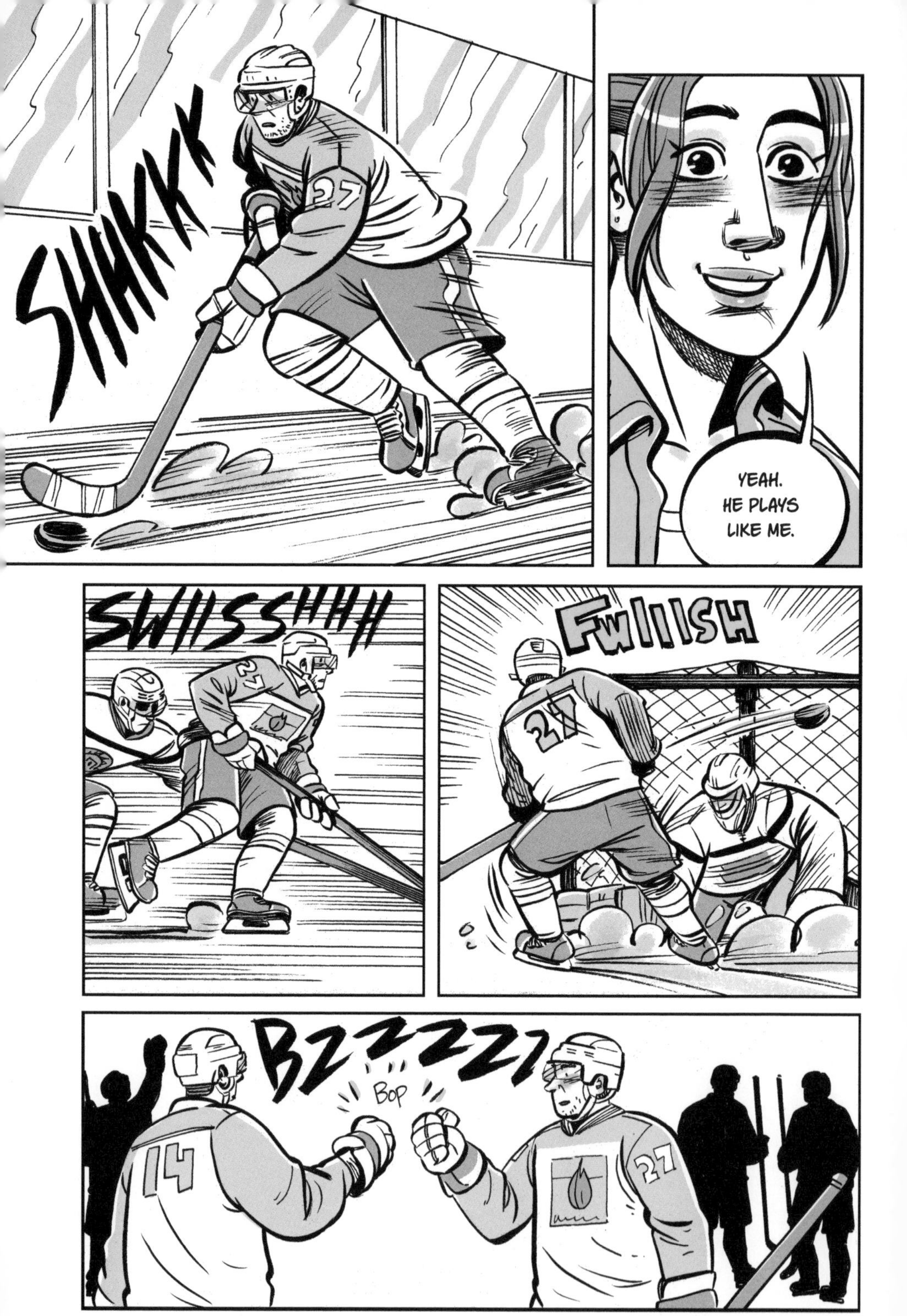
SHHKKK
YEAH.
HE PLAYS
LIKE ME.
SWIISSHHH
FWIIISH
BZZZZZ
Bop

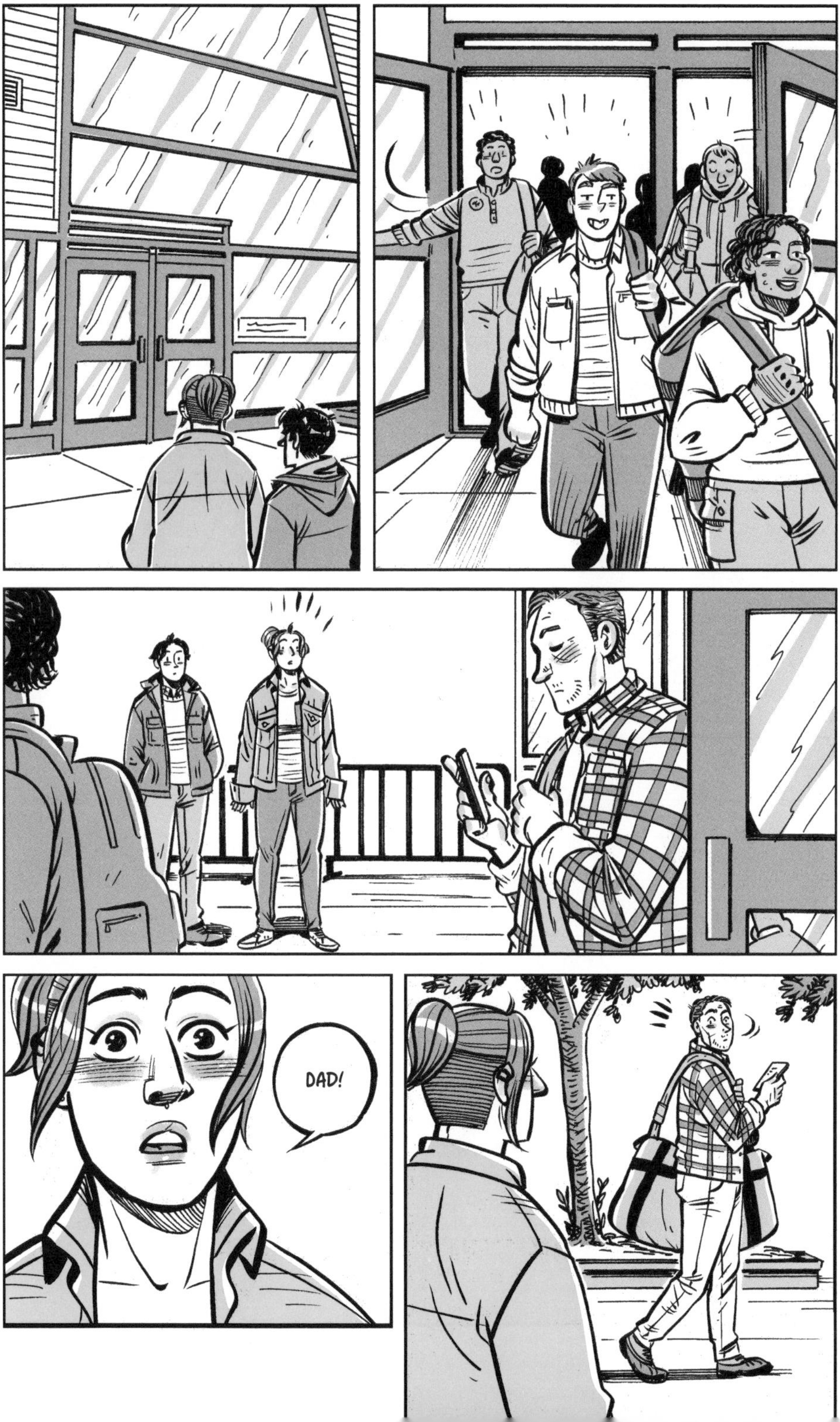
DAD!

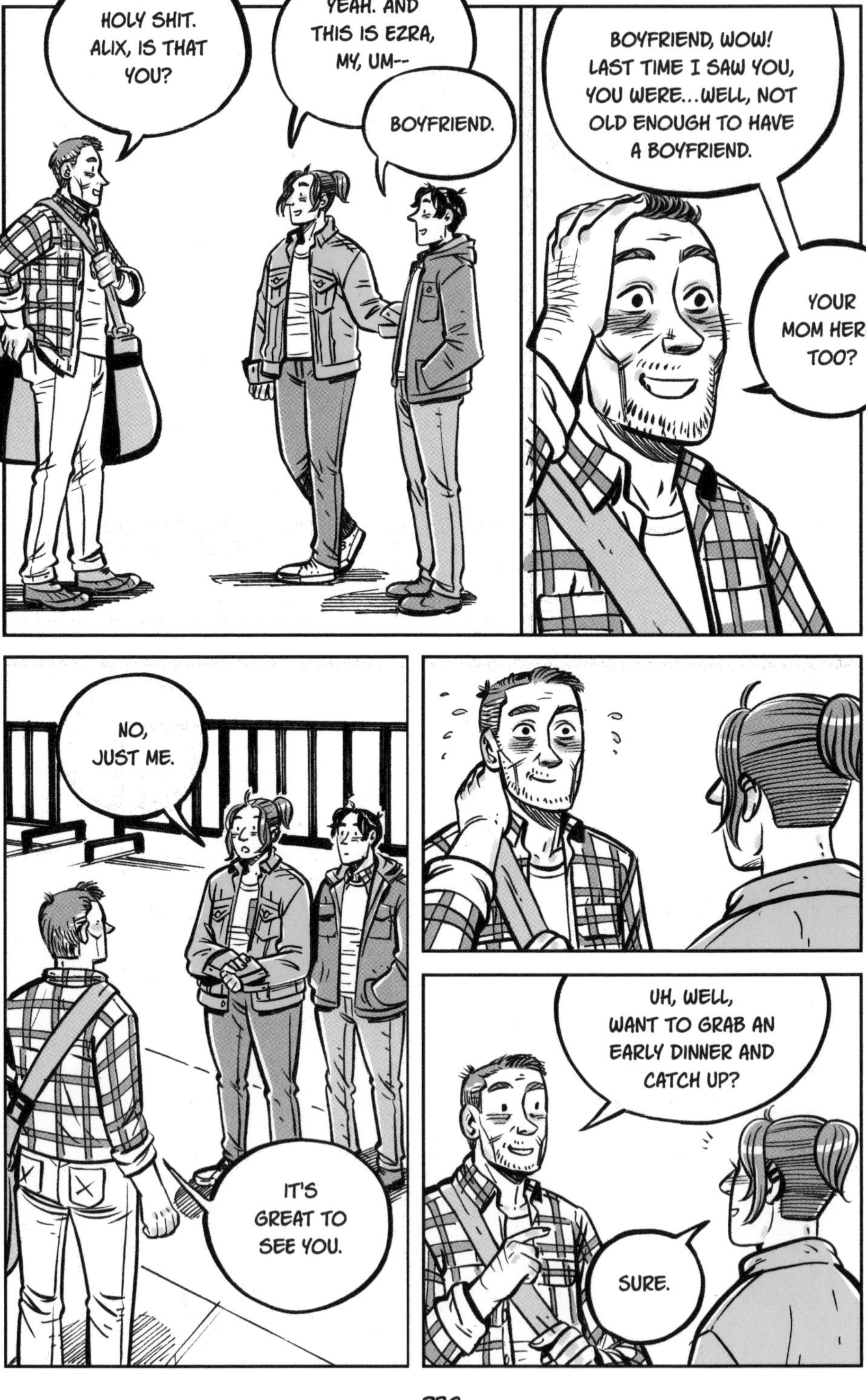
HOLY SHIT. ALIX, IS THAT YOU?
YEAH. AND THIS IS EZRA, MY, UM--
BOYFRIEND.
BOYFRIEND, WOW! LAST TIME I SAW YOU, YOU WERE...WELL, NOT OLD ENOUGH TO HAVE A BOYFRIEND.
YOUR MOM HERE, TOO?
NO, JUST ME.
IT'S GREAT TO SEE YOU.
UH, WELL, WANT TO GRAB AN EARLY DINNER AND CATCH UP?
SURE.

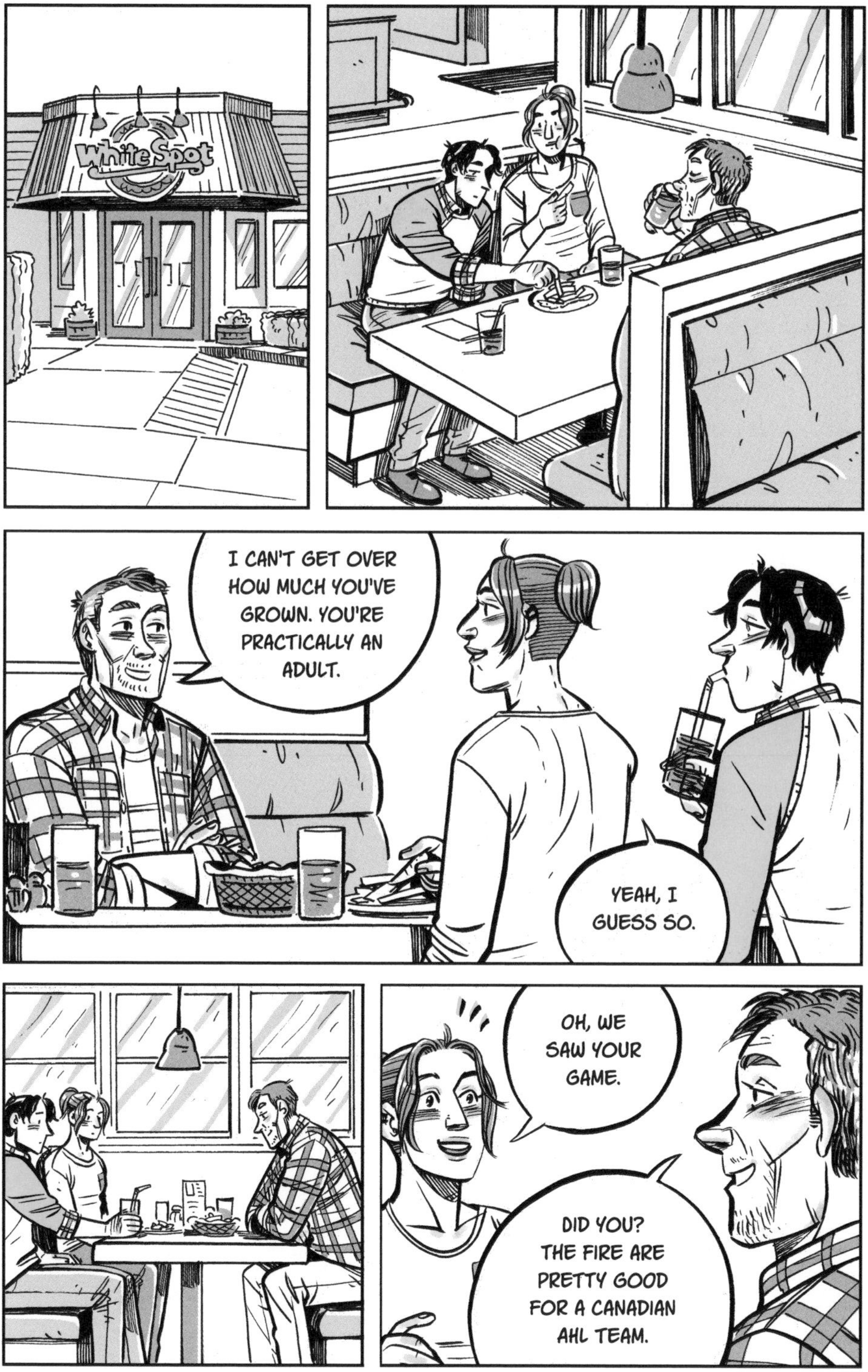
White Spot
I CAN'T GET OVER HOW MUCH YOU'VE GROWN. YOU'RE PRACTICALLY AN ADULT.
YEAH, I GUESS SO.
OH, WE SAW YOUR GAME.
DID YOU? THE FIRE ARE PRETTY GOOD FOR A CANADIAN AHL TEAM.

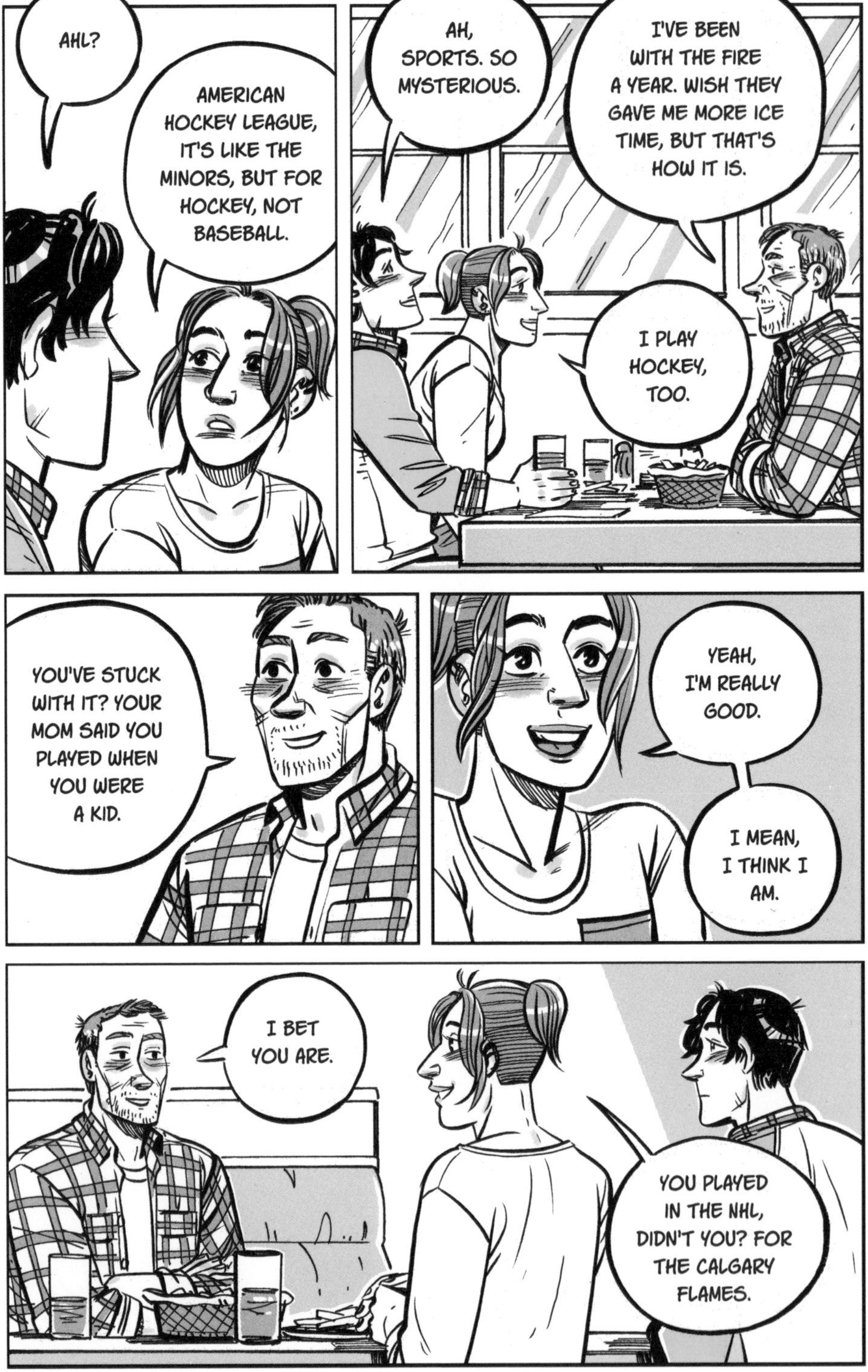
AHL?
AMERICAN HOCKEY LEAGUE, IT'S LIKE THE MINORS, BUT FOR HOCKEY, NOT BASEBALL.
AH, SPORTS. SO MYSTERIOUS.
I'VE BEEN WITH THE FIRE A YEAR. WISH THEY GAVE ME MORE ICE TIME, BUT THAT'S HOW IT IS.
I PLAY HOCKEY, TOO.
YOU'VE STUCK WITH IT? YOUR MOM SAID YOU PLAYED WHEN YOU WERE A KID.
YEAH, I'M REALLY GOOD.
I MEAN, I THINK I AM.
I BET YOU ARE.
YOU PLAYED IN THE NHL, DIDN'T YOU? FOR THE CALGARY FLAMES.

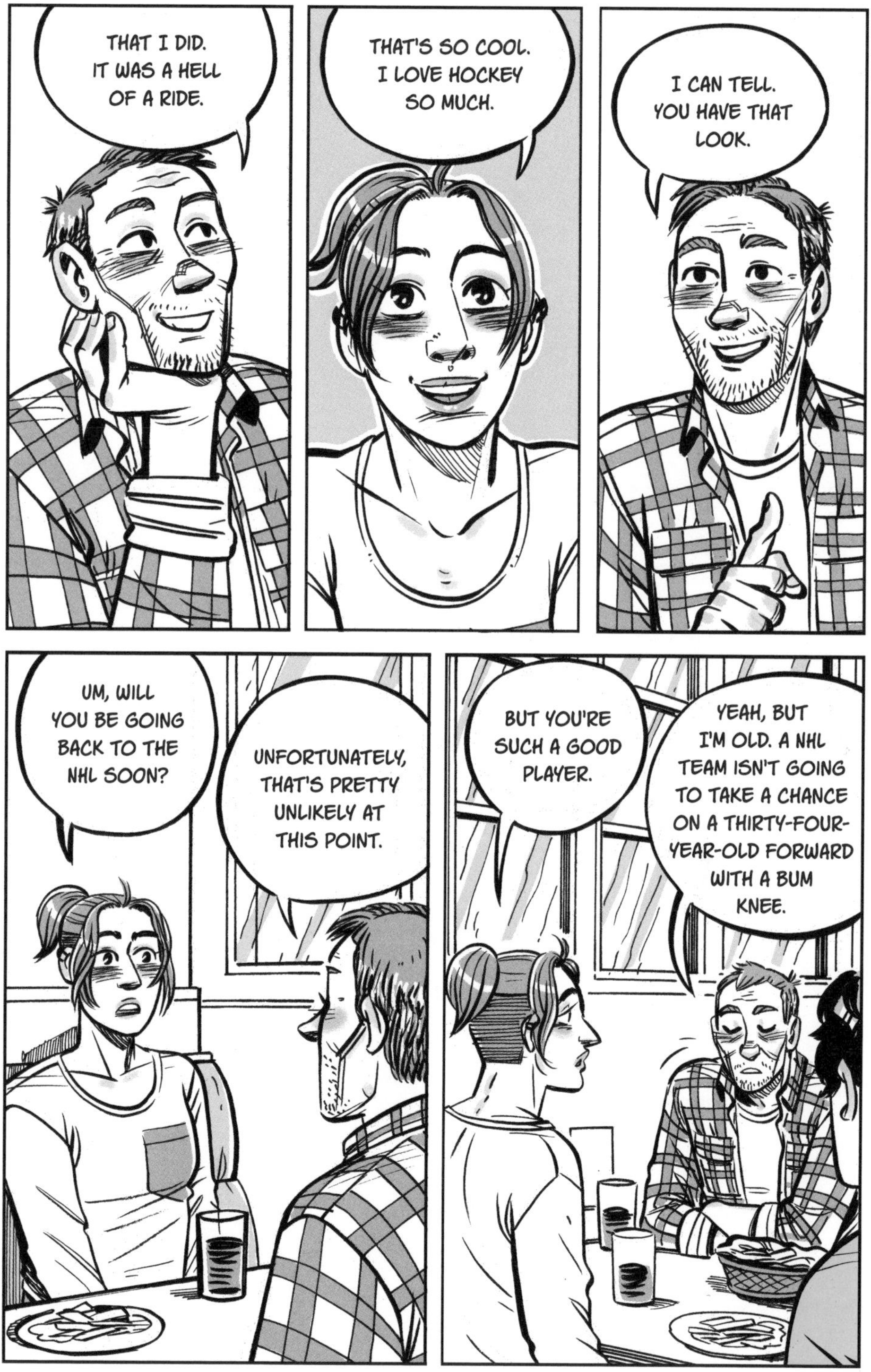
THAT I DID. IT WAS A HELL OF A RIDE.
THAT'S SO COOL. I LOVE HOCKEY SO MUCH.
I CAN TELL. YOU HAVE THAT LOOK.
UM, WILL YOU BE GOING BACK TO THE NHL SOON?
UNFORTUNATELY, THAT'S PRETTY UNLIKELY AT THIS POINT.
BUT YOU'RE SUCH A GOOD PLAYER.
YEAH, BUT I'M OLD. A NHL TEAM ISN'T GOING TO TAKE A CHANCE ON A THIRTY-FOUR-YEAR-OLD FORWARD WITH A BUM KNEE.

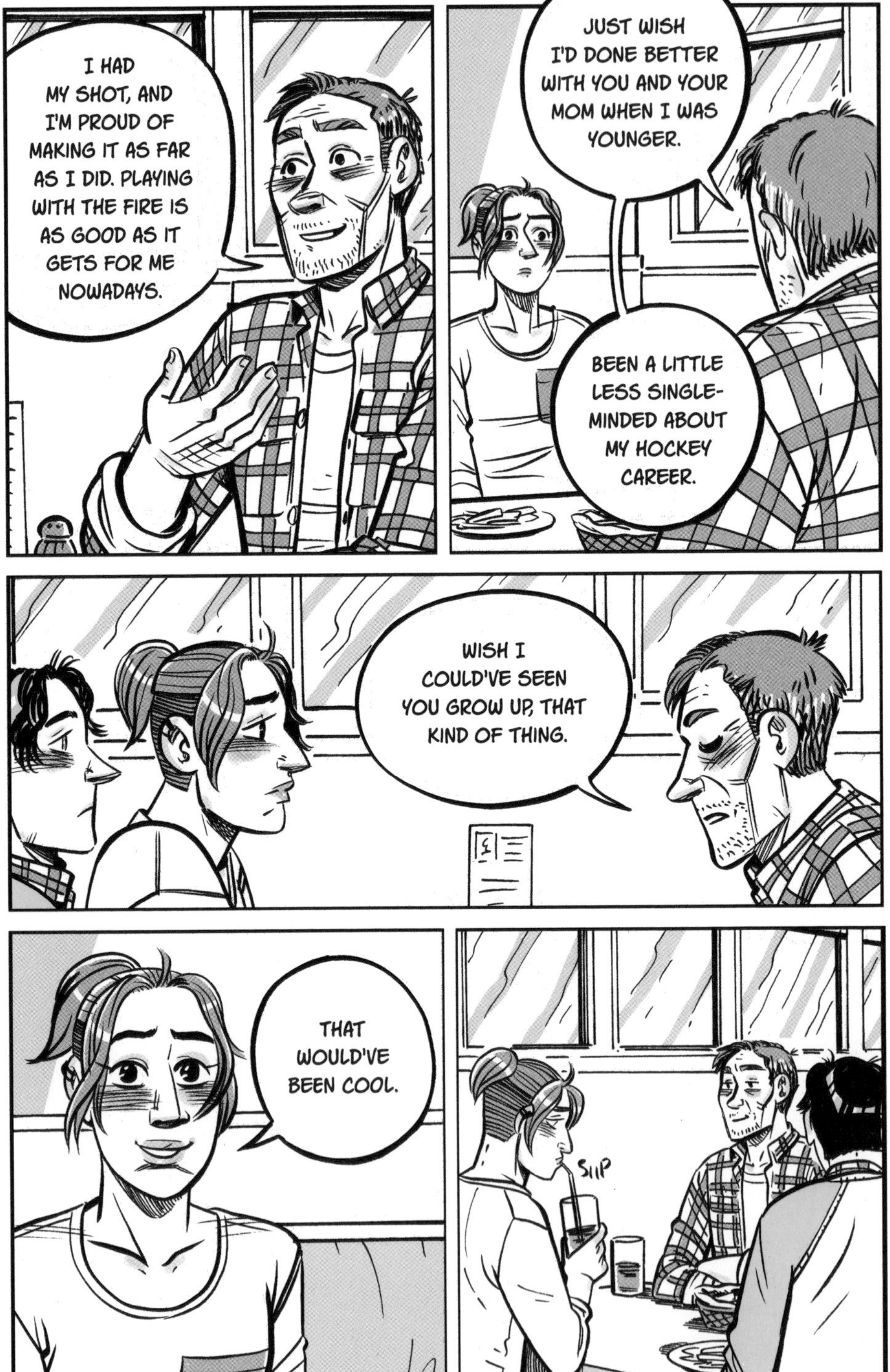
I HAD MY SHOT, AND I'M PROUD OF MAKING IT AS FAR AS I DID. PLAYING WITH THE FIRE IS AS GOOD AS IT GETS FOR ME NOWADAYS.
JUST WISH I'D DONE BETTER WITH YOU AND YOUR MOM WHEN I WAS YOUNGER.
BEEN A LITTLE LESS SINGLE-MINDED ABOUT MY HOCKEY CAREER.
WISH I COULD'VE SEEN YOU GROW UP, THAT KIND OF THING.
THAT WOULD'VE BEEN COOL.
SIIP

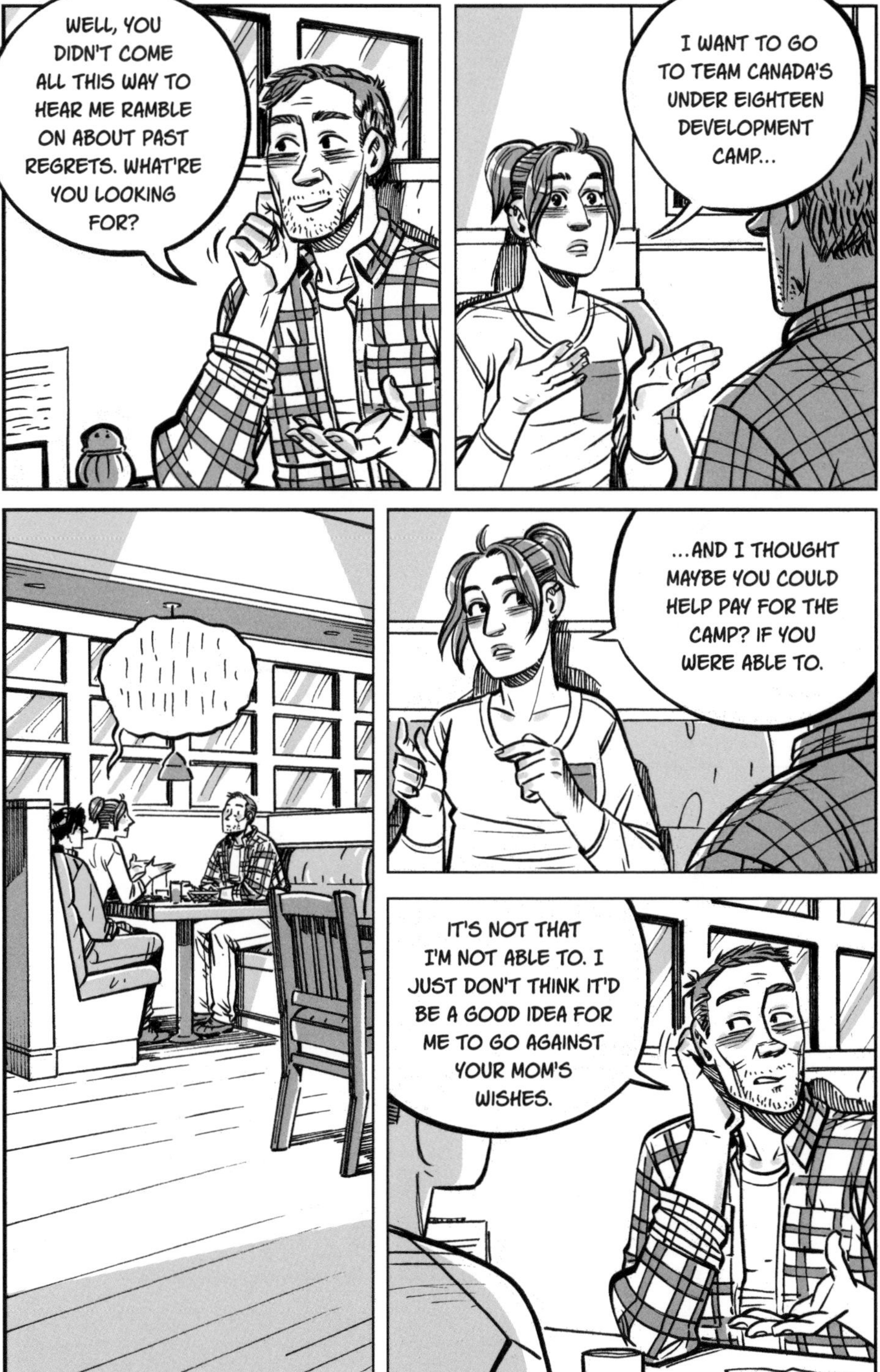
WELL, YOU DIDN'T COME ALL THIS WAY TO HEAR ME RAMBLE ON ABOUT PAST REGRETS. WHAT'RE YOU LOOKING FOR?
I WANT TO GO TO TEAM CANADA'S UNDER EIGHTEEN DEVELOPMENT CAMP...
...AND I THOUGHT MAYBE YOU COULD HELP PAY FOR THE CAMP? IF YOU WERE ABLE TO.
IT'S NOT THAT I'M NOT ABLE TO. I JUST DON'T THINK IT'D BE A GOOD IDEA FOR ME TO GO AGAINST YOUR MOM'S WISHES.

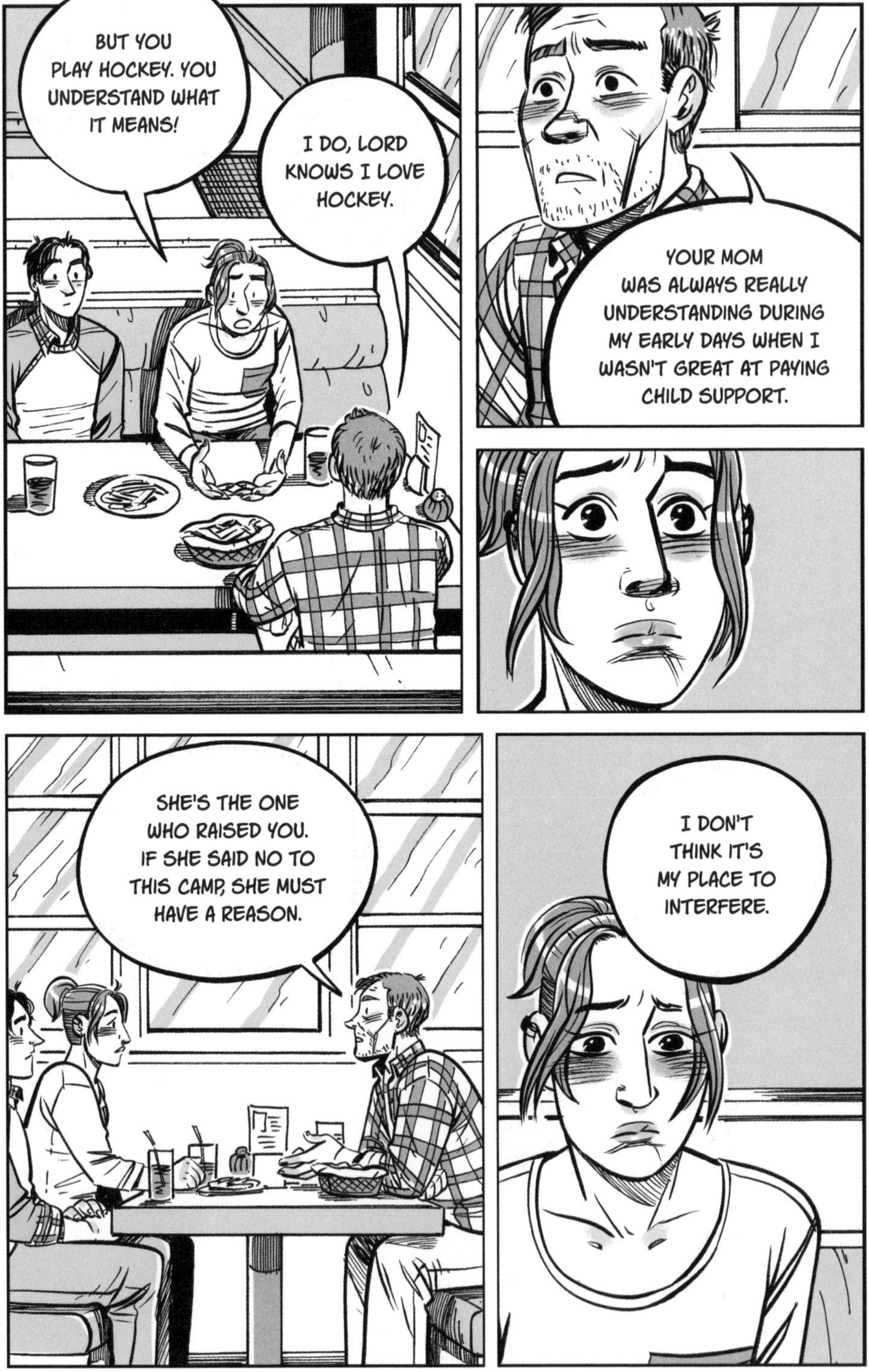
BUT YOU PLAY HOCKEY. YOU UNDERSTAND WHAT IT MEANS!
I DO, LORD KNOWS I LOVE HOCKEY.
YOUR MOM WAS ALWAYS REALLY UNDERSTANDING DURING MY EARLY DAYS WHEN I WASN'T GREAT AT PAYING CHILD SUPPORT.
SHE'S THE ONE WHO RAISED YOU. IF SHE SAID NO TO THIS CAMP, SHE MUST HAVE A REASON.
I DON'T THINK IT'S MY PLACE TO INTERFERE.

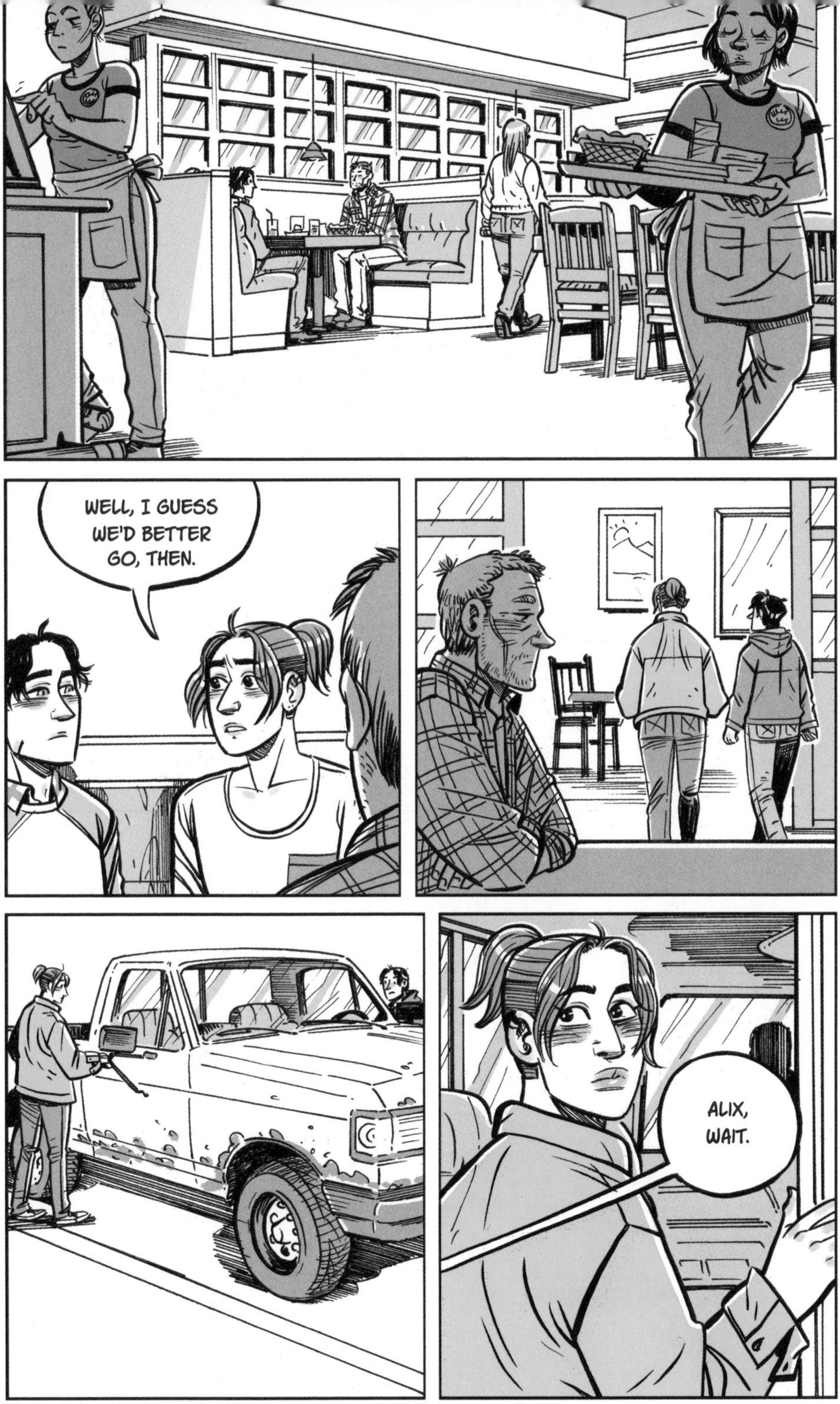
WELL, I GUESS WE'D BETTER GO, THEN.
ALIX, WAIT.

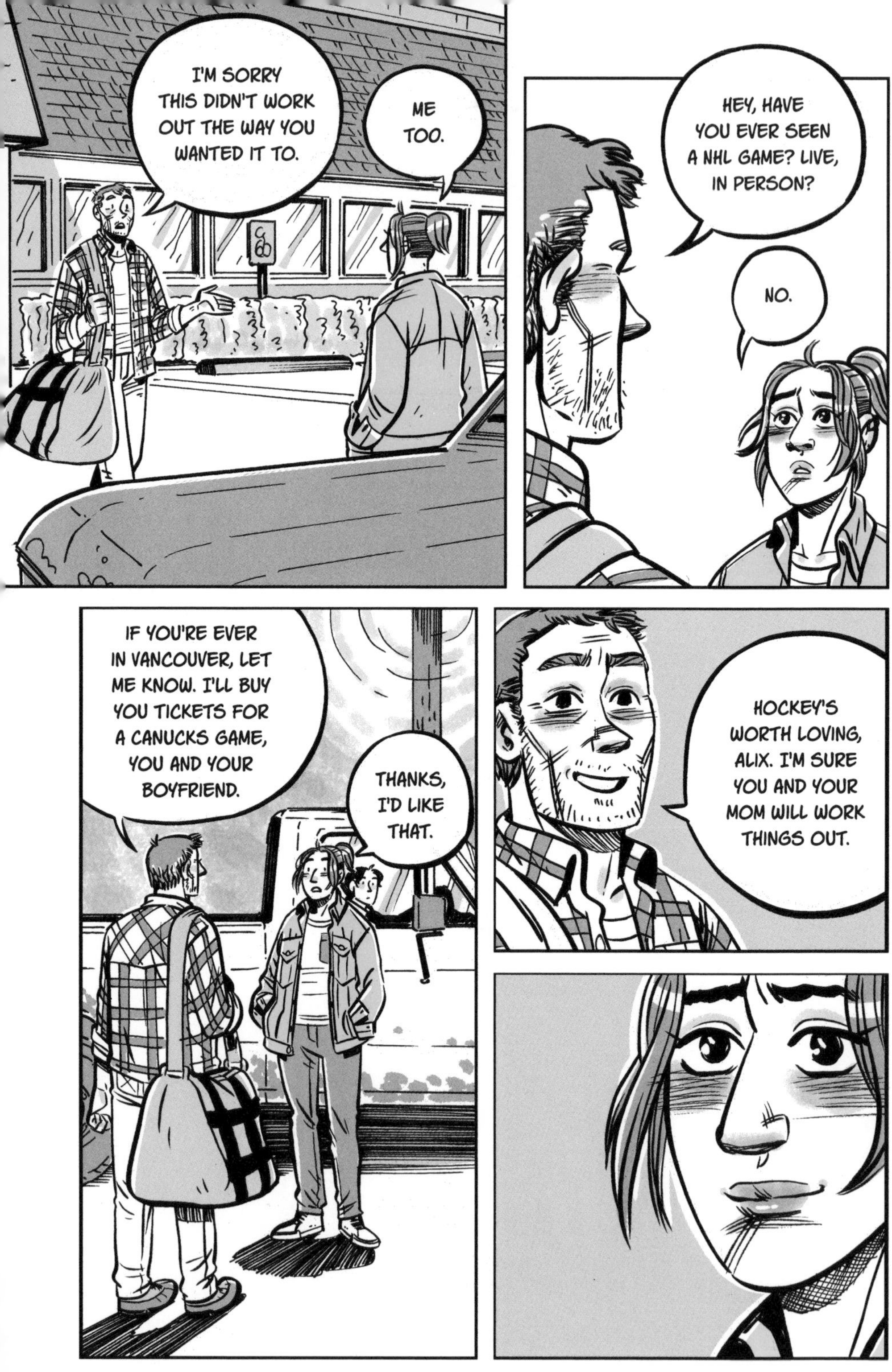
I'M SORRY THIS DIDN'T WORK OUT THE WAY YOU WANTED IT TO.
ME TOO.
HEY, HAVE YOU EVER SEEN A NHL GAME? LIVE, IN PERSON?
NO.
IF YOU'RE EVER IN VANCOUVER, LET ME KNOW. I'LL BUY YOU TICKETS FOR A CANUCKS GAME, YOU AND YOUR BOYFRIEND.
THANKS, I'D LIKE THAT.
HOCKEY'S WORTH LOVING, ALIX. I'M SURE YOU AND YOUR MOM WILL WORK THINGS OUT.

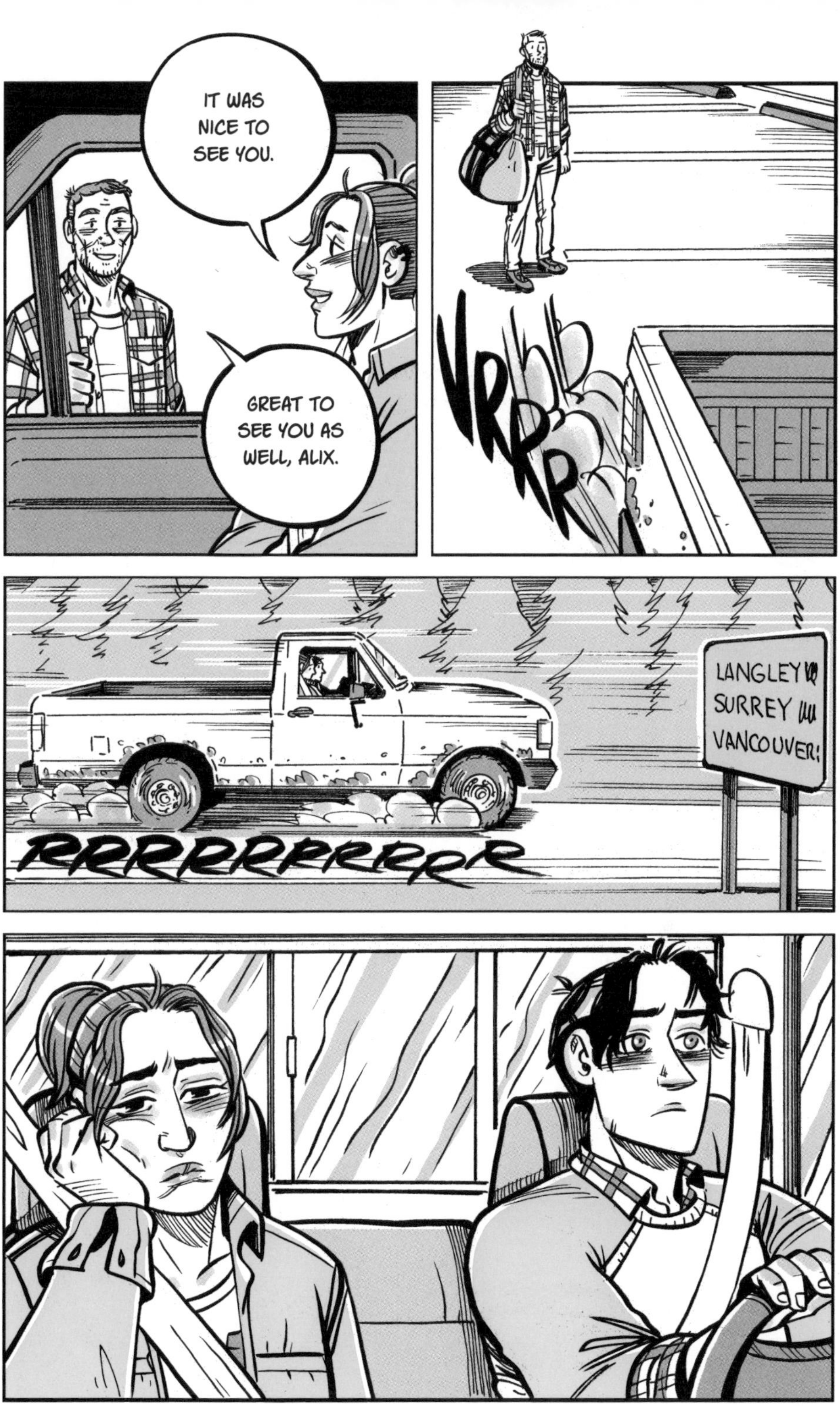
IT WAS NICE TO SEE YOU.
GREAT TO SEE YOU AS WELL, ALIX.
VRRRR
RRRRRRRRRRR
LANGLEY
SURREY
VANCOUVER

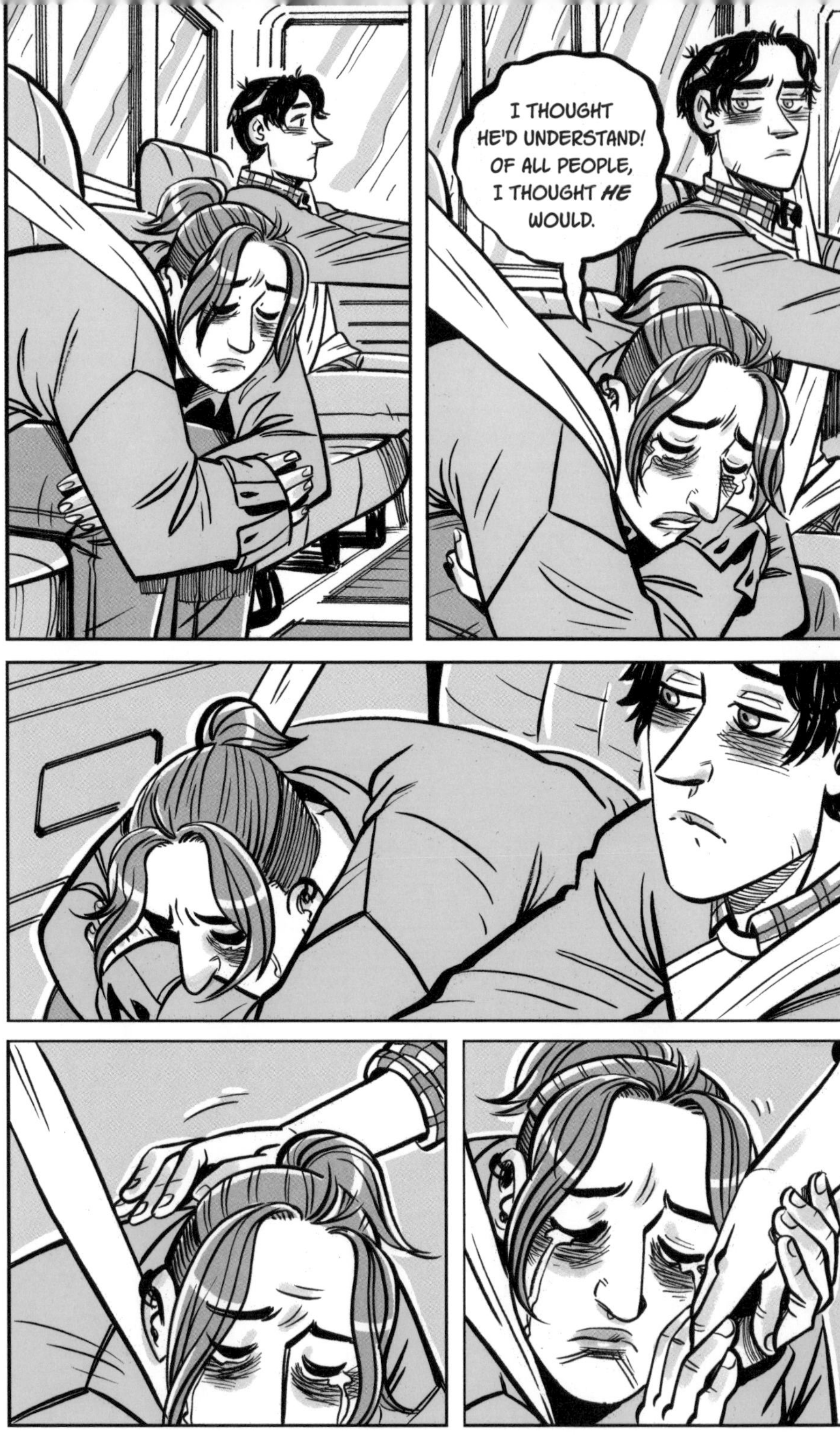
I THOUGHT HE'D UNDERSTAND! OF ALL PEOPLE, I THOUGHT HE WOULD.

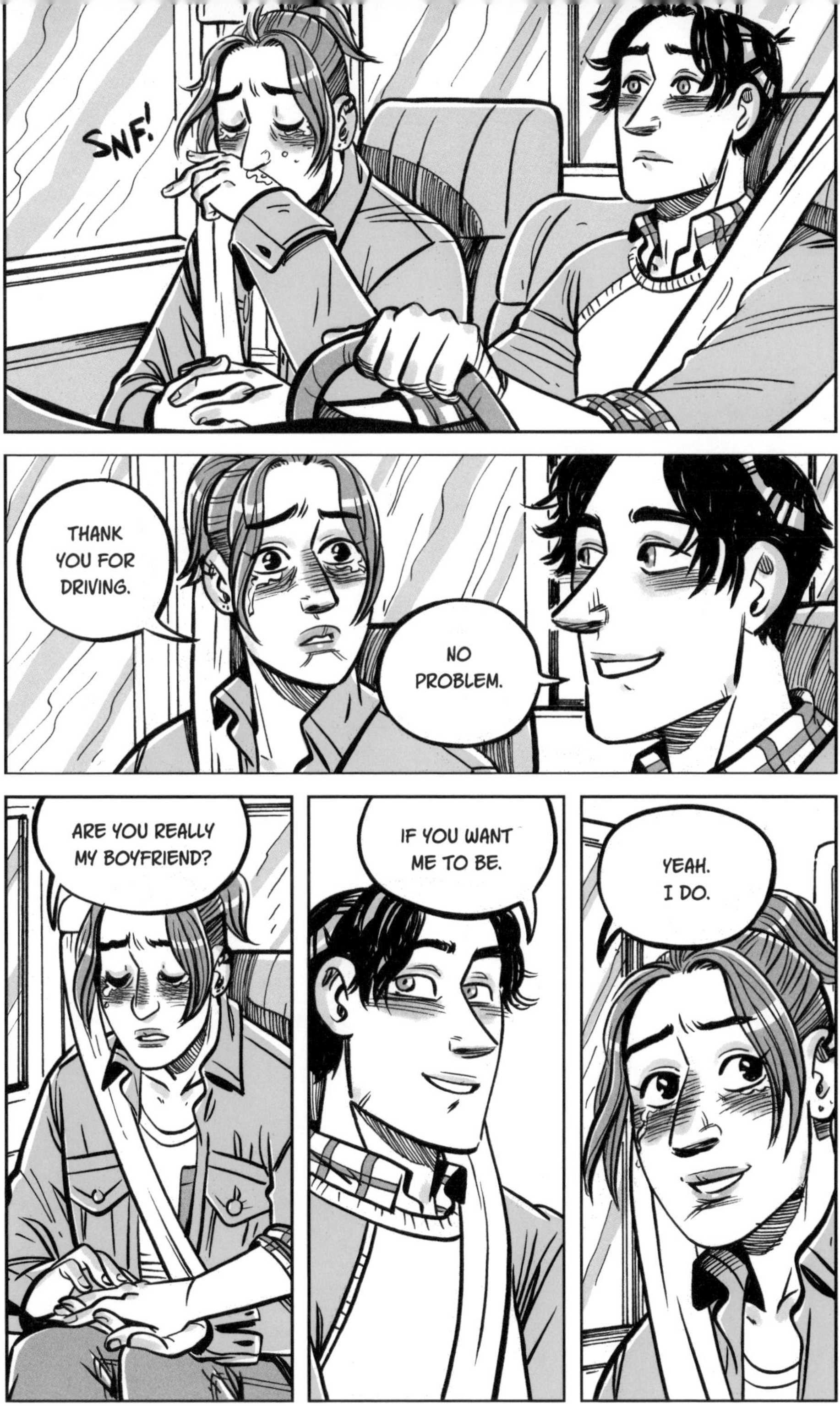
SNF!
THANK YOU FOR DRIVING.
NO PROBLEM.
ARE YOU REALLY MY BOYFRIEND?
IF YOU WANT ME TO BE.
YEAH. I DO.

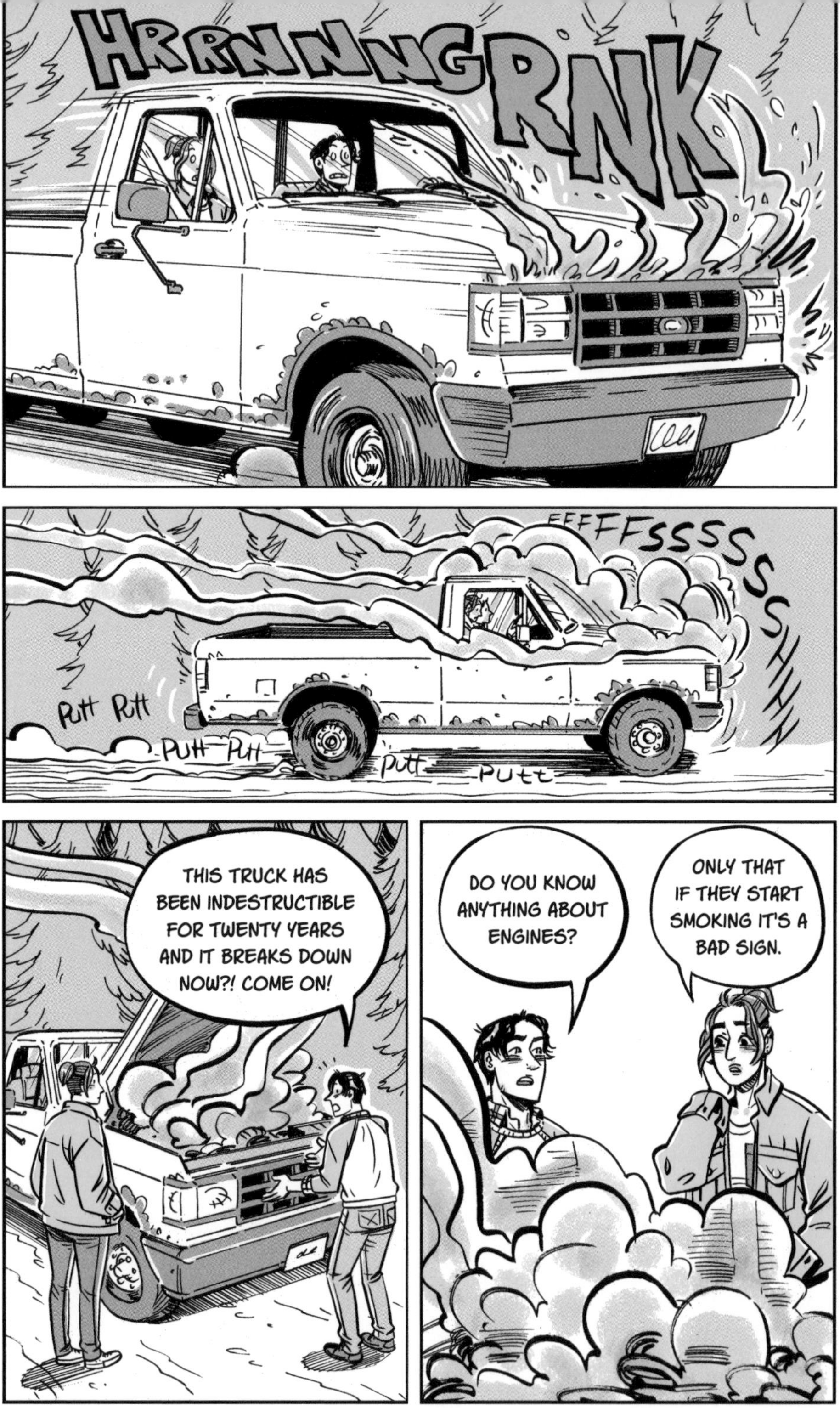
HRRNNNGRNK
EEFFFSSSSSSSHHHN
PUTT PUTT
PUTT PUTT
PUTT
PUTT
THIS TRUCK HAS BEEN INDESTRUCTIBLE FOR TWENTY YEARS AND IT BREAKS DOWN NOW?! COME ON!
DO YOU KNOW ANYTHING ABOUT ENGINES?
ONLY THAT IF THEY START SMOKING IT'S A BAD SIGN.

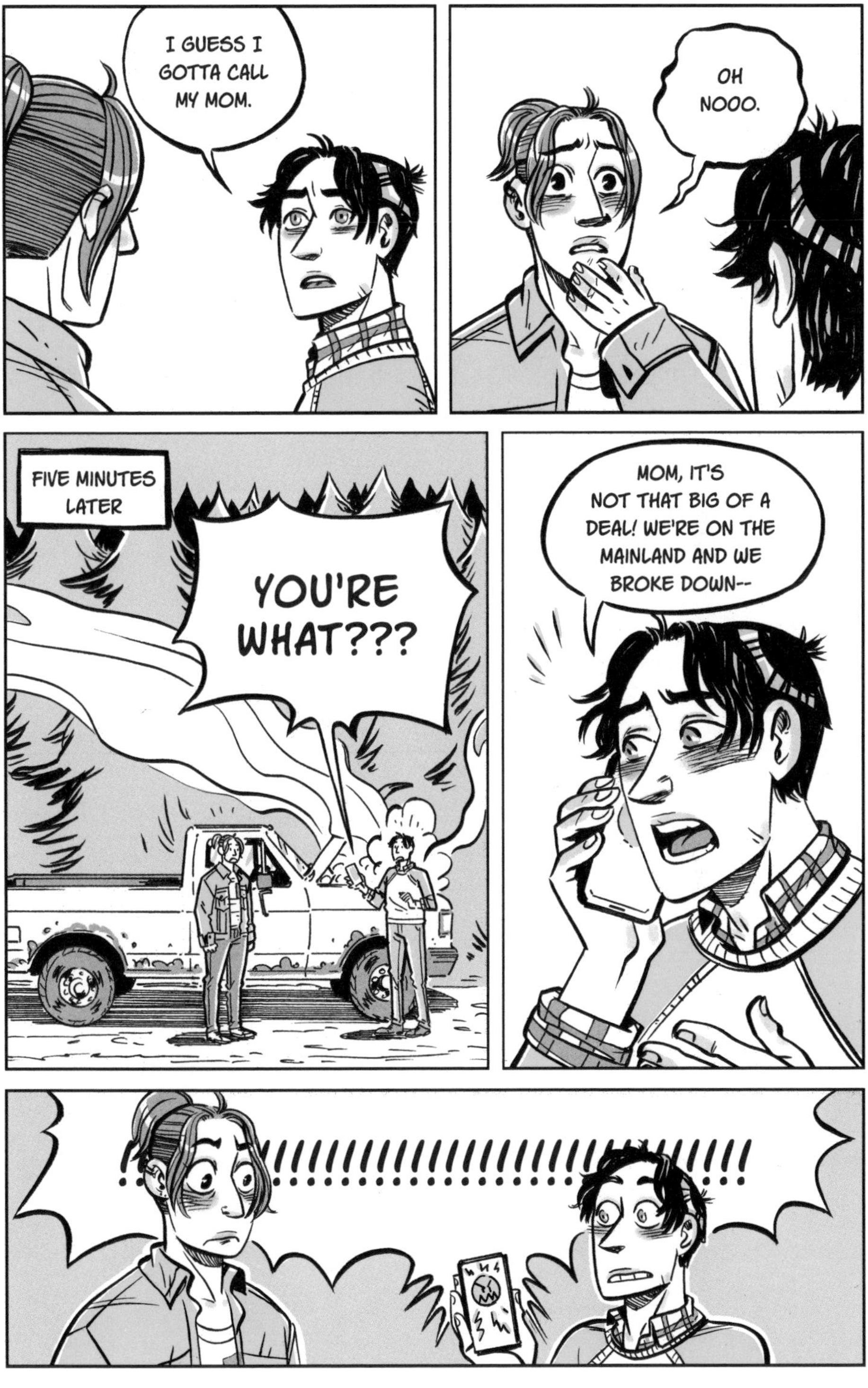
I GUESS I GOTTA CALL MY MOM.
OH NOOO.
FIVE MINUTES LATER
YOU'RE WHAT???
MOM, IT'S NOT THAT BIG OF A DEAL! WE'RE ON THE MAINLAND AND WE BROKE DOWN--
!!

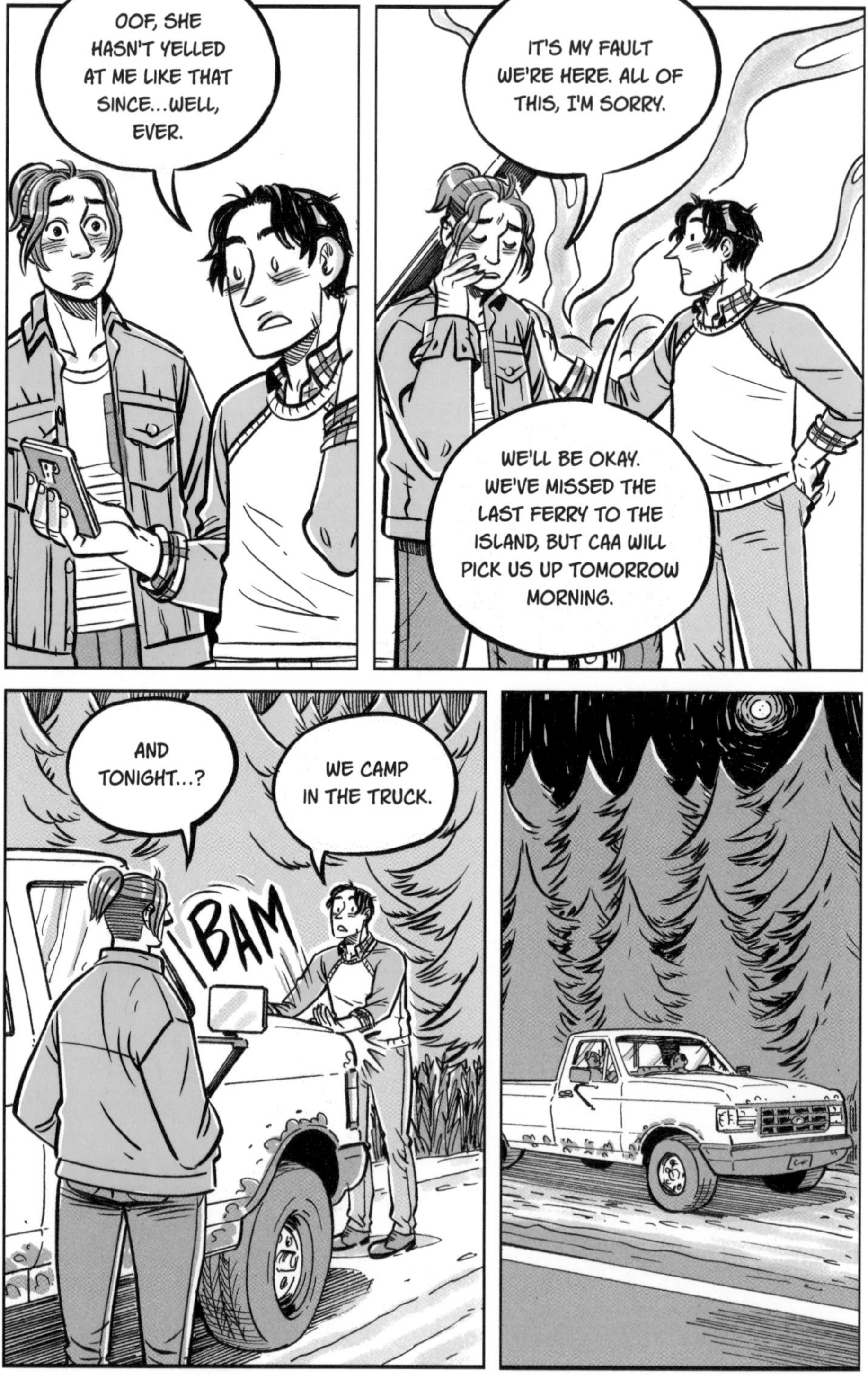
OOF, SHE HASN'T YELLED AT ME LIKE THAT SINCE...WELL, EVER.
IT'S MY FAULT WE'RE HERE. ALL OF THIS, I'M SORRY.
WE'LL BE OKAY. WE'VE MISSED THE LAST FERRY TO THE ISLAND, BUT CAA WILL PICK US UP TOMORROW MORNING.
AND TONIGHT...?
WE CAMP IN THE TRUCK.
BAM

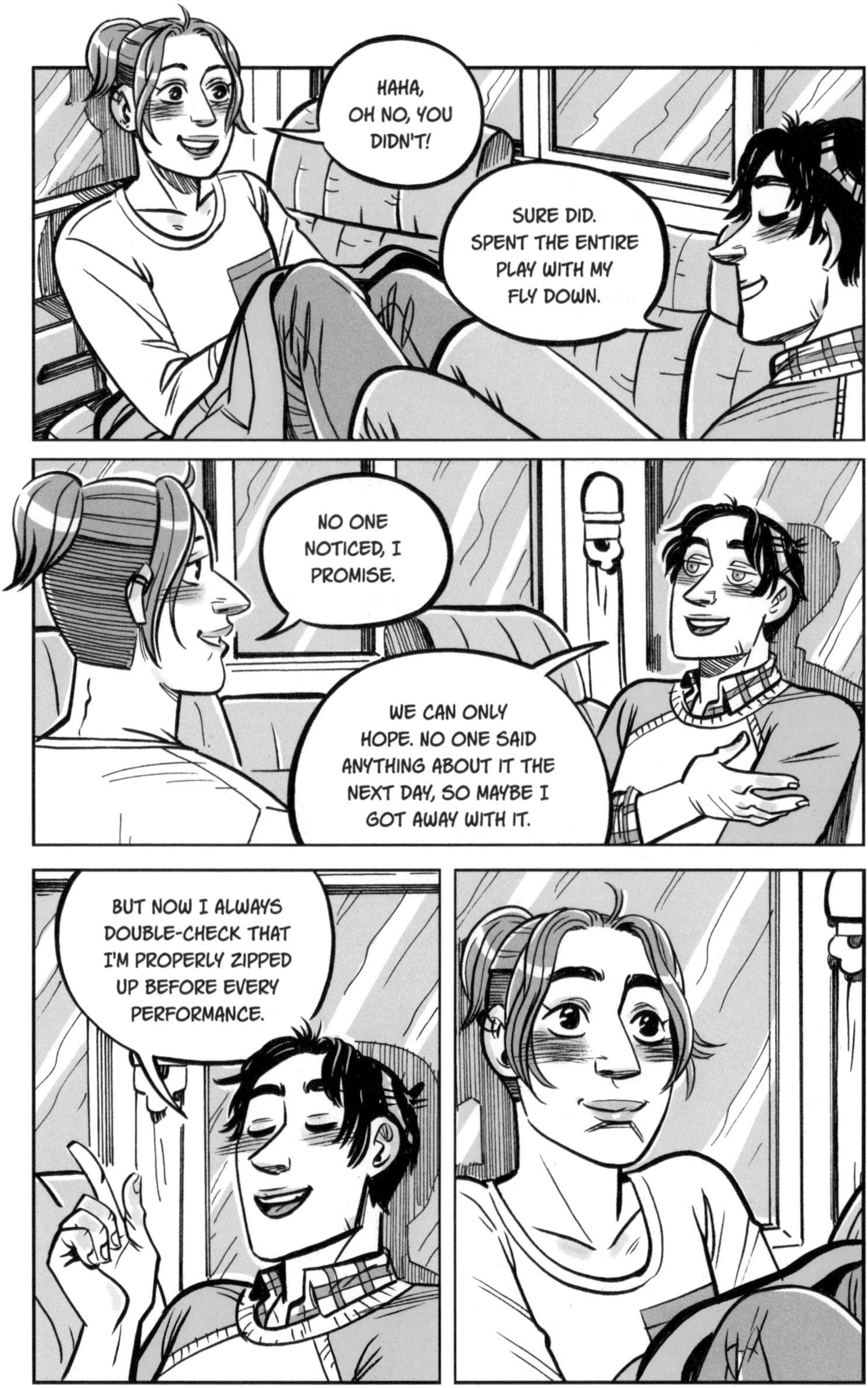
HAHA, OH NO, YOU DIDN'T!
SURE DID. SPENT THE ENTIRE PLAY WITH MY FLY DOWN.
NO ONE NOTICED, I PROMISE.
WE CAN ONLY HOPE. NO ONE SAID ANYTHING ABOUT IT THE NEXT DAY, SO MAYBE I GOT AWAY WITH IT.
BUT NOW I ALWAYS DOUBLE-CHECK THAT I'M PROPERLY ZIPPED UP BEFORE EVERY PERFORMANCE.

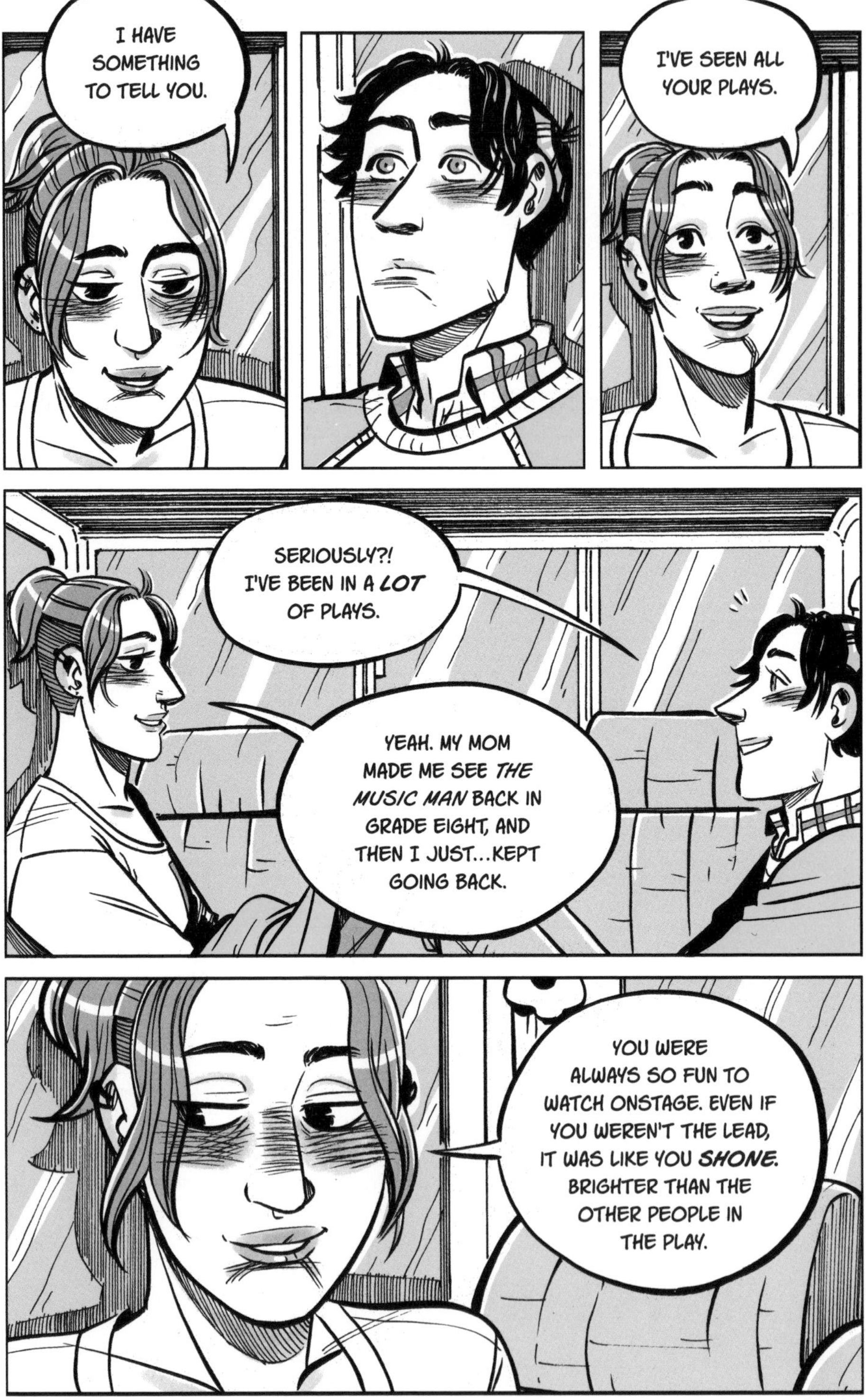
I HAVE SOMETHING TO TELL YOU.
I'VE SEEN ALL YOUR PLAYS.
SERIOUSLY?! I'VE BEEN IN A *LOT* OF PLAYS.
YEAH. MY MOM MADE ME SEE *THE MUSIC MAN* BACK IN GRADE EIGHT, AND THEN I JUST...KEPT GOING BACK.
YOU WERE ALWAYS SO FUN TO WATCH ONSTAGE. EVEN IF YOU WEREN'T THE LEAD, IT WAS LIKE YOU ***SHONE***. BRIGHTER THAN THE OTHER PEOPLE IN THE PLAY.

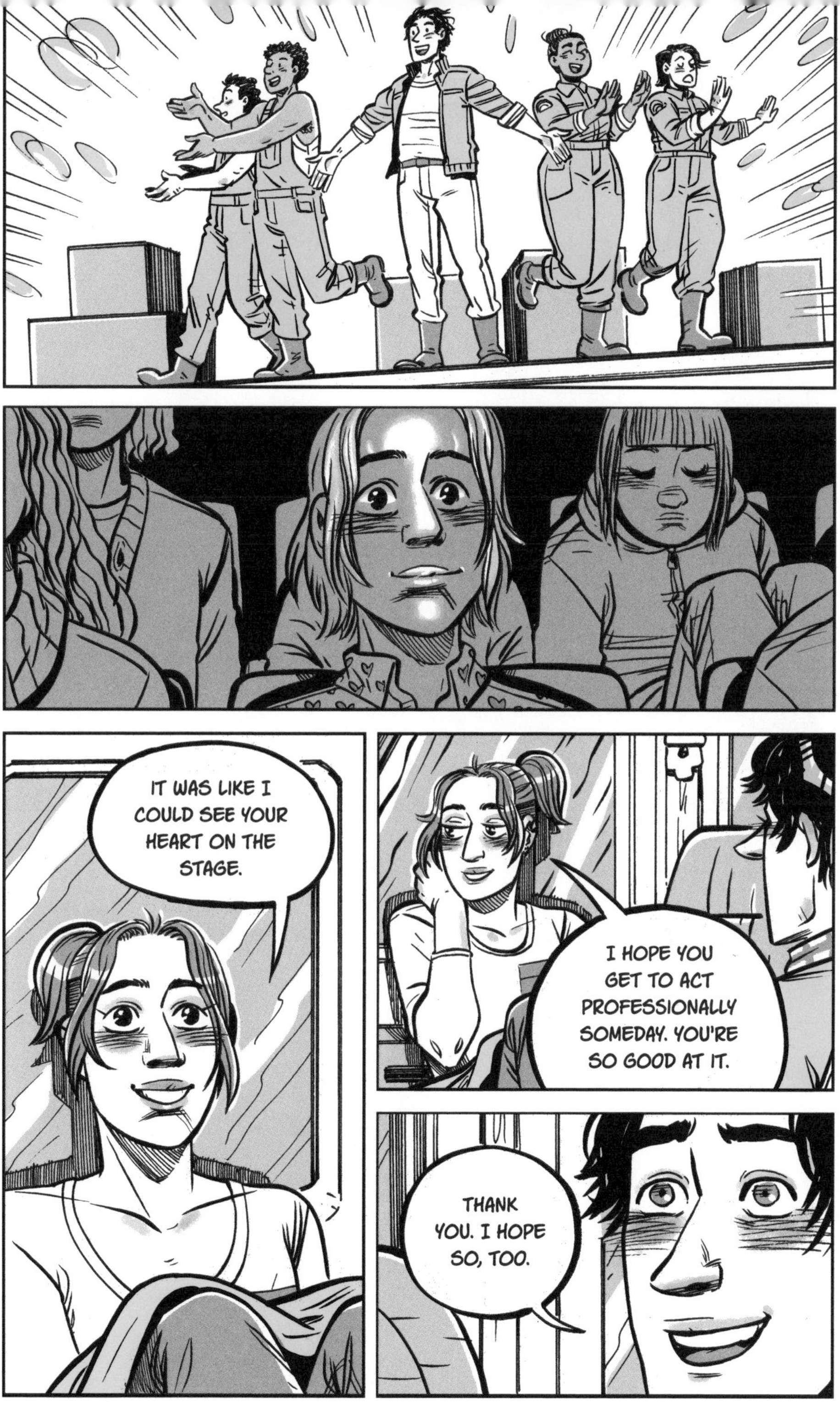
IT WAS LIKE I COULD SEE YOUR HEART ON THE STAGE.
I HOPE YOU GET TO ACT PROFESSIONALLY SOMEDAY. YOU'RE SO GOOD AT IT.
THANK YOU. I HOPE SO, TOO.

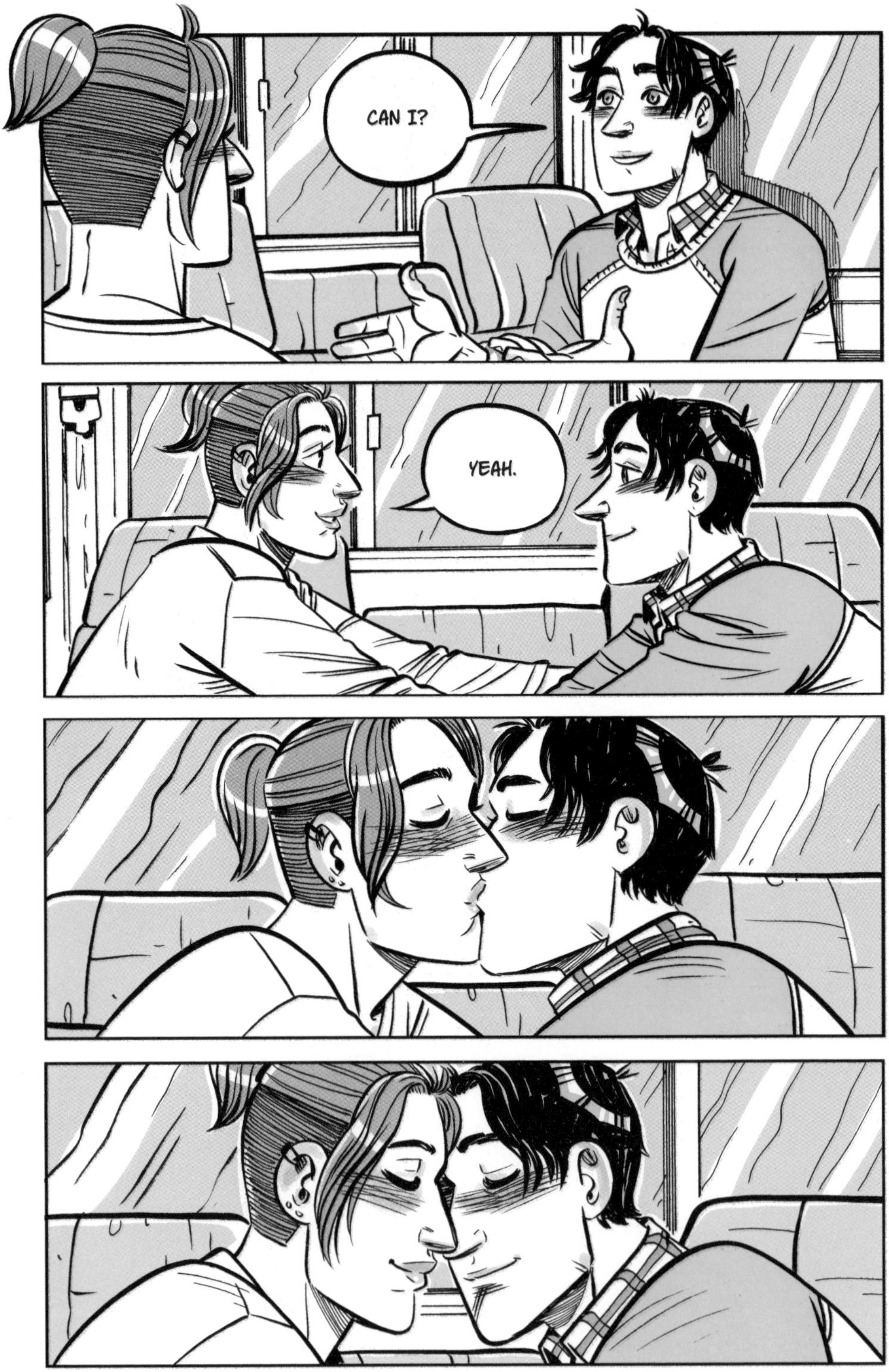
CAN I?
YEAH.

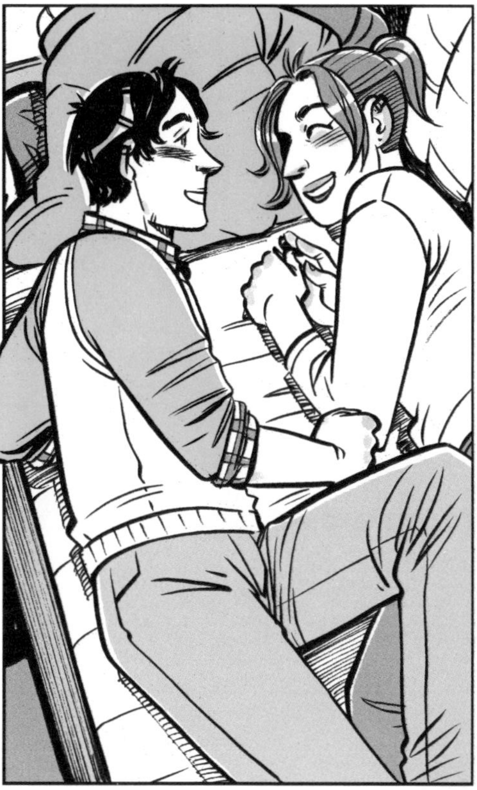

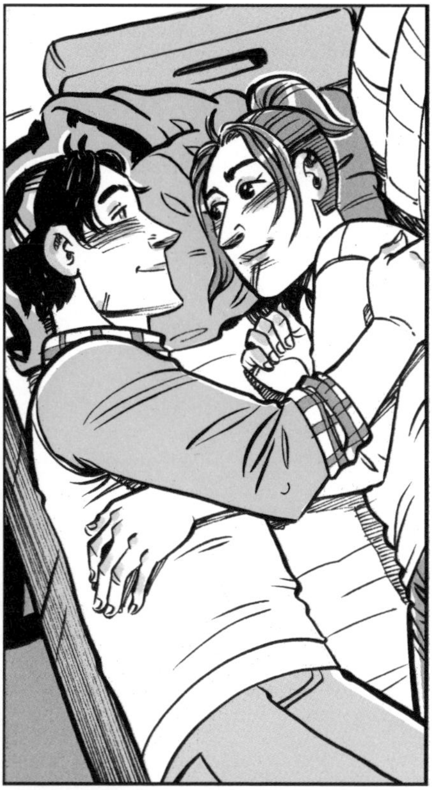

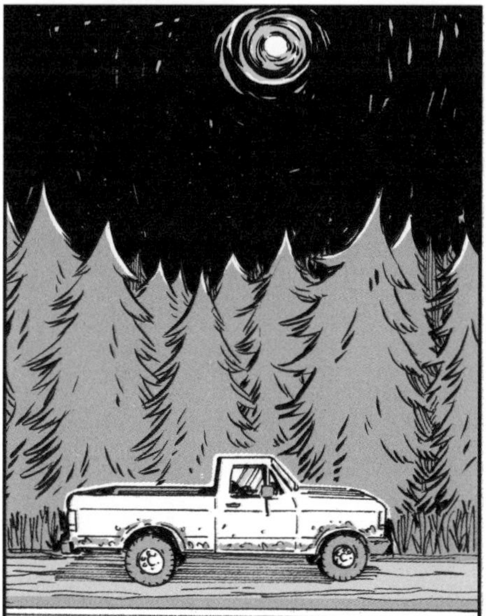

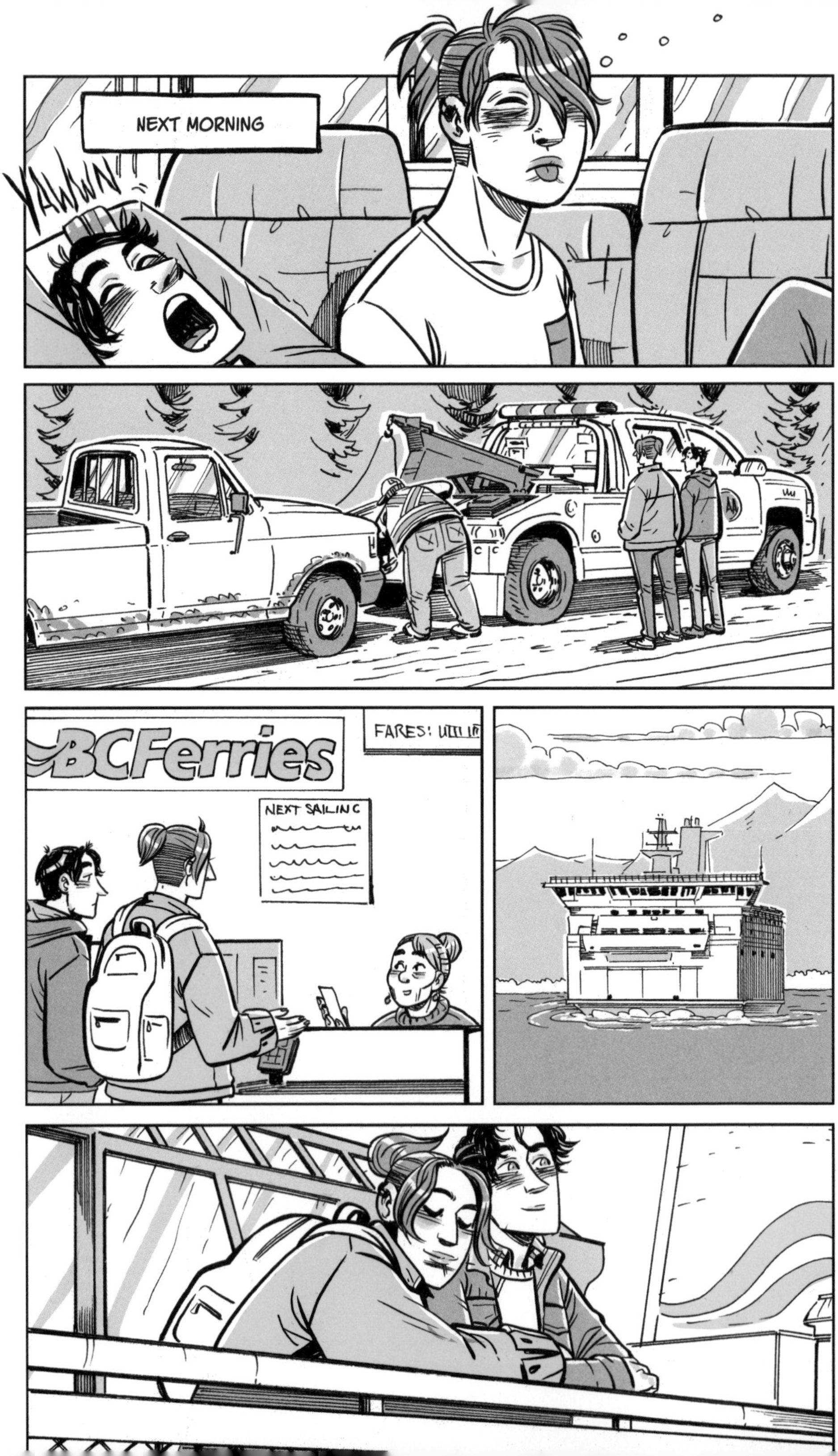
NEXT MORNING
YAWWN
BCFerries
FARES:
NEXT SAILING

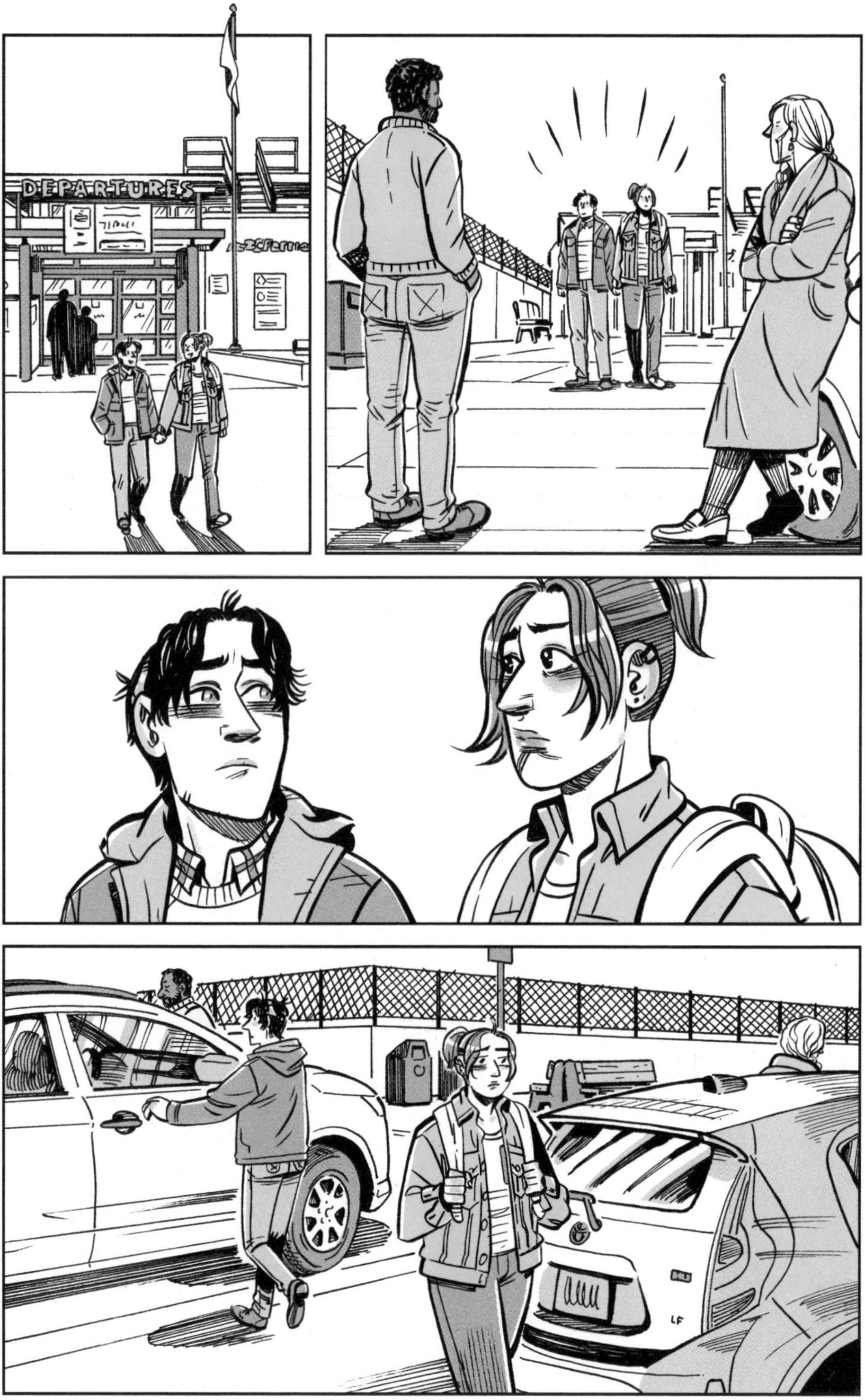
DEPARTURES

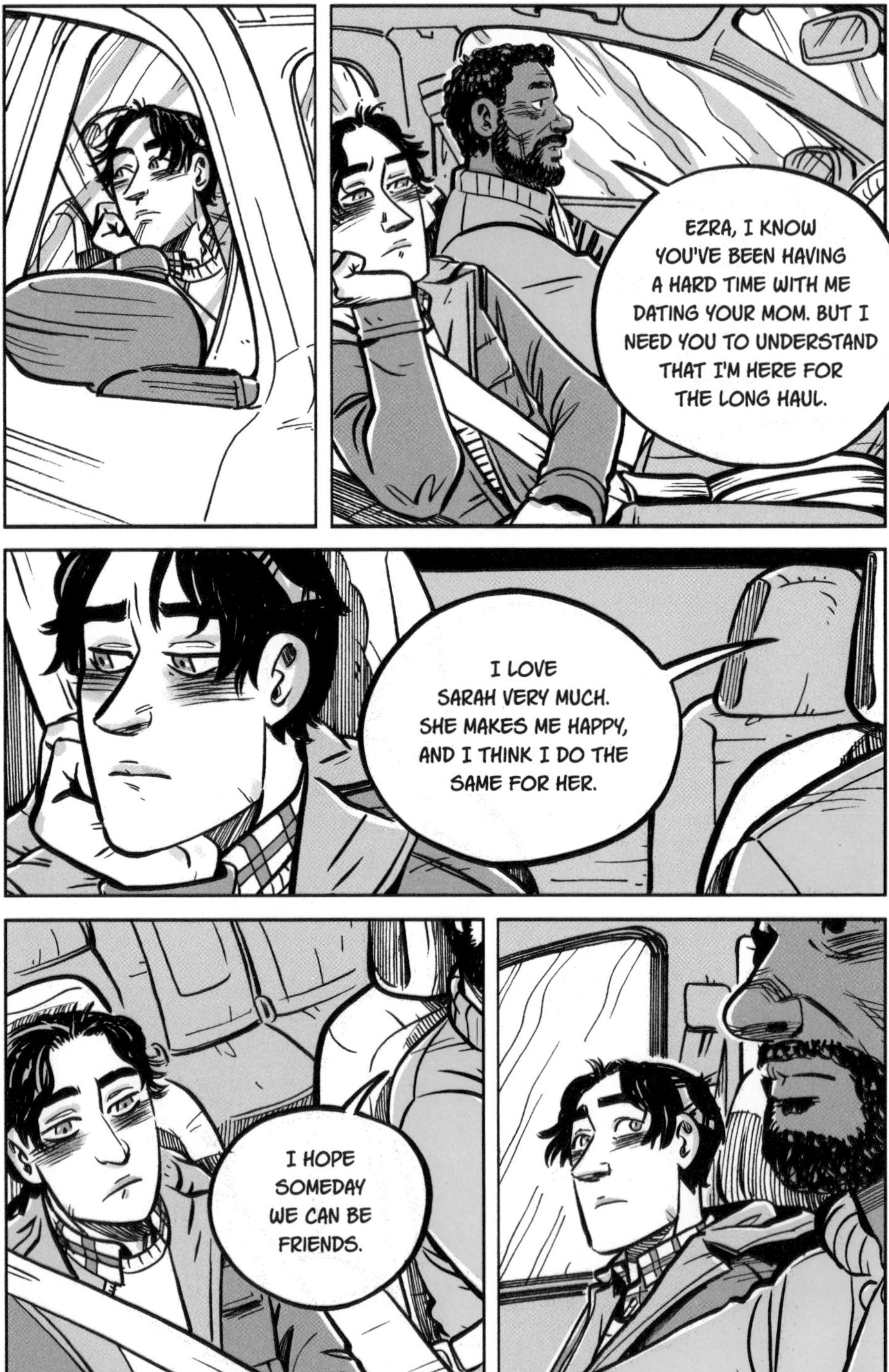
EZRA, I KNOW YOU'VE BEEN HAVING A HARD TIME WITH ME DATING YOUR MOM. BUT I NEED YOU TO UNDERSTAND THAT I'M HERE FOR THE LONG HAUL.
I LOVE SARAH VERY MUCH. SHE MAKES ME HAPPY, AND I THINK I DO THE SAME FOR HER.
I HOPE SOMEDAY WE CAN BE FRIENDS.

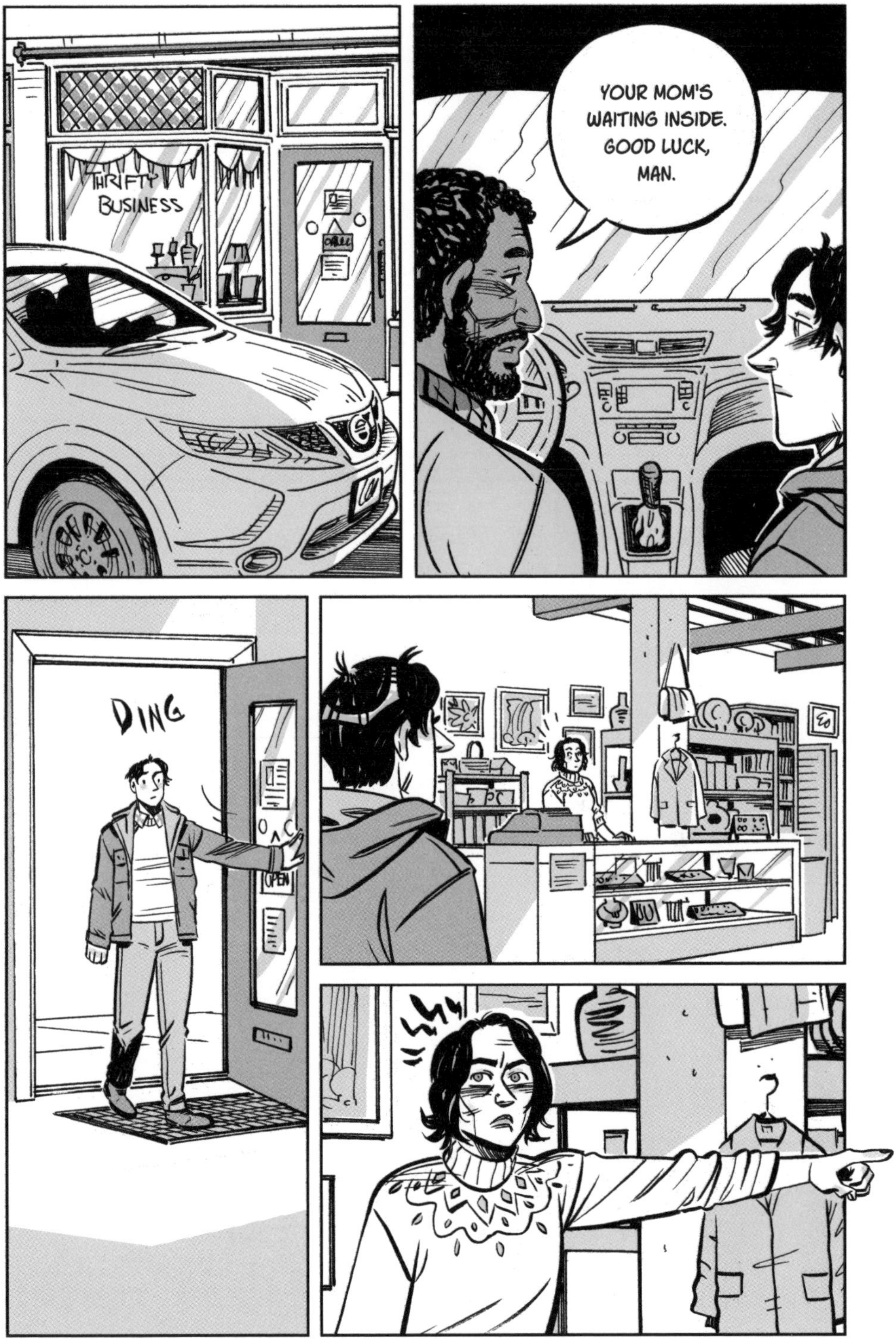
THRIFTY BUSINESS
YOUR MOM'S WAITING INSIDE. GOOD LUCK, MAN.
DING
OPEN

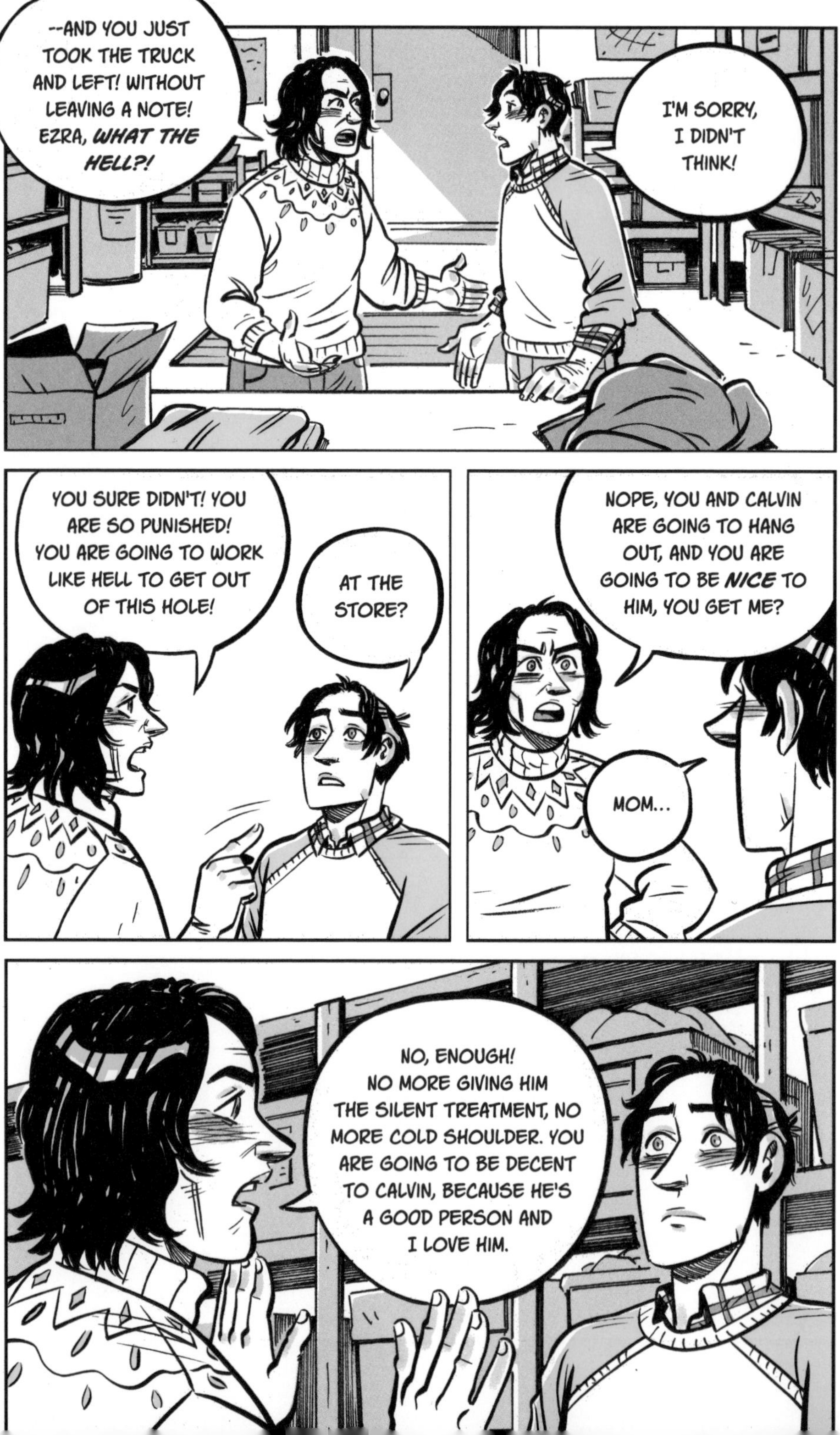
--AND YOU JUST TOOK THE TRUCK AND LEFT! WITHOUT LEAVING A NOTE! EZRA, WHAT THE HELL?!
I'M SORRY, I DIDN'T THINK!
YOU SURE DIDN'T! YOU ARE SO PUNISHED! YOU ARE GOING TO WORK LIKE HELL TO GET OUT OF THIS HOLE!
AT THE STORE?
NOPE, YOU AND CALVIN ARE GOING TO HANG OUT, AND YOU ARE GOING TO BE NICE TO HIM, YOU GET ME?
MOM...
NO, ENOUGH! NO MORE GIVING HIM THE SILENT TREATMENT, NO MORE COLD SHOULDER. YOU ARE GOING TO BE DECENT TO CALVIN, BECAUSE HE'S A GOOD PERSON AND I LOVE HIM.

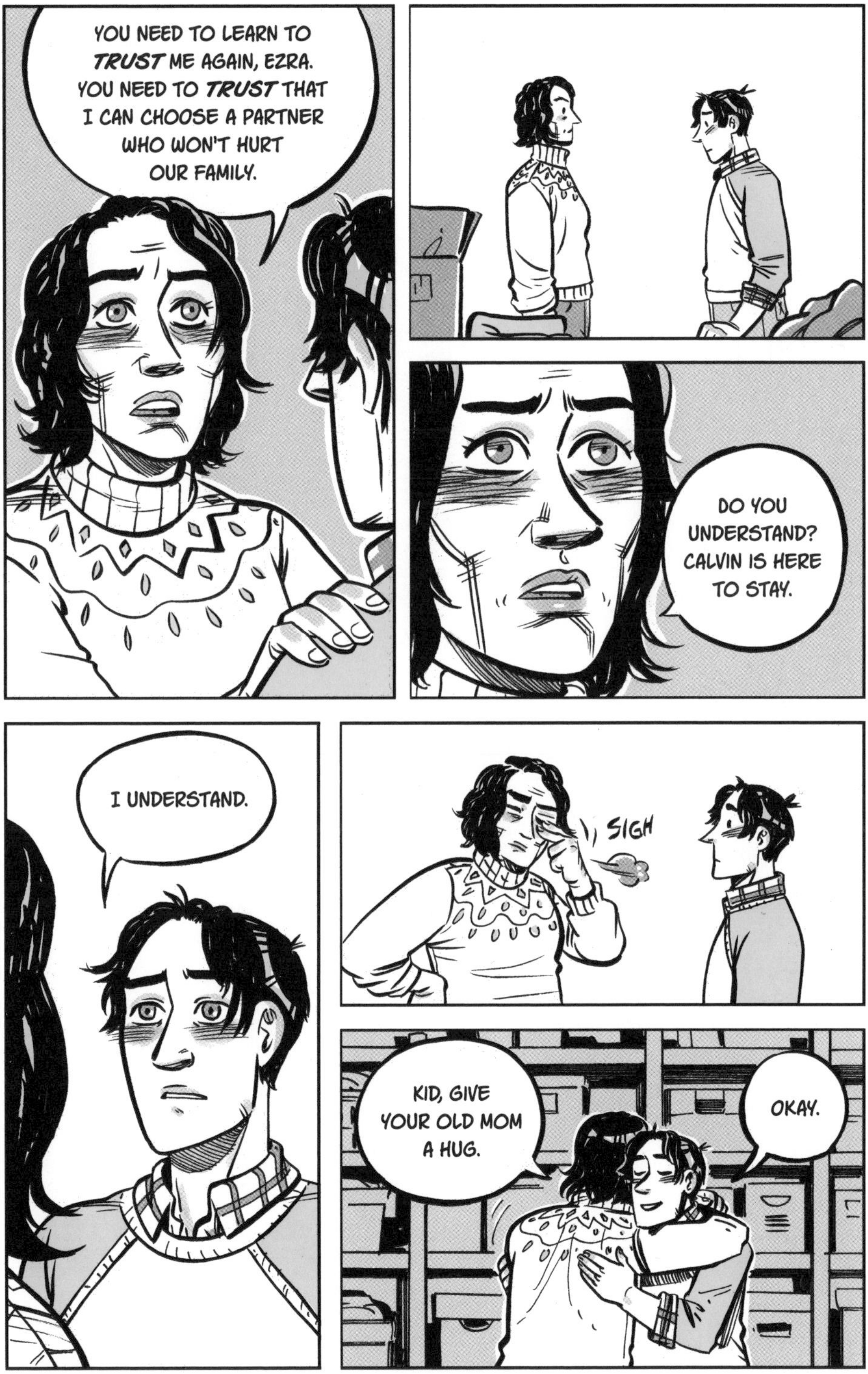
YOU NEED TO LEARN TO *TRUST* ME AGAIN, EZRA. YOU NEED TO *TRUST* THAT I CAN CHOOSE A PARTNER WHO WON'T HURT OUR FAMILY.
DO YOU UNDERSTAND? CALVIN IS HERE TO STAY.
I UNDERSTAND.
SIGH
KID, GIVE YOUR OLD MOM A HUG.
OKAY.

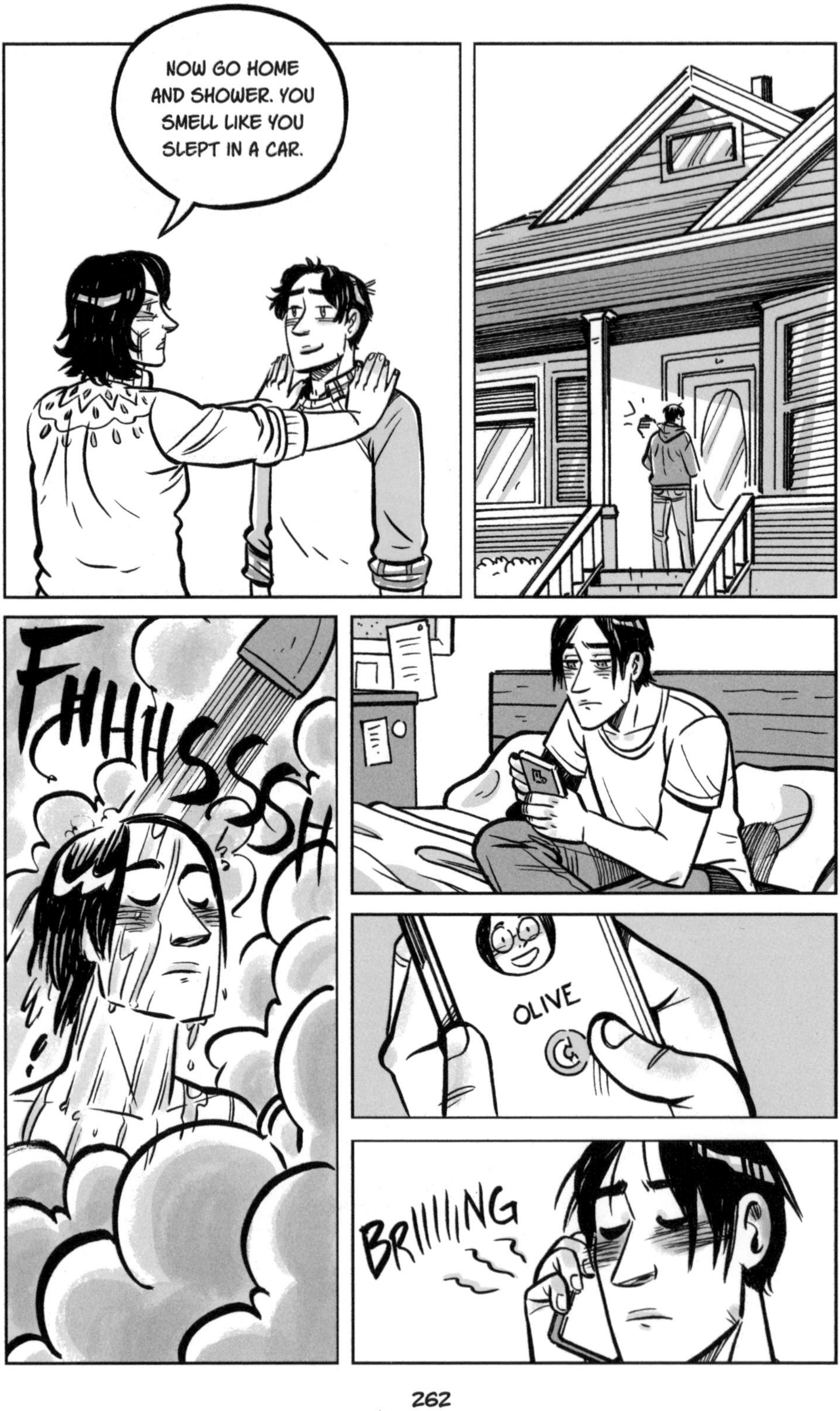
NOW GO HOME AND SHOWER. YOU SMELL LIKE YOU SLEPT IN A CAR.
FHHHSSSH
OLIVE
BRIIIING

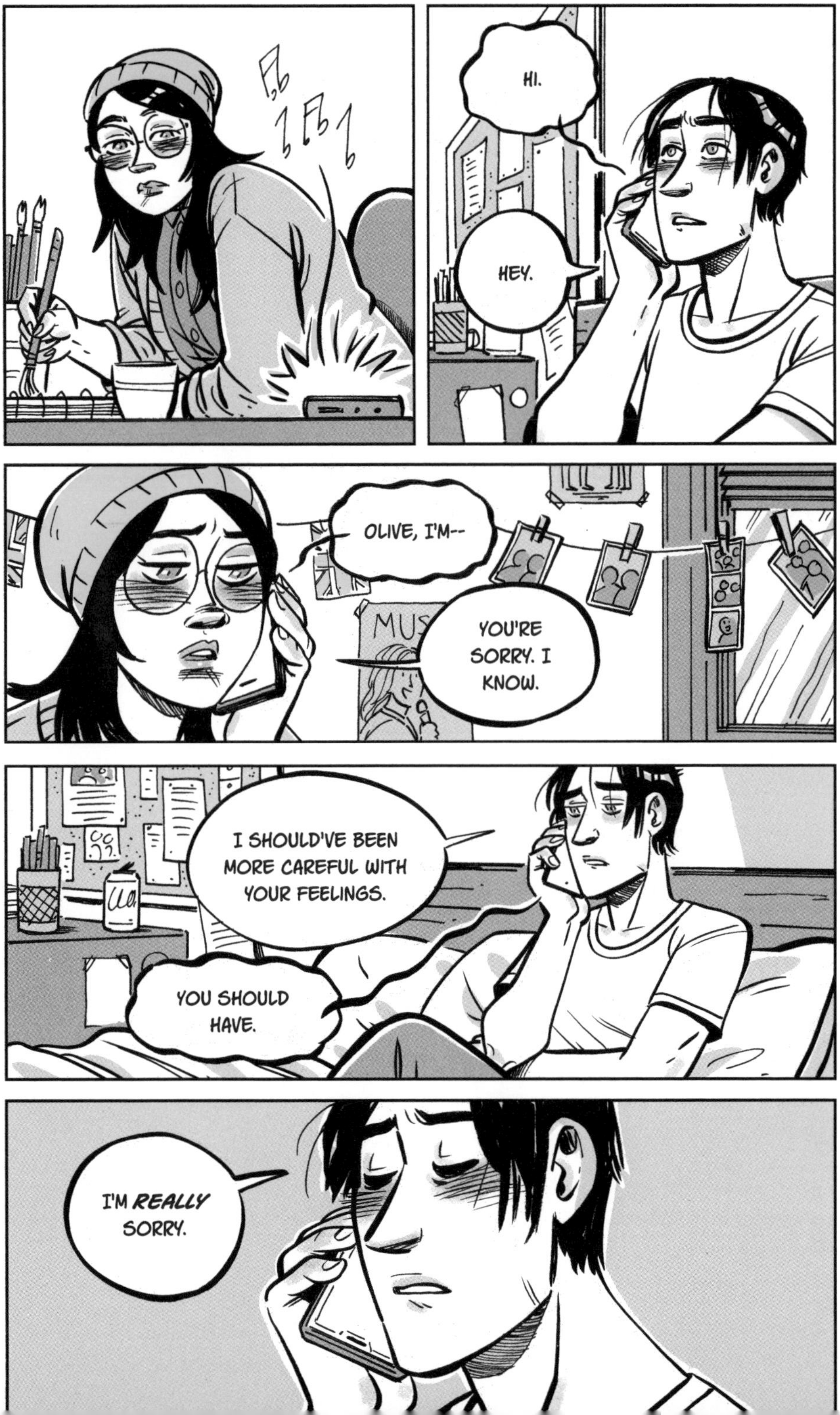
HI.
HEY.
OLIVE, I'M--
YOU'RE SORRY. I KNOW.
I SHOULD'VE BEEN MORE CAREFUL WITH YOUR FEELINGS.
YOU SHOULD HAVE.
I'M *REALLY* SORRY.

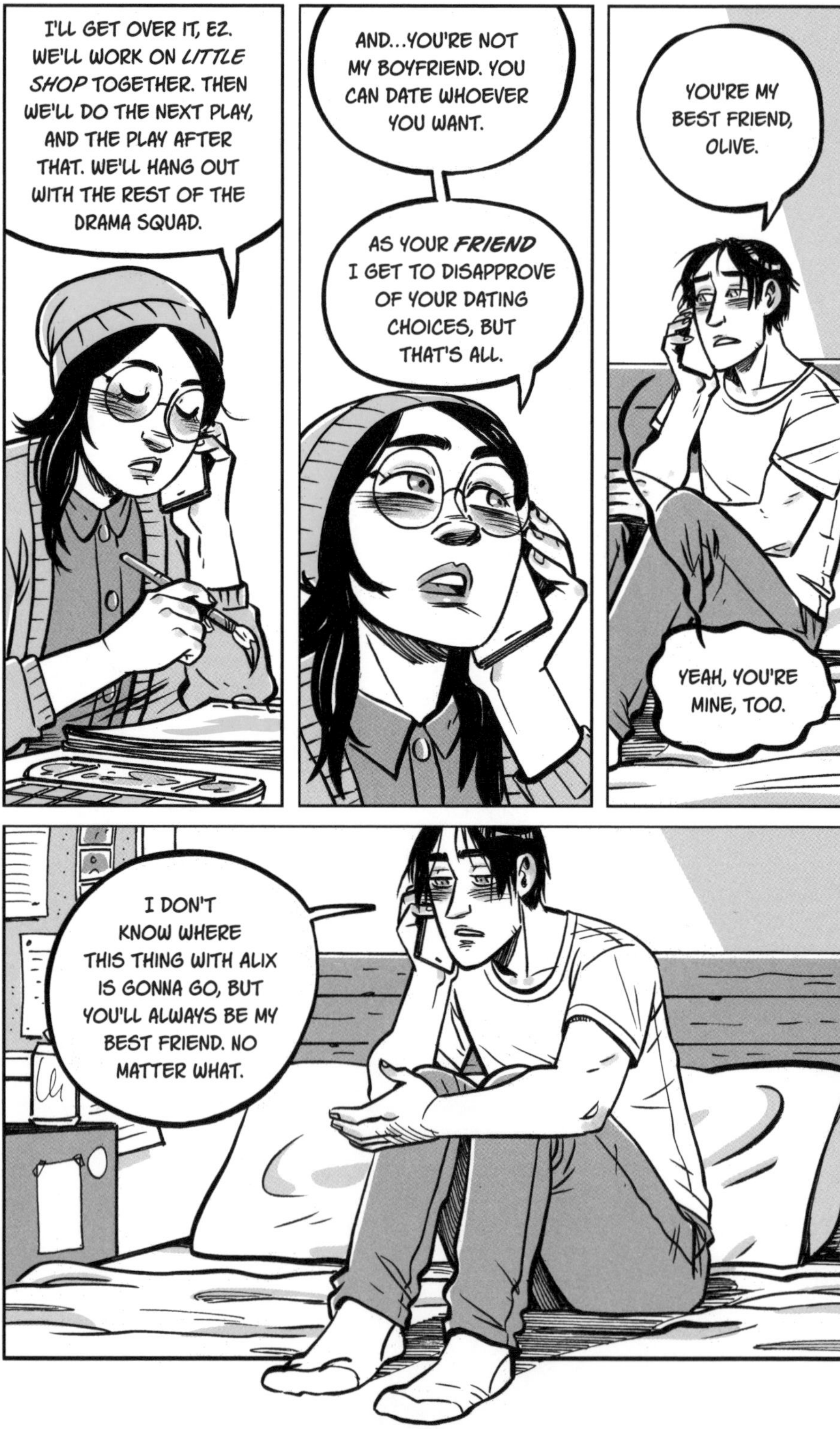
I'LL GET OVER IT, EZ. WE'LL WORK ON *LITTLE SHOP* TOGETHER. THEN WE'LL DO THE NEXT PLAY, AND THE PLAY AFTER THAT. WE'LL HANG OUT WITH THE REST OF THE DRAMA SQUAD.
AND...YOU'RE NOT MY BOYFRIEND. YOU CAN DATE WHOEVER YOU WANT.
AS YOUR *FRIEND* I GET TO DISAPPROVE OF YOUR DATING CHOICES, BUT THAT'S ALL.
YOU'RE MY BEST FRIEND, OLIVE.
YEAH, YOU'RE MINE, TOO.
I DON'T KNOW WHERE THIS THING WITH ALIX IS GONNA GO, BUT YOU'LL ALWAYS BE MY BEST FRIEND. NO MATTER WHAT.

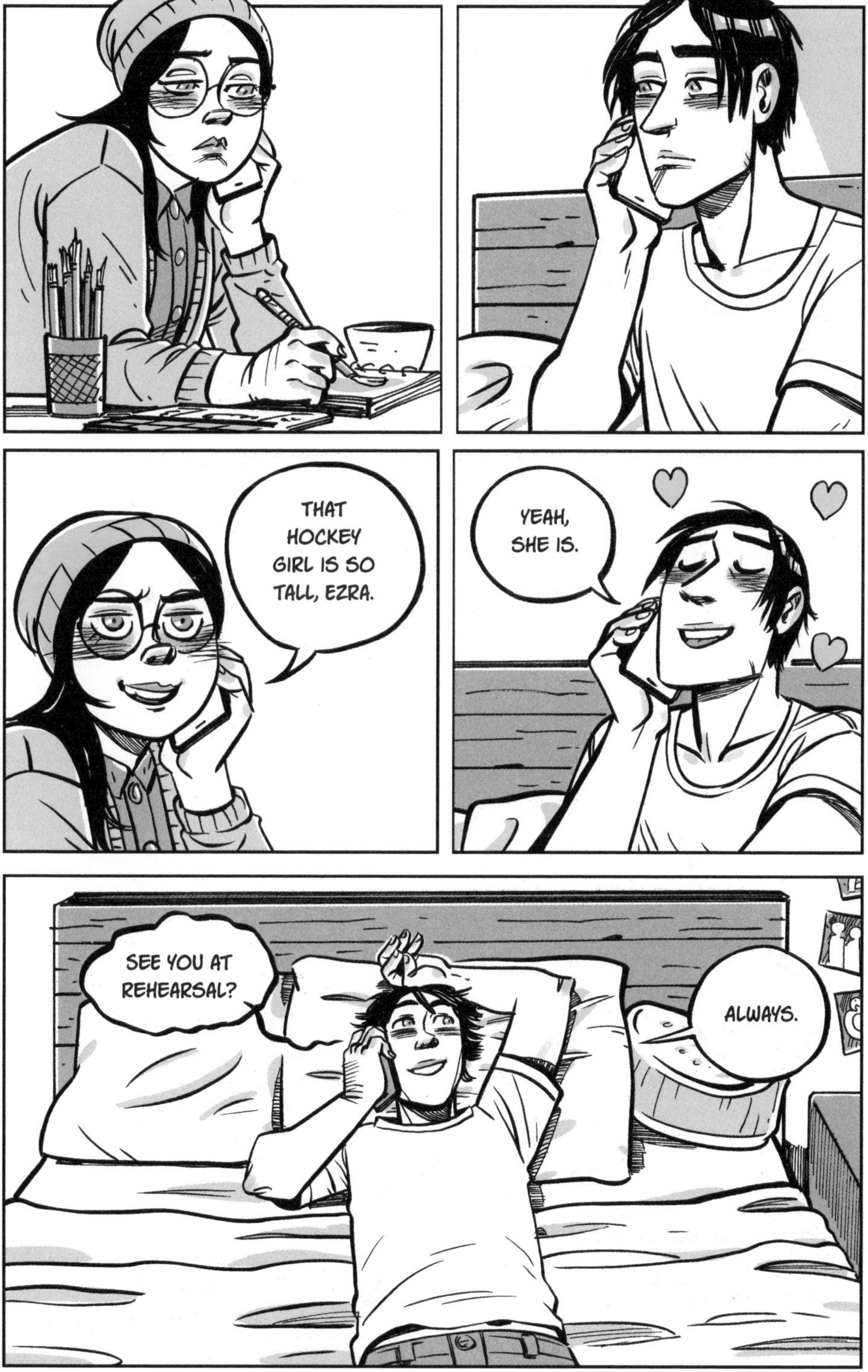
THAT HOCKEY GIRL IS SO TALL, EZRA.
YEAH, SHE IS.
SEE YOU AT REHEARSAL?
ALWAYS.

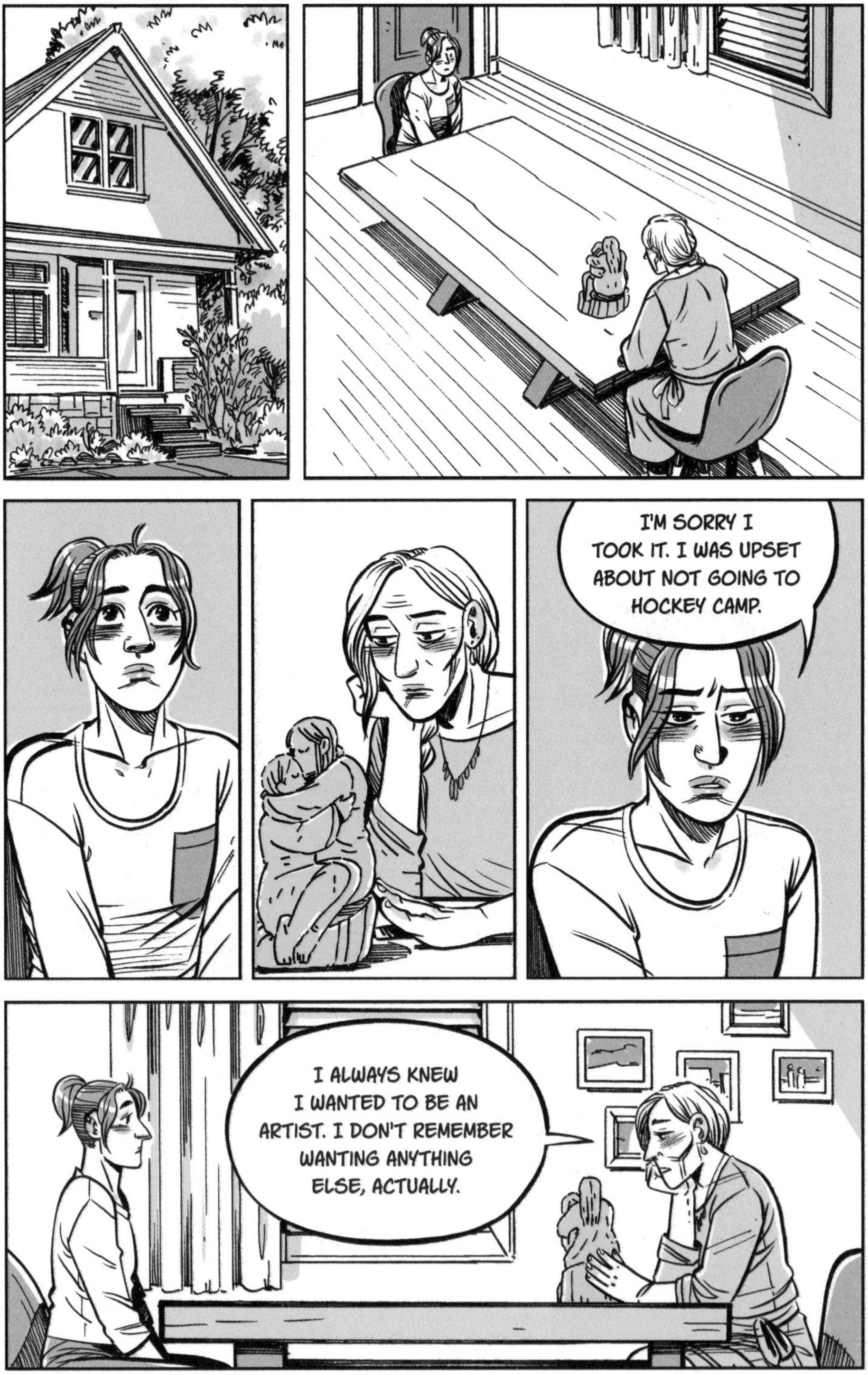
I'M SORRY I TOOK IT. I WAS UPSET ABOUT NOT GOING TO HOCKEY CAMP.
I ALWAYS KNEW I WANTED TO BE AN ARTIST. I DON'T REMEMBER WANTING ANYTHING ELSE, ACTUALLY.

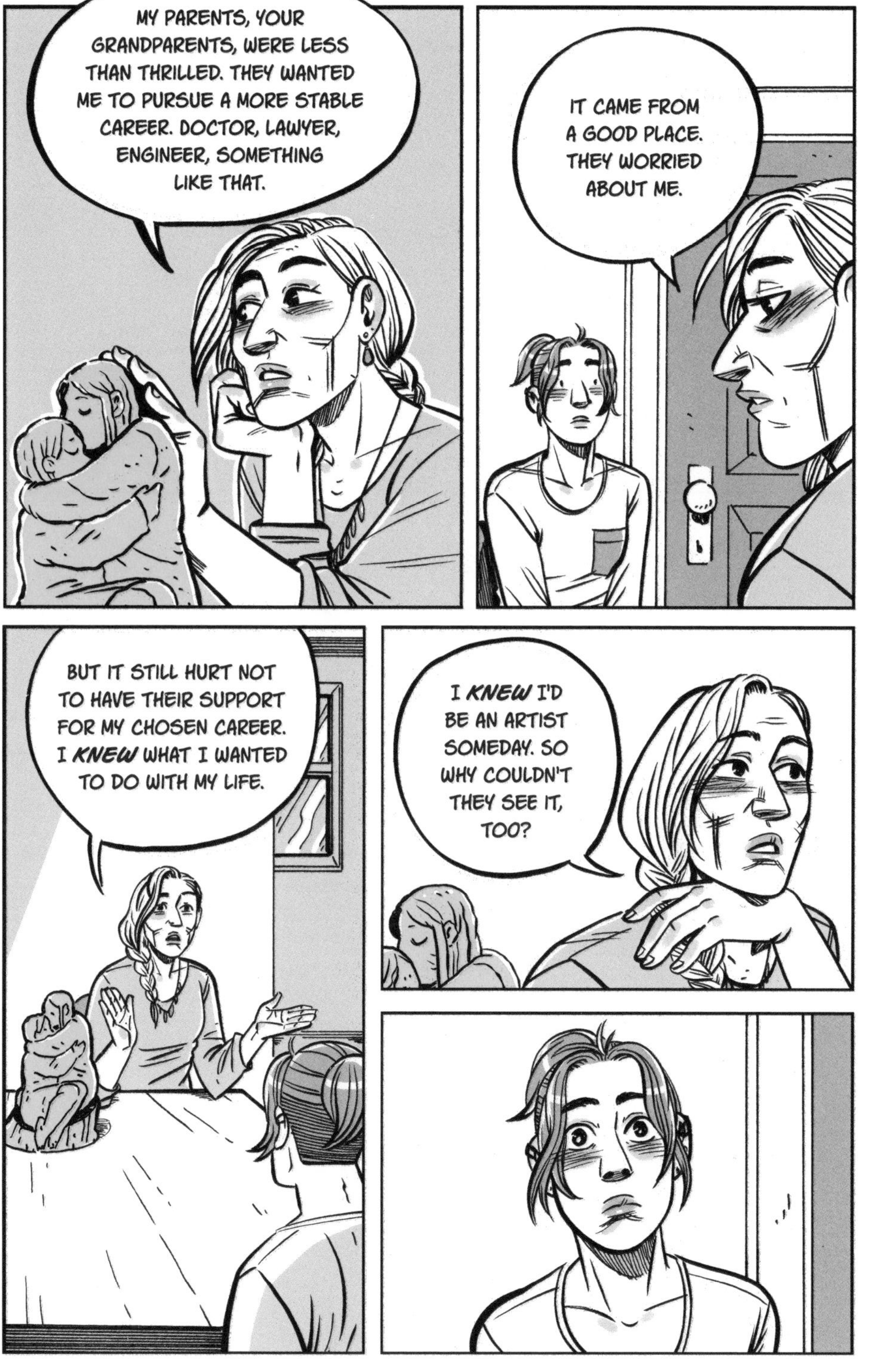

MY PARENTS, YOUR GRANDPARENTS, WERE LESS THAN THRILLED. THEY WANTED ME TO PURSUE A MORE STABLE CAREER. DOCTOR, LAWYER, ENGINEER, SOMETHING LIKE THAT.
IT CAME FROM A GOOD PLACE. THEY WORRIED ABOUT ME.
BUT IT STILL HURT NOT TO HAVE THEIR SUPPORT FOR MY CHOSEN CAREER. I *KNEW* WHAT I WANTED TO DO WITH MY LIFE.
I *KNEW* I'D BE AN ARTIST SOMEDAY. SO WHY COULDN'T THEY SEE IT, TOO?

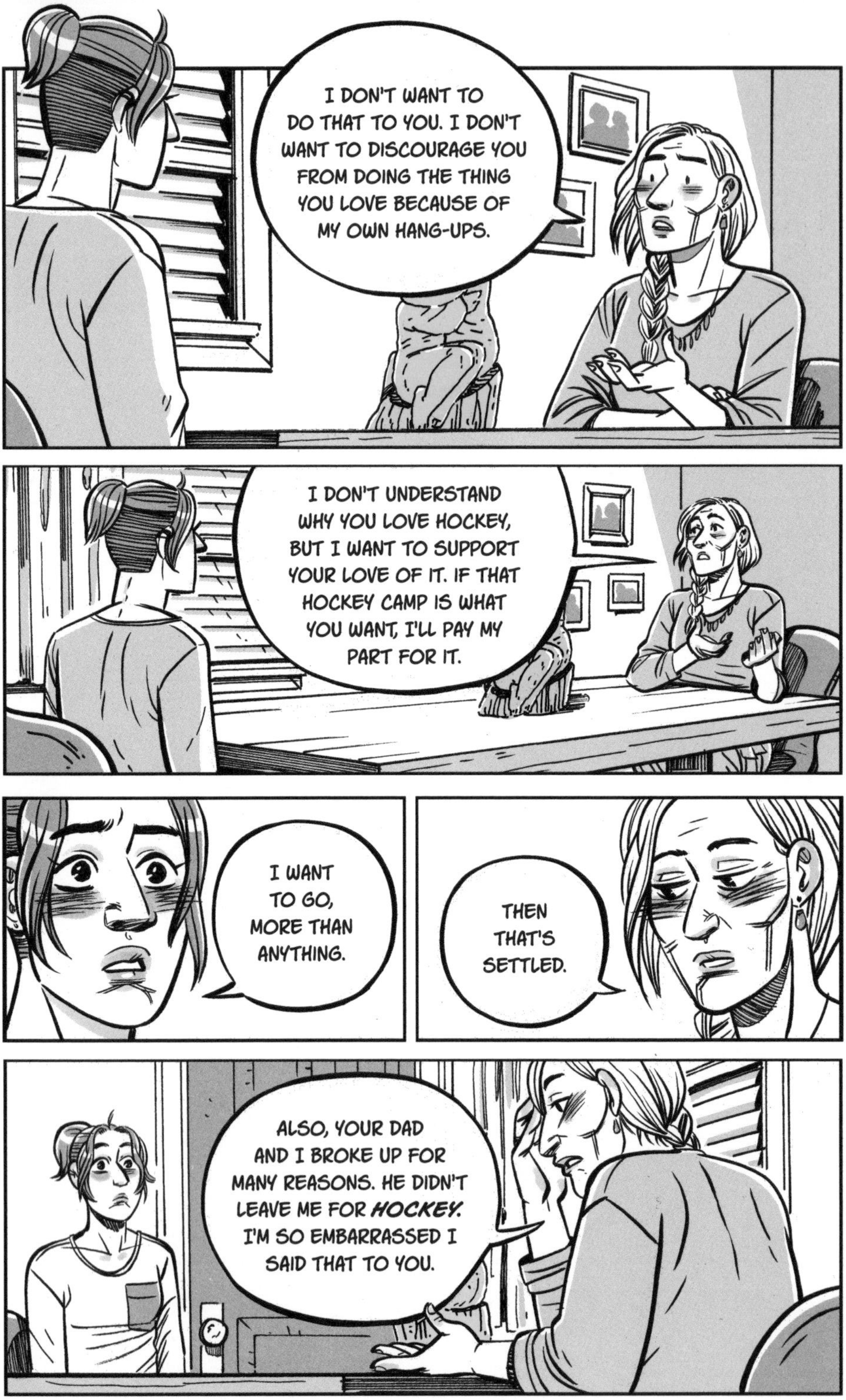
I DON'T WANT TO DO THAT TO YOU. I DON'T WANT TO DISCOURAGE YOU FROM DOING THE THING YOU LOVE BECAUSE OF MY OWN HANG-UPS.
I DON'T UNDERSTAND WHY YOU LOVE HOCKEY, BUT I WANT TO SUPPORT YOUR LOVE OF IT. IF THAT HOCKEY CAMP IS WHAT YOU WANT, I'LL PAY MY PART FOR IT.
I WANT TO GO, MORE THAN ANYTHING.
THEN THAT'S SETTLED.
ALSO, YOUR DAD AND I BROKE UP FOR MANY REASONS. HE DIDN'T LEAVE ME FOR *HOCKEY.* I'M SO EMBARRASSED I SAID THAT TO YOU.

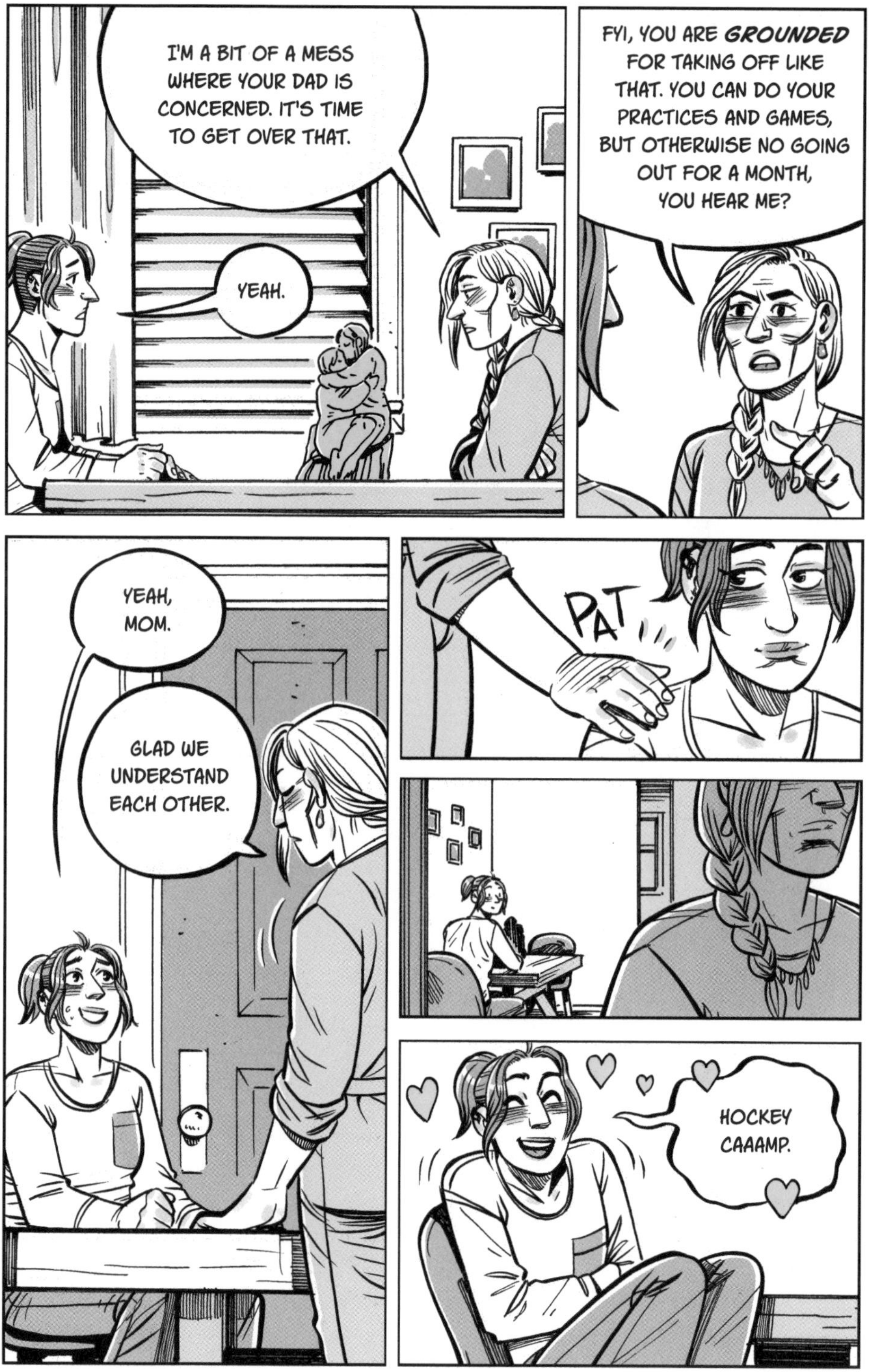
I'M A BIT OF A MESS WHERE YOUR DAD IS CONCERNED. IT'S TIME TO GET OVER THAT.
YEAH.
FYI, YOU ARE **GROUNDED** FOR TAKING OFF LIKE THAT. YOU CAN DO YOUR PRACTICES AND GAMES, BUT OTHERWISE NO GOING OUT FOR A MONTH, YOU HEAR ME?
YEAH, MOM.
GLAD WE UNDERSTAND EACH OTHER.
PAT
HOCKEY CAAAMP.

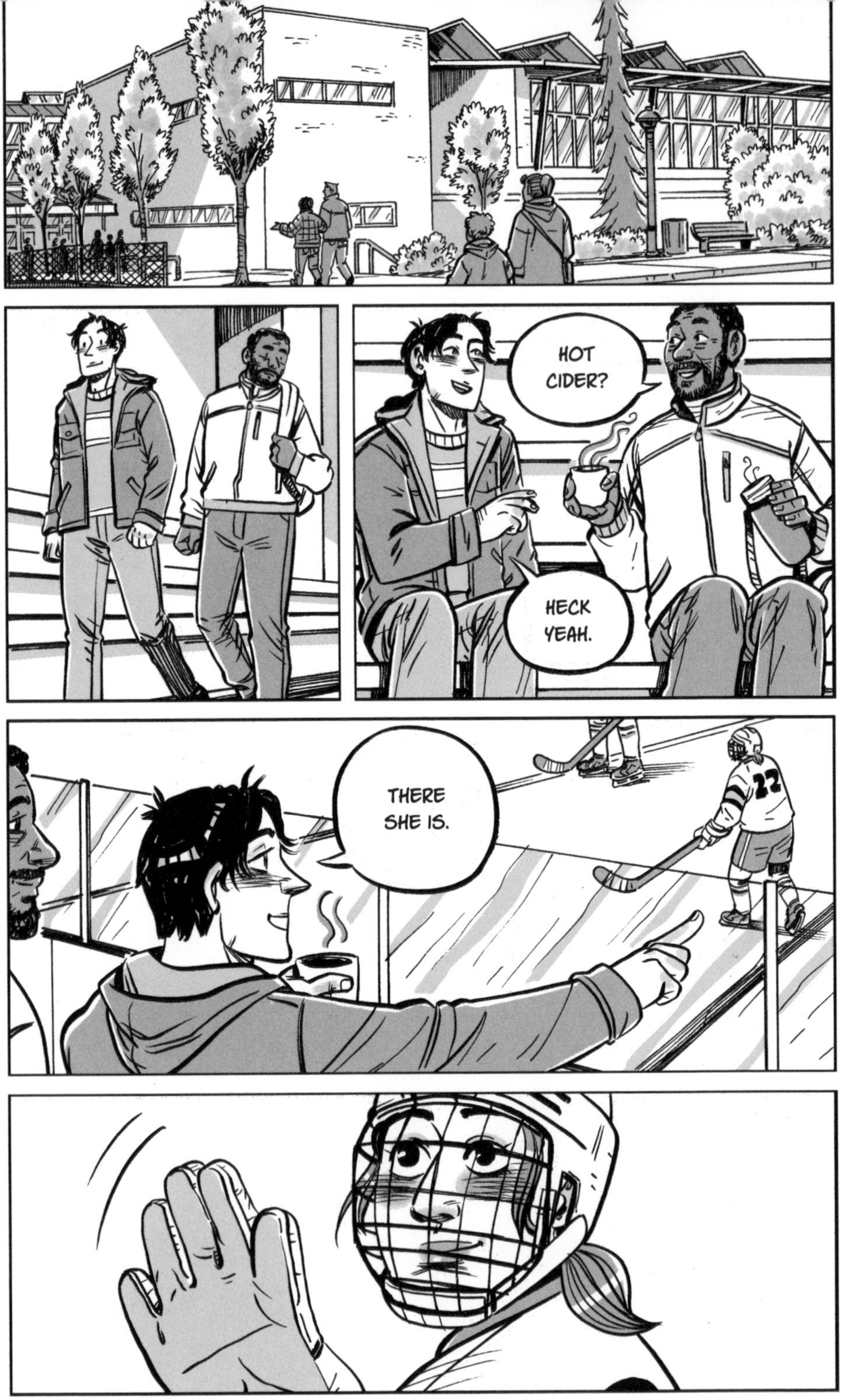
HOT CIDER?
HECK YEAH.
THERE SHE IS.

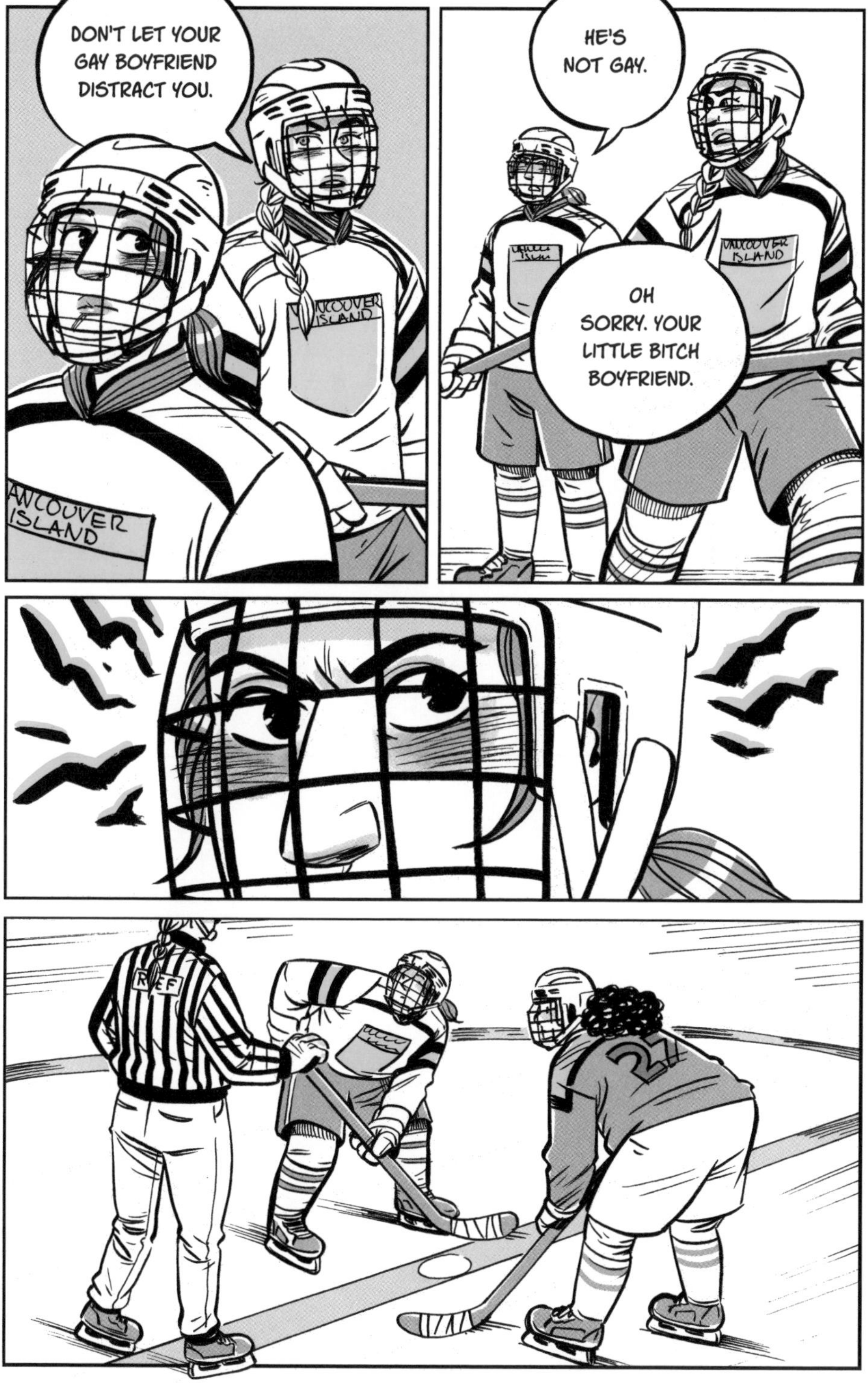
DON'T LET YOUR GAY BOYFRIEND DISTRACT YOU.
VANCOUVER ISLAND
VANCOUVER ISLAND
HE'S NOT GAY.
VANCOUVER ISLAND
OH SORRY. YOUR LITTLE BITCH BOYFRIEND.
REF
27

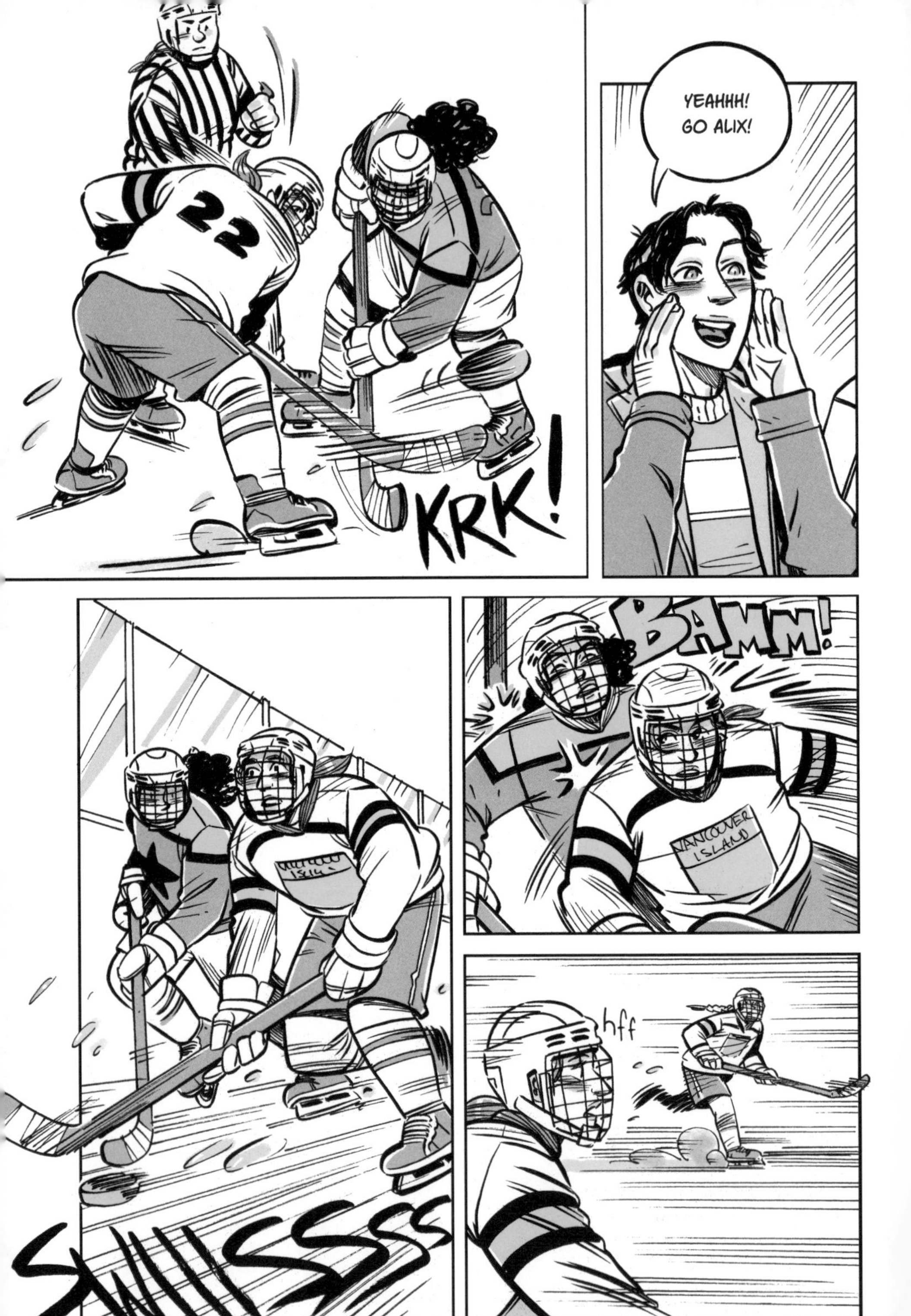
KRK!
YEAHHH! GO ALIX!
BAMM!
VANCOUVER ISLAND
hff

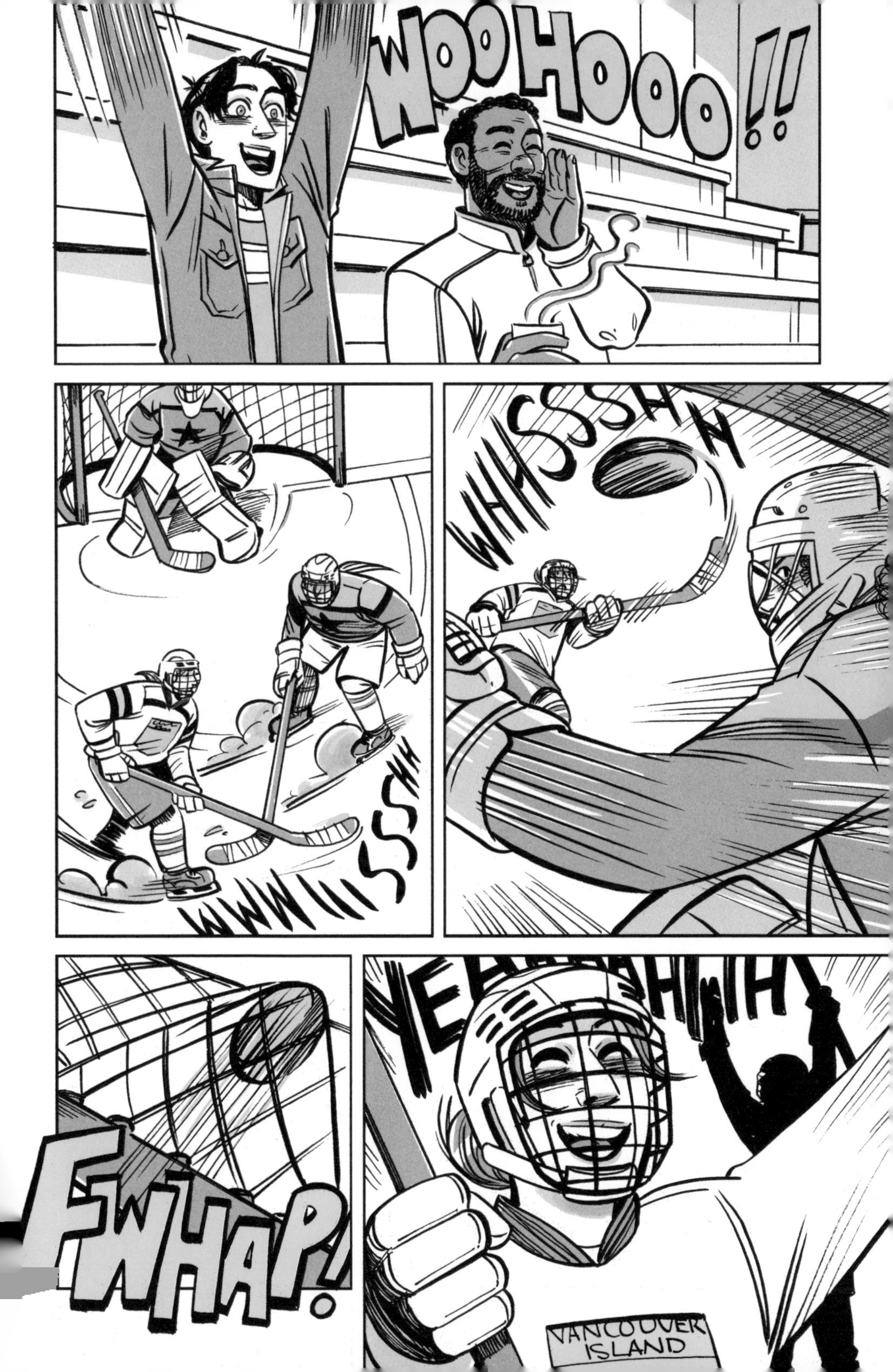
WOOHOOO!!
WWWIIISSSHH
WHHSSSHH
FWHAP!
VANCOUVER ISLAND

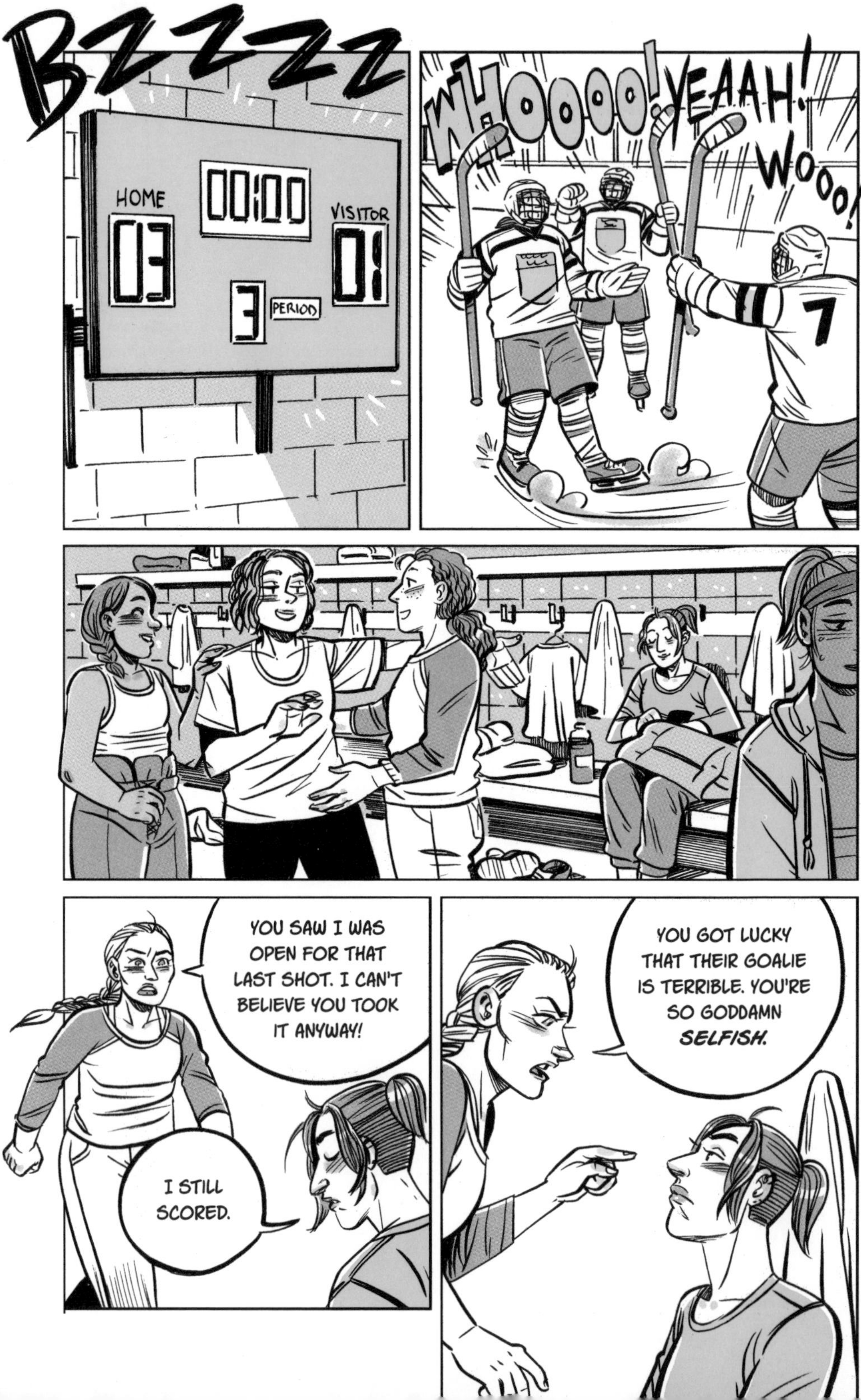
BZZZZZ
HOME
00:00
VISITOR
03
01
3
PERIOD
WHOOOO!
YEAAH!
WOOO!
7
YOU SAW I WAS OPEN FOR THAT LAST SHOT. I CAN'T BELIEVE YOU TOOK IT ANYWAY!
I STILL SCORED.
YOU GOT LUCKY THAT THEIR GOALIE IS TERRIBLE. YOU'RE SO GODDAMN *SELFISH.*

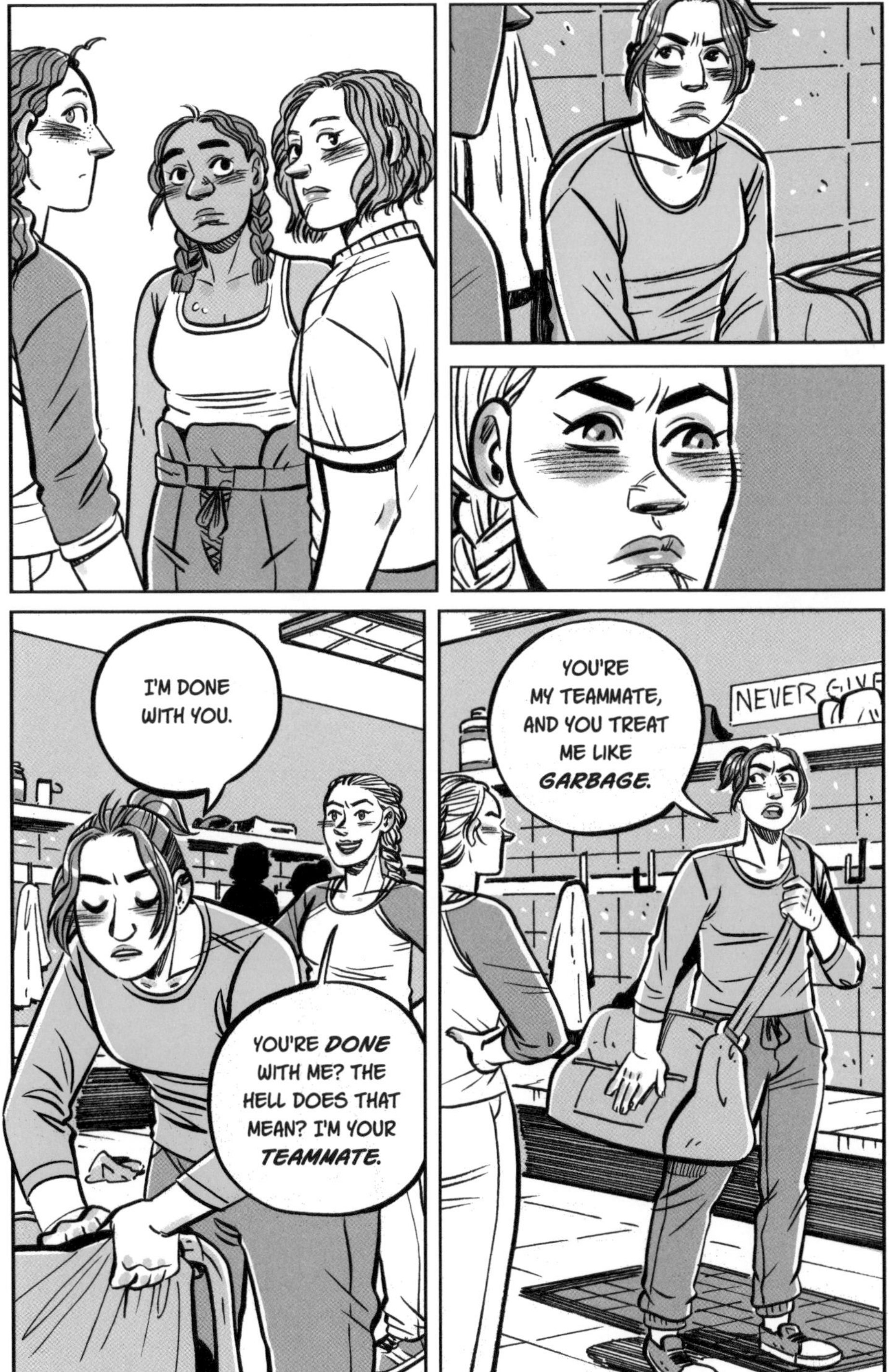
I'M DONE WITH YOU.
YOU'RE *DONE* WITH ME? THE HELL DOES THAT MEAN? I'M YOUR *TEAMMATE.*
NEVER
YOU'RE MY TEAMMATE, AND YOU TREAT ME LIKE *GARBAGE.*

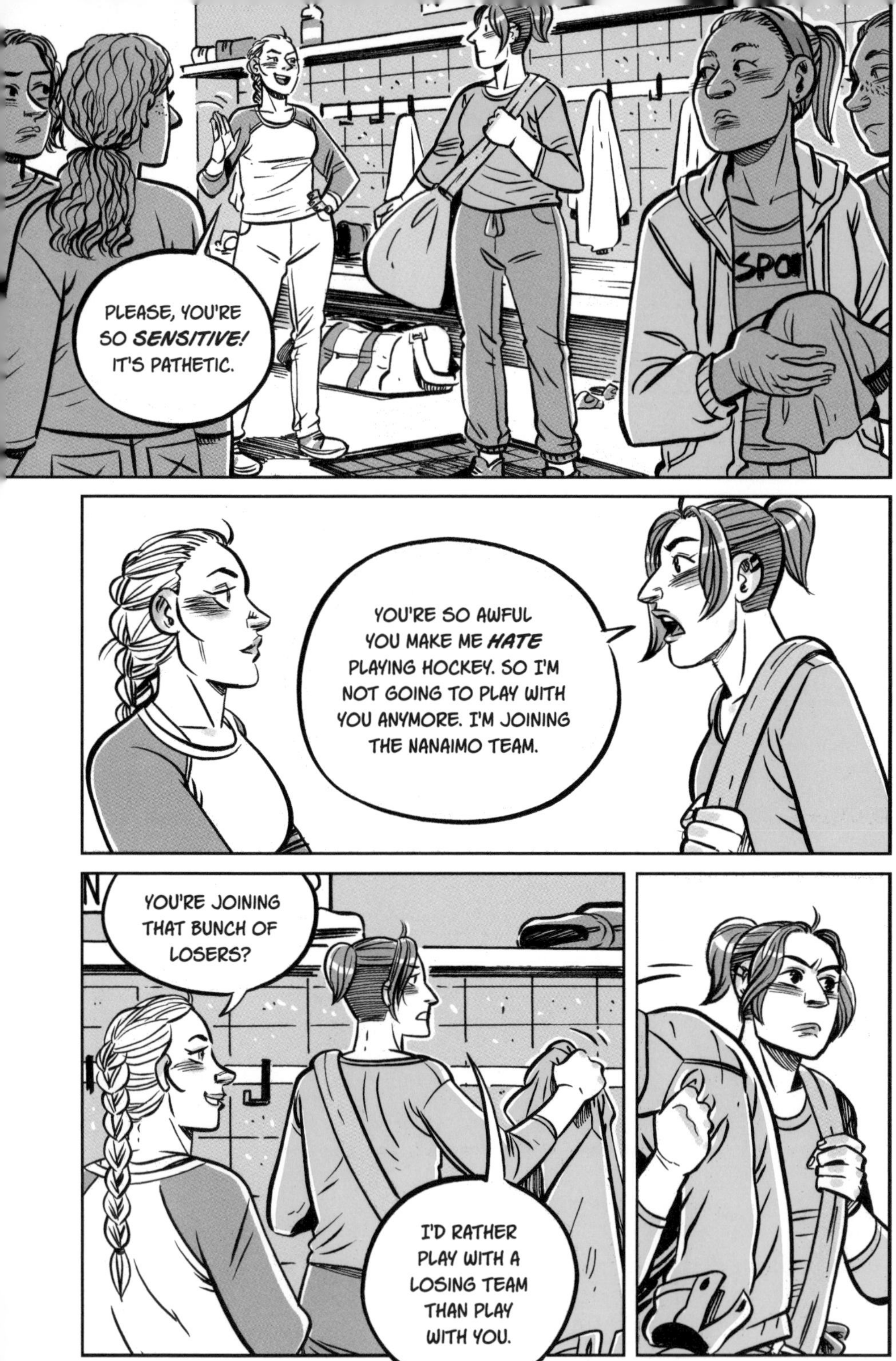
PLEASE, YOU'RE SO *SENSITIVE!* IT'S PATHETIC.
SPO
YOU'RE SO AWFUL YOU MAKE ME *HATE* PLAYING HOCKEY. SO I'M NOT GOING TO PLAY WITH YOU ANYMORE. I'M JOINING THE NANAIMO TEAM.
YOU'RE JOINING THAT BUNCH OF LOSERS?
I'D RATHER PLAY WITH A LOSING TEAM THAN PLAY WITH YOU.

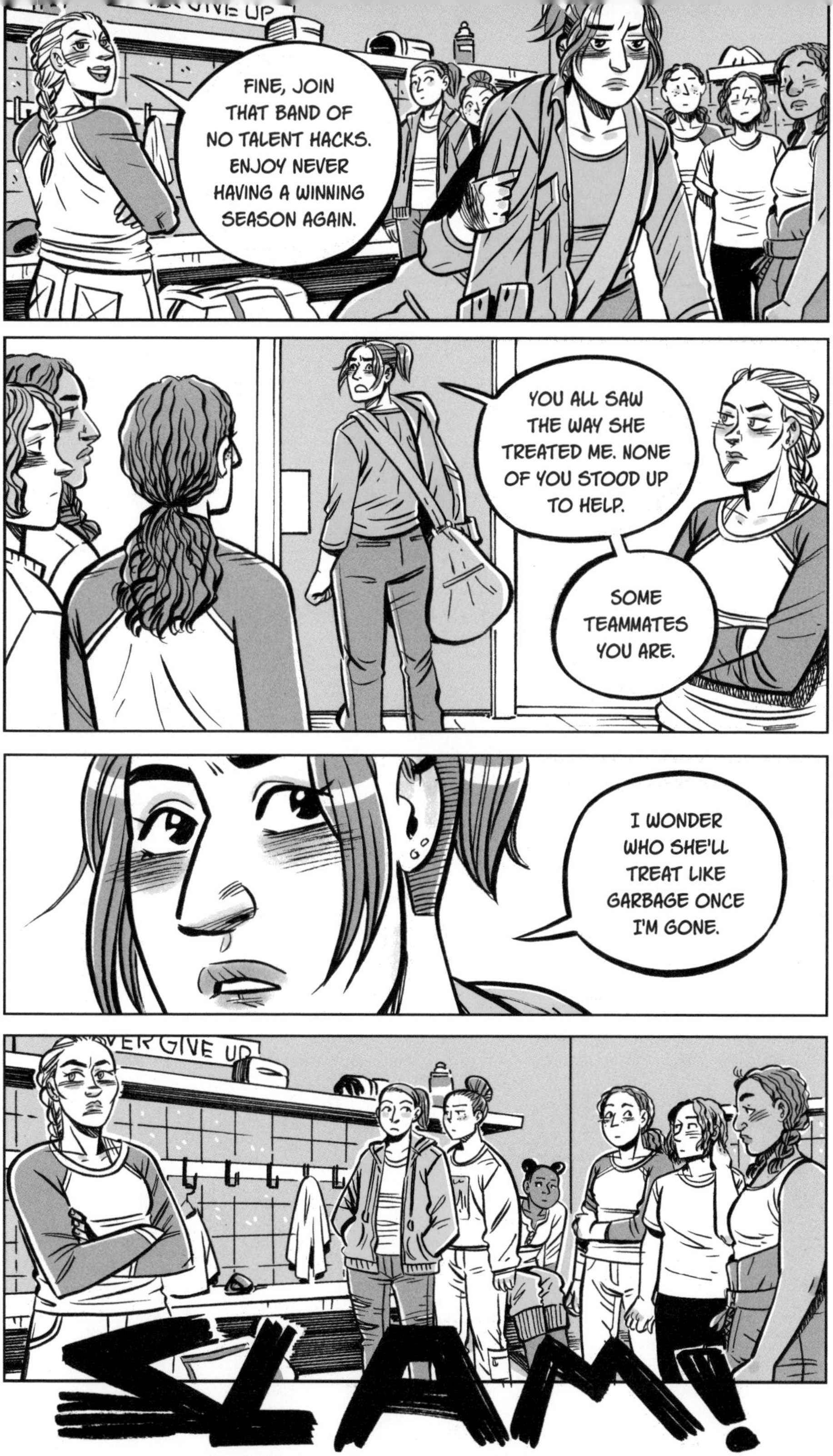
NEVER GIVE UP
FINE, JOIN THAT BAND OF NO TALENT HACKS. ENJOY NEVER HAVING A WINNING SEASON AGAIN.
YOU ALL SAW THE WAY SHE TREATED ME. NONE OF YOU STOOD UP TO HELP.
SOME TEAMMATES YOU ARE.
I WONDER WHO SHE'LL TREAT LIKE GARBAGE ONCE I'M GONE.
SLAM!

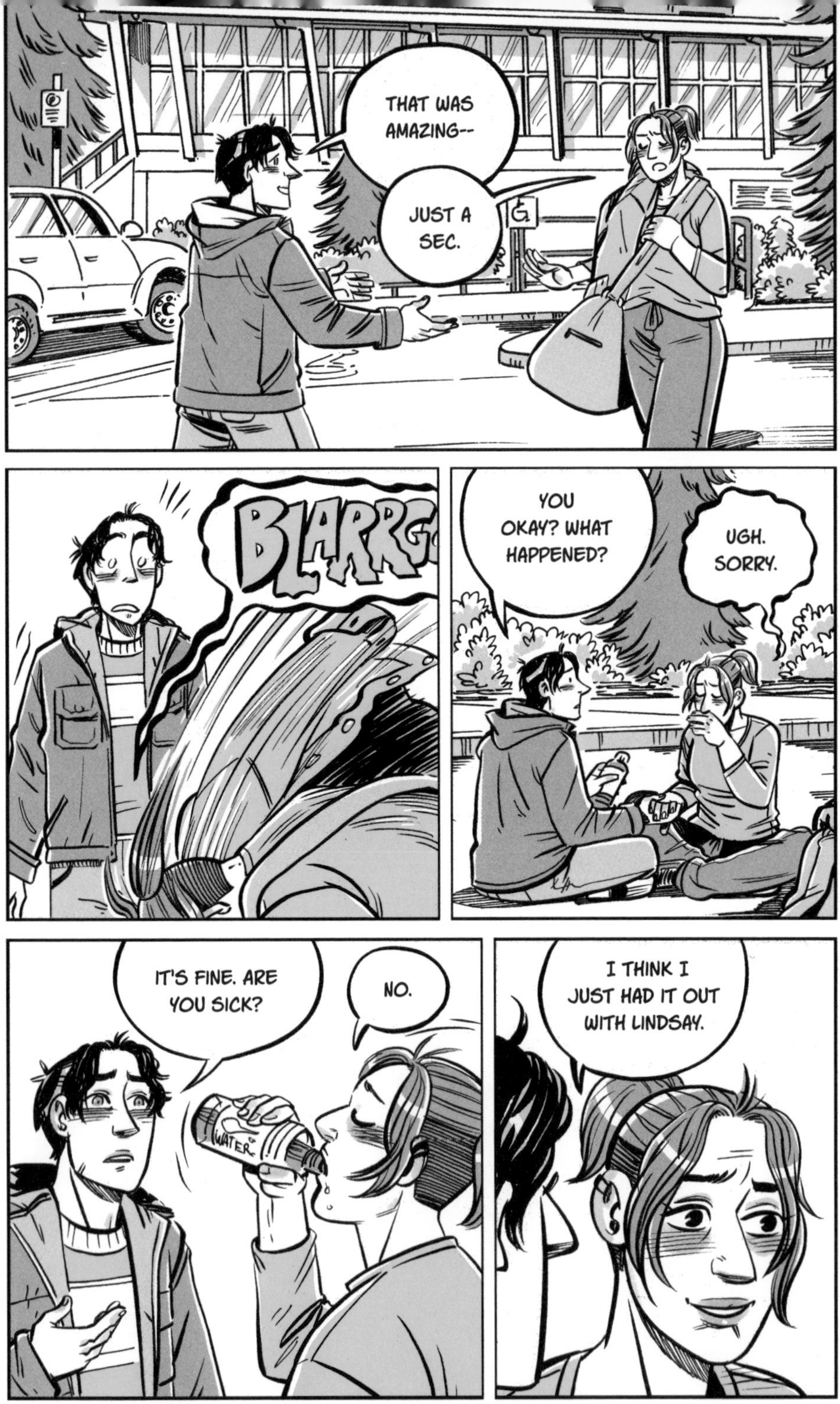
THAT WAS AMAZING--
JUST A SEC.
BLARRG
YOU OKAY? WHAT HAPPENED?
UGH. SORRY.
IT'S FINE. ARE YOU SICK?
NO.
WATER
I THINK I JUST HAD IT OUT WITH LINDSAY.

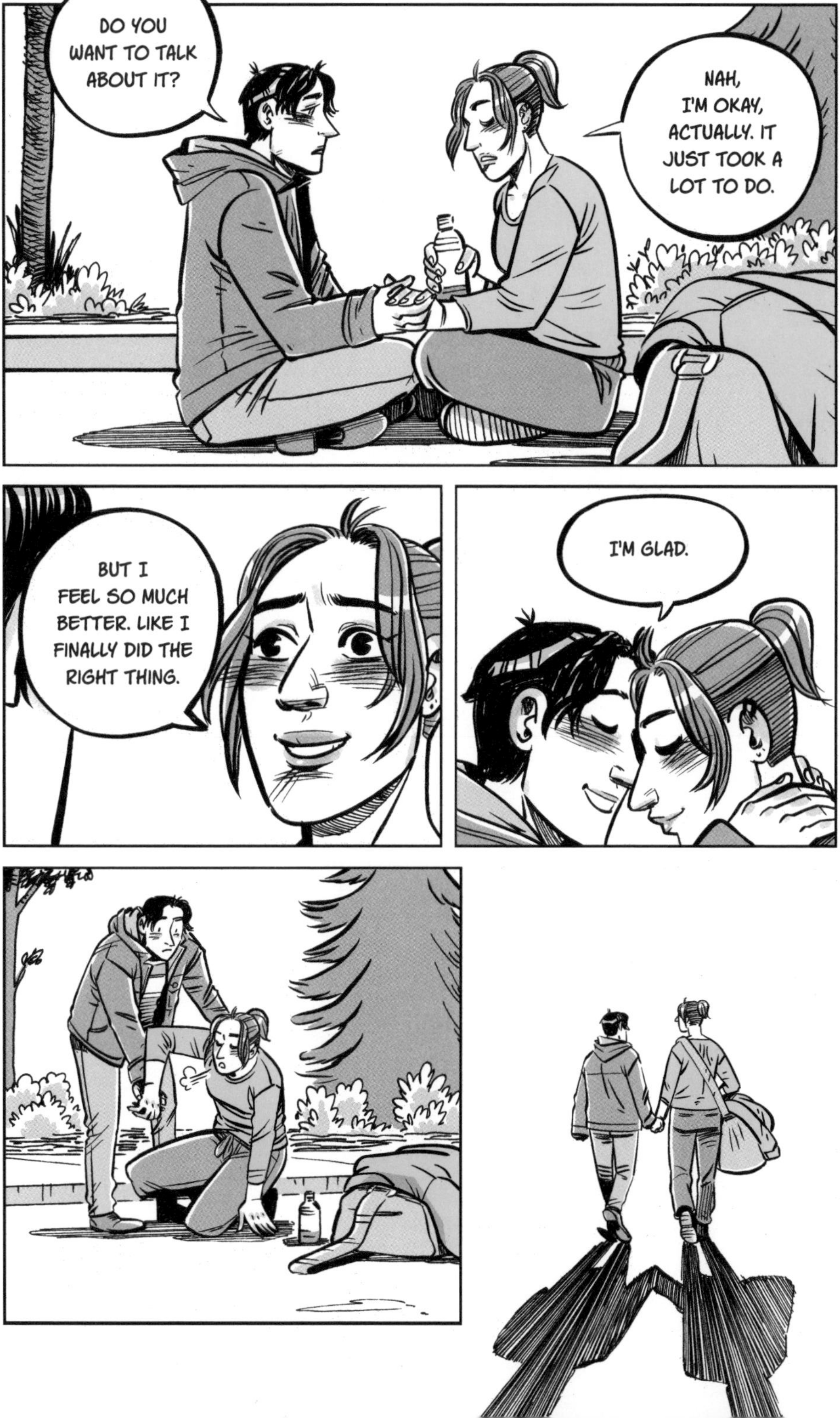
DO YOU WANT TO TALK ABOUT IT?
NAH, I'M OKAY, ACTUALLY. IT JUST TOOK A LOT TO DO.
BUT I FEEL SO MUCH BETTER. LIKE I FINALLY DID THE RIGHT THING.
I'M GLAD.

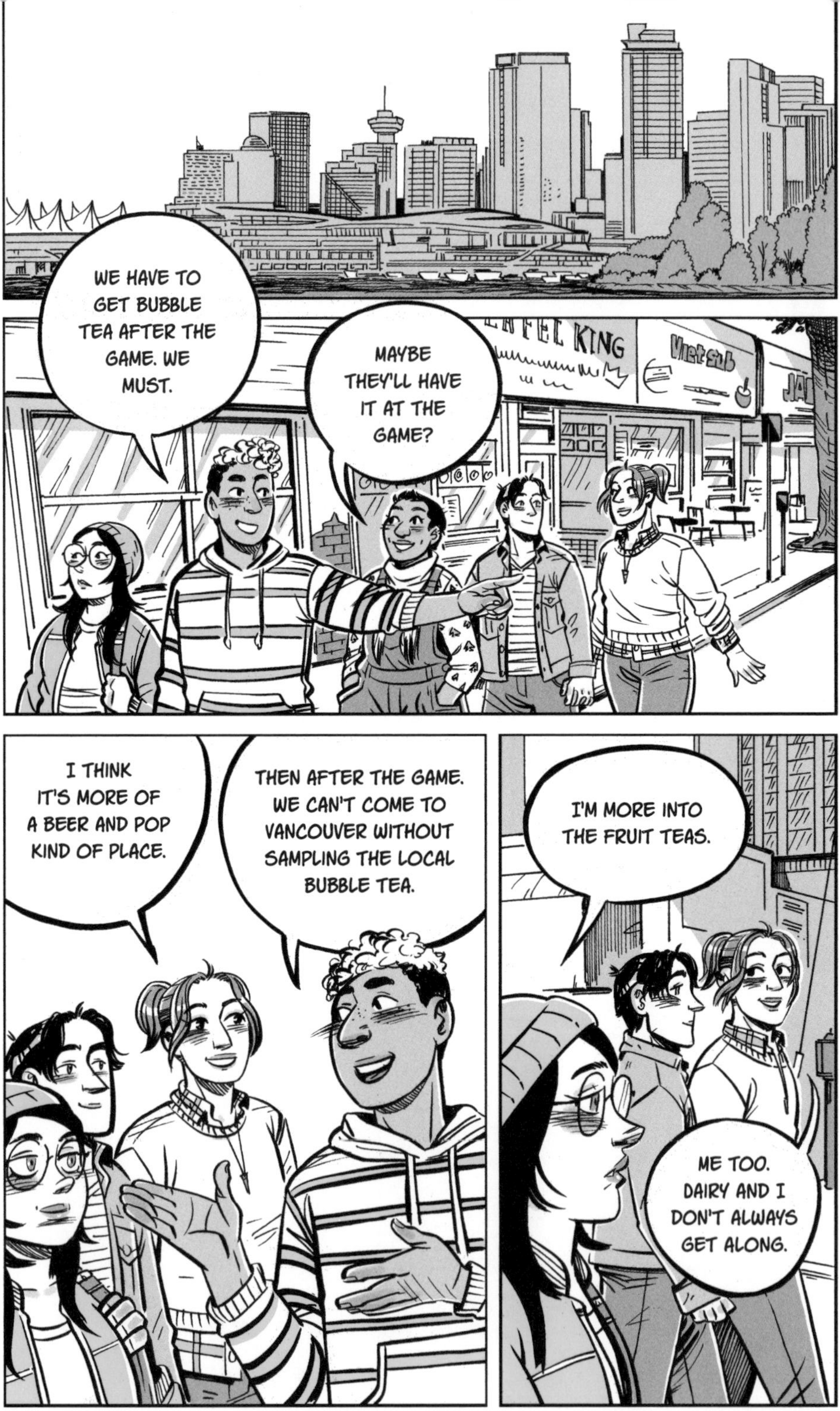
WE HAVE TO GET BUBBLE TEA AFTER THE GAME. WE MUST.
MAYBE THEY'LL HAVE IT AT THE GAME?
I THINK IT'S MORE OF A BEER AND POP KIND OF PLACE.
THEN AFTER THE GAME. WE CAN'T COME TO VANCOUVER WITHOUT SAMPLING THE LOCAL BUBBLE TEA.
I'M MORE INTO THE FRUIT TEAS.
ME TOO. DAIRY AND I DON'T ALWAYS GET ALONG.

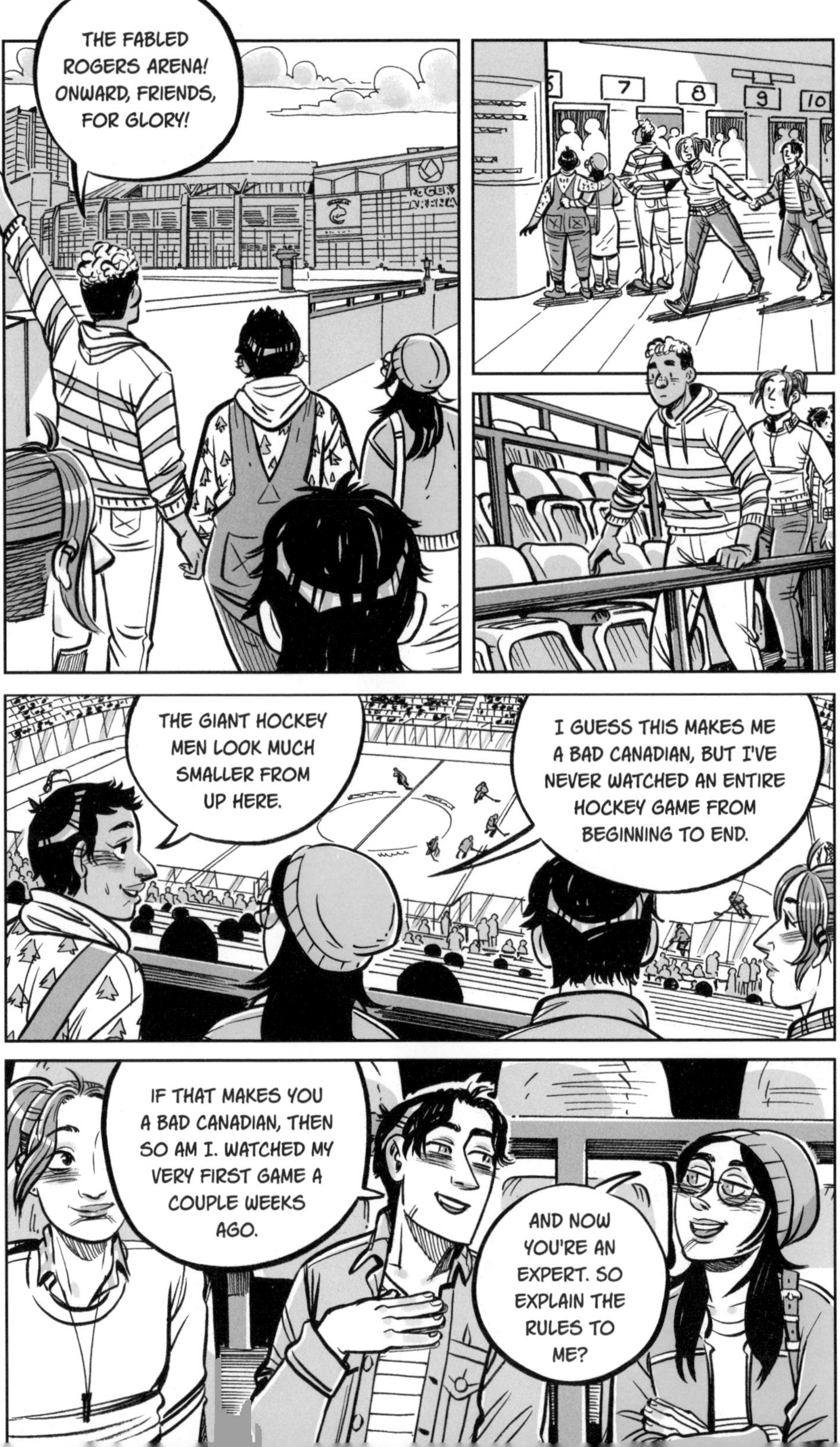
THE FABLED ROGERS ARENA! ONWARD, FRIENDS, FOR GLORY!
7
8
9
10
THE GIANT HOCKEY MEN LOOK MUCH SMALLER FROM UP HERE.
I GUESS THIS MAKES ME A BAD CANADIAN, BUT I'VE NEVER WATCHED AN ENTIRE HOCKEY GAME FROM BEGINNING TO END.
IF THAT MAKES YOU A BAD CANADIAN, THEN SO AM I. WATCHED MY VERY FIRST GAME A COUPLE WEEKS AGO.
AND NOW YOU'RE AN EXPERT. SO EXPLAIN THE RULES TO ME?

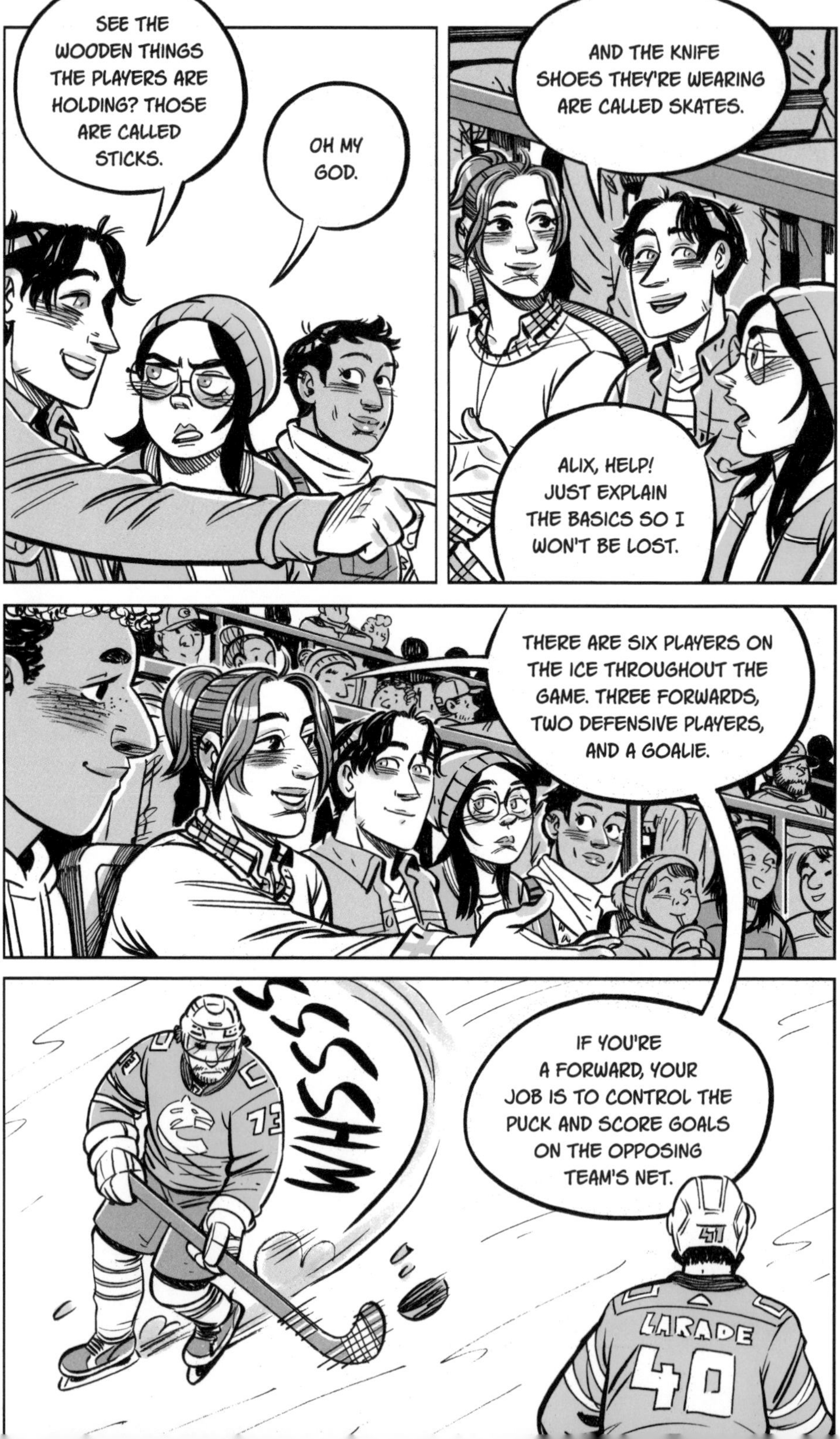
SEE THE WOODEN THINGS THE PLAYERS ARE HOLDING? THOSE ARE CALLED STICKS.
OH MY GOD.
AND THE KNIFE SHOES THEY'RE WEARING ARE CALLED SKATES.
ALIX, HELP! JUST EXPLAIN THE BASICS SO I WON'T BE LOST.
THERE ARE SIX PLAYERS ON THE ICE THROUGHOUT THE GAME. THREE FORWARDS, TWO DEFENSIVE PLAYERS, AND A GOALIE.
IF YOU'RE A FORWARD, YOUR JOB IS TO CONTROL THE PUCK AND SCORE GOALS ON THE OPPOSING TEAM'S NET.
WHSSSS
73
LARADE
40

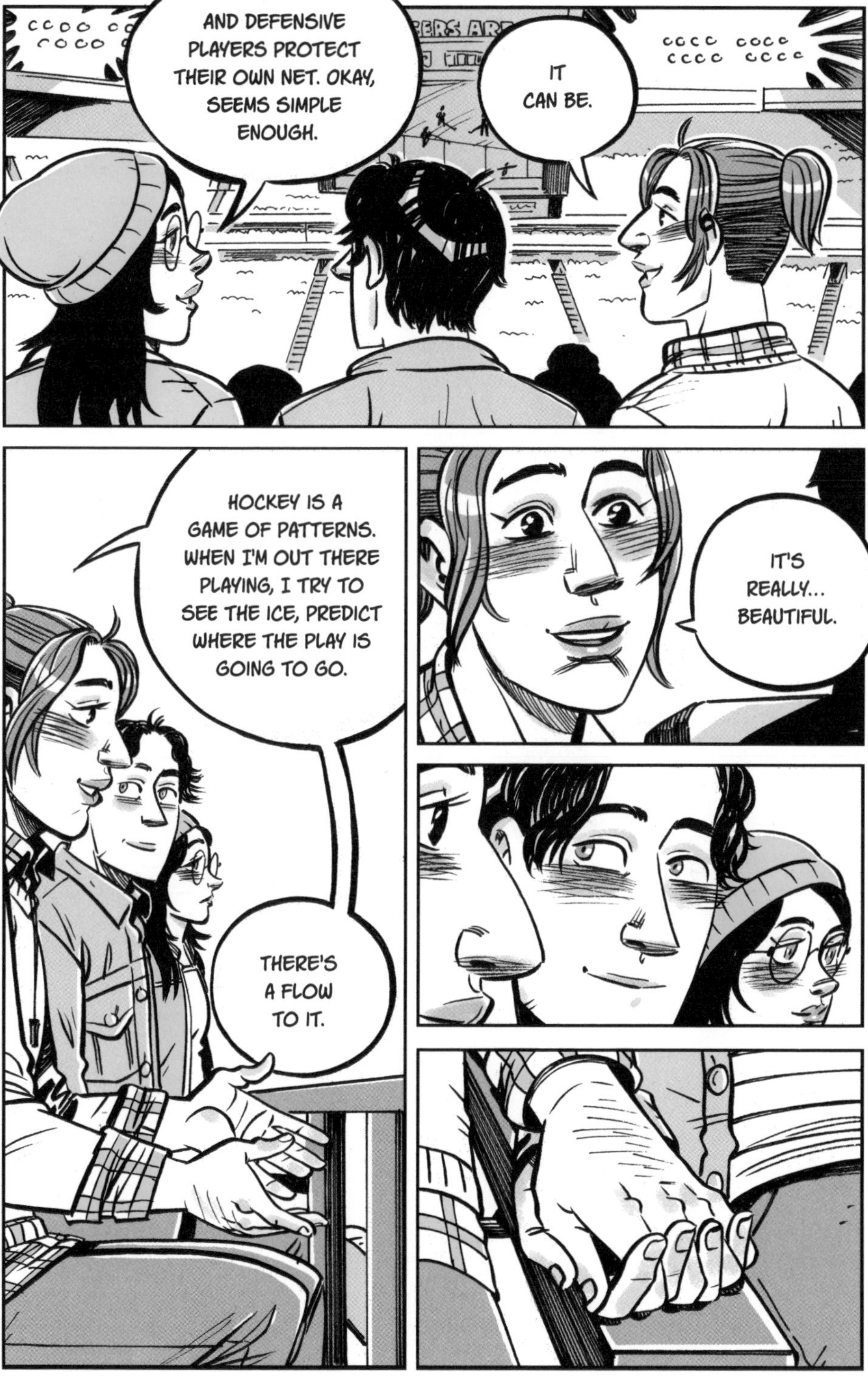

AND DEFENSIVE PLAYERS PROTECT THEIR OWN NET. OKAY, SEEMS SIMPLE ENOUGH.
IT CAN BE.
HOCKEY IS A GAME OF PATTERNS. WHEN I'M OUT THERE PLAYING, I TRY TO SEE THE ICE, PREDICT WHERE THE PLAY IS GOING TO GO.
THERE'S A FLOW TO IT.
IT'S REALLY... BEAUTIFUL.

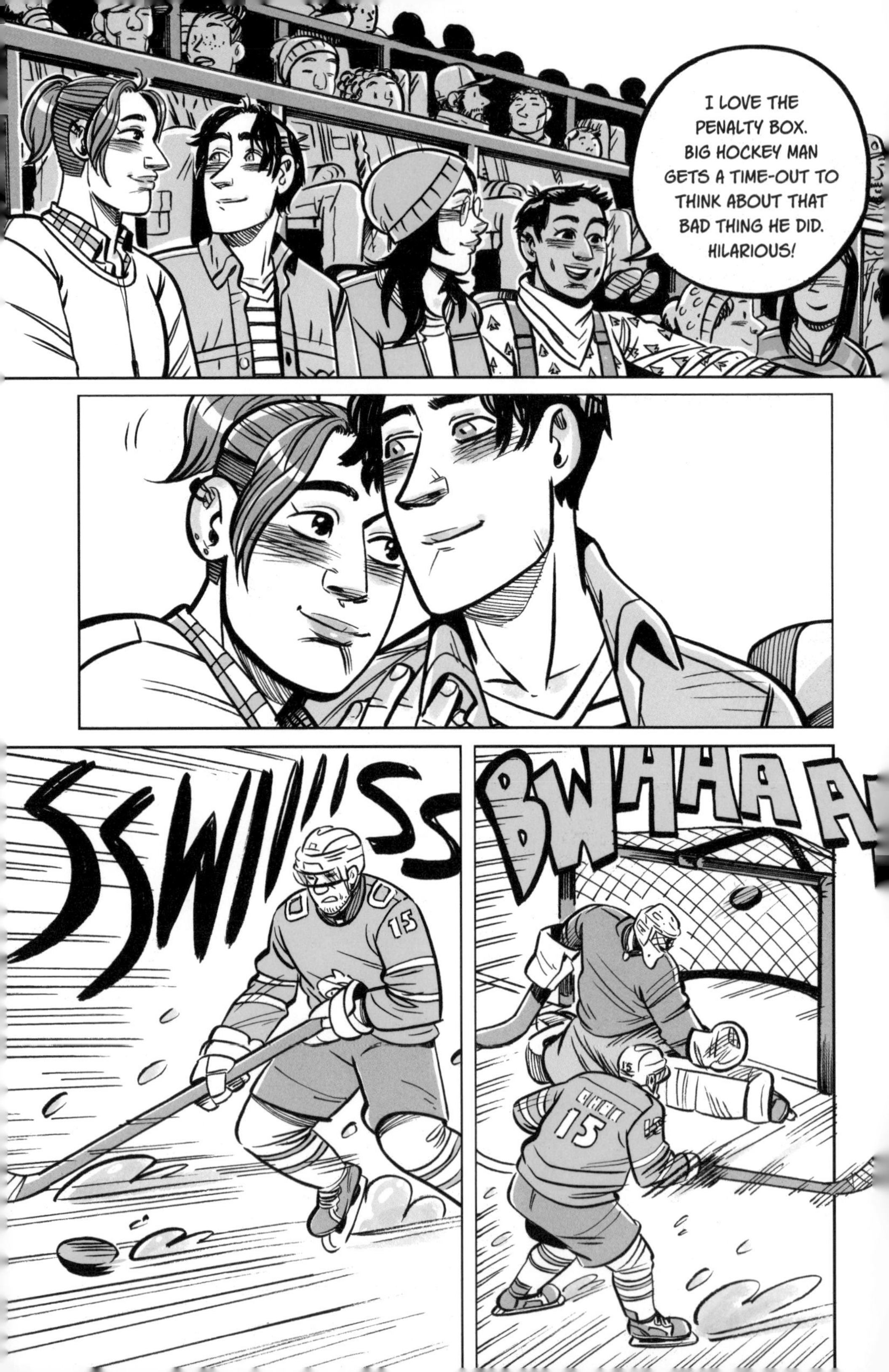
I LOVE THE PENALTY BOX. BIG HOCKEY MAN GETS A TIME-OUT TO THINK ABOUT THAT BAD THING HE DID. HILARIOUS!
15

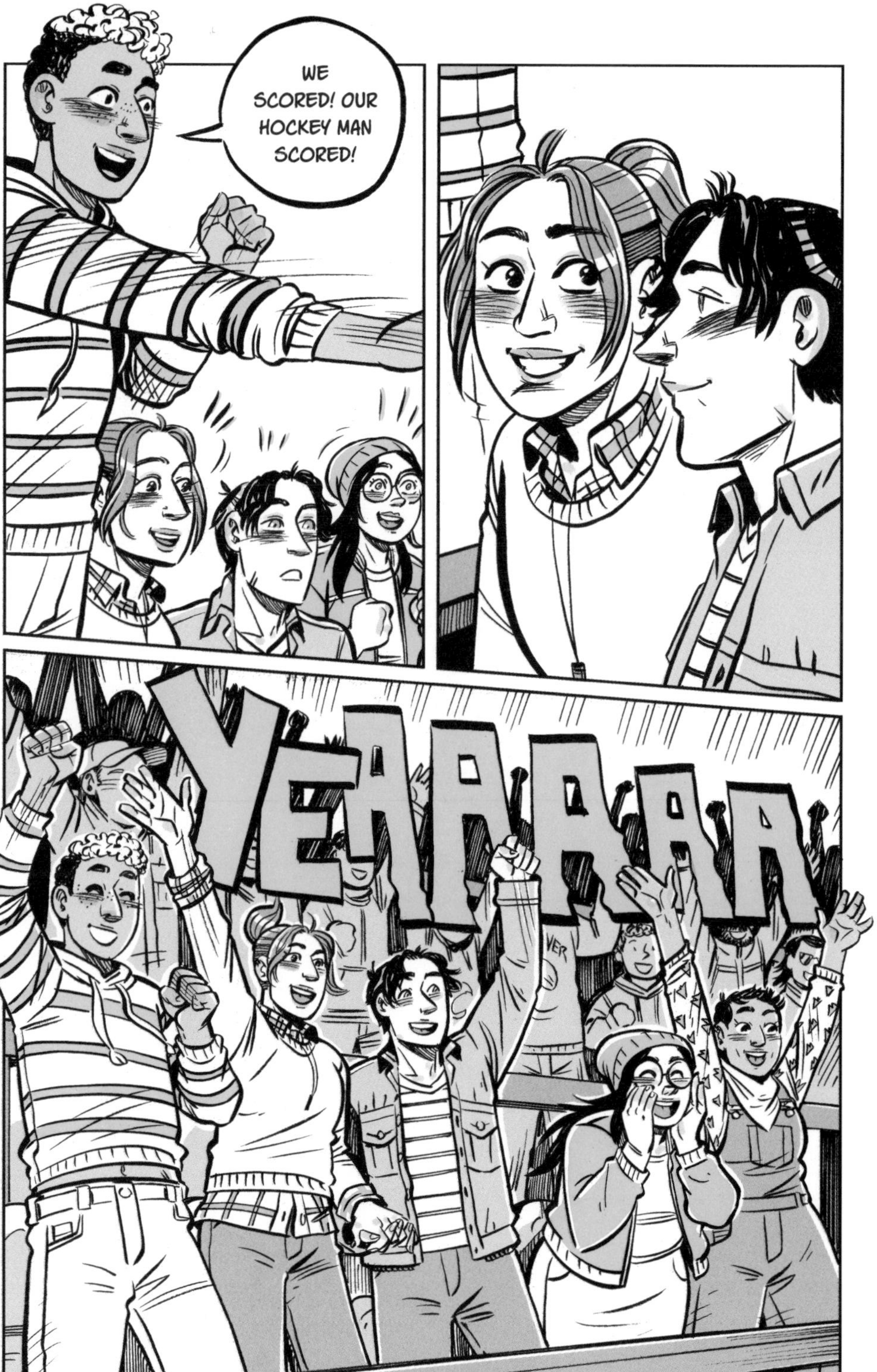
WE SCORED! OUR HOCKEY MAN SCORED!
YEAAAAA

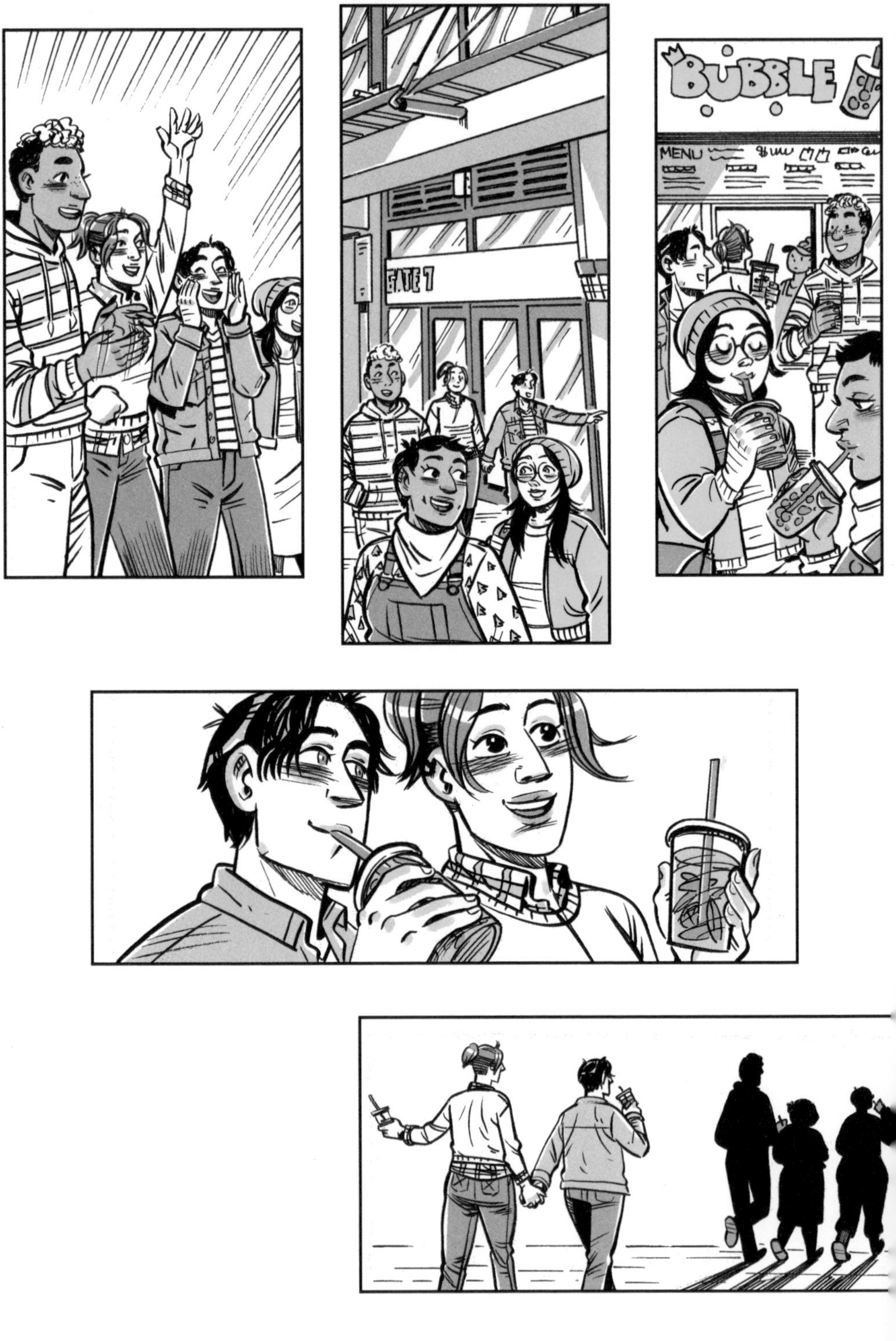
GATE 7
BUBBLE
MENU

ACKNOWLEDGMENTS

I am Canadian, but I have always been terrible at ice skating. I have a childhood memory of trundling around the ice at my local community center during an empty daytime skate session, believing that no one was faster or a better skater than I was. That feeling was quickly quashed when I joined friends at a crowded night-time public skate, only to see real skaters tearing lightning fast across the ice. They could skate backward, sideways, diagonal, every which way, while I was stuck trying to keep up and feeling miserable about it. Despite rumors to the contrary, Canadians aren't born with an innate ice-skating ability, we actually have to practice (which I did not).

I have also never played hockey, so thank you to my friend and fellow cartoonist Shelli Paroline for her invaluable insight into what it's like to be a Hockey Girl. Shelli took me on an incredible tour of her experiences as a teenage (and older) hockey player, telling me about the joys and complexities of that world. This graphic novel would be much poorer without her insight, so thanks to Shelli for sharing with me. I also want to thank my husband (and former hockey player), Tim Larade, for answering questions when I lacked knowledge of this complicated, amazing sport. Tim also looked over my drawings of the hockey scenes in this graphic novel, to make sure they were portrayed as authentically as possible. Any remaining mistakes in those drawings are mine, of course.

Making a graphic novel is like running a years-long marathon, so thank you to my amazing support team that cheered me on to the finish line while I drew this comic: Calista Brill, the editor of my heart, you make me the best cartoonist I can possibly be. Here's to the next decade of working together. Thanks to Kiara Valdez and Kirk Benshoff, for their invaluable assistance, especially when it comes to navigating the mysteries of the two-color Pantone process. Thank you as well to Steve Foxe, for his excellent authenticity script read for Ezra, which was so helpful in deepening the character of a young queer person.

This graphic novel was written and drawn during a time of great difficulty for humanity in general, and I feel very fortunate that I was able to bury myself in comics throughout the past two years. Thanks to my family, my friends, my colleagues, and especially my partner, Tim, for all your support during, well, everything. I love you all so much.

—FAITH ERIN HICKS, 2022

EXTRAS

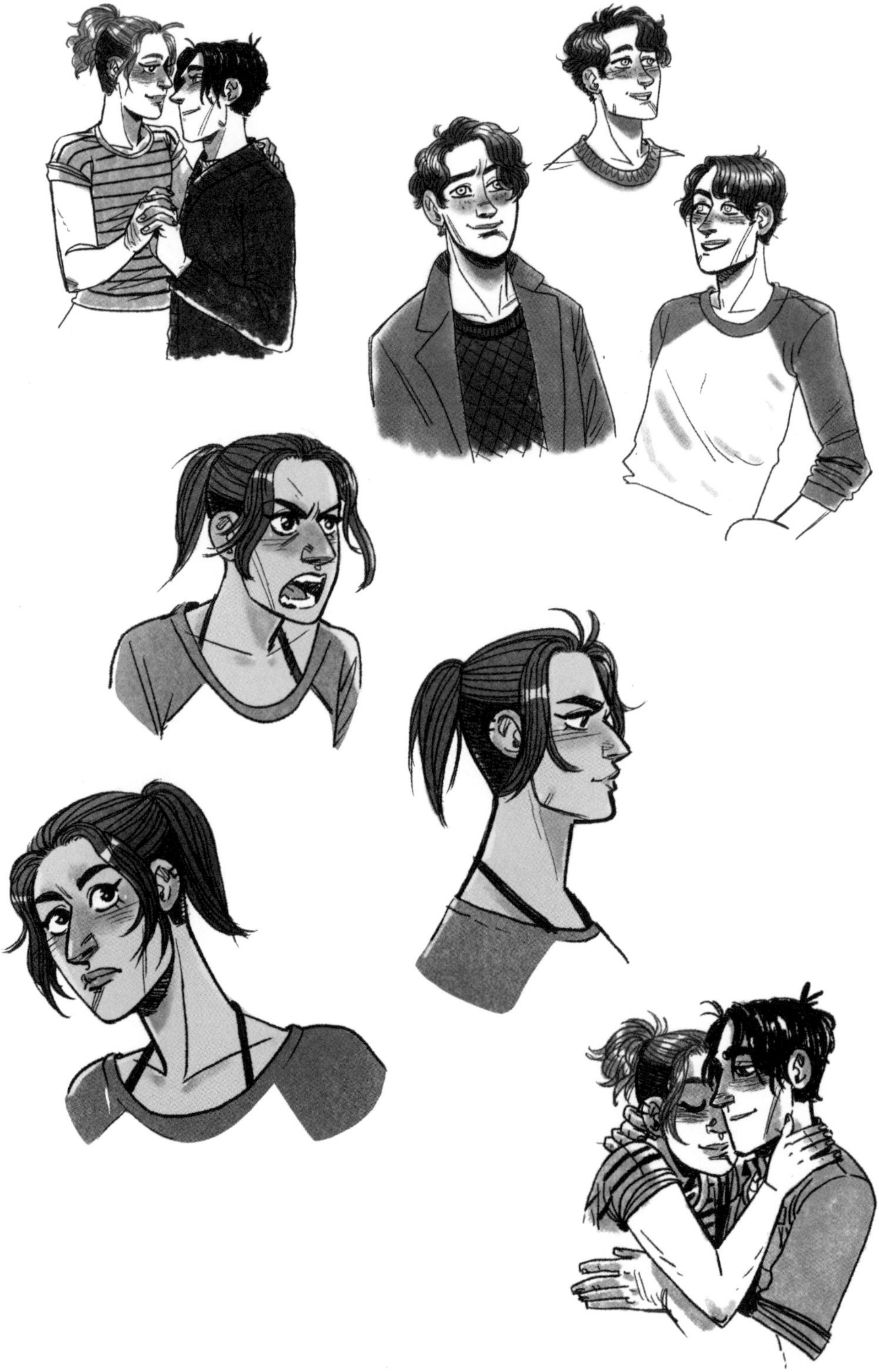

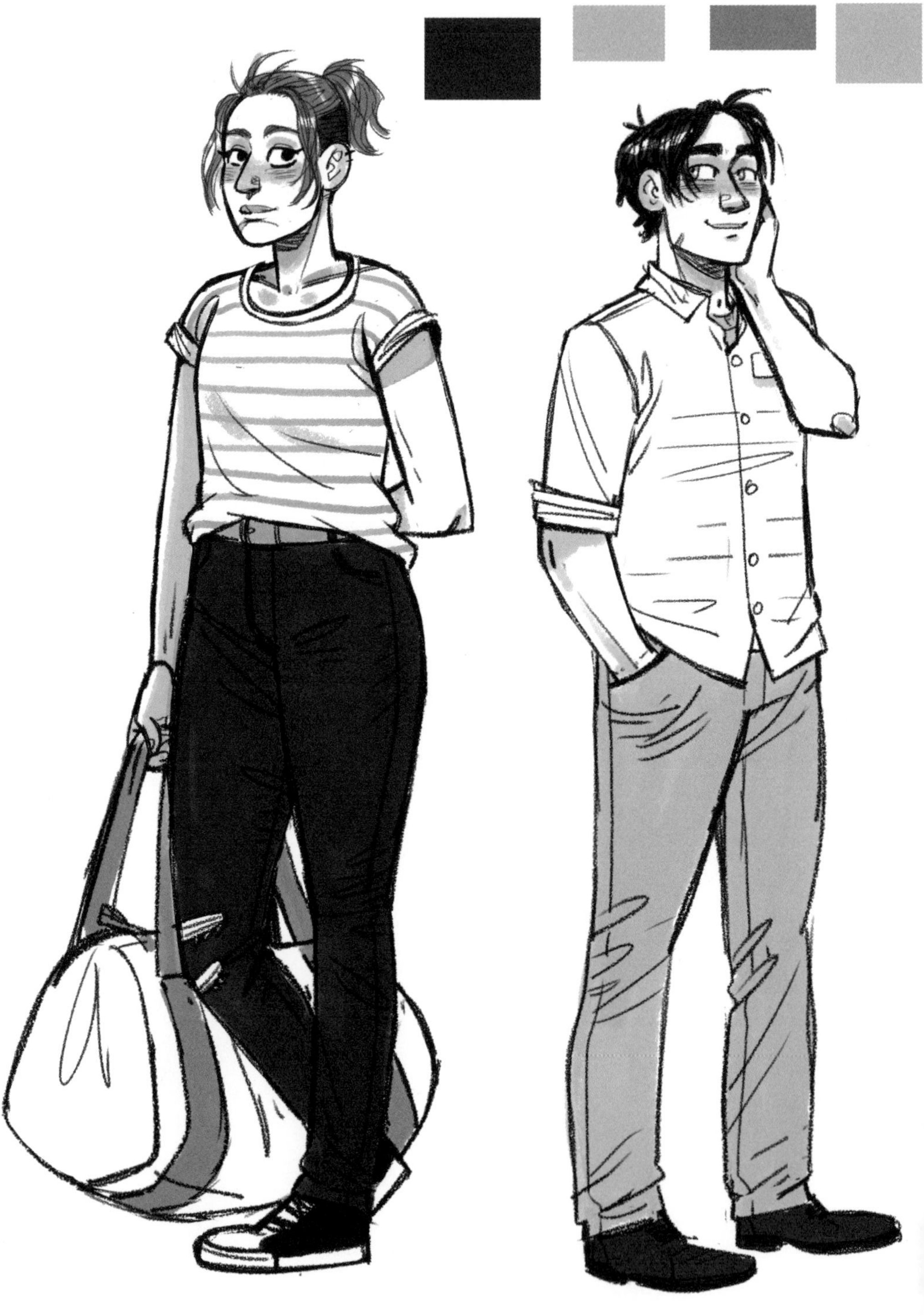

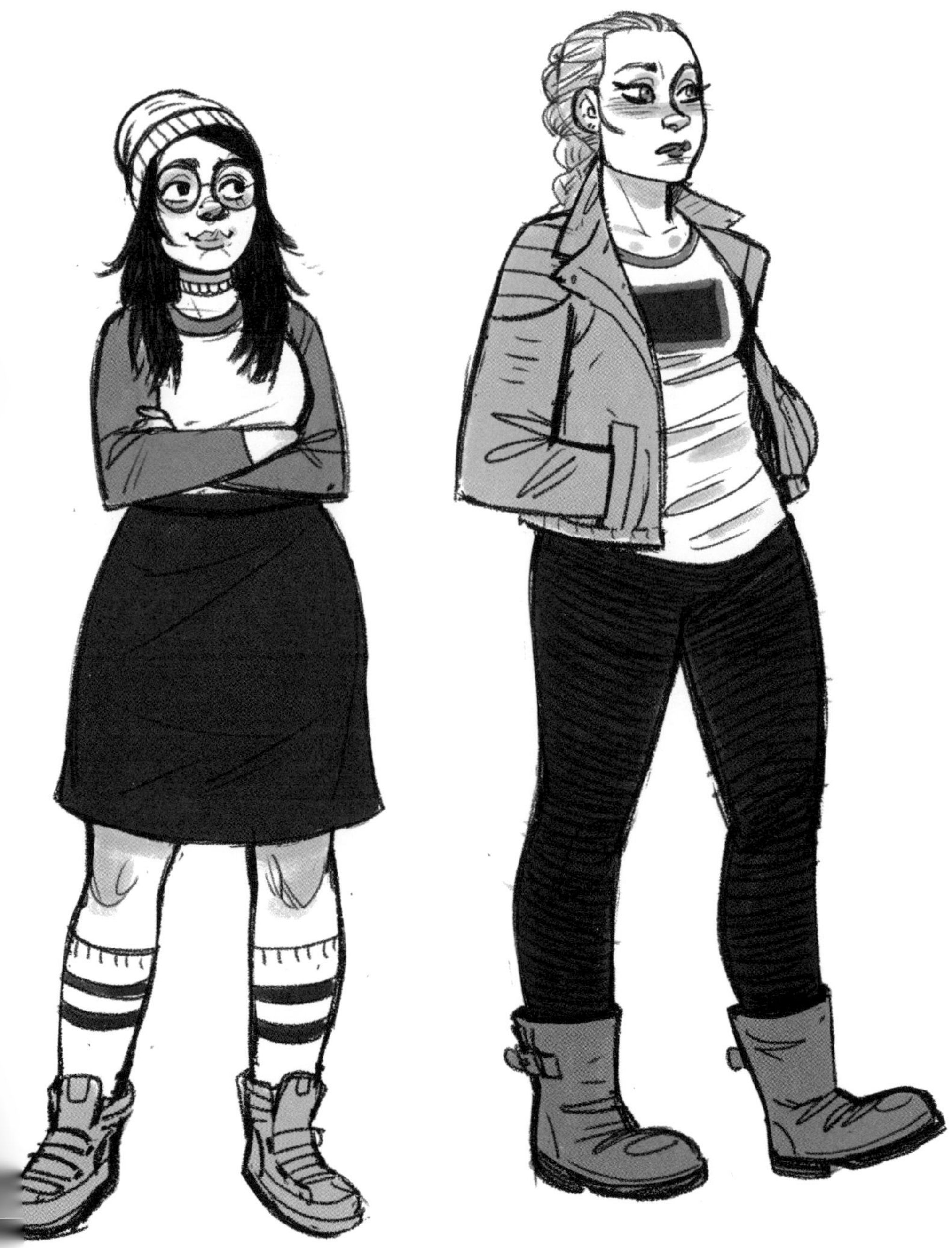

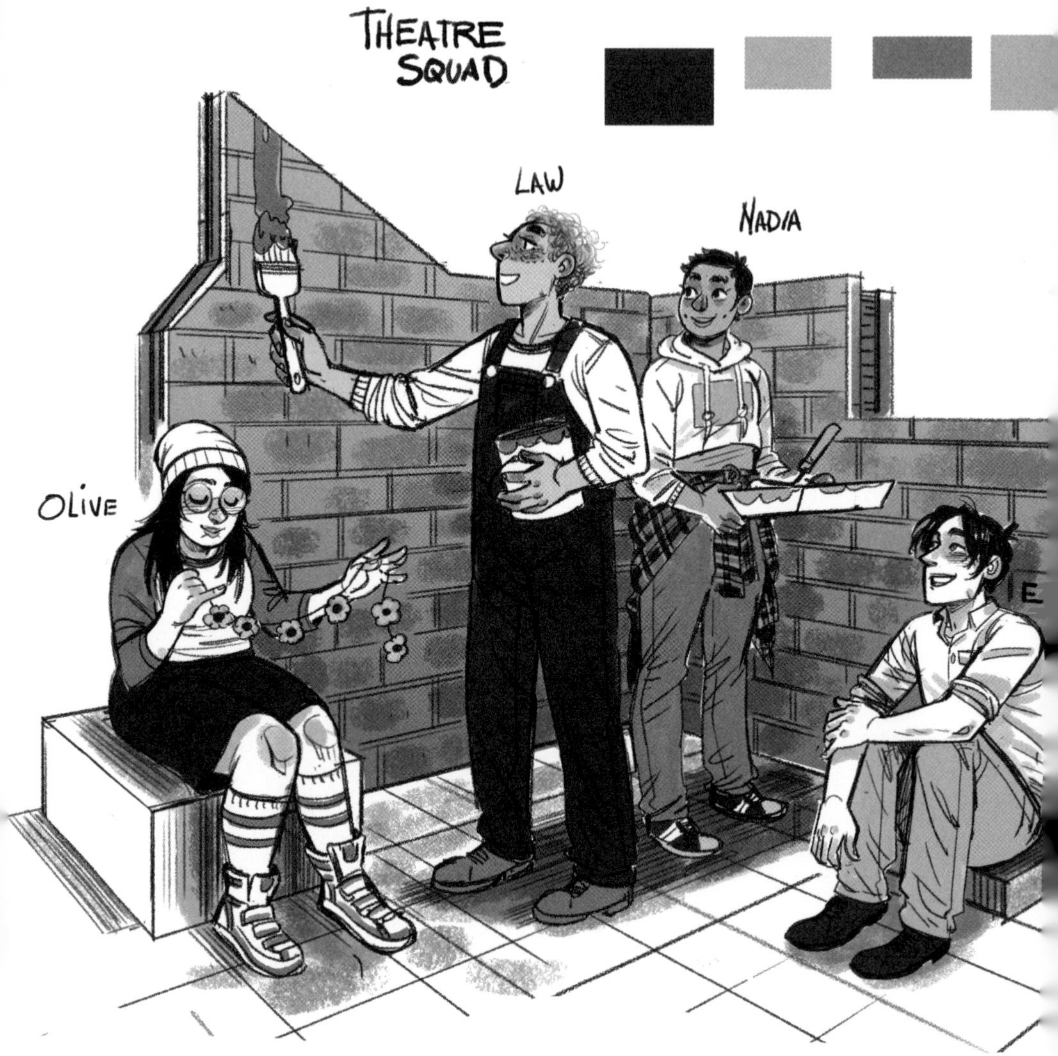

THEATRE SQUAD
LAW
NADIA
OLIVE

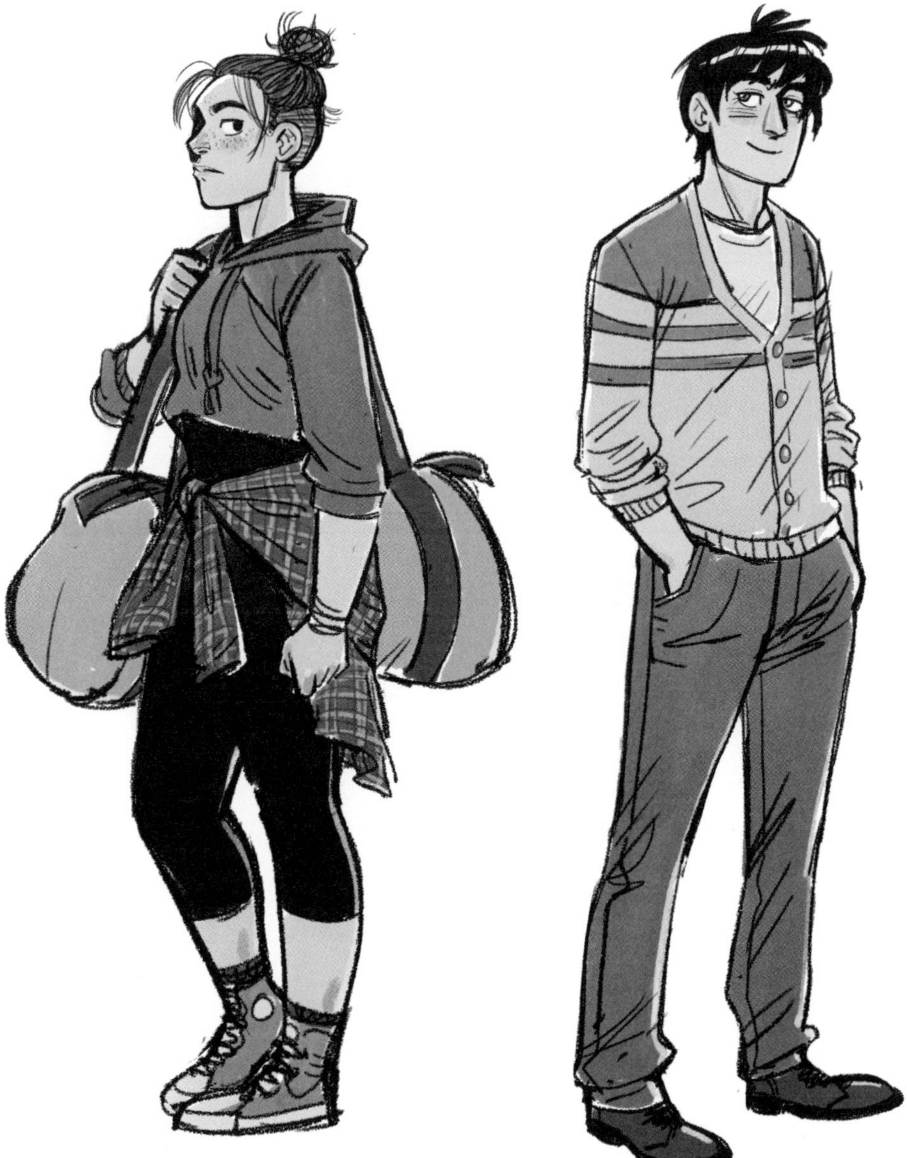

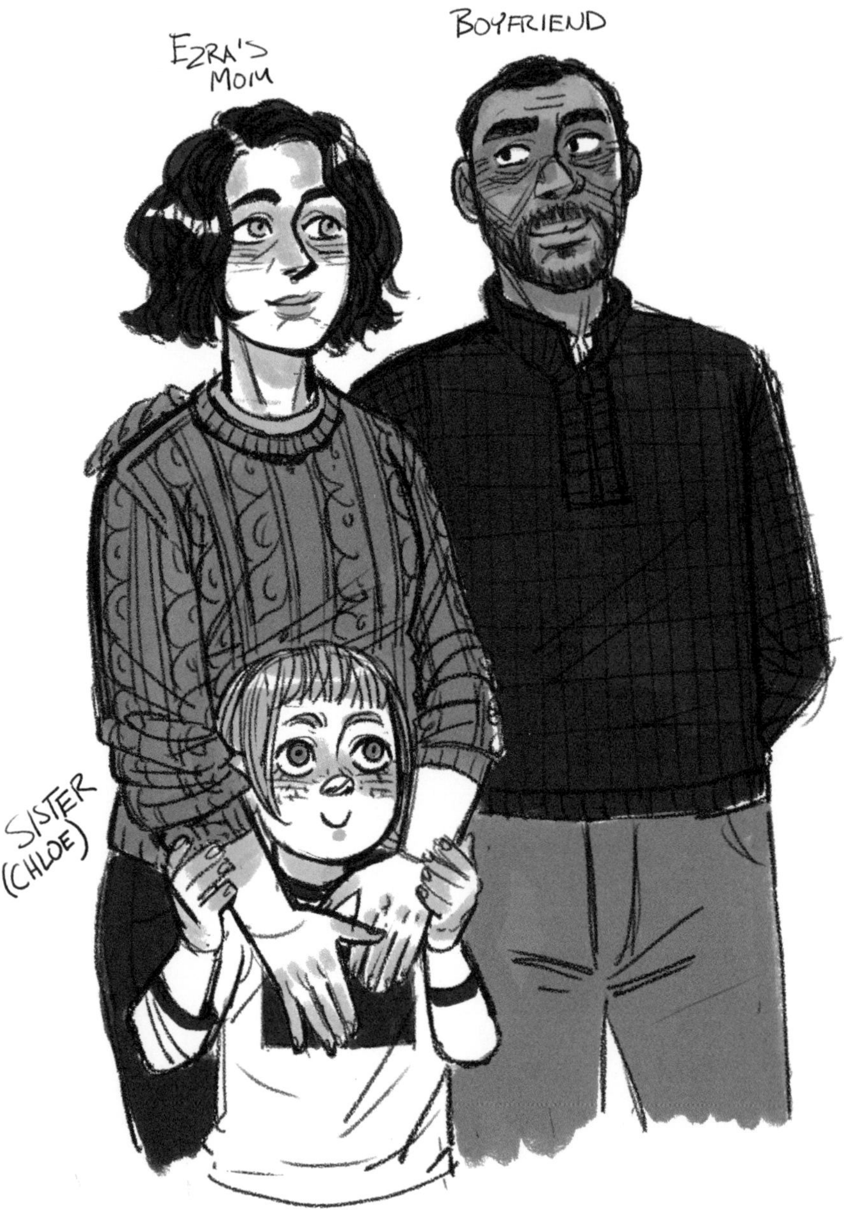
EZRA'S MOM
BOYFRIEND
SISTER (CHLOE)

ALIX'S
MOM

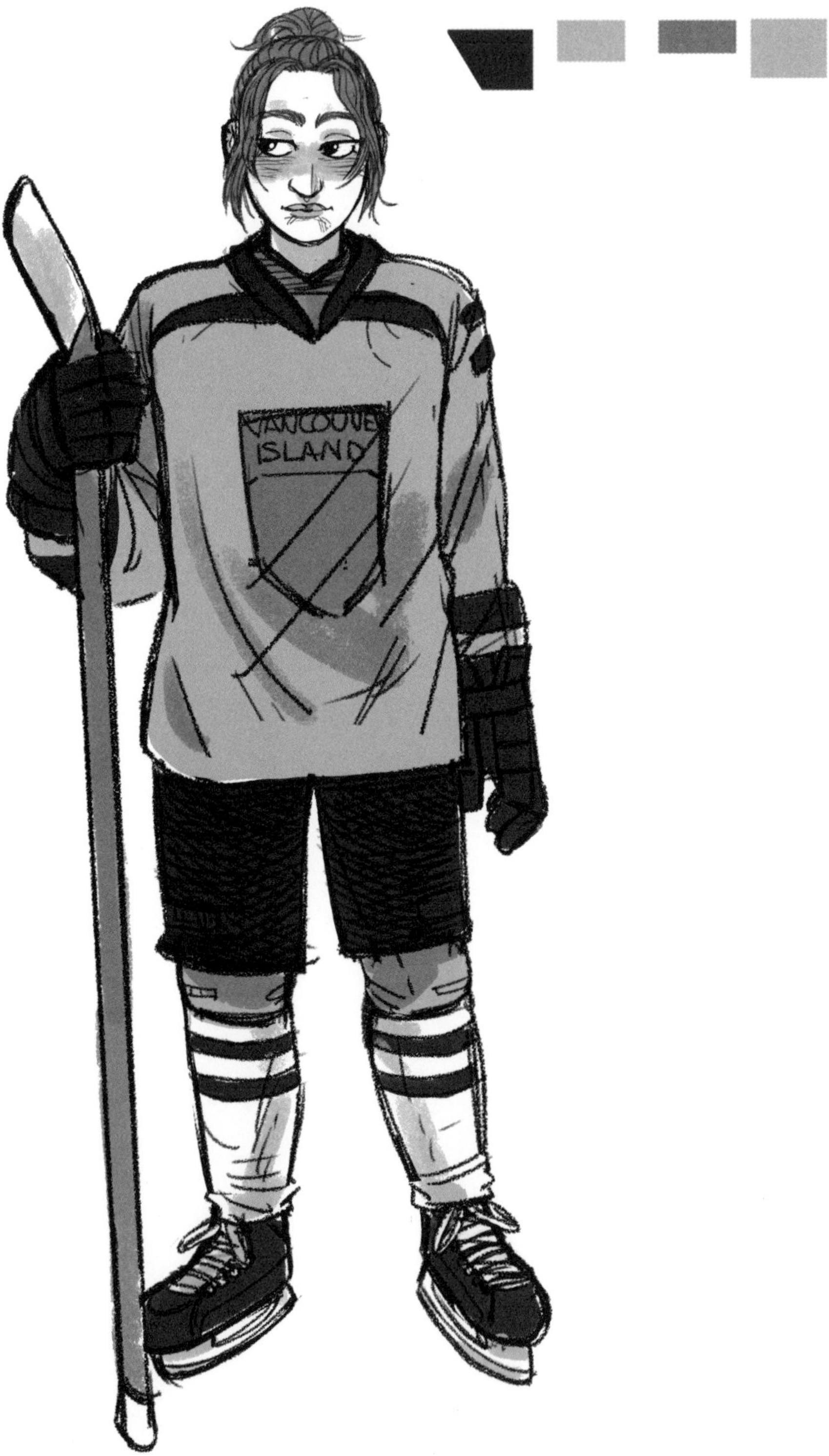
VANCOUVE
ISLAND

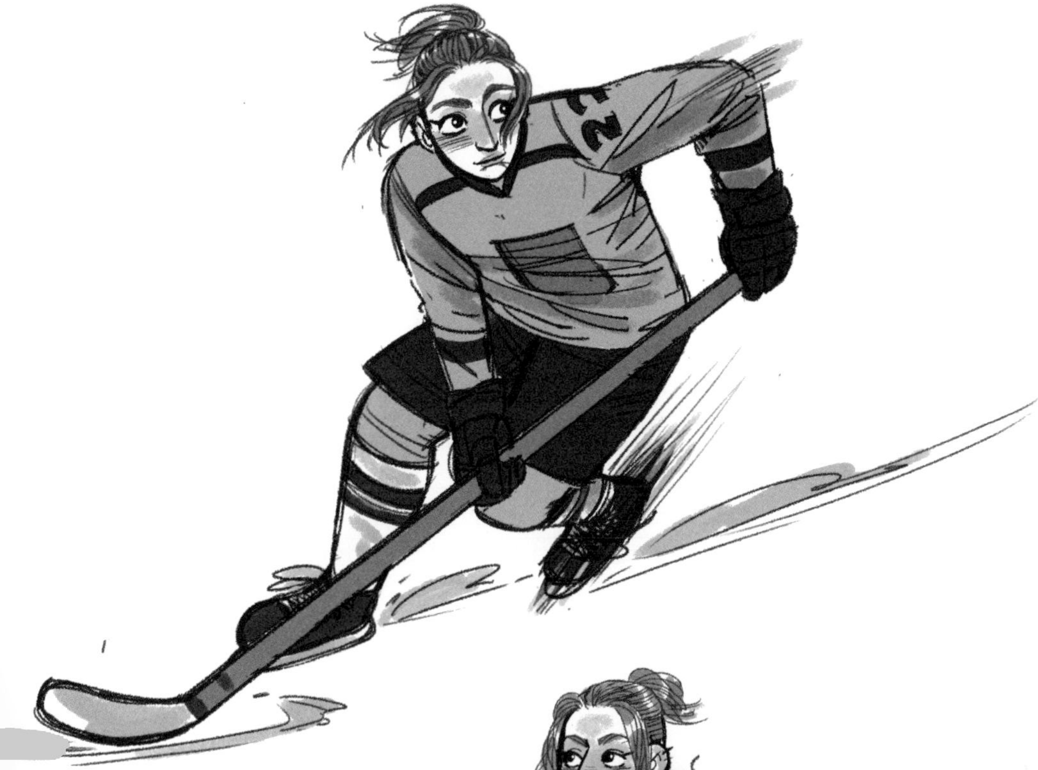

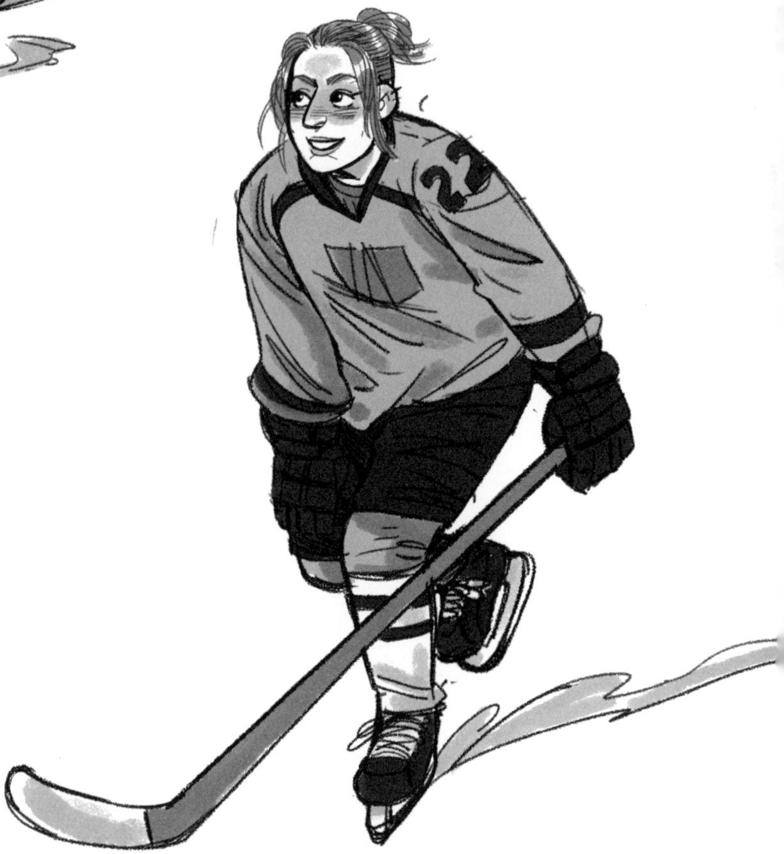

:01
First Second

PUBLISHED BY FIRST SECOND
FIRST SECOND IS AN IMPRINT OF ROARING BROOK PRESS,
A DIVISION OF HOLTZBRINCK PUBLISHING HOLDINGS LIMITED PARTNERSHIP
120 BROADWAY, NEW YORK, NY 10271
FIRSTSECONDBOOKS.COM

LIBRARY OF CONGRESS CONTROL NUMBER: 2022920382

OUR BOOKS MAY BE PURCHASED IN BULK FOR PROMOTIONAL, EDUCATIONAL, OR BUSINESS USE.
PLEASE CONTACT YOUR LOCAL BOOKSELLER OR THE MACMILLAN CORPORATE AND PREMIUM
SALES DEPARTMENT AT (800) 221-7945 EXT. 5442 OR BY EMAIL AT
MACMILLANSPECIALMARKETS@MACMILLAN.COM.

FIRST
EDITION

FIRST EDITION, 2023
EDITED BY CALISTA BRILL AND KIARA VALDEZ
COVER DESIGN BY KIRK BENSHOFF
INTERIOR BOOK DESIGN BY SUNNY LEE
PRODUCTION EDITING BY AVIA PEREZ
SPECIAL THANKS TO STEVE FOXE

DRAWN IN MANGA STUDIO ON A WACOM CINTIQ. PRINTED ON STRATHMORE BRISTOL PAPER
AND INKED WITH A RAPHAEL KOLINSKY WATERCOLOUR BRUSH AND KOH I NOOR INK.

PRINTED IN CHINA

ISBN 978-1-250-83872-8 (PAPERBACK)
1 3 5 7 9 10 8 6 4 2

ISBN 978-1-250-83873-5 (HARDCOVER)
1 3 5 7 9 10 8 6 4 2

DON'T MISS YOUR NEXT FAVORITE BOOK FROM FIRST SECOND!
FOR THE LATEST UPDATES GO TO FIRSTSECONDNEWSLETTER.COM AND SIGN UP FOR OUR ENEWSLETTER.

BY ART
WE LIVE